Keeping Kyla

Joan Crombie

All Scripture quotations are taken from the *Holy Bible, New International Version*®. NIV®. Copyright © 1973, 1978, 1984 by International Bible Society. Used by permission of Zondervan. All rights reserved.

FIRST EDITION

ISBN: 978-1-946466-89-1

Library of Congress Control Number: 2020909364

Published by

3741 Linden Avenue SE | Grand Rapids, MI 49548

Printed in the United States

Dedication

This book is dedicated to my mother, Dorothy, who modeled what it means to follow Jesus and who inspired me to write. And also to my husband Steve, who has cheered me on in this journey.

Prologue

Dr. David Grant strategically moved his shoulder to scratch his back against the rough bark of the oak on which he leaned, waiting. He crossed his feet, staring ahead with contentment, unconsciously watching the farmers work their fields in the valley beyond him, opposite from where he rested on the upper bank of the river near the edge of the Tynnbury Hall gardens. The fields in the distance were a patchwork of soft spring greens. Before them, a short walk down the bank, the silvery flow of the Cherwell glided by. Dozens of noisy birds gathered there, poking their beaks into the stones and mud of the shore in their search for their food, ignoring the couple on the grass so near them. Grant shifted again, looking to where his petite companion dozed on the blanket beside him, lulled to sleep by the sound of the water and the powerful April sun which warmed her back. Her blond hair fanned out over her tan arms on which she rested her head. Grant sat patiently, not willing to hurry the day and waiting until the right moment to share his news with her.

He thought back to when they had first met—such an unlikely convergence. It was near the end of his first year as guest lecturer at Oxford. Both of them had been invited to be panelists at the University for a Symposium on British History and the Arts, an event sponsored by a movement of purists concerned with responsibly portraying their national history accurately through film. Grant had been selected as one of the two historical scholars on the panel, and Marilee Montayne, having been recently catapulted to fame after her leading role in the historical film *Galleghent,* represented the Actors Guild. She and two film producers, also invited, had taken the train up from London that day to donate their entire day to an event that would end up a bust. The symposium, as it turned out, was poorly attended by those interested in anything to do with history and its portrayal in the arts. However, throngs of students crowded in with another purpose

5

in mind—meeting Ms. Montayne and seeking her autograph—and the day ended with the event chair accusing her of hijacking the function for self-promotion.

Unaware of Montayne's plight, Grant was simply happy that the sorry meeting had come to a close, politely making conversation and shaking hands with his colleagues before skirting out of the hall to retrieve his briefcase and suit jacket from the anteroom. He could see from the narrow window in the door that the mob waiting for the movie star among them was still crowded around the meeting hall's main double doors. Grant took the back stairs, intending to cut through the basement to the side door nearest the parking lot. At the bottom of the stairs he rounded the corner into the first hallway to see Ms. Montayne trying the door of a locked closet. She noticed him approaching and quickly turned to lean casually against the wall.

Curiously, Grant stopped. "Are you lost? This place can be a maze down here."

She shook her head. "I'm fine—thank you." Her hair was short back then, and dark.

Grant studied her for a moment, then continued to the end of the hall, where he suddenly turned back toward her.

"If you *were* lost," he said, "I would tell you that the way back upstairs is right back that way and to the left. Now, if you were looking for a quiet side entrance, you could follow me this way, and I would show you a way out of here. Plus," he added with a small smile, "I just happen to know a guy with a car who could take you anywhere."

She smiled back, pushing off the wall to follow him. Such a simple beginning to such a deep friendship.

Grant rested his arms on his knees, absently fingering a blade of grass. The breeze ruffled the edge of the blanket against her arm and Marilee stirred. He looked down at her where she lay so relaxed on the blanket. He wondered how she would feel about the changes ahead. After being together two years now, he didn't want to think about a life without her.

"Are you watching the time?" her muffled voice came from beneath her arms.

"Yeah," he said, checking his watch.

"What time is it?" she asked. "I don't want to miss our tour."

"We've got time," he assured her.

She sat up, stretching. "I don't want to be late, and I don't want to have to hurry."

"Marilee, we've got time. The tour doesn't start for half an hour," he said.

She sat cross-legged on the blanket, facing both him and the mansion across the gardens behind him. She loved this place. It held so many pleasant memories. As a child she would walk past the stately iron gates set so securely in the long brick wall surrounding the Tynnbury Estate on the way to and from her grandparent's cottage to visit the little shops on the outskirts of Banbury. Each trip past she would stop and peer through the scrolls of wrought iron, studying the mansion's many windows, dreaming of what it must be like to live there.

"Haven't you already seen this place a dozen times?" Grant asked her.

"Yes," she said, "but *you* haven't. I want you to see it."

He moved to the side to get a better view. "She's kind of an eyesore," he said honestly, "like the setting for a movie I wouldn't let my kids watch. If I had kids."

The house, he observed, was an enormous, sprawling red brick structure, three stories tall, with thirty-three white-framed windows on the front of the house alone. Stone chimneys dotted the flat roof like random Lego stacks, and a wrought iron parapet wound around the perimeter above. Top and center of the house rose a small peaked roof, with a single octagonal window centered high on it. The mansion's grand entrance was a set of ornate double doors under an arched portico, with a few broad stone steps leading up to the doors. The backside of the house was very similar, with an added concrete patio nearly the length of the house. Probably the most attractive feature of the house, Grant thought, was the fountain in the center of the manicured gardens. That he could appreciate.

She wasn't offended by his comment. "Yes," she admitted, "but isn't it charming too?"

She gazed at the house fondly, which was a museum now. She knew it didn't compare to other stately English mansions, but she had always been attracted to it.

"This is my dream house, David. If I could pick anywhere in the world to live, I'd pick here."

He studied her face. "Seriously? Here in Banbury?"

She shrugged. "I guess it's not so much Banbury as it is the house. I've always loved it. Sentimental reasons mostly."

Grant stood, brushed off his blue jeans, and reached out his hand to help her up. "Well, my dear, it's time to go see this monstrous pile of brick that has so captivated you!"

They dropped the blanket off in the car before joining the eight others gathered in Tynnbury's broad paneled foyer. Marilee had donned a hat and a pair of brown-rimmed cosmetic glasses, keeping her manner aloof, as was her custom in public, but there were still whispers, and by the second room of the tour a young woman shyly approached her.

"Excuse me," she said. "Are you Marilee Montayne?"

Marilee smiled and nodded.

The lady gave a small squeal of excitement. "I knew it! I love your movies!"

Marilee thanked her as Grant moved in close, his hand protectively on the small of her back, smiling kindly as he leaned toward the woman to say, "We're here for the tour of Tynnbury Hall."

She blushed. "Of course."

She sidled away, rejoining her friends, but the whispers and furtive stares continued throughout the tour. The couple had learned to both be careful of people and ignore them simultaneously.

Their guide was a winsome man in his sixties, a glad volunteer for the grand museum house. As they stood in the enormous drawing room, he gave them an animated history of it, from when the house was built in the early 1800s, through the various wealthy families who had lived there up until its requisition for the war in the 1940s. Slowly they passed through one room after another as the gentleman pointed out various historical and architectural features — the paneled walls, the recessed windows, the ornate marble fireplaces, and so on.

"See? Don't you love it?" Marilee whispered.

For Grant it was mostly a very large, old house, complete with a very large, old-house smell. But he had to admit as a historian that he did like the library, its walls lined with rare leather-bound collections from floor to ceiling, the windows framed with heavy velvet drapes, the hulking desk of old ship wood, and the furniture arranged around a massive hide of some sort of exotic African deer. Their guide lingered in the room, accommodating Grant's interest in the books.

"There's been many a fellow that's gone through those all, one by one," the guide said, gesturing toward the shelves. "Searching for the treasure. In them, around them, behind them." He chuckled.

"Treasure?" Marilee asked.

"Oh, yes!" the guide said, leaning his hand on the brass pole from which the heavy cord blocking them from the displays hung. "No place like this is complete without its legends and mysteries!"

"Shortly before the war," he continued, "they evacuated national treasures from London to secret locations in the north for safekeeping. All sorts of things were transported up here from the museums in London. Even the Palace. They spread those valuables out all over to various places—a highly organized system of protection. And Tynnbury Hall was one of those locations."

"I didn't know that," someone said.

"Unfortunately, some of the treasures sent away for safekeeping have never been recovered. Even some of the royal family jewels—for one, a little princess crown of the queen's that she wore as a baby—you might know it if you've seen her childhood photos. And a pile of other fine jewels. Never been found."

"Stolen?" another asked in surprise. "How did they not anticipate that happening?"

"Oh, but they did!" the gentleman asserted. "They had made copies, excellent fakes to divert from the real objects. But this time somehow the real pieces disappeared, leaving only the facsimiles. The authorities at the time had strong reasons to believe that the items disappeared here, at Tynnbury. Some people think that they are hidden here somewhere, even to this day."

Grant frowned. "You would think they would have torn this place apart!"

"Oh, certainly they did!" he exclaimed. "Believe me—there's not a corner here that hasn't been searched, even with ultrasound technology. Yes, and every inch of that garden has been upturned too." He rocked on his heels, adding, "Personally, I think they're long gone, stashed away in some forgotten German cellar." He lifted his hand to the door. "Shall we move on?"

Toward the end of the second floor Grant started to grow a little impatient, glancing at his watch. The tour was taking longer than he expected, and he wanted to be sure he had enough time to talk to Marilee before she had to catch the train back to London. Halfway up the stairs to the third floor Grant stopped her on the landing, letting the rest of the group go on ahead. He pulled her back slowly and turned her around, drawing her near, touching his nose against hers.

"Look," he said quietly, "I like this place, and I can see why you love it. But right now I would rather be down there—with you." He jerked his head toward the window and the fountain in the gardens below.

"Oh, you!" She sighed, pursing her lips and frowning at him for a moment. "Okay," she conceded. "Let's go. I'm surprised you lasted this long!" They started down the stairs, abandoning the tour.

He told her his news outright when they got to the fountain. Both of them were sitting on a dry edge away from the spray from the breeze. He could tell she was disappointed.

"When did you find this out?" she asked, speaking loudly over the sound of the water. She had known his time at Oxford was temporary, his three years there ending next month. But she had not known about the job opportunity in the United States. She had assumed he would be looking for something else here in England, not back in his own country.

"Only this morning," he answered. "Right before I picked you up at the station. I didn't want to spoil our day by telling you right away."

She was thoughtful, looking down at her feet.

"It's a really great offer," he explained, sincerely, "and it's a really great private school. Taiton College. Hard to pass up. I would have a lot of opportunities in the department there." He paused for a brief moment, adding, "But the thought of leaving you rips my heart out."

"Then I'll come with you," she announced.

He wrapped his arm around her shoulders, giving her a quick side squeeze.

"We could make it work," she continued. "Of course, I'd have to leave when I'm doing a film, but the rest of the time we'd be together."

"I don't want to be away from you either, Marilee. But your life is here. You would be walking away from everything—your family, your dream. I certainly couldn't ask you to compromise your career. Not now. We could talk every day, and you could visit some; then I could come here during the summer—"

She looked up, somewhat irritated with him. "David, people *do this*, you know! It's not unheard of. We could make it work! If you get this job, I'm coming with you. Period. I don't want to be apart from you. It's hard enough seeing you only on the weekends here!"

He smiled slowly. "In my wildest dreams I was hoping you would say that." He kissed the top of her head and continued. "And I was also hoping that if I asked you to marry me you would say yes."

She pulled back in surprise. "Are you serious?"

He held up the diamond he'd been carrying in his pocket.

She laughed out loud. "Well, if that isn't strategic bribery!" She gave him a little push backward. "But yes, of course!"

"Careful!" he cautioned. "Don't make me drop it in the fountain!"

He put the ring onto her finger and kissed her.

She buried her head happily in his chest, murmuring, "So when do you leave for your interview?"

"Tomorrow night."

The afternoon was gray, but it had stopped raining, the blustery winds drying up the runway and the roads. Large, billowy clouds passed swiftly across the sky. Dr. Grant's jacket and necktie whipped around in the gusts as he followed Gary, his driver, to the silver minivan in the airport parking lot. The college had sent the elderly gentleman to meet him and bring him to his hotel near the Taiton College campus in New Hampton, half an hour's drive away. Grant had rested on the plane, but he was bone tired and eager to get some real sleep once he arrived at his hotel. He got into the front seat and buckled in, ready to make conversation on the drive.

They chit-chatted lightly about traveling and airports, rough landings, getting married, and British accents. The old-timer was friendly and talkative. Grant kept up a steady supply of subjects to keep him going, paying attention to most but also finding himself painfully sleepy from the lull of the driver's monologue. Suddenly he was jolted out of his exhaustion by a directional road sign tucked in the trees beside the road that read, "Wynnbury House, four miles." An arrow pointed left.

"Did that say 'Wynnbury House'?" he asked, looking back down the road toward the sign.

"Yeah, 'Twinbury,' they call it," the driver replied.

Grant looked at him questioningly.

"'Wynnbury,' 'Twinbury.' It's a nickname for the place. I guess it was built to look just like one of those rich houses in England. It had a similar name."

"No kidding!" Grant said, turning to him. "You wouldn't mean 'Tynnbury'? As in 'Tynnbury Hall'?"

Gary, the driver, shrugged. "Ah, I'm not sure what it's called. Some place in England is all I know. It's like a museum now or something."

"No kidding!" Grant repeated.

"Yeah, I guess it was built by some GI who'd been stationed in England in the '40s. The kid used to be a farmer and comes home to build that! Only had one kid in that huge house, and he didn't even live past forty. It's a shame. Been sittin' empty for years. Just went on the market."

"Is that right?" Grant said curiously.

Gary paused at a stop sign, shaking his head. "You know, I never understood that place—why a simple guy would go to that much trouble to build that big of a house, and an eyesore at that. What the heck was he thinking?"

"Indeed," Grant replied thoughtfully.

Two days later Grant called Marilee on his way back to the airport. He knew it was night there and that she'd be sleeping, so he left a message.

"Hey, darling—I know you're sound asleep, but I wanted you to be the first to know—I got the job! And you'd never believe what else—I put in an offer for a house! Yeah, you heard me right! Just wait until you hear about it! See you soon."

Chapter One

The wipers skipping obnoxiously across her windshield had tested Kyla DeKane's sanity for the last ten minutes, and she was relieved to finally turn them off. The storm front that had whipped in with a deluge left as quickly as it had come, and now the afternoon sun glinted blindingly off the wet pavement, straight into her eyes as she waited for the eternal traffic light to change. With one hand she rummaged through her purse on the passenger's seat to find her sunglasses, then pulled the visor down to check her eyes in the mirror before donning them. The puffiness from crying had gone down a little. Perhaps her pounding headache would go away soon too, now that she was out of the house.

Drumming her thumbs on the steering wheel, she considered that maybe going home was a mistake. It wasn't as though her dad could do anything about what she was going through. Plus she couldn't really afford to be throwing away time with finals starting on Monday. But she was over halfway to Stanton now, and she couldn't go back to the apartment. She needed someplace to go, someplace to run away to, someplace to think and get a grip—someplace to collect herself so that she didn't blow up on someone! Life and final exams would have to wait. She just couldn't stay there one more minute—just couldn't handle one more joyous celebration in someone else's life when the bottom had fallen out of hers.

Kyla sniffed and found a napkin in the cupholder to wipe her nose. She had never been in theater, but she had to admit she had done a pretty good job of acting an hour or so ago, coming out of the bathroom with the trash tied up in the Walmart bag to the squealing of beautiful and buxom Ashley Buckley, showing off the flashing new diamond on her left hand, beaming as each of the girls in the house rushed to congratulate her. She was the third of the five college senior roommates sharing the town house to be engaged in the last few months. First had been Stacy at Christmas, then Jessica on her birthday in March, and now Ashley. Her other roommate, Mary, was much too in love with her chemical engineering major to even date. And then there was her, Kyla, who, although she hadn't exactly thought she would be engaged before graduation, assumed her relationship with Alex was going somewhere eventually. But not so. Emphatically not so. Their breakup had already been a week ago, but what she learned today—she sniffed, wiping the tears off her cheeks again—what she learned today had made her livid! But how could *they* know—she hadn't even had a chance to tell her roommates anything yet. So for Ashley's sake she sucked it up, playing her part well, pasting on the happy face, giving the warm hug of congratulations, listening to every detail of how Paul asked her, and gushing over the ring.

But after a point she had to get out of there. She knew she couldn't hold in her misery for long, and why spoil her roommate's happy moment? Nor could she mask her jealousy of the glow on Ashley's face. All her roommates, for that matter. All of their dreams were coming true—yes, even Mad Scientist Mary's—when Kyla's were going down the toilet. She could not listen to another minute of wedding or career talk and maintain her composure. Kyla told herself that the kindest thing was just to get away, to let Ashley have her day, and let them in on her depressing drama when she got back tomorrow. It was her problem anyway. And besides, sometimes she got a little snippy when she was stressed out, so it was probably kinder to just bolt. So here she was sitting in her steaming hot car on her way home.Impatiently she held her hand out over the vent, feeling its burst of warm air as the car sat idling. Now that the rain had stopped, she could finally open her front windows to breathe and get some air movement on her sweaty body. The air conditioning hadn't worked at all this spring, just one more thing to add to the list of reasons she hated her car. At least her hair was up off her neck, she thought, glad she had thrown it up into a loose bun for her presentation.

Beside her a large dump truck rumbled past her in the left turn lane, grinding and hissing to a stop. Kyla coughed and swung her head away from its cloud of diesel exhaust, noticing in the right lane next to her the eyes of two thirty-something men gawking across at her from the seats of their Park and Rec utility truck. She looked away, shifting in her seat, feeling a drip of sweat roll down her back.

She knew it was her dress. It was the effect they had hoped for when she and her two classmates planned their outfits for their communications class final presentation that they gave this morning. The idea was to illustrate the effect of power dressing—and to add a little oomph without going over the line. Jenn Hadley had drawn the scanty red dress—the "hooker dress," they called it, giggling over it when they bought the three together. Kyla had hoped to draw the pink power suit, as it would have been useful over the summer at Alex's dad's firm, but instead she drew the little black dress, which fit perfectly snug over her curves, except that Kyla had more than a "little" on top, which, according to her friends, bumped her from looking great to looking sizzlin' hot. At the time the choice was a good second best, as she knew it would drive Alex wild. But that was all before everything went down, before the breakup, before she got the accidental text, and before she learned the eye-opening bits of information about her ex-boyfriend and the red hooker dress. Oh, would she like to—

The long blare of a car horn behind her jolted her—the light had finally turned green. Kyla moved her foot off the brake to the accelerator, but nothing happened until a certain point when her Chevy jarred roughly into motion. "Probably the transmission slipping," Alex had said a couple weeks ago. Kyla had called her dad about it, but he asked if she could hold out just a few more weeks until after graduation, after which he would take her car to the mechanic. She had gotten mad at him, for she wanted to move up to Bridgewater right away after school to get settled before she resumed her summer job at Alex's father's law firm for the third summer in a row. She shook her head, marveling at how close she had been to going back there, naive to Alex's trysts. The pain surged through her stomach and chest again. Well, she definitely wasn't going to work at his parents' firm now! And until she found another job, she would be back home in Stanton with her dad. Indeed, so much had changed so quickly.

Moving to an inside lane, Kyla got up to speed, glad to be out on the last stretch of highway. Even with heavy traffic, the way home across the metro area was so familiar that she didn't have to think about it. Her mind was reeling with enough other things now. Like a summer job. Like a post-college career. Like living at home again. Like hurling Molotov cocktails through Ashley Stormer's windows. Kyla let out a long breath, pulling her mind back to the road. Crud—she hated breaking up. She couldn't think of anything much worse.

The crazy part was that she had spent all of last week stewing over every little detail of how the actual breakup had gone down. She was irritated that Alex hadn't even seemed to be that affected by her calling their relationship quits. For the whole week she had pictured his face over their table that night, intently eating away on his sandwich during their talk, wiping his mouth with his napkin, drinking his Coke. She had wanted to throw it at him. He hadn't looked hurt or even disappointed, and that made her mad. In hindsight, there were so many things about him that infuriated her now. Things that she wished she had seen before. All the flirting with other girls—boy, had she been blind! She wondered if her roommates had noticed that about him, and if they did, why the heck hadn't they warned her? She had adored him! *How in the world did this happen?* she asked herself.

Embroiled in her thoughts, the hour-and-a-half drive through city traffic flew by, and soon she was home. She set her sunglasses on the dash as she threaded her way through the narrow streets of her old neighborhood, guiding her car under the shaded canopy of newly leafed maples to the corner lot at the end, where she pulled into the driveway beside the white rambler where she had grown up. Just parking the car in her old driveway was a comfort. She wanted to run inside, to retreat to her familiar nest, to lick her wounds in the safest place on earth she knew. And she was anxious to see her dad too, although she wasn't sure what she would say to him. From the beginning she knew that Alex Duvall wasn't the kind of man her dad approved of. He had never voiced that to her. No, he had never communicated anything but acceptance the whole two years they had dated. Still, she knew.

Kyla's dad, Kendall Lee, was technically not her real father. Her real father, or "biological father," as she referred to him, had moved out a month before her fifth birthday, and only the faintest memories of him remained. About a year after he left, Kendall Lee moved in, a handsome, full-blooded Korean who was as American as apple pie, born and raised in America by Korean American parents. Four years later, when she was ten, he married Kyla's mother and legally adopted Kyla as his daughter, though he insisted to her mom that she keep her birth surname, since "Kyla DeKane" sounded far better to him than "Kyla Lee." He also insisted that Kyla call him "Dad," which took some getting used to for her. He had always been a great guy for the four years he had lived with them, but from the adoption onward Kendall had taken pains to actually be a dad to her in every way, especially so when her mom had gotten sicker. And then two years later when she died, navigating grief together drove their manmade bond deeper. It was a bit easier to call him "Dad" then—he was all she had.

Kendall was definitely not a perfect father, especially as an inexperienced rookie starting out with a "tween," but he was immovable in his commitment to Kyla. Neither was she an easy child. As a teenager she was embarrassed and annoyed by him, brutal to him with her words, sassy and headstrong, to say the least. But her powerful volleys had met their match in him, for Kendall was steady and stronger, and thick-skinned through her tempestuous, emotional outbursts. He did all he could to keep life normal for her, if there was such a thing after one loses his or her mom at the age of twelve. He was the homework police and the dad who showed up for every school conference and every basketball game she played. He was the dad who monitored her television shows, the king of *you're-not-wearing-that* and the dad who wouldn't let just anybody give her a ride home. Somehow she grew up and turned out mostly nice. And somehow they were still together as father and daughter, and she did respect and appreciate him, despite the many things about him that bugged her.

Kyla opened her door and got out, stretching her legs and breathing deeply, thankful for the fresh breeze. The lawn had just been cut, and the air smelled like heaven. After adjusting her dress down around her hips, she reached back into the car for her pink-striped canvas purse. Shouldering it, she made her way to the front door along the perfectly edged sidewalk, suddenly aware that this would be a surprise visit. She paused by the door, thinking that she probably should have called her dad to let him know she was coming, but it was too late. At the same time she noticed the empty pocket on the outside of her handbag and realized she had walked out of her apartment without her phone. Even if she had thought of it, she couldn't have warned him anyway.

With a click of the latch and a forward shove, Kyla pushed open the door and stepped in onto the tiled foyer. A rush of the familiar met her as she entered the widened entry hall, where dozens of her photos lined the walls. It smelled like home and dad. And coffee. The light was on in his study to her right, and she was relieved that he was home—another factor she hadn't considered.

"Hi, Dad," she said, dropping her purse with her discarded shoes, stepping around the edge of the French doors. "It's me!"

Kyla looked directly into the face of a stranger, who rose hastily from her father's leather couch. He was tall, with a tousle of blondish hair, wearing jeans and a T-shirt, and his mouth dropped open in surprise as his eyes swept over her and landed back on her face. He extended his hand.

"Hello," he said. "Um, your father is—"

"Kyla? Is that you?" her dad's voice came from behind her.

Kyla turned to look down the hallway toward her dad's call and saw him step out from the kitchen doorway, a pair of empty coffee mugs in one hand.

"Hi, Dad," she answered, going for her best fake of cheerful. "Surprise!" She was disappointed that he wasn't alone. She hadn't thought of that either.

"It's Thursday," he said without moving, his brow knit together. "What are you doing here? Is everything okay?"

"Yes, Dad—everything's okay. I just decided to pop home for a night."

He stared at her for a moment longer. "I'll be right there."

As he disappeared into the kitchen, Kyla glanced back into the study. On the wooden coffee table were two Bibles lying open, one in front of her dad's chair and the other in front of the blond guy who looked a few years older than her and who now extended his hand toward her for the second time.

"Hello—I'm Peter," he said, "a friend of your father." He had an indistinguishable tattoo on his bicep and the telltale white line of a summer haircut on his neck.

"Hi," she replied curtly, shaking his hand and looking away. She had the brush-off down to an art with these guys.

That was one of the things about her dad that drove her nuts. Ever since she had gone away to college, he had started meeting with guys like this at the house. He told her he had started having a few young men over to study the Bible and talk now and then, but there were more than a few, and it was more than now and then. They hung out there. They grilled with him. Or worked together in the yard. Stuff like that. On her college breaks she never knew who she would find in the house evenings or on Saturday mornings. Regularly she would find at least four pizza boxes stacked by the kitchen trash. This guy was perhaps a little less geeky than some of the others, but for the most part they were all about the same—weird. Religious. Everything about them made her bristle. They were always a little too friendly, a little too nice, and a little too eager to do things for her. And most annoying of all was her dad's not-so-subtle efforts to set her up with a few of them. Thankfully she had always had Alex to fall back on whenever one of them approached her to ask her out, and she would give her standard sorry-I-have-a-boyfriend reply. She would need a new excuse now. She shifted her bare feet, standing awkwardly beside him on the patterned rug.

Her dad suddenly appeared in the doorway, blinking with confusion at her dress. She could feel her cheeks grow warm, a frustrating trait of hers, and she hoped he wouldn't ask her any embarrassing questions. After a brief hug and a careful look at her face, he turned, extending his arm as he introduced her.

"Kyla, my guest, Peter Watkins. Peter, I would like you to meet my lovely daughter, Kyla."

He tipped his head. "It's nice to finally meet you. I've seen your picture and heard your dad talk about you a lot." His eyes were blue and his voice sincere.

She gave a polite nod. That was another thing that bugged her. She hated when her dad talked about her to his friends, but he did it anyway. It seemed to her that he found a way to weave her into any conversation. The Twins, the Brewers, the Cubbies, and "my daughter, Kyla." Nice new car, crazy weather lately, and, "Oh, have I told you about my daughter, Kyla?"

"Peter goes to the university downtown," her father was saying. "He's studying horticulture. We go to church together and connect during the week to talk about the Word."

"Uh-huh. I see." She stuck to crisp responses that didn't invite further comments.

As was her intention, the conversation stalled out, and the three stood together quietly for a moment. Her father turned back to her. He was dark-haired and handsome, with smooth olive skin and creased eyes that made him look perpetually happy. At five-foot-eight, wearing dress slacks and a button-down shirt, he almost looked small next to Peter's taller, more muscular frame.

His eyes studied her face. "I had no idea you were coming."

Kyla let out a breath. "Yeah, sorry about that. I forgot my phone so I couldn't call."

"And everything's okay?"

She lifted a shoulder defensively. "Yeah, everything's fine! I just felt like coming home for a night."

"Okay." He paused. "Well, the two of us were just about to get a bite to eat. Would you care to join us?" He gestured toward his friend.

"No, no," she said hastily. "No, you go ahead. I'm not really hungry."

"No?" Her father frowned. "You sure? Why don't you just come sit with us?"

She shook her head. "I had a late lunch. You go ahead. I'll just hang out here until you get back."

She had skipped lunch, but the rest of it was true—she had no appetite at all. Furthermore, she was in no mood to make chitchat with some guy she didn't know who was apparently having difficulty taking his eyes off her.

19

Plus she was quite ready to be done faking it for the day. It was wearing her out. She stepped off the rug of her dad's study to the cold tile floor of the hall, leaving without acknowledging her dad's guest again.

"Are you sure?" Kendall repeated to her departing figure. "You're welcome to come with us!"

Kyla lifted her arm to wave behind her. "No, Dad—I'm fine! You go ahead. I'll hang out here and rest a little, then study. We can catch up later when you're home."

She waited by the kitchen sink, watching them leave together in a large, white pickup truck that she hadn't noticed was parked across the street from the house until now. After it rumbled away, she sighed and walked through the empty house, depressed. She had probably been right in thinking that she shouldn't have come. But here she was.

Now that she was home, Kyla regretted her hasty departure from the apartment. She hadn't brought a change of clothes, makeup, or anything. Anything. And her dad didn't exactly keep feminine products on hand in the bathroom anymore. Thankfully she found a stash in her bedroom. She also found a change of clothes and wriggled out of the little black dress, exchanging it for a bra that was slightly too small and an old volleyball T-shirt from high school and shorts. Feeling somewhat more comfortable now, she draped the dress over the back of the chair that sat in front of her antique white desk under the window.

Her bedroom was undisturbed from spring break two months ago, the last time she'd been home. Adolescent posters still covered her lavender walls, overlooking her bright purple-and-blue bedspread with its pile of decorative pillows. Everything about her room screamed "high school," except that the stuffed animals that used to cover her bed had been packed away in the back of her closet for a few years now. She plopped her purse on top of the dress on the chair and pulled up the white metallic window blinds to let in some of the evening light. As she sat on the edge of the bed, her eyes were drawn to the photo of her and Alex on the end table. She stared at it. Both of them looked so happy. Amazing how quickly things could change!

He wasn't her first boyfriend by any means. She had never been one of the popular girls in high school who had boyfriends galore, but she'd had a couple. Nor was Alex the first one she had given herself to. Her freshman year in college she had stepped over that line, but that was a mistake with a capital "Mike." After that episode was when her roommate had shared with Kyla what her mother had always told her—*You don't give yourself to just anybody, only someone really, really special.* If Kyla had had a mother, she would have no doubt gotten that advice too and avoided being defiled by that creep altogether. Oh, did she learn her lesson! Of course, her dad staunchly believed an unmarried young lady shouldn't be having sex at all, but that was her dad—Mr. Religious. His beliefs were a little archaic and unrealistic, given the fact that it was a normal part of dating nowadays. One just had to be smart about it. When she met Alex, he was special. *Really, really special.*

She met him at a basketball game. By chance she had sat in the row ahead of him, and somehow over her shoulder he had read her student ID.

"Your name fits you," he said out of the blue, tapping her shoulder and leaning his face down toward her. He was dark-haired and handsome, with a full, dark beard.

"How so?" she asked him curiously over the crowd shouts and the squeak of tennis shoes and referee whistles on the court.

He had made her blush with his reply. "It sounds as beautiful as you look."

Of course, he was razzed later for the lame pick-up line, but it worked on Kyla. She couldn't concentrate for the rest of the game. Then after the final buzzer, as she made her way through the crowded gym, he caught up with her and invited her to the student center for pizza. She said okay, and they talked until the center closed and they were asked to leave.

Yes, Alex was special. He had such a way about him. At first he would simply ask her questions and listen to her talk and smile at her and tell her she had beautiful eyes, beautiful skin, beautiful hair. And after a week he suddenly reached over to hold her hand. And then he would play with her hand and look at her in a way that made her weak, and she wanted him to kiss her. Then he kissed her in a way that left her wanting more, baiting her. It wasn't long until she wanted him so badly that she could hardly stand it, and she very willingly gave herself to him. Two years they had been together. Two years. And up until a few short weeks ago she had been happy. Naive, but happy. All until she suspected that she was pregnant, which was a mystery to her given that they always used protection. And actually she was happy then too. It was only after her talk with Alex that things changed.

She already knew that she wasn't pregnant before their conversation—she had taken a test in the Walgreens bathroom, and it was negative, but the thought that she *might* have been made her think. *What if,* she wondered. *What then?* Her imagination brought her down several roads all at once, and she couldn't stop asking the question. She wanted to know. So she asked him.

Her question came out that night, snuggling with him in his room on campus, their secret sign on the door signaling his roommate to stay out.

"So do you ever think about our future?"

"Yeah," he murmured. "I'm going to be lawyer and make truckloads of money. You're going to—well, you're going to find a job doing something."

What was that supposed to mean? she thought, feeling slightly insulted.

"No, seriously, Alex," she said. "Our future, like you and me."

"Not really," he said, pressing in to her with heated focus.

She pushed him away a little. "You're not listening."

"What's this about?" He was obviously irritated at the interruption.

Kyla drew herself up, pulling the blanket around her. "I'm serious. I just want to know what you think."

"I think that you shouldn't think about it." He took her wrist and pulled her back to kiss her.

"Like what if I got pregnant?"

He stiffened and leaned back suddenly. "What? Are you pregnant?" His voice was filled with accusation.

"No," Kyla answered defensively.

After a moment of hesitation, he gave a long sigh of relief. "Crap! Don't scare me like that!"

"But what about us?"

Alex exhaled impatiently, his expression dark. "Seriously, Kyla, what is this all about? You want to get married? I don't think either of us are ready for that!"

His words cut, and she didn't know what to say. She had hoped he would give her an *of-course-someday* answer. It was his manner that told her what she didn't want to hear.

Reaching out to her again, he sighed and pulled her close, his tone softening. "Okay—I'm sorry. Come here, baby. Look—we have a good thing going. I love you. You love me. We love each other. We have fun together. Let's not make it complicated, okay?"

"Yeah," she answered numbly, but something inside had turned off. Reluctantly she gave in to his advances.

"And for heaven's sake, don't get pregnant," he murmured, his face buried in her.

"Or what?" she asked, looking at the ceiling over his shoulder.

"Well, let's just pray we don't have to go down that road!"

That began the tailspin for Kyla as she replayed the conversation over and over in her mind each day for a week, still waiting for her period, vacillating wildly about what to do—until she convinced herself firmly of what needed to happen.

"You don't love me, Alex," she told him in the student center when she broke up with him. She hadn't wanted to meet there, where they'd had their first informal date, but he said he was starving hungry, so she picked a quiet corner by a window. Very few other students were there because it was so late. "You don't even know who I am," she said to him. "You only love yourself and what you can get from me."

He said nothing until he had finished the remainder of his sandwich; then he looked at her and waited, as if he expected more. But she was finished.

"So that's it?" he asked. "You're not going to freak out on me?" His bearded jaw was set, like he was steeling himself for a blast of verbal buckshot.

"So that's it?" she countered. "You have nothing to say to me?" No *Please, Kyla—let's talk about this*. No *I've been a dink, and I don't want to lose you*. No *You're absolutely right, and I'm sorry*. She was determined to break up but had hoped for a heartfelt response nevertheless. *Please,* she begged him silently, *please convince me to stay with you*.

He leaned with his elbow on the table and rubbed his forehead with his hand. She had kissed that forehead a thousand times. "Kyla, sometimes there are things that happen that you regret, but you can't do anything about them. Some things can't be undone."

Kyla's stomach twisted, and her cheeks grew warm. She assumed he meant he regretted his relationship with her. How long had he felt stuck? She swallowed. Her chair squeaked across the floor as she rose, reaching for her book satchel. No, the past couldn't be undone—but the future was about to change.

"Good-bye, Alex," she said and walked away.

She kept her composure until she got outside, then cried her entire walk back to her apartment in the dark. All night she tossed and turned, glad to have it done with, yet hoping desperately for her phone to ring, longing for him to call or text her as a part of her wished he would come to his senses and want her back as much as she wanted him.

In the morning when she awoke she had a surge of hope when she saw two text notifications, but they were from Jenn Hadley and Becca Monson, wondering where she was—the three of them were supposed to work on their class project together. She had to skip her shower and breakfast to meet up with them.

That was the beginning of another miserable week.

But the clincher had been this morning in the stairwell of Seibrend Hall when Kyla got the text from Alex while she and Becca and Jenn were on their way to give their communications class presentation. Becca, with her laptop in her stylish leather tote, was admiring how perfectly her borrowed heels matched the pink of her power suit and declared it had made her day lucky. Her roommate's friend had lent them to her. As they turned up the next set of stairs, Jenn retorted she was done lending any of her clothes out again, telling the two of them how disgusted she was that the armpits of the skanky red dress she was wearing had been stained by her friend Ashley, who had borrowed the dress a few weeks ago for a date and returned it to her dirty. Becca defensively replied that she always took care of the things she borrowed, at which Jenn reemphasized her point. Kyla was tired and quiet, staying out of the conversation. She hadn't slept well since the breakup. Besides second-guessing her decision to break up with Alex, her period was almost three weeks late, and she was now very worried. In her purse was another pregnancy test she had gotten from the campus nurse that morning to take after their class. That was when she heard her phone chirp. She pulled it out of her bag, startled to see that the text was from Alex.

Hey, Ash, it read. *How 'bout you wear that hot red dress again when you come over tonight?* It was followed by three tiny text icons of wolves howling.

Confused, Kyla stared at it for a moment, pausing on a stair. Then she turned her face toward her friend Jenn. "So who'd you say borrowed your dress?"

"Ashley Stormer, that punk sophomore who hangs out with Kade Colburn. She asked me for it again this morning, but she's not gettin' it!"

Kade Colburn was Alex's roommate. Kyla's stomach turned over, and her body suddenly felt weird, like she was far away from herself. A strange rushing sound filled her head as she studied the text again, slowly shaking her head in disbelief as everything became clear.

Somehow—she called it a miracle—somehow she managed to make it through the entire hour of their senior presentation and do her part well, despite her mind spinning with the newly acquired information. It had caught her completely off guard, but it wasn't like it changed anything. She had already broken up with Alex. She wouldn't have to do it twice. But had she known the full story, she certainly would have had a lot more to say to him. Oh, a lot more!

She bit her lip, staring blankly at Jenn in that sexy red dress as she talked so confidently to the class with their graphics up on the screen. *Unbelievable!* Mentally she replayed her last conversation with Alex, seeing it in a completely new light. He had expected her to chew him out. No wonder he hadn't said much—he was entirely guilty! What could he say? His big, sloppy sandwich had been merely a buffer between them, something for him to concentrate on so he didn't have to look her in the eyes. *Wow—he got off easy*, she thought. No doubt she had probably seemed unusually nice to him, given what he had done. She wondered how long they had been seeing each other. Glancing at the clock in the back of the room, she calculated where he was on campus. Part of her wanted to go find him, barge into whatever class he was in, and ream him out like he deserved. She didn't care what kind of scene she made! Another part of her never wanted to see that scumbag again. One thing she knew—she had made no mistake in breaking up with him!

Right after their presentation Kyla went straight home to her apartment and straight into the bathroom to take the pregnancy test, although at this point it was unnecessary, for it was suddenly very evident that she was not pregnant. *Finally!* Nevertheless, she wanted to be absolutely, positively, and completely sure and took it anyway. She had been coming out of the bathroom with her evidence hidden in a plastic bag right when her roommate Ashley Buckley walked into the apartment with her engagement news.

Now back at her dad's house Kyla sniffed, still gazing hollowly at the photo of Alex and her on the bedside table. From where she sat on the edge of her bed, she reached over for the frame and carefully opened the back, removing the picture. With deliberation she slowly tore it right down the middle of his face.

Across the house she heard the bang of the front door closing and moments later the creak of her bedroom door as her father peeked in.

"That was quick," she said. "Some seriously fast food."

"We cancelled," he replied, stepping into the room. "I had him bring me home so I could find out what's going on. But I got this." He held up a bag of submarine sandwiches.

"I told you I'm not hungry."

"Okay." He stood there for a moment. "So what's going on?"

"Nothing."

He huffed. "Baloney." His eyes dropped to the torn photo she held inconspicuously between her knees. "Did Alex break up with you?"

"Nope." She shook her head. "*I* broke up with *him*." She turned her head away so he wouldn't see her new flood of tears.

"Ah, honey." He set the sandwiches on the desk and came to sit beside her on the bed.

She sniffed again and wiped her cheeks, then lay down and curled up on the bedspread, crying freely into the ruffled pillow sham. He placed his hand on her leg and sat there quietly.

"What happened?" he asked softly after a while.

She shook her head. She couldn't tell him anyway.

"Obviously you had a reason. Are you okay? Did he hurt you?"

Her voice was muffled by the pillow. "I don't want to talk about it."

"Okay. Well, I'm here." He rested his hand on her leg for a while longer, then with a sigh stretched out onto the bed beside her, crossing his feet and folding his hands on his stomach.

Kyla lay on her side with her back to him, hugging her pillow, crying harder now. *How did this happen? How in the world did this happen?* They had been such good friends at the beginning. She had adored him! While they had dated she had actually felt proud that so many girls flirted with him, like somehow she was special because she got Alex, the handsome prize, and he wanted *her*. How naive she had been! Oh, he always had thrived on the attention of others, especially pretty girls, but she had never been threatened by them because she never doubted his love. She had never doubted him. Somehow in her mind sex had equaled love, and she had given it freely. And sex, to her, had meant she had his loyalty. Her stomach gave a painful twist. At this point it was a toss-up for which felt worse—his betrayal or her blazing stupidity. She felt like she could die from both.

"It hurts, Dad," she moaned into the pillow. "It hurts so bad!" Heartache was a real, agonizing phenomenon, she discovered, as her heart felt like it was being wrung out. Her whole chest pulsed and ached horribly.

"Yeah, darling, I know. It hurts." He set his hand on her hip, waiting as she cried herself out.

Eventually she needed a tissue, and she had to sit up to reach the box on the desk. She blew her nose several times and yawned to unplug her ears. After several deep breaths, she lay back down beside him facing the ceiling, as he was. She wished she could tell him the whole story, the whole truth, but she knew how he'd react, how disappointed he would be in her.

Oh, *thank God* she wasn't pregnant!

"Breaking up stinks," she said finally.

"Yes, it does. Are you having regrets?"

She gave a bitter laugh. "Yeah, I'm having regrets, all right! I regret my whole relationship with him! I regret how blind and stupid I've been! I wish I'd seen this long ago." She sniffed. "It's just so embarrassing! I feel so stupid. And angry. He's so—so—! He's such a"—she uttered an angry sound—"such a stupid jerk!"

"So what happened?"

She sniffed, pursing her lips.

He turned his head to give her an inquiring look.

"I can't talk about it."

"Why not?"

"I just—can't."

After another long silence, Kyla heaved a sigh. "My life sucks. Everything bad happens to me. I am the poster child for a pitiful life."

"Nonsense!" he protested.

"My roommate Ashley Buckley just got engaged today. Everyone is taking their big career steps or getting married, and I'm breaking up and without a job. My life is a train wreck."

"It is not!"

"Oh, Dad—it is too!" she spouted impatiently. "What am I going to do for a job now?"

"Look, hon—just because you broke up doesn't mean—"

She raised her hand, sharply cutting him off. "I'm not working with him, Dad! I can't! I hate him!" She sniffed again, shaking her head. "Everything's changed. I've lost *everything*. Why does God always do this to me?" She brought a hand to her forehead.

He frowned. "What is that supposed to mean? God's not against you, Kyla."

"Yes, he is."

"No, he's not!" he replied just as firmly.

Kyla gave another loud sigh and dropped her arm heavily on the bed, looking up at the ceiling.

He curled on his side toward her. "You know, Kyla, not everything painful in life is a bad thing."

She bit her lip, shaking her head imperceptibly. *Here it comes.*

"Going to the dentist hurts. Having babies hurts. And raising a kid like you." He poked her in the arm. "But they're not bad things. They're just hard things. You've had some very painful things happen in your life, but it's certainly not a train wreck, and everything bad doesn't happen to you. You broke up, and it hurts a lot. But you're gonna be okay. God is not against you."

He was in his irritating fix-it mode, so there was no sense in arguing with him.

"It took some courage to break up," he added. "The right choice was a painful choice."

She shot him a hard look, trying not to react. "You never liked Alex, did you, Dad?"

His mouth opened, but he hesitated. She could tell he was trying to choose his words wisely.

He let out a breath. "Kyla, I care about you. I don't want to see you get hurt." He looked her in the eye. "Alex was a nice young man, but I know that unless you're following God in your relationships, there's going to be pain at the end of the line. Guaranteed."

Kyla groaned. "Oh, Dad—don't make this about religion. Please." She cringed when he went off talking about God. She did not share his love for religion, and everything in her struggled to be respectful. Plus he always talked like he assumed she agreed with him, and that irked her.

"This isn't about religion—it's about saving you from heartache. Kyla, honey, I want God's best for you in all the areas of your life. I don't want to see you settle for less. If you trust in God, he will connect you to the one who is right for you."

Kyla gave a huff of frustration. "I thought Alex *was* the one! I thought I was going to marry him!" More tears. She wiped her eyes. "We were such good friends, Dad! It started out so good! I don't know what happened, but I don't want to go down this road ever again. It hurts too bad!"

He tapped her hand. "That's what I'm saying, honey. You gotta find a man who loves God. Someone who understands what love really is. Someone who will make hard choices to do what's right. There are some good men out there, Kyla. Men like Peter."

Her face scrunched. "What? Who?"

"Peter, the young man who was here this afternoon."

"Oh, geez, Dad, stop!" She rolled her eyes. "Do not even go there!" He was doing it again!

"I'm not—" Kendall lifted his hands helplessly. "I'm just saying there are some good ones out there."

"Oh, well—thanks a lot! That's really helpful at the moment!" Her sarcasm was thick.

His hands dropped, and he said nothing. The two of them lay there in silence until the room began growing dim as the day grew later. Finally Kyla sat up and switched on her bedside lamp. Kendall also slid off the bed and stood up.

"What am I going to do for a job now?" she asked glumly, looking down at the rug.

He rested his hands on his hips. "Kyla, darling, there are always jobs. Don't worry about that today. You'll find something."

Her expression said she didn't believe him.

"Would you like me to pray for a job for you?" His eyes brightened.

She shrugged. "Sure." *Whatever you want, Dad,* she thought. It wouldn't make any difference anyway.

He nodded. "All right. I will then."

She pulled the bag of sandwiches off the desk. "You should probably do something with these."

"Come on," he urged. "Let's go eat. It might help you feel a little better."

Reluctantly she rose, and he held the door for her as they made their way to the kitchen.

❖ ❖ ❖

Chapter Two

Early in the morning Kyla's father tapped on her door, waking her up. He was showered and dressed for the office and carried a small brown bag and a large disposable coffee cup. Kyla pulled herself awake and sleepily sat up, suddenly aware of the wonderful aroma filling the room.

"Good morning," she murmured.

"Sorry—I was hoping you'd be awake."

She gave a long stretch and a yawn, watching him set them on her desk. "That's okay. I need to get up anyway."

"How was your night? You doing okay?"

She moved the covers to put her feet over the edge of the bed. "Pretty good. I slept like a rock."

Indeed, she had slept better that night than she had in the last two and a half weeks, with no bad dreams, no trying to figure everything out, and no tossing and turning with worry that she was pregnant. She had found it comforting to be back in her own quiet bedroom, in her own familiar bed, between her old, favorite sheets.

"Good. I'm glad." He nodded. "I have to head out. Will you be here at noon? I could take an extended lunch. Maybe meet you somewhere if you want."

She shook her head, yawning again. "No, I should get back. I've got a lot to do before finals on Monday."

"Okay. Thought so. I just wanted to say good-bye before I left. And bring you this." He gestured to the coffee.

"Thanks, Dad." She rose to give him a hug. "Thanks for everything. For listening and letting me talk last night."

"You're my girl," he said, squeezing her tightly. "I'm glad you came home."

"Me too."

He kissed her cheek. When he stepped back, his hand went to rest on the back of the chair over which the black dress still lay draped. His eyes dropped to it a moment, and then he brought his gaze up to her again. Immediately Kyla tensed. She knew what he was thinking and what he was about to say. She couldn't count the number of times she had heard it—*Kyla, you don't have to twist your tail or dress like that to get attention. You are beautiful just as you are, and any boy who can't see that doesn't deserve you.* She wanted to tell him she wasn't in high school anymore. She knew it was futile for her to explain the dress, for it would only make things worse, since she had worn the dress to manipulate her grade, and he would freak at her juvenile behavior.

"Honey," he started, then paused, shaking his head, "you looked absolutely stunning in that dress yesterday."

She swallowed. Sometimes the things her dad said surprised her. "Thanks," she replied.

"What was the occasion?"

Kyla shifted awkwardly. "It's a long story. I had to dress up for a class."

His head lifted in a nod. "Huh. Well, you are a beautiful woman, Kyla."

She felt his sincerity. But she could see a dozen other statements in his eyes too—concern, the worry of a protective father, dreams and desires for her life. *Be careful*, his eyes said. *Be careful.* Reaching into his shirt pocket, he retrieved a small hot-pink object the size of a domino. A flash drive.

"I want to give you this," he continued, holding it out to her. "From your mom. I think it might be time to try again."

She met his eyes, then looked at the flash drive. She knew exactly what he had put on it. Before she had died, her mother had recorded five video messages for Kyla to watch when she was older. She took it, closing her palm around it.

"I'll try."

He nodded. "You're gonna be okay. I'll be up next Saturday to help you move out. And in the meantime I'll be praying for your finals. And for everything else, of course."

"Thanks."

"Bye, sweetheart," he said, kissing her again. "I love you. Call me if you need me, okay?"

"Love you too, Dad. I will."

A cautious sip confirmed that the steaming brew left on her desk was Kyla's favorite specialty coffee from the local donut shop in downtown Stanton. Closing her eyes, she inhaled deeply its wonderful smell. Her dad was awesome about remembering little things like that, and it made her feel special. She set it down and rustled open the paper bag, discovering a sesame bagel wrapped in tissue, toasted perfectly, just the way she liked it. Not only had he remembered that the combination was one of her favorite things in the world, but he had also gone to the trouble of going out early to get them for her. It was like she was holding love in her hand, she thought. Comfort food in the truest sense. She tossed the dress onto the bed so she could savor every bite seated at her desk.

Yes, she was glad she had come home. At twenty-two she still needed her dad. Hanging out with him last night had been a great diversion from Alex, and this morning he had surprised her with his compliments about the black dress. She had fully expected the modesty lecture from him, but instead his affirmation was a salve to her stinging heart. Alex's fling had dealt her self-esteem a hard blow, causing her to question everything about herself. Her dad was not one to flatter someone with an insincere compliment—even her. And he had no ulterior motives in saying she looked nice. But when he spoke those words—that she was a beautiful woman—it was like it stopped the awful tumbling inside and set her on her feet again. At least for a little while. Right now Kyla was very grateful for him, and their time together had allayed some of her gnawing apprehension about their bond.

Sometimes she worried that her relationship with her dad would run its course, that someday he would feel as though he had fulfilled all the obligations of raising her to adulthood and cut her loose. Not that he had ever hinted at such an idea, but still, it was one of her greatest fears—having no one in life. He had his own life now, with his pack of eager young bucks, and she'd had hers at college with her friends and Alex. It scared her that the two of them might drift apart. What if he lost interest in her? Perhaps it was an irrational fear, but nonetheless, she could not shake it.

That's why she tried to be extra careful about their differences. Or difference, really, she admitted, since it was primarily one thing that kept them at odds. God was his core value in life. Kyla, on the other hand, couldn't do the God thing anymore, and that's where things sometimes got dicey. Her dad was always asking her, encouraging her, urging her to do things God's way, which in his eyes was the right and best way. Kyla struggled with his strong opinions, but she recognized how tied her dad was to his faith and was afraid to push back too hard. It was difficult for her to see what was so wrong with people making their *own* judgments about what was best. Who made God the happiness guru? Her dad's life certainly wasn't perfect, despite his earnest efforts to follow him! In their discussions over the years Kyla could acknowledge that God existed, but she had a hard time with anything after that. God demanded too much of her. And she was afraid he would bring more pain into her life, so it was best if God and she just kept their distance from one another.

As for her own core values, she wasn't quite sure what they were. All she knew is that she wished her life could be normal, the opposite of what it was now. And by "normal" she meant she wished she had a real family—a father *and* a mother. Siblings would be nice. And grandparents, aunts, uncles, cousins. But she didn't. What she had was a Korean American father who had adopted her. Period. So she tried to cut him slack when it came to his obsession with God and just put up with it. She tried to.

As Kyla savored the bagel with her coffee at her desk, she regarded the little pink memory device that lay before her. No doubt her dad thought she needed to hear some words of wisdom from her mother on men. Offering her the flash drive was perfectly logical. What girl wouldn't want to hear her mother's advice? It was a jealousy she fought daily—observing mother-daughter relationships all around her. *Hey, Mary—your mom called. Sorry, Kyla—I can't do lunch. My mom is in town. My mom and I went dress shopping last weekend.* No matter what the situation, passing statements like that produced perpetual ouches in the mother-void chasm of her heart like blisters from ill-fitting shoes she could not take off. Almost always she would think about what life would have been like if her mother hadn't died. Certainly she would have had visits, phone calls, and shopping dates with her mom as well. She was surprised that she hadn't become calloused to those mother-comments over time. Maybe she would eventually. It had only been ten years.

Indeed, mothers were everywhere, and most people took them for granted. They were like the paint on the walls on which life hung, providing the color of normal for everyday interactions and experiences. "Normal" had changed for Kyla at the age of ten when her mom got sick. For most girls, that would be all the more reason to treasure a series of short video clips that your mother made for you before she died. Kyla did treasure them. She just couldn't watch them. It was too difficult for her. Someday, she told herself, someday.

It wasn't as if they were kept from her, held by her father until some magic date, although they sort of were at first. Kyla had been aware of them when her mother, Evangeline DeKane, had made them for her while she was sick, but she wasn't ready for them then. So they were saved on her dad's computer—five clips in all, listed by subject: *God, Girlfriends, Boyfriends, Having Babies & Stuff,* and the last clip, *Forgiveness.* When she was fifteen Kyla courageously watched the first one on God. It was only seven minutes long, but those seven minutes unleashed a hurricane of confusion and grief that left her reeling and caused her to miss a week of school. The barricade in her heart against God was fortified after that, and she refused to go to church with her dad again. She hadn't watched any of the other clips since, despite her dad's urging over the years. Eventually he tired of her persistent balking and let it rest. Until this morning.

Relishing her last chewy bite of bagel, Kyla put the little flash drive in the zippered pocket inside her purse. She was glad she had it, but she wasn't going to stress about it. It wasn't likely that she would be watching any of her mother's video messages any time soon, since she knew she needed every single minute between now and Monday to study for her finals and finish her papers. Which is why she'd told her dad she would *try* to watch them, rather than that she *would* watch them. That way she could honestly say she simply couldn't fit them into her schedule.

She wished learning came easily for her like it did for her four roommates, who were always acing their classes with seemingly little effort. Three of the four were graduating with honors. Kyla, on the other hand, had always had to study extra hard for good grades. With her dad, she jokingly called herself a straight-*A* student—*A* for average. She blamed it on missing too much class in middle school and high school during her mom's illness and death and the subsequent visits to the school counselor's office. It was inevitable that she would fall behind. To her moaning about her difficulty keeping up in high school, her dad would say, *It is what it is. Just do your best. That's all you can do.* After high school he insisted that she go to college, and here she was, finishing her senior year already. She was practically over the finish line. She hoped to do well on her finals, but she knew she would have to focus hard—Alex seemed to be prominently stationed in the front of her brain waving his arms for every ounce of her attention.

Downing the last of her coffee, Kyla was ready to go, happy to get off to an early start. She exchanged her old volleyball shirt for a white V-neck from her dad's dresser drawer to wear with her shorts back to school, and since she had showered last night and had nothing to pack, she grabbed her purse and the black dress and headed out, stopping to write a note to thank her dad for the breakfast. She drew a large heart around it and put it beside the newspaper on the counter in the kitchen, where she knew he would see it after work.

Outside, their driveway was still shaded from the morning sun, and Kyla could tell it was going to be another unseasonably hot day for the end of May. She put her long hair into a ponytail so it wouldn't blow around if she had to drive with the windows down, then threw the dress into the back seat and got into her old Chevy, relieved to have it start right up. Threading her way out of her neighborhood, she got back onto the highway to join the steady morning commuter traffic all the way through the clustered cities of the metro area on her way to Bakerton, on the far southern side.

Behind her a burnt orange muscle car, sleek and low to the ground, approached at a high speed and glided past her. It made her think of Alex and the handful of other rich kids at school whose daddies bought them cars, something she would never have. Oh, she had enjoyed his hot, little Camaro with him, yes, but now every sports car reminded her of what he was like. Just like that car, she thought. Selfish, attention-seeking, faster-and-better-than-everyone Alex. How foolish of her to have once actually admired him!

The awful pangs of separation set in again, and she clenched the steering wheel, wondering what he was doing this very minute. Glancing at the clock in the car, she guessed he was probably getting ready for his first class of the day. Then he would study at the library until noon, where they always met to walk to the student center for lunch before her afternoon class. She wondered what he had been doing for lunch now without her. Lunchtime for her had been a daily struggle since their breakup. Kyla marveled at how many tiny parts of life could be connected to one person. At least today was the last day of class and graduation was next weekend. Just one more week. She could tough it out that long.

About a half hour into her drive, road construction slowed the traffic and funneled every vehicle into one lane. Kyla found herself trailing a pop-up camper pulled by a minivan, with two children's bikes cabled to a rack on the back of the van and two kayaks bungeed to the luggage rack on top. Summer vacation had obviously begun early for that family. Kyla wondered if they were going to Tamran Lake. She had driven by its nearby exit regularly but had never been there. As a general rule she didn't do lakes. Lakes and rivers and all the activities on them made her nervous. Scary things lived beneath their surface, and boats were dangerous—people died in boating accidents all the time. As far as it was in her power, she stuck to enjoying natural bodies of water from the shore and swimming in clean swimming pools. Once, however, her family had vacationed on a lake. The camper ahead of her reminded her wistfully of that sweet week, the one and only time she had ever been camping, if staying in a cabin on a lake counted as camping. It had been one of the happiest weeks of her life. Some days she imagined that if time travel were ever possible, that family vacation would be the first place and time in history she would retreat to.

Her mother hadn't wanted to go. She said she was too tired. Too *overtired*, she said, like she couldn't get enough sleep. She had always preferred to stay home in the first place, though she was a happy person, not depressed as you would expect someone with such a strong recluse personality like hers to be, and she was unapologetic about it, claiming she liked her nest with her family better than anywhere else. But Kendall — they weren't married at the time — had made her go. He said what she needed was some rest and relaxation out in nature. He booked the cabin and made all the arrangements, shopped for all their food in advance, and packed up their family of three.

Their two-bedroom cabin had been rustic and private, tucked in a thick woods of sweet-smelling pines, overlooking quiet Wilkes Lake, near which a makeshift stairway of rock slabs and tree roots led down a steep embankment to their own six feet of waterfront. On the cabin's covered porch hung a squeaky wooden bench swing where Kyla liked to sit sideways with her feet up, and near it were two white Adirondack chairs where her mom and Kendall had sat watching her play or watching the sunset over the lake. Every family photo taken captured the happiness they felt that week. One particular treasure was a picture her mom took of Kyla and her dad beside their rather pathetic sandcastle they had built on their tiny beach. Kyla was flat chested, with the thick belly of a ten-year-old and an ear-to-ear smile of crooked teeth — pre-braces, of course. Kendall was wearing navy swim trunks and looking at her with delight. Another *save forever* photo was a candid of her sitting on the arm of her mother's Adirondack chair, holding hands with her while they relaxed together.

And yet another image of that trip that Kyla would never forget was not in the photo album but burned only in her mind. Neither Kendall nor her mother were aware that she was watching when she peeked out from beside the latch of her pine bedroom door their last night in the cabin. She was supposed to be in bed, but she could hear their soft talking and was curious. They were coming in from the porch, and Kendall took her mother in his arms and kissed her in the doorway in the dark. Kyla heard her tell him that she didn't deserve him, and he replied he had no plans to go anywhere but would stay with her forever. That was music to Kyla's ears because she had hoped and hoped for that very thing. In the same conversation Kendall told her mother that when they got back to Stanton, he was taking her to the doctor. That was the point at which Kyla tiptoed back to her pink sleeping bag on the bottom bunk of the log bed. And that was also the point she preferred to stop remembering, for that doctor's appointment had brought her happy world to an end.

To stay with her forever. Maybe that moment etched in her memory was what caused her to finally see Alex so clearly for what he was. *Do you ever think about our future, like you and me?* In her heart she wanted to hear him say that he had no plans to go anywhere but would stay with her forever. That's all she wanted—for Alex to love her and want her with him for all their days. But "forever" had never been in Alex's plans, even from the beginning. He was concerned only about what he could get from her, and he had a smooth way of making it happen. No doubt he had worked his same charm with Ashley Stormer.

The camper had turned off the highway some ways back, and Kyla was now long beyond the road construction, with traffic back up to full speed. Her mind turned toward the week ahead of her and the long list of assignments and tasks she had to do, the first and worst of which was sharing her latest with her roommates. For a second she wondered if she could get by without telling them anything, for she had already dominated the drama spotlight last week with her big breakup. Once again they would all feel sorry for her, and oh, how she hated that! Or maybe, she thought, maybe she could just text them all—or write it on the whiteboard by their front door: *Hey, guys—by the way, that skunk Alex was two-timing on me. Yup. So that's all. Have a nice day!* That way it would be done and over with, and she wouldn't have to deal with the looks on their faces that confirmed to her she was the most pathetic, unfortunate creature on the planet. Yet their solemn roommate code dictated that personal things were shared in person, as agreed on at the beginning of the school year when they moved in by the five of them laying their right hands on a dusty old dictionary, the largest, most official-looking book they could find on the spur of the moment. And since Kyla lived with four very busy girls, she would probably get to share her woeful information on four separate occasions.

Ashley Buckley's was the only car in the driveway when Kyla arrived at the apartment. Reminding herself to call her dad about the check-engine light on the car, she parked on the street and grabbed her stuff, heading up the walk. When she entered the house, Ashley was in the foyer preparing to leave. At the sight of Kyla, she straightened up quickly from putting on her shoes, her eyes wide.

"Kyla DeKane, where have you been?" The shake of her head made her curls bob.

Kyla took a breath to speak, but Ashley didn't wait for her answer.

"Are you all right? We've been calling *everyone* and looking *everywhere* for you since last night! You left your phone, but your car was gone, and no one knew where you went! My God, we thought maybe you even—" She gave a horrified shudder. "You scared the daylights out of us! Where *were* you?"

"Sorry," Kyla said guiltily, tossing the black dress and her purse onto the bench near her friend. "I went home to Stanton for the night and forgot my phone. To see my dad. I didn't mean to make anyone worry."

"Yeah, well—too late! You freaked us out! We were all looking for you last night, but when you still weren't home this morning—well, Stacy said if you weren't home by noon she was going to file a missing persons report!"

Kyla made a little sound of protest. "Sorry. I honestly didn't even think about you guys. I just had to get away for a little bit. Besides, it's not even ten yet."

Ashley took her by the shoulders, frowning into her face. "And why didn't you say anything about the thing with Alex yesterday?" Her words came with accusation.

"Holy cow, Ashley—chill!" Kyla pulled away and backed a step. "I needed some time. I needed to process things by myself. How do *you* know about it? Who told you?"

Her head waggled a bit. "Well, a few people brought it up when we were calling around looking for you—that Alex has a new girlfriend, um, has had one for a while now, it appears." She shot her an apologetic look.

Kyla pursed her lips and flayed her hands. It was easier than she thought—they already knew.

"Why didn't you say anything to us? We're your friends! We'd have been there for you!"

"Uh-huh!" Kyla rolled her eyes. "Right, like I would do that to you, Ashley—spoil your engagement news with a big downer in front of everyone! It could wait. I just needed to get away to think."

Ashley gave a little sigh. "I understand. I'm just glad you're all right." She leaned in and gave her a hug.

Kyla's throat constricted, but she held back her tears. Of her four roommates, she felt the closest to Ashley, with whom she had roomed last year also. Both of them had started dating around the same time, and both were quite accustomed to playing second fiddle to one another. Paul had been Ashley's priority, and Alex hers, and they had been good with that.

"I only found out yesterday on my way to class," Kyla said when they had separated. "By accident."

"Well dear, sorry, but word's out." Ashley turned back to putting on her shoes, leaning down over the gray mat on the floor that was crowded with nearly a dozen pairs of women's sandals.

Tiredly Kyla reached for her purse on the bench. "Well, let the others know I'm back now, okay?"

Behind her the front door suddenly burst open, banging loudly against the closet door behind it as their roommate Mary appeared on the threshold, her eyes fixed hard on Kyla, who looked back in surprise.

"Where *were* you?"

Two down, Kyla calculated with an inward sigh, *two to go*. She started in with the apology first and then her story.

Turns out Mary had known what had been going on for a few weeks. She had heard rumors in the cafeteria about Ashley Stormer wearing some "hot red dress" borrowed from Becca Monson for her study sessions with Alex, but by the time she had worked up the courage to say something to Kyla, she had already broken up with him. She figured she already knew, so she hadn't bothered to say anything.

It was salt in the wound. Kyla was struggling to stay calm. It was time to go. She picked up her purse and the dress from the bench, trying to keep things light until she could get away. "Well, thanks for your support, guys. Again."

Ashley stepped forward, laying her hand on her arm. "Look, Kyla— no one thinks badly about you!"

"Yeah," Mary said in agreement. "If anything, it shows Alex for the jerk he is."

Kyla gave a little smile. "Thanks, guys. Who knows? Maybe if I try hard enough I can drum up some new drama for next week too!"

Mary and Ashley gave a sympathetic laugh, and their little group dispersed. Kyla crossed the house to her room, which was the smallest of the three bedrooms, but she had it to herself unlike the others, who shared theirs. On her unmade bed in the corner was her laptop, where she had left it yesterday before she had bolted, with a sticky note in Stacy's large handwriting firmly attached to the screen, scolding her for not telling anybody where she had gone. She pulled it off and threw it into her wastebasket. Her phone, which was nearly dead, had fifteen texts, seven unanswered calls, and five messages, all from her friends. She plugged it in and dug a change of clothes out of her closet, pausing by the little vanity to debate whether or not to wear makeup for the day.

Behind her the phone suddenly chirped with another incoming text. Kyla looked back to see that it was from her roommate Jessica.

"Hey K, glad you're home. Sorry about what jerk-face did to you. Love you." An angry emoji and a broken heart followed. Immediately another text arrived. "P.S. Can I borrow your black dress next weekend for a family dinner?"

Kyla shook her head in annoyance. She wished she could make all those dresses go away! Buying them was such a stupid mistake! What were they thinking?

She texted a simple reply. "Thanks. Sure."

On top of her fury and disgust with Alex and Ashley Stormer, the red dress had now made campus gossip. That meant everyone probably knew Kyla's connection to it, and how embarrassing was that! That also meant there was the possibility of the information getting around to her professor too. For the first time it occurred to Kyla that their ploy to up their score had the potential to backfire. What if her grade actually suffered because of what they had done? Her face puckered with the thought. She needed all the points she could get in that class! She hoped never to see that stupid red dress again. And certainly she hoped she would not run into Ashley! She did not know what she would say or do to her, but she knew it would probably be ugly.

At the moment she didn't want to run into *anybody*. She wanted to melt into the carpet of her bedroom and disappear from the earth. She wanted to run away to the woods of Wilkes Lake, where she could play carefree on the beach with her mom and dad watching over her from their Adirondack chairs on the cabin deck. Unfortunately, that was not an option, and her finals would need some preparation before Monday. So Kyla decided against makeup. Pulling out her tote from its slot beside her bed, she packed up her laptop and textbooks, phone and charger, a wad of Kleenex and some mascara for later. Retrieving her keys from her purse, she collected her things and made her way through the now-quiet house toward her car in the street to drive to her last class as a college senior.

Her car wouldn't start. She swore at it, tinkering angrily with it until it revved up on her fourth try. In the middle of her efforts, her dad called. She let it ring, but before she drove off, she listened to his message.

"Hi, hon. Just checking in to see how you're doing. I want to encourage you that God is at work in what you're going through. I'm praying for you. You don't need to call me back. Bye."

Kyla gave a huff of frustration, dropping her phone into the cup holder next to her. God was at work—oh, right! He was at work watching another part of her life crumble to pieces—no, God was at work watching it *blow up*—while doing absolutely nothing about it! What did he do up there all day? She pictured him leaning back somewhere with folded arms enjoying her squirm from the pain of betrayal and humiliation now, on top of everything else she'd had to deal with in life! Her car bogged again at the next intersection. Angrily Kyla punched the accelerator, and the car squealed noisily as it spun out. Guiltily her eyes flicked to her rearview mirror, scanning the street for police, but only a few bystanders had turned their heads to observe her little temper tantrum. Her dad and his prayers! He was so delusional! Plus he always *called* her—he would never text, no matter how many times she asked him to with simple messages like that!

"Dad," she breathed, "sometimes you are just *so clueless!*"

Chapter Three

Sometimes a week can go by in a blink. For Kyla, finals week went by in one hundred sixty-eight painfully slow hourly increments. Nevertheless, the sun continued to rise and set, and each day did pass into another day that week as Kyla kept her focus on systematically completing her next necessary task, one after another. *Just do the next thing*, she told herself.

Being genuinely swamped with cramming for tests and finishing essays somewhat helped corral her emotional pendulum swings of anger and mourning. When she was studying she was too occupied to think about Alex. However, every moment of filler time—while she was getting dressed, brushing her teeth, driving to class, walking down a hallway—was crammed thick with haunting questions that ate at her: *Had Ashley initiated things with Alex? Or had Alex initiated things with Ashley? Had he been flirting with her or meeting up with her for a while? Or had it been just a one-time fling, an accident that turned into something? Did he really like Ashley or was he dating her now only because Kyla had broken up with him? Did he think Ashley was prettier than her? Or was it that Kyla was not smart enough? What was wrong with her? Had she become boring to him? What was he doing right this very second? Did he even think about her anymore?*

Two years was a long time to date someone. Everything on campus had an association to him. Melbourne Hall was *his dorm*. The second table from the end on the far right side was *their table* in the cafeteria. The towering maple in the center of the green was where they met every Thursday between classes. The side door in the library was where he had first kissed her. She just couldn't turn it off! Everywhere she turned she bumped into the powerful, invisible Alex.

Especially difficult was thinking about their last conversation, their breakup, for something he had said kept resurfacing in her mind. He had said something about things happening that he had regretted and being unable to undo them. At the time, she thought he meant their relationship. But now in retrospect, Kyla wondered if he had meant his fling with Ashley. Was he saying that he regretted it? *It shouldn't even matter!* she scolded herself. *Stop thinking about it!* She had already clearly and firmly decided to break up with him long before she knew *anything* about Ashley Stormer. *So don't you even go there!* Nevertheless, she wondered if he had been starting an apology. What if? *What if* he was regretful? *What if* he was sorry and wanted her back? She knew she was crazy, but there was still a tiny part of her that wished he would call her, wished he was sick with the thought of losing her, wished he would beg her to come back. A few times Kyla was even tempted to call him; however, she quickly told herself that it wouldn't be smart. Still, she kept her phone near—but Alex did not call or text, and Kyla determinedly did not seek him out. It mystified her that she could be twenty-two years old and graduating from college and feel so adolescent, like a confused high schooler again.

Her roommates helped. They went out of their way to talk with her, invite her to lunch, ask her how she was doing, and text her at odd times to let her know they were thinking about her. She tried her best to act like she was fine. Every night around ten that week, they would crowd together like cats in their cozy living room, where boxes were beginning to collect around the edges in preparation for moving out, and the bottles of wine began flowing in commemoration of their diminishing time together before graduation. Kyla went through the motions, laughing and crying intermittently with the sharing of memories, then giggling with her friends as the toasts got sillier and sillier through the evening. Below the surface, though, her heart was a mess, and she was never more grateful to get into bed each night to end the day. Soon enough the week was over, and all her projects completed and handed in. Graduation was Sunday, now just two days away. Next on her list was packing up to move home, which she was less than thrilled about, though she was more than ready to get out of there.

Her dad had called almost every other day since she had been back to school. She texted to let him know that she probably wouldn't be able to answer most of the time because of her need to study, so he left several short messages to encourage her, mostly reminders that he was praying for her and requesting her to check her email, at which she fought annoyance, for he certainly made up for his texting deficit by the abundance of electronic mail sent her way. He wrote that he was trying to help her out by starting to job search for her, sending her leads and notices of all different sorts in an effort to find something before the university students got out to flood the job market. Kyla ignored them all until Friday, her first free day after her last final. She slept in until mid-morning, then spent the day packing, perusing his emails on breaks.

"Don't worry about getting the perfect job right away," he wrote. "It takes time to find a good fit. Just look for something simple to start with while you're searching for where you want to be."

Right. Kyla closed out of one email and opened another. The problem was that she had no idea of where she wanted to be. She knew only where she *thought* she would be—at Duvall & Ross, Alex's dad's law firm. But she wasn't.

Scrolling down, she perused her dad's suggestions of interim jobs, complete with links to apply online—grocery store clerk, bank teller, optical technician, server at a high-end restaurant, summer activity coach for elementary students, Bible camp counselor, road construction flagger. She rolled her eyes at the Bible camp counselor link. It was just like him to drop that in there, like *that* was an option! But the last one made her laugh out loud. *Really, Dad?* she said in her reply. *Road construction?* She wondered what he would do if she actually went for it! Kyla sighed, opening her dad's next email. Each of his recommendations was a far cry from the position she'd had at Duvall & Ross. That had been her ideal job. But that was now her former job.

Late in the afternoon Ashley poked her head into Kyla's room to invite her to come with her to a senior party, one of several that weekend. She had on a navy-and-white chevron dress, and her hair was done up cute. Kyla had barely made it out of her pajamas.

"It's in the courtyard behind Brandt. We're grilling."

"Sorry," Kyla told her. "I just can't."

A week ago she had been so angry that she was ready to find the party that Alex was at, get whopping drunk there, and try to sleep with one of his friends just to spite him. She would have never done such a thing, of course, and that she'd had such extreme thoughts alarmed her. Only crazy, whacked-out chicks did that! But then the pendulum swung the other way, and now she didn't want to go out at all, not to anything. She didn't want to take the chance of running into him, knowing he wouldn't miss a single event, since he had to be the center of everything. It made her kind of sad. Had she still been with Alex, she would have been at all of the parties with him, enjoying life in his shadow.

Ashley nodded silently in reply. Then she came in and sat on the edge of the bed. "Would you like to talk? We could go for a walk or something. I don't mind going to the party late."

Kyla was on her knees in her closet where she had just packed all her shoes in a box. She turned to face her, sitting on the floor. "Thanks, but I'm on a roll here packing. I'll think I'll keep working. Is Paul picking you up?"

"Yeah," she said. She crossed her legs and bounced her foot in the air. "I should be packing too. I'll have a lot to do in the morning, I guess. I'll have my mom help me. My parents are coming in tomorrow."

"My dad is too," Kyla replied. "Just to get my stuff. But he'll come back again for graduation."

Ashley nodded again. She looked at Kyla for a bit and then cleared her throat. "Do you remember last year when Paul and I broke up for a few months?"

Kyla nodded. "Yeah. Sorry I wasn't more sympathetic."

Ashley smiled grimly. "I was invisible to you."

Kyla grimaced. "I'm really sorry. But hey—look at you now. The two of you are engaged! It all worked out!" She could tell Ashley was getting ready to share some of her advice, and she wasn't crazy about hearing it. "So maybe Alex will come to his senses and want me back—is that what you're going to tell me?"

"Of course not!" Ashley said with a bit of a scowl. "No, I wanted to tell you that when we broke up, I couldn't see anything good happening at the time. Life sucked for quite a while. But my mom shared something with me that really helped me through it. I know you don't have a mom, Kyla, so I want to share this advice with you from my mother. I think it might be helpful."

Don't have a mom. From my mother. It was like being snapped by a rubber band each time one of her friends talked about their wonderful mothers. Kyla wished she had a mother too, but she didn't, thanks to God, who took hers away. She said nothing, waiting for Ashley to finish.

"She told me I needed to know my own value, apart from Paul, that I needed to focus on being a healthy individual. She said that when I get that part, everything else will flow together more smoothly."

Kyla's smile stiffened. "Thanks, Ashley. That's good stuff." *So you're saying I don't know my value apart from Alex? Thanks a lot!*

"I know your dad has probably given you some great advice too," she added, "but sometimes you just need a mom's input. I don't want to make you feel sad, sweetie, but I wish you had a mom. You look like you could use a lift. I wish she were here to give you advice."

"Yeah, you and me both. Thanks." *Now go away, please*, Kyla added inside. It was an uncomfortable, unchangeable subject that she preferred not to talk about.

After an awkward silence, Ashley sighed. "Are you sure you don't want to come to the party with Paul and me?"

She nodded. "I'm sure. Thanks for asking, though. It means a lot."

Ashley left, but Kyla didn't move from the floor. Instead, she leaned back against her closet door, rubbing her hand unconsciously across the carpet, thinking of the little flash drive in her purse that her dad had given her last week. She had always told herself that she didn't need to hear her mother's advice on boyfriends, that she was doing fine with Alex, so that she didn't have to watch it. But here she was. Things hadn't worked out so well. Perhaps she *did* need a mother's advice. Her *own* mother's advice, not Ashley's. She was going through one of those floundering moments in life, and her mom had purposely left her a video clip about boyfriends. If any time was appropriate for her to watch it, it was now. Plus everyone was gone for the night, and she would be alone in the house. *Why not just watch it?*

She knew her problem wasn't with seeing her mother. Her problem was with God. She still had a huge difficulty understanding why God would take such a beautiful person away and leave her motherless. Since the day she passed away, every moment and experience of her life had been accentuated by what it *should* have been, what it *could* have been if her mother had lived. Watching her girlfriends with their moms, she was conscious of the enormity of life experiences she had missed out on without her, even tiny, simple ones. Kyla knew she was insecure; she knew she struggled in so many areas of life because of her unsureness of what to do. If she'd had a mother, she would know what to do. She wished she could just pack away those feelings and live in denial, but it was impossible—it was a void that was constantly there, like having an enormous empty photo frame filling the most prominent wall of your house, a continuous reminder of someone who wasn't there. *How could God do that to her?*

Kyla closed her door and sat on her bed with her laptop. Removing the flash drive from her purse, she fingered the device, hearing her dad's voice reminding her that not everything painful in life was a bad thing. She hoped he was right in this case. Steeling herself, she plugged it in, and the short menu filled the screen. For now she would watch just one. Only the clip on boyfriends. Her eyes dropped to the other titles, and she shuddered with the thought that she could be watching, with good reason, the clip titled "Having Babies & Stuff." She wondered what her mom meant by *stuff*. Someday she would probably find out, but for now Kyla double-clicked on the icon "Boyfriends."

A flood of memories and emotions rushed back as her mother's face filled the computer screen, and Kyla stared at her still image. Her stomach lurched as she observed her mother's pale skin, her hollow cheeks and dark, sunken eyes, the straight brown-haired wig her mother couldn't stand because it was so scratchy on her scalp. For a moment she looked away, reconsidering her decision. Did she really want to go there? But she had to, she decided. It was time. She had to go there.

Forcing herself to look back, Kyla gnawed on her cuticles, a nervous habit, while her eyes lingered on her mother. How she hated cancer and all its associations! Her mom had fought so hard, tried to remain so positive, so strong. It had been terrible watching her grow thin and weak and waste away. Kyla's mind swirled with images from that era: the mechanical beast of a hospital bed that dominated their living room, the blue wheelchair always parked beside the fireplace where it was out of the way, the large, square toilet chair that was always awkwardly in the way, the smells of medicine and urine and bad breath and casseroles, the pink foam mouth swabs and Styrofoam cups of chipped ice, the steady flow of church people and hospice volunteers in and out of her home, whispered conversations in the kitchen, and pitiful glances from visitors toward herself, a girl of barely twelve. Without a doubt, she knew that's where her aversion to feeling pitied came from.

"How is she doing?" she would hear them ask her dad about her in hushed tones. "The poor thing."

"We are managing the best we can," Kendall would reply.

Kyla looked up at the ceiling, took a deep breath, and blew it out. Then she clicked "play," and the image on the screen began to talk.

"Let me know when you're recording," her mother said, shifting in her hospital bed where their couch had previously sat. She had on a blue short-sleeved nightgown. Her arms looked like sticks.

"It's going," she heard her dad's voice reply. "Go ahead!"

Eva, her mother, looked up at the camera and smiled. Kyla immediately teared up at the sound of her voice. Her face was beautiful, her eyes bright with so much life.

"Hi, Kyla! So, this is my third video. I guess we're on a roll!" She gave a thumbs-up. "I hope someday you will appreciate these and that they'll be helpful to you. It's the best I can do for you under the circumstances. I wish more than anything I could see you grow into a young woman." Then her voice quavered, and she looked above the camera. "Ken, can you pause it?"

There was a gap long enough to for Kyla to sniff and wipe her cheeks before the video seamlessly resumed, her mother again composed. "I want to talk to you about boys and boyfriends." She cleared her throat, as if readying herself for a prepared speech. "First off, Kyla, I want you to know that finding that special someone can't be the goal of your life. You need to know that you are a special person all by yourself, created with gifts and talents. And God's got a fulfilling life in store for you. Period. So don't be too obsessed with having a boyfriend. Follow God first. Do things his way. He'll give you what you need in the right time."

She paused, concentrating on drawing a deep breath before continuing. "I wish you could know me, and the irony of me sharing this. Everything about my life is a picture of what *not* to do. I'm so ashamed. You could never understand how wrong I lived. I don't deserve anything good, but you are the jewel that came out of all those ashes, and I thank God for you." She smiled, showing a mouthful of beautiful teeth. "And Ken— Ken is a pure miracle from God.

"If it were up to me, I'd keep you from dating altogether. Seriously, most of it ends in trouble or heartbreak. I made so many mistakes." She paused for another deliberate breath. "So, don't date anyone you couldn't see yourself married to. Make sure he loves God. For real. And when you find a guy you really like, be sure that he respects you—that he respects who you are as a person, and that he respects your body—your mind *and* your body. God wired your bodies to want each other. It's natural. But you need to know that it's hard to reverse things once you start—well, you know. It's like trying to crawl up a water slide—it's just meant to go the other way. So be careful."

"Eva, she's eleven!" her father's voice interjected.

Her mom looked to where he stood. "She'll be older someday."

She turned her face back at the camera. "Don't let guys just have you. You're worth more than that. He should marry you if he wants you. And as you're searching for love, I hope you find your value first from God. Imagine you're someone really important—like a princess—because you are. You're worth having a guy respect you and treat you right." She had a short fit of coughing and reached for the Styrofoam cup beside her bed to drink from the straw.

"So, Kyla, behave yourself. Don't flirt and throw yourself at boys.

Don't dress like—well, be sensible with how you dress. Boys notice things you might not realize. Follow God with all your heart. Remember that sin will lead you down a hard and costly path, even if you don't think so. And if you screw it up, like I did, well, you can trust that God is able to fix the mess. He truly can. The key to—" Her voice became strained, and she held her finger up, as if to pause the conversation while she worked to clear her throat. "Forgiveness," she said finally, "forgiveness is the key to a fresh start."

With another fit of coughing, she looked away from the camera. "Ken, I think that's all I can do for now," she said, and the clip ended with her mother in mid-cough.

Kyla sat motionless on the bed for a while, frozen in time as an eleven-year-old again with a powerful longing for her mom, the scab once again ripped off her awful wound. Back was the familiar ache of emptiness that clawed for relief that would never come. She felt starved for her mom's love, her voice, her touch. How she wished she could crawl into the video and lie next to her mother on the bed, as she had done so often until it had gotten too painful for her! How could the hurt still be this fresh? *Her face! Her beautiful face!* Emotions tumbling, Kyla got up and roamed through the house. In the kitchen she stopped to get a drink from the refrigerator and ended up lying with her head down on the countertop, crying into a dishtowel with deep, howling sobs from her belly. Grief was a beast that wouldn't die. It was kept alive by love.

When she had finished crying herself out, Kyla wandered into the living room and sat tiredly on the arm of the puffy green couch, absently staring out the large window at the wooden fence border of their short and plain backyard. She felt a slight comfort in her mom's self-admitted failures, that apparently Kyla wasn't the only one who had dated a loser who didn't respect her. Her mom's advice lined up with what Ashley's mom had told her—to know her own value. To see herself as being worth having a guy treat her right. She pursed her lips as she thought about Alex. That was the problem, and she felt a twinge of shame and regret about it—she had given herself far too easily to Alex. No, he hadn't respected her body or her mind, but she was just as much at fault as Alex in their relationship, for she had definitely wanted all of him, a willing partner, through and through. She wondered what her mom would say about her and Alex if she were there to talk to face to face. Would she be sympathetic and comforting? Or would she be frustrated with her?

Lost in her thoughts, Kyla slid down onto the couch, pulling her legs up to hug them. One thing she had forgotten was how religious her mother had been at the end of her life. Ordinarily she thought of her dad as the religious one and remembered her mother mostly as she had been before she got sick. Up until her mother's diagnosis, Kyla could not recall ever going to church as a family. After her mom had learned she had cancer, it was one of the first things she had done. *God is punishing me*, Kyla had heard her mother tell Kendall, and she needed to go make things right. She had asked him to come with her, but he wasn't interested. For a long time he stayed home, but Kyla had no choice in the matter. Her mother brought her to church with her regularly. Kyla always wondered why she wanted to go so much, because every week for a long time, her mother would only cry while she was there, throughout the entire church service, until one Sunday when the pastor talked to her for a long time after church and prayed with her. After that, Kyla remembered her mother being happier than she had ever been. She started singing church songs at home and reading her Bible until she got too sick to do either.

Several months after her mom started going to church, Kendall finally agreed to go too, but only to quell her persistent urging. Ironically that's when he changed too—even more so than her mother. It wasn't entirely bad, Kyla decided, because that's when he immediately married Eva and adopted Kyla. From Kyla's point of view, her parents' religion had helped both of them cope with her mom's illness. It was fine for them, but for her it was only confusing. And maddening. When she was fifteen, Kyla decided that she couldn't trust God—after watching her mother's video clip about him. That was when she told her dad she wouldn't go to church with him anymore, although he tried his hardest to make her go.

Preoccupied with her thoughts, Kyla chewed on her thumb, feeling a bit guilty. She longed to hang on every word her mother spoke in this one of her final messages, but simultaneously she also felt herself pull away, conflicted. Part of her, she had to admit, was a little disappointed. Her mom had filmed the video message ten years ago, and Kyla wasn't a little girl anymore. Yeah, most of it was good advice, and she was grateful for it, but times had changed. The princess part was downright corny, and seriously, no one waited until marriage to have sex anymore, even if that *was* in the Bible. Her mother was just like her dad. They really were a pair. They didn't just mention God casually and business-like, but they talked about God with feeling, with—with *love*, which both mystified and grated Kyla. Her jaw tightened stubbornly as she hugged her knees. She didn't want God. As far as Kyla could tell, God must have it in for her, for she saw herself like a magnet for things that could go wrong. From her perspective, her life had been one long, continuous string of unfortunate circumstances, courtesy of a God who was not as powerful as he made himself out to be.

Kyla had once heard that a person never fully recovers from the loss of a mom when she dies young, and she believed it. And from what she had studied in her psych classes, she could clearly testify about anger as a stage of grief, sort of like the debris and mess left after a hurricane or flood. Sometimes people never bounced back. She got that. She was angry, all right. God had taken her mother, and she resented him for it. Her bitterness toward him was something that she had grown accustomed to living with in the last ten years. For the sake of her relationship with her dad, Kyla had learned to dial it in some, showing him respect for the way he was. But she didn't want anything to do with God personally.

And yet her mother loved God so. That meant Kyla had to close herself to a part of her own mother. It was a terrible dichotomy to resist the very one she mourned for. In some ways this made her even angrier with God. And in some ways it made her feel terribly sad and guilty. It was like she was split in two, as if in her mind there were two toddlers in full meltdown—one bawling, in need of comfort, while the other raged with a temper tantrum. Who could understand the war inside her? Who could she talk to about it? And who could fix it? No one.

With a sigh, Kyla got up and returned to her bedroom. The flash drive was still protruding from the side of her laptop, and she humored herself with the thought that if she wanted to be really miserable, she could watch her mom's video on girlfriends! Relationships with friends had often been challenging for her, and she knew she had a lot to learn. More than likely the video on girlfriends would accentuate her feelings of failure in her friendships as well as her relationship with Alex! Why not be a well-rounded failure in every area of life? Snickering to herself, Kyla ejected the drive and returned it to her purse. Then she turned on her music and packed more of her stuff, leaving out the clothes she needed for the next two days.

Eventually the sun went down and it grew dark outside. Kyla usually stayed up much later, but being the only one home was strange for her, and it made her sleepy. After a quick shower she got ready for bed. Right before turning off the lights, she checked her phone and was jarred awake—she had a text from Alex!

"Can we talk?" was all it said.

Kyla felt the breath sucked out of her. Checking closer, she noticed it had come earlier that evening, probably while she had been crying in the kitchen. She stared at the phone in her hand, adrenaline surging through her body. *Now you want to talk?* she thought. *After leaving me hanging all this time?* Flustered, she paced restlessly around her room, her thoughts going haywire. Finally she texted "no" in reply, although she decided that if he asked again she would say yes.

But her phone remained silent all night, and Kyla lay awake wondering what her mother would counsel her if she could poke her head into the room and come sit beside her on the bed. Sometimes love was complicated.

Chapter Four

As promised, Kyla's dad came late Saturday morning with a borrowed truck to help her move out of her apartment. Together they dismantled her bed and hoisted it into the back of the truck, then jigsaw-puzzled her other furniture and boxes around it. True to his nature, after Kyla's belongings were packed and loaded, he spent the rest of the afternoon helping the other girls' fathers and boyfriends haul the rest of the heavy things out of the house too. Meanwhile Kyla and her friends divided up the refrigerator and cupboard items and cleaned the house, vacuuming to the corners. They were sweaty and spent when finished.

For dinner Kendall had Kyla choose the restaurant in Bakerton that she would miss the most now that she was finished with her college years. She chose a local burger joint where she had worked her sophomore year, since she knew her dad would like it. They left the truck at her apartment and he drove her car, and she was glad, for on the drive to the restaurant he saw firsthand how her car was behaving, firmly declaring it unsafe. Her engine would need to be looked at first thing next week, he said, and he expected it to be a major repair. Then he expounded on how her car had always been a money pit and that he regretted buying it. He said it was time to think about selling it and looking for another used vehicle. That would be great, Kyla thought, except for the accompanying car payments, which weren't exactly something she could afford right now.

Car payments and student loan payments—two of the harsh realities of being out of college. Everything cost money. The last two summers Kyla had moved directly up to Bridgewater after school to live with Alex's sister Kate in her summer house for free while she had worked for their dad's firm. With few expenses, Kyla had raked in the cash. Kate had a pool, and oh, did they have some great times there, especially when Kate wasn't home! It had been a carefree time. Kyla shook herself from thinking about

Alex again. All her future plans had been built around him, and now those idyllic days were over. Change was hard.

"Have you had a chance to look at the emails I sent you?" Her dad broke into her thoughts as he parked the car in the restaurant lot. "I hear the new medical claims company in town is hiring. I sent you their information."

"Yeah?" Kyla mused. She hadn't seen that one. "That's a possibility—although I kinda had my heart set on working road construction." She shot him a crazy look, and they both laughed.

"Yeah, I got a kick out of that one too." He gave her a wink and turned to get out of the car.

"I was thinking of maybe not getting a job at all." Opening her door, Kyla breathed in the luscious smell of grilled meat and French fries.

"Oh?" He gave her an inquiring look over the top of her vehicle.

"Yeah. I'm going to stay home and watch movies all summer. I'll be a hermit."

"Ah, I see," he said. They crossed the parking lot, and he held the door open for her. "And how will you pay your rent?"

"Since when have you ever charged me rent?"

"Starting tomorrow night when you get home." He had a glint in his eye.

Kyla furled her brow playfully. "In that case I'm moving out. I'm going to move somewhere and live off the land instead."

Kendall laughed out loud. "Right! I would have a hard time picturing that! What in the world would you eat? Kyla, the pioneer woman! You'd be rummaging through dumpsters somewhere in the first week."

"Shhh!" she said, looking at the people around them.

"I take it this same place would also be off the grid with the U.S. mail service, so you wouldn't get notice of your delinquent student loans, right?"

"Of course!" she answered. "But I'd let you come visit me now and then."

"So nice of you!"

At their table he leaned forward on his arms, smiling. "Look at you. You used to be five. You used to play with dolls and sit on my lap and read books with me. Where did the time go? I can hardly believe that my little girl is graduating from college tomorrow!"

She returned his smile, glad he had considered her his girl from the very beginning of their relationship.

"I'm proud of you, hon," he continued. "This is quite an achievement.

I know you worked hard. You've proved yourself to be one smart and capable young woman."

"Thanks," she said, adding wryly, "I wish it were a better ending. Kinda feels like the plane crashed the runway on the landing. It's been a rough couple of weeks."

He handed her a menu, shaking his head sympathetically. "Ah, yes. But you know, in the long run this thing with Alex will pass and you'll move on. It doesn't change the hard work you've put in to accomplish what you've done here. I'm very proud of you. Your mother would be too."

He turned to study the menu, pulling his glasses out of his shirt pocket. He always dressed so classily, even for loading a truck. His old jeans were clean and his shirt neatly pressed. His hair had a few more gray flecks around the edges than she remembered. Kyla looked at him briefly, conscious that he didn't know the half of what she was going through. He certainly wouldn't be very proud of her if he knew the full story, she thought. She wondered what it would be like living at home again now that she'd had a taste of living on her own.

"I listened to Mom's advice on boyfriends last night," Kyla told him.

He glanced up from the menu over the top of his glasses. "Yes? How did it go?"

She gave a little shrug. "Hard."

His cheek twitched in acknowledgment. "Well, good for you."

Their server passed their table, stopping to give them water. Kendall put his menu down, and they ordered their food right away. Then he adjusted the blinds on the window next to their table so that the sun was not in his eyes.

"So how did you know that Mom was the one?" she asked him after he had finished. "Give me the details of how you got together again."

He took a drink, setting the glass back down onto the same circle of condensation. "I'm surprised you don't remember it yourself. Back when I managed the Stanton Senior Care facility, I walked past Skillings Park on my way home from work every night, and she'd be there pretty often. There she was—this beautiful woman with the cutest little girl. She'd hang back and watch you play, always wearing a sunhat and sunglasses, even if it was cloudy. And she always sat by herself. So mysterious and aloof. I kept thinking she looked like she needed a friend. So one day I got brave and asked her out."

Outings to Skillings Park had been a normal part of Kyla's childhood, since it was the nearest to their home. She did remember her mother always keeping to herself, but that was how she was. She could not recall when Kendall had entered their lives.

"So where did you go on your date?"

"Nowhere!" He laughed. "She said no! But I thought I'd keep trying, so I made a point of saying hello to her whenever I saw her, and I'd stop to push you on the swing a little. Eventually she started to smile when I'd come around, and we'd sit and talk a bit."

"And you asked her out again?"

He shook his head. "No, not for a long time. I would just play with you, and then we'd chat. Almost every evening for quite a while." His eyes twinkled. "I even faked that I was coming home from work on my days off."

Kyla didn't remember that part of the story. "So what happened?"

Kendall chuckled. "Well, the season changed. In the fall it got cold and rainy, and she didn't bring you to the park for a week. I was driving to work then, but I'd stop every evening on my way home and wait to see if she would come. And sure enough, one day she did—the two of you were there in the park, standing out in the rain, both of you with umbrellas, and you bundled up in a puffy coat. It was so cold that day. That's when I knew she had come there for me." He was looking down at the table with a wistful smile on his face.

"Huh." She paused, giving him a moment. "Glad you were patient."

"Me too." He gave her a wink.

Kyla fiddled with the tape that held her bundle of silverware in the napkin. Alex had been patient too, at the beginning of their relationship. How was she to know they would crash and burn?

"I wish there were some kind of warning system with guys that made dating easier and saved you from crap down the road. Like a little light on their foreheads that only dating prospectives could see. Red light—stay away from him! Yellow light—proceed with caution!" She stopped and dropped her hand. "What? Why are you looking at me like that?"

Her dad had a broad grin on his face. "There is! I know just the thing!"

She tipped her head. "Okay, what?"

"The Word of God. It's quite a good warning system if you—"

She made an impatient sound. "That's not what I had in mind!" She shook her head. "Besides—you and Mom had nothing to do with religion, and the two of you were soul mates."

He gave a nod. "True. But both of us would agree we weren't truly complete until we started following Jesus."

Kyla blinked and clamped her lips together.

"Send the guys my way first," he added. "I'll prescreen them for you."

Kyla bit her lip and shook her head.

"You know, your grandparents had an arranged marriage," he said, continuing. "Although my dad sort of cheated, because he made it very clear to his dad who he was in love with, and it worked in his favor. That was right before they moved to Seattle."

That story she remembered. "Please tell me you're not offering to arrange a marriage for me," she said dryly.

Her dad gave a twisted smile. "No, but I could if you'd like. I know some green light men."

"Dad, stop."

"This young man that I've been meeting with for the last year—"

"Dad!" Kyla sat back abruptly against the back of the booth. "Do *not* set me up with one of your guys! I've been down that road, and it wasn't fun. I mean it! Seriously, if you say one more thing about how great this guy or that guy is, I am going to walk out of this restaurant and drive away without you!"

He laughed and held up his hands. "Okay! All right! I'm sorry! I'm done." He let out a breath and grew serious, reaching his arm across the table toward her. "Kyla, honey, I can see this thing with Alex is eating you up. Just forgive him. Forgive him and let him go. You carry so many things inside, so many burdens. You need to forgive and let those things go. Life will go on, and you'll be okay."

She ignored his hand. "It's not that easy to just 'let it go.' I can't. And your pat answers don't help any. I'm just—I'm having a hard time."

He was silent, looking thoughtfully at her. Finally he pulled his arm back. "Okay. I'm sorry." He sighed. "Look—why don't you come home with me tonight? We can go to church together in the morning and be back here in plenty of time for your graduation ceremony."

"I can't. I have a senior brunch in the morning." It was true, so she had a valid excuse for once.

Just then their burgers arrived, and the subject changed.

After dinner they returned to her apartment, and Kyla walked her dad to the white pickup truck parked in the street. Before he left they made plans for the next day—what time he should be at the field and where they would meet up after the graduation ceremony tomorrow. As usual, it would be only the two of them, as her mother had no relatives, and her dad's parents wouldn't be coming from out West. Then she hugged him good-bye, and he gave her an affectionate peck on the cheek before climbing into the truck and bringing it roaring to life. She waved him off, then turned back to her apartment.

Coming in, Kyla met her roommate Jessica, who was just leaving with her fiancé to meet up with both of their parents at a fancy restaurant downtown. She was wearing heels and the black dress borrowed from Kyla, which looked completely different on her, given that she was pencil thin and less endowed. Her fiancé was wearing a suit and tie. Kyla greeted them, admiring them both.

"Kyla, what timing!" Jessica said, dropping her lipstick into her purse and snapping it shut. "Someone was just here asking for you!"

She would have told her straight out if it were Alex. "Really? Who was it?"

"I don't know—he didn't say. Older guy, like maybe forty-something. Seriously, just a few minutes ago! You just missed him!"

"Huh, okay. What did he want? Did he say?" Alex's dad. Perhaps it was Alex's dad.

"No, he just asked to see you. Said he'd try to meet up with you tomorrow." Jessica tipped her head down and leaned in close to Kyla. "I'll tell you one thing—he must be rich, because he had one super-hot car!" She laughed, and then the couple left.

Ashley was heading out right behind her in her tight leather pants and hair in a stylish updo. "Big party at Jimmy Sykeston's tonight," she said. "Keep it under the radar, though!" She raised her eyebrows at her.

"Got it," Kyla said as Ashley swept past her out the door.

Another night of parties she would not be attending.

"Hello?" Kyla hollered into the apartment from the living room, but no one else was home.

Void of furniture, the apartment looked spacious now. She hadn't noticed before how worn and stained the carpet was. Only a few scattered suitcases and boxes remained here and there, plus whatever necessities were needed for morning showers in the bathroom. Some of the empty kitchen cupboards gaped open, revealing bare shelves. There was nowhere to even sit but the floor. Kyla stood there alone, feeling as empty as the house.

She had left her pillow and comforter on the floor of her room to sleep on. Turning on her light, she sat against the wall, setting her laptop on her loosely closed suitcase, which she slid up next to her. In her open closet hung her favorite black-and-white dress and her graduation gown, ready for the morning.

It was still early, so she decided to take the next hour to look through her dad's emails again and to apply online for at least five jobs, a number she randomly picked that sounded good to her. Opening her email, she studied the options so far. Her dad had sent her over a dozen leads, too many to seriously consider all of them, so she quickly began the process of elimination, deleting non-options, applying for the possibilities, and dropping the "maybes" into a file, labeling them so she didn't forget about them.

Late last night her dad had sent three new emails, and she opened those too, the first one from the medical claims company. Definitely one to pursue, she decided, filling out the online application and sending it in. The second email was notice of a job fair. Opening the last one, she found a forward of a forward from another person. At the top of the page was a note from her dad:

"Kyla, passing this along. Here's an unusual job. Could be an adventure. Or not! See you in the morning. Love, Dad."

Then below, from the sender, "Perhaps your daughter would be interested in this."

She scrolled down further to the original email. "Colleagues," it said, "below is an ad my wife and I placed recently, but I'm sending it out through the department as well, in the event that one of you may have the perfect referral for us. Word of mouth is always best, they say. Best regards, D. H. Grant, Ph.D."

His ad followed, "Midwest couple seeking full-time, live-in nanny for summer months for two children. Secluded home. Submit résumé with application. References required." A link to an application and an email address followed.

Kyla studied it. She wondered where in the Midwest. Secluded home—what did that mean? And two children. Two infants? Two angelic ten-year-olds? Two demonized thirteen-year-olds? Kyla agreed with her father's comment with slight amusement. It could be an adventure, she concurred—or a nightmare. Kyla put the nanny job in with the "maybes" as a last resort. Then she closed out of her email, picked a movie, and downloaded it to watch on her laptop.

An hour into her movie Kyla realized she was daydreaming about lounging on an Adirondack chair watching ten-year-old girls from the deck of a secluded cabin in a woods of sweet-smelling pines and birches. *Wouldn't that be a dream!* She wished she knew where the job was. With effort, she pulled her attention back to the movie, but in a short while she was thinking about the email again, wondering what it would be like to nanny. She had little experience with children, but *How difficult could two kids be?* she mused. That could be a very relaxing summer. Finally, on a whim, she paused her show, going back to the email to pull up the application. After studying it briefly, she filled it out and sent it in with her photo and résumé before she could change her mind. She could always turn it down once she found out more, she reasoned. And *Heck,* she thought, *it's only a summer.* Good or bad, she could handle a summer. That's if she even got the job, which, considering her luck in life, was pretty unlikely.

That was the problem. For her, even situations that started out good turned out bad—like Alex Duvall. She remembered the awkward conversation with her dad over dinner about "forgiving" and "letting go." With him everything was simple—like a formula. Forgive, let go, trust God. Pray, release it, trust God. Even when things went wrong—feel it, give thanks, trust God. For Kyla, nothing, *nothing* was ever that easy!

"God," she said suddenly out loud, her voice echoing in the empty room, "I don't get what you have against me! I didn't do anything to you—I was just born! I wouldn't mind having just *one great thing* happen in my life! Like how about something going really right for a change? Then maybe I would be open to giving you a chance!"

She felt silly after saying it, as if she expected something to happen, but there was nothing but blank walls surrounding her. With resignation Kyla shifted her focus back to her movie, settling down on her pillow to watch. She dozed off before it was over, waking up later to turn off her lights and close her laptop before going back to sleep.

The next morning Kyla awoke to the rumbling of thunder and raindrops pelting against her bedroom window, but by the time she and the other girls were ready to leave the house for their champagne brunch at the nearby country club, the storm had passed. A gray line in the distance was all that was left of the dark front, and the brilliant sun in the fresh morning sky promised a pleasant day. The five roommates crowded around a table for four on the club's terrace, while waitstaff in crisp, white shirts hurried around them with broad platters, serving china plates of spinach quiche, sausage links, and peach brioche while pouring coffee and keeping the champagne glasses filled. The girls talked about summer plans, job plans, wedding plans, and reunion plans, and although Kyla didn't have much to offer, she listened to her friends and engaged in the conversation. Despite the last few miserable weeks of school, it had been a good senior year. She was genuinely thankful for her roommates and would miss them a lot. She wasn't sure what was ahead for her, but she could do nothing about it today. She smiled to herself, sipping from her glass as she listened to her friends. Most assuredly the champagne contributed to her sense of peace.

Beside her Ashley commented to her privately. "You okay? You're quiet."

Kyla shrugged. "Just enjoying the morning."

Ashley lifted her chin. "Well, you look nice today. And happy."

Sometimes Kyla could hear a compliment like that and wonder if the person really meant it or if it was their twisted way to say that every other day she looked plain and unhappy. Today she decided to let it go and relish the moment.

"Thank you," she replied, observing the dark rings under her friend's eyes. "You look—like you partied hard last night."

"I know!" Ashley burst out. "I did! I know I must look like a wreck, but it was so fun! You missed out on a good time!" She popped open a compact, inspecting her face in the small mirror.

Kyla was perfectly fine with having missed out. She relaxed and leaned back, listening to the singing birds and the clinking of glassware on the tables mixed with the sound of chatting women.

Around noon the girls gathered back at the apartment one last time for a final clearing-out of miscellaneous belongings and to carpool down to their graduation ceremony. Mary collected all their keys to turn in to the landlord later that evening when she did the final walk-through. Kyla loaded her suitcase and bedding and the rest of her belongings into her trunk, then donned her cap and gown, ready to head out.

Traffic near the athletic field was crazy, as expected on graduation day, but Kyla found a good parking spot off campus in a nearby residential area just a few blocks away from the football field where the commencement ceremony would be held. Excitedly the girls piled out of the car, perusing their information sheets once again to confirm their designated meeting places for the class lineup.

Crowds of people were starting to gather in the stands. Kyla searched the bleachers for her dad as she followed the line of black gown-clad students all the way back to the front of Harran Hall, a majestic four-story limestone building on the hill above the field, where the Ds were gathered on the sidewalk and on the lawn. She checked in with the underclassmen student guide and found her place in the line, recognizing the unmistakable back and shoulders of Alex Duvall a short distance away from her. At the sight of him her stomach gave a nervous jolt. Alphabetically he was only sixteen classmates away from her, and this was the first time she had seen him since their breakup. She kept her back to him, pretending she hadn't noticed him, chatting with the other Ds around her.

"Hi, Kyla." His voice came from behind her. She suspected he might try to talk to her, but his approach was a lot sooner than she'd expected.

She turned to face him, folding her arms defensively. "Hello, Alex."

He looked taller in his black gown, and it made his eyes look darker. He'd had his hair cut and trimmed his beard some. Kyla thought he looked powerfully handsome, even for a former boyfriend. Briefly she met his eyes and looked away.

"Hey," he said, with a quick glance around at the students near them. "I was hoping I'd see you and get to talk to you." His voice was low.

Right. Like this was his first opportunity. Kyla waited for what he had to say.

"I—I'd like to talk to you. Do you think we could meet sometime?"

She blinked, shaking her head slowly. "Um, no. I don't think so."

He let out a breath. "Kyla, please. I need to talk to you."

"I'm right here. What do you want?"

He frowned. "You know what I mean."

"Alex, why would I want to meet with a snake like you?"

"I know." His head jerked uncomfortably. "But I wanted to tell you—" He paused, looking away, then back at her. "I wanted to tell you that I'm sorry I hurt you. I was an idiot."

Kyla didn't know what to say. What was *that* supposed to mean? Where was he going with this? "It's over, Alex," she said coolly.

"Yes, I know." He nodded. "But I wanted to tell you that. Good luck to you." He gave her a curt wave and turned on his heel, and she watched as he strode to his place back in line on the grass.

Kyla continued on in conversation with the others around her, but she had no idea of what they said or what she said back. Alex's unexpected apology rang in her mind. She wished she hadn't cut him off so abruptly. Was he telling the truth—was he *really* sorry? Or was he playing games with her? Did *sorry* mean he wanted her back? Of course, she was glad for the apology, that he owned what he had done—sort of—but it didn't take away what happened. How could they get past all that? It would be very, very difficult to forgive him. She didn't know if she could ever trust him again. He stood only sixteen classmates behind her, but she could still feel him right there, as if he were breathing down her neck. To her relief, the brass at last began their melody from the field below, rescuing her from her thoughts as slowly the class began its march down the hill.

The graduation ceremony came to pass. First the faculty processed onto the athletic field to take their places, followed by the senior class while staff, families, and friends watched from the stands. The band played their emotional tunes, all the speakers spoke their humor-laced wisdom, and then the long, long line of students crossed the stage one by one, receiving diplomas and shaking hands with the dean and the president, and the ceremony was over. With a resounding hurrah, the class moved the tassels on their caps to the opposite side, becoming alumni. Kyla had graduated.

Beaming from ear to ear, Kyla's dad found her in the crowd and hugged her proudly, handing off the modest bouquet of red roses he had bought her. All around the field her classmates posed for final pictures with roommates, friends, and family. Then came the tearful good-byes with hug after hug until at last the crowd began to thin out and disperse. High with the emotion of the day, Kyla was in no hurry to go, but when the maintenance crew began backing their trucks out onto the lawn, loading chairs and disassembling the staging, the remaining friends finally parted.

"Well, girl," Kendall asked her, "do you need to go back to your apartment for anything?"

Kyla shook her head. "Everything is in my car. I already turned in my key. I'm good to go." It felt strange to be completely finished with college—with classes, with her apartment, with the town. She would not be coming back.

"So where shall we celebrate?" he asked. "Would you like to have dinner here somewhere or at home?" Home was an hour and a half away, but this time of day on a Sunday afternoon the traffic would not be congested.

She was tired. "How about takeout at home in our comfy clothes?" she suggested.

"Sounds like a great plan," he said in agreement. He pointed toward the street, and she could see his silver Toyota toward the end of the block. "I'm right over here."

She jerked her head in the other direction. "I'm parked down there but not too far."

"Do you want to meet me and drive together?" he asked, his keys in hand.

"No," she said. "How 'bout you go straight to Stanton and pick up the food when you get there? I'll be right behind you, and I'll meet you at home."

He told her to drive carefully, and they parted.

Kyla's car was three and a half blocks down the street, but it was a pleasant walk as several families in the neighborhood were outside grilling or mowing their lawns, and the air smelled as wonderful as it felt against her skin. Her open graduation gown billowed out behind her as she swiftly cut across a street, the bouquet of roses still tucked in her arm. These were her final moments in Bakerton, she realized. This was good-bye to a chapter of her life, and she was at peace with it, although her encounter with Alex earlier had mixed her up a little. He had sounded so—so sincere in his apology, and it confused her. Was that chapter *really* at an end? She was starting to wonder if perhaps she should have agreed to meet with him somewhere and hear him out. She couldn't imagine his having anything to say that would change her mind about him, but it was possible—improbable, but *possible*—that she didn't understand the full story.

Up ahead near the end of the block she saw her vehicle parked by the curb. When she had arrived there earlier in the afternoon, the narrow, tree-lined street had been crowded, and she had felt lucky to find a spot. Now the street was empty, except for the snazzy car parked directly behind hers, a sharp red Mustang convertible, shiny and clean, with a wide black bar running the length of the side and a matching black top folded down. It was nice. *Some people have money*, she mused, eyeing the luxurious gray leather interior as she came down the walk. She tried to imagine how much a car like that must cost. The stark contrast between it and her own old car was glaring.

A tiny movement startled her and caused her to suddenly notice a man leaning up against the tree under which the convertible was parked. He was drawing on a cigarette and right then looked up to see her too. He watched her for a moment, then straightened, pulling himself off the tree and stepping out onto the grassy boulevard to face her as she approached, a smile appearing on his lips. Immediately on guard, Kyla's eyes darted to the nearest house, relieved to see a few people out on their deck a short distance away. This man was bold about showing his interest in her, but she did not recognize him, and she had nothing but her car keys, flowers, and a few seldom-rehearsed moves for self-protection.

Nearly at her car, Kyla lifted her chin and quickened her pace, walking steadily forward with an air of feigned confidence. Shooting him another look, she observed him smoothly flick his cigarette away and shove his hands into the pockets of his dark suit pants, still staring at her. He made a little noise between his tongue and teeth. *Almost there,* she told herself, double-clicking her fob to unlock her doors, *just a few more steps. Just get to the car and get in!* Thoroughly creeped, she stepped into the street on her way to the driver's-side door.

"Kyla DeKane?" came his voice.

In surprise, her eyes rose to his over her car. How did he know her? He did not look familiar, but he obviously knew who she was. He made no movement toward her but stood on the grass near the tree with his hands in his pockets watching her, his smile fixed on his face.

"I've been looking forward to meeting up with you," he said amiably.

With her hand resting on the door handle and the car between them, Kyla observed him warily. He was forty-ish, with dark eyes and short, dark hair, his face weathered, with pronounced lines. His suit fit him well, and she thought him handsome in a rugged way, for a middle-aged guy. Kyla glanced at the Mustang, her mind connecting the dots.

"I take it that it was you who stopped by for me yesterday at my apartment," she said.

"Yes," he said with a tilt of his head, "that was me."

As they sized each other up, he made no effort to walk toward her. Kyla stood still by her car, cautious but curious. She kept trying to think of whether she should know him.

"My roommate said you had a really hot car," she offered in explanation.

He tipped his head again. Then removing one hand from his pocket, he held out a square black key fob from which dangled a key. When Kyla did nothing, he extended it further toward her.

"It's for you."

Kyla looked at him, bewildered. "What?"

His hand remained extended. "The car—it's for you."

"What?" Confused, Kyla looked around her, her long hair tossing side to side on the back of her gown. She wondered if this was some sort of prank. "What's going on here? Who are you?"

In an unhurried way, he stepped forward off the curb to stop in front of her car, leaving some distance between them. Again he offered her the key.

Kyla pulled her door open, stationing herself behind it. She shook her head. "I think you must have me confused with someone else."

"You're Kyla DeKane? Kyla *Evangeline* DeKane?"

It gave her goosebumps. "Who are you?"

He smiled broadly, gesturing with his hand. "The car is for you."

Her brow creased. "Um, I don't get it. What's this all about? I didn't order a car. I don't know anything about this."

"No, of course!" His voice was soft, almost winsome. "No, it's all my doing. I'm giving it to you."

This was too strange. It was time to leave. In her mind Kyla heard her dad's voice speaking, "If it seems too good to be true, it probably is."

"Look," she said, "I don't know you, and I'm sorry, but I gotta get going. I'm going to need you to move, please."

He didn't press her, but he didn't move. He simply stood in front of the car, watching her. She knew she could go nowhere with him standing there. She glanced again to the house nearby where the people on the deck talked and laughed, unaware of the two of them.

"I'm not going to hurt you, Kyla. Don't worry about nothing like that. I just wanted to see you."

"I don't even know who you are," she said with growing aggravation. "Seriously, what is this about? Who are you?"

"Yes, of course! I'm sorry. I *am* being rude." He spread his hands open apologetically. "Please forgive me. I was a friend of your mother's. I've been thinking of her lately and decided to track you down. You favor her. Same beautiful face, same eyes." He shook his head, his eyes locked on her face.

Kyla felt uncomfortable. "Excuse me," she persisted. "Do I know you?"

"My name is Robert DeKane." He pursed his lips, watching her reaction.

Kyla's breath caught in her throat, her mouth dropping open. She stared at his face, his eyes, his jaw, feeling her skin prickle with recognition.

"Well, Robert DeKane," she said, when she could finally speak, "I think you might not be telling me the whole truth. I believe you were a lot more than a friend to my mother."

His eyebrows rose as he nodded. "You are correct."

Kyla stood, looking into the eyes of her biological father. It had been so long that she hadn't even recognized him.

She hadn't seen her real father since shortly before her fifth birthday, when he took his clothes and left with their only car. Kyla didn't know what had happened, only that her mother was hysterical with crying to the point that it frightened her. Kyla cried too, and tried to find out from her mother what was wrong. Her mother told her that she had made him leave the family, that he *needed* to go. She never explained why, but only said that it was far better that way for all of them. That was the last time she had seen Robert DeKane, and he hadn't been talked about at home after that.

When she turned ten, right after her mother was diagnosed with cancer, her biological father showed up again, but Kyla did not get to see him. From her bedroom late one night she heard a commotion in the front entryway of the house. Curious and a little frightened, Kyla cracked her door open, peering from her dark room into the hall, wanting to go out into the hallway to see around the corner to the front door, but the arguing scared her. She didn't know who her mother was talking to, but their voices were quite agitated and carried through the house.

"I just want to see her," came a man's voice she didn't recognize. "I have a right—"

"You have *no* rights," her mother told him emphatically. "None at all! I asked you to stay away from her. Completely. That means *completely*!"

"Eva, shhh," Kendall's voice came softly, trying to calm her down.

"The last thing I want for my daughter is to have *any* association with you," she continued, her voice growing louder.

"Eva—" Kendall interjected again. "Eva, calm—"

The stranger's voice rose over his. "You seem to forget that she's my daughter too!"

"Yes, that may be the case," her mother snapped, "but if you break your end of the deal, I break mine! I promise you—if you ever come near her, I tell everything! I have nothing to lose!"

"You—"

There was a crash of the front door slamming against the closet door behind it and a scuffle of movement. Kyla heard her mother cry out, followed by another scuffle and Kendall's voice resounding low and stern, "Stop right there, DeKane! Don't you touch her! I want you out of this house this instant, and don't you *ever* come back!" Kyla had never heard his voice sound like that before or since.

It was suddenly quiet, except for the pounding in Kyla's chest. Too quiet. She heard an unintelligible mumble from the man and then the sound of the front door closing. And just like that he was gone. Her mother cursed loudly, but Kendall shushed her.

"Stop, Eva," he urged. "Kyla is sleeping."

Her mother began to cry, but Kendall's voice consoled her, "Come on, Eva. It's okay. Come on, darling. He left. He's gone now."

Then she heard her mother speak through her tears, begging him: "Ken, if I die from this, please don't let him have her. Please don't let him have her when I'm gone."

Kyla scooted back into her bed quickly as their voices approached and passed her room. She lay awake for a long time that night, confused and frightened. She couldn't remember what he looked like, but from what she had overheard, she gathered that her biological father was a bad, bad man and that it was good he was out of her life.

After that was when Kendall gave in to her mother's urging and started going to church with her. Then the justice of the peace married them in their neighborhood park on a beautiful day. Kyla was her mother's bridesmaid, wearing a white dress similar to her mom's and carrying a miniature version of her mother's bouquet. And very soon after, they all stood before the same judge in court, where Kendall legally adopted her. That day he gave her a heart-shaped locket with a tiny picture of her mother and him in it, telling her that, as this locket held their photo, he would always carry Kyla in his heart. She still had it, somewhere in her jewelry box, but she hadn't worn it for a long time because its chain was too short.

Around the time the videos were made, when her mother's cancer returned and she started to decline, Kyla's mom gave her a photograph of her real father that she had saved for her, so that she would know what he looked like and wouldn't always wonder, she told her. Kyla buried the envelope with the photo in it on the bottom of her dresser drawer under her socks and underwear. She had brought it out to study it once or twice during her early teen years but then forgot about it. She hadn't thought about the photo—or him—in years.

The light breeze stirred her graduation gown around her, brushing the back of her legs as Kyla stood with her hand on her open car door, staring at her father.

He cleared his throat, finally breaking the long silence between them. "I suppose I should have asked to see you or tried to contact you in some way to let you know I was in the area."

Kyla gave an involuntary sound, shaking her head. "Oh, yeah? I don't know—showing up at my car on a street in an obscure neighborhood seems to work fine for me." She shrugged.

His face fell, stung by her sarcasm. "I know. I'm sorr—"

"And a car?" Her face puckered. "Seriously? What the heck!"

"I wanted to give you a gift. For your graduation."

"Oh, right!" She nodded her head, tossing the bundle of flowers into the passenger's seat. Then she quickly pulled off her graduation robe, bundled it loosely and threw it over her seat into the back. "Like, 'Hello girl—here's a Mustang for your graduation—and oh, by the way—I am your father!'" With that she climbed into her car and shut the door, pulling the seatbelt across her chest.

In a second he was leaning over her window, tapping on it.

"Kyla, wait!" he said through the glass. "I'm sorry! I wasn't thinking! You're right—it was wrong of me to show up like this."

She started the engine, biting her lip, refusing to look at him.

"I only want to talk with you," he continued. "Kyla, please! Would you give me a chance?"

She drew a long breath, staring straight ahead with her hands on the steering wheel. Finally she turned and looked at him through the window. His face was earnest, his eyes appealing her. She lowered the window a few inches.

"What do you want?"

His brow was knit together, his expression pained. "I would like to meet you somewhere. To talk, connect, *explain*. Not right here, of course." He gestured to the street where they were. "But somewhere, sometime soon. Maybe tomorrow?"

"I don't know," she said warily. "I have to think about it."

He held his hands out to her, as if in surrender. "That's all right! You can think about it!"

"And I want to talk to my dad about this," she said.

"Of course."

She was silent, looking away from him. She heard the scrape of his shoes on the pavement as he shifted his feet, waiting.

He cleared his throat, offering a suggestion. "Look—today is Sunday. How about on Tuesday morning we meet up at a McDonald's or something and give it a try? If it doesn't work, you can go." He looked pathetic, bent over beside her car, leaning to look at her through the gap in the window.

"I'll think about it," she said, "but I'm not promising anything."

DeKane nodded. "Okay. Good. You think about it."

After another pause, Kyla added, "I don't live here in Bakerton."

"I know where you live," he said quietly, and their eyes met briefly.

Yes, you do, she thought, realizing he had been to her house before. It was unsettling to think what else he might know about her.

"So Tuesday then." He stepped back from the car. "How about at the McDonald's in Stanton near the tire shop on Fourth?"

He knew Stanton well, she noted. She gave a short nod. "Maybe."

He pointed his finger at her. "I will definitely be there. And Kyla—"

She had her hand on the shift.

"Congratulations on that!" He jerked his head toward the athletic field where her graduation ceremony had been. "Good job!"

"Thanks," she said numbly. Her hands were shaking on the steering wheel as she drove away.

Chapter Five

"You can't be serious!" Incredulous, Kendall stepped back from the peninsula that separated their kitchen from their dining room.

Kyla had predicted her dad's adverse reaction to the news, which is why she waited until she arrived home to tell him about her encounter with her biological father rather than call him on her drive. He stared at her in disbelief and then began to pace the tile floor, shaking his head.

"That rascal actually showed up after your graduation! You've got to be kidding me! You've got to be kidding me!"

Still in her dress, Kyla set her keys and purse onto the counter and slid onto the swivel barstool while her dad moved agitatedly about the kitchen. The whole room smelled like egg rolls and broccoli and lo mein, their Chinese takeout untouched in the paper bag beside her.

At the refrigerator Kendall turned with his hands on the back of his head. "And you say that he was already parked right behind your car when you walked up?"

She nodded. "I guess he came to the apartment last night too. One of my roommates said an older guy with a hot car was there asking for me right before you and I got back from the restaurant."

"No kidding!" Kendall breathed out heavily and shook his head. "Unbelievable."

"I tell you—it was the strangest thing ever!"

"Well, I should say!"

Running a hand through his hair, he frowned and asked her again to tell him what happened. Kyla leaned onto the counter, replaying the scene with him detail by detail. Over and over he shook his head.

"And the car," he said angrily, "what was that? Some kind of a bribe or something?"

"He said it was a graduation present."

Kendall's cheek twitched. He was no doubt insulted by the extravagance of the gift. "I would be really careful, Kyla," he cautioned. "I don't trust that man for nothing."

"That's why I wanted to talk to you," she replied.

It was certainly a lot to process for both of them. To her advantage, she'd had an hour and a half on the drive home to work through the initial shock and think about the situation. Unlike some of her friends whose fathers were sporadically in and out of their lives, making grandiose promises they never kept, Kyla's biological father had been consistently absent. Gone, period. By choice he had become a stranger to her, someone to whom she had no emotional ties. So it wasn't like her *daddy* had finally come home and she felt the need to reconnect. No, she decided, that wasn't a need. However, Robert DeKane had offered an *explanation*, and that, Kyla thought, that would be nice. His seventeen-year absence had left a seventeen-year-sized question mark that begged for answers. It would be nice to know why he had left. Had there been another woman? Would he blame her mother? She didn't even really care, Kyla realized. She just wanted to know why she wasn't worth a moment of his time in all those years. She wasn't even sure of what she would ask him. But that was the reason she told her dad—her dad, Kendall—that she had decided to go through with it on Tuesday. She felt like she needed to do it.

"But I didn't commit to anything," she added, "so I still have time to think about it."

Kendall rubbed his chin, brooding.

"So you need to tell me what I need to know," Kyla continued. "I don't know a thing about him."

He gave a shrug. "I don't have much information to give you."

"Well, you know a lot more than I do!"

"Not much," he admitted. "Your mother was pretty tight lipped about that part of her life."

"Then how do you know he was a rascal? I'd like to know why he left—at least Mom's side of the story."

He spread his hands. "Honestly, Kyla, I don't really know. She refused to talk about him or anything else in her life before I came along."

Kyla frowned. "How can you *not* know? She must have said something! Surely you must have asked!"

"Well, of course, I did! But he was out of your lives, and she never would talk about him, so I let it go." Kendall leaned against the counter. "I did meet him once, though. He showed up here one night, a long time ago. He came by to see you, but your mother wouldn't let him. You were probably about—"

"Ten," Kyla stated. "I remember sneaking out of bed and listening from my bedroom. I was terrified for months that some stranger was going to abduct me! I didn't even know what he looked like!"

His eyebrows rose. "Were you? I suppose. I'm sure your mom didn't know about that!"

"I was afraid to tell her! I thought I'd be in trouble for listening in, so I didn't say anything."

"That was a long time ago. I didn't know what to think then. Your mother was quite upset that he showed up here. She was adamant that he was not to be anywhere near you. Or her. As far as I could tell, all the guy wanted was to see his own daughter. But your mother wouldn't have it. Not at all."

"Why not?"

He shook his head. "I'm not sure. She wouldn't tell me. Like I said, she wouldn't talk about it. I learned to accept it and not ask questions."

Kyla leaned back, folding her arms. "Well, there must have been some reason she didn't trust him."

"Yes, obviously so. That's why I don't trust him as far as I can spit!"

She sighed. "I wish I could remember back before he left, but I don't recall much about him. Nothing bad anyway. Maybe he drank too much. Or had an affair or something. Or maybe he was abusive to her, and I just didn't know it."

Again he shrugged. "I've wondered the same, but I don't know. Those were dark days back then, around the time he showed up. Right after we found out she had cancer." He looked downward in reflection.

"Well," she said after a bit, "as odd as it was the way he showed up today, he didn't appear to be dangerous. And he offered to meet me in a public setting. I feel like I should do it. Hopefully I'll find out a little more about the situation."

"Yes, perhaps you will."

After another pause in the conversation, Kendall reached over to touch the side of their takeout bag, as if suddenly remembering they had food.

"This is probably getting cold."

"Yeah," Kyla said. "We should probably eat before we have to reheat it."

While her dad removed the cartons from the paper bag, she got two plates from the cupboard and two serving spoons from the silverware drawer.

"This has been the craziest day," she said, inserting the spoons into the open containers. "Kinda all over the place emotionally—with graduation, saying good-bye to my friends, and the thing with Alex. Then this!"

"The thing with Alex?" Her father turned his face toward her. "What happened with Alex?"

"Oh, I didn't tell you! You wouldn't believe it—he apologized to me! In the lineup before the graduation ceremony. Out of the blue, he just walked up to me and told me he was sorry."

His forehead wrinkled. "Did you—you didn't get back together—?"

"No, no."

"Interesting," he said simply, but Kyla noticed a touch of relief in his voice.

The two of them sat side by side on the peninsula with their spread of choices laid out before them. Her father prayed to bless the food, as was his habit, and they began to dish up and eat. Kyla filled her plate first.

"It was unexpected for sure," she said, sliding the food closer to her dad. "The thing with Alex, I mean. It really caught me off guard."

"Uh-huh." He was focused on filling and arranging his plate.

She unwrapped her chopsticks and picked up a bite, pausing with it in midair. "I must confess, he sure got me thinking about the forgiveness thing, what it all means to let it go and stuff."

"Oh, yeah? What do you mean?"

"Well, he actually sounded sorry. I'm still pretty angry with him, but maybe he really does regret what he did. It made me think. I guess even big jerks can have a change of heart. Or at least a teeny nice streak."

"I guess," he replied, shooting her a look. "That's if he really is sincere. You'd want to see some good, hard evidence of that."

"Yeah." She nodded, chewing her food, wondering if she should mention that Alex wanted to talk.

They ate in silence for a little while.

"So here's what hit me on the way home." Kyla paused, looking up at her dad. "What if my birth father has regrets for whatever happened back then between him and Mom? What if he has changed from the way he was back then? What if he's not the same person anymore?"

Kendall tilted his head thoughtfully.

"I mean, who knows? It could happen!"

He nodded. "I guess it's possible."

"I mean, *you* changed, didn't you—from being one kind of person to another, didn't you? Maybe *he* has too." Kyla was referring to how Jesus-crazy he'd become when he started going to her mom's church. "I guess I'm curious to find out what he's like. And what he wants. He could be really nice now—you never know."

"Yes, I did, and you're right," he said, bowing his elbow toward her in acknowledgment. "That's a good point. You'll have a chance to find out, huh? When you meet with him."

"Well, that's what I was thinking."

Kendall nodded. "Okay. But I'd still be careful."

"Of course."

He took a drink. Then he reached back for his glass again and raised it up toward Kyla with a smile. "By the way, this was supposed to be our celebration dinner, so I'm offering an official toast with our finest tap water: To you, my only daughter, who is now a college graduate—may you find true love and true treasures in life!"

Kyla's eyes narrowed as she held her glass but didn't raise it. "Am I supposed to read between the lines on that one? I take it you are not in favor of me getting back together with Alex. Don't worry, I'm not. But what did you mean by treasures?"

Kendall frowned, still extending his glass. "I promise you—Alex did not enter my mind."

"Oh. Then I'm sorry." Swiftly she raised her glass to his. "Okay—thank you. I receive your wish for true love and treasures. God knows I need both! And in return I offer a toast to you, Daddio, cosigner of all my student loans—may you never tire of me, and may your money tree always flourish!" She giggled.

He shook his head as they clinked glasses and sipped their water. "You goofball," he said, poking her gently in the bicep. "I was quite serious about my toast."

Kyla pinched him back with her chopsticks. "Yeah? Well, why are you in such a hurry for me to find true love? I'm ready to take Mom's advice and not date at all. It's going to be a while until I'm ready to go down that road again, Dad."

"What? Who says I'm in a hurry for you to date? That wasn't on my radar either!"

"Well, what did you mean then?"

He turned his face toward her. "Honey, most college grads are intent on making money and finding love. I am praying for you to find *true* love and *true* treasure, and I believe both are found in Jesus. That's my prayer for you."

Kyla blinked at him. She should have known. "Geez, Dad, you're getting pretty sneaky. Your toast was like a religious code! I feel tricked."

"Tricked?" He crinkled his brow and shook his head, turning back to his plate. "My dear, I would hope by now you'd know me, that I want only the very best for you in everything."

Inwardly she rolled her eyes, turning back to her food.

After they finished their dinner, the two of them lounged in front of the television set in the living room with their feet up, unwinding from the day.

Later, on their way to bed, Kyla paused by her door and said to him, "Please assure me, Dad, that I'm not going to wake up and find some dude in our house tomorrow."

He laughed and waved her off on his way down the hall to his bedroom. "Nope, one is gone for the summer, and the other is on vacation."

Back in her old room, Kyla got right into bed. She was tired. The encounter with her birth father had been a lot to navigate. Things with him could really go any direction, and her mind was tired from trying to figure out all the scenarios of what their meeting might be like on Tuesday. Musing about the day also made her think of Alex again, her mind slipping into the familiar track of missing him, being furious with him, longing for him, hating him, wondering if he wanted her back, wondering what she would say if he called her right now. Plugging in her phone into the charger, she opened her contacts and looked at his number.

"Stop it right now!" she told herself firmly and set the phone down, turned off her lamp, and made her nest.

In the morning Alex was still on her mind. Kyla woke up dreaming of him, turning sleepily and finding herself longing for him. Longing for his body. She cozied into her blankets, remembering snuggling up to his warm back after their nights together. Her heart ached. She missed sleeping with him. *Should she call him and offer to talk?* His apology yesterday replayed in her mind, and she wondered again if it meant he wanted her back. With a long stretch, she opened her eyes to the morning light, not in any hurry to get up. So strange, she thought, that she could know how wrong Alex was for her yet still want him—almost as if she were tied to him. Maybe they were meant to be together. Maybe that was why she couldn't let him go.

She missed the feeling of belonging that she had when they were a pair. Perhaps she should call him. Would he be up?

Twisting in her bed, she reached for her phone on the end table to see what time it was, surprised to find that it was a lot later than she had thought. She must have needed the sleep. There were also two texts that she hadn't heard come in, and she opened them. The first was from her dad saying that he was going to work and would see her when he came home for lunch. The second was from her roommate Mary.

"So my mom and I are at Chetty's in Bridgewater having breakfast and guess who's here? Yup, AD and AS. Two tables away. Couple of slime buckets!"

Kyla gave a groan and tossed the phone back onto the end table. *Great!* Like she needed to hear that! She wasn't even out of bed yet and already Alex had rained on her day. How in the world was it that just a moment ago she was feeling sentimental about him? Alex was a jerk! He had not really known her or cared for her—how could she think that their intimacy was special to him and he would want her back? It had been a stupid thought. With reality thrown in her face any sparks of desire for Alex were now kicked and scattered in the dust. She wished she could just forget him altogether!

It made her think of her mom and the "Boyfriends" video. Maybe it would be smart to watch it again, even with her mom's religious bent. She wished Alex had respected her like her mom said—body and mind—but wishing didn't make it so. It only made her more frustrated. She would have to be way more careful in the future when she dated again. Her mother's advice had been to avoid being obsessed with having a boyfriend. Kyla knew she was right, but her main issue at the moment was being obsessed with her *ex-boyfriend*. She wished she could stop thinking about him. Why was it so hard to break free? If only her mother had included that subject in her clip. And if only her mother weren't so fanatical about God. It was such a negative.

She sighed, pulling herself out of bed. It was time to get up. Padding through the empty house in her slippers to the kitchen, she found the coffeepot full and still hot in the kitchen. She glanced at the clock, calculating how long ago her dad would have made it. Holding it up, she gave it a sniff, then dumped it into the sink to start over. While the new pot was brewing, she found a package of Pop-Tarts in the cupboard and toasted one perfectly dark, just the way she liked it. When both were ready, she carried her mug and plate to her father's study to enjoy her breakfast in her favorite spot in the morning sun.

She loved his room and everything about it—the multi-paned French doors, the wall of books behind her dad's mahogany desk, the masculine woolen rug, the leather furniture centered in front of the new fireplace, a feature he'd added last year. Despite the fact that it was electric, it was a really nice fake and the perfect finish to his study. Kyla wished it weren't already too warm to turn it on this morning. Her dad's well-worn Bible rested on the end table next to the lamp, between the couch and his chair— his "Sword," he called it, at which Kyla rolled her eyes with its cheesiness. Why did he have to be like that? She believed in God, but privately and tastefully, and didn't feel the need to talk about him all the time. She set her coffee on a coaster beside it and sank onto the end of the couch where the sun shone in from the windows, tucking her legs up under her and pulling a throw blanket over her bare legs while the leather warmed to her skin.

Her dad kept his desk neat. This morning there were only five items on it: a classic desk lamp with a green glass shield; a globe, which she had gotten for him for Christmas two years ago, with a mahogany pedestal that matched his desk; his laptop; a small stack of mail; and a framed eight-by-ten of Kyla's high school graduation portrait, with a tiny card tucked into the ornate, gold painted frame near the bottom. Scrawled on it in her father's handwriting were the words from Psalm 102:28: "The children of your servants will live in your presence; their descendants will be established before you." It was a verse he said he claimed for her. Once she took the card off and threw it away, but he made another one and put it in the exact same spot without saying anything to her. On the floor behind his desk, below a section of the hanging bookshelves, was a little cupboard with a dark countertop which held his printer and a few organized piles of papers.

Comfortable in her spot with her plate on her lap, Kyla noticed a new bronze-like sculpture in the center of the coffee table between the couch and the fireplace. It was a resin cast of two life-sized hands carefully cradling a pearl the size of a cherry. It was classy. An engraved inscription on a thin plate attached to the marble base read, *The Pearl of Great Price*. On the table beside it was a note on a plain card, which Kyla craned her neck to read since the handwriting was upside down from her place on the couch: *Kendall, thanks for your friendship and the prayer cover. Peter.* The hands must be from him, she guessed, since its box was still on the floor in front of the fireplace. She remembered him, recalling the awkwardness of surprising each other when she had popped home that ugly day she had found out about Alex and Ashley Stormer. She should have expected her dad would have someone over—he always did, and she had to admit she was glad he had friends, even if most of them were a little strange. She didn't want him to be lonely living by himself in the house. *At any rate, you have good taste, Peter Whoever-You-Are*, she credited him. The sculpture was nice.

With her hands cupped around her mug, she sipped her coffee, considering the week ahead of her. Two mountains loomed before her, which she faced with reluctance. First was her job search. She needed to follow up on the places where she had applied online and look around herself for good possibilities that her dad might have missed. What Kyla wanted was a real job, a stable, high-paying job, but it took connections to get into those places, which is how she'd gotten the job with Alex's dad. But she couldn't see where such a job was to be had in Stanton.

"You worry too much," her dad had told her the previous evening. "Just relax and take your time! *Pray* for what you want!"

Right! Like that would get her a job! She knew she just needed to get out there and start looking.

The second mountain she had to face was the meeting with her biological father coming up the next morning. Those were uncharted waters. She had no idea of what to expect. She wondered what to even call him. *Father?* He certainly wasn't a father! *Dad?* Absolutely not. Kendall was her dad. Should she call him *Robert?* That felt weird too. *Maybe I could call him something like "Bio Dad,"* she thought, but that evoked images of a sci-fi robot or of biowaste containers at the doctors' office. And then she imagined having to outfit herself in a hazardous materials suit every time she went to meet him. Nope, not *Bio Dad*. She could see him now, leaning in and tapping on her car window as he strained to talk to her, completely at her mercy. He had looked so forlorn. Kyla swirled her coffee in her cup. What on earth does a person say to someone who's been absent from his or her life for seventeen years? It was a mystery to her as to how she could be hurt by someone she had no feelings for. Yet she had to admit that she was angry.

So who goes first? she thought, playing out an imaginary conversation with him. *Do you want to tell me what you've been up to for the last seventeen years, or should I start? Me? Okay. Well, I can read now. And I know how to ride a bike and swim and play tennis. I can put my hair up into a ponytail all by myself, and I even have my own checking account! Now how about you? Why don't you start with why you left me and didn't bother to say good-bye.*

She bit her lip. Maybe it was a bad idea to meet up with him. What good could possibly come from it? Where would they even start? How could she trust herself not to be totally mean to him?

And yet the empty space in her heart shouted to be filled. It was awful having no family except a dad who had adopted her. Sometimes she felt like one of those mylar helium balloons with no anchor, no string, just floating through the world all by herself, alone and held by no one, belonging to no one. Where did she come from? Why did she have no relatives? Perhaps her birth father would give her answers. Downing the last swallow of her coffee, she reflected on her last night alone in her apartment just a few days ago, the very night before her father showed up unexpectedly. She had challenged God. Maybe, just maybe this was the *one great thing* she had asked for. Maybe God had actually heard one of her prayers. Maybe.

Setting her empty cup on the coffee table, Kyla went to her bedroom to rummage through her dresser drawer of old socks and underwear. The yellowed envelope from her mother was still there where she had last put it years ago, and in it the photo of Robert DeKane. She studied his face. He was the same person, all right. Just older in real life than in the photo. She held it up to compare her face to his in the mirror, examining their facial features closely. She knew she looked more like her mother, but she could definitely see a resemblance to him too.

Her phone rang suddenly, vibrating on the bedside table, causing her to jump and drop the photograph. She unplugged it from her charger and looked at it. It wasn't Alex. The number was unfamiliar, but she took the call.

"I'm looking for Miss Kyla DeKane," a male voice declared.

"This is Kyla," she said cautiously, wondering at first if it was her biological father or if the call was somehow connected to him. Was he stalking her, and now he had her phone number too?

The man was very businesslike. "Hello, Kyla. Dr. David Grant here. I received your application over the weekend for our nanny position."

Kyla frowned in confusion at first, but then her mouth opened in surprise as her memory was jarred. "Yes?" she replied, fully alert now.

"Well, if you're still interested, I was wondering if you had time to discuss it."

"I am," she replied, "and I do! I have time right now!" Quietly she yanked the shallow drawer of her desk open, scrambling for some paper to write on.

"Great," he replied. "Just a few initial questions: Do you know who I am?"

Should she? Kyla wondered. She swallowed, racking her brain to remember details from the email. She had read over so much information that night. All she could think of was that the job was watching two kids in the secluded woods, or something like that. She debated faking it but decided against it.

"Ah, I'm sorry, I do not." She could feel her cheeks grow warm. *Crap*, she thought.

"Do you know who my wife is?" he asked and waited.

Now she really felt foolish. She didn't remember reading anything about the couple.

"No, I'm sorry," she admitted. "I applied through an email, and it only said the last name 'Grant' with some initials. I didn't get very much information about this job." Kyla scrunched her face at how lame it sounded. What message did that send? *Sorry, I didn't bother to research anything about you or this job.* Her interview had gone south quickly. She had blown it on the first two questions. That didn't take long.

The man responded cheerfully, "Well, Miss DeKane, I'm happy to hear it, because I'm looking for someone who is serious about the nanny job more than whom she's working for."

Kyla looked up at herself in the mirror, confused. She didn't know what to say.

He continued: "Is it possible for the two of us to connect online? I would love to be looking at your face during our interview."

"Sure," she replied. "Could you give me five minutes?" She was still in her pajamas, and she would need a hairbrush and some makeup.

Half an hour later Kyla was lying on her bed in disbelief, her eyes closed and her hands over her mouth. The blouse she had quickly thrown on for the interview clashed horribly with her pajama bottoms, but she didn't care. She'd just found out that she had a chance for what sounded like a dream!

The nanny job, she learned, was for the two young sons of Dr. David Grant, professor of history at Taiton College in New Hampton, only three hours away, and his wife, Marilee Montayne. For real, Dr. Grant assured her—*Marilee Montayne, the famous actress from London!* Kyla was stunned when she heard it and was glad she was sitting down. Although she was screaming on the inside like a crazy fan wanting an autograph, Kyla kept it together during the entire video chat, trying to appear nonchalant, as if watching the children of famous movie stars was something she did on a regular basis. Ms. Montayne, he explained, would be away for several weeks on a movie shoot back in England, and at that same time he would be teaching a summer session at Taiton. Their former nanny had gotten married recently and had moved away, and they were in need of someone to live full time at their mansion home on the backwaters of the Mississippi for the summer to help Dr. Grant care for the boys.

"I need you to understand how important anonymity and privacy is for this job," Dr. Grant told her. "I cannot stress this enough, so if you cannot comply, tell me now."

Kyla learned she would not be able to receive visitors or even tell her friends whom she was working for. She assured him she was all in! Of course, it wasn't a career step, she admitted. It was definitely a temporary job. But the opportunity, Kyla thought, and the connections she could make! Plus the salary he named made her mouth gape. She wanted the job. She wanted, wanted, wanted the job!

Kyla was out of the house to meet her dad the moment he arrived home for lunch.

"You will never believe what happened this morning!" she announced to him as he got out of his car. "I might have a job—a really amazing job!"

"Already?" He closed his car door and turned to face her on the driveway, his eyes dropping to her owl print pajama shorts and back up to her face. "Okay. Well, that's cool. Where at?"

Kyla blurted everything to him while they walked together up the sidewalk into the house. Kendall held the door for her.

"Now, who is this again?" he asked.

"Marilee Montayne," she repeated with emphasis, listing off some of her most popular films. "You know—*Sing Canary Sing, Lilliana, Fervent, Godwin Dreams*—?" She held out a hand, waiting for him to recognize one of the titles.

He raised his brow and shook his head, unimpressed. "Sorry, hon."

She folded her arms and shook her head. "Well, all my friends know who she is! You're getting old!"

He gave a half shrug, continuing on down the hall toward the kitchen. "I don't watch too many movies anymore. But that's great, hon. I'm happy for you. And I bet your friends are excited for you too!"

Kyla let out a loud breath. "They would be *so jealous* if they knew! I wish I could tell them, but I can't!" At her dad's look she added, "I'm not supposed to tell anyone anything about this. But you, of course. They don't want the public to know the kids are there. She's so famous—I guess photographers are prowling about everywhere she is, always trying to get pictures of her or the kids."

"I see." He nodded. "That's interesting. How old are the kids?"

She frowned. "Um, he didn't say. But it's two boys. And he said they're young."

"He didn't say? Also interesting." He raised his eyebrows at her, then went to the refrigerator and began setting items on the counter. "Care for a sandwich? Or the takeout leftovers?"

"I'll have the Chinese, if you don't mind. But I'll heat it up later."

"Okay." He looked up at her, pausing with an open jar of mayonnaise in his hand. "So where did you say this job is again?"

"Outside of New Hampton somewhere. On the Mississippi. In a mansion. He said if I get the job he will give me all the necessary details of where he lives."

"Uh-huh," he replied. "And this famous actress lady—she won't actually be there over the summer?"

"No. She's in England, shooting a film."

"So you won't actually meet her."

"No."

"And who will actually be there?"

"The kids. And the professor—Dr. Grant—part of the time. When he's not teaching. He's the one I interviewed with today."

"Just the two of you? And you're okay with that?"

"Well—" She wasn't sure how to answer him.

"This professor is decent? Trustworthy?"

"He seemed nice. Decent, yes. And I'll be watching the kids for the summer, not chumming with him. He's going to be at work."

"Okay," he said, nodding thoughtfully. "Just a concern, I guess."

He turned his attention to construct his sandwich, carefully layering pastrami and Swiss on his bread. When he had finished, he set it on a plate and came to stand across from Kyla at the peninsula. He narrowed his eyes at her a bit. "Since when are you interested in taking care of kids? It seems a little uncharacteristic of you."

Kyla blushed, looking downward. That was the weak link in all of this. She knew she was not very experienced with children, but she was determined that she could do it. She hoped that detail was not too blaringly obvious on her résumé or in the interview.

"I know I can do it, Dad," she said.

"Yeah, I'm sure you'll do fine," he agreed, raising his sandwich in preparation for a bite. "It's just kind of surprising to me—that's all. And I wish it weren't just you and him and the kids. How soon will you know?"

Kyla gave an excited shiver. "Hopefully this week. He said he had a few more interviews to conduct and that he would contact me soon either way." Her stomach fluttered with the anticipation. "Dad, will you pray for me to get this job?" She couldn't believe what she was asking him to do, and she felt like a little kid. But she wanted the job.

"Why don't *you* pray?" he asked her back.

"I—have been," she lied.

"Good," he said, enjoying his sandwich. "God hears you too, you know."

Chapter Six

Tuesday morning came—the big morning when she would sit down with her biological father and find out who she was. She was surprised at how calm she was about it. She had even slept well last night. Her nanny job possibility was a healthy distraction from thinking too much about her upcoming encounter, and that helped. But more than that, *How could a stranger hurt her?* Kyla asked herself. At least she couldn't be hurt more than she already had by him! There was nothing to lose in the meeting.

Kendall, on the other hand, was the one having the more difficult time. He insisted on taking the day off work to be near, just in case he was needed. He let her know it when she got up.

"I don't think it's going to be like that, Dad," she called to him in reply out her open bathroom door, her toothbrush poised in her hand as she stood before the sink in her pajamas.

Nevertheless, he stayed home from work. She made eggs and toast for breakfast, but he said he wasn't eating. When she pressed him as to why, he told her he was fasting, something he did on Tuesdays anyway. He said he was determined to cover her in prayer and spent the morning alone in his study until Kyla was ready to go. She had long ceased trying to understand some of the strange things he did, so she let him be and ate her eggs and toast by herself in the kitchen.

"You're sure you don't want me to come?" he asked when she knocked on his door later to say she was leaving. "I could just sit in the car in the parking lot."

"No, Dad." She was tempted to chide him for worrying about her, but she realized that in his eyes that moment she was still the ten-year-old girl that Robert DeKane had tried to visit in the night long ago. She held up her finger. "You know what? I almost forgot something. I'll be right back."

She set her purse on his coffee table and returned to her bedroom. Searching through her jewelry box, she found the gold heart locket he had given her at her adoption and slipped it on a longer chain, which she then draped over her neck.

"I'm back and ready to go now," she said, reentering the study and going to his chair to hug him good-bye. "Remember this?" She held out the locket. "I want you to know I'm wearing it today."

His eyes told her that she couldn't have said she loved him in a better way. He swallowed and nodded. "Okay, then," he said, waving her off. "See you when you get home."

They hadn't picked a specific time to meet. He had simply said he would be there. *We'll see if he keeps his word*, Kyla thought, entering the McDonald's parking lot beside the tire shop on Fourth Street. She strategically chose to go later in the morning, wanting to be there when it was busy, with plenty of people around, but not too busy in case she got emotional. Her eyes scanned the parking lot for the red-and-black Mustang, but she didn't see it.

She parked and went inside, slipping past a crowd of five chattering nine-year-old girls and their mothers as they waited at the counter to place their orders. One of the little girls wore a birthday tiara over her elaborately braided blond hair. The others carried girly pink gift bags overflowing with colored tissue paper. Behind the counter employees bustled and shouted over a backdrop of frying grease and beeping machines. Stepping into the dining room, Kyla saw her biological father there in a corner booth facing the door, a newspaper and a coffee before him. He immediately stood when he saw her, obviously glad to see her but reserved.

"Can I get you something?" he asked as she approached. "Would you like something to eat? Or a coffee? Soda?"

For being so confident that she couldn't be hurt, Kyla was surprised at the sudden eruption of animosity she felt against him, finding herself wanting to ask for seventeen years' worth of ice cream cones and Happy Meals, but she held it in and calmly requested a coffee. He nodded and left, and she sat down to wait for him, glancing around at the people near her—a foursome of retired men with their coffees, a technician of some sort in his polo shirt with his laptop open before him, a mom with two toddlers, an elderly couple eating quietly without speaking to one another, a gray-haired woman with red glasses at the edge of her nose reading a novel at a booth by herself. The birthday girl and her frenetic friends noisily slid two tables together in the middle of the room right in Kyla's line of vision and then argued over who got to sit where while they waited for their mothers to bring their food. Kyla observed the birthday girl, remembering having her hair braided nice like that once when she had stayed overnight at a girlfriend's house in high school, and her friend's mom had done it for her.

Robert DeKane returned with her coffee and a refill for himself and slid into the booth across the table from her. His eyes darted around, unsure of where to look, revealing to Kyla that she was not the only one who was nervous.

"Thank you for coming," he said, folding his hands on the table.

"Sure." She gave a polite smile and popped the lid off her coffee so that it would cool faster.

He was thin and of average height. His dark hair was neatly trimmed and peppered with more gray than she had remembered from two days ago, certainly more than her photo of him as a young man. His eyes were dark, like hers, and he was freshly shaven, his skin weathered, rough, and sort of wrinkled with deep lines in his cheeks. He was wearing blue jeans with a button-down, navy shirt, untucked, and he looked nice, she thought, even healthy—except for his teeth, which were stained. Smoker's teeth. He was older than her dad, Kendall, certainly. Kyla thought he looked—normal. Somehow she had always imagined her biological father to be some kind of a druggie or down-and-outer, someone who couldn't hold a job, but that wasn't the impression he gave today. She wasn't sure why she had made that judgment.

"I—I don't really know where to start," he said, appearing far less confident this morning than he had beside her car on her graduation day, most likely because of how she had responded then. "I guess I was thinking about your mother recently—as I told you the other day—and I decided to look you up. Found out you were graduating from college. That's really a great accomplishment."

"Thanks," Kyla responded simply. She wasn't sure what to say yet, so she just sat holding her latte.

He suddenly let out a breath, shaking his head. "Oh, man—I can't get over how much you look like your mother! You even talk like her. And you have her same dark eyes. And mouth. Everything!"

The way he said it made her feel embarrassed, and she wished she hadn't worn lipstick.

"She wore her hair long and loose like yours," he continued, gazing at her. "The same color brown. She was beautiful."

Kyla cleared her throat uncomfortably, looking down at the whipped cream melting on her coffee.

"Sorry," he said, pulling himself back into the present. "So anyway, I just wanted to see you, to tell you that finishing college is really great."

She smiled and gave another polite nod, then took a sip of her coffee, setting the cup onto a napkin and twisting a circle into it with the bottom of the cup, waiting for him to lead the conversation. They sat quietly for a few moments.

He made a little sound sucking air between his tongue and teeth. "So, here we are," he offered into the silence finally. "I know this is a little awkward for both of us, but I thought I'd give you the chance to ask me any questions that you want." He opened his hands to her.

"I would like that," she responded.

He dipped his head. "Ask away."

"Okay," she said thoughtfully, a question immediately in her mind. "Where do you live?" The idea that he may have lived right under her nose during her whole childhood bugged her. She might even have to leave if that were the case, and she wanted to know first thing.

"I'm from Illinois," he replied with a curt nod, acknowledging the validity of her question. "I'm only up here for a job."

"So you never lived here?"

"Only with your mother."

She nodded, slightly relieved. "And what do you do?"

"I'm in investments." He looked down at his hands, which hugged the side of his paper coffee cup.

"How did you meet my mother?"

He was calm and straightforward. "We met on a job."

"On a job?"

"Well, actually we met in a bar, but I asked her to work for me. That's where we got to know one another."

Kyla tipped her chin downward. "Did you love her?"

"Oh, yes, I loved her! She was a beautiful woman." He paused, nodding. "We had a good thing going. I loved her. She loved me. We loved each other. We had fun together. Then it just got complicated."

She blinked. *Right.* Those words sounded too familiar to her. She had heard them before out of the mouth of Alex Duvall and had replayed them many times in her mind.

"Complicated," she echoed. "Let me guess—with me?"

Her father smiled wryly. "Sort of. Having a kid did change things. But it wasn't only that. It was a lot of other things too. Like I said, it was complicated. Things just didn't work out."

Having *a kid*. Not, having *you*. A kid was a generic human, someone's genderless offspring. *Having a kid* meant an interruption in someone's all-too-important life.

Their attention was suddenly drawn away by a large family entering the dining area, the mother carrying a baby nested in a car seat and corralling a toddler with a missing shoe. The father set a tray stacked high with their food on a table and dispersed drink cups to their three older children. He sat to watch the baby while his wife secured the toddler in his booster seat. Searching a large tote bag for a pacifier, she found it and gave it to her husband, then hurried to contain their giggling children playing with the ice at the soda machine. Kyla observed the man starting to make goofy faces at the baby. *Maybe meeting here was a mistake,* she thought. It was always hard being around families whose mothers and fathers were engaged with them.

She turned her face back to her biological father. "So you left and never came back — because of me."

DeKane lifted his hands, defending himself. "Whoa — I didn't say that! That's not how it was!" He shook his head, his eyes wide. "Yeah, we had you, but *you* were the lucky dice in the cup! It was everything *else* that went haywire."

Kyla regarded him dubiously. "Everything else?"

He hesitated. "Look, I could never explain it in a way that you could understand it all, but you must certainly know that my leaving was not all about you."

"What was it about then?"

He shrugged. "Well, there were a lot of reasons why I had to leave."

"Had to leave? What *were* the reasons?"

He shook his head, looking around. "Like I said, it was complicated. Trust me on this."

She narrowed her eyes. "Excuse me, but did you just tell me to trust you?"

He opened his mouth to speak, then closed his lips, resigned. "You're absolutely right. I'm sorry. What do you want to know?"

"Well, I want you to answer my question," she pressed. "Why did you say you had to leave?"

He looked down, struggling to answer. "Okay," he said reluctantly, leaning forward in his seat, "it had to do with"—he tapped his fingertips lightly on the table—"with things I was involved with at the time. My line of work was, um, stressful. Your mother insisted that I leave. And she was right. She was right."

Kyla frowned. "Weren't you in investments? What was so stressful in that?"

"Well—"

"What were you involved in?"

He toyed with his empty coffee cup.

"Did you go to jail?" Kyla remembered that frightening night when her mother threatened him that she would "tell all." Had he been—or was he now—a drug dealer? She studied him carefully—his eyes, his mouth, his skin. He looked clean to her.

"No." He shook his head.

She waited, watching him shift a bit in his seat.

"What did you do that you were asked to leave? Were you abusive to my mother? Or to me? Did you have an affair? I have a hard time understanding why you left and never ever came back."

He let out a long sigh. "Look, Kyla," he said, his voice quiet. "I'm sorry. I can't exactly talk about it. But I never hurt her, and I never laid a hand on you. Honest. I wouldn't have. It's been a long time since then. I want you to know there hasn't been a time when I've seen a little girl that I haven't thought about you. But I can't turn back the clock."

Both of them were silent. He met her eyes. He was evasive, yes, Kyla observed, but she had to decide whether it was worth it to pressure him for answers. After all, did it matter? She took a drink of her coffee.

"So why now, after all these years?" she asked.

He pressed his lips together, nodding. "Right. I guess—I guess I just decided to look you up. I was thinking about your mom—"

Kyla made a little sound. "Uh-huh. So you showed up exactly on my graduation day, exactly after the ceremony. At my car. Don't give me a line of crap that you were just thinking about Mom and decided to look me up! This all took some planning!"

His eyes widened.

"You bought a car. You came to my apartment. You had to follow me to know where I would park! That feels really creepy!"

He straightened defensively. "Well, I knew I couldn't show up at the house! I know your stepfather! I figured meeting you after your graduation was my only chance."

"Chance for what?"

"Well—" he hesitated.

"What do you want?" Her voice rose with irritation.

"To give you—" He stopped.

She frowned. "To give me a new car?" Her cheek twisted. "Seriously? Like that's what you think I want from you? A measly greeting card would have been a lot cheaper and fine by me!"

Robert DeKane glanced quickly around them, then back at Kyla. He lowered his voice. "I was never there for you. I was hoping—"

Kyla scrunched her face, cutting him off. "—that buying me a new car would make up for seventeen years of being out of my life? Um, I don't think so, mister!"

He tried to speak, but Kyla wasn't done.

"But you're absolutely right! You were never there for me, and *you* missed out." She pointed her finger accusingly across the table. "Do you know how many days seventeen years is? It's about six thousand, two hundred-some days. That's a lot of trips to school and soccer games and dance recitals. That's a lot of trips to the dentist. And a lot of lunch money, and clothes, and Friday pizza and movie nights. Those are only a few things. Let me tell you—you missed a lot! And in all of those six thousand-some days, you never even once acknowledged my birthday—that I was a person who you had a part in bringing into the world. Not once. You had seventeen chances! Do you even know when my birthday is? Did you ever think of me on that day?"

His shoulders drooped as she glared at him, and he leaned back, his mouth closed. A deafening silence fell between them. Then, in the most awkward of timing, the group of little girls across the room chose to sing "Happy Birthday" to their braided blond princess friend, crowding in around her chair while a large pink cupcake with a burning candle was presented to her by her beaming mother. Every head in the restaurant turned to watch them sing the chorus, some joining in, until the song was over and the little princess blew out her candle. DeKane's eyes moved from the birthday scene back to Kyla's face. His countenance was pale and drawn, and he looked utterly beaten. Once again, she found herself feeling sorry for him.

"Kyla," he said hoarsely. He cleared his throat and began again, slowly and quietly, "Yes, everything you said is exactly as you say. You are completely right. I missed out. The past cannot be changed, and I cannot make it up to you. But I am sorry." He paused, making the sound between his teeth and tongue. "I'll be honest—I'm here to fulfill an obligation I made to your mother. Yes, it's been seventeen years, but I'm here because I don't want it to be eighteen, nineteen, or twenty years."

Another silence fell between them. She saw his eyes drop to her locket for a moment.

"Words are cheap—I get that," he continued. "And I understand that this is difficult for you—it's hard for me too. But I was hoping that you would maybe be open to building—" He stopped again, shaking his head, looking out the window toward the parking lot. "I don't know. This get-together was just a first step."

She waited.

He looked back at her. "Perhaps we could try to have a relationship. If you're willing."

Kyla gave a heavy sigh. That was what she was afraid of. "You're like a random stranger off the street to me. I don't know you."

"I know." He nodded, moving his coffee cup to the side. "I realize it feels that way right now. But I'm not."

She looked at him, considering his request.

"And I know it's a sore spot to you and probably seems like a joke, but I really do want you to have the car. I understand I can never make up for my past mistakes with you, Kyla. But this is fulfilling a commitment I made to your mother, and I guess it's kind of my way of making at least one great thing happen in your life, even if it *is* from me."

Kyla's breath caught. *One great thing.* She blinked at the words.

"I mean, how often does it happen that someone gives you a new car?"

She stared at him. *One great thing.* It was part of her half-ways prayer challenge to God. Still, this was the man who walked out of her life with absolutely no contact for seventeen years. How could she receive a car from him? She didn't want *anything* from him!

"I can't accept that," she said firmly.

"Right," he said, nodding. He held up a finger. "I figured you would say that. So I've thought about this, and I've decided that I'm not going to give it to you anymore. I'm going to sell it to you."

Like that made a difference. Again Kyla shook her head no. "No, I clearly can't afford—"

"Ten bucks."

She sat back against her seat.

"Ten bucks," he repeated, tipping his head.

Kyla looked at him in disbelief. "What?"

"I brought the title. I'll sell you that car for ten bucks."

Kyla frowned, realizing that he was serious. "Wait, are we still talking about the Mustang? The red and black one—"

He laughed. "Yes, the Mustang. The same one you saw the other day. I'm not doing the old bait-and-switch on you! Yes, I'll sell it to you for ten dollars. Then when people ask you about it, you can simply say that it was used. You bought it from a second party and got a heck of a deal on it."

At that Kyla laughed. She couldn't help it. He laughed too.

"So what do you say? Deal?"

She hesitated. *Was this for real?* It was such an inappropriate gift! Yet she thought about the slipping transmission in her car, and the offer loomed attractive. It was way too good to be true. But to be sure, she had flung out a request for one great thing. Was this car a sign from God? What were the odds of someone *giving* her a new car?

"It's brand spankin' new," DeKane added. "I just drove it off the lot. I'll sign over the title, and it's yours, free and clear. Do we have a deal?"

What did she have to lose? Reluctantly she agreed. "Well—okay."

"Wonderful!" DeKane seemed genuinely happy. Immediately he got out his phone and sent a text. "All right. The car is on its way! I'll sign it over to you and follow you home in your old car. My buddy Rich will pick me up at your house, and we'll make our getaway before your stepfather kills me."

"He just might," she admitted with a smile. "I did notice that the car wasn't in the parking lot when I arrived."

"Didn't want to scare you off." He set his phone down on the table and folded his hands in front of him.

"So, where do you get money to buy a car like that? You must have a pretty awesome job."

His lip curled into a smile. "Investments. I've done well."

Out of the blue, Kyla's phone went off in her purse. She had meant to silence it but had forgotten. Since their conversation seemed at a natural break, she pulled it out of her purse to check the call. With a surge of adrenaline she recognized the nanny job number.

"Oh, my goodness! Sorry," she told her father over the table as she quickly slid out of the booth, "this is important—I've got to take this! I'll be right back." She answered her phone on her way out of the restaurant to talk on the sidewalk, where it was quieter.

It was Dr. Grant, calling to offer her the job if she was still interested.

Kyla told him she was and closed her eyes to silently shout the word *yes!* She got the job! He asked how soon she could start, and she told him it would be nice to have a few more days at home. He said he would really love it if she was there by Saturday, and Kyla replied that she could do that. They agreed that she would arrive to meet him at one o'clock Saturday afternoon at Wynnbury House, his mansion in New Hampton. He described it briefly, and they talked for a little while longer. Then he said he would email her details and directions and that he had to go. Kyla hung up and raised her arms in celebration. *She got the job!* She could hardly believe her luck! She wanted to shout with happiness and had to pace the sidewalk to walk out her joy a bit before going back inside.

After a brief visit to the restroom, Kyla returned to her father's table, surprised to see that another man had arrived already during the short time she'd been out. He was sitting there next to her father, and she noticed him check her over as she approached the table, as she did him. In contrast to her father, he was thickly built, with dark hair and a high receding hairline and a full dark beard.

"Kyla," her father said, "meet my buddy, Rich Connors. Rich, my beautiful daughter, Kyla DeKane."

Kyla was not sure how she felt about the way he called her his *beautiful daughter*. It sounded way too familiar for what he had earned thus far in their relationship, even if it was technically true. She hoped he didn't think that just because she accepted the car his seventeen-year absence was no big deal to her anymore. And she hadn't expected a third party to join them. She nodded her hello as she slid back into the booth.

"As you can see," her father continued, "Kyla is obviously very happy to be the new owner of my Mustang convertible."

"All right! Congratulations!" Rich congenially offered her his hand. "That car is a beauty! I'd be grinning from ear to ear too."

"Thank you," she said, shaking hands with him.

The man turned to her father, jerking his head toward her. "Just look at her face—you made her day!"

Her father was beaming.

"Well," Kyla offered, "it *is* very nice, and I *am* happy about it, but I just found out some great news that has also made me happy. That phone call was from a summer job that I applied for, and the guy wants to hire me!"

"Yeah?" her father said. "That's great, baby! What's the job?"

Baby? Okay, so her father was feeling a *lot* more confident about the two of them—the pet names were coming out! It kinda bugged her.

"Um, I got a job taking care of two kids."

"You're babysitting?"

Babysitting! Well if that didn't suck the glamor out of the job! His look and his tone made her feel like a loser. "No," she replied defensively, "I'm going to be nannying for two boys. I'll be living in a mansion on the Mississippi River called Wynnbury. The parents are"—with a jolt she suddenly remembered the strict agreement for anonymity and privacy—"very rich," she trailed off.

Connors cocked his head. "Wynnbury?" he asked. "Over by New Hampton?"

"Yes," Kyla replied, surprised.

He sat back. "I know the place!"

She swallowed, hoping she hadn't said too much. "You've been there?"

"No. You can't get in. But I know the place!"

"That's—cool." She wasn't sure what to say.

"'Twinbury,' they call it," he continued. "Supposedly it was built as a copy of some place in England, some Tynnbury House or Manor or something. One of those large country homes for rich people way back when. I guess the houses look identical."

"How do you know this?" she asked cautiously. "I've only just learned of the place!"

"Through my cousin." He laughed. "My cousin would entertain me with all these mysterious tales of the other side of his family. Supposedly his great-grandfather on his father's side was partners with the original owner and builder of that house, but it was bad news between the two of them. Some argument over something between them in the war. World War II. Lots of rumors about that place."

Kyla frowned. "Oh?" Was there something she should know?

Rich Connors folded his arms, studying her face. "So you're working there this summer."

"What kind of rumors?"

He shrugged. "Oh, just crazy stuff. I guess the builder's only son died suddenly and mysteriously, although he was young and in good health. Then shortly afterward, my cousin's grandfather passed away suddenly too, in a strange accident. Stuff like that." He paused, his eyes lingering on her face. "And other things."

"Other things like wha—"

"Stop it, Rich!" DeKane said, jabbing him with his elbow. "You're freaking her out! Don't listen to him," he told Kyla, rolling his eyes. "Believe me—he's always got a tale!" He gave Connors a little scowl and turned back to Kyla. "Anyway, congratulations on getting the job. I'm very happy for you. I'm sure you're going to have a wonderful time there."

Then he slid a small piece of paper halfway across the table and pulled a pen out of his shirt pocket. The title of the Mustang.

"I need a smoke," he said, clicking the pen, "so let's do this! Do you have ten dollars, or do I need to float you a loan to buy my car?"

Chapter Seven

Kyla took the long way home in her new car. It was one nice ride, she had to admit. She had never driven anything like it. And the interior was gorgeous. With one hand on the wheel, she slid her other hand over the silky-smooth seats, the tiny cords of red piping at the edges providing a classy pop of color to frame the milky gray leather. Gorgeous! Her roommates would be drooling with envy if they could see her. Who wouldn't be? With the top down, her hair blew wild in the wind, and it felt exhilarating. She took her time through the business district, accelerated on the straightaway, then detoured to wind along the curves in Skillings Park near her home, enjoying every bit of how the car handled.

Meeting her eyes in the rearview mirror, she smiled at herself and shook her head in disbelief. As of fifteen minutes ago, she — Kyla DeKane — owned a new car! A nice car. A hot car, even! *Was this for real? Pinch me!* she thought. What a crazy twist of events! A week ago she never would have imagined that her biological father would show up out of the blue, much less show up and *give her a car*, of all things! It was unreal! She wondered how her new relationship with him would play out. He seemed as if he genuinely wanted to try. At the moment she was unsure about things, but she would give it some time. At any rate, things were off to a very interesting start!

But there was a deeper question nagging at her. Kyla wondered what God's role in all of this was. *One great thing.* Had God orchestrated all of this? Or was it just an amazing coincidence? Had he brought her and her biological father together again? Did that mean that things were going to be good between them? Was God responsible for her getting this car? It was hard to think otherwise! The thought both intrigued her and sort of frightened her. She preferred God to keep his distance. And if it was him that had brought about these events, why? Was it a sign that other things in her life might work out too? Or would there be another heartache right around the corner, as always? She never quite knew what to believe when it came to God, and none of her questions had answers.

Kyla rounded the final curve in the park's winding trail and glided out the exit onto her street. Reducing her speed, she crept up the narrow lane toward her house at the end of the drive, mentally preparing herself for how she would explain the car to her dad. As she looked down toward her home, a jolt of adrenaline hit her as she recognized a familiar car in the driveway. A yellow Camaro. Gah! Alex Duvall! *What was he doing there?* Her dad was in the driveway talking with him, and she could see Alex standing with his hands in his pockets looking at the ground. *How dare he show up like this!* Perturbed, she pulled over and stopped in front of her house, her tires scraping the curb. Both men turned their heads and gawked at her as she shifted the shiny red-and-black Mustang into park and got out. She slammed the door, cutting determinedly across the grass to where they stood.

With his jaw hanging, Kyla's dad turned to her in confusion. "Kyla, what in the world—?"

She did not respond to him. Her eyes were fixed on Alex. "What are you doing here?" she demanded.

Alex tore his eyes from the Mustang. "Holy cow—what's with the car?"

She squared her shoulders at him. "I asked you a question!"

He gestured, as if it were obvious. "I came to talk with you."

"There is nothing to talk about," she replied abruptly.

Alex shifted his feet, shooting her an irritated look. "Kyla, seriously—I came all the way from Bridgewater to see you! At least hear me out—"

She lifted her chin. "Then you've wasted your time."

Beside her, Kendall stiffened, blurting out, "Now what's this? What on earth is going on here?" He was looking into the street.

Kyla glanced behind her, where Robert DeKane was pulling up in her old car behind the Mustang on the curb. Closely behind was Rich Connors in his car, who slowed and stopped in the middle of the street. From behind the windshield DeKane gave the three of them a small, acknowledging salute.

"Tell you in a bit, Dad." She turned back to Alex.

His jaw was set, his eyes appealing her. "Come on. Please talk to me."

She shook her head angrily. "You can't just show up here and think

I'm going to drop everything and talk to you! I have a phone, you know!"

"I wanted to talk face to face. Besides, you wouldn't answer if I called you anyway!"

"Uh-huh." She folded her arms. "So why didn't you bring Ashley with you on your little drive?"

"Oh, knock it off!" He scowled back at her. "I'm not seeing her anymore! That was a mistake, and that's why I'm here. Look—can we go somewhere?" He cast a glance toward Kyla's dad, who was closely watching the arrivals in the street.

Kyla's lips were firmly closed, and she shook her head no. From a distance she heard her old car door open as Robert DeKane got out and transferred to the other car in the street, but her eyes remained fixed on Alex, who returned her stare.

"I told you I was sorry, and I meant it," he said quietly, reaching out for her arm. "Can you just settle down so we can talk?"

She pulled away. "Alex, you are so full of it!"

His mouth opened.

"You're such a liar! If you're not seeing Ashley, why were you having breakfast with her yesterday at Chetty's? Mary Finn saw you both together!"

He gave a sound of protest. "Yeah, well, I was breaking up with her! Did Mary Finn tell you that too? The nosy little—" He leaned his face in close to hers. "I want to talk to you!"

She backed a step.

Again his eyes darted to Kendall and back to her. "Kyla, please," he appealed. "I can't stop thinking about you. I need you."

She raised her eyebrows. "I know what you *think* you need, and apparently you can easily get it elsewhere."

He threw her a dark look. "Can't you just forgive me? It was a stupid fling. She didn't mean anything to me."

"Neither did I, I'm guessing."

"That's not true! That's not true at all!" Kyla could see the vein on his brow that appeared when he was angry. "I came all the way up here for you—don't humiliate me!"

She cocked her head. "Oh, right, Alex! So nice of you to think of yourself! If you want to talk about feeling humiliated, I have a lot I could share with you. I did a pretty intensive study on it my last week of college!"

He let out an impatient breath. "Dang it! What do I have to do to get you to talk to me?"

She leveled her gaze at him. "Answer me this, will you—was Ashley the only one?"

His hesitation was a moment too long, and he spoke through his teeth, "Can't we talk about this somewhere else?"

"Oh, geez." She pointed to his vehicle on the driveway. "There's your car. You need to leave."

"At least let me expla—"

"Go!"

"Okay—" He held out his hand. "I know you're angry. Understandably so. But if we—"

"Alex!" She jerked her hands out. "How many times do I have to tell you no? You need to leave! Go! Now, please!" She pointed him to his car again.

He scowled, silent for a moment, then jerked his head toward the street. "So whose car is that?"

Kyla shot him an incredulous look. "That is none of your business!"

"You have a new boyfriend. It's his, isn't it?"

She blinked.

He nodded, biting his lip, giving her a long look. "And you're mad at *me* for messing around!" He turned on his heel and got into his car.

"You don't know anything!"

He started the car, then turned to ask through his open window. "So who is he?"

"How do you know that car isn't mine?"

"Oh, right!" He gave a sarcastic laugh. "There's no way either of *you* could ever afford a car like that!" His eyes flicked to Kyla's dad, who was at the moment turning to look at them.

His insult stung. As he started to back out of the driveway, Kyla yelled toward his open window, "Well, guess what, Alex! Surprise, surprise—that car is mine!" She pointed to her chest. "I bought it! I bought it used from someone with my own money, and I got a heck of a deal! I bet you're so jealous!"

Kyla was startled at how good it felt to spout that statement, and the shocked expression on his face made her doubly glad she had said it. He stared at her a moment, then with a grunt drove away without looking back at her, following Rich Connor's car out of the neighborhood.

"The coward!" Kendall spat angrily.

"Gah! He is a total rat!" Kyla agreed, infuriated. "He's got a lot of nerve to show up here! What is he thinking—that he can lie to me and actually think I'll want to get back together with him? How long was he here?"

Kendall turned his face to look at Kyla. "I was referring to the man who left your car and ran away."

She met his eyes.

"So what's going on? What's this business with that car?" He pointed his thumb behind him toward the street. "Why did you come home driving that? I thought you refused it. And what's this nonsense about you buying it?"

Kyla sighed loudly, rubbing her forehead. "It's a long story, Dad, and I promise to tell you everything. But first, how long was Alex here? And what did the two of you talk about?"

Kendall fixed his hands on his belted waist. "Okay, let's talk about Alex. What did he do that warranted the way you talked to him just now?"

"You don't know the half of it, Dad," she responded tiredly.

"Well, Kyla, you—" He paused, pursing his lips.

"What?" she said sharply, unable to hide the irritation in her voice.

"You shredded the guy!"

"What? Are you kidding?" She tossed her head defensively. "Don't make this about *me*, Dad! He is such a jerk! He—he really hurt me! I'm mad at him!"

"Yeah, that's obvious! I'm not saying he didn't do anything wrong, but he came here to try to make things right with you. And you—you were pretty hard on him."

Kyla could feel her cheeks grow hot as she stared at her dad.

"He just wanted to *talk* to you! You could have been a little nicer about it—poor guy."

"Oh, poor, poor Alex!" she spouted angrily. "Why are you taking *his* side? What do you know about Alex and me? Did he tell you some sob story or something? You don't understand anything about what happened!"

He held up his hand. "No, I don't, and I'm not taking his side. In fact"—his brow furled—"after hearing your conversation I wouldn't mind a few more words with him right now! But aside from that—jeepers, Kyla, you were downright hostile!"

With an angry huff, she turned her face away from him.

"I get that you're angry," Kendall continued fervently, "but his character flaws are about *him*. What I care about is *you*! You're twenty-two! For heaven's sake, you need to learn how to keep your dignity, Kyla Evangeline. Your anger is unbecoming!"

Fuming, Kyla clenched her teeth, remaining stubbornly silent. She would not look at him.

After a long pause Kendall exhaled heavily, dropping his arms. "Okay. I'm sorry, hon. You probably didn't need that on top of everything else."

She stood unmoved, her arms folded.

They stood next to each other in the empty driveway a few moments before he cleared his throat. "All right, all right," he said finally, "I know you're bugged, but listen—I truly am on your side. It's been a hugely emotional week, but you're going to be okay. Now come on—show me this new car, and you can tell me what happened and how it went with your father. I'd like to hear about it. Then you can take me for a drive."

Kyla gave him a long look, then took a deep breath, reluctantly letting her offense go. Together they walked across the yard to the Mustang while Kyla reported what went down during the morning with her biological father. Kendall listened patiently while he walked around the vehicle inspecting the tires and the body finish, but he was nevertheless grim and distrustful. At last when she opened the door for him and let him sit in the driver's seat, he slowly began to soften. Even he had to admit it was a beauty of a car, admiring the luxurious interior, the stereo system, the shape of the seats, and enjoying the feeling of the sun on his shoulders. Kyla told him about her biological father's idea to have her purchase the car, and then showed her dad the transferred title, which he examined thoughtfully.

"He said he really wanted me to have it," Kyla concluded. "It's odd, for sure, but I think he means well."

Kendall handed the title back to her, which she returned to her purse.

"Well," he said, shaking his head, "who would have ever thought something like this would happen?"

"I know!" she said in wonder. "It's like the first great thing that has ever happened in my life!"

He gave her a strange look. "What are you talking about? I certainly wouldn't say that! But it *is* nice. And I'm glad it went okay with your father."

She leaned her head back against the gray leather headrest, her arm resting on the door. "He said he wants a relationship."

Kendall said nothing, exploring the dash.

"I suppose I'm obligated now, huh?" Her mouth curled into a sheepish smile.

He raised his eyebrows and nodded. "Yeah, I'd say so. When will you see him again?"

"I'm not sure. We didn't make any plans." Kyla suddenly realized that they hadn't even exchanged phone numbers. She wondered if Robert DeKane had discovered the same thing yet. She hoped he remembered that she was leaving this weekend. And that jarred her memory.

"By the way," she said, suddenly reaching over to grab her dad's arm, "guess what—I got the nanny job! Dr. Grant called this morning while we were at the restaurant!"

He leaned away from her, surprised. "No way! Are you serious? Well, that's great news!"

She shot him a look. "What? You didn't think I'd get it?"

He held his hand up in defense. "Now, now! I knew you had as good a chance as anybody, but I think I know one young lady who will be taking a crash course on caring for youngsters!" He winked at her.

She giggled. "That's probably a really good idea!"

Later, after they had gotten out of the car and were walking to the house, Kyla's dad brought up Alex again.

"So you asked earlier what Alex and I were talking about." He stepped up onto the concrete porch and reached for the door. "He told me he had really messed things up with you and wanted to talk with you to make it right. But that led into a really good conversation about God."

Kyla gave him a startled look. "You were talking about God?"

"Yeah." He nodded. "I wish we would've had just a few more minutes together. I was talking to him about Jesus, and he seemed to be really responding. Then you came."

He motioned her to enter the house ahead of him. "It's too bad you weren't just a few minutes later."

"Huh," Kyla replied, turning her head so that he couldn't see the amusement on her face. The thought of Alex trapped in one of her dad's God speeches gave her great enjoyment. For once she was glad her dad was the way he was!

❖   ❖   ❖

Kyla's week turned into a frenzy of activity, with registering and insuring her new car, unpacking from college, repacking for the summer, shopping for summer clothes and shoes, and the predicted crash course on caring for kids under the age of eight, complete with a scouting trip to the toy department of the local Target to see what toys were now popular with little boys. In a box in her closet she knew she had an old babysitting handbook, which she dug out and threw into one of her bags just in case. With the handbook she found a brand-new box of color crayons, which gave her the idea to go online to download various coloring and activity sheets. She wasn't sure if boys were into that sort of thing, but just in case, she would be prepared. She added them to her box of fun things for the kids.

While online Kyla decided to do a search on Dr. David H. Grant, immediately finding a short biography and information on his current position at Taiton College but also learning he had connections to Oxford University in England and with Cornell University, his alma mater. No mention of family or his marriage to Marilee Montayne was made.

On a whim she also typed in "Wynnbury House." Nothing surfaced. She tried to remember the place her father's friend Rich had mentioned in England—"Winbury"? "Wonnbury"? She experimented with a several different spellings until it came to her: "Tynnbury." The search produced one photo and a minimal description. She studied the image, impressed with the size of the house, though it was less impactful when it came to its aesthetics, being a rather plain brick building with a large number of windows and an enormous fountain in the garden. She wondered if the house in New Hampton was as much like it as her father's friend had indicated. Dr. Grant had told her the setting was gorgeous, tucked amongst the bluffs and inlets of the Mississippi. Kyla decided to stop trying to imagine what it would look like—she would be there soon enough!

Though she was busy, Kyla tried spending as much time with her dad as possible, knowing she wouldn't see him for a good share of the summer. Every evening when he got off work they went for drives in the new car and walks and out to eat. She even tried to honor him by watching her mom's videos, knowing it would make him happy and also be good for her, but none of her attempts panned out. Twice she started the clip on forgiveness, but both times she was interrupted by phone calls, and then afterward the moment just wasn't right.

She also considered her dad's scolding about the conversation, fight, or whatever it was that she'd had with Alex. She hated to admit that her dad was right, and it stung like crazy to be corrected. She could have been a lot nicer and still as firm, but after getting that text from Mary about him she had been so angry that she hadn't wanted to hear a word Alex had to say. She didn't know why she was like she was—always getting so riled up— but sometimes things just came out of her. She regretted her hostile manner toward him and wondered if she should have taken the time to hear him out. She felt so guilty about it that she almost called him but then realized how foolish that would be. The last thing she needed was for him to have false hopes for them as a couple. Kyla decided that perhaps sometime she would do an online search on how to keep your sanity when having difficult conversations. She amused herself by thinking of typing "how not to turn into a monster when your ex-boyfriend doesn't get that it's over" into the search bar. But now more than likely her interaction with him had come to an end after their conversation in the driveway. She hoped so. The pain of breaking up was awful enough without having it strung out. She was more than ready to be done with it.

If only she could stop thinking about him! Why did she still mourn him? Why did his rejection still sting? Why did she keep wondering what she could have done differently that might have possibly prevented his stupid choices to fool around with Ashley? As always, she wished she had a mother to talk it all through with.

Then, like a flash, Kyla's week of gearing up for her summer adventure came to an end, and she still had not heard from her biological father. Certainly by Friday she had expected that he would call her or somehow try to get in touch with her, but she had not heard from him since Tuesday, when they had met at McDonald's. Why hadn't he called? Hadn't he thought of her at all? Surely he must have realized they had no way to contact one another! She wasn't sure what the next step was supposed to be now, with no way to get in touch with him. *Left hanging again*, she thought. She tried not to let it bother her, although it was hard not to think about it. Having the new car was now a constant reminder of having her biological father in her life. Or of *not* having him in her life, depending on which mood she was in—it swung both ways.

On Saturday morning Kyla dressed in a smart miniskirt and summer blouse and packed up her car while Kendall was out for breakfast with a group of men from his church. He came home from his meeting a little early to see her off.

"I'm going to miss you," he said, giving her a long, affectionate hug. "It's been great having you home. Please call me to let me know you arrived safely."

She promised him she would call him as soon as she got there, and after finishing their good-byes she climbed into her new car and left for New Hampton, a three-hour drive from Stanton, according to her phone's GPS. She allowed herself a full hour of extra time so that she would be unhurried to her one o'clock appointment.

The morning was already warm and the air heavy with humidity, but the sun was shining—a perfect day for driving with the top of her car down. Plugging her music into the car's sound system, Kyla found her favorite playlist and cranked it. *Nice*, she thought, digging the pulsing bass through the speakers. Life was good—at the moment anyway. For once she felt that luck was on her side, and she was excited for what lay ahead. Here she was in her new car, with her hair flying in the wind, on her way to a great job for which there were surely others more qualified than she was. She was glowing with happiness.

Part of the thrill, she knew, was working for someone rich and famous—still an amazement—but it wasn't entirely that. Part of it was just getting away from Stanton and starting a new chapter in her life. A new chapter minus Alex Duvall. A new chapter in a new setting, a brand-new place. Plus—this job was an adventure! Kyla was well known to her friends as one who played it ultra-safe in life, finding her refuge in the familiar and predictable. She'd had enough stressful situations in her twenty-two years than most people have in their lifetimes—she certainly didn't need to invite more of it in. But she was up for this adventure! Of course, she admitted, there was more than a bit of romance in the thought of living in the large house, Wynnbury House. Who wouldn't want to live in a mansion? And as for the only loose end that hadn't been tied up—her biological father—well, he would just have to figure things out himself. The onus was on him to contact her. Maybe he would even have to ask her dad where to find her. She tried to imagine that. *Whatever.* She wasn't going to worry about it. He'd had his chance.

The Saturday morning city traffic was light, flowing steadily along. In time she passed through familiar Bakerton and soon after was outside of the metro area into the country, passing cornfields and hayfields tucked between patches of hilly woods. About three-fourths of her way to her destination, the vehicles before her suddenly began to slow, eventually coming to a complete standstill. Road construction. Miles of it! Eventually the long double lines of cars began to file into one lane and crawl slowly forward for what seemed like eternity. Frustrated not only with her GPS's lack of redirection but also with the new prospect of getting tar on her brand-new car, a first-time-ever concern, she settled glumly down into the snail-like drive, knowing there was nothing she could do about it.

Puffy clouds had begun floating across the sky, competing with the sun, and the brief moments of overcast felt good. She rested her arm on her door, enjoying the freshness of summer, relieved that she had given herself extra time, and thankfully, though her margin had vastly diminished, the GPS indicated she could still make it on time. But then a closed exit further pushed her arrival time back, and by the time she got onto the main highway headed toward New Hampton, Kyla tried to hurry.

Eventually, after missing a turn and backtracking a few miles, she saw a sign pointing left to Wynnbury tucked in the trees along the highway. Almost there. Four miles to go. In a short distance she turned at the T in the road and began winding downward through a forested area for a few miles. Passing a sign for a public landing, she could tell she was near the river. The house must be very close by, she presumed, and the thought gave her body a zing of adrenaline.

The road straightened out for a bit, now following a high, red brick wall for some distance until suddenly there it was to the right—not the house yet but the great wrought-iron gates she was told she would see, ornate and imposing, with the name "Wynnbury" on a great arch spanning over them. She pulled alongside the brick station in the center of the driveway to find the electronic keypad. Double-checking the combination on her email printout, she punched it in, surprised that her hands were a little shaky. Nerves. *Here we go,* she told herself, *the point of no return.* As the gates closed behind her, she proceeded slowly down the wooded driveway, hugging the side of a steep bluff, the trees a cool canopy over her on the narrowed pavement. She reminded herself to breathe.

Then as Kyla navigated the car around a curve alongside another bluff, the woods suddenly opened to expose a flat and grassy plateau, and there in the center stood Wynnbury House, a mammoth three-story brick mansion stretched out lengthwise like a large red rectangle, with more than a dozen white-framed windows all across its front. Symmetrical and austere, it spread out wide over the plain trimmed lawn, reminding her somewhat of a college dormitory but absent of its flurry. Up above, around the entire perimeter of the roof, wound a short, wrought-iron railing, like a parapet, and in the middle third of the roof an attic peak rose up with an octagonal window high in its center. She wasn't prepared for the sudden pit in her stomach as she approached it, for its size and appearance were overwhelming and rather intimidating, as if the structure itself was an entity with a personality. It's just a building, Kyla reminded herself. A big, fancy house. But she found her dreams and imaginations morphing into trepidations and questions, like a sudden minor key in the score of a movie.

A small stone patio with a set of handsome double doors over which an arched roof jutted out a short distance over the driveway indicated the home's entrance. Kyla pulled up slowly, stopping beside the house and behind a small gray Honda, which was parked partially under the portico. On the lawn nearby were a garden tiller and shovel beside a cluster of potted shrubs that looked ready for planting. She walked up the steps, admiring the large and freshly planted pedestal patio pots, the telltale garden tools, and short stacks of disposable plastic containers scattered nearby. She didn't even bother to check her phone to see what time it was as she knew she was hopelessly late. Ringing the doorbell, she waited. After a minute she tried it again, this time knocking firmly on the door too. Still no answer. After her third attempt she looked back at the other car, debating what to do. Someone must be home. She decided to take a chance. Carefully she opened the door.

"Hello?" she called timidly.

Gingerly Kyla stepped into a broad and richly paneled foyer onto a colorful rectangle of rug. Straight ahead past the foyer and across a wide hallway, her eyes were drawn to a huge and beautiful sitting room where a wall of tall and elegantly draped windows rose a full two stories on the far side of the house. She stared at them in awe for a moment before looking around her. Beside her, to her left in the foyer, was an open closet-like room, a small oak-paneled cove with a coat rack, hooks, and compartments, like an old-fashioned cloak room. To her right, on the opposite oak-paneled wall, hung an enlargement of an old black-and-white photograph of Wynnbury House in a dark antique frame, in which a smiling young couple posed for the camera, dwarfed beside the house. Looking more closely, Kyla guessed the picture was most likely taken when the house had been newly built, as the trees around it were very young. Next to it in a matching frame hung a close-up of the couple, with the woman now holding a child and the man dressed in a smart military suit. *Kennedy*, the name read, sewn on the upper right chest of his uniform. She could read it from where she stood on the rug.

"Hello?" she called again.

Still there was no response. Cautiously she walked to the end of the foyer, pausing before the grand entrance of the sunken sitting room to take in her surroundings. She guessed that she could probably fit her and her dad's whole house into this one room! Well, maybe not, but it was enormous enough that it felt like it! Before her, arranged throughout the white-carpeted room, were several varied but coordinating sets of furniture, which made up several sizable sitting areas. No doubt it had seen some very large parties! The spaciousness of the room reminded her of the study lounge in the student center at college, although this furniture was elegant, quite the opposite of dilapidated college furnishings. Yet the room had a homey, comfortable feel, its accents no doubt reflecting the professor and his wife's good tastes.

Flanking the great sitting room were two impressive open staircases, one on either side, both with red woolen runners neatly attached to each ascending stair with thin brass rods. An ornately carved wooden balustrade curved gracefully down both sides of each stairway, its spindles spiraling outward on each side where the two sets of stairs met the wide ceramic-tiled hallway where she stood, which itself ran the entire length of the house. Down the hallway to her left was a spacious kitchen and dining room, behind which she could see a small corner of what she assumed were patio doors on the back side of the house. To her right, the wide hallway continued to where, just past the stairway on that side, two sets of magnificent, beautifully-grained oak pocket doors faced each other on either sides of the hall, indicating grand entrances to additional large rooms there, although both sets of doors were pulled closed. The hallway continued on, with several doors to the left and right farther down in the shadows.

Kyla stood awkwardly in the center of the hall, unsure of what to do, when at last she heard some movement and quiet singing from above her, upstairs on the second floor, which was open to the large room before her but hidden from where Kyla stood underneath at the end of the foyer.

Relieved, she called again, more loudly this time, "Hello!"

"Hello!" came a woman's surprised reply. There was another scuffling of movement, then around the landing of the stairway to her right appeared a pleasant-looking woman of about fifty, with round hips and a short, brown sugar-colored bob, carrying a scrub bucket filled with rags and a trash bag. She was wearing elastic waist jeans and a cotton button-down camp shirt.

"Hi there! You must be the nanny." Her smile produced rosy apple cheeks.

"Yes. I'm Kyla DeKane."

"Susan Gordon. I clean for Dr. Grant." She set the bucket down and extended her hand to Kyla. "I think he expected you a lot earlier."

Kyla winced, shaking her hand. "Yes, I–"

"He was here at one. He came home from work to meet with you but went back into town when you didn't arrive."

"Road construction," she said, feeling her face turn pink. She didn't think she was *that* late.

"Ah, that's too bad." The woman smiled sympathetically. "Well, I'm sure he will be back before too long. Go ahead and make yourself comfortable." She shifted the trash bag, gesturing toward the sitting area.

She glanced into the fine room. "Okay."

"Any other day I'd join you, but I was just on my way out, and I'm kinda in a hurry." She turned to glance at the ornate grandfather clock near them in the hall. "I have to watch my grandchildren while my daughter goes to work, and I'm running late."

"No, that's okay," she offered. "I'll just—hang out."

"Yeah, it shouldn't be too long." She stooped for the bucket. "I'm really sorry to rush off on you."

"No problem. Just glad you were here."

She smiled. "Well, it was nice to meet you, Miss Kyla, even briefly. I'm sure we'll see each other again soon."

Kyla nodded. "Yes, nice to meet you too."

Susan Gordon hurried down the hall beyond the kitchen and disappeared into another room. There was the slam of a door, and soon after, Kyla heard the little car in front of the house start and drive away.

The house was so quiet. Kyla stepped into the sitting room, choosing the set in the center of the room where two angular, modern sofas of textured cream upholstery faced one another, with brightly colored silk accent pillows. A glass coffee table on an exquisite polar bear rug separated them. It looked real. Kyla slipped off her sandal to feel it with her foot, guessing that she was right. From where she stood she could see all the way through the family dining room into the kitchen, as behind the staircase there was no wall, allowing an open view of that part of the house. As she had thought, off the dining room was a set of glass patio doors. Behind her, on the far wall of the sitting room was a towering fireplace of some kind of light, creamy stone, and above it hung a long, silky tapestry, a multi-colored batik of leaf patterns, with tassels at its bottom corners, the fabric's brightness accentuated by the room's clean, white walls. To the side of the fireplace, behind the other staircase, a nine-foot grand piano of shiny mahogany looked perfectly modest in the large room. It was beautiful. Kyla turned to look upward, seeing another balustrade railing across the exposed hallway of the second floor, and up along the wall behind it were three sets of French doors, evenly spaced across the broad open balcony.

Setting her purse down on the couch near her, Kyla walked to look out the expansive wall of windows, examining the yard beyond the concrete patio on the back of the house. She found it much like the front—

very plain, a simple flat lawn, extending far out to a defined edge where the woods began again and where she could tell the land started its slope downward toward the river. Beyond the yard she could see a few slivers of water through the trees. She wondered how far it was to walk to the river and if the banks were wild and natural or if they were manicured. Would the professor allow her to take the kids there? She brought her gaze to the patio right outside the window, where she noticed more large pots that had been freshly planted. They looked nice. And parked off to one side near the house and mostly out of sight, Kyla could see the back of a white truck piled high with something dark. Wood mulch perhaps, she thought.

She turned, surveying the clean and quiet room again, noticing that there were no toys anywhere. She bet the boys were not allowed to play there. And that made her wonder where those little boys *did* play. She took a deep breath, aware that she was nervous. Not only was she stepping out of her comfort zone to care for the two kids, but this house was something else! What had she gotten herself into? Wandering back to the sofa, she settled down on one edge where she could see the front door and dug her phone out of her purse. Checking the time, she decided that now was probably a good time to call her dad, before the professor got home. She dialed, then brought the phone down from her ear to see why it wasn't ringing. Two little words spanned the tiny area where normally there were bars of reception: no service. With a sigh she returned the phone to her purse. Her dad would have to wait, as she would have to wait.

Chapter Eight

Half an hour went by as Kyla sat on the spotless sofa, the house completely still except for the steady ticking of the grandfather clock in the hall. Absently she bounced her leg, looking around the room, thinking. Outside the sun had disappeared, and the sky was now overcast and gray, as if it wanted to rain. And she was hungry. The road construction had taken so much extra time that she hadn't stopped to get anything for lunch. Having the kitchen right in view made it worse, and after a while she scrounged in her purse for some gum, hoping it would help. She yawned, crumpling the wrappers and dropping them into her bag. Tracing the design on one of the pillows with her finger, she thought about how good it would feel to lie down. After a few more minutes she succumbed, laying her head on one of the pillows and putting her feet up. The weather had made her sleepy, and a few minutes of rest would do her good.

The loud bang of a door in the distance jolted her from her doze. Kyla's eyes popped open, and quickly she swung her feet down and sat up with no idea of how long she had been asleep. Someone had come in the house—a male who was intermittently whistling and singing loudly off-tune. Kyla recognized Dr. Grant's voice from their previous video interview together. With a quick breath she shook herself awake and swiftly stood to meet him as she heard him move into the hall.

"Hello," he said, entering the kitchen with an armful of grocery bags, greeting her across the house through the open dining room. "I see you let yourself in." He looked to be in his early forties, of average height, trim, with a head of dark, wiry curls, and he was well dressed, wearing a blue-and-black nylon golf shirt with black dress slacks.

"Hello," she responded, adding guiltily, "The housekeeper was here."

"Ah. Well, come on over." He jerked his head toward one of the high-backed chairs across the granite countertop on the kitchen peninsula and began putting his groceries away.

The spacious kitchen had ample cupboards and countertops and new-fashioned appliances, complete with an industrial-looking stove on the far end of the room. A long kitchen island sat slightly off center, a workspace that sort of doubled as a divider from the wide hall that ran the length of the house. A peninsula with high barstool-style chairs with curved backs separated the family dining area from the kitchen. Kyla cut through the side of the living room area and around the table, noticing two child booster seats buckled onto the chairs there.

"Miss DeKane!" he said, extending his hand to her across the counter. "Dr. David Grant. Nice to finally meet you in person. Coke?" He offered her the soda that he held in his other hand.

"Sure." Kyla took it, sliding onto the stool at the counter.

He filled a glass from the cupboard with ice from the dispenser on front of the refrigerator and set it down in front of her.

"You know," he said, popping open his own can with a hiss and taking a sip, "if you were one of my students, I would mark you tardy." He raised his eyebrows.

Kyla swallowed. Any excuse sounded lame, even the truth. "I'm sorry, sir. I had good intentions, but I was nevertheless very late." Then she felt foolish that she had called him "sir." She felt like a freshman again, asking for an extension on her first late paper.

He studied her face for a moment, then shrugged. "It's okay. It just meant that you had to wait until I got back."

He took another long drink, gave a little burp, then set the can on the edge of the peninsula, turning to finish putting the cold goods in the refrigerator. The rest of the items were left on the counter beside it for later. Finished, he came to stand opposite her.

"So, Miss Kyla DeKane." He spoke her name slowly, emphasizing each syllable as he retrieved his soda. "Welcome to Wynnbury. What do you think of my house?"

"It's big," she replied. She didn't know what else to say.

"Yeah." He gave a short laugh as he nodded his head in agreement. "Yeah, it's big, all right. So do you think you're ready for this?"

Kyla's breath was tight in her chest, but she tried her best to appear confident. "I think so. I mean, I've been really looking forward to coming. I'm up for the challenge."

"Good. Glad to hear it." He gave a brisk nod. "Well, let's get started. This"—he reached over to pick up a framed portrait from the underside of the cupboard near the coffeepot, setting it down firmly in front of Kyla—"is my wife, Marilee. You already know who she is, but so we're clear, we're married, and I love her, so don't get any funny ideas."

Kyla immediately felt herself blush and was speechless, fixing her eyes on the actress in the photograph.

"This is her house, our house. I want to be clear on that too, in case you think you might have a better way of doing things."

"I—I understand."

"Good," he said, putting the photo back into its place of prominence. He swung the chair beside Kyla around the corner of the peninsula and straddled it, facing her, resuming in a business-like manner. "As you know from our previous conversation together, I'm teaching a course at the college during the summer session, which starts this coming Monday. I'm gone every day except Fridays and the weekend, so I'm counting on you to watch my boys, Howard and Henry. And that entails everything—dress them, feed them, play with them—you know, the whole works."

Howard and Henry. It was the first she had heard their names. She nodded, taking mental notes, unwilling to interrupt him for a pad and pen.

"I leave early, and don't usually return from town until about 1:30 in the afternoon, after which I am planning on working outside in the yard on some special projects for the summer. Late afternoons I try to connect with Marilee in my office before she goes to bed, and evenings are when I plod through student essays, which you are more than welcome to help me with, if you happen to be proficient in your history of the Ottoman Empire." He tilted his head at Kyla with dark, questioning eyes.

Ottoman—what? Was he serious? She shook her head.

His face dropped in mock disappointment. "As I expected."

His glance suddenly flicked past her to the patio doors. Kyla followed his eyes and saw that it was starting to rain, the drops beginning to accumulate on the glass.

"So what I need from you, Miss DeKane," he continued, "is for you to more than watch my boys, but to engage with them. I don't want their summer to be a free-for-all where they are barely supervised and survive on a diet of macaroni and cheese, if you know what I mean."

Kyla nodded, turning back to face him.

"Keep them safe, play with them, feed them nutritious food, and make sure they eat something green once in a while."

"Right."

His eyes narrowed. "You *can* cook, yes?"

"Yes," Kyla said. "Nothing fancy, but I have abilities beyond operating a microwave." One of the advantages of growing up with a single dad. There weren't many other advantages.

His head tipped approvingly. "I'm glad to hear it. You'll feed the kids while I'm gone, of course, but for dinner in the evening the two of us will trade off. Can you manage that?"

"Yes," Kyla nodded. She hoped he was not particular about his food.

He took another drink of his soda, pursing his lips at the carbonation.

"We don't watch TV. We read books and play with toys. And we play outside. I expect you to exhibit maturity in seeing that that happens, as they might try to convince you that they are in charge of what they do. Make no mistake—I have put you in charge of them, not the other way around."

"Okay." Her stomach gave a little twist.

"And all that being said," he added, "I am still their dad, and being a good father is important to me. I never had a close relationship with my father, and I don't want to repeat that with my own sons. I love being with my boys. I intend to put them to bed most nights. I like to give them their baths. I like to play with them, sometimes at random times of the day. So anytime I'm there with them, I'm in charge. Whenever I'm not there with them, you're in charge. Is that clear?"

"Yes." The bare skin of the back of her leg stuck to the chair as she shifted in her seat.

"This"—he pulled up a photo on his phone and held it for her to see—"is Mrs. Gordon. Susan. She comes twice a week to clean."

Kyla recognized her. "We met. She was here when I arrived."

"Ah, yes. Good. Well, add her number to your contacts right now."

Kyla looked at him in surprise, then reached for her purse to retrieve her phone.

"Susan is not only your housekeeper, but she is also your personal shopper. If you need something while you're here—anything—you text Susan, and she will bring it the next time she comes."

"Okay," Kyla said with curiosity, tapping the number into her contacts.

"You need butter?" Dr. Grant held up his phone, pretending to text. "Susan, bring me two pounds of butter. Done. Susan, we need milk, eggs, vanilla, popcorn, and toothpaste. Sparkly White brand, please. Done!"

"I really don't mind going shopping," Kyla offered, setting her phone down onto the granite countertop. "In fact, I kind of enjoy—"

"Ah!" He lifted his finger to interrupt her. "So here's the deal! My children may not go into town. Period. I don't want the paparazzi snapping their pictures and plastering them all over the Internet, or anything worse to happen to them. They are preschoolers, and this is enough of a world for them. They stay here, and so do you. It's part of your job. I would like you to be at my disposal at all times—forgive my poor metaphor. I want to be free to do what I need to do without having to coordinate schedules and wait around for you."

Kyla's eyes widened as she sat back in her chair. "Okay. I understand," she answered. She wasn't going to argue with him, but surely she wouldn't be on lockdown for the entire summer, would she? She wasn't sure how she felt about that.

"Remember, though—Susan comes only twice a week, so keep that in mind. Make sure you plan ahead for the weekends."

"Right. Got it."

"But if you find you really need something, and she isn't coming that day," he added, gesturing with his hand as if to accommodate her, "you can call or text me at work, and I can stop to pick it up. But let that be an exception, okay?"

"Okay." Her head bobbed with another nod.

From down the hall behind Dr. Grant came the sound of a door closing, followed by the stomping of feet from another person who had entered the house. A few moments later into the hallway walked a tall, young man with blondish hair, damp from the rain. He was in his stocking feet, wearing dusty work khakis and a T-shirt spotted with dark, wet blotches. When he saw Kyla he broke into a grin. Instantly she recognized him from the day he had been in her father's study at her home, and her mouth opened in bewilderment.

"Ah, Peter!" Dr. Grant turned in his chair to greet the newcomer. "Good timing! Come on over—I'd like you to meet Miss Kyla DeKane." He waved his arm toward her.

"Kyla," Peter said, tipping his head.

Kyla frowned, blurting out, "*You!* What are *you* doing here?"

Dr. Grant leaned back in surprise. "You're already friends?"

"No!" Kyla said immediately, while at the same time Peter answered, "Yes."

Dr. Grant tilted his head in question, looking from one to the other.

"He knows my dad," Kyla explained quickly.

Peter joined them at the end of the counter, happily explaining, "Yes, I'm friends with her dad. In fact, I helped her get the job. Her dad told me she broke"—he halted suddenly, flicking a glance at Kyla—"um, that she was out of a summer job, so I forwarded him your email about needing a reliable nanny."

"What?" She blinked, turning her head toward him. "That was from *you*?" Her indignation rose at the discovery.

Peter cocked his head in confusion.

"And excuse me," she continued, her eyes narrowing, "how do you know so much about me? I wasn't aware that my personal life was any of your business!"

Peter drew back in surprise. "I—um, I'm sorry. Your dad—" He trailed off, obviously uncomfortable.

Dr. Grant slowly folded his arms, his eyes darting from Kyla to Peter and back. He cleared his throat, speaking into the awkward silence, "All right then, my friends. Miss DeKane, Peter is my gardener and groundskeeper this summer. He's living here at Wynnbury. Is there going to be a problem with the two of you working here together? 'Cause if so, I need to know it. Otherwise this could be a very long and unpleasant summer for all of us."

"Of course not," Peter answered immediately.

Dr. Grant turned to Kyla.

Living here! What the heck! Had her dad arranged this? He was so in trouble, *so in trouble!* She shook her head. "No, it's all right. Sorry. I was just caught off guard." She met Peter's gaze, then quickly averted her eyes. *So in trouble!*

"Well, all right, then," Dr. Grant repeated. He leaned forward, resting his elbows on the countertop.

Peter brought a hand to his waist, addressing Kyla, "So hey—can I carry in your things from your car for you?"

She lifted her chin, her voice brisk but light. "No, that's okay. I'll take care of it."

Dr. Grant was silent, observing her curiously, and Kyla felt her cheeks grow hot as she read his unspoken question. She could see it probably looked very rude of her to refuse Peter's help, especially given the quantity of things she would have to carry in herself.

"You sure?" Peter asked again.

"Oh—all right," she conceded hastily. "Yes, I would very much appreciate it. Thank you for offering." She couldn't look at either of them.

"Now that's more like it," Dr. Grant said, turning to give Peter a thumbs-up. "Do you know which room is hers?"

"I'm happy to," Peter said to Kyla before turning to Dr. Grant. "Yes,

I do. I'll let the two of you finish your conversation." He left, padding silently down the hall in his socks back the way he came.

Kyla watched him leave, then turned back to discover Dr. Grant studying her.

"So what's going on? Are you and Mr. Watkins in some sort of conflict?"

Kyla shook her head. "No, nothing like that. It's just that he and my dad—" She stopped, not knowing what to say. She shrugged. "It's—it's a long story. I'm sorry. I was just—caught off guard. It's all good. I'm fine."

"Okay," he said, nodding thoughtfully. "Okay."

Kyla took a drink of her soda.

The professor took a long breath. Laying his hands on the table, he blew it out loudly, rising to his feet. "Well, my dear Miss DeKane, unless you have any questions about what we've discussed so far, I think we might be ready for our tour."

"Just one question," she said, rising with him. "Where are the kids?" She felt a bit foolish asking.

"The kids!" He lifted his hands, feigning surprise, as if he had forgotten about them. "Actually, that's a great question! Right now they are"—he studied his watch—"still in the air on their way here, but not for long. They've been with their aunt and cousins since Marilee left for London—for two weeks now. My sister is delivering them from Texas and flying back home tomorrow morning. I'm going to be leaving for the airport in just a little while to meet them, and we'll be staying overnight in a hotel, where I promised I'd take them swimming tonight. We'll be home in the morning sometime. Now come on, my dear—I'll show you around."

Dr. Grant led her back in the direction of where she'd come in, commenting along the way. "We call this the Great Room," he said, indicating the spacious living room. "When we bought the house we called it the 'Great Mess.' It was filled with debris. The whole place was a shambles, with holes knocked in nearly every wall in the house. So far the first two floors have been completely redone."

"Holes in the walls? Why?" she asked. "From what?"

"We're not sure," he said simply, eyeing her carefully.

"Huh," she said. The walls looked fine now. "Are the kids allowed in there? I didn't notice any toys."

He raised his eyebrows. "The toys are picked up and put away when they're finished playing with them."

Kyla nodded. "Right." His reply embarrassed her, but her question was answered.

They passed the foyer and Great Room to pause at the majestic, oak pocket doors in the hallway beyond the stairway.

"This," he said, pushing back one of the heavy doors into its slit in the wall to reveal a very large, old-fashioned library within, "is my favorite room in this whole, behemoth house. We often leave these doors open, just to break up this long hall. And because I love the room."

With another shove the other door rumbled back, creating a large opening into the hall from which the smell of books and ink filled the air. He waved her in. The entire perimeter of the room was lined with book-filled shelves. Kyla craned her neck to read the titles, recognizing many antique sets among his collection. A fireplace dominated one wall, and before it was a set of comfortable reading chairs on each side of a love seat, all atop a patterned Persian rug. Near the windows on the far side of the room was a large oak table for studying, and before it, in the room's center, were two shorter double-sided bookcases filled with children's books and educational toys. Puffy beanbag chairs and a child-sized table were nearby.

"This is—this is awesome!" She couldn't hold back her delight. She gestured to the children's furniture. "So the kids are allowed in here too, I see."

Dr. Grant seemed pleased at her interest in the room. "Of course! Absolutely! Encouraged, actually. Enjoy it. But keep in mind there is no 'Marian the Librarian' that will come and put away your books and toys for you!"

She smiled. "Understood."

He then turned quickly to the opposite set of doors across the hall, pulling one to the side.

"This is my office, my personal study." He held out an arm, motioning her in. "Get a good look, because neither you nor my boys are allowed in here unless I'm here to invite you in. There are very few rooms in this house that are entirely off-limits, and this is one of them."

Kyla entered timidly. Its large windows looked out to the front of the house with a view of the driveway and the mammoth bluff. She observed his rugged desk stacked full of files and papers, his collection of books lining the walls, his leather furniture near the fireplace. It was very similar to her dad's study, only on a grander scale, a bit more cluttered, and with a definite air of academia rather than repose.

Dr. Grant pulled the heavy door shut behind them. Then Kyla followed him down the hall back toward the kitchen, where he paused to open inwardly a set of double doors across from the kitchen island, revealing a formal dining room, which also looked out over the front of the house. Kyla breathed out, taken with the room's beauty. A delicate blown-glass centerpiece stretched down the middle of an elongated mahogany table, over which hung a sparkling chandelier from the ceiling. To the left, a wide mahogany cupboard showcased Marilee's delicate china, and on the opposite wall was a sizable matching buffet, where a large soup tureen from her set was flanked by tall silver candlesticks on either side.

"Nice," she breathed softly. "Very beautiful."

"As you can probably guess, we don't let the boys in here," he said, closing the doors behind him, "but you might enjoy it sometime when you get a little time to yourself. Feel free."

They continued down the hall beyond the kitchen, where he showed her a long and narrow pantry and the laundry room, off of which was a restroom. Across from them at that end of the house was a large side entrance room, smaller and less formal than the grand foyer where Kyla had initially come in. A long, padded bench sat against one wall next to an area for coats, which had narrow oak built-in compartments above with oak drawers below for hats and gloves. At the base of the drawers were cubbyholes for shoes. Beside the wall on the mat next to the door rested a pair of work boots which she assumed were Peter's. In the corner of the room nearest her was a stairway leading upward, and beside it one going down.

"Goes up to the second floor," Dr. Grant said, pointing, "a shortcut to the upstairs hall leading to your room. And that"—he pointed again—"takes you to the cellar. The dungeon-type, so you know. We don't use it much."

"Outside on the west side of the house is our carport," he continued, indicating with his head toward the window. "You probably saw it when you arrived. That is where we usually park, and you can move your car there. We use this door to come and go. Keys go here." He pointed to a rack on the wall.

"Got it," Kyla replied.

He looked at his watch. "All right. Let's keep moving. I'll take you to your room the regular way."

She ambled after him back through the house, down the long hall, past the first staircase toward the second in front of his office. Beyond them the hall continued, dark and formidable.

"Down there"—he gave a curt nod toward where she looked—"is a fitness room, our home theater, and other rooms, but you'll explore all that soon, I'm sure. For the sake of time, let's go up. You can use either stairs."

He motioned to her and then followed her up, where they paused in the hallway at the top. The distance in the hall between the top of the two stairways made a wide balcony from which they looked down over the balustrade to the Great Room below them. It also offered an excellent view of the backyard and a thin line of the river beyond it through the Great Room's wall of windows, but because it was raining Kyla couldn't see very much of it.

"Wait until morning," Dr. Grant said. "It's gorgeous in the morning sun." He then turned, facing the three sets of French doors opposite the balustrade on the balcony.

"Okay—this will be your and the kids' suite," he told her. "These three rooms are all connected inside. Your room is there." Dr. Grant pointed right to the first set of doors across the hall from the top of the other stairway. The middle set of French doors, he explained, was normally the children's playroom, adjoined to hers, and the third set was the entrance to the boys' bedroom, which was across the hallway from the other stairway, up which they had just come. Dr. Grant said they wanted the boys close to them, motioning to Marilee's and his bedroom, next to the stairway and diagonally across the hall from the boys' doors.

"Except that this summer, while their mother is gone," Dr. Grant said, "I have flip-flopped their rooms so that they will be sleeping in the middle room next to yours. That way"—he looked at her sideways—"you will hear them if they wake up in the night."

"I see."

"The rooms on that side beyond your room"—he gestured down the dim hall—"are guest rooms that we have closed off so that we don't have to heat them or cool them unless we have company. The stairway leading down to the side entryway by the carport is at the end of that hall. You are welcome to use it. This side of the house"—he turned and gestured behind him—"is all open. Peter's room is right over there, and next to it is a restroom." He indicated to several doors beyond the third set of French doors. "The other three rooms down there are unoccupied, and there's an identical back stairway which leads down to the main floor at the end of the hall."

He pointed to a door across from Peter's room. "And right there are the stairs to the third floor, which, as I said before, is unfinished. I'm not taking you up there today, but feel free to explore to your heart's content as you have opportunity. I doubt there's ever been a piece of furniture on that floor, and some days I doubt there will ever be." He gave a small chuckle. "Who knows? Above the third floor is an attic. You'll find a stairway to it, but I wouldn't recommend going up there unless you have a fondness for bats."

"Then you won't find me near it," Kyla informed him.

"And now," Dr. Grant said dramatically, moving to open the door immediately to his left at the top of the stairs, "I know you're dying to see it, so I'm going to right out show you the bedroom of my wife, Marilee Montayne, to satisfy your curiosity. After this I would ask you to please respect our privacy and not snoop around in it when I'm not here." He motioned her inside with his hand. "Please."

Kyla hesitated.

"Ah, now's your chance," he said. "Go ahead—take a look at anything you'd like!"

Embarrassed again, Kyla didn't have a reply. Indeed, she was curious, but now so explicitly invited in, she felt uncomfortable, knowing this was also his room. She leaned forward to gaze within, its modesty surprising her compared to what she had expected, but she liked Ms. Montayne's style and taste. Dr. Grant pointed out his wife's dressing room on the other side of their master bath, complete with clothes and shoes, but Kyla would not enter the room any further, aware of his presence close beside her. She stepped away, backing awkwardly into the hall, thanking him, her cheeks warm. Dr. Grant didn't close the door but remained there, his hand still on the lever.

"I'm afraid I'm going to have to leave you on your own at this point. I really should grab a few things and be getting on my way to meet my sister and the boys. I wouldn't want to be late." One eyebrow rose slightly as he emphasized the last sentence.

Inwardly she winced. It was her strike one, she realized, and he was keeping tally.

"You okay here alone overnight? I know this place can be a bit overpowering. Peter will be here, of course."

"I'm fine—thank you," she said.

"Okay. Well, Miss DeKane, welcome to Wynnbury. Tomorrow then." He gave a little salute and disappeared into his bedroom, leaving her in the long and shadowy hall.

Chapter Nine

Kyla entered her bedroom, found the light, and leaned back against the wall. *What was I thinking?* she wondered. Since she had arrived at Wynnbury that afternoon, her previous ratio of self-confidence over fear had reversed itself, leaving her with blaring self-doubt. All the expectations for which she felt unqualified loomed before her, and Kyla knew there would be no faking it with Dr. Grant, for he was particular. She had the distinct impression that she was in over her head. The excitement she'd had about living in a mansion had waned—not that she didn't think the house was beautiful, of course, for it was more beautiful than she'd imagined—but it was also unfamiliar, dark, and daunting.

From where she stood, Kyla studied her room. It was lovely, situated on the front of the house, straight over the foyer below. Long sheer curtains of peaceful blue swirls lined the entire far wall from ceiling to floor, pulled back from each of the four windows with ties, and framed above with a darker padded valance that spanned the length of her whole room, trimmed in matching cord. Tasseled shades were pulled halfway down over each of the windows, out of which she could see that it was still drizzling. A high four-poster bed with a darker blue toile coverlet and colorful contrasting pillows dominated one side of the room, and on the other side an antique style settee and two wing-backed armchairs framed a fireplace, its dark mantel topped with a vase of yellow silk tulips. Cobalt blue tiles comprised the hearth and decoratively lined the ornate iron fireplace opening. Near one of the windows was a small drop-leaf table with two chairs. Neatly arranged behind the armchair nearest the door were her bags and luggage. She had not seen or heard Peter bring any of it into the house. He must have used the back stairs in the side entryway.

On her left, in the center of the wall near the bed, was a little hallway, which she observed led to the boys' adjoining bedroom. Between their rooms was a bathroom on one side and on the other a sizable closet for her. Peeking into the boys' room, she saw two twin beds covered in a retro cowboy print. Above each bed was a giant "H" on the wall, decorated with a miniature set of cowboy boots, a cowboy hat, and a red bandana. *Howard and Henry*, Kyla repeated to herself. Such old-fashioned names. Toys were put away neatly in baskets on shelves. A package of diapers on one of the dressers gave Kyla a sudden jolt, as she for the first time considered that area of childcare. She knew nothing about diapers or toilet training, and tomorrow her little charges would arrive. She bit her lip, realizing the boys must be younger than she anticipated.

Beyond the boys' bedroom was their playroom, where Kyla noticed various stations of activities—a painting easel, and shallow indoor sandbox, a low table with a castle with knights and royal-subject play figures, a collection of construction vehicles, wooden blocks, various kinds of balls in a large bin, a tub of stuffed animals, and a tall shelf filled with more toys. There would be no shortage of things to do, she observed.

Kyla returned to her bedroom. In her mind she heard Dr. Grant's voice asking, *So do you think you're ready for this?* The question carried a little more meaning now, and she sighed. Everything around her seemed foreign from her small, familiar world. Just one week ago today she was moving home from her apartment and graduating, without even the slightest idea that in such a short time she would be here! She sank into one of the armchairs by the fireplace, clicking on the curved floor lamp beside it, admiring the silky lampshade, thinking of how classy this room was compared to her overly purple teenage bedroom at home. What a contrast the entire house was from her modest home in Stanton, excepting that, although Wynnbury was beautiful, it felt anything but cozy to Kyla. It shouted refinement, neatness, and perfection, everything that she wasn't. She felt like a fish out of water, admitting to herself that perhaps she *wasn't* ready for this.

Her thoughts of home reminded Kyla that she was supposed to have called her dad to let him know she arrived. He would have figured that out by now, she presumed. Her purse and phone were still downstairs in the kitchen, but she was in no hurry to get up. She was irritated with her dad anyway. It was pretty obvious that he and Peter What's-His-Face had been discussing a little more than the Bible in their meetings together. Unbelievable! She wished she could go online and look again at the original email from Dr. Grant, but she knew without the Wi-Fi password it would have to wait. Her dad must have known Peter was here! Her jaw tightened at the thought. Why hadn't he said anything to her? She would have words with him about that! And Peter! She let out a breath and shook her head, thinking of him in the kitchen. Eager, geeky-happy Peter. He had acted entirely too familiar with her, and it bothered her. She certainly hadn't expected him to be here, and it was difficult for her to warm up to the idea of being stuck with one of her father's flaky friends for the entire summer.

Indeed, nothing was as she had expected! What a disparity between Wynnbury House and her fantasy vision of Adirondack chairs on a quaint cabin deck in the piney woods. Kyla stared ahead into the cold fireplace, wondering what she'd gotten herself into. For certain, this nanny job wasn't going to be a summer vacation. She was reminded of the strange arrangement Dr. Grant had with his housekeeper and frowned. *What the heck!* How could she endure a summer with no shopping? No little trips to town even? Not even to pick out her own deodorant or a personal stash of sour gummy worms? It seemed unreasonable!

Feeling hungry again, she finally pulled herself out of the chair and ventured down the stairs to the kitchen, where her things were right on the counter as she had left them. Outside the thunder rumbled, and raindrops still pelted against the patio door there, the gloomy weather darkening the house prematurely. Searching for the lights, Kyla found a switch that illuminated one side of the kitchen. *Good enough for now*, she thought, turning to the refrigerator for something to eat. She chose an apple in a drawer and some peanut butter, leaving a half-eaten box of pizza undisturbed. Starting tomorrow she would have to feed the kids. She peered back into the fridge with that in mind, again reminded that she would have to order groceries through the housekeeper. What did kids eat besides macaroni and cheese? She didn't even know what to ask for.

The light above the sink reflected on the photo of Marilee Montayne. Kyla studied it in the dim light, eating her apple, admiring her flawless beauty and her perfect hair, wondering if she would ever meet her. What would Dr. Grant tell his wife about the new nanny, she wondered. From what Kyla could tell, he was an exacting man, very clear about what he expected. Would Marilee hear complaints? Would he regret hiring her?

"I hope I can handle your kids," she said, peering at the photograph.

Kyla finished the apple and threw away the core, then reached for her phone across the kitchen peninsula. Five notifications lit up across its face: a missed call and a text from her dad, a missed call and a message from a number she did not recognize, and—she sighed in annoyance—a text from Alex.

"Oh, Alex," she breathed, opening it. "You just can't get a clue, can you?"

"I don't blame you for hating me," his message read. "I'm texting you because my dad really wants you back at your old position. Will hold for you. Please reconsider. I promise to respect your space."

Kyla felt the breath sucked out of her. She stared at the text, reading it again. Was he serious? Or was he manipulating her? The moment she asked herself the question she knew the answer. She closed the text. "Nice try, Alex," she murmured.

She opened her messages to listen to the one the unknown caller had left and held her phone to her ear.

"Hello, Kyla. Richard, here. Richard Duvall. I'm calling in regard to your pos—your old position here at the firm. I understand things are a bit tense between you and my son, but would you please call me? I'd like to talk about a way this could work. And I'd like to make it worth your while. Give me a call, hon."

She stood frozen by the counter, staring at her phone for a full minute, stunned by the sudden option. *This could be her out!*

Now Kyla wanted to talk to her dad, wanted his advice. Resolutely, she grabbed her phone and pressed his name to call him, but like earlier in the day, her phone would not dial out. Still no reception. *Dang it! What was the problem?* She obviously had *received* those calls and texts! She tried standing close to the window, then walked slowly around the kitchen holding her phone in crazy angles, but still nothing. She tried the same in the dining room and along the patio doors, holding her phone up high, then stepped into the eerie darkness of the Great Room to try it there along the wall of windows. Nothing! A little noise from upstairs caused her to quickly turn and look upward toward the balcony, but she saw nothing but the dim hallway above. Was it Peter? She peered upwards, waiting to hear the sound again, but there was nothing. It had spooked her, though, and she decided she was done with messing with her phone in the shadows. Resigned, she left the light on above the sink in the kitchen in case she needed to come back downstairs later, then took her purse and went upstairs.

The reception wasn't any better in her room. Nor could she text, as it failed to send after each attempt. Abandoning her phone, she sat before the fireplace again, staring at the tiles thinking. She knew she was caught in a web. It scared her that the offer was even a temptation. With her hands behind her head, she weighed out both the issues that would be solved and issues that would be created if she left. Inside she knew what her father would most likely advise, but she wasn't sure if that was the right choice for her. This would have to be *her* decision. But it wasn't easy.

Twenty minutes later Kyla dug through her purse for a quarter, holding it out on her fist.

"Okay, God—how 'bout you decide this?" she murmured, flipping it high into the air. "Heads, I stay."

She missed the catch, and the coin bounced off her hand, falling with a *tink* onto the tile hearth and rolling onto the light rug, facing heads up.

It was clear then what Kyla wanted to do, regardless of the coin toss. Decisively she shouldered one of her tote bags and took her largest suitcase, maneuvering it toward the door. She would need to make several trips to load her car. Spying her car keys on the small table near the armchair, she scooped them up, suddenly noticing under them a scrap of paper with a scrawled note from Peter.

"Kyla, I put the top up on your car and wiped down your seats. Should be fine."

"Ah, my car!" she groaned, her hand popping to her forehead. It was enough for her to remember her car windows, much less the top of a convertible! Mentally she calculated how many hours it might have been sitting open in the rain if he hadn't closed it up. Grateful, she debated also leaving Peter a note of thanks in the kitchen before she left, beside the note she would leave for Dr. Grant. It would be strange if she said nothing to him at all. She would write both their notes on her way out.

Quietly and carefully, she opened her door and lugged the bulky suitcase down the staircase to the broad hall, pulling it over the rug in the dark foyer to the heavy front door, which she opened to the rainy night. She blinked. Her car was not there. Then she remembered the carport. Peter had probably moved her car to the carport for her. It bugged her that he drove it without asking her, but since he did save it from being saturated by the rain, she supposed it would have to be okay. She wondered how far she would find the seat moved back. He had long legs.

Softly she shut the door, tugging the suitcase back across the rug and down the dimly lit hall to the side entrance beyond the kitchen, the rollers rattling noisily across the tile of the floor. Leaving the entry room lights off, she pulled her bag across the mat in the dark. Opening the side door, she heaved it over the threshold and down the three steps to the driveway, jerking the heavy suitcase around the edge of the house. The glow of the streetlight in the yard revealed her car there, parked neatly with its top up in the carport, and behind it, completely blocking her in, was a large white pickup truck, its bed covered with a tarp. *Right.* She shook her head, recognizing it from the day her dad moved her out of her apartment. Peter's truck.

Her shoulders sagged in disappointment as she stared at the vehicle, the rain splashing off the edge of the carport, dripping onto her head. She couldn't leave. Not unless she asked Peter to move his truck, and *that* wasn't going to happen! Reluctantly, she pulled her suitcase into the house again, closing the door quietly behind her. Running a hand through her wet hair, she shook it out and looked down at her soaked blouse, taking a few moments to catch her breath before retracing her steps upstairs. Then right as she grabbed the handle of her bag, she was startled to hear Peter's footsteps coming through the house. *Oh, great,* she groaned inside, dreading meeting him. He had probably heard her dragging her suitcase through the house and had come to investigate. Or to possibly "help." She waited in the dark for him to appear in the doorway, trying to think of an explanation.

He did not come into the entryway. After hearing him singing to himself in the kitchen, opening cupboards, and moving about for a few minutes, Kyla realized that he did not know she was there. With her hand, she covered her mouth in the darkness, barely breathing, wondering what to do. What would he think if he saw her trying to leave Wynnbury? It wouldn't matter a bit if he didn't know her dad. But what could she say to him now if he saw her, suitcase in hand? She could never live down the embarrassment. She couldn't even fib that she was bringing in her things.

Panicky, she eyed the shadowy opening of the back stairs that led to the second floor. Hesitating only for a moment, she quickly hefted her bag onto the first step, then silently repeated the motion until the room below was out of sight, working her way up into the eerie darkness until reaching the door of the second-floor hall. On the other side she stopped to catch her breath, her heart pounding. Fixing her eyes on the lighted balcony ahead where her bedroom was, she hoisted the heavy suitcase up against her chest, wrapped her arms around it, and tiptoed hurriedly down the vacant hallway to her room, letting herself in as quietly as possible.

Finally out of Peter's earshot, she deposited the bag onto the carpet near the others where it had sat before. Panting, she stood there, wanting to cry from frustration. Nothing was working out! Nothing was going her way! She was soaked from the rain and stuck in this place! Defeated, she bent down and unzipped her suitcase, rummaging through it to find her pajamas. The night was still young, but what else was there for her to do with no phone, no Internet, and no television set in her room? When she was finished getting ready for bed, she surveyed her room once more. With effort, she dragged one of the armchairs across the carpet, positioning it tightly against the center of the French doors. Then she locked the door to the boys' bedroom, and leaving the light on in the bathroom, Kyla went to bed.

The faint smell of coffee is what finally caused her to stir. Kyla rolled back in her bed, disoriented at first until she remembered where she was. Her stomach growled, and she stretched to check the clock on the end table, discovering that she had slept later than she thought. Probably because her room was still dark. Or because the bed was so comfortable. Or because she'd had trouble falling asleep from thinking about how much she wanted her old job back.

Slipping out from between the covers, she opened one of the tasseled shades to see the hazy morning sun shining through a thin layer of clouds. Before her towered the steep bluff around which she'd driven yesterday and beside it the driveway winding out of the woods into the yard, splitting, with one path leading to the portico below her and the other to where she knew the carport to be, although from her window it was out of sight. Through the trees on the left edge of the yard she could see the beginning of a little wooded ravine, leading, she assumed, downward toward the river. Quickly she threw on a pair of shorts and a hoodie, then returning the winged back chair to where it belonged, she went to get herself some breakfast. She was starving.

As she opened her bedroom door, the view stopped Kyla short, and she lingered at the balcony railing to take it all in through the tall windows of the Great Room. Beyond the broad and grassy backyard she could now see a slice of the silver river tucked down beneath the verdant wooded bluffs that surrounded it. Dr. Grant was right—the sun on the bluffs was beautiful. She had to stay a few minutes to enjoy it before continuing on down the stairs.

In contrast to its gloomy dimness yesterday evening, the house was now very bright, though still very quiet and empty. Kyla made her way to the kitchen, finding the coffee she had smelled upstairs. *Thank you, Peter Whatever-Your-Name-Is*, she mused. A carton of coffee creamer was nearby, the top still opened. In the cupboard above it she found a mug and poured herself a cup, setting it on the peninsula, and then one by one Kyla opened cupboard doors in the kitchen, exploring until she found the breakfast cereal. She poured herself a bowl, adding milk from the refrigerator, and slid onto one of the swivel chairs at the counter. Beside her she noticed the patio door slightly ajar, allowing in the cool and fresh air from outside. The slight breeze felt nice on her legs.

Kyla was halfway finished with her cereal when she heard the scrape of footsteps on the patio. Peter appeared, pushing open the sliding door to let himself in.

"Good morning," he said, his eyes brightening when he saw her. He was freshly showered and had on a clean T-shirt. He slid his cell phone into the front pocket of his jeans.

"Morning," Kyla replied, looking up briefly with her mouth full of cereal.

"How was your night? I hope you were able to sleep." He came around to the kitchen side of the peninsula and paused to face her.

Kyla swallowed her cereal. "I slept well—thank you." Without looking at him, she sipped her coffee and set it down, applying her technique of offering nothing further.

It didn't seem to work with him.

"Great! I'm happy to hear it," he responded. "And I'm glad I caught you before I left. I'm going into town, and I wanted to be sure you were okay here alone for a bit until Dr. Grant gets back this morning. This place can be—" He shrugged, looking around.

"I'm fine," she returned coolly but couldn't help asking, "Where are you going?" So *he* could leave but *she* couldn't?

His eyes lit up. "I'm going to church. You would be welcome to join me, but—"

"Ah, I think Dr. Grant expects me to be here when he gets home," she said hastily, cutting him off.

"Yep." Peter nodded. "That's what I was thinking."

She remained quiet.

His fingers bounced silently on the countertop. "Well, I should probably get going," he said.

He left, skirting around the dining room table behind her into the Great Room. Kyla turned her head to see him fetch a Bible from an armchair in the corner and an empty coffee mug from a coaster on the end table, which he brought to the kitchen sink. How very much like her dad, she thought, watching him rinse the mug. He shut the water off and turned to face her, wiping his hands on a towel.

"Hey, um, I want to apologize for yesterday. You're right—your stuff is none of my business." He set the towel on the counter.

Kyla lifted her chin defensively.

"And just so you know," he continued, moving to stand across the peninsula from her, "even though I sent your dad that email, I didn't know you got the job until yesterday."

"Huh." Her eyes lifted to his briefly, and then she looked away.

He sighed, pulling his car keys from his pocket. "Okay. Well, I wanted to tell you that. And I want you to know I think it's pretty cool you're here."

He tapped his knuckles on the countertop, picked up his Bible, and headed down the hall to leave through the side door. Kyla remembered her car as she heard his truck start. She probably should have thanked him for putting the top up in last night's rain, but she had thought of it too late. She was taking her bowl to the sink when she heard him come back into the house again. He came swiftly through the hall, pausing by the island.

"Hey," he said, holding up a finger, "just a quick thing I want to let you know—in case you need to use your phone. The best place for reception is at the edge of the yard out in back."

Immediately her cheeks turned pink as she thought of all of her contortions as she had tried to call out last night. Had he been spying on her from the balcony or some other dark corner of the house last night?

"Were you watching me?" she asked.

He cocked his head. "What?"

"Were you watching me?"

"Watching what? When?" He frowned, shaking his head. "What are you talking about?"

She folded her arms, giving him a look.

Peter raised his hands, his eyes wide. "Look—all I'm saying is that the reception here is terrible! I go to the edge of the yard to make my calls." He gestured outside. "That's all I wanted to tell you! That's where I was this morning—outside on my phone!"

Kyla shifted, a bit embarrassed. "Okay," she replied with a nod. "Thanks."

He stared at her, bewildered.

She cleared her throat, unfolding her arms and plunging ahead awkwardly, "Um, I should probably thank you for closing up my car last night. And for moving it to the carport for me."

He gave a slow nod. "You're welcome." He looked at her a bit longer, then took a breath. "Well, I should go. See you later." He held up his long arm in a wave as he turned and left the same way he came in.

Kyla blew out a long breath and looked toward the ceiling. There was no way being with him for a summer was going to work. He was definitely one of her dad's good 'ol boys. What was it about them that made them so weird? Everything about Peter was just—just—! She shuddered, unable to determine what it was that bugged her.

But now that he was gone, Kyla realized that his truck was no longer blocking in her car. Her eyes lifted to the balcony over the Great Room. She could gather up her things right now and leave. Adrenalized, she hurried up to her room, where she quickly made the bed and threw her things into her suitcase. She grabbed her phone off the end table to pop it into her purse but paused, glancing out the open French doors to the backyard through the Great Room windows. She supposed she ought to at least call her dad before she left.

Knowing she had only a window of time, Kyla bounded down the stairs and out the patio door, crossing the damp grass to the edge of the yard where the woods started, as Peter had indicated to her. She had forgotten to plug her phone in last night, and it was only halfway charged, but it was more than enough charge to call her dad. She dialed and was delighted to hear it ring. But he did not answer. The call went straight to his messaging. She looked at her phone in disappointment. At least she had been able to call out! Perhaps he was talking with someone—she would wait and call him in a few minutes.

With a sigh, Kyla put her hands into the front pockets of her hoodie and turned to look at the backside of the enormous house before her on the lawn. The concrete rail of the patio that spanned nearly the length of the house gleamed white in the sunlight. Several large planters of flowers and greens were spread across its surface, arranged in complimentary groups. Near the sliding door were a grill and a patio table surrounded by chairs. Next to it, and partially in front of the Great Room windows, was a metal pergola covered by a canvas shade canopy, under which was a set of comfortable outdoor furniture with green-and-tan-patterned cushions. On the far side of the concrete deck, opposite of where she had come out, was another set of patio doors. The house looked rather nice in the morning light, Kyla thought.

The discordant squawk of a blue jay suddenly pulled her attention to the trees near her. In the woods before her a short distance from where she stood, she saw that the ground dropped sharply downward. She peered down into the brush, looking for the river, which she could smell but not yet see. The jaybird squawked noisily again, and Kyla strained to find him in the trees. She followed his call, walking to her right toward the east side of the yard, where she could now see into the ravine that she had noticed earlier from her bedroom window, observing that it broadened and deepened as it continued down the hill. It was a lovely view. As she gazed into the woods, she suddenly noticed two deer far below her standing in the mud of a little stream, their heads erect, studying her with their dark, round eyes. She stood very still, watching them, the young does poised and alert, staring back, their tan hides blending into the soft underbrush. Then the blue jay squawked again, followed by the chattering reply of other birds, and startled, the deer bounded downward through the gully.

Pleased with the unexpected surprise, Kyla peered into the woods after them, wondering how close the river was from where she stood. She listened carefully, unsure if she could hear the water or if it was just the rustling of leaves. Either way, it was peaceful. She took her time walking back along the edge of the yard, trying to see through the trees, when suddenly, through a clearing, she saw what she was looking for—the river, although it wasn't the wide, swift-moving main current of the Mississippi. She knew these were the backwaters, which more closely resembled a narrow lake. She gazed at the dark water below, framed by the oaks and maples all around, and breathed deeply. Beautiful. Just beautiful. As she kept following the edge of the woods, it opened up more, and she could see on the hillside across the river a modest home, which overlooked a similar view and Wynnbury House from the other side. A short distance out from the opposite shore there was an island.

Then Kyla noticed a large, square, wooden structure at the edge of yard that jutted out toward the river. Curious, she approached it, discovering a long, winding staircase of lumber built right against the side of a steep drop-off. As she stepped out onto it and looked over, her breath caught. Below her at the bottom of the wooden stair was a small sandy patch of beach on the riverbank on which sat a pair of white-painted Adirondack chairs. She stared at them. They weren't the only chairs there, as there was a chaise lounge nearby too, and a hammock strung between two trees, but still—there they were! Two of them, positioned next to each other on a trimmed grassy area. On the shore a canvas-covered boat bobbed gracefully alongside an aluminum dock. As she leaned on the railing surveying the scene, a sudden movement overhead caught her eye, and she looked up to see a bald eagle glide across the river to its thick nest of sticks high in a tree on the little island. The sight took her breath away, and she stood there for several minutes, watching it in wonder.

Then the blue jay was back, squawking up a fuss, calling her to attention again. That's right—she was trying to leave, she reminded herself. She needed to keep moving. Kyla retrieved her phone from her pocket and called her dad again. Still no answer. It hit her then that it was Sunday, and he too would be at church. Feeling foolish, she called once more to leave a message, but as it rang she debated what to say. It would be odd to tell him in a recording that she was quitting before she even started and to expect her home later that day. She decided to keep it simple. His recorded message began.

"Hi, Dad," she said into her phone. "Just letting you know I made it. Sorry I didn't call you yesterday, but I couldn't get reception. Hope we can talk soon. Love you!" That way, she reasoned, he wouldn't worry when he got the message, and she could explain everything else when she got home.

She hung up and put the phone into her pocket, gazing out thoughtfully again at the water and the two white chairs below. At that moment she heard the sound of a vehicle enter the yard behind her. Turning, she glimpsed a shiny blue SUV coming through the woods, disappearing for a moment and reappearing to park at the carport beside the house. Dr. Grant was home. Kyla watched him get out and open the side door of his vehicle, out of which a young child jumped onto the driveway, laughing and running in his excitement to be home.

Kyla knew what she had to do. It didn't have to be complicated. *I'm not a nanny,* she concluded. *What in the world made me think I was?* She would simply be mature about it and tell him she was not cut out for the job and that she had gotten another offer that was better. He didn't need to know anything more. Surely he had other applicants who would be glad to take her place. Determinedly she cut across the yard to the house.

Chapter Ten

From a distance Kyla heard both yelling and crying through the patio screen as she approached the house. Dr. Grant and his two boys were already inside when Kyla stepped into the dining room through the patio door. A whimpering child, red-eyed from crying, was perched on the granite peninsula with his short jean-clad legs dangling over the side, holding up an injured hand while Dr. Grant searched through a narrow cupboard over the sink. The little boy sniffed, wiping his tears with his good hand, then rubbed it across the mud-streaked belly of his yellow T-shirt. When he spotted Kyla, he gave a startled cry and reached his arms toward his father. It was apparent to Kyla that this wasn't the time to make her straightforward announcement.

"Good morning," Dr. Grant said to her cheerfully, finding a box of Band-Aids and picking through it for one the right size. "Just a little wipeout on the edge of the carport. Gotta do a little first aid."

He found one, peeled it open, and leaned over the toddler's hand. "All right, kiddo. Show me your scrape."

From far down the hallway Kyla heard the smacking footsteps of the other boy running on the tile while shouting, "I'm home! I'm ho-o-o-me, I'm ho-o-o-me!" all the way to the kitchen.

"That's enough, Howie!" Dr. Grant called to him over his shoulder.

The excited brother suddenly noticed Kyla and stopped running, finding shelter behind his father's leg and eyeing her cautiously while he caught his breath. Simultaneously with the bandage applied, the crying tapered off as the younger boy sniffed and studied the cartoon graphics on the colorful strip.

At the sudden quiet, Dr. Grant gave Kyla a look of relief. "Now that's more like it! Boys"—he hoisted the child off the counter into his arms—"I'd like you to meet Miss Kyla DeKane. She is going to be your nanny."

The younger son gave a jerky breath, watching her guardedly, his cheeks still wet with tears. He was blond and fair-skinned with long eyelashes.

"Miss Kyla," Dr. Grant continued, placing a hand on the older child's head, "this is my son Howard, named after my father. He's four, but he's going to have a birthday in August. Right, Howie?"

Howie, short for Howard, and four, Kyla noted. The child smiled timidly from beside his father. He was lean, with dark hair and brown eyes like his dad. He was wearing blue jeans with a zippered athletic jacket.

"And this is Henry," Dr. Grant said, turning to the son in his arms and reaching up to wipe his nose again, "named after Marilee's father. Hank just turned two last month. Boys, say hello to Miss DeKane."

With a sniff, Hank curled into his father's neck. Howie said hello very softly, peering out a bit from behind his dad to get a better look at her.

"It's very nice to meet you," she told them, smiling at them both. *Hank and Howie, ages two and four.* They were handsome boys.

"Who would like to tell Miss Kyla about the surprise we brought for her?" Dr. Grant continued, his eyes moving from one of his sons to the other.

Kyla gave Howie a questioning look. "You brought me a surprise?"

His head dipped toward the floor, and he whispered something unintelligible.

Dr. Grant looked down at him. "What was that? Speak up!"

"We brought you a donut," he repeated shyly, glancing up at her.

Kyla's eyes widened. "Are you serious? Donuts are my favorite!"

Howie looked pleased, and with the prospect of having his treat he began climbing into his chair on the far side of the table. Dr. Grant deposited Hank in the booster seat on the end by the patio door and then handed Kyla a rectangular box of pastries, which she opened and set on the table.

"Coffee?" he asked, holding up two to-go cups in a cardboard carrier.

"Yes—thank you," she said, taking the one he handed her.

Kyla slid into a seat beside Howie, who was already standing in his chair, leaning over the donut box with one knee on the table, pointing out which donut belonged to each person by touching each one. He held up a pink frosted donut with sprinkles for her.

"I picked this one for you!" he told her, admiring the donut. "Do you like pink?"

"Thank you," Kyla said, taking it from him. "Yes, I do."

"Why?" He picked another donut out of the box and held it up flat on his palm, looking at her while he stood in his chair.

"M-i-i-i-ne!" Hank gave a panicked squeal from his chair, his hands outstretched. "My donut! Mine!"

"Why do you like pink?" Howie asked again, oblivious.

Dr. Grant appeared at the table, whisking the donut off his hand and giving it to his brother, who quieted and eagerly turned his attention to it.

"Howie, have a seat," Dr. Grant said. "Which one is yours?"

Howie pointed, settling in his chair. His father gave him his chosen donut and went back to get the kids their drinks.

"We get chocolate milk," Howie told her, pointing to the small plastic drink bottle his dad set before him.

"Nice," Kyla replied. "You must be special!"

Dr. Grant finally sat down with his own coffee, turning to Kyla. "How was your night?"

"Good—thank you," she replied.

"Your room is okay? You found something to eat?"

"Yes, I did, and the room is beautiful."

"Hey!" Howie said. He was standing again and leaning his face in front of Kyla's. "Did you know that this is my house?"

Dr. Grant turned to him. "How is your sprinkle donut, mister? How 'bout you sit down to work on that while I visit with Miss Kyla?"

Reluctantly Howie settled into his chair and took a bite, watching Kyla curiously. Hank, at the end of the table, had already finished eating the frosting off the top of his donut and was examining the colored sugar beads stuck to his palms.

Dr. Grant nodded to the open patio door. "I see you have been out enjoying the beautiful morning."

"Um, sort of," Kyla responded and slipped her phone out of her pocket to hold it up briefly. "But, yes—it's lovely out too."

He gave a knowing look, the corners of his mouth turning up. "Ah, that. Yeah. I forgot to mention it yesterday." He peered into the pastry box and selected his own donut. "I really hope you aren't one of those phone addicts who needs to be looking at it all day long. You'll go into withdrawals if you are. Wynnbury seems to be completely off the grid when it comes to phone service. There's one or two places in the house that are hot spots, otherwise out there is best." He jerked his head to the backyard and took a bite of the donut.

"Peter told me," she said, returning the phone to her pocket.

"Who's Peter?" Howie asked into his chocolate milk.

"You know, this would be the perfect little spot if you were into anything illegal," Dr. Grant said. "You could train a terrorist army here, and no one would ever know! We are quite tucked away from satellites and civilization."

"Who's Peter?" Howie repeated, licking his lips.

Dr. Grant wiped his face with his napkin and replied to Kyla's startled look, "Oh, don't worry—there's nothing shady happening here!"

Kyla asked, "How close is the nearest neighbor?"

"Not far." He nodded outside. "Right there."

Kyla frowned. "What? Like, there across the lake?"

"Who is Peter, who is Peter, who is Peter—" Howie was rocking to and fro with his chocolate milk.

"River. Yes, they're the closest. Otherwise two miles by road, and you have to go out the gate. That's not unusual for country living. Howie, please!" He turned, holding up a hand, indicating for his son to stop. "Peter is the name of the guy staying with us this summer to help Daddy with some things outside in the yard."

"Where is he?" he asked, looking behind him into the Great Room. "Is he a kid or a grown-up?"

"A grown-up," Dr. Grant answered. "And I don't know where Peter is."

Howie's face fell. "Aww, I wish he was a kid!" He set down his milk and turned back to his donut.

"He went to town to go to church," Kyla offered.

"Ah. Did you hear that, Howie?" Dr. Grant lifted his hand. "Peter went to church." He took another drink of coffee.

"What's church?"

Dr. Grant's eyes met Kyla's over his cup. "Finish your donut, please."

He turned to Kyla with a questioning look. "What about you? Are you one of those types?"

"Those types?"

"I figured maybe since you're friends with Peter you might also share his interest in religion."

"We're not friends."

Dr. Grant lifted his head. "Oh, that's right. Your father—"

"Yes, he's my dad's friend," she said. "And I'm afraid Peter's religious interests might be due to my dad. My dad is, ah, a little over the top."

"I see. And you—you're not into that? Or do you go to church too?"

She shook her head. "No, I'm not. Just my dad. I went with him for a few years, but I stopped going quite a while ago."

"Huh." He nodded, frowning. "Okay. Mind if I ask why? Just curious." He glanced over to check on Hank.

Kyla held her fingers before her lips while she finished her bite. "I guess there are some things I question about God. Some things I don't get. Like why he let some things happen."

The professor paused with his coffee in mid-air, his head tipped in question. "But you *do* believe in God?"

She raised a shoulder. "Well, I guess so. I mean, I'm pretty sure there *is* a God. It's just that he's—well, I'm disappointed by him. Sort of. I don't know. I guess I have a lot of questions. It seems he's not very fair. And other things."

"Okay, okay," he replied, thoughtfully. "I'm not trying to pry. I've just always been a little fascinated by what people think and believe. My hypothesis is that religion is kind of a family thing—you know, passed down from the parents. Personally, I have no need of God, but I can respect your views. Peter, now, he's *very* enthusiastic about God! But to each his own." He raised his eyebrows and lifted his coffee mug out toward her before drawing it in to drink.

Hank suddenly piped up from his chair, where chunks of his destroyed donut were spread across the table before him. "All done!" He held his hands up, fingers outspread. Frosting covered his face, and his broad smile revealed a mouthful of baby teeth. Kyla couldn't help smiling at him.

"That's my boy!" Dr. Grant said, chuckling at the sight. He threw Kyla a look, rising from his chair to clean him up. "I've had a break from this for a couple of weeks. I forgot that there's no such thing as relaxing with a cup of coffee with these two."

Returning with a washcloth for Hank, he continued. "So today our objective is to get to know one another. I'd like you to simply follow me around and watch how we do things around here. It's pretty clear that one of these two munchkins has warmed up to you already, and I'm confident the other will too before the day is out."

"Sounds good." Kyla nodded in agreement, turning her attention to Howie, who was patting her sleeve with his sticky, chocolate-smeared hand to get her attention, leaving a streak of frosting on her arm.

"Hey, hey—want to play castle?" he asked. "I'll be king, and you can be the princess—"

"Ah, Howie, look what you did!" Dr. Grant frowned at the chocolate mess on her sleeve. "Sorry about that!" He turned to his son. "Listen, young man—keep your little paws to yourself! Also, you may call her 'Miss Kyla' or 'Miss DeKane,' but her name is not 'hey, hey.' And now if you're finished with your snack, you may be excused to go wash your hands."

Howie gave Kyla an embarrassed smile. Taking one last drink of his chocolate milk, he climbed down from his chair, starting toward the bathroom beside the laundry room. Halfway there he stopped.

"Hey," he said, then rolling his eyes, he giggled. "I mean, Miss Kane. Wanna come with me to wash my hands?"

Kyla rose to follow him. "Sure—I'd be happy to."

Standing on a stool, Howie was able to use the sink by himself. With a squirt of liquid soap on his palms, he rubbed his hands together under the faucet and rattled nonstop to Kyla about playing pretend castle with his girl cousins in Texas, specifically highlighting that he got to be both the king and a knight of a very large castle. Above his head, Kyla met her own eyes in the mirror, reflecting on how it was becoming more and more difficult to tell Dr. Grant that she wasn't cut out for this and would be leaving for another job. So far the timing had been completely inappropriate, but she hoped an opportunity would present itself soon, as it seemed so wrong to carry on like she was.

"So do you *have* to be a nanny?" Howie asked her, drying his hands on the towel.

"Do I *have* to be a nanny?" Kyla echoed, looking down into his brown eyes, wondering how he could possibly know her conflict within. His question startled her, and she struggled for what to say. Indeed, she did have choices.

"Yeah," he continued, his head cocked. "Don't you want be a princess instead?"

She gave a little snort, suddenly reminded that he was four. She reached out to muss his hair. "Today I have to be a nanny in real life for your dad, so I can't really pretend for your castle game."

"You can't be a princess?"

"Maybe. I need to be a nanny first."

"So you can, just not today?" he asked.

"Yes. Kind of."

With damp hands he struggled to open the bathroom door, and Kyla got it for him. "Me and my cousins made a castle. Do you have a castle?" He wiped his hands again across his stomach.

Kyla looked into his upturned face, his nose brushed with light freckles. Today her home in Stanton would have to qualify as one. "I do. It's not very large, but it's nice."

"Can I see it?"

She nodded. "Perhaps sometime."

Back in the kitchen Howie seemed to forget the subject, turning to his dad to ask if he could join Hank, who was now running down the hallway. Dr. Grant waved him on.

"Yes, fine—go on and run until it's time to settle down." He shook his head, glancing at Kyla. "Just a word of advice—have your kids while you're young and still have the energy to keep up with them!" He gave a short laugh.

As he had requested, Kyla shadowed the professor for the day. Together they brought the boys' luggage upstairs, and she assisted him in putting their things away while the boys scurried back and forth between their bedroom and the playroom showing Kyla their toys one by one. Dr. Grant showed her the closet where all the puzzles and other toys with small pieces were kept. Howie then insisted on building a large tower out of Legos. Kyla sat nearby on the floor watching him while helping Hank transfer miniature cars from one plastic bin to another and back again.

Shortly after noon Dr. Grant showed her the corner of the pantry that was stocked with an abundance of kid food, along with a list of meal and snack suggestions posted near it. Kyla offered to make quesadillas, which they ate with grapes outside on the patio table. After lunch they read books in the library until Hank fell asleep, and Dr. Grant carried him up to his bed for a nap. Then he clipped a nursery monitor to his belt and suggested that the three of them walk down to the riverbank. On the way he snatched up a toy dump truck beside the patio and brought it with, and Howie played in the sand with the truck while Dr. Grant and Kyla sat on the wooden deck chairs looking out over the water and talked about daily routines, sibling rivalry, and behavior modification.

Later on their way back to the house, the professor showed Kyla another way up other than the steep stairway, a longer but more scenic trail that snaked upward through the woods and entered the yard on the west side near the carport. They walked slowly, lingering as Howie pushed his truck up the trail, hauling loads of dead sticks and leaves to various locations along the way. As they reached the edge of the yard, they noticed that Peter was back from town and was out in the carport with a hose and bucket, washing his truck. Beside it was Kyla's car, which she could see was already washed and polished. Spying the running hose, Howie excitedly turned to his dad to ask permission to help the new guy wash his truck, then abandoning the dump truck in the grass, he took off running toward the carport.

"Huh, would you look at that?" Dr. Grant said, swooping up the toy from the lawn. "It appears our man Peter has just washed your car. I'm guessing that might be a little penance for whatever was the issue between the two of you last night." He turned his head to look at Kyla.

She could feel her cheeks grow warm. "It's very nice of him," she responded, her eyes fixed ahead. She knew it was futile to even attempt to explain anything to Dr. Grant regarding Peter.

He looked away. "Ah, well, I suppose I should go rescue the poor guy from my son and make some formal introductions." He unclipped the baby monitor from his belt and handed it to Kyla. "Would you mind checking on Hank? He should probably get up so he'll go to bed tonight at a decent time."

On her way through the carport, Kyla was polite and thanked Peter for the car wash. He smiled, explaining that the side of her car had been splattered with dirt and grass clippings from the rain coming off the edge of the carport and splashing up from the ground.

"Ordinarily I would have asked first, but I thought it would be a pretty obvious answer," he said, standing over Howie, who had a hold of the hose and was ready to spray everything in sight.

Kyla kept the conversation short, and with another polite nod went to get Hank up.

The rest of the afternoon passed quickly. Both of the boys were enamored by Peter, who, after letting them help him wash his truck, pulled out a soccer ball and began to play with them, having them take turns kicking the ball to him, then awing them with his fancy footwork and silly moves. Both Hank and Howie giggled at his antics. Although invited to play, Kyla watched from the steps under the portico by the front door. Later Peter brought Howie's bike out of storage and helped him ride, while Hank scooted across the driveway after them on his tricycle. Finally Dr. Grant called them to the patio, where he had finished grilling dinner.

Having played with the kids, Peter was now of celebrity status, and at the table the boys couldn't keep their eyes off him. Howie insisted on sitting beside him and couldn't stop talking to him or touching his arm. Soon Dr. Grant had to remind Howie to keep his hands to himself and respect the grown-ups at the table by letting them talk with each other.

"You may talk, but you need to listen very carefully first and let the grown-ups lead," he told him, after which Howie gave a great sigh of disappointment but was much quieter and more attentive.

Their dinner conversation centered mainly on education. Dr. Grant talked a little about his career as a history professor and how he eventually got the job at the history department at Taiton College. Then he described the courses he had taught the last semester and the one was teaching over the summer. On Kyla's request he shared about his teaching term at Oxford and meeting his wife there, drawing her and Peter in with story after story, all of which were a pleasant mix of both interesting and funny.

At a certain point Howie began clearing his throat, focusing his eyes patiently on his talking father until he finally couldn't hold it in any longer. "Excuse me!" he announced loudly.

Dr. Grant turned to his son. "Yes?"

Howie looked around the table, speaking to Kyla and Peter, "'Marilee' is my mom's name. She's at a place called England making a movie, but we get to talk to her on my dad's computer."

After a few seconds of silence Dr. Grant gave a nod. "Yes, my son is absolutely right. And that, Howie," he added, turning back to the boy, "is again why Miss Kyla is staying with us this summer. You are going to have to be extra nice to her because, if you haven't noticed, she is the only girl."

Howie's eyes grew round as he looked at Kyla, then around the table at each person.

Dr. Grant slid down in his chair somewhat, crossing his leg and turning toward Kyla. "So now that I've been boorish and have dominated the conversation with stories about myself, let's hear about you, Miss DeKane. Congratulations on your recent graduation. Why don't you tell us what you're interested in and what your plans are for the future?"

Kyla shifted uncomfortably in her chair, disliking being the center of attention and especially conscious of Peter's eyes on her. "I don't have much to tell," she said, setting her water glass on the table. "I graduated with a degree in social work, but I'm not sure of what I want to do. My initial dreams and goals have changed." *More like vaporized, thanks to Alex,* she thought, feeling that familiar twist in her heart. She didn't know what to say beyond that, especially since Peter apparently had an inside scoop from her father. "So I'm here in the interim while I get some vision for the future." She shrugged. "There's nothing terribly interesting about me. I'm just an average person, I guess. Average height, average life, average grades, average house, average everything," she finished lamely.

"Huh." Dr. Grant narrowed his eyes at her across the table. "Certainly you underestimate yourself. Your car, for instance. For being so average you sure have a dang set of wheels. I'm sure there's a story behind that!"

She gave a small smile and quipped, "I bought it used from someone for an incredible deal."

Kyla noticed Peter's sharp glance, but he said nothing.

"No kidding!" Dr. Grant said. "Well, good for you!"

"Excuse me," Howie said loudly, charging into the conversation with something to say. "I know something about Miss Kane! Miss Kane told me she only has a small castle, but it's nice." He turned to Peter next to him, adding in explanation, "Miss Kane is kind of a princess."

"Is that right?" Peter's head rose at the words. He threw a quick look at Kyla, then he turned his head away toward the yard, a lopsided grin on his face. Kyla felt a flush creep up her neck, and she turned to face Dr Grant.

He laughed out loud, holding up his hands defensively. "Don't look at *me!*"

She blinked, looking back at Howie. "What the heck? You were trying to get me to play pretend with you!"

Dr. Grant leaned in toward her. "Hey now, lighten up—he's four! He's been playing with his little girl cousins for two weeks now, and I wouldn't be surprised if he wanted to marry you too before the week is out."

Howie stood up in his chair, leaning on Peter's arm. "What was funny? Can I be done eating, Dad?" He turned to Peter. "Wanna play with me?"

The professor sat back. "Well, I think that's our cue that dinner is officially over. Subject to be continued at another time. Yes, Howie, you can play now, but it's your bedtime soon. And let's give Peter his grown-up space, okay?"

"Thanks for dinner," Peter said. He abruptly gathered his dishes and took them to the kitchen.

Dr. Grant eyed Kyla as he took Hank out of his chair.

"From the mouths of babes," she said lightly.

"Yeah," he repeated, "from the mouths of babes. At the hotel this morning he asked a pregnant woman why she was so fat."

"At least she was pregnant," she offered with a smile.

"Yes, much to my relief!" he replied, his eyes growing wide.

After dinner Peter did not reappear. Dr. Grant read the newspaper in the Great Room while Kyla and the kids played on the floor with a bin of large toy animals. The boys were having an animal parade, lining them up single file in a long row that wound under the coffee table and chair legs. After a while Dr. Grant leaned out to check the time on the grandfather clock in the hall.

"All right," he said to Kyla. "It's bedtime. We start this process around eight, regardless of whether it's still light out. Sometimes it's quick—sometimes it's not."

He made the announcement, and soon the boys were charging up the stairs. Kyla went up too, filling the tub in the bathroom between their rooms for them, which soon held two naked little boys. After their baths Dr. Grant dressed them in their pajamas and helped them settle down in their room, preparing to read them a bedtime story. Howie was the first to be tucked into his bed, but little Hank wiggled away from his dad, running away giggling into Kyla's room. Plopping the book onto Howie's chest, Dr. Grant commanded him to stay put and went to retrieve his younger son. When Kyla entered her room behind them, the professor had Hank in his arms, but his head was turned, observing her luggage still neatly packed and sitting near the door. He pivoted, his brow drawn together.

"Your things," he said, gesturing.

Kyla's mouth opened as she paused beside her bed. "I—was really tired and got distracted last night and haven't unpacked yet."

"I see," he said, his eyes studying her face. "Okay."

He left with Hank, and Kyla stayed in her room, settling down on the settee by the fireplace, listening to Dr. Grant's muffled voice through the walkway while he finished putting his kids to bed. Eventually the room next door got very quiet. Kyla waited. Then she heard a couple of taps on the French doors that opened to the balcony. One of the doors squeaked open, and Dr. Grant poked his head in. Kyla twisted toward him in her chair.

"I think they're down," he said to her in a low voice, "but we'll see."

She nodded. "All right."

"I'm going to be in my office preparing for my class in the morning, but you're welcome to hang out wherever you'd like—downstairs in the Great Room, the library, the fitness room—"

"I'm fine here—thanks."

He paused, briefly glancing again at her bags near the door. "Regarding tomorrow—I leave around six-thirty every morning, but the boys will sleep later than that. I'm sure it will go fine. Don't stress out—it's just the first day. You'll get used to each other, and I think you're going to

149

do fine with the kids. They like you." He smiled. "And the most important thing for me is for *you* to like *them*."

She smiled back. "Thanks. I think they're sweet kids."

"Good night." He tipped his head and closed the door.

Tiredly, Kyla sank back into the chair, propping a throw pillow behind her head and putting her feet up on the other arm, thinking. After a while she pulled her phone out of her pocket where it had been all day, observing that it carried barely a charge, certainly not enough to call her dad at the edge of the yard.

The text from Alex begged her to open it again, which she did. She had thought all day about it and the phone call from his dad. All day. His dad would hold the job for her. She wondered how long. Closing her eyes, Kyla pictured herself working at her old desk at the prominent spot in the office foyer, at an angle from Alex's small office and right across from Alex's dad's large, windowed board room. She had felt so important there. His dad had doted on her, giving her attention and special privileges and surprise gifts of cash here and there to shop with. Fun money, he called it. All because she was his son's girlfriend. It had been great. Who wouldn't love wearing smart, expensive clothes to work? She thought he was going to be her father-in-law and that she would work there forever. Or at least until she and Alex had kids, when she could stay at home with them. That was mostly what she had wanted for her future. A family. A house of her own.

Maybe I didn't love that job, she considered glumly, setting the phone down onto the coffee table. Perhaps she mostly loved the idea of a future with Alex and his family. She had loved them too, not just Alex. His parents. His sister, who had become like a sister to her. They had lived together the last two summers—like really bonded. And now she too was out of her life without even a good-bye. All of them gone, not just Alex. Alex had broken her heart, but in the process Kyla's heart felt ripped away from the rest of the family too. "I promise to respect your space," he had texted. Of course, that would be necessary if she returned, Kyla reasoned, but not enough. All of the relationships had changed. Everything. How could she go back? There wasn't any way Mr. Richard Duvall could make it work for her.

She had cried in hurt and anger over Alex many times, but now another variation of pain gripped her chest, and tears of sorrow streamed silently down her face. Kyla did not bother to wipe them but let them flow, down past her ears into her hair. *How long does grief last?* she wondered.

Howie's small voice from near the bathroom suddenly cut into Kyla's sadness. "Miss Kane? I need a drink."

Quickly she sat up, pulling her T-shirt up to wipe her face. He stood squinting in the light of her room, rubbing his eyes, dressed in his little cotton summer pajamas. She took him into the bathroom and gave him a cup of water, which he drank noisily, watching her over the glass.

"Were you crying?" he asked, breathless, scrunching his nose.

She nodded.

"Do you miss your mom too?"

Kyla's throat constricted. "Something like that."

He wiped his mouth on the sleeve of his pajamas and his arm. "My dad says it's okay to cry. I tell him when I get sad, and then we talk to Mom on his computer."

He turned, padding back to bed. Kyla followed and tucked the blankets around his small body. The sound of Hank's even breathing came from his bed across the room.

"Maybe you can use my dad's computer," he whispered, "to talk to your mom."

"Okay, thanks, Howie," she replied. "Good night."

Kyla closed the door between their rooms again and stood in the dim walkway with her hands pressed against her cheeks. His innocent statements had pierced her heart. After a moment she splashed her face with water in the bathroom and then set about the task of unpacking her things.

❖ ❖ ❖

Chapter Eleven

When Dr. Grant arrived home in the middle of the afternoon the next day, he was mobbed by his boys, who pulled him to the table to see their crafts, chattering excitedly about their day with their new nanny. He set his briefcase on a chair and hoisted Hank to his hip, who was eagerly waving a coloring page in his face on which the form of an animal was scribbled completely orange.

"Nice, Hank," he said, pulling it back to where his eyes could focus on it.

"I see everybody survived thus far," he said over his shoulder to Kyla.

"No blood or vomit," Kyla replied playfully, rinsing two sippy cups in the sink.

He gave a short laugh. "That's good, that's good. Seriously, it went okay?" He turned to see her face. At her nod he continued, "Good. Well, I'm sure you're more than ready for a break. I'm going to have the kids talk to their mom in just a bit here—why don't you go relax somewhere and be off duty for a while?" He waved her off.

Kyla didn't realize how grateful she would be to hear those words. She had gotten up early to plan out activities and meals for the kids, anxious to start out firmly in control, but most of those ideas ended up being scrapped since Howie, who was still glad to be back in his own home again, had plenty in mind to do. Happy to have a new playmate, he pulled Kyla and his little brother along into several pirate adventures aboard furniture ships on the high seas of the Great Room carpet, in which no princess characters were necessary. Kyla accommodated his preferences and played along until he tired of them, after which she pulled out her activity list. To her relief, Howie was compliant to her direction and requests, proving to be an agreeable kid, and she liked him. By afternoon, however, his incessant talking and many questions had worn her out, and although she did find his inquisitiveness more endearing than annoying, she was ready for some quiet time.

Hank, of course, was irresistible. He spent most of his time observing and imitating his older brother and was more than willing to do anything that Howie was doing. Though his words were few, they were sugar sweet, causing her to either melt with their cuteness or to laugh. As the day unfolded, Kyla could see him drop his reservations of her, and by noon he was boldly calling out to Miss Kane for more food on his plate.

Eager now for time apart, Kyla grabbed the book from Dr. Grant's library that she had set aside for herself while the boys had played there earlier and headed away from the little voices, out the patio doors to the waterfront. The afternoon sun was warm on the wooden staircase, and the hum of Peter's riding lawnmower in the front yard all but disappeared on her way down to the little area of sand below. She hadn't seen Peter all day, apart from late morning, noticing him through the window working out in the yard, planting shrubs along the back of the house. He'd already gone outside by the time she and the kids came down for breakfast, and he had taken his lunch alone in the kitchen while she and the boys had been upstairs in the playroom. His Bible and coffee mug in the corner of the Great Room had not escaped her notice, however, as she was barely able to whisk the partially filled cup out of Hank's curious hands in time to avoid it spilling on the carpet. She made a note to mention it to him later.

On the sandy waterfront she stripped down to her camisole and pulled one of the Adirondack chairs forward, angling it to sit fully in the sun. She hoped for a little color on her early-summer skin. Kicking her shoes off, she got comfortable and started the book. Without her sunglasses, the brightness of the paper strained her eyes, so she stopped and readjusted the chair, centering the pages in her shadow. She continued reading, but before long she began to yawn. The warmth of the afternoon sun and the calming sounds of the birds and the water made her sleepy. Setting the book down on her lap, she leaned her head back, and using her hand as a visor, she gazed out over the water at the house across the way and the shoreline below it, studying the gnarly oaks and searching for the eagle in his nest that she had seen the other day. Below her the boat made little bumping noises against the dock as it bobbed in the water. *This was nice.* Relaxed, she closed her eyes. *Not bad for the first day*, she thought.

Last night had been a turning point. After her cry about Alex's family, she finally came to terms with staying at Wynnbury and was done with vacillating. She knew there was no going back to anything related to Alex, and she deleted his text. She could see it now—her own personal neediness—and it made her feel foolish and embarrassed. His affection and his family's affection, or perhaps simply their attention, had filled a cavernous longing in her soul that she so badly wanted filled. So badly that she had convinced herself that being used by Alex was being loved. The problem now was that in spite of seeing it, she still couldn't stop thinking about him, wondering how he was, or what he was doing. And even despite her most determined willpower, she still found herself longing for him. Then she'd get angry with herself and go down the road of accusing him and making speeches in her head. He wouldn't go away!

Her new chapter at Wynnbury was going to be good for her, even if it was a mere summer. She needed a completely fresh start away from her old world, and this was just the place. Dr. Grant carried himself with authority, and Kyla feared him, but he was also kind and a good parent. She liked him. Watching the kids would be a challenge, but it was a *job,* and she was being paid well, so she would give it her best shot. And as for Peter and all his weirdness—she would just have to put up with him. It was only a summer, and so far she had barely seen him. So Kyla declared it out loud as she put her last articles of clothing in her closet last night, "Okay—I am all here!" Then she slid the suitcase into a narrow upper shelf and closed the closet door.

After Howie's comments about missing her mom, she had even considered re-watching the Boyfriends clip of her mother's on her computer, but she had too much to get organized in her room. Laying out the coloring sheets for the morning, she contemplated her mother's bit about envisioning herself as a princess, which she thought was ironic in view of Howie's awkward statement to Peter at dinner. She knew what her mother had been trying to say, but it just sounded so hokey. She was far more familiar with feeling bad about herself than feeling special. She supposed that's what came with losing her mom at a young age. Since she had died, Kyla's life had been tainted with insecurity—ten years of emptiness and wondering what she as a girl should be, do, and say. Ten years since God had so cruelly broken the rudder from her ship, leaving her anxiously drifting to figure life out on her own and envious of friends who seemed to know exactly where they were going in life.

Before she had gone to bed, she wrote herself a note to ask Dr. Grant for the Wi-Fi password, then closed her laptop where she had set it up on the drop-leaf table under the window. How strange her last month had been, with so many things to deal with! First, everything had suddenly gone haywire with Alex, then the grief of losing her mom had been freshly dredged up again after watching her video, and on top of it all there was the confusing appearance of her biological father. What was she supposed to do now about him? What was she supposed to feel? *Hello—I'm your father that you haven't seen in seventeen years. Good-bye.* Everything combined was a lot to navigate through, like a sloppy glop of emotional spaghetti that had suddenly been dropped on her brain, a big mess for her to untangle. It was hard work!

But that had been last night, and having been busy since morning with the little boys, she found the emotional net over her mind had loosened a little today. It had been a good day, full of welcomed distractions, and she was happy to soak in the momentary peace of the sunshine and nature around her.

After a while Kyla dropped the book beside her shoes on the sand and sat up, hugging her knees, breathing in the fishy smell of the water, mixed with the aroma of the freshly cut grass in the yard above her. At her movement two gray squirrels in a nearby oak stopped their scrambling after one another to scold her loudly. Amused, she peered into the tree until she found where they sat on their leafy branches, shaking their tails at her in their angst. Then she remembered the deer from yesterday morning and craned her neck to the right, wondering if she could see where the stream flowed into the river from where she sat on the lounge chair, but the thick trees and underbrush blocked her view. Maybe she would take the boys for a walk in the woods to explore the ravine some day this week.

Without a watch or phone on her, Kyla guessed that perhaps an hour or more had passed since she had left the house. She wasn't sure how long Dr. Grant meant when he had said to take a break, but it was probably time to go back. If he was still busy with the boys, she could at least prepare dinner. She got up and stretched, retrieved the book, and slipped her shoes and shirt back on. Starting up the stairs, she counted the steps out of habit as she went. After every six steps there was a short landing and the steps turned. She stopped to catch her breath at the landing below the last set and looked up, surprised to see Peter at the edge of the yard near the top.

"Hello," he said as she topped the stairs, as if he'd just noticed her. His jeans had flecks of grass around the bottoms near his boots. He was sweaty everywhere, and his cheeks were flushed. At his waist he held a set of black binoculars in one hand. "That's a long ways up!"

"Hi," Kyla replied, leaning over slightly to catch her breath. "Yes, it is!" Twenty-four steps, she had counted. Then seeing the binoculars, she asked, "What are you doing?"

"Just mowing," he replied, gesturing to the riding lawnmower near the house.

"What are you doing with those?" she asked, indicating what was in his hand.

Peter looked at the binoculars and back at her. "I was—" He hesitated, shifting his feet. "There was, um—there is an eagle's nest on the island over there. I was just checking it."

She was silent for a moment, observing him. It was almost like—*No way*, she thought to herself. Her eyes narrowed. "Were you using those binoculars on me sunning down there?"

"What? No!" He straightened defensively, his brow suddenly knit together. "I didn't even know you were down there!"

She shook her head, giving him a perturbed look. "You are such a loser!" she muttered under her breath and with a toss of her hair behind her back continued on her way to the house. Behind her she heard him make a sound of exasperation.

Conversation was minimal between the two of them at dinner that night, although Kyla responded politely to Peter's compliments on the meal she had made. She was grateful that Dr. Grant had a lot to say about his new summer school students and the interesting discussions they had had today about the Middle East. He then began a diatribe about how most of the younger generation today were consumed with social media and gaming and didn't have a clue to what was happening in the world. Peter contributed some to the conversation, but Kyla mostly listened. After dinner Dr. Grant retreated to his study to prepare for the morning, asking Kyla to take the kids until their bedtime. Peter again disappeared. Nestled all together in the large library armchair, Kyla read the boys a sizable pile of storybooks until across the hall the professor's door slid open and he gave the announcement of bedtime.

"I got this tonight," he told her, hustling the kids toward the stairs. "You don't need to join us."

"I'll be 'Marian the Librarian,'" she replied, setting a hand on the stack of books beside her to put away.

The boys screamed and scrambled upward as their dad pretended to be a hungry bear on his way to devour them. Kyla smiled and took her time placing all the books neatly back on their shelves, then went to get her phone to go outside to call her dad. She stood at the edge of the yard, leaning on the lumber railing of the staircase while his phone rang, overlooking the colors of the fading day on the river below her. The water was calm, but she could see the current moving swiftly along, the flow a dancing purplish blue. Around her trilled what seemed like a thousand birds in their evening chorus.

Kendall sounded glad to hear from her when he answered. She apologized and explained why she hadn't called him until now, but he said he figured she had a good explanation and knew that she was busy. Then he told her he was out on their patio at home just finishing a late dinner, a steak he had grilled for himself. He asked for a report on her trip down to New Hampton and wanted to know how the new car handled and how she was doing with the Grant kids. Kyla had a lot she wanted to tell him, but she wanted to get one thing out of the way first.

"Dad, did you know that Peter Watkins was here?" Her tone was accusatory. Agitated, she turned and walked along the edge of the woods on the line in the grass where Peter had stopped mowing.

"Yeah!" her dad exclaimed, as if a miracle had occurred. "Isn't that something? He called me Saturday morning right after you had left to check in with me. I told him I had just seen you off on your way to New Hampton, and lo and behold, I find out he's spending the summer there too, in the very same place!" He laughed. "What a small world! We were both so surprised!"

"Honest, Dad? You're tellin' the truth?"

"What? Well, of course I am!"

"You didn't set this up?"

He made a sound of protest. "How in the world would I set up something like that? I don't even know the doctor."

"He's a professor."

"What?"

"He's a history professor, not a medical doctor."

"Right. Whatever. I did not set anything up. Peter called me, and that's how I found out you were both there. I think it's fantastic!"

Kyla rolled her eyes. "Well, I wish you wouldn't talk to him about me!"

"Talk about you? We don't talk about you, sweetheart."

She gave a little snort. "Yeah, Dad, *you do*! He knew about my breakup with Alex."

"Oh, yeah," Kendall replied, dismissing it. "Well, we pray for each other."

"Right. Well, I don't want him in my business, okay?"

"I guarantee he's not in your business," he assured her. "Now come on—tell me about that mansion you're at—is it as opulent as Peter says it is?"

She turned to regard the brick structure in the deepening dusk as she described it to her dad. Several lights were on inside, and she could see Peter working out in an exercise room on the main floor in an area of the house she hadn't explored yet. He was shirtless, and his back was to her, and even from a distance she could see the form of his muscles in his arms and back. A tattoo covered one bicep and another covered his back between his shoulder blades. It made her think of her own secret tattoo, hidden from her dad, who insisted she wait until she was twenty-five to make *lifelong decisions like that*. She turned away to face the woods, unconsciously sauntering along the edge of the yard toward the ravine, catching him up with her report of life so far at Wynnbury. Her dad shared with her a few bits of news from his work and his plans for the coming weekend. When they had finished talking, Kyla promised to call again soon, and they hung up.

She turned back to examine the large house again from the corner of the yard where she stood. The uninhabited top floor appeared cold and dark, its black bar of windows across the house accentuating the tall illuminated ones of the Great Room below, where she could see inside all the way to her bedroom doors beyond the railing of the balcony above it. On the main level the exercise room where Peter had been while she'd been talking was now dark. A figure moving across the patio revealed Dr. Grant taking a seat on the furniture under the canopy. Peter, she saw, had just come out the patio doors near the kitchen too and was joining him. He sat in a chair across from Dr. Grant, his back toward Kyla. Leaning against a nearby tree, she watched them a bit, their voices low and indistinguishable from where she stood hidden in the dusky shadows. Around her the rhythm of the crickets blended with the tapping of leaves in the breeze. She lifted her head, thinking she had caught the faint smell of tobacco smoke, but as she inhaled she found the air was sweet with the scent of the freshly cut grass and moist dirt.

Now that the sun was down, the air felt damp. Kyla shivered and decided to go in, cutting across the lawn to the patio steps on the ravine side of the house. Halfway there the men's voices suddenly became more audible.

"—checking her out, I tell you! I saw him looking at her!" Kyla

159

heard Peter say to Dr. Grant, as she approached.

"How do you know he was looking at her," came the professor's voice, "and not something else?"

"Oh, I know he was! I could tell by how he stood there!" Peter's voice was insistent. "And by the look on his face."

Dr. Grant spoke again, but the sound of her sandals squeaking on the dewy grass drowned out his words. Ascending the far stairs of the patio, she paused curiously beside a potted plant near the concrete railing, listening.

"—couldn't have been the Hancocks," Dr. Grant's voice continued. "In our few years here, I have never known our neighbor Gene to be snoopy, even with Marilee here. Unless maybe he saw you and was wondering what *you* were doing. I mean, it puts me in an awkward place. What do you want me to do—call him and ask if he's been spying on our nanny?"

Kyla felt a twinge of adrenaline where she stood in the dimness.

"No, but you could ask if he's seen anyone around," Peter replied.

The professor sighed. "Yeah. Yeah, I can certainly do that. I'm positive it's not him. It's got to be someone else. So how did Kyla respond to this?"

"I didn't say anything to her."

"You didn't tell her?"

"Of course not!" Peter replied. "I didn't want to freak her out!"

"That's probably—"

At that moment Kyla appeared beside them, her shoes silent on the concrete. Both their heads turned upward in surprise, and both fell suddenly quiet.

She looked from one to the other. "Tell me what? Am I interrupting something?"

"No, no," Dr. Grant said, rising quickly from his chair as if remembering his manners. "Have a seat; have a seat, please. Beer?" He held his up, gesturing toward the two bottles on the end table.

"Thank you." She took one and sat on the edge of a chair across from Dr. Grant and at an angle to Peter, noticing that he sat without a drink. He had showered and smelled like soap and was wearing black athletic shorts and a tight T-shirt.

Dr. Grant returned to his seat, and a pregnant pause elapsed between the three of them. Kyla glanced again from the older man to Peter, who sat chewing his bottom lip, avoiding her eyes.

"Um, so what's going on?" she asked. "Did I hear something about a Peeping Tom?"

Dr. Grant cleared his throat, setting down his beer. "Kyla, Mr. Watkins here tells me he noticed a person—a man—on the bank across the way, who seemed to be"—he paused, dipping his chin and raising his eyebrows at her—"'checking you out' this afternoon. He has expressed some concern for your safety."

Kyla shot a look at Peter. "So you *did* know I was down there."

He twisted in the chair, meeting her eyes. "Yes, I did. But I was trying not to alarm you."

She pursed her lips, waiting.

Peter leaned forward, his arms resting on the sides of the chair. "I was edging the yard with the weed whip, and I just happened to look out to see this guy standing there, way on the other side of the river. I looked closer and could tell that he was holding something up—binoculars. He stood there for quite a while, and it just felt—funny. So I went to get our binoculars, and when I came back, he was still there in the same position. It looked to me like he was watching you."

"It wasn't someone checking out this house?" Kyla inquired. "It's not your average country home, you know. Or maybe someone birdwatching—keeping an eye on the eagle's nest?" She tipped her head, sending him a knowing look.

He looked away and shook his head, his jaw rigid. "No," he said soberly, turning back to Dr. Grant. "Birdwatchers watch birds, which move around in trees. This guy—he was fixed."

The professor looked at Kyla. "Did you notice anything while you were down there today?"

She shook her head. "No."

She remembered looking across to the other bank at first, but only briefly, having mostly read or rested in the chair with her eyes closed. She wondered how long the man had been looking at her and how long Peter had been above on the ledge. Kyla didn't know what to say. Peter, too, was quiet.

"Why didn't you say something this afternoon?" she asked him finally. "Or during dinner?"

"Sorry. I didn't want to scare you. It's just that"—he shifted uncomfortably in his chair, gesturing with his hand—"er—well—I have a sister." In the light of the Great Room on the patio, Kyla thought his face looked flushed.

Dr. Grant's eyes lingered on Peter for a moment, then he bowed his head in a nod and turned to Kyla, repeating him, as if she hadn't heard,

"Right. Peter has a sister." He paused, looking into her face. "Which would mean he's looking out for you." He tipped his beer toward Peter, then turned back toward Kyla. "So here's the deal, folks. We don't know who this guy was, but my guess is that it's probably a gawker who found out somehow that Marilee lives here. She's had stalkers before, although never here at Wynnbury. I'm guessing that he was expecting to see her and was a little confused at seeing *you*."

"Do we contact the police?" Peter asked.

Dr. Grant cocked his head. "We could, but that's usually an exercise in futility at this point. The guy's gone. There's no crime. They typically don't do anything unless we report someone trespassing or unless the person is discovered lurking around here a few times."

He raised his beer to his lips for a sip and continued. "I will contact Marilee's people, and usually what they do is give her a little more press — make a big deal about her going to a party somewhere and blow it up in the entertainment news. Then whoever this is will know that she's not here. I expect that will curb his enthusiasm." He ran a hand over his head. "That the guy was out there in broad daylight says something. He's probably a rookie. Or possibly just some clueless person with a set of binoculars."

He turned to Peter. "Do you think he knows you saw him?"

Peter shrugged. "Hard to say, but I think so."

He nodded. "That helps."

Kyla waved an insect away from her neck as the three sat in silence for a moment. Dr. Grant finished his beer. The bottle clinked as he set it on the glass table beside him. He turned in his chair toward her.

"Look — I know you're probably spooked, but sooner or later this creep will realize that Marilee isn't here. Perhaps he's already discovered that. Like I said, he showed up in the daylight and on the other side of the river — more than likely that's where it will end. Wynnbury House is not impenetrable, but it's surrounded by a pretty serious brick wall, and no one's going to just wander in. To get in here you need the combination to the gate. I'm confident we're safe here, *but*" — he lifted his finger as he emphasized the word, looking straight at her — "if for any reason you feel otherwise, would you please let me know right away?"

"Thank you," Kyla replied. "I will."

"And meanwhile our man Watkins will keep his eyes open." He swung his head toward Peter.

"Absolutely," he said, nodding his agreement to Kyla.

Dr. Grant leaned back and suddenly chuckled, crossing his legs with his ankle resting on his knee.

"What's so funny?" Kyla asked.

"I was thinking that our description doesn't exactly narrow down our suspects—a tall guy with a dark beard!" He laughed again. "I could just see you, Peter, giving the UPS driver the third degree—poor guy!"

The two laughed together.

"Okay—I'll try not to overreact," Peter said with a smile.

"A dark beard?" Kyla echoed. She hadn't heard that part mentioned.

Their conversation was interrupted by the click of the patio door handle and the small sound of the door being pulled open. The three of them turned to see pajama-clad Howie poking his head out, looking quite pleased to find all the grown-ups in one place.

"Daaad," he said, drawing out his name, "I need a drink."

"Ah, that kid!" Dr. Grant muttered under his breath, tipping his head back on the cushion for a second before calling across the patio, "Young man, what are you doing out of bed? Go back to bed now, okay? Miss DeKane is going to help you. Good night!" Then he turned to point his index finger at Kyla. "Nanny DeKane, this one's for you!"

As Kyla went to take Howie back to bed, Peter also rose and reached the patio door ahead of her, sliding it open for her.

"Look, Kyla—I'm sorry. I should have said something out there this afternoon."

"It's okay," she said coolly, taking Howie's hand and stepping past him into the house. She felt a little guilty for misjudging him, but it felt too awkward to say anything about it, and she was stubborn about keeping her distance.

Howie was wide-eyed at seeing Peter. "What are you guys doing outside? Can I stay up with you?"

"Nope," he answered him, tapping him on the shoulder. "It's late. Even the grown-ups are on their way to bed."

"Good night," Peter said to Kyla as she led the boy through the dining room.

"Good night!" Howie answered back, and Kyla lifted her hand in a brief wave without looking behind her. She heard him go back out onto the patio after she left.

After Howie was back in his bed, Kyla immediately lowered the decorative shades over the windows in her room, unsettled by the blackness outside. *A dark beard*. She folded her arms in thought. It was highly doubtful that Alex would come all the way to New Hampton to talk to her again. Not after the way it ended in her driveway. But it was *possible*. She reviewed Peter's strange story, thinking of herself at the waterfront, thoroughly naive of what was happening around her. It did make her feel uncomfortable. But if it were Alex, she thought, she would not be afraid of confronting him again.

Pulling her pajamas over her head, another scenario occurred to her—what if the whole thing wasn't true? What if Peter had made it all up? Perhaps he had expected Kyla to tattle on him to Dr. Grant about his spying on her with the binoculars and had fabricated the story to avert anticipated trouble. Kyla played it out in her mind for a bit, then looking at her jean shorts and summer blouse on the floor of the closet, decided that probably wasn't the case. They were certainly nothing to look at. It didn't make sense. Perhaps if she had been wearing a swimsuit, maybe. It was hard to know what to think. Locking her door, she went to bed.

Chapter Twelve

The week rolled along, and every day Kyla grew a little in self-confidence as she developed her own rhythm of caring for the kids. Their routine usually started with something fun for breakfast to set a happy tone for the day, like smiley pancakes or French toast sailboats, followed by playing in their room for a short while after they got dressed. Then she would take them outside for fresh air and then bring them in later for an art project at the kitchen table while she prepared lunch. After lunch it was reading time, and if she was lucky, Hank would fall asleep. Then she and Howie could do something special for a while until Dr. Grant came home.

Since the occurrence of Peter sighting the man with the binoculars, Kyla kept to the yard with the kids, riding bikes on the driveway and playing games on the patio or in the grass. The few times Howie asked to play in the sand down by the water, Kyla made up creative excuses, which he accepted without protest. Once or twice she went out to the top of the deck stairs near the overhang in the backyard to scrutinize the shore on the other side, but she didn't see anyone or anything unusual, except for the delight of discovering eaglets in the eagle's nest on the island. Peter, too, was watchful all week, checking daily at odd times, but he reported nothing—except for the eaglets too, on the same day Kyla saw them, which also made him happy. Kyla hoped that Dr. Grant's theory was right—their curious watcher had gone away, done with his peeping.

Later on in the week Kyla found herself home alone. Dr. Grant was at school, and Peter had run to town to buy more shrubs for the front of the house and some perennials for another area he was landscaping. Feeling more free to poke around with them gone, Kyla decided it was a good day to finally explore the house a little more, so with Howie as her guide, they ventured down the hallway past the library and Dr. Grant's study to find the little fitness room where she'd seen Peter working out from the yard. The room was unlocked, and the three of them walked around on the mat looking at the treadmill and the other exercise equipment. They soon discovered that the room was not suitable for little ones when Hank accidentally pinched his fingers in one of the weight machines. He cried hard, calling over and over for his daddy, and Kyla comforted him. When he finally stopped crying, she hustled the kids out, deciding to come back again during her alone time, that is, if Peter wasn't using the room.

Across from the weight room was a long recreation hall with a pool table and a ping pong table, a dart board, and a few antique pinball machines. On one side of the room were several recliners and a large TV monitor mounted on the wall, the focus of an elaborate gaming system set up below it. *Alex would be in heaven*, she thought. Though she let them look, Kyla explained to the little ones that these were toys for the grown-ups. Howie insisted that he was old enough, but Kyla told him they'd have to talk to his dad about that, and they left the room. Next door at the very end of the hall was a small home theater with very comfortable-looking furniture and windows covered with heavy velvet drapes, which completely blocked the light. She would definitely come back there too, she decided, closing the door.

At the end of the hall was a narrow back staircase, similar to the one in the side entryway on the opposite side of the house. Kyla took Hank's hand, pointing for the boys to go up.

Howie shook his head, informing her, "This isn't the stairway we use."

"It goes to the same place," she said, starting up with Hank.

He balked. "I don't like these stairs. My dad says we don't have to walk on these stairs."

"He says that, does he?" Kyla found his objections strange and unreasonable. The staircase was plain and narrow, with painted wooden steps, but it was adequate and perfectly functional, not scary in the least.

"I do it! Hard work!" Hank said happily, holding Kyla's hand and lifting his leg high for each step as they made their way to the top.

"Hank, you're such a big boy!" she said, encouragingly.

"I don't like these stairs," Howie insisted, still at the bottom. His small arms were folded, his bottom lip bulging out in a pout.

"Come on!" she urged. "What's with you? Hank and I are almost to the top!"

But he stubbornly refused.

"Fine," she conceded. "How 'bout you go back and use your own stairs, and we'll see who gets upstairs first. Hank and I will try to beat you!"

His face lit up at the idea, and he took off running back down the hall.

Kyla and Hank stepped into the upstairs hall right as Howie reached the top of the stairs opposite his room. Both boys screeched in delight and began running toward one another, falling down together as they met in the middle. Giggling, they began to chase each other wildly up and down the hall. Rushing past his brother, Howie banged into one of the closed guest doors with his hands extended. With a loud boom, the door burst open, smacking against the wall behind it.

"Howie!" Kyla exclaimed, but he wasn't hurt. He was rolling on the floor laughing, and Hank soon piled on top of him. The two began wrestling in the doorway. Kyla separated the boys and made them go out, glancing at the room's beautiful furnishings before she closed the door.

"Watch me! Watch me, Hank!" Howie called to his brother and did it again, this time against Peter's bedroom door, which also popped open. He couldn't stop giggling.

"Hey—that's enough!" Kyla called out.

Corralling them, she made the brothers sit down quietly opposite each other in the hall to settle down. She closed Peter's door, noticing his loosely made bed, a few clothes on the armchair, and his laptop open on a heavy antique desk in the corner. His room was considerably smaller than hers, but it was nice. After counting out three full minutes, Kyla let the boys get up, but she would not allow them to run.

"Can we go up here?" Howie asked, patting the door across from Peter's, which led to the third floor.

"No," she answered.

"Why not?" His little eyebrows furled together. "Why can't we go up there?"

"Have you ever been up there?" she asked.

He nodded. "Once. With my dad. It's kinda messy. I'll show you! Please—can we go up?"

Kyla hesitated, first because Howie had just refused taking the back stairs, and now he wanted to go up to the third floor—? It seemed a little contradictory to her, and she wondered if he would chicken out halfway up. Second, Kyla wasn't crazy about going up there herself. It always looked so dark and eerie from outside in the yard. In her short week at Wynnbury Kyla had ignored that there was a third floor, pretending it wasn't there. Of course, practically speaking, so did the rest of the household—for no one used that floor. She was too skittish to go up there herself and too embarrassed to ask Dr. Grant to go with her. And she certainly wasn't going to ask Peter!

"Please?" Howie asked again.

She paused, considering it. At least with Howie and Hank she would not be alone.

"Okay," she said, and Howie clapped happily. Hank clapped excitedly too, unaware of what was happening.

Opening the door, they were immediately met by a waft of old-house smell. Trudging up the hollow-sounding wooden stairs, they came to a landing halfway up, where a filmy window overlooked the backyard, providing an excellent view of the river and the ravine, a beautiful sight. Kyla held each of the brothers up to look out, while she herself scanned the scene before her for any suspicious figures or Peeping Toms. She set Howie down, and they continued up to the third floor hallway, where she discovered all the doors along it opened, spilling stripes of light across the dimness of the hall, giving a brighter, more airy feel up there than in the hallways on the lower floors. From the top of the stairs she could see the bluff beyond the front yard of the house through the window in the room opposite. Peeking in the doorway, Kyla stopped short and gasped, shocked to see all four of its walls polka-dotted with holes in the drywall, having been hacked and punched evenly about every foot around the room, probably with a crowbar or a large hammer. The wooden floor was dusty and streaked with obvious marks from a broom, no doubt from the efforts to clean up the crumbs of debris from the demolition.

"Yikes! What happened here?" Kyla exclaimed, gazing around her.

Howie said, "I told you it was messy! But not over there on that side!" He pointed down the hallway to the other side of the house. "There's some rooms with no holes over there."

Bewildered, Kyla walked from room to room, viewing the similar damage done to each one she saw along the way, until they got to one long, large room in the center of the house, exactly above the Great Room. Here only half of the room was destroyed. Even despite the wreckage, it was a lovely room, painted a sunny yellow, with beautiful woodwork and crown molding and recessed alcoves around the windows. Matching the windows in the Great Room below, the windows in this room were larger than the ones in the other rooms, going lower to the floor and rising higher in the wall. Hank quickly ran to look out, leaning both his hands and his face on the glass, pressing his nose against the pane, peering out again over the backyard, now from a slightly higher viewpoint than previously on the stairs. Kyla, with her hands on her hips, shook her head, surveying the room, both mystified and curious at who would do such haphazard damage to the walls. *What a shame!* she thought. *And why only half of this room?*

"See? This place got wrecked," Howie said. He was busy pulling loose pieces of debris off the wall.

"I'll say!" Kyla replied softly.

Hank moved to the next window, leaning his face against it again, a little circle of moisture forming where he breathed on the glass. Suddenly he pointed outside. "Look! Look it, Kane!"

Kyla had just noticed a large black stain spread out on the wooden floor, and it gave her the creeps. She stared at it. Was that from blood? She glanced around the room again, rubbing the goosebumps on her arms, suddenly very uncomfortable.

"Kane!" Hank repeated, turning to beckon her. "Look!" The tot came to get Kyla from where she stood, taking her hand to pull her to the window. "Come!"

"What are you showing me, Hank?" she asked, following him.

"Guy outside! Look!"

"Is Peter back?" She peered outside for his white truck but could not see it. Nor could she see anyone in the yard, from the patio straight below her all the way to the edge of the woods and beyond.

"Look!" Hank still pointed out the window but then stopped, peering down with a bewildered look on his little face. "All gone! No more guy." He stood still, staring downward into the yard.

Behind them Howie sighed heavily. "Can we go? Let's look at the other different rooms. The ones that aren't wrecked."

Hank had followed Kyla away from the window and was now hugging her leg. She paused, combing his light hair with her fingers and noticing that his little blond eyebrows were wrinkled. He didn't look happy.

"What's the matter, Hank?" she asked.

"Down," he said, his bottom lip turning out.

"Are you done in here too?" Kyla didn't mind. She was more than eager to end their tour. "Okay—let's go look at the other rooms really quickly."

"Go down," Hank said, starting to cry, "go down!" He reached up for her, asking to be held.

She frowned. "What happened, Hank? Did you get hurt?" She knelt to check his hands over but didn't see any pinches or scrapes, apart from the one he got downstairs in the fitness room.

"Go down!" he whined, stamping his feet and reaching for her.

Was he afraid? Kyla wondered. He was acting afraid! Over her shoulder she glanced outside again, scanning the yard for any unfamiliar person, any person at all. He must have seen Peter, she guessed, who then probably went into the house. She tried to calm him, but soon Hank's whimpering escalated to full-out bawling. Spooked, Kyla was done with seeing the third floor. Picking him up, she carried him out of the room, hurrying back the way they came.

"Howie, we're leaving!" she called over Hank's loud wails. "Hank needs to go."

He trailed along grudgingly, protesting that they didn't even get to see the rooms that weren't wrecked, to which she replied that they would have to do it another day. Rounding the corner of the landing, they tromped hurriedly down the remaining stairs to the second floor, where Kyla, winded from carrying the two-year-old, closed the door behind them. Hank clung hard to her when she tried to put him down, so she held him a little longer, walking the hall with him until his crying finally diminished to jerky breathing and sniffling.

"You are having one rough morning, aren't you?" She set him on the low dresser in his room to wipe his nose. But when she put him down he stayed near her, which was unsettling to her.

Needing a distraction for all of them, Kyla decided on an impromptu snack time, taking the boys down to the kitchen with a promise of treats. After doling out trail mix into tiny bowls, she got them situated at the table and then scooted out to check the carport for Peter's truck, finding herself a bit surprised at its absence. Where was he? *Certainly he must be somewhere*, she thought. Back in the dining room with the kids, she moved to the patio window to check for the truck in the backyard again, when she stiffened, suddenly noticing the sliding patio door standing open about six inches. Kyla felt herself break out in a sweat, distinctly remembering that she had pulled Hank away from it earlier that morning and closed it firmly—right before they had gone looking for the weight room. Both Dr. Grant and Peter had already been gone at that time. Kyla stared through the open gap, and her heart began to pound in her chest. Nervously she looked over her shoulder through the house. Had someone come in? Surely it was Peter. She peered outside but could not see his vehicle in the backyard either.

"Peter?" she called out feebly toward the Great Hall.

There was no answer, but he wasn't normally in the house to begin with, she told herself.

"Why do you want Peter?" Howie asked, trying to poke the straw in his juice box. "Is he having snack time too?"

Her mind racing, Kyla looked at Hank picking the raisins out of his snack mix and building a little pile of them on the table. Had he seen someone outside? Could it have been the same man Peter had seen? Had he come in through the patio? Was he inside now?

At that moment Kyla was startled by the form of a person who suddenly stepped into the kitchen from the back hallway, and instantly she responded with a terrified shriek. Both boys jerked with fright, and Howie's bowl went spinning off the table, sending peanuts and raisins bouncing over the floor. Immediately Kyla recognized Mrs. Gordon, who had simultaneously released a startled cry, her hand popping to her chest. In her other arm she clutched a bundle of bedsheets. She stood with her mouth open, gaping at Kyla.

Kyla's hands flew over her mouth. "I'm so sorry!" she said. "I had no idea you were here!"

"Oh, my goodness!" Mrs. Gordon panted, her hand over her heart. "I didn't know you were here either! I didn't mean to scare you!"

Hank burst out in a loud wail, screeching in panic and reaching out for Kyla, who grabbed him from his chair.

"Sorry, Hank," she said, feeling terrible and pressing his small body close against her.

"I hope I didn't give you a heart attack!" she said to Mrs. Gordon over his sobbing. "I'm *so sorry*! I didn't hear you come in."

Howie's shoulders were tight, and he too looked as if he might cry. With his face puckered, he said forcefully to Kyla, "Don't do that! You scared me! Why did you scream?"

"I'm sorry, Howie," she told him. "I didn't mean to scare you!"

Adrenalized, she walked Hank around, trying to calm him down, reminding her own self to breathe too. Hank kept twisting in her arms, looking fearfully at Mrs. Gordon, who stood by helplessly.

"You know me, Hank! Hey, now! It's Miss Susan!" She leaned toward him and patted his arm, clicking her tongue. "Poor little fella. It's okay, it's okay."

Hank pulled his arm away from her.

She turned to Kyla. "I came in a little bit ago and stripped the beds. I thought no one was home. I must have been in back folding clothes when you came in. Were you outside?" Her tawny hair was parted on the side and pulled back with a tortoiseshell barrette.

"We were upstairs—way upstairs." Kyla pointed upward.

"Oh, I see," she replied, lifting her chin. "That's why I didn't hear anyone!"

"Were *you* outside?" Kyla asked. "In the backyard?"

"I was on the patio a little bit ago. Shaking the rugs," she answered.

Kyla breathed an enormous sigh of relief. Mrs. Gordon had left the door open! And it must have also been Mrs. Gordon that Hank had seen, she surmised.

At last Hank's crying subsided, but he would not let Kyla put him down, clinging to her tightly.

"Goodness, goodness," Mrs. Gordon said, smoothing her hand across the linens. "Nothing like getting the old circulation moving!" She laughed. "Well, I suppose I should take these up and finish the beds. I'll leave you to enjoy your lunch." She started for the stairs and then stuck her head back around the corner. "Maybe next time when I come I'll wear a bell around my neck!" She laughed and went to finish her work.

Kyla glanced at the clock. It was still a bit early for lunch, but not by much. With Hank in her arms, she rounded out the boys' snacks with some cheese and vegetables, which he ate sitting on her lap. When finished, Howie asked to be excused so that he could start reading books in the library. Kyla let him go, and when Hank was finished, she carried him to the Great Room, where they snuggled together under a soft throw on a chair in Peter's corner, the toddler leaning his head against Kyla's chest.

Peter's Bible, a small journal, and a pen were prominently on the corner of the end table, in the same place as they were every day, but Kyla could tell that he'd used them, for they were always in a slightly new position. She had never actually seen him read there, and she wondered what time he got up. Kyla had read the Bible once too, a long time ago, when her dad made her go to a certain class for kids at his church. It was a purple one that he'd bought for her, with a soft, embossed floral cover. She still remembered many of the stories, but so much of the Bible seemed disjointed to her from one part to another, and she felt like she never really got the point of what she had read. Her father, on the other hand, loved—really loved—his Bible, something she had always found hard to understand. What did he get out of it? Kyla could tell from the wear on the side of the pages that Peter was into his too. Apparently he had caught some of her dad's zest for it. Their early-morning reading was certainly a strange routine, she mused. She certainly couldn't ever see herself preferring that over sleep.

As Kyla expected, Hank soon fell asleep in her arms. She enjoyed holding him for a while, his body warm and relaxed and breathing deeply against her chest. After a while she carefully wriggled out from under him and laid him down on the love seat, not wanting to risk his waking if she carried him up to his bed. As she finished tucking the blanket around him, she heard Mrs. Gordon on the stairs again, who soon rounded the corner with a bag of trash and a bucket of rags, heading through the house. Kyla watched her from behind. The last woman Kyla had talked to, she realized, had been one of her roommates on her graduation day. Her world was filled with men and boys. Not that it bothered her. She felt she was managing fine as the only female in the household, but it did seem special having Mrs. Gordon here, who was friendly and seemed nice. Kyla met her in the kitchen while she was emptying the trash under the sink.

"Have you had lunch?" Kyla asked her. "Would you like to join me?" It seemed like a very grown-up gesture, she thought. One that would probably make her mother proud, had she a mother.

"Oh, I'm on a special diet," Mrs. Gordon answered. "So I'll pass on lunch. But I would certainly take a cup of tea!" She shook open a new trash bag and fit it into the can.

Kyla smiled and hurried around her to fill the tea kettle, pulling the most feminine mugs she could find out of the cupboard for the two of them. Mrs. Gordon sat on one of the bar stools, facing Kyla in the kitchen while Kyla found the tea canister and a sleeve of shortbread cookies.

"Oh, my—shortbread!" She chuckled when Kyla set the package on the counter. "My weakness! Those aren't on my diet, but I might have to have one or two—just to be polite!"

Kyla joined her at the counter, pouring the hot water from the tea kettle into their cups. Mrs. Gordon watched, and when Kyla had put the kettle down on a hot pad, she folded her hands together on the counter.

"I'm glad we can visit," she said, "because I wanted to ask you about something."

Kyla chose a tea bag from the canister and dropped it into the hot water, listening expectantly.

"I know it's none of my business, but as I emptied the trash in your room, I couldn't help noticing that you had thrown away a letter to someone."

Kyla's eyes flicked up at her. The last few nights she had written out letters to Alex, trying to untangle herself from him, never intending to actually send any of them. Then last night, mentally tired of dealing with it, she had thrown them all away.

"You're struggling with your feelings for someone?"

"Yeah," Kyla said simply.

"Not Dr. Grant, I hope," she asked. Her smile was fixed, but her eyes were focused intently on Kyla's face.

Her eyes widened. "What? Dr. Grant? No, of course not!" she said quickly. She could not deny thoughts of admiration for him as an intelligent, kind man and an excellent father, and he was indeed handsome, but feelings for him were certainly off her radar. Her summary was that the invisible Marilee Montayne had found a good one.

"Well, that's good," the housekeeper replied, "because that would break up his family, and we wouldn't want to be responsible for that, would we?"

Kyla took a deep breath, shaking her head. "I assure you, there is nothing—nothing—inappropriate going on with me regarding Dr. Grant."

"Oh, I'm glad," she said, apparently satisfied. She picked up her spoon and pleasantly twirled her tea bag in her cup. "So it's the *other* fella—what's his name again?"

"What—you mean Peter?" Kyla laughed and shook her head. "No, definitely not him! No, I broke up with my boyfriend from college a while ago—Alex. Alex Duvall. I'm just having a tough time getting him out of my head, so I tried writing all my frustrations out in a pretend letter. It hasn't worked."

"Ah, I see," she nodded, removing her tea bag from the cup, setting it down on her napkin.

"He really hurt me. I can see now that we weren't right for each other, but it seems like I can't shake him loose because I still want him. It's so strange." Kyla looked down at her tea, feeling suddenly vulnerable with how much she had shared.

"Mmm, the power of a soul tie," the housekeeper murmured under her breath. "That's tough. I'm sorry, honey."

"What did you say?" Kyla tipped her head curiously. "Did you say 'soul tie'? What's that?"

Mrs. Gordon sipped her tea and set her cup down on the granite counter. "You know, I didn't mean to pry into your personal business, and I don't want you to think that I sift through the garbage around here. I was simply looking out for David—Dr. Grant. I've worked for their family since they moved to the states."

"Oh, I understand," Kyla replied. "It's all right."

Mrs. Gordon smiled at her, silent.

"So what is it—the 'soul thing,' or whatever you said?"

"Oh, it's something that I've heard taught at our church," she said. "It's like a bonding that's out of order, that's not God's way. Sort of like gluing two pieces of paper together that aren't supposed to be. They're not going to come apart very easily."

That's exactly what it felt like, Kyla thought. Gently she blew across her tea before taking a drink of the hot liquid. It burned her tongue.

"You were sleeping together?" Mrs. Gordon asked.

Kyla stiffened. "Of course. We dated for over two years."

She simply nodded in reply.

Kyla gave a short defensive laugh. "What are you saying? That we shouldn't have had sex? Yeah, right." Mrs. Gordon apparently had the same puritan values as her father.

"Well," Mrs. Gordon tilted her head toward Kyla in a motherly way, "you asked me what a 'soul tie' was."

Kyla was silent, looking down at her cup, conscious of wanting to show the older woman respect.

Mrs. Gordon folded her arms, leaning on the counter, speaking kindly. "I know it seems like a natural thing to do nowadays, and I'm not judging you." Her hand opened in gesture. "So many people today give away more of themselves than they should, and then the boyfriend ends up getting all the rights of a husband but without any of the responsibility. God designed sex to happen in a marriage—you know, where there's commitment to one another and emotional protection. In the Bible it says the 'two become one.' Like the pieces of paper. The two of you bonded. Deeply. But it was not in marriage, how God intends it to be. When you broke up with your boyfriend, part of him stayed with you, and part of you has stayed with him. That's a soul tie."

Kyla considered her words. The paper was meant to stay glued. But she didn't want to stay glued to Alex. She met Mrs. Gordon's eyes. "Sometimes I hate him."

She shrugged. "Hate, desire, indifference—it doesn't matter. You bonded. It's a soul tie."

Howie suddenly appeared at Kyla's side, leaning tiredly on her leg. "Miss Kane, when are you coming to read to me?"

Kyla had forgotten all about Howie waiting for her in the library, yet she wanted to finish the conversation with Mrs. Gordon. Feeling a bit guilty, she turned to him. "Howie, I'm visiting with Mrs. Gordon right now. Do you think you could play by yourself for a little while longer?"

"Aww!" He heaved a dramatic sigh and walked away with his head hanging back, starting for the Great Room.

Kyla intercepted him. "Hey, hold on! Hank is sleeping in there! Don't you even go near your brother! You'll wake him up!"

With a pout Howie redirected his path and trailed back to the library, dragging his feet.

Kyla turned back and leaned in toward the plump woman sitting across from her. "So you're saying it all has to do with having sex?"

She nodded. "Well, yes." Then she tipped her head to the side, her bob bouncing out from her chin. "Well, actually, no. I mean, not only sex. You can have a soul tie with anyone—it would be kinda like a codependency, you know, where you're too intertwined with each other emotionally. That's not healthy either. God doesn't want us emotionally dependent on our friends or anybody. Or any *thing*. He wants us dependent on *him*." Her eyes sparkled even when she wasn't smiling.

She made it sound so simple. Kyla bit her tongue, thinking, trying to separate what Mrs. Gordon was saying with the part of her that automatically recoiled at the subject of God.

"Do you believe in God?" Mrs. Gordon asked.

Kyla looked down at her mug where a thin film had gathered on the top of the liquid. She wasn't crazy about tea, she decided.

"I think so," she answered, "but let's just say that I'm pretty sure he's not on my side. And so because he doesn't seem to care for me, I don't really want him either. Does that offend you? I guess I'm angry with him."

"Of course not, honey," she replied. "You probably have a good reason why you feel that way. Maybe sometime we can talk about it. If you want. Some other time." She turned back to her tea, swirling her cup around a little.

"So how are things going with the kids?" she asked, changing the subject. "Are you managing okay? Be sure to let me know if you need anything. No one's asked for diapers for a while."

Kyla's eyes widened. "Diapers! I never thought about those! Yes, please bring diapers next time! And anything else you think I should need. Seriously. I'm new at this!"

She laughed. "Oh, I think you're going to do just fine here."

They visited about the children for a little bit, after which Mrs. Gordon stood to her feet, thanking Kyla for the tea, and telling her she needed to get back to work.

"I'm on the job, you know," she said. "I hope we can talk again someday."

"Me too," Kyla told her.

Mrs. Gordon retrieved the bucket and bag of trash, starting back toward the laundry room.

"Mrs. Gordon," Kyla said, following her.

She turned.

"If you don't mind my asking"—Kyla looked up toward the ceiling, feeling awkward—"what does a person do about this 'soul tie' thing? Like, how can a person get 'untied'—or 'unglued,' whatever you call it?"

"Of course, I don't mind!" Mrs. Gordon replied. "I'm certainly not an expert, but I'd be happy to share with you what I know." She rested the bucket on the kitchen island. "Soul ties need to be broken and healed. Through Jesus. He's the only one strong enough to cut those bonds and heal our hearts. So first, you have to go to him and make things right with him. Don't be ashamed—we've all done things the wrong way. You simply admit that to him and ask him to forgive you for your sins against him—for not doing things as he has directed in his Word. If you ask him, he will forgive—"

"Sorry," Kyla interjected, cutting her off, "I'm really not into the God thing."

"Oh." The older woman stopped, surprised. She looked at Kyla, waiting.

Kyla shifted her feet. "Could you just tell me the part I need to know?"

Mrs. Gordon lifted her hand to move her hair behind one ear. "Well, I'm not quite sure what to tell you, honey."

Kyla frowned. "What—so it's a big secret? You can't tell me because I'm not in the God club?"

"Oh, no, no, no! Nothing like that!" The older woman shook her head, clucking her tongue. "I guess it's a matter of letting the Fixer fix you. Sort of like if you needed a doctor, you would go to the doctor. If you needed your teeth filled, you would to go to the dentist."

Kyla stared at her blankly.

Mrs. Gordon smiled. "It's *Jesus* who's the doctor! He's the soul tie healer. You don't need to be afraid of him, Kyla. He loves you and wants to set you free."

Kyla stood still, unsure of how to respond. It all sounded very strange. If what Mrs. Gordon said about the so-called "soul ties" was true, then she knew it applied to her. The thought of being separated from Alex was appealing, but the way to get there was frightening if it was through God, and she didn't care what Mrs. Gordon said—she was wary of God. She couldn't take that step.

"I see," Kyla replied politely. "Well, people have been breaking up with each other for a long time. I'm pretty sure that eventually I'll get through this. Thanks for listening to me."

"Of course, you will, darling," Mrs. Gordon said. She gave Kyla a brief hug and kissed her on the hair. "You have my phone number. You can call me anytime you want to talk." She smiled and continued on to the laundry room to finish her cleaning for the day.

Kyla went to find Howie, her mind busy processing thoughts about separating glued papers.

Her afternoon turned out to be long. Hank woke up early from his nap in a cranky mood, and Dr. Grant had to work much later than usual, giving her no afternoon break at all. Crabby, Hank clung to her leg while she tried to cook dinner, but Peter happened by and took the boys outside to play for a bit so that she could finish more easily. Because it was so windy out, Kyla decided they'd eat inside at the dining room table, and she had just finished putting the food on when Dr. Grant walked in, declaring loudly how glad he was to be home, how hungry he was, and how happy he was to smell food. Kyla was glad to see him too, relieved that it wasn't just Peter and her at the table with the kids. The professor gave Howie a mock punch on the arm and tousled Hank's hair in greeting before taking a seat.

"How was your day?" he asked Howie, handing him the plate Kyla had filled for him.

"Very, very bad," Howie answered with a scowl on his face. He scrutinized the food on his plate, choosing first the dinner roll.

"Oh?" Dr. Grant raised one eyebrow. "What was so very, very bad about today?"

"Everything," he announced crossly. "First, Hank got hurt, and then Kyla screamed really, really loud and made him cry. And she wouldn't read to me."

Both Dr. Grant and Peter looked at Kyla, who was staring at Howie, her mouth open.

"That's 'Miss Kane' to you," she told him stiffly. Hastily she turned to Dr. Grant. "I didn't hear Mrs. Gordon come in this morning, and we startled one another. I screamed, and it scared Hank. And earlier he pinched his fingers in the weight room. We were exploring."

Dr. Grant set his knife on his plate and wiped his mouth with a napkin. "Relax. I'm not accusing you of anything."

Howie leaned into Peter, whispering sweetly, "We saw your room."

Kyla dropped her fork, which clattered on the table.

"*Did* you now?" Peter straightened, turning his face toward Kyla.

"Why, you really *were* exploring, weren't you?" Dr. Grant said, his eyes twinkling.

Kyla was speechless, her cheeks pink. She didn't even know where to begin.

Dr. Grant gave her an amused glance. "This ought to be good."

Chapter Thirteen

After her long day Kyla was ready and eager for a break, but after dinner Dr. Grant pushed his plate back and turned to her with a request to put his kids to bed that night.

"Sure," she replied, a bit surprised. "Of course, I can do that." She had expected to have the night off after such a full day.

"Thank you," he said. "I have something important I need to take care of."

Kyla nodded. "No problem."

No sooner had she answered him when Dr. Grant pivoted in his chair toward Peter to ask if the two of them could meet together for a little while in his office. The pair rose and disappeared down the hall, where Kyla heard the heavy doors of the study open and close. The exclusion stung as Kyla sat abandoned at the table full of dirty dishes with two sticky-fingered children who were overtired and disappointed that they couldn't play with their dad. Internally she complained that she wasn't paid enough for her job, but she checked herself, knowing that wasn't true—she was being paid very well for what she did. So she rallied through her fatigue, first tidying the kitchen and then bathing the kids and helping them into their pajamas, all the while wondering what was so important between Dr. Grant and Peter.

Hank, however, refused to go to bed, fighting each attempt of Kyla's to put him down with a display of hysterics. She held him and paced with him in the dark bedroom, waiting for him to relax so that she could try again, but her efforts were futile.

"What is your problem tonight?" she asked, lifting the bawling child from his bed again.

"Sometimes my dad lays down with him," Howie suggested. He was lying on his back sideways in his own bed, kicking his feet against the wall.

"Put your feet down!" Kyla said impatiently. "You're not helping things, Howie."

Hank's forehead did not feel warm, and he shook his head no when she asked if he had an "owie" or if his tummy or his ears hurt him. Finally she took Howie's suggestion and lay in his bed with him. He sat up beside her and cried while she rubbed his back, but eventually his head dropped down to the mattress, and the crying turned into feeble whining interrupted by long yawns. Kyla lay still for a long time beside him until his breathing became deep and even. Finally, with both children asleep, she was able to slip off the bed and tiptoe out of the room.

The boys' delay in getting to bed made her regular phone call to her dad much later than usual, but she knew he would still be up. In the dusk she went out to her spot in the corner of the yard beside the oak to talk to him, but it was hard to hear him, for the wind was still very strong, thrashing the branches above her. He told her the news of his day and reported that Kyla had gotten a wedding invitation in the mail, which he would forward to her, but she had to ask him to repeat himself several times, and they finally cut the call short. Drained from her day and her mind still sorting out her conversation with Mrs. Gordon, Kyla decided that she was ready for bed.

As she entered the house and headed for the stairs, she heard the rumble of the solid doors to Dr. Grant's study as they were pushed back, and the two men appeared, smiling broadly. The professor reached to shake Peter's hand, who looked flushed, almost giddy.

"Well, tomorrow then," Dr. Grant said, releasing Peter's hand and leaning back on his heels.

Both of them saw her as she rounded the corner, tipping their heads to acknowledge her, but neither spoke.

"Good night," she said, eyeing them curiously.

"Good night," they chorused in reply.

Kyla's night was miserable. Not long after she had gone to bed, Hank woke up crying, and she had to walk with him again to settle him down. As a just-turned-two-year-old, he was starting to get heavy, and her arms ached the longer she held him. "Bad guy," he whimpered in his tired delirium, "bad guy outside." His words made her shiver as she paced, his head resting on her shoulder and his breathing jerky from crying. Was he simply having toddler nightmares, she wondered, or was he genuinely afraid of something—someone—that he had seen from the third-floor window? She wished there were a way to explain to him that it had been Mrs. Gordon—if indeed it *had* been Mrs. Gordon. Perhaps their binocular man was back, she wondered. Or perhaps another person. Why else would Hank be so afraid?

Something had frightened him, and that something now caused Kyla to feel nervous as well.

She rocked him until he fell asleep and deposited him back in his bed. Two hours later he was screaming again, and she had to repeat the same routine, walking and rocking him in the night. This time the moment she laid him down he awoke, crying and reaching for her again. Exhausted, Kyla brought him into bed with her, where, near her, he was finally content, and though his little body was right smack in the center of the bed, leaving her little room beside him, they both fell asleep.

Despite the interrupted night, Kyla was wide awake at her normal time in the morning. Both boys, however, remained sound asleep, Howie in his own bed and Hank lying on his side pressed up tightly against her, facing her chest. She lay still, studying his full cheeks, his little lips, and his gorgeously long eyelashes. His light hair swooped down on his forehead, and she wanted to move it to the side with her finger, but she didn't dare touch him and accidentally wake him. He was breathing deeply, making little sucking motions with his mouth every now and then. *What a beautiful boy!* she thought. And what a beautiful moment, even with so little sleep!

Still gazing at his little face, Kyla wondered if she would be a good mom someday. Her mind flitted briefly to several childhood memories of her own sweet mother. Suddenly she had a flashback of how afraid she had been that day in the Walgreens bathroom taking the pregnancy test, flooded with questions and uncertainty of what to do. Her mind lingered there, determining that if she had found herself pregnant with Alex's baby now, she would keep the baby for sure, even without him in her life. And then she realized that Alex was in her brain again—and the day had barely started.

Alex. Kyla pursed her lips. What Mrs. Gordon had said yesterday made a lot of sense to her, both the concept of having "soul ties" and that dealing with them was out of reach for her—by her own choice admittedly. She wasn't sure quite what that process would be, but she knew it entailed surrendering to God, and that she couldn't do. There were just too many questions that she had about him. Nevertheless, she hoped that she would have another opportunity to talk with Mrs. Gordon about it. For some reason, despite that she was religious, Mrs. Gordon felt safe to talk to.

At that moment Hank took a deep breath and shifted, sprawling onto his back. Kyla took the opportunity to slide out of bed without disturbing him. She donned her robe and sneaked silently out her door, glad for some quiet time alone before the little people arose. On her way down for her morning coffee, however, Kyla was surprised to hear Dr. Grant's and Peter's voices conversing below in the kitchen. She then recalled that it was Friday, Dr. Grant's day off.

"—to keep track of every place we dig on a grid," she heard him say.

"Right," Peter replied. "So we can already mark off where the shrubs went in yesterday. And the flower beds in the back. I had to turn the soil pretty deep."

"Okay—that's a start. Now if you look at the photograph you can judge about how far out the fountain is."

"Yeah. Looks like about fifty feet. I can draw it out to scale if you want," Peter offered.

"It's gotta be there. It's the only part of this house that's different than the other one. I think Kennedy didn't put it in on purpose."

"That makes sense. I can start staking it off as soon as we get the rest of the shrubs in."

"Kennedy, old boy, what's your secret? You gotta speak up—"

"Good morning," Kyla said pleasantly, entering the kitchen.

"Good morning," Dr. Grant replied, smiling at her from his chair on the peninsula. He was wearing faded blue jeans and a T-shirt, the first time Kyla had seen him out of his normal work attire. His hand moved to close a manila folder before him on the counter as he sat back.

"Good morning," Peter echoed, his eyes dropping quizzically to her robe, then to his coffee.

His look wasn't unnoticed. Kyla pointed to her robe. "Sorry for my fancy attire. I didn't expect anyone to be down here, and the boys are still asleep."

Dr. Grant extended his arm. "Hey—make yourself at home."

Kyla poured herself a coffee, glancing at the file on the counter. "I forgot it's Friday. So what's going on here?"

"Oh, we're just planning a little project," Dr. Grant said, "a little surprise for Marilee when she gets back."

"Oh?" Kyla got herself a bowl of cereal and joined them at the counter.

"Yeah," Dr. Grant said. "We're putting in a fountain. Right in the middle of the backyard."

Kyla lifted her eyes to the patio door and the yard beyond. "A fountain?"

"Yes, a fountain. And we're starting today. Did you know that Peter here is one smart cookie?" Dr. Grant turned in his chair toward Peter. "He will graduate next year with a degree in horticulture and plant pathology. But he also knows a lot about landscape design. He is going to spearhead my project."

"I didn't know that," Kyla replied, glancing at him. She remembered her dad saying that Peter went to the university. She added lightly, "So I guess if any of your houseplants are found murdered, I'm sure to be a suspect." She realized that a pathologist was not a forensic scientist, but she still thought her joke was funny.

Peter gave her an amused smile through the wisp of steam rising from his mug. He hadn't shaved, and his hair was curly from being uncombed. His eyes matched the blue of his T-shirt.

Dr. Grant continued: "What I'm saying is that I've got a gold mine for the summer, and I'm going to utilize him. Up till now we've spent most of our time working on the inside of this place, and this summer we're going to transform the yard. I want my wife to be impressed when she gets home."

"Nice," Kyla said.

Peter set his cup down and leaned on the counter with folded arms. "I grew up working in my parents' nursery."

"Watkins Nursery," Dr. Grant added.

Kyla recognized the name. She set her spoon down and wrapped both hands around the warm mug. "So I overheard you talking about the house as I was coming down the stairs."

Both Dr. Grant and Peter said nothing.

"My father has a friend who's heard of this place," she continued. "My biological father," she specified with a flick of her eyes to Peter.

Dr. Grant tilted his head in interest. "Is that right? What did he say about it?"

"Not much. Just that it was built to be exactly like a place in England and that it was sometimes called 'Twinbury' for fun."

"Ah, well, he's exactly right," Dr. Grant said. "The house in England is called 'Tynnbury Hall,' and my wife's grandparents lived very near it. She walked past it often when she stayed with them and was very fond of the place. That's a large part of why we're here."

"Huh," Kyla said. "That's cool. I found a picture of it on the Internet."

"Really? That's nice," Dr. Grant nodded, shifting in his chair. "Did they have anything else to say about the house?"

Kyla pursed her lips, thinking. "Um, yeah. There was something to do with World War II and the guy who built the house being in a conflict with someone. Supposedly the builder's son died young, and that was suspicious. And then the other guy died too. I don't know. I can't remember exactly. But he said there were lots of rumors about this place." She laughed and shrugged. "I guess that doesn't tell you much."

Dr. Grant leaned back in his chair, folding his arms on his chest. Kyla glanced up at Peter, who was also watching her intently.

"So who is this guy—your father's friend? And how does he happen to know this?" the professor asked.

Kyla looked from one of the guys to the other. "Is this important?"

The professor shrugged. "Oh, you know—I find house history fascinating. These places are full of stories, and you never know what's true and what's not. But it sort of fits in with things I've heard."

She nodded. "Well, his name is Rich Connors, and apparently his cousin's grandfather was partners with the builder of this house—what's his name?"

"Kennedy. Michael Kennedy. There's an old photograph of him hanging in our foyer."

"Yes, I noticed that," Kyla said.

Dr. Grant was thoughtful. "So, your dad's friend's cousin's grandfather. How very interesting."

Kyla leveled her gaze at Dr. Grant. "Yes, interesting. So what are the big rumors about this house? Certainly you've heard them, and I would like to know. Yesterday I was upstairs on the third floor—goodness, what *happened* up there? It gave me the creeps! Did Kennedy's son die up there? Was he murdered?"

"Whoa now!" Dr. Grant held up a hand with a short laugh. "The official record was that both Kennedy and his son died in accidental deaths on separate occasions, and neither in this house. And also for the record, this entire place looked like the upstairs when we bought it, just so you know. I believe I told you that already. We don't know what happened here. Maybe there was an infestation of some sort. Or maybe—"

"It looked like someone was searching for something," Kyla cut in, "in the walls."

"Perhaps, perhaps," Dr. Grant replied slowly, tapping his fingers on the countertop. "But then that's where the rumors come in. Look—there's no reason to be frightened here. These things are weird, yes, but this is not a haunted house. It's my home. I certainly wouldn't raise my sons here if there was any reason to be afraid." He raised his eyebrows at her as if asking if she understood.

Kyla looked up, challenging him. "Well, Hank couldn't sleep last night, and I think it was because he was scared. Yesterday when we were up there on the third floor, he acted like he saw someone outside, and in the night he cried about a 'bad guy.'" She gave a half shrug. "Actually it might have been Mrs. Gordon, but still—he was freaked out!"

Peter frowned. "He saw someone outside?"

"I'm not sure," Kyla answered. "I didn't see anyone myself. And Mrs. Gordon said she had been outside on the patio. But Hank knows her, and I thought it was strange how upset he got. He was on the edge all day and up several times during the night."

Peter shot a glance at Dr. Grant, who studied Kyla thoughtfully. "All right. Thank you for telling me that. We'll keep our eyes peeled today. But that doesn't have anything to do with the house."

"Maybe not," Kyla said, "but we were up there when it happened. It's creepy up there!"

Dr. Grant cleared his throat, shifting in his chair. "Not to minimize my son's fear, Miss DeKane, but Hank is afraid of the giant in our *Jack and the Beanstalk* book. So we don't read that book. Kids get scared. Don't take him up to the third floor. He's two! He doesn't need to be up there, and neither do you. I think everyone got a little spooked earlier this week with our binocular man, and what has come of that?" He spread out his hands. "No one has seen him since."

Except maybe Hank, Kyla thought, but she remained silent. There was no way to know. It might have simply been Mrs. Gordon. Across from her, Peter looked wordlessly at Dr. Grant. From upstairs Kyla could hear the opening of a door, followed by the pitter patter of feet and the sound of one of the boys on the stairs. Her morning was about to kick into gear.

She sighed. "You're probably right," she conceded. She gathered her dishes and put them into the sink.

"So what's with this?" she asked, gesturing again to the file on the counter between the two of them.

Dr. Grant blinked. "We're putting in a fountain for my wife."

At that moment, a very rested and happy Hank entered the room, hurrying across the floor in his pajamas to his father, who scooped him up with a hearty greeting.

Howie was beside himself that his dad was home for the day. After breakfast when it was time to get dressed, his bed became a trampoline on which he jumped wildly, singing silly songs to Hank, who giggled at him while Kyla wrestled to get him dressed on the floor. Attempting to divert Howie's attention, she urged him to put on his clothes so they could go outside, but instead he picked up his pillow and whipped it down at his little brother, who again roared with laughter. He repeated the action with a stuffed monkey, only this time he snagged the edge of the large "H" hanging on the wall behind him, and it came crashing down between the bed and the wall. Howie looked nervously at Kyla.

Her brow went up. "See what happens? You should have listened! Now get dressed!"

Obediently he went to his dresser while Kyla pulled the cowboy decor out from behind the bed. It was undamaged, but they had lost the brad on which it had hung. Hank was still sitting in the middle of the floor laboring to put on his own socks, so Kyla told the boys she was going downstairs to get a new nail from the cabinet in the laundry room and would be right back. She hurried, but when she returned neither of the boys was in the bedroom.

"Miss Kane! Miss Kane, come and look!" came Howie's muffled voice from the hallway.

She followed their voices to find them in the guest room next to their parents' room, standing on an armchair together, looking out the window. Howie had pants on, but no shirt.

Seeing her enter the room, Howie pointed outside. "Look!"

Hank opened and closed his hand to beckon Kyla, then also pointed below, echoing his brother, "Kane! Come—look at the cows!"

Howie giggled and poked him. "It's deer, Hank, not cows!"

Kyla followed their pointing to the grass at the edge of the yard below where four deer had ventured out of the woods and were nibbling on the thick green carpet. The scene was intriguing, for just a short distance away in the center of the yard stood Dr. Grant and Peter in animated conversation. Dr. Grant was talking, gesturing to the house and to the ground in front of them, while Peter stood with his hand on the hip of his khaki work pants, also drawing invisible lines with his other hand. Nearby the deer grazed, undisturbed, as if they were unaware of the men.

"Aren't they beautiful?" Kyla said softly. She had the boys count them, and then pointed out their feet, ears, and tails for them to observe.

Suddenly the head of one deer shot up, as if startled by something below, the other three following in kind, their bodies poised to run. Then all four disappeared back into the woods, bounding upward through the ravine in the direction of the bluff. Kyla peered toward the woods to see what had spooked them.

"Aww," Howie complained, but then distracted by the men in the yard below, asked, "Hey, Miss Kane—can I go help my dad and Peter work?"

Kyla responded that no half-clothed boys would be allowed to help, after which he quickly jumped down from the chair to run back to his room for the rest of his clothes. On the way he charged his body against Peter's door, popping the door open, laughing as he did. Kyla chided him, guiding Hank out of the guest room and closing both its and Peter's doors.

Outside it was impossible for Dr. Grant and Peter to accomplish any work with the kids around. Kyla tried to confine them to playing on the patio where they could watch, but Howie hung his arms over the fat concrete railing and fired off constant questions and commentary toward the busy men. She tried moving them to the front of the house, but their curiosity overpowered them, and they began to make a game of escaping to the back yard. Then Kyla packed up a snack bag and tried to take them on a hike down the ravine, but Hank cried and refused to go because of the "bad guy outside." Kyla remembered what Dr. Grant had said and didn't fight him. Hank's comments had made her feel eerie, and she was only too glad to abort the plan.

Running out of ideas, Kyla brought the boys back into the house, and since it was a nice day, decided to take them down to the river. Quickly she threw on her swimsuit and put her shorts and blouse back on. She slathered the boys in sunscreen and dressed them in their two-piece swimsuits to protect their fair skin. As the boys led the trek, the group crossed the yard and headed down the wooden staircase to the tiny beach below, Kyla's arms loaded with supplies. She plopped the towels onto one of the chairs and tucked the bag of snacks under another in the shade, then dumped the toy bag out onto the sandy dirt. This was the first time she had been down to the waterfront since the binocular incident, and it had been even longer for Hank and Howie, who were immediately immersed in play.

In only an hour it was lunchtime because of their late start. Already the tots had devoured their snacks and sucked their juice packs dry, but they appeared satisfied. Since it felt as if they had just gotten there, Kyla decided to let them play longer, which they were eager to do. She sat in the sand playing with them for part of the time, but after a while they were content to dig and pile on their own, so she spread her towel on the chaise lounge and situated herself to sunbathe. Every once in a while she peered across the river to the wooded rise on the other side, scanning for any mysterious watcher, but she saw no one. Even the eaglets were hidden from sight in their nest from her position on the shore where she reclined.

In the warmth of the sun Kyla felt very relaxed, and the sound of the boys' laughter mixed with the splashing of water was very pleasant. After a while she flipped onto her stomach, leaning her head on her arms on the footrest, watching the kids with her feet up in the air. They thought she looked silly and took turns pouring water over her bare back to cool her off. It felt icy cold, and she wasn't crazy about the sand that dribbled out of the bottom of their cups, but eventually it dried, and she brushed it off later with her towel.

As the morning moved into afternoon, the boys' shade disappeared, and it was starting to get hot. Both Howie and Hank, filthy with sweat and dirt, were busy playing, filling their sand buckets with water and pouring it into holes they had dug, creating lakes and rivers in the muddy sand. Kyla was resting with her eyes closed when she heard the sound of footsteps coming down the wooden staircase. Looking up, she saw that it was Peter, with two water bottles tucked under his forearm. Immediately she snatched up her shirt from the ground beside the chair and threw it on over her head. It crossed her mind that she would have never done the same with Alex, but with Peter it felt different. She sat up.

"Hey," he said, coming off the last step to hand her a water. "It's getting hot out. I thought you might need some help bringing the troops up." He inclined his head toward the stairs behind him. "I sprayed the trail in the woods last night, so you probably should stay off it yet."

Kyla thanked him for the water, but he didn't hear her. He was already down on one knee, cheerfully greeting the boys who excitedly ran to him, convinced that he had come down solely to play with them. He helped them share the water bottle, which they drank thirstily, taking turns back and forth. Howie asked if they could have the empty plastic bottle to pour more water into their rivers, and Peter tossed it into the hole they had dug. Both rushed to retrieve it, each squealing to have it. Kyla sighed and handed her empty bottle to Peter, who passed it on so they could now have two.

"Thanks for the water," she repeated. "The kids are still having fun. We're gonna stay out a little longer."

His eyebrows rose. "It's pretty warm out."

"They're not ready yet." Kyla tipped her head toward the boys as if to prove her point. The two were holding their new bottles under the surface of the water, laughing at the noises and bubbles coming out of them as they filled. Then they inverted the bottles to pour the water over their feet and legs. Hank shrieked with joy, stamping his feet in the splashes.

"Mind if I join you?" Peter asked. "We're taking a break."

Without waiting for an answer, he moved the towels and sat down on a nearby chair, stretching his arms up behind his head as he leaned back to relax, his long legs crossed in front of him. His eyes narrowed as he scanned the shore on the far side of the river; then his face grew pleasant as his eyes rested on the boys splashing at the edge of the shore.

"It's nice out," he said.

"Yeah," she responded. She wasn't sure what to say to him.

"Have you talked to your dad lately?" he asked.

She knew he was just making conversation, but she didn't want to talk with him about her dad. It bothered her that the two of them were so chummy. She answered coolly, "Yeah, we talked last night," but she didn't offer anything more.

It shut him down temporarily. A few moments passed before he made his second attempt, as if searching for another way to initiate polite chitchat. "So. Your dad seems to be pretty proud of you graduating from college."

And how would he know that, Kyla surmised, unless the two of them had been discussing her?

"Yes," she said, adding quietly under her breath, "one of the many facts you seem to know about me."

He frowned, shooting her a look. "Was that a jab? What was *that* supposed to mean?"

"Nothing." She shook her head, making a fuss of adjusting her ponytail and twirling her hair into a loose bun.

He looked back at the boys. "Kyla, when you are with a person for a while you learn things about them. Your dad thinks the world of you and talks about you a lot."

"Apparently so. How long have you known my dad?"

"Known him? Well, I met him—a while ago, but we started meeting together once a week around the beginning of last summer. We've gotten closer over the last year."

"Huh," she replied, her chin jutting forward. "He's never mentioned you." It was true. He hadn't.

Feeling the barb, he glanced at her, then looked out across the water, shaking his head slightly, saying nothing. A short silence passed.

"So what do you guys talk about?" she asked. "Besides me."

He let out a breath, closing his eyes in a long deliberate blink. "We talk about God," he said. "We talk about the Bible. We talk about life. We talk about me. *Rarely* about you. I like your dad a great deal. He's helped me through some tough times. You are blessed to have him."

She was quiet, and he said nothing too. In front of them Howie began pouring water over his little brother's head. Hank caught his breath from the icy chill of the water, then laughed, so Howie filled the bottle to do it again.

Peter brushed some sand off his khakis, trying again. "Do you and your dad ever talk about God?"

"No, not really," Kyla replied matter-of-factly. "I'm not into religion like he is. But don't get me wrong—I love my dad and can accept the things that he's into, and as you said, he loves me for who I am. We get along just fine. We have a great relationship."

Peter folded his hands in his lap, chewing his lip thoughtfully. He studied the tree near him, waiting a bit before he replied. "Well, it's about a person, not about a religion. A beautiful and wonderful person."

Kyla blinked. She knew what he was referring to, and it bugged her that he was just like her dad. "You know, Peter," she said abruptly, "I don't really want to talk about it. I'm just not like you."

He frowned and swung sideways on the chair to face her, bringing his boots to the ground in front of him. "Which is—? I'm like *what?*" he asked curiously.

Kyla's face puckered. "You're so—so—so *clean*. So squeaky clean and perfect. So excessively good and overly nice. It's like a priest lives in the house!"

His jaw grew slack, and he turned his face away from her with a little laugh. "Now *that's* a switch! I've been called a lot of things, but never *that* before!" He rose to his feet. "And I'll take that as my cue. See you later. Call me if you need help." He jerked his head toward the kids and pivoted toward the steps.

"I won't need any help!" she called after him as he trudged up the stairs.

He held up his arm in a wave. "I'll be up top. Just call."

Kyla was shaking. She hadn't meant to be so mean, but it was like she couldn't help it. It was like the beast within her had to strike out. He was downright wacky with his faith, and it irked her. She glanced upward after him, but he was gone, probably back to work with the professor. She fidgeted on the chair, trying to get comfortable again but was too agitated. Her peaceful reverie had disappeared, and now she fought both irritation and guilt.

Within minutes both children were crying. Hank accidentally dropped his full water bottle on Howie's foot, who screamed in pain and then angrily shoved his brother to the ground. Kyla quickly got off her chair to intervene, helping Hank up, who was now wailing and rubbing his eyes with dirty hands while Howie's bawling grew louder, vying for her attention. Carefully she examined his foot, which appeared to be fine, though likely bruised, but Howie insisted that it was broken. Overtired and completely worn out by the sun, the preschoolers had reached their limit. Just like that, it was beyond time to go.

Hastily Kyla popped on her shorts and shoes, gathering up everything but the toys in one large bag. The boys, however, refused to put on their shoes. Howie said his foot hurt too badly, and Hank just sat on the ground and cried. Remembering his interrupted night's sleep and realizing how deliriously tired he must be, she hefted him into her arms and tried to comfort him, but it wasn't working. He was a mess.

"Come on, Howie," she said. "Let's go up to the house." She shifted crying, sweaty, and sandy Hank and swung the bulging bag over her shoulder, starting for the stairs.

Howie whimpered, remaining on the ground, "I can't walk! My foot really, really hurts!"

She turned to look at him through steely eyes, demanding firmly, "Howie. Stand up, please. We are walking to the house. Right now!"

At her stern tone, he burst out crying again. Reluctantly he stood to his feet, walking slowly toward her, his face red and dirt-streaked with tears. She took his hand and led him to the stairs. After a few steps he bawled that the stairs were too hot and hurt his bare feet, but she pulled him along up to the first landing, where she had to set Hank down to catch her breath.

Then from above her came the tromp of boots again. Dismayed, Kyla closed her eyes and braced herself for Peter's comments, her face bright pink from exertion and embarrassment. Which would it be? *I told you so! I knew this would happen! So—you won't need any help?*

He ignored her.

"Hey, fellas—what's going on?" he said to the boys. "Anyone want a ride to the top?"

With a veiled glance at Kyla, he hoisted Hank to his shoulders, fixing his little arms so that he held onto his head. Then he swept Howie up off the step under his arm, and with one hand on each kid, climbed the rest of the way to the top of the staircase. Kyla paused a minute where she stood on the landing to finish catching her breath and to compose herself. By the time she reached the house, the boys were standing under the carport naked, and Peter was rinsing out their sandy suits with the hose.

Chapter Fourteen

All three of them—Kyla and both boys—napped hard that afternoon, the boys waking with rosy pink faces and forearms. Dr. Grant asked Kyla to deliver them to his office when they awoke to video chat with their mother, and later he also cooked dinner, allowing Kyla a few hours of welcomed time off.

Peter was absent when they sat down to eat. He had gone to town later in the afternoon and returned right when they finished their meal, pulling a trailer behind his pickup with a skid loader on it, which Kyla learned he had arranged to rent for a few weeks from his parents' nursery. The little boys were round-eyed with awe staring at it. Dr. Grant made them sit on the step by the front entrance while he and Peter unloaded it onto the driveway. Then Peter taught the professor how to drive and operate it, giving rides to Howie and Hank in the process. Kyla watched them for a little while, then went to sit in the evening sun out on the patio, where it was quieter and where she was on the opposite side of the house from Peter.

After the kids were put to bed, she went out to her tree and made her routine call to her dad. On her way back to the house, Dr. Grant and Peter were lounging outside in their usual places on the patio furniture. The clinking of glass and their voices carried across the yard.

"Now wait," Dr. Grant said. "So you're telling me that you believe all people are basically evil? 'Cause I can't buy that!"

"What I'm saying," came Peter's voice in steady reply, "is that all people have sinned against God—that at their core, people will consistently choose their own way rather than God's way."

Kyla groaned inwardly. She had heard this spiel so many times from her dad.

"That can't possibly be true!" Dr. Grant came back. "How can you say that? I would like to believe that people, *at their core*, as you put it, are basically *good*."

"It's a noble thought," Peter replied, "but let's take children, for example. No one has to teach a kid to lie or be selfish. It's just in him. Hank is a sweetie, but I've seen him haul off and whack his brother. That's a sin nature right there!"

"It's called *instinct*," Dr. Grant replied, flaying open his hands, "pure survival instinct! As they grow their morals develop. Deep inside the good is there."

Peter smiled, lifting his finger. "Ah, but here's the deal — you want to define goodness on *your* terms rather than by what *God* calls good. So in effect you are choosing your own way rather than God's. Case in point!"

Kyla scraped her feet on the concrete deck on purpose so they could hear her as she approached. Both men turned. Even in the dim light Peter's eyes were shining, as if he were enjoying the discussion very much. His arm rested on the side of his chair, holding a Coke.

"Kyla DeKane, there you are!" Dr. Grant said. "You have been elusive today! I've barely seen you! Care to join us?" He pointed to an empty chair, beer in hand.

"No thanks," she said, glad that she could opt out. "I'm calling it an early night." She cast a quick glance at Peter, who was watching her from where he sat.

"Suit yourself," the professor replied. "Get some sleep. No doubt those kids will be up early. They're pretty nuts about that machinery."

"Good night," she said, heading toward the patio door.

Behind her she heard him ask Peter, "Okay, so where were we? Right — this concept of sin. So tell me why you think right and wrong have to be defined by God. Don't you have any faith in humanity? For instance, I like to think of myself as a good person. I have high moral standards. I keep myself healthy. I don't smoke. I drink in moderation — most of the time. I think I make a good contribution to society by what I do — I'm good to my students, I'm good to you, I'm raising my kids to be good. But I don't share your views on God. So where does someone like me fit on your sin grid?"

"That's a great question," Peter answered. "Let me ask you something — have you ever told a lie?"

Kyla pulled the door shut behind her, cutting off their voices.

As predicted, the kids scrambled out of bed in the morning, eager to watch the "quipment" in the yard, but Kyla told them they couldn't go outside until they had eaten and were dressed. And then when she saw how pink their sunburns still were, she wished she hadn't said anything about going outside, for it was clear that they would have to stay out of the sun for the day. She felt a twinge of guilt that she hadn't paid more attention to their fair skin yesterday.

When she had their breakfast prepared, she had to pull them off the furniture in the Great Room where they stood with their noses pressed against the glass watching their dad and Peter outside. After they had eaten, she didn't even try taking them upstairs but let them climb back onto the couch while she went up to get their clothes. She wondered for a second how Marilee Montayne would feel about her kids climbing and standing on the backs of the furniture the way they were, but then, Marilee wasn't here and she didn't know.

Back in the Great Room Kyla recognized that she would need to be creative to occupy these active boys in order to keep them in the house on such a nice, sunny day. Impulsively, she pulled three armchairs across the carpet and made a tent with a couple of blankets. Creating a door, she crawled inside with the boys' clothes and waited. After a bit Howie turned and noticed her under the blanket canopy.

"What are you doing?" he asked in open curiosity. "Can I go in there too?"

That was all she needed to fill the next two hours with play. The boys asked to bring toys down from their playroom upstairs, and Kyla said yes and let them fill a box, which she carried down. The tent started as a house, then turned into a fire station, later becoming a volcano, until it finally morphed into a cave of wild animals. Kyla, of course, had to protect Hank from the wild bear who would rush after him when he sneaked up to look into the mouth of the cave. He squealed and ran to jump into Kyla's lap where she sat on the floor. She then threw her arms around him to save him.

"This is the best game!" Howie said breathlessly, crawling back under the tent. He turned and smiled at Kyla through the opening. "I like you because you're nice. And because you play with me."

Kyla smiled back at him. "I like you too, Howie."

At that moment Hank threw his arms around Kyla's neck from behind her, laying his head against hers, his chin on her shoulder.

"Hank wants you to say you like him too!" Howie said.

Kyla reached up for Hank's arms. "I do, Hank! I like you so much!"

"So much!" Hank said as he hugged her tightly.

Her chest felt a flood of happiness. There was something especially sweet about love coming from these children. It was love unmixed with pity for her life, and it seemed so genuine, so pure. Kyla's heart was filled with affection for the kids.

Within seconds the moment passed, when Howie decided that he and his brother should be alligators and that the tent should be their home in the swamp. Kyla left them playing contentedly and went to prepare their morning snacks. She got what she needed from the refrigerator and stationed herself on a chair at the peninsula to spread peanut butter on little celery pieces, topping them with raisins. While she worked, she pulled the photo of the boys' mother out from its place beside the coffee maker and searched for the boys' features in her face.

"Miss Kane," Howie called, "look!"

She turned to see the cushions of the armchairs stacked on top of Hank, who was peeking out from underneath them.

"Kane," Hank cried, imitating his brother, "look at me!"

She gave them the attention they needed.

Pleased, Howie held up one of the cushions. "Can we take these in the tent?"

Kyla gave them the green light, and they disappeared.

She looked back at the beautiful woman in the photo with her perfect hair, perfect skin, perfect lips, and perfect eyes. She wondered what it was like to be a movie star and a mother. To see her children through a computer screen and not be able to touch their little bodies or snuggle with them. To live in a world of lights and cameras and miss her boys' bath times and story times.

"You're missing out, Marilee Montayne," Kyla breathed softly. "You have some really great kids."

Beside her the patio door suddenly opened and in walked Dr. Grant, who grunted a greeting to her on his way to the refrigerator, where he found a cold bottle of Coke. Swiftly Kyla slid the frame back to its place while his back was turned. After a long drink, he took a breath, pausing with the bottle up in the air and his other hand on his hip. He was sweaty, and his hair had flecks of something brown in it, like tree bark. He cleared his throat and took another drink, looking at her over the bottle.

"You were looking at my wife," he stated.

"Yeah," Kyla said, "just thinking."

"Thinking? What were you thinking?" He wiped the sweat off his forehead with the back of his arm.

She wasn't sure how to answer that. She hesitated a moment, glancing at the photo, then back at him. "Just that she's missing out. On that." She pointed her thumb over her shoulder toward the boys' tent behind her and their soft laughter coming from inside it. "And so much more. It's a shame."

Dr. Grant set his soda down with a firm bump on the granite counter and leaned in toward her, speaking bluntly: "Miss DeKane, someday when you're older and you find someone and have kids of your own, you'll see that life is sometimes—complicated. Don't judge her." His penetrating eyes fixed hard on hers.

Kyla squirmed and wished she hadn't said anything.

"One thing I've learned," he continued, "is that life doesn't come in a perfect box, nice and square and tidy. Life is like a tree. You know—living, growing—except it's not symmetrical. It's all over the place—like a vine, chasing after what it thinks it should be doing and trying to cover all the bases it can."

She swallowed. "I'm sorry. I didn't mean to be critical. It must be very difficult for both of you."

His brow was wrinkled. "Well, it's easy to form an opinion about something you know nothing about." The bottle hissed as he opened it and took another drink.

Kyla gave a little sigh. "Actually, I *do* know. I grew up without a mother. For part of my childhood at least."

Dr. Grant stopped mid-drink to look at her.

"And without a father, for that matter," she added. "Kinda."

His demeanor changed. He set his drink to the side and faced her with interest. "Tell me," he said.

She shifted again in her chair, her bare legs sticking to the wooden seat.

"Well, as you say, it's complicated." She gave a half-smile. "My biological dad left for good when I turned five, and my mom died when I turned twelve. But my mom had remarried, and her husband legally adopted me. So he's my dad, and he raised me. By himself. He's Asian—Korean, actually. So I've been without a mother for a long time."

He was silent, listening.

"I know it's not the same for your boys," she added. "They *do* have a mother, and it's great that they get to talk to her. I'm glad for them."

"I didn't know that about you," he said sympathetically. "That must have been really tough. I'm sorry for what you've been through."

Her eyebrows rose as she gave him a nod. "And if you want to know what 'complicated' is, my biological dad, whom I haven't seen since the time he left, showed up a couple of weeks ago at my college graduation. Just out of the blue! He gave me that car outside and told me he wants to have a relationship and then left without any way for me to connect with him!"

Dr. Grant blinked in astonishment. "After how long?"

"Only seventeen years—that's all! So in the meantime while I'm wondering when and if I'll ever see him again, I have a whole new batch of questions in my mind—like 'Did you even think of me that whole time you were away?'" She felt her throat constrict. "Sometimes I feel like an orphan, all alone, wondering where I belong in life. And talking about it like this only makes it worse, because then I wonder how people feel about me, whether they like me only because they feel sorry for me." She wished she hadn't added that last part.

Dr. Grant slid the box of Kleenex in front of her. She took one and quickly dabbed her eyes.

"Sorry." She took a deep breath and blew it out.

He shook his head slowly from side to side. "Don't be. This is no small thing. I'm glad you told me this."

She sniffed, wiping her nose while he stood silently across from her.

"It's just hard to figure it all out," she said finally.

"Yes. I get that. I do get that." He slid his Coke to the side, setting his hands on the counter. "I had a stepdad too, since I was nine. Two actually, but the first one was out of my life within a year. The second was an okay guy. Anyway, I grew up going between my mom's place and my real dad's place, and yes, it was hard to figure it all out. Sometimes both places felt like home, but most of the time *neither* place felt like home. Whosever place I was at, I felt like I was a visitor. Like I was always missing out on stuff. So I get what you're saying about belonging. Anyway, I never really got to know my dad until I was almost thirty. All that time together, and I never appreciated him or took the time to really talk to him until then. But I found out that he was actually a great guy. A really great guy. And three years later he died." He paused reflectively. "I regret not getting to know him sooner. Seriously, it's one of my biggest regrets in life. I blew it. Here I could have had a great relationship with him for so much longer. I should have pursued him sooner. I wish I had made the effort and pressed through."

"I'm sorry," Kyla offered.

He lifted his hand. "Yes, and likewise, I'm sorry for what you've gone through. That *would* be confusing."

Another space of silence passed between them.

"You know, Kyla," Dr. Grant said finally, "when you first came here, I sort of got the impression that you didn't like it here. I even thought for a moment that you might leave."

She felt her cheeks grow warm. "Well, you're right. I considered it. My ex-boyfriend's dad wanted me back at my old job. But I couldn't go back." She added meekly, "Thanks for not saying anything."

"I figured you would make up your mind one way or the other." He winked at her, reaching for his soda. "I'm glad you stayed."

Her eyes dropped to the celery bites on the plate in front of her.

"I'm serious," he said. "You're a great fit here. And Marilee would like you."

Kyla swallowed. "Thanks."

"This isn't easy for us," he admitted, "but we're trying to make it work, and you're a part of that. I think you're doing a fantastic job."

She smiled. "I like the boys a lot."

"Oh, it's mutual—it's mutual." He took a quick drink of his Coke, then wiped his mouth with the back of his hand. "Last night Hank insisted that he needed to sleep with Miss Kane when I put him to bed." Then he pointed to the plate before Kyla. "So what's this, may I ask?"

"This? Alligator food, of course." She grinned. "You didn't recognize it?"

"Oh, right! For our alligators." With a look of amusement he finished his soda and threw the empty bottle into the trash. "Okay then. Well, our Mr. Watkins is probably wondering what the heck happened to me, so I"— he clapped his hands—"am going back out to work."

He grabbed a cold soda for Peter and left through the patio door, closing it behind him with a hard thump.

Howie heard the door and popped his head out of the tent. "Dad?" he called, looking around. He asked Kyla, "Is my dad here?"

"Sorry, bud," she answered. "He just went outside."

"Aww, I wanted to see him!" He skipped over to where Kyla sat and saw the snacks on the counter. "Can I eat these?"

"Yes, it's alligator food."

"For real?" His eyes grew wide. He ate one, licking the peanut butter off his fingers.

"Where's our other alligator?" she asked.

"He fell asleep in the tent."

By the middle of the afternoon Kyla was running out of energy and out of indoor activities for the kids. They had tired of the fort and book time in the library, and they'd had their room time and—unfortunately—their wild time in the hallway, running and smacking open doors. Kyla thought back to her own childhood to some of the favorite things she did with her mother while she was alive, then pulled two sturdy chairs from the kitchen table to the counter in the kitchen, where she started the brothers in a simple chocolate chip cookie baking project, with lots of measuring and pouring. It was a winning distraction, and so far they were agreeably working together. Furthermore, she had somehow managed to keep both of them from licking their fingers until they were actually shaping the little dough balls for the pan.

As the first sheet of cookies came out of the oven, Kyla heard the side entry door of the house open, followed a minute later by the sound of movement upstairs in the hall. *Hmm—was it Dr. Grant or Peter?* Probably Peter, she guessed, but then she heard footsteps rapidly coming down the stairs and entering Dr. Grant's study. Wrong. It would have to be Dr. Grant.

"Your daddy is here," she told the boys. "You can surprise him and give him a cookie!"

Both boys strained to see him from their chairs. A moment later Kyla heard the heavy doors close and the sound of shoes on the hallway floor. To her surprise, Peter came around the corner, a scroll of white paper and a few other items in his arms. He sniffed the air in an exaggerated way, then greeted everyone amiably, including a brief nod at Kyla.

"So what's going on here?" he asked the boys. "Something smells incredible!"

"Cookies!" Hank said, pointing down at the counter.

"Want one? I made this!" said Howie, excitedly extending a cookie to him, which promptly slipped off his hand and dropped onto the floor. "Aww!" he groaned, looking down at the crumbled pieces.

"Mine!" Hank hollered as Howie reached for another cookie, elbowing his older brother away from the ones in front of him.

Peter laughed. "Hey, now! That's okay, guys! I'll have some later."

He set a child's half-full cup of milk with a lid and an opened bag of fruit snacks on the counter. "I found this on my bed just now." He gave Kyla a little smile. "No biggie."

She grimaced. "Sorry. The boys have started this thing up there—

running and pushing open the doors. I keep telling them to stop."

"No biggie," he repeated, tapping the scroll of paper absently on the counter.

It was the first time they had spoken since yesterday afternoon at the waterfront, but his eyes betrayed no grudge from her put-downs. How he could always be so nice baffled her. She determined to keep things light.

She eyed the paper. "What's that?"

"Drawings for the fountain," he answered, holding it up. "And of the yard."

"Ah." She turned back to guide Hank as he lumped a large chunk of cookie dough onto the baking pan.

"It's gonna be a big, big fountain!" Howie said, stretching out his arms. "My daddy says!"

"Have you ever built a fountain before?" Kyla asked.

"I've done a couple. With my dad, for the company. Nothing this big."

She recalled his family's large nursery business. "Why aren't you working for your dad now?"

He didn't answer right away, watching the kids finger the dough. "Well, a couple reasons," he said finally. "Better pay here, for one. But mostly that I'm still earning back some trust with my dad. For some things I'm not so proud of."

She glanced up quickly.

He gave a wry smile. "Everyone has their secrets, huh?"

She raised her eyebrows and looked away.

"And speaking of secrets," Peter continued, lowering his voice, "does Grant know that you smoke?"

Her mouth opened in surprise. "What?"

He gave her a knowing look.

"I don't smoke," she assured him.

Peter frowned, rolling his head at the boys, who were listening. "I only mentioned it because he made it emphatically clear to me that he didn't care for it. He didn't want the boys being around it whatsoever. I wouldn't want you to lose your job over it."

She shook her head.

He gave her an amused look. "Right. Kyla, I mow the yard. There's no hiding the little pile of cigarette butts behind the tree over where you talk on your phone."

Kyla frowned at him. "Well, they're not mine!"

His jaw twitched, and he looked down, bouncing the paper on the edge of the counter again. "Anyway, I should probably get going." But he stood where he was, his eyes on the granite surface.

Finally he looked up, straight into her eyes. "So, it's been a long week, and you've been really busy. Would you want to go to church with me tomorrow?"

Kyla felt a twinge in her stomach. *What was that?* Did he just ask her—it was almost like he was asking her out on a date—but to *church? Was he joking?* She was so startled by the question that it took her several seconds to answer. "Um, no—I don't think so," she said.

He smiled, unfazed by her answer. "Are you sure? It would be a nice change of scenery, and you could have a little break from these guys. The people are super nice, and we could maybe do lunch afterwards, or pick something up to bring here for everybody."

By his face she could tell that he was completely serious. Kyla unconsciously moved her hand to the back of Hank's chair. So far she had been proud of herself that for once she'd been able to have an almost normal conversation with him, but now she fought to stifle the desire to jab him again. Church? Yeah, right! Apparently he did not know how different she and her dad were!

She shook her head. "Sorry," she said. "I'm not into that. And Dr. Grant already promised me I could sleep in."

"Okay," he said simply. "Maybe some other time." Then bopping each of the boys lightly on the head with the paper tube, he told them good-bye and headed out the back door.

The timer went off, and Kyla took the second sheet of cookies out of the oven, her mind spinning in multiple directions. He had asked her to church. Yes, to *church*—but still he had asked her to go there with him! That felt strange. Automatically her heart reached out for Alex, and with it came the pain of mourning their relationship again. Over the chatter of the boys, she slid the cookies off the sheet onto the rack. It had been a long time since she had felt sought after, and she had to admit a small part of her felt gratified to be asked by Peter, even if she would never go anywhere with him. It made her feel desirable again. Of course, it was just Peter. It wasn't like it was someone special. But she was getting used to him, learning to keep her boundaries and tolerate him. Aside from his religious weirdness, there was no denying that he was a nice guy. Maybe *too* nice. And he wasn't bad looking either. If only he wasn't, well, so much like her dad.

And then the thought occurred to Kyla that perhaps Peter's request wasn't about her at all—perhaps it was more about *him* and his need to talk about God. Maybe he felt like she was an easy target, a candidate to convince of his beliefs. Or—another more logical thought hit her—maybe her dad had urged Peter to invite her to church. She bit her lip, nodding to herself. The more she thought about it, the more she could see that happening. Yes, she bet her dad probably had something to do with it! Oh, it bugged her when they gossiped about her! She would definitely bring it up the next time they talked.

She surveyed the mess before her on the counter. Hank was clapping and rubbing his hands together in the air, dough crumbs flinging into his hair and all over the chair and floor below. Howie was busy rolling his dough into snakes. One thing that Peter was right about was how nice it would be to have a little break. A change of scenery, as he put it. How she would love to order from a menu somewhere, anywhere! She felt a teeny tiny twinge of regret. But church? It was out of the question! She just couldn't trust that Peter wouldn't trap her with his talk about God. Maybe, she thought, maybe she could ask Dr. Grant if she could go to town by herself, just to get away for a couple of hours. Then, thinking of Dr. Grant, she felt a little bad for making up the bit about her sleeping in and hoped that it didn't come back around somehow.

Hank was helping Kyla sweep the kitchen when Dr. Grant came to take the boys to his office to talk with their mother. He gave her a warm greeting, and they exchanged a look of deeper understanding from their talk earlier as Dr. Grant put aside Hank's broom and led him down the hall. Howie had already run ahead, slapping his hands noisily against one of the broad pocket doors, which rumbled in its place. Kyla watched them go, recognizing the importance of this time together for each of them, even if only by video. She finished wiping down the kitchen and went outside.

Exiting by the front door, she paused on the step to inhale the sweet smell of summer, realizing that this was her first moment outside all day! Certainly she must let the boys play outside after their time with their mother, now that the sun had lost its midday strength. The large pots of flowers that had been freshly planted on her first day at Wynnbury were starting to fill out a little. She bent to examine the different blooms closer, fascinated by the variety of plants nested together in the container. Planting was an area she knew nothing about. Her dad had majored on keeping their grass thick and weed free, but if she'd had a mother, then she would know how to plant.

Peter seemed to know what he was doing. Though on the small side at this point, the shrubs and hostas he had put in at the beginning of the week looked great against the red brick of the house. They would grow and fill out with time. He had also cut out an area in the yard the shape of a large kidney bean and planted it with bushes, green plants, and flowers, arranged in just the perfect way, with wood mulch covering the ground, a similar look to what he had planted in the beds below the concrete rails on the patio in the back of the house. The guy was talented—it looked really classy. Probably taught by his mother, she guessed. Which reminded Kyla of what Peter had said earlier that afternoon about his father—about regaining trust with him. She wondered what he meant by that. She definitely had some questions to ask her dad.

She took another deep breath, gazing upward to the top of the bluff in front of the house, following it visually to the left to where the land sloped sharply down into the ravine. She still hadn't explored either yet, as they weren't exactly activities conducive to preschoolers, but she wanted to. The view from the top of the bluff was no doubt spectacular, and cell phone reception guaranteed, she chuckled to herself. She wondered how a person could get to the top. Just as she was about to walk up the blacktop road around the side of bluff to check the terrain, out of the corner of her eye a little movement caught her attention. She turned, spying Peter's broad shoulders and the back of his head on the far side of his truck in the carport, where he leaned against it. He was looking toward where Kyla knew her car was parked. Though it was out of sight, she could tell that he was admiring it, and she didn't blame him. It was a dream car for anybody.

Her car. What a strange affair that car was! She had barely driven it. But there it was. An odd reminder that her biological father actually had showed up in her life for a brief moment, leaving an extravagant down payment on a promise of relationship, then abandoning the deal. If her old car hadn't already had two wheels in the junkyard, she might have thought of refusing the new one. At the time it just seemed too good to be true. She wondered where Robert DeKane was this moment, what he was doing, if he had thought of her much since that day at McDonald's. She wondered where he lived, what his house was like, if he had a family, maybe other children, half-siblings to her. Did he spend time with them? Did he remember their birthdays? Did he have parents who were living? If so, that would mean she had grandparents. Did they know about her? Did they wonder about her? All these were thoughts and questions that hadn't mattered until a few weeks ago.

Beside the truck, Peter suddenly stretched and then left around the corner of the house, probably back to work somewhere in the yard. Briskly Kyla started off toward where the road came out of the woods at the foot of the bluff. She hoped that she would have time enough to explore a part of it. As she reached the opening, however, she heard her name called from behind. Turning, she saw Dr. Grant with Howie and Hank at the front of the house, where she'd just been.

"Miss Kane! Where are you going? Can I come?"

"Kane! I come?"

She sighed. The little Grant brothers would be joining her on her walk. Maybe tomorrow she would have a space of time to explore the bluff. For now, however, her power walk had suddenly turned to a leisurely stroll with tots.

After dinner that night Dr. Grant took the kids to read to them before their bedtime. Free again, Kyla ran upstairs for her phone to call her dad early. She opened her door and crossed her room to the drop-leaf table under the window where she kept her phone near the charger and stopped short to see a small vase filled with a few cut flowers from the yard in the center of the table, next to her computer. Her shoulders slumped as she let out a breath.

Oh, geez, Peter. She shook her head. First inviting her to church, then this. This just took things to a whole new level of uncomfortable. Again she shook her head, rubbing her forehead. She wasn't quite sure if he was saying he liked her or if he was schmoozing her to get her to church, but either way he was trying way too hard. It was almost like because he knew her dad he thought he had an *in* with her. She sighed, options of how to respond flitting through her brain. Nice guy or not, somehow she needed to communicate that she was a dead-end street where he was concerned. Perhaps she would just have to be blunt. She definitely didn't want to encourage him. Meanwhile, just seeing the flowers there bugged her. It was like he was looking at her from the table. Kyla picked up the vase and put the flowers on the floor of the bathroom, next to the waste basket. Then she went outside to call her dad.

She leaned against the wooden railing of the staircase in the humid evening air waiting for him to answer, performing her customary scan of first the opposite shoreline, then the riverbank below. No one. The water was still tonight.

"Okay, Dad, so who is this Peter guy?" she asked him after they had greeted one another and got caught up with news. She had moved out to walk along the edge of the lawn to her tree at the far corner. "Where did he come from? What is his past?"

"Ah, Peter Watkins is one decent guy," Kendall said. "There should be more like him."

"Yeah, so who is he? What's his story?"

"He goes to the university downtown."

"You didn't answer my question." Kyla moved her sandal to avoid a small thistle in the grass.

"What was your question?"

She gave a little sound of impatience. "Well, tell me about him! Like, how did you meet him? What is his past?"

"Oh, now," he replied in his easygoing way, "everyone has their story, you know."

She pulled back her phone, looking at it incredulously, as if the instrument was her dad. "What do you mean by that? Why won't you answer my question, Dad?"

He paused. "Well, sweetheart, it's not my story to tell. If you want to know his story, then ask him. Let *him* tell you about his life."

Like that was going to happen.

"Was it something bad? Can't you just tell me?" she pressed.

Her father was quiet.

She breathed out in silent frustration. "So did you tell him to invite me to church?"

"Did he invite you to church?"

She rolled her eyes. "Yes, Dad, he did. Was that your idea?"

"Are you going to go? I think you'd like it."

"No, I'm not!" She gripped her phone tighter. "And I would like to be off-limits in your conversations with Peter Watkins, please! How many times do I have to ask you? Don't talk about me!"

"Kyla, come on! It's not like you think! He cares about your eternal destiny. And I didn't ask him to invite you, hon. He apparently thought of that himself. I think it's a good idea, though. You should consider it."

Kyla couldn't even respond.

When he spoke again, he brought up that he had gotten her old car fixed and was about to sell it. The subject of Peter Watkins was officially closed.

There was still plenty of daylight left when she went back to the house. Near the stairs she could hear the sound of the television and exercise equipment from the weight room down the hall. Peter was working out. She went up to her room and plugged her phone in. Next door Dr. Grant and the boys were doing their bedtime routine. She liked the sound of his voice and the way he talked to his sons. He was a good dad. Tired and ready to put her feet up, Kyla cozied into the settee, listening to them while she considered what she might do for the evening. Perhaps she would continue reading her book. Or start it again, rather, as it was tough getting into it with so many interruptions.

Howie appeared in her doorway. "Miss Kane, would you get me a drink?"

She took him in the bathroom and gave him a cup, observing that his pajama shirt was tight and strained at the buttons, and his pants were very short. It looked like he was wearing Hank's pajamas. Howie didn't seem to notice or mind.

"Howie, whatcha doing?" Kyla heard Dr. Grant's voice come from the door behind her. "Let's keep it moving, kiddo."

Through the mirror Kyla watched him step into the room. Then she saw his expression change as he spotted the vase of flowers on the floor. He looked up at her, his forehead puckered in confusion.

"Now that's a strange place to keep flowers," he said. "You don't like them? I picked them myself."

Kyla could feel the color rush up her neck. "No, I do! I just thought—" She stopped. What could she possibly say? Should she make up something about allergies?

He cocked his head, still staring at her bewildered. "You thought—?" He turned and looked at the flowers, then back at her, the revelation slowly unfolding. "Ah! You thought they were from Peter!"

She could feel her cheeks burning, and she had nothing to say.

He shook his head. "Holy cow. Miss Kyla DeKane, you are—you are—" He didn't finish. "Come on, Howie, let's go to bed."

Kyla put the flowers back onto the table beside her computer, wishing she could die. She felt foolish on so many levels. What did the professor think of her? She was embarrassed that she had gone down a crazy road in her mind over an invitation to church! *He cares about your eternal destiny*, her dad had said. Of course. It was so obvious that she felt stupid. Peter had one goal, and he had been proselytizing her! She only wished Dr. Grant hadn't walked in on her error in judgment! She was still standing there when she heard a soft knock on her hallway door.

"Yes?" she called quietly, conscious of the boys in the next room.

One of the French doors opened, and Dr. Grant leaned in. "The flowers were to show you that I care about you losing your mom and all the stuff with your father." His eyes flicked briefly to the bouquet back in its place on the table. "I thought I would clarify that, just in case you had any other crazy ideas."

Kyla blinked. "Thanks. They're nice." She realized how lame it sounded at this point.

He closed the door and opened it again. "One more thing. I had a conversation today with Peter about the importance of down time. His theory is that everybody should take a weekly day of rest. He's convinced me. So I just wanted you to know that I'm going to take the morning to myself in my study. You got the kids."

"Got it." She gave a nod. *So much for sleeping in,* she mused.

"Good night," he said, closing her door.

Chapter Fifteen

The weekend passed, and a new week was well underway. Dr. Grant was back to work, leaving early for school before Kyla got up. Since the night Kyla had let Hank sleep with her, the two-year-old liked to come into her room mornings to snuggle with her before they started the day, that is, if Kyla wasn't already up and downstairs. Then he would come looking for her to have morning snuggles wherever she was, whether in the dining room or the Great Room. Howie, on the other hand, wanted to find his dad first thing in the morning, so the days Dr. Grant was at school, he started his day with a bit of disappointment. Peter was second best, so after finding that his dad was gone until afternoon, Howie would ask if he could go play with Peter, to which Kyla routinely said no. Occasionally, though, Peter would take them for a little while to entertain them, just for fun.

Wednesday was one of those days. Kyla had made scrambled eggs and blueberry muffins for breakfast and was just cleaning up when Peter stopped in the house briefly. He was in cargo shorts and athletic sandals rather than the work jeans and boots he normally wore.

"Miss Kane, can I go help Peter?" Howie asked. He was getting dressed for the day on the bottom step of the stairs, where he had brought his clothes from his room. He pulled on his jean shorts and buttoned them over his superman undies.

"No, Howie," Kyla answered, "Peter's got things to do."

"But I can help him!" he protested, pulling his shirt over his head.

"Sorry, bud," she repeated, wiping down the table with a wet cloth. "We'll go outside later. Maybe we can go down to the river."

"Aww, I want to be a worker!" His face dropped into a pout as he folded his arms in front of him.

Peter had just passed by the kitchen on his way back outside, but he stopped, peeking his head back around the corner, his sun-bleached hair accentuating his tan face. His sunglasses hung on the neck of his pocket T-shirt. "He can come out with me for a while," he offered.

Howie's face lit up. He turned to Kyla wide-eyed. "Can I?"

Kyla turned to Peter and shook her head. "You don't have to do that. I know you're busy."

"Actually," he said, leaning on the wall with his arm, "I'm not that busy right now. And I'm doing stuff where he could tag along. Seriously, I don't mind."

She shot him a look. "Are you sure? It's not part of your job description."

"I would enjoy it." His blue eyes sparkled at Howie.

Kyla raised her brow at her young charge. "Did you hear that? Get your shoes on, young man!"

"Me! Me! Me!" Hank shouted, reaching his arms up with his fingers spread out like two starfish. He started to stand up in his chair, dressed only in a diaper and pajama shirt.

"Hank, you get to stay with me," Kyla said quickly.

Immediately his face fell, and he began to cry.

"Naw, I'll take them both," Peter said.

"No, really," she protested, turning to look at him, the soggy dishcloth still in her hand. "He'll get over it. He can stay with me."

Peter leaned his hand on the kitchen island looking at her with a playful smile. "I'll tell you what," he said. "I'll take both of these guys until noon if you go to church with me next Sunday."

She leveled her eyes at him. "No. Nice try, but no dice." The reality of his intentions had been confirmed multiple times since the flower fiasco. Boy, was he like her dad!

He snapped his fingers in disappointment. "Come on, buster," he said to Howie, brushing him on the shoulder, "let's go do some man work." Then he tipped his chin up and said to Kyla, "Bring Hank out when he's dressed."

Howie ran ahead of him to the back door.

Kyla turned back to Hank with a smile. "Hank, you lucky duck! You get to go outside with Peter! Quick—let's go get you dressed!"

"Yay!" The little boy beamed and clapped his hands.

Kyla had just delivered Hank to Peter and was returning to the house when Mrs. Gordon arrived, parking her silver Honda in her usual spot. She was reaching into the backseat to retrieve a large bundle of Dr. Grant's dress shirts fresh from the cleaners as Kyla approached and greeted her.

"Good morning!" Mrs. Gordon replied pleasantly. "It's nice to see activity around here today! I won't have to worry about scaring anybody."

"Don't remind me!" Kyla said as they both laughed. "That wasn't my best day." She saw the groceries in the vehicle and moved to help. With her arms loaded down, she tapped the car door shut with her foot. "You're here early," she observed.

"I am!" Mrs. Gordon replied. She had on tan capris with a matching leopard print shirt and tan orthopedic sandals. "I have no grandkids to watch today, so I thought I'd come right out and get a jump on things." She held the back door open for Kyla, then entered the back room behind her. "Thanks, hon! I can get the rest—you go watch those sweet boys."

"Actually, Peter offered to take them for a while. So momentarily I have no kids to watch either!" She lugged the bags into the kitchen and set them on the island.

"Really? How nice! A little free time to yourself!"

Mrs. Gordon busied herself with putting the cold items in the refrigerator. Kyla stood near and handed them to her, then took the rest of the food to the pantry.

"Would you like a cup of coffee?" Kyla offered. "I was just about to enjoy mine minus the little people. It'd be nice to talk to another woman!"

Mrs. Gordon had a box of laundry detergent under her arm and was headed toward the laundry room. "Sure," she said over her shoulder. "I would love a cup of coffee—if you have some. But don't make any on my account."

"Already made," she answered.

"Great!" The housekeeper paused and turned. "Mind if I strip the beds and get the first load of sheets going? Then we can sit down and visit while they're in the washer."

Kyla agreed. "Sounds like a plan!"

By the time Mrs. Gordon returned to the kitchen, Kyla had opened up the formal dining room and had set out three of Marilee Montayne's Wedgwood plates, one each for the two of them and one to hold four of the muffins left over from breakfast. The matching coffee cups rested on little saucers. She couldn't find any fancy napkins, so she took the everyday ones from the other table, as well as the regular silverware from the kitchen.

Mrs. Gordon gave a little sound of delight when she saw the table. "How lovely!"

Kyla poured the coffee when the older woman sat down. "Dr. Grant invited me to use this room if I wanted to. It's my first time." She set the carafe down onto a hot pad. "Of course, the boys aren't allowed in here, so this is truly a rare occasion!"

Mrs. Gordon chuckled. "I'll bet!" She fingered the porcelain handle of the cup. "Mmm—Miss Marilee has such fine taste. It's a shame she isn't here with us. She's really a very wonderful lady. I hope you have the opportunity to meet her sometime." She raised the cup to her lips to take a careful sip of the steaming brew. "And how has your week been?"

"Busy," Kyla answered, "but good. And yours?"

"Oh, busy all right!" Mrs. Gordon said. She cut one of the muffins in half and spread it with butter. "We celebrated all the June birthdays in the family over the weekend, so my elderly parents and all the kids and grandkids came over. Everyone except for one of my daughters, who decided not to come. It's so rare to get all the kids together at the same time when they get older, you know, with work schedules and all. We sure had a houseful! It was fun to see everyone, and we even got a few family pictures. But boy, I tell you—was I ever worn out Sunday night! I'm not as young as I used to be!" She laughed and held up the coffee. "I'm still tired!"

"How many children do you have?" Kyla asked.

"We have eight children," Mrs. Gordon replied. "Three girls and five boys. All grown up, of course. And right now I have seven grandchildren, but there's one more in the oven, so eight this fall."

"Eight kids, eight grandkids," Kyla echoed. "Wow—that's a lot!"

Mrs. Gordon chuckled. "Yeah—especially at Christmas! You don't hear of many families that large nowadays. But I'm number ten of a family of eleven."

"Eleven!" Kyla's eyes grew wide. "Yikes!"

The woman set the cup down with a little clink on the saucer. "Folks had more kids back when my parents were young. How about your family?"

Kyla had hoped she wouldn't ask. But she had. She braced herself for the coming expression of pity on Mrs. Gordon's face. "My family is about as opposite as you can get from yours. We're very small—just my dad and I." Next Mrs. Gordon would ask about her mom, after which Kyla would drop the bomb and the pity-look would appear. It happened every time.

"Oh," Mrs. Gordon tilted her head, enjoying the muffin. "Then you must be very close."

Kyla studied her face, nodding. "For the most part."

"Hmm," she said. "So what does your dad do?"

"He's an administrator in a health clinic. Same job as long as I remember."

"I see," she replied. "Sounds important!" She held up the muffin half. "These are very moist."

"Thank you. It's just a mix." Kyla waited. Surely she would ask about her mother.

"So tell me about your father. What's he like?"

"My dad?" Kyla frowned. "Well, he's Korean. He married my mom and legally adopted me. My family is a little odd."

Mrs. Gordon pulled her head back slightly. "Oh? How so? What does that have to do with being Korean?"

"Nothing." Kyla shook her head. "It's just such an oddity for an American child to be adopted by a Korean. Usually it's the other way around."

Mrs. Gordon nodded. "Yes, I suppose so. But I don't think that matters. Was he a good dad? Did you know that he loved you?"

"Yeah, I guess so," Kyla admitted, regretting that she had made an issue of his ethnicity. "He did his best. He stuck with me when I was just awful to him. He loves me. It's just"—she paused—"it's just that with him it's like a neon sign flashing 'Ask questions here'! And then I have to explain everything, and then people feel sorry for me." Inwardly she kicked herself—*Why did she always say things like that? That was way more than she needed to share!*

Mrs. Gordon's mouth opened as she gave Kyla a look of concern. "My dear, that is nothing to be embarrassed about! And nothing of the sort entered my mind! In fact, I was thinking that he must be a great guy because you turned out very well. It's hard raising girls!"

"Thanks," Kyla said, looking downward. "He *is* a great guy. But we're so different."

"How so? You mean culturally? 'Cause he's Korean?"

She shook her head. "No, no. He's American, born and raised. But he's super religious, and I'm—not." She stopped, suddenly remembering that Mrs. Gordon was religious herself.

"Ah, I see," Mrs. Gordon said. She reached for the other half of the muffin, preparing it as she had the first.

Kyla threw her an undercover glance. Was she offended? She wasn't sure. If she was, she hid it well. Uncomfortable, Kyla, too, turned her attention to her muffin, pulling it apart and taking small bites.

Mrs. Gordon set the knife across her plate, looking thoughtfully at Kyla. "So can I ask you a question?"

Kyla shrugged. "Sure."

"You mentioned you're not super religious. I try not to be super religious either. I just try to be conscious of God and stay connected to him through the day. What about you? Would you say you feel connected to or disconnected from God? If you don't mind my asking."

"Mmm—that's a strange question, but I guess I don't mind." She pulled a blueberry out of the muffin to eat it separately. "I would say disconnected. Definitely."

Mrs. Gordon pursed her lips. "And why do you think you feel that way? Is that where you want to be?"

Kyla took a sip of coffee, considering her answer. "I've actually thought about this recently. I'm disconnected from God probably because I'm angry with him. He does not seem like the loving deity everyone talks about. To me he seems cruel and arbitrary."

"Huh." Mrs. Gordon leaned her chin on her hand. "And why is that? Might it have something to do with the absence of your mother?"

Kyla let out a breath of surprise and started in on her explanation like a well-rehearsed speech. "Yes, as a matter of fact! When I was ten my mom got cancer and went through treatment. At that time she started to go to church. She took me with, and eventually my dad started going, toward the end. When I was twelve her cancer came back, and she died. It's just a bad association, I guess. I have a hard time understanding why God let her die and why he would deprive a young girl of her mother. He doesn't seem very powerful to me. Anyway, I stopped going to church with my dad. He is even more religious today, though. He's always—seriously, *always*— talking about God! Like, it consumes his life! I can't handle that! I mostly just try to ignore him."

"Ah." Her mouth twisted, and she nodded, silent.

"It seems like everything has gone wrong in my life," Kyla continued. "It's like God is against me!"

"I see," Mrs. Gordon said thoughtfully. She narrowed her eyes at Kyla. "And you feel like a psych patient when people hear about your mom because they show you pity. Is that what you meant earlier when you said people feel sorry for you?"

"Yes!" Kyla said, surprised to hear her say it. "Exactly! I've felt that way for ten years, and I *hate* it!"

Mrs. Gordon's brow creased sympathetically. "Do you think about your mother a lot?"

"Every day," Kyla said, her throat tightening. She didn't understand why she was suddenly feeling so emotional. "Almost every day I wonder what my mom would have thought of something or advised me to do. Every day I watch people with mothers, and I'm aware of my loss. Every day I am unsure about things that I think I should know—things that mothers teach their daughters—except I never had that. You know what I mean?" She sniffed. "I've had to figure out everything on my own. Everything! Like shaving my legs. And learning to wear makeup. Those kinds of things. Do you know how embarrassing it is to have a friend's mom offer to take me bra shopping because she can see mine doesn't fit me very well? That's why I have a hard time with God!"

"Oh, hon, I'm sorry." Mrs. Gordon's expression was soft. "And I say that as someone who cares about you, not because I pity you. But those things aren't God's fault."

"Well, if you were in my shoes, I bet you would think otherwise!"

The older woman clicked her tongue. "I hear you, sweetheart. Sounds like you've had some terribly difficult circumstances, and that would be tough." She patted Kyla's arm and sighed. Resting her elbows on the table, she was quiet for a bit. She rubbed her cheek thoughtfully, then leaned forward, continuing in a kind voice, "I don't mean to minimize what you've had to deal with in your few years, honey, but I think I should warn you to be careful not to make the loss of your mom the defining feature of your life."

"What do you mean?" She shifted in her chair, blinking back her tears in her determination not to cry.

"Well, I know some people who have experienced tragedies who wear them like daily clothing. Their tragedy has become their filter for life, and they camp there, focused inward on their loss. They can't see beyond it, and they lose out on so much. Your life is about a lot more than your loss. It doesn't take away what happened, but you have a lot of living to do."

Kyla swallowed. "You don't understand. It's been hard not having a mother."

"Absolutely, hon! But keep it real! Stay in reality. Be careful not to make a monument in your heart toward something that didn't exist. You know, something that you think should have been but never actually happened."

"What? What do you mean?"

Mrs. Gordon leaned on the table with her arms, gesturing with her hands. "All of your imaginations of what your life *would* have been like with her are just that—imaginations!"

Kyla drew back. "My mother was wonderful! It would have been great!"

"I'm sure she was, honey!" She reached out to touch Kyla's hand, but Kyla pulled back, folding her arms across her chest.

"I don't get what you're saying."

The woman looked upward, thinking. "Oh dear. Okay. So I had three daughters, right? Let's say I wanted four, but the rest of my babies were boys. It would have been foolish to resent my sons, wishing one of them had been a girl. Wisdom says to accept what I have and be thankful for it."

Kyla blinked. "I'm sorry—I am not following you. Are you saying I shouldn't grieve my mother?"

"No, of course not!" Mrs. Gordon laid her hand on the table. "In fact, you'll feel that loss all your life! Cherish those memories! Write them down in your journal so you don't forget! I'm just saying to grieve what actually *was*, not the fantasy of what *could have been*. You have made up a life that you have lost—but it's all in your imagination! It's a false reality that you're pining over. There's no way to know how it would have been!"

Kyla listened soberly.

Mrs. Gordon went on. "Every mother dreams of a great life with her kids, but I have one daughter who hasn't talked to me in three years! Two of my girls think I'm wonderful. The other thinks I'm the worst mother in the world. All of them argued with me growing up. All of them sassed me. That's reality! That's *real* motherhood! In real life there probably would have been a few things about your mom that bugged you. Life's not always the way it plays out in your imagination. How do you know how things would have been with your mother? The way it is with my daughter is not my choice. It hurts, but it's out of my control. I don't like it, but I have to accept it. I pray for her daily."

Kyla was silent, fingering the edge of her napkin.

"It sounds to me like you have built a case against God for the life you didn't have—which is something that *didn't exist*. Very real in your mind, but a fantasy, nonetheless. But it also sounds to me like what you *did* have was pretty good—an awesome mother who died way too young, and a man who cared for you enough to want to adopt and raise you. A guy who kept a steady job and loved you."

A tear slipped down Kyla's cheek. She let it fall without wiping it.

"Death is not one of my favorite subjects, but none of us can escape it! All of us will face it sometime or another. It's especially hard when it's a tragedy, like a mom with kids or a little child who dies. It's a heartbreak plain and simple." She shook her head sympathetically. "Life is fragile, and we take these beating hearts of ours so for granted. I'm sorry your mom had cancer, Miss Kyla. Cancer is horrible, but you need to know that God didn't give her that. God's not the author of sickness and evil. It's part of the broken world we live in. And it sounds to me like your mom found a lot of peace in God. Your dad too."

Kyla swallowed and nodded.

"If you look at your life, what you had was better than what I see some families with two parents have. Don't you be ashamed of your daddy! He did a courageous thing raising you!" Mrs. Gordon set her plate to the side. "I realize I'm kinda in speech mode, but I hope you'll hear my heart. We've all got hurt, honey. Don't let that eat you up and spoil your future. You need to let go of what wasn't and isn't and be thankful for what you have. You have a great future ahead of you!" She pointed at the muffins. "Your life is like a recipe, and you're in charge of adding the ingredients to make something great. You're a lovely young lady. You're beautiful, smart, fascinating, and I've watched you with those kids—you're good with them! I think you'll be a great mother someday. That's if you have kids, you know."

"Thanks." Kyla choked. She wiped her eyes and blew her nose on her napkin. "It's a lot to think about." She took a deep breath and looked up at Mrs. Gordon, adding daringly, "A couple weeks ago I thought I was pregnant. I was scared to death. My dad—my dad would have been so disappointed in me."

Mrs. Gordon tilted her head. "Your old boyfriend?"

Kyla nodded, looking down at the table.

The housekeeper reached for Kyla's hand again. This time Kyla let her take it. "Honey, your daddy might have been disappointed, but I'm sure he would have supported you. If he loves Jesus, I guarantee it." She squeezed her hand. "Your boyfriend dumped you because of that?"

She shook her head. "No, he actually never knew about it." She let out a sigh. "It's complicated. Let's just say the situation caused me to open my eyes to see the depth of our relationship. Or the lack of depth in our relationship, I should say. He also cheated on me."

Mrs. Gordon made a sour expression with her mouth. "Ouch." She held on to Kyla's hand. "Sweetheart, God made you to want to be your man's only one. That's the way he wired you. It's the image of God—but in marriage! Remember our conversation the other day?"

Kyla gave a meek nod.

Mrs. Gordon shook her head. "Oh, I see so many young girls looking to fellas for love. You need to know how much God loves you, sweetheart, how very beautiful you are to him! He can fill all those empty places inside!

So you're not pregnant? And there's nothing else wrong?"

"I'm okay," she said.

Mrs. Gordon searched Kyla's face for a bit. Then letting go of her hand, she finished her coffee and set the cup down on the saucer. She smiled. "I'm glad it worked out for us to talk. I've been praying for you."

Any other time Kyla would have been irritated by those words. Today she just wanted to think. From down the hall she heard the click of the washer as it finished the spinning cycle.

Mrs. Gordon heard it too and glanced at her watch. She breathed out a sigh. "I certainly didn't intend to get this personal when I sat down with you this morning. I hope you're all right."

Kyla gave a tired smile. "I'm okay. It's a lot to think about. But I should probably let you clean. We've been talking for a while now."

"Yeah, I suppose." Mrs. Gordon moved forward in her chair. "I'm the one who's been chatty. But this has been very nice! Your muffins were delicious!" She picked the edge off another one and popped it into her mouth as she rose. "Let me help you clear the table."

Together they carried the dishes to the sink. Then Kyla went back to wipe off the table while Mrs. Gordon disappeared into the laundry room. She heard the slam of the dryer door and the sound of it starting as she closed up the dining room doors. Soon Mrs. Gordon appeared with a caddy of cleaning supplies and her usual bucket of rags.

She smiled. "I usually start upstairs, so I guess I'll see you later."

"Okay," Kyla said with a nod, and Mrs. Gordon left.

Kyla loaded the dishwasher with the breakfast dishes. *You need to know how much God loves you and how very beautiful you are to him.* Mrs. Gordon's words rang in her mind. She scrapped the dried egg off the skillet, deep in contemplation. As she finished tidying up, she peered out the window above the sink, searching for Peter and the kids in the backyard, but didn't see them. She expected that any moment they would probably appear for their morning snack, so she prepared two cups of chocolate milk and set out a banana to cut in half when they came in. *How very beautiful you are to him.* She paused with her hand on the milk jug. How would she know that? How could Mrs. Gordon know what God thought about her? After standing there a while lost in thought, she caught herself and put the milk back in the refrigerator.

On a whim Kyla opened the doors and went back into the formal dining room, glancing out into the front yard, but the boys were not in sight there either. Ahead of her the bluff beckoned. She had time to herself—

would she dare go for it? She was free—now was her chance to walk up the driveway to see if she could climb it from the other side. She wasn't sure how soon Peter would want to pass back the kids to her, but for the moment at least she had a little bit of time. She studied the bluff thoughtfully for a minute, then closed the dining room doors and went upstairs.

Mrs. Gordon was in her bathroom, bending over, scrubbing the toilet. She looked up at Kyla standing in the doorway. "Yes? Did you need something, hon?"

Kyla took a breath. "Right now is one of those moments that I wished I had a mother to know if it would be improper or bothering you if I just hung out with you while you were cleaning."

Mrs. Gordon tipped the toilet lid down on the brush and straightened up, wiping her hands on her khakis. "Well, then, this is one of those moments when I would tell you that even a girl *with* a mother would probably wonder the same thing. So rather than feel insecure or like you're missing out on something, you could just ask if it's okay. And then I'd say yes, I'd love to have you hang out. But here—" She smiled and handed her a spray bottle. "You can start on the tub."

Kyla looked at the cleaner and at the tub. "Now I automatically wonder if I'll clean it the right way."

The woman brought her hand to her hip. "Good grief, girl! Who says there's a right way to clean? Do it your own way!"

"I'm just letting you know what it's like for me not to have had a mom."

Mrs. Gordon nodded. "Okay—I get it. But I hope you'll think about what I said today. I think if you retrain your thinking, you'll be much less burdened. God wants to set you free." She turned back to the toilet. "And I'd be happy to help you along the way, just so you know. In case you were wondering if it was proper to ask." She leaned back and winked at Kyla.

She smiled. "Thanks."

Peter didn't return with the boys until a bit before noon. Kyla had just said good-bye to Mrs. Gordon and had returned to finish vacuuming the Great Room carpet for her, when through tall windows she saw them top the wooden stairs at the cliff with Hank on Peter's shoulders and Howie under his arm. Kyla stopped the vacuum and watched him plop Howie to the ground and saunter with long steps across the yard to the patio with the youngster trotting hurriedly beside him, talking the whole time. Peter looked focused, the boys ecstatic. Howie slid open the door, and holding Hank's legs, Peter crouched down low to enter without bumping Hank's head on the doorframe. Kyla found herself anxious to see them.

"Fish! Fish!" Hank cried out excitedly from Peter's shoulders when he saw her.

"Miss Kane!" Howie said, running to her in the Great Room, his eyes aglow. "Guess what! We caught a fish!"

"Really?" she replied with a brief questioning look at Peter. "Howie, remember we take our shoes off before we come in here. Were you guys fishing down on the dock?" She squatted down to help him remove his shoes.

"No, we goed out in the boat!" He held out his foot for her, gesturing with his hands. "It was this big!" Since he had mentioned fish, Kyla could now smell it on him. His chin was streaked with dirt. Or something—she hoped it was dirt.

"Big, big fish!" Hank echoed from his perch. "I touch it!" His little arms opened wide, then quickly he clutched Peter's neck again.

"We *went* out in the boat," Kyla corrected Howie, frowning at Peter. "You took these guys out in the boat?" A slew of childhood fears flooded her mind.

He raised his eyebrows, giving a twisted smile. "And we had a great time!"

Kyla's face puckered disapprovingly. "Did Dr. Grant say you could do that? It's not very safe for children!"

Howie was breathlessly patting her arm. "Miss Kane, the fish was this big—" He gestured again. "But we put it back in the water. Peter says that we can go fishing again sometime and try to catch him again! Right, Peter?"

Kyla looked down into Howie's eager face. "How big? Wow, that's huge! How awesome!" She shot a dark look back at Peter, who was still standing at the edge of the dining room.

Peter jerked his head. "What do you mean?" His voice betrayed annoyance. "Of course, it was safe! They had life jackets on! And I was watching them!"

Kyla's jaw was set, and she shook her head. "Well, Dr. Grant put me in charge of his kids, and I would never take children out in a boat by myself. I wouldn't take that risk! There are too many things that could happen." Behind her the grandfather clock in the foyer began to chime.

"Yeah?" Peter gave Kyla a smug smile as he reached up and swung the tot down to the floor. "Well, I *did*, and we had a great time, didn't we, Hank?" He bumped him playfully in the diaper. "Did you have fun, Hank?"

"Fun in the boat!" he said, running happily to Kyla.

"And guess what," Peter continued, looking down at her through narrowed eyes. "I watched them all the way to noon. I think you owe me, remember?"

Kyla's mouth dropped open. "What? No, I did not agree to that deal!"

He laughed, throwing up an arm. "I'm teasing you! Anyway, these two are starving. I thought I'd better deliver them in a hurry. I'm going back down to take care of a few things and then put away the boat. I'll see ya later."

Howie turned to him with adoring eyes. "Can I come with? Please? I could help!"

"Nope, not this time." Peter gave Kyla a little salute and left.

As Peter had predicted, the boys were indeed very hungry and ate their lunch eagerly. Hank, however, began yawning halfway through, and before he could finish his food his eyes were rolling back. Carefully Kyla cleaned him up and carried him to his bed. By the time she had come downstairs, Howie had finished and had washed his hands. She sat with him in the big chair in the library reading books to him while he snuggled up to her. Down the hall she could hear the clatter of dishes in the kitchen. Peter was back in the house, making himself lunch.

"I know how to put a worm on a hook," Howie said in the middle of the story Kyla was reading. "Peter showed me."

She paused. "You're brave, Howie. Worms gross me out."

He smiled at her and looked back at the book. Kyla continued reading.

"But you have to be very careful with the hooks," he said, interrupting her again. "They are really, really sharp!"

"Yes, you do," she agreed, pausing the story and looking down at the top of his head. He was looking at the page, so she resumed reading.

She hadn't gotten very far when he blurted, "Do we have any books on fish?"

She paused once more. "We can look. Did you like fishing with Peter?"

Howie nodded, stretching a bit. "Yeah, it was great! And we played a good game in the boat."

Kyla frowned, alarmed. "I hope you weren't running around in the boat."

"No, Peter wouldn't let us walk around. We had to sit by him."

That's good, she thought. "And what was this game you played?" She closed their book.

"It's called 'God's Crayshun.'" He straightened, looking up at her.

Kyla shook her head. "I don't know that game. How do you play it?"

"It's fun!" he said. "I tell Peter something that I see outside, and he tells me things you can learn about God from it."

"Ah, 'God's Creation.'" *Very clever, Peter,* she mused.

"Yup, 'God's Crayshun.'" He leaned back against her, yawning.

"And what did you learn about God?" She wondered what Dr. Grant would think of Peter's little game with his boys.

"Um—that he's really big, and he made everything, and he's happy, and"—he yawned again—"I can't remember all the things. But I know he made fish! They are really cool. I got to touch one. They have these hard things on their skin called scales. And they have little teeth that are really sharp. And these pink things on the side for breathing in the water."

"Gills."

"Yup." Howie nodded. "Gills, so they can breathe in water. God made them that way." He pulled his head away from her arm, looking up at her. "So do we?"

"Do we what?"

"Do we have a book on fish?"

"I'll see," she replied, pulling away from him. "Come—you can help me look."

"I'm too tired," he said, lying across the chair after she rose.

Kyla knelt beside the children's bookshelf in the center of the room and flipped through the books. "Well, I'm glad you had fun this morning. And I'm glad you guys wore your life jackets and didn't do anything risky."

"Just one kinda dangerous thing," Howie said, patting the chair cushion, a little smile on his face. To Kyla's questioning look he whispered, "Peter let me drive the boat. But I'm not supposed to tell anybody."

"Did he?" Kyla's eyes grew round. "I see. And is there anything else you're not supposed to tell me?"

"Umm—" Howie frowned. "Only that we found another different boat. In the ravine. A little one, kind of hidden under some tree branches." Then his face grew worried. "But don't tell Peter that I told you. He told me not to say *anything* to you!"

Chapter Sixteen

From the floor of the library Kyla stared with confusion at Howie in the large armchair for several seconds. Why would Peter not want her to know anything about finding a boat in the ravine? It hit her with a surge of adrenaline. Alarmed, she rose hastily from the floor and headed directly for the kitchen to pump Peter for information, but when she got there, he was already outside again. She set her hands firmly on her hips, her jaw taut in frustration. Why did he not include her in what was going on? She turned to look for him outside and saw him talking on his phone at the edge of the yard, facing the river with his back to her. In his free hand was a sandwich, which rose and fell as he gestured.

Howie appeared at her side, looking up at her nervously. "Are you mad at Peter?"

Kyla took a deep breath, trying to stifle her displeasure. "I just need to ask him a question about something."

Quickly Kyla went to retrieve her sandals from the library, but by the time she returned to the patio doors, Peter was off the phone and walking determinedly toward the ravine in long strides. His head and shoulders disappeared as he entered the woods and the valley below, and she could see him no longer. For a moment she considered going after him but changed her mind when she heard Howie in the side entrance, also fetching his shoes. She didn't want to take him with her, nor did she want to leave him there by himself.

"He's gone, Howie!" she called after him. "We missed him! I guess we'll have to talk to Peter another time."

He stood in the hallway holding a shoe in each hand, looking confused. "We're not going outside?"

"No, it looks like he's busy now," she said. "I can ask him my question later. Let's go back and see if we can find a book about fish."

Crestfallen, Howie dropped his shoes in the middle of the floor and reluctantly followed Kyla back to the library. Kyla knelt and resumed looking through the books, but Howie stood stiffly beside her.

"Are you mad because I drove the boat?" he asked her soberly.

Kyla sighed, pulling him near to give him a little hug. "I'm not mad at you, Howie."

He drew away. "Your *face* looks mad."

She smiled tiredly. "You didn't do anything wrong. Don't worry. I'm mostly thinking about something else right now."

He seemed satisfied, kneeling down to join her in the task of finding a book on fish.

A short time later when Kyla had gone upstairs to play with Howie in the playroom while Hank finished his nap, through the window she saw Dr. Grant's SUV come up the driveway. Glancing at the clock confirmed her sense that he was home much earlier than usual. She watched him pull up to the carport and waited for his footsteps through the house downstairs, but she didn't hear him come inside. On a whim, Kyla left Howie and crossed the hall to the guest room across from Peter's room to get a view of the back yard, and there they were—Dr. Grant and Peter together, walking to the edge of the yard by her oak, where they both stood looking into the ravine. Peter moved his hands and pointed while Dr. Grant stood fixed, his hands on his hips. Kyla tried to see beyond where Peter was pointing, but the trees were too thick.

"Howie, can you play quietly by yourself a bit?" she asked, popping her head into the playroom. "I need to run downstairs. I'll be right back."

She went down to wait in the kitchen. Sure enough, within a few minutes she heard the two men come in through the back entryway, talking with each other. She faced them squarely as they entered the hall, standing by the kitchen island with her arms folded.

Dr. Grant came in first, a line etched between his brows. He was holding his briefcase, his suit jacket draped over his arm. "Good afternoon," he said, then seeing her stance and the scowl on her face, stopped to look at her in surprise. Peter, close behind him, stopped too, eyeing her. He looked very much in need of a shower. His shorts and T-shirt were dirty, and his calves and arms were streaked with mud in a few places.

"All right," Kyla demanded. "I would like to know what's going on!"

Dr. Grant blinked, speaking under his breath to Peter. "From the sounds of it, one of us is in trouble, and I'm betting it's you."

Kyla gave a sound of exasperation. "Seriously, I'm not stupid, and

I'm not blind! I want to know what's going on! I saw you both out there!"

Dr. Grant shifted the briefcase in his arm. "Well, if you insist. Our man Peter found a boat hidden in the ravine."

"I already heard about that!" Kyla pinned Peter with her eyes. "A little birdie told me!"

Peter shook his head, bewildered by her fuss. Dr. Grant frowned, watching her through narrowed eyes for so long that her cheeks began to burn. Finally he continued, matter-of-factly, "Miss DeKane, this bumps our Peeping Tom to the category of a stalker. But we're not going to talk about this right now with little ears in the room."

Kyla was suddenly aware of the boys coming down the stairs. Dr. Grant nodded to Peter, who continued down the hall toward the study. As Howie appeared around the corner, Dr. Grant moved to set his briefcase down on a nearby chair, revealing a set of dirt-encrusted binoculars hidden under his jacket. Kyla stared at them, feeling punched in the gut.

Howie ran across the floor to his dad. "Dad! I didn't know you were home!"

Dr. Grant leaned down to greet and embrace his son, meeting Kyla's disturbed gaze over Howie's shoulder. Hank then made it to the bottom of the stairs and ran toward them, but he trotted past his father to reach for Kyla. She picked him up, and he nuzzled into her, his hair damp with sweat from his nap. With his arms around Kyla's neck he smiled sweetly at his father.

"Oh, right!" Dr. Grant waggled his head. "I have now become chopped liver!" He reached over to give Hank a playful squeeze on his ankle. "Look," he said to Kyla. "I need to meet with Peter right now, and then afterwards Marilee—" He gestured to the kids.

Her face fell at being put off again. Eyes flashing, she piped up. "I think I have a right to know what's—"

"Yes, yes!" Dr. Grant held a finger over his lips. "All in good time! Dang, DeKane! Dial it down a bit! And cut Peter some slack! He's looking out for you!"

Kyla closed her mouth, feeling the heat in her cheeks.

"What are those?" Howie asked, suddenly noticing the binoculars.

"They're called 'binoculars,'" his father said, swiftly snatching them up before his little hands could touch them. "People use them to watch birds—and stuff." He emphasized the last word, his eyes meeting Kyla's for a second. A clod of dirt fell off them onto the floor and exploded into tiny pieces.

"Can I hold them?"

"No."

Kyla touched Howie's shoulder. "Tell your dad what you did today," she suggested, helping to change the subject.

Howie swung his face toward her guiltily.

"The fish," she reminded him.

"Oh!" he said, turning back to his dad. "Me and Peter and Hank went out in the boat, and we caught a fish! A big one! I got to look at it and touch it!"

"Fish!" Hank echoed, suddenly animated, holding up his arms.

"No kidding! How big?" Dr. Grant asked. Then to Howie's measurement he replied, "Sounds like a nice sized fish." He reached for his briefcase. "Boys, I need to have a meeting now in my office, so I'd like you to go play. I'll come for you when it's time to talk to Mom." He put his hand down for the boys to slap his palm, then poked them each in the belly after they did. Then he retreated down the hall.

"Come on, boys," Kyla said, waving her arm. "Let's go outside and ride bikes on the driveway."

"Yes!" Howie exclaimed, now charged with energy. "Is Peter coming with? I like it best when he helps me ride."

"Peter's busy," Kyla replied.

"Aww!" Howie folded his arms and gave his best pout. "I like Peter better than you!"

From down the hall Kyla heard a loud laugh from Dr. Grant. "Now you know how I feel!"

The three remained hard at play until a few hours later, when it started to sprinkle. Kyla was just bringing the boys into the house when Dr. Grant came out to fetch them to talk with their mother. He whisked them away, and Kyla was alone in the back entrance room straightening the boys' shoes when Peter came down the back stairs, clean and dressed in fresh clothes. His hair looked darker when it was damp. He didn't see her at first, heading straight for the door, pausing to take his keys from the rack on the wall. He opened the door, but when he saw it was raining he turned back for a baseball cap. That was when he noticed Kyla kneeling on the floor.

"Oh, hi," he said. "I didn't know you were there."

"Hello," she said and flipped her hair off her shoulders to her back.

He stood for a second, tapping his hat onto the hand that held his keys.

"Kyla, I'm sorry you're in the dark about all this."

"'In the dark.'" She sat back on her knees with her hands in her lap.

"Yes, *that* would be an accurate description. I wish someone would explain what the big secret is!"

"It's not a secret. The boat—I was just trying to protect Howie from knowing—"

"Oh, now *that's* ironic, isn't it?" She spoke over him. "Since he was the one who told me that you guys found a boat hidden in the woods!"

"Yes, but he doesn't *understand*!" he replied just as aggressively in return.

She could think of a few things to say, but she bit her lip, making herself stay silent.

He sat down on the nearby bench, leaning toward her, his forearms resting on his legs. "So this morning," he started, "I took the kids out in the boat, and we fished for a while over by—well, never mind—the point is, when we were coming back in, we passed the mouth of the ravine. I noticed the muddy footprints there first and could see a cut in the mud that seemed strange. So we went closer, and I saw a boat, pulled up and hidden under some branches by the shore. You could barely see it."

"What kind of boat? It's not just some old boat junked in the woods, is it?"

He shook his head. "No, it was an aluminum rowboat. And they were freshly cut branches. So anyway, I brought the kids in—"

"—so you just need to find out whose boat it is," Kyla said. "Did you see a license number?"

He held up the hat. "Let me finish!"

Kyla held her fingers over her lips.

"So I brought the kids in to you and went back out to look at the boat, and when I got there it was gone."

"What?" Her eyes grew wide. "In that short amount of time?"

He nodded, his brows creased.

"So do you think someone saw you out there looking at it?"

"Maybe," he said. "I kinda think so."

Kyla gave a little exhale, looking down at her hands. "Creepy."

"Yeah."

"And this is at the bottom of our ravine." She cocked her head in that direction.

He nodded. "Uh-huh. So I docked our boat, then came up to the house to get my phone to call Grant."

"So someone's been in our ravine."

"Yes," he said, "and get this—so after I talked to Grant, I went down there on foot to look around, and what do I find?"

"The binoculars," Kyla said with a shiver.

He nodded, chewing his lip. They were both silent for a bit.

"I think he must have lost them some time ago, because they weren't near where we saw the boat," he said. "And they were embedded in the dirt."

"Creepy," Kyla repeated. "Do you think it's the same guy as before?"

"I'm sure of it," Peter said, jingling his keys absently. "Has to be."

She knew that if the binocular man were Alex, he would have been at their door within a day. Kyla knew without a doubt that it was not him.

Her brow wrinkled. "But I don't get it. What does he want? Marilee isn't even here." She paused. "But maybe he hasn't figured that out yet!"

"Or—" Peter stopped, looking at her face.

"What?"

"Or maybe it's you." His expression was sober.

Her pulse quickened. "Me? Yeah, right! Like I look like Marilee Montayne!"

"No," he said, "but maybe it was someone who was looking for her and discovered *you* instead. Or," he added, "perhaps it's someone who has his eyes on the boys."

Kyla felt a stab of fear. Her face must have showed it, for he suddenly put his hand over his face.

"Oh, man, I'm sorry—I shouldn't have said that. It's just what I was trying to avoid—you being afraid. I'm sorry."

She rubbed her arms, suddenly feeling cold. "And Dr. Grant knows all this?"

"Yes, of course." He took his phone out of his pocket and checked the time. "Actually I'm running into town right now to meet up with a security rep for him, and I should probably go so I'm not late." He stood and put his hat on. "I'm really sorry this got weird."

She rose too. "Well, as the nanny I think when something like this happens I should know about it, shouldn't I?" She struggled to keep the irritation out of her voice. "I mean, if I'm in danger or the boys are in danger, don't you think I should be one of the first to know?"

Peter opened his hands.

"Next time just tell me instead of mysteriously slinking around."

He gave a snort. "What was *this*? I just did!"

"Well, I was the last to know!"

Peter's face twisted. "What? You're kidding me! Kyla, there's you, me, and Grant. I have to talk to *him* first. And what do you mean *next time*? Like we're planning this again—?"

She opened her mouth to speak, but he held up his hand to stop her.

"No. Just—" He made a face as he shook his head. "I gotta go. Good-bye."

He left, shutting the door behind him. Kyla heard the rumble of his truck as he drove away.

If I had a mother, she thought to herself, *I would ask her how to handle guys like Peter.* He seemed to bring out the very worst in her. She sighed. Perhaps that would be a good topic for Mrs. Gordon the next time she came.

Dr. Grant was thoroughly distracted for the rest of the day, asking Kyla to occupy his kids while he took care of other business. After dinner he again had Kyla take them, give them their baths, and put them to bed. When she came down he asked to see her in the kitchen, where he sat correcting a stack of student essays while he waited for her there, because it was raining outside and they couldn't meet on the patio. Peter had returned from town and joined them at the table.

"So I understand Peter caught you up on what happened," he said. He looked weary, with deep lines on his face. His dress shirt was untucked, and he was in his socks.

Kyla nodded.

"So it looks like it's official—we have ourselves a stalker. And what lovely timing!" He plopped his pen onto the pile of student papers and pushed them to the side. "I'll have you know people who do this bug the hell out of me! We had to deal with this once in London, and it was a pain in the you-know-what." He glanced at Peter. "Anyway, we've learned from a few actor friends of Marilee's who've been down this path to take it seriously. I've been in touch with the authorities, but like I said before, without an actual person apprehended there's nothing they will do about it. Peter has arranged for a security representative to come out tomorrow afternoon to look over the place and discuss some options." He sighed and ran a hand through his wiry hair, adding under his breath, "Old Mr. Kennedy might be surprised to find that even his Great Wall of China can't keep all the weirdos out!"

"Huh?" Kyla asked.

"Kennedy—the guy who built this place," Peter said quietly. "He built that huge brick wall along the highway."

"Ah," Kyla said, remembering it now and looking back at Dr. Grant. "So what does this mean for me? Do I need to change how I watch the boys?"

"I don't know. I'm not sure." He folded his arms, leaning on the table. "That will be determined tomorrow sometime with our guy—what's his name—?"

"Justin Marsden," Peter murmured.

"Yeah, him—Mr. Marsden. This is a very unusual situation, as Marilee isn't actually here. I really thought we had dealt with things, so it's a little strange to me. So we're going to look at some camera options, possibly a fence or an alarm system. And maybe security personnel."

"Have you talked to the neighbors?" she asked. "Do we know for sure it's not just some hiker or someone exploring the river?"

"Great question," Dr. Grant said, pointing his finger at her. "I like how you think. Yes, I did talk to them and no, it doesn't look like it. But it doesn't rule out the possibility. However,"—he held up a hand—"the Hancocks across the way say they have seen someone from a distance. They just assumed he was from Wynnbury. No details except that he's a white male with a medium build. They did not notice a beard."

Peter moved agitatedly in his chair. "Really? Did they say how many times they've spotted him?"

"Is he prowling *their* place too?" Kyla asked at the same time.

"It doesn't appear so," Dr. Grant answered Kyla, and then meeting Peter's eyes, "Several."

Kyla shuddered. "Oh, God—I am never going outside again!"

Peter placed both hands on the table. "We'll set a trap!"

Both heads turned to look at him as he stared down at the table, as if visualizing his plan.

"We'll set a trap and apprehend him. Then we'll know he's gone."

Kyla leaned back. "That's going to be kind of hard to do if we're out there installing a fence or cameras."

"No, we'll use bait and—".

"Bait?" Kyla asked, her face contorted. "Like what? Or should I say, like *whom*?"

Dr. Grant held up a hand. "Now hold on! We're going to discuss this all with the security company tomorrow. This is what they do."

The three sat quietly for a moment until Dr. Grant reached out to lay his hand on the stack of papers and pull them near.

"All right, folks—I hate to be a party pooper, but I need to go through these by tomorrow and prepare for my class in the morning." He turned to Kyla. "You doing okay?"

She wrinkled her brow. "It's a little creepy for me," she admitted. "I'll be locking my door."

Dr. Grant nodded. "Tomorrow I hope to have our security system in place. Or at least in progress. As for tonight, don't worry your pretty little head. You're safe. I have enough work to keep me up half the night, and by the looks of it, this guy is too jacked up to sleep!" Dr. Grant jerked his head at Peter, then gathered the essays and rose. "I'll be in my study. Good night." He left.

Peter remained where he sat at the table, looking down with his hands extended before him, tapping his thumbs in thought. Kyla rose from her chair, wishing she could call her dad and tell him everything. But she would have to wait until tomorrow, for through the patio door Kyla could tell that it was still raining steadily.

She slid her chair in, feeling slightly aggravated. "One thing that bugs me about this place is that you can never make a phone call without standing in the yard! I just want to call my dad!"

Peter looked up at her. "You could go upstairs and try. The reception's a little better up on the third floor in some places. It's still pretty sketchy, but it's better. I'll go up there with you, if you want."

"Oh, geez," she said. "No, thanks. I'd rather stand out in the rain than go up there!"

He shrugged. "Just offering."

Kyla went to the sink for a glass of water to take upstairs. "All right—I'm heading up to my room. See you later."

"Good night, Kyla."

Dr. Grant had left his office doors open, and Kyla could hear his voice as she approached the foot of the stairs. She paused and glanced over to see him standing beside his desk with his hands in his pockets, staring at the rows of books on his bookshelves. He was talking to himself.

"Dang it, Kennedy!" she heard him say, "Would you help me out a little? If a guy's gonna hide something, where would be the best place for—" He must have heard her, for he turned on his heel and met her eyes. "Yes?"

"Good night," Kyla said, suddenly embarrassed. She started up the stairs.

"Good night, Miss DeKane," he replied.

Chapter Seventeen

The rain continued steadily through the night. In the morning Kyla was surprised to find both Howie and Hank sound asleep in bed with her. Vaguely she remembered Hank crawling in, but not his brother. Craning her neck to see the clock, she noted that the boys and she had slept really late, for the morning sky was darker than usual. At her stirring Howie moved and yawned, sleepily opening his eyes and extending his skinny arms in a stretch. He rolled over onto his side and smiled at Kyla. She noticed his freckles were darkening a bit from all his outdoor play.

"I fell asleep," he said in a raspy voice.

"I didn't hear you get in bed with me," she said.

"Peter said to go find you," he said. "You and Hank were sleeping, so I decided to get in bed with you until you woke up."

On the far side of the bed Hank lifted his head and looked sleepily at Kyla and Howie, his hair puffed out on one side. Howie giggled at him.

"You saw Peter this morning?"

He sat up cross-legged beside her. "I got up, and I thought you were downstairs. Peter gave me some cereal and read to me from the, um, the— his book."

"The Bible?"

He nodded. "Yeah. Then he told me to go find you." He added, "My dad has to work at college today."

Hank crawled over Howie's legs and laid his head on Kyla's belly. She rubbed his back, in no hurry to move, but soon she laughed when she heard his stomach growl.

"Hank, are you hungry?" she asked.

"Yeah, I hungry," he said.

And then Kyla discovered that he was also very wet. She groaned. "All right! Everybody up!"

❖ ❖ ❖

The rainy weather made for a slow-moving, gloomy day of playing inside. Kyla wasn't sure what playing outside would look like from there on out due to the discovery of their presumed prowler, but the weather made it a nonissue for them, and no one complained about it—at least for the first part of the day. When the boys got restless, she let them play running games up and down the halls for a while, then spent what was left of the morning upstairs in the playroom. After lunch, however, Hank, having slept late that morning, refused his nap, and Kyla had to ramp up her creativity to keep the two of them occupied.

The kids had barely started finger painting at the kitchen table when their father arrived home from work—in full business mode. He greeted his sons briefly but headed straight for his study, explaining that he had to buckle down to finish a few things before the scheduled appointment with the security company. Peter, who had spent the better part of the day out in the tool shed, came in to join him there, and the doors were closed. Kyla felt a little jealous of Peter, always being on the inside of things with Dr. Grant. Here she was again, stuck with the kids.

Howie apparently felt similarly. His face fell when his dad and Peter closed the doors behind them.

"My dad is really busy," he said sadly, examining the paint on his hands.

He wiped his goopy hands on his belly, leaving a wide streak of green across an old shirt of hers that she had him wear. Hank's face was smeared with blue where he had rubbed his eyes. She wiped most of it off, but he still resembled a little raccoon.

"Can we be done?" Howie asked. At the moment he was carefully sticking his fingers together, then pulling them apart, fascinated with the texture of the paint.

"We just got started," Kyla said, feeling a bit impatient, but when Hank started to lick the paint, she too was ready to quit. "No sir!" she said, catching his hand, which splattered droplets of paint across the front of her shirt and down her bare leg.

Howie went to the bathroom to wash his own hands, but Kyla cleaned up Hank and put him down to play. Starting to run, the brothers each rounded the corner of the peninsula and smacked into one another, knocking each other to the floor. Hank's lip quivered as he wound up to cry, but Howie thought it was funny and started to laugh hysterically, lying down on the floor, gripping his stomach. Soon Hank was giggling with him.

"Come on, Hank—let's do it again!" Howie said.

"No!" Kyla interjected. "That's a good way to get hurt!"

"Aww!" Howie closed his eyes and hung his head back, his mouth hanging open. "You never let us do *anything* fun! Can we go outside?"

Kyla pointed to the door. "Look—it's raining out."

"So!" He pouted, wandering aimlessly down the back hall.

Kyla glanced at the clock. There was a lot of afternoon left. As she cleaned up the painting debris, she remembered all the hours she had spent at the park near her home playing with the neighborhood kids without having to be entertained by her mother. Right now she felt as if she would do anything for a dry public park.

"Hey—someone's here!" Howie called from the back of the house.

Kyla poked her head into the side entry, where Howie stood with his nose on the side door. Joining him to peek over his shoulder, she saw a young man in a dark windbreaker getting out of a van in the driveway. She was immediately startled by how much the man looked like Alex from behind—tall, with thick, dark brown hair and a full beard. Hurriedly he slid open the van's side door in the rain to retrieve a black briefcase, then turned and started quickly for the front door. Kyla also turned and hastened through the house to meet him in the front foyer, hearing the doorbell on her way. Howie trotted along with her, asking if he could be the one to open the door, and Hank, sensing the sudden excitement, came too.

He looked older than Alex and a bit taller and was so attractive that Kyla could hardly squeak out a hello. He introduced himself as Justin Marsden from the security company. She invited him in and took his rain jacket, acutely aware of the mess on her shirt and blue-faced Hank peering at him from behind her speckled legs. Howie began firing off questions—why was he there, why did he have a van, and why didn't he use an umbrella. Mr. Marsden smiled and remained quiet, holding his dark briefcase while he waited for Kyla to hang his dripping jacket in the little cove closet. Mustering up a shred a dignity, she smiled at him and led him to Dr. Grant's study, where he was swallowed by the heavy oak doors of the command and control center. She stood in the hall outside the closed doors, looking down at herself, mortified by her appearance. Through the doors she could hear Dr. Grant's firm voice, and for a second she was tempted to put her ear up against the door.

Howie took advantage of her lingering there by throwing his small body against the oak panels, resulting in a resounding boom.

"Howie!" she scolded in a hushed voice. She grabbed his arm and whirled him to face her.

The door opened, and Dr. Grant's scowling countenance appeared. "What's going on?"

"That was an accident!" Kyla said, embarrassed. "I'm very sorry. We're leaving."

After finishing clearing the mess in the kitchen, Kyla took the boys in the library to do some craft projects at the table, but they were soon bored. Leaving the table, Howie climbed onto one of the armchairs and began dropping books from up high, laughing as they smacked flat against the floor. Hank soon crawled up with him and tried to copy, but Howie wrenched the book out of his hands, hurting Hank's arm and making him wail. Kyla hurriedly pulled the doors of the room shut to contain the sound. Then before she could stop him, Howie jumped from the chair to the floor and threw himself against the pocket doors, laughing at its loud reverberation. Kyla scolded him again, but at this point the boys seemed out of control. They had been cooped up in the house way too long.

"I've got an idea," she said. "Maybe if you're very, very quiet we can go run around under the carport outside. Want to?"

Immediately she regretted saying anything. Fresh air or not, she realized it was a recipe for them all inevitably getting soaked, but the boys cheered at the prospect of going outside.

Hank had heard the word *run* and pressed up against Kyla as she carefully slid open the library's pocket door. The moment he was able, he slipped out into the hall and began running noisily toward the kitchen. Howie, excited, joined him, hollering that they finally got to go outside. Kyla tried to shush them, but neither listened, and turning at the island, they began their return back down the hall toward her, ending with Howie banging against his dad's study doors again.

Strike two, Kyla thought, closing her eyes.

Sure enough, the doors opened, and Dr. Grant appeared again with a look of acute annoyance. "What the heck?" he snapped quietly.

From where Kyla stood, she could see Peter and the Justin Marsden fellow sitting around a large sheet of paper on the coffee table. Both of them were stretching their necks to see beyond Dr. Grant's figure in the doorway.

Her hands flew over her mouth. "Sorry! They're just a little stir crazy from playing inside all day. I'm taking them out to the carport."

Dr. Grant glowered at her, muttering under his breath, "For Pete's sake, we're trying to have a meeting here!"

"Sorry," she repeated. Promising not to disturb them again, she resumed moving the boys down the hall, then stopped and went back to present an idea.

"Excuse me," she said, knocking briefly and poking her head in a crack of the door. The professor had joined the others in his chair in front of the coffee table. "Would it be okay if I took these guys to an indoor park in town?"

All three heads rose to look at her and said simultaneously, "No!"

Surprised, Dr. Grant looked at his partners, then back at Kyla. He sighed. "I'm sorry. We just don't know what we're dealing with yet. And I don't bring the boys into town."

"Oh, yeah. Sorry. Got it." Kyla backed away, feeling foolish. How had she forgotten that? She closed the door.

It opened a second later, and Peter emerged, saying over his shoulder that he would return in a bit.

"Go upstairs," he said quietly to Kyla, closing the door behind him. "I'll meet you up there in a minute." He took off for the side entrance.

Her eyes followed his retreating figure. She saw him tap Howie on the shoulder and point him upstairs as he passed him on his way outside. She had no idea of what he was up to, but nevertheless Kyla took Hank's hand and led him upstairs, waving Howie to come up with them. Hurriedly she grabbed a clean shirt from her room and a washcloth for her leg and to remove another layer of blue from under Hank's eyes. A few minutes later Peter appeared at the back stairway at the end of the upstairs hall. From the balcony in front of her bedroom doors she saw him navigate both of the kids' bikes through the doorway and down the hall to where she stood. Howie and Hank stood open-mouthed, staring.

"What in the world—?" Kyla asked. "Are you sure this is this okay with Dr. Grant?"

Peter's eyes sparkled. "Shhh—Grant doesn't need to know!" He jerked his head toward the door across from his room. "Open the door—I'll take these up, and they can be as crazy as they want." She could see by the grin on his face that Peter thought he was pretty clever.

She hesitated.

He jerked his head again. "Come on! It'll be fun!"

"Wait a minute!" Squirming, she shook her head. "I really don't feel comfortable up there!"

But Howie had figured out what was happening and could hardly contain himself. "Hank, we get to ride our bikes—in the house!"

Kyla knew she was outnumbered.

In his excitement Howie shook his brother by the shoulders, causing him to fall and bump his head against the wall. Hank winced and looked as if he were about to cry, but Kyla quickly picked him up, distracting him.

"Come on! Hurry up—let's go!" Peter urged. "You're a big girl, Kyla—you can do this!"

Her protests were futile, and before she knew it she was on the third floor of Wynnbury House with two kids riding bikes down the hallway and in and out of the rooms, free to yell as much as they liked. Peter left, giving her a thumbs-up and telling her there was nothing to be afraid of, but she wasn't convinced. Fresh in her mind were memories of the last time they were up there, and now she was almost certain it was not Mrs. Gordon that Hank had seen. Kyla shuddered at the thought.

It was truly what they needed, however: an area to work off all their energy where they wouldn't bother anybody or break anything. After racing up and down the hall for quite a while, the large room right above the Great Room became the place where the three gathered to wind down. With the taller windows and more natural light, it felt more inviting than the other rooms. At first they all spent some time looking outside at the gloomy rain clouds pouring onto the canopy of leaves in the woods and the river in the distance, but soon the boys lost interest and turned back to their bikes. Kyla stayed at the window to watch the rain drizzle down the glass, fighting to keep the uncomfortable feelings she had about this place from dominating her thoughts.

Rooms were made to be occupied, not empty. There was something so unnatural and creepy about an entire floor of empty rooms. Another whole family could live up here in this amount of space, Kyla reasoned. But maybe that was the intention, she thought. Perhaps Mr. Kennedy wanted his son and family to live with them. How depressing to know that he had died early in life, his family tree cut off!

The room had become quiet. Kyla turned to see that Hank had flipped his tricycle over in the middle of the room and was on his knees, turning the wheel with the pedal by hand, observing how it worked in his curious toddler way. Howie was in another corner of the room, picking dangling chunks of sheetrock off of the edge of a hole in the wall. A big piece came loose, but in his wiggling to separate it, the piece dropped down into the wall.

"Aww," he said to himself, peering into the hole.

He stuck his skinny arm down in to retrieve it and pulled out the chunk, glancing back in to make sure he got it all. He paused, leaning in.

"Hey—there's something in there!"

With his forehead wrinkled in concentration, he reached his arm back into the opening, stretching and fishing around until he came up with a small rectangular piece of paper in his hand.

"Ah—I got it!" he said triumphantly. "Hey, Miss Kane—look at this! A picture!" He held it up for her to see.

Kyla crossed the room to look at it, discovering that he had found an old postcard with a photo of a house that looked like Wynnbury. She flipped it over and read the words "Tynnbury Hall, Banbury England" in the upper left corner. *How cool!* she thought. The card was hand-addressed to Marna Kennedy at a New Hampton rural route address, and in the area for the message there was merely a scripture reference, nothing else—Luke 7:13–15. There was no signature. She strained to read the date, but she couldn't make out the last number. It was definitely 1940-something.

"Nice job, Howie!" Kyla told him. "Your dad is going to appreciate this! This is an old postcard!"

"What's a postcard?"

"It's like a way to send a short letter with a picture of a place that you've visited."

"What does it say?" he asked.

Kyla shrugged. "Nothing much. Just 'Tynnbury Hall,' the name of the house. See—it looks very much like *your* house!" She wondered who Marna Kennedy was. His wife? Mother? Sister?

Howie beamed, straightening and pointing to his chest. "And I found it myself!"

"Me see! Me see!" Hank was there in a moment, looking on, needing to be part of the action. "A house!" he said, touching it with his wet finger. Satisfied, he went back to his trike.

Howie agreed to let Kyla hold it for safekeeping, turning his attention to poking his little arm into all the holes he could reach in the walls. Kyla let him but warned him to be careful of nails and sharp edges. Before long he grew bored and returned to riding his bike, pedaling fast down the hall, then skidding on the brakes to leave a white line in the dust of the hallway floor.

After a while Kyla saw movement outside. It had stopped raining, and the three men were walking along the edge of the yard. The handsome Justin Marsden carried a clipboard and wrote on it now and then. She watched him do his job from above until unexpectedly Peter turned and looked up, lifting his arm in a wave when he saw her. She lifted her hand, then stepped away from the window.

Without a watch or her phone, she had no idea of the time, and the gloomy skies gave no reference to help her. She was hungry, however, and if *she* was, then the boys would most certainly also be hungry very soon.

"What about our bikes?" Howie asked when she told them it was time to go downstairs.

"Let's park them in the hall by the stairs. Peter will get them later," she said.

Howie wanted to show his dad the postcard right away, but Kyla told him he was not allowed to interrupt his meeting with Mr. Marsden. She put it next to the photo of his mother in the kitchen, but Howie took it and put it in the napkin holder on the table so he wouldn't forget to tell his dad about it at dinnertime.

The evening, however, turned out to be much like the previous one, with Kyla caring for the kids while the men did their business. She and the kids ate alone, and when Dr. Grant, Peter, and Justin Marsden came in from outdoors, they went directly into the study. Before long it was time for her to take the kids up to bed.

"I didn't even get to play with my daddy today," Howie lamented.

Yes, and because of it I didn't get one moment to myself, Kyla thought, pulling his sheet up and tucking him in. She assured him that it would be better tomorrow, since his dad didn't work on Fridays. She hoped that was true, feeling a bit overworked herself and feeling rather piteous for being left out of the man powwow downstairs. She sat in her room with her bare feet resting on the tile table, worn out. How do mothers do it, she wondered, parenting all day without a break?

Her musings turned her to own mother, who would have given anything just to have lived to see her grow up, which then brought to mind Mrs. Gordon. They had only talked yesterday, but so much had happened since then that it felt like days ago. The more Kyla pondered the older woman's words, the more she could see how right she was, which was a little hard for her to face. It was a bit of a mystery that Kyla could even listen to her talk about God without reacting—maybe even the first person ever in that regard. Kyla liked her. She seemed warm and motherly, not pushy. *Maybe,* Kyla thought, *maybe Mrs. Gordon could adopt me as kind of a daughter—not officially, of course, but in relationship.* She stared at the fireplace tiles absently, considering that idea for a while until she remembered what Mrs. Gordon had said about creating fantasies. Then she decided that maybe Mrs. Gordon could just be Mrs. Gordon to her, exactly who she was, the cleaning lady who had become a friend. A wise and motherly friend.

A tap on her door interrupted her thoughts. When no one responded to her call, she got up and opened the door. It was Peter, standing a ways out with his hand on the balcony rail.

"Marsden left. Grant wants to know if you're available."

Dr. Grant was in the process of baking a frozen pizza for Peter and himself when Kyla entered the kitchen. The timer had gone off, but he decided to leave it in a little longer, pulling a couple of beers out of the refrigerator while he waited. As usual Peter requested a Coke instead. Dr. Grant offered the beer to Kyla, but she also declined, sliding onto a stool at the peninsula facing him, leaving an empty chair between Peter and herself.

"Mr. Watkins, help me bring this little lady up to speed," Dr. Grant said, his hands in oven mitts. "My brain is absolutely fried."

Peter turned to her, his tan arms stretched out on the granite counter. The bottom of his tattoo protruded from below the sleeve of his T-shirt, and for the first time she could make out part of the design, recognizing the bottom of a scroll with the words *of sons* on it.

"So can I give it to you in a nutshell? Then you can ask us any questions you want." He blew out a long breath. "It's been a long day."

"Okay," she agreed.

He sat up, leaning his elbows on the counter, cradling his chin in his hand. "So then, as you know, we met with the security guy and told him what was happening, and he asked us a million questions, and then we discussed a million options, after which we walked him through the yard and got his recommendations. So what it boils down to is that tomorrow their people are coming out to install security cameras—"

Kyla was adjusting her hair, twisting her ponytail into a bun. "No, seriously?" She laughed and shook her head. "So we're gonna be like one of those suspense dramas, with a security guard in a room full of monitors?"

Dr. Grant set the pizza on the counter before them, eyeing Kyla tiredly. "Yeah," he said, "we are. Do you have a problem with that?"

Kyla looked back at Peter.

He shrugged. "Yeah, we are, actually. But it's all on one computer monitor. We can check it here too, but Grant's paying to have them monitor it at their office complex. The cameras are highly sensitive infrared, with night vision, so their guys can watch our place twenty-four-seven."

Kyla's eyebrows rose.

"That only took us"—Dr. Grant looked at his watch—"five-plus hours to determine. That's five hours of time I can't get back. Pizza?" He handed Peter a paper plate and offered one to her.

"No thanks," she said.

"Today sophomores and security reps are on equal footing for drawing out a matter eternally longer than it need be. I was up until almost two last night grading those essays. Then Marsden this afternoon. I am dog tired." He pulled a piece to his plate and lifted it to his mouth.

"It mostly took a while to figure out the best places for the cameras," Peter added, looking down, intent on his food.

"So then—what does this mean for me? When do I resume life as before?" she asked.

"Now," Dr. Grant said, taking a large bite.

"Seriously? That's it?"

He lifted a finger, chewing and swallowing his food. "Basically, yeah. I mean, of course, you'll observe normal common-sense precautions." He frowned. "And that reminds me—I would like to know what the hell you were doing with the kids this afternoon that caused such a racket!"

"That was your son!" she declared. "Howie would not listen to me! He's got this habit of busting into doors—I've tried to get him to stop!"

"Sheesh—sounded like a bomb went off in the hallway! Oh, crap!" Dr. Grant looked down at a drop of tomato sauce on his chest. "There goes another shirt."

Kyla moved to get him a napkin, but he was already around the edge of the peninsula, pulling one off the table. Howie's postcard flipped out and tumbled out before him. Dr. Grant froze in mid-reach when he saw it, then straightened.

His tone changed. "Where did *this* come from?" Ignoring the spot on his shirt, he quickly wiped his hands and carefully picked up the postcard.

"Oh, yeah!" Kyla had forgotten all about it. "Howie found that upstairs—way upstairs, in the room above the Great Room. He wanted to show it to you. I thought you'd find it very interesting."

Dr. Grant shot her a look. "Howie found this?"

"Yes," she continued. "We went up there to—um, to keep our noise from disrupting your meeting." She threw a glance at Peter. "Howie put his arm in one of the holes in the wall to pull out a chunk of plaster, and that was down inside."

"No kidding! Seriously, down inside the wall?" He looked back at the postcard, turning it over.

Peter stood, regarding the postcard in the professor's hands. Kyla saw them exchange a look.

"It's Tynnbury," she said, "the other house like this one. In England."

Dr. Grant tilted his head to the side. "I know! I've been there! I proposed to my wife right there, sitting on that very fountain." He frowned, peering at the writing. "Marna Kennedy."

"His mother," Peter said softly.

Dr. Grant tapped the writing, looking up at Peter. "You're the Bible guy around here. What is this—Luke something?"

"Hang on." Peter strode across the room to retrieve his Bible from his corner in the Great Room, opening it and turning pages as he walked back toward Dr. Grant. He shook his head. "That's a strange one. I have no idea what this means." He held the book toward Dr. Grant and pointed to a place on a page.

He frowned, reading under his breath. "'Do not weep . . . touched the bier . . . Young man, I say to you, arise . . . the dead man sat up and began to speak, and Jesus gave him to his mother.' Huh. Now that's an odd thing to write home to your mother." He looked up at Peter, who shrugged and spread his hands.

"What's the date on that?" he asked.

"I couldn't read it," Kyla answered from her chair behind them.

Dr. Grant scrutinized the card under the light. He handed it to Peter. "You're younger. See if you can tell."

Peter studied it, turning the postcard in various directions. "Can't read it. 1940-something. Could be '41? '42? Hard to tell. Could be anything." He handed it back. "We'll use the magnifying glass."

Kyla cleared her throat. "Excuse me. Is there something significant about this postcard? This can't be what they were searching in the walls for. What's the big mystery here?"

Dr. Grant briefly met Peter's eyes before setting the postcard on the table. "No mystery. Just a personal fetish of mine. I collect things connected to the history of this house." He took another napkin, dabbing his shirt as he returned to his place on the other side of the peninsula. "That is utterly fascinating." He nodded to the card on the table. "Quite a find! I'd love to have you show me where you found it."

Kyla gave an inward sigh, resigned to remain in the dark. "Sure. But not tonight, please. I am exhausted from watching your kids all day. And I haven't talked to my dad in a while, and I'd like to tonight, if it isn't raining again."

"Right," Dr. Grant replied. "Of course. Maybe tomorrow."

"It's not raining," Peter said, glancing behind him at the patio door, then turning back to his plate.

Kyla hesitated. "Is it safe?"

"Sure—I think so," Dr. Grant replied. "Nothing out there tonight but drowned rats. Even the coons don't want to come out when it's this wet."

"Well, then"—she slipped off the chair—"if you don't mind, I think I'll go make my call now."

"You're a real trooper, you know," Dr. Grant said after her as she moved toward the door.

She looked back at him curiously. "For what?"

His eyes were bright. She noticed he was suddenly in a much happier mood. "Oh, putting up with little kids all day, putting up with knuckleheads like Peter and me, putting up with having to go outside to use your phone—"

Kyla's mouth twisted up at the corner. "Well, it's about time someone noticed!"

"Oh, I appreciate you," he said. His eyebrows rose while he helped himself to more pizza. "I appreciate you a great deal!"

She waggled her phone. "See you later."

"Leave the door open a little," Peter said. "It's stuffy in here."

It was late. The rainclouds had begun moving out, and looking up, Kyla could see stars right above her and to the west. All that was left of color in the sky was a hue of deep indigo on the horizon. The lights of the Great Room behind her lit her walk across the wet grass to the staircase, where she leaned on the rail and waited for her dad to answer, her eyes on the dark shadows of the river below. The air was cool and very damp and still. Around her chirped a loud chorus of crickets and frogs happy from the rain.

There was a lot for Kyla to tell about in her phone call. Kendall was concerned when she told him about the boat in the woods and the need for security, but he was also relieved to hear what measures were being put into place. She told him about the new fountain, and bringing the bikes up to the third floor, and Howie's discovery of the postcard. She even shared a bit about her conversation with Mrs. Gordon, careful not to divulge anything too personal. She wanted this to be her thing, without his commentary, whether good or bad.

"She's really nice," she said. "You would like her, Dad. She's a person of faith like you. And it's nice to have a woman around. We've had coffee a couple of times now. Technically, it was tea the first time, but you know what I mean."

"An answer to prayer," he said. "I'm happy for you."

Kyla had turned as she spoke, rubbing her back against the scratchy two-by-fours of the rail. In the distance she could see that Dr. Grant and Peter were back to examining the postcard under dining room light.

"I have something to tell you too, sweetheart," her dad said, "something you should probably know about."

"Oh, yeah? What's that?" She had found a good spot on her back.

Kendall paused. "Well, honey, Alex showed up here."

"What?" Kyla blinked. "Alex? Like *my* Alex?"

"Alex Duvall—yes."

"When? Today?"

"No, the day after we talked last. And I've started meeting with him."

She gave an angry exclamation, suddenly adrenalized. "What? Are you kidding me? Oh, Dad, *please!*" She started pacing down the lawn, rubbing her forehead with her free hand. "How many times do I have to tell you—*stay out of my business!*"

"Kyla, we're not meeting about *you*."

She rolled her eyes in the dark. "Yeah, right! I've heard *that* before!"

"Well, he wanted to talk to me about something and then ended up giving his life to Christ."

Kyla huffed. "Dad. Listen to me! Alex is a snake! He's just using you to get to me. I know some things about him that you don't know."

"Well, Kyla," her dad replied carefully, "I know some things about Alex that *you* don't know."

His comment hit her in the gut, and she bit her lip, feeling vulnerable. Had Alex told her dad about the two of them?

"He wants to get his life right with God," Kendall continued, "and I'm going to help him."

She exhaled quickly, shaking her head in the dark. *Yeah, right—that sounded like Alex all right!* "Well, be careful, Dad," she said. "He's untrustworthy. And don't you even dream of trying to get us back together again!"

"I can promise you that," he said firmly. "I just wanted you to know."

Her dad then changed the subject and talked about a few other things from home, to which Kyla responded lightly and politely, entirely distracted by the thought of Alex meeting with him. And in her own house! Finally the phone call came to an end.

"Love you, sweetheart," her dad told her.

"I love you too, Dad," she replied automatically.

She hung up and stood there in the dark by the familiar oak, facing the house and breathing heavily, her hands on her hips. She was furious. The nerve of that guy, she thought, preying on her dad like that! She gripped her phone tightly in her hand, tempted to call Alex right that moment. Oh, would she like to tell him—

Suddenly Kyla lifted her head, recognizing the undeniable and strong odor of cigarette smoke lingering heavily in the air around her. It confused her for a second, and she wondered why she would smell cigarette smoke by her tree. Who would be smoking out here—? Then she stiffened, her heart slamming in her chest with the knowledge that someone was in the woods behind her. She swallowed and as smoothly as she could turned sideways, her eyes scanning the darkness around her, trying to appear nonchalant, as if she didn't notice anything unusual at all. Taking a nervous step backward, she wondered if she should yell for Peter or Dr. Grant or if she should just run like heck back to the house. Or both.

Then from the darkness came a barely perceptible squish of a footstep in the wet underbrush. Her breath caught, and with one shaking hand she swiped open the flashlight app on her phone, ready to shine it into the intruder's face to blind him in the dark, if necessary. A twig snapped, and Kyla jerked with fright, bumbling the phone, which slid out of her hands into the wet grass.

"Who's out there?" she croaked into the darkness, fear clawing through her.

The same instant she spoke she was grabbed from behind, and a hand clamped down hard over her mouth. With lightning speed another arm whipped vice-like around her chest, and she was pulled roughly against her assailant, her head crunching tightly against his breastbone, the button of his shirt cutting into her cheek. Terrified, Kyla immediately twisted, clawed, and kicked with all her might, her attempted screams muffled under his steely grip.

"Quiet! Be quiet!" he ordered in a low voice, shaking her slightly. "I'm not here to hurt you, but you need to be quiet!"

Violently she struggled against his crushing hold.

"Please!" he repeated sternly, "I need you to be quiet, and I'll let you go!"

Parting her lips, she searched the inside of his hand for any piece of flesh her teeth could find, then bit down with all her might. Cursing, he jerked his hand away, and Kyla let out a dreadful shriek for help. With his grip compromised, she twisted and flung herself out from his arms, falling away from him onto the grass. On her seat she scrambled backwards on her hands in a clumsy crab walk to escape him.

"Kyla, stop!" the man commanded urgently. "It's me—your father! I'm not here to hurt you!"

Chapter Eighteen

With her palms embedded in the muddy grass, Kyla gave another awful scream as Robert DeKane's form appeared over her in the darkness. She cringed, poised to kick him if he came closer.

"Shhh! Damn it, stop screaming! Kyla, baby, it's me! Stop your screaming!" Then he looked over his shoulder and swore loudly. "Oh geez—call off your dogs!"

Behind him Kyla heard Peter hollering as he tore across the yard toward them. Her father turned and backed a step, raising both hands high as Peter arrived with a hefty, sharp-edged scraper from the grill raised in his hand, poised and ready to strike. His face was hard, and Kyla could tell he meant business.

"Peter, stop!" she cried. "Stop! I know him!"

Peter positioned himself between Kyla and DeKane, breathing hard, every muscle taut. Immediately after him Dr. Grant hustled across the lawn, speaking jerkily to an emergency dispatch over his phone as he approached. Robert DeKane stood motionless with his hands up and spread.

"It's my father," Kyla said again weakly from the ground. "Don't hurt him!"

"What's going on?" Dr. Grant demanded breathlessly, holding his phone a little out to the side. "Who are you, and what are you doing here?"

Kyla's father answered submissively, "My name is Robert DeKane. I have been trying to locate my daughter, Kyla—"

"Stalking her, more like it!" Peter said, stepping forward with his club, his nostrils flared.

"Peter!" Kyla cried out as DeKane flinched away from him, his hands still outstretched.

"Come out on the lawn where we can see you!" Dr. Grant ordered, pointing. "Right out here!" With his eyes locked on DeKane, he stepped up to lay a hand on Peter's shoulder. Peter glanced at him, then lowered the tool slightly.

"Yes, sir! Absolutely." DeKane complied, backing slowly out into the clearing. "I mean no harm!"

"That's good! Stay right there!"

Peter sidled around behind him. Tucking the tool under his arm, he patted him down, and when he had finished, he nodded and motioned to the professor.

Dr. Grant's phone made a sound, and he drew it to his ear. "Hold on—I don't know yet. Kyla," he asked, his eyes still on DeKane, "are you hurt?"

Gingerly she moved her wrists. "I don't think so."

"And," Dr. Grant continued, his voice low and even, "would you please explain to me what happened here?" Without turning his head, he extended his hand to help her to her feet.

Kyla wiped her muddy hands on her shorts and brushed herself off, explaining that she had just finished her phone call when she noticed the smell of cigarette smoke. "I knew someone was there," she said. "And then he grabbed me from behind. Hard! I had to fight to get away!" She glared at her father in the dark.

Dr. Grant cocked his head.

DeKane shook his head defensively. "This is exactly what I was trying to avoid! I didn't want to cause alarm and frighten anyone! I was just trying to reconnect with my daughter!"

"Reconnect—what?" Kyla said hotly. "You hurt me! You grabbed—you—you *assaulted* me!"

"I didn't want you to scream—"

"*Who does that?*" she spat angrily. "Someone who wants to connect says, 'Hey, Kyla—it's me!'"

DeKane gave a twisted smile, waggling his head. "If I had done that, you would have screamed bloody murder, and I would have been shot! Or bludgeoned to death." He cast a sideways glance at Peter, whose eyes bore into him from where he stood.

"All right!" Dr. Grant raised his hand for him to stop. He paused, his eyes narrowing. "Are you aware that you are trespassing on private property?"

"Why, yes—of course, I am!" DeKane answered. "But here's the deal—the last I talked to Kyla, my daughter, whom I hadn't seen in seventeen years, she said she would be at a residence called Wynnbury near

New Hampton." The words *seventeen years* were given special emphasis. "I happened to be here working in the New Hampton area, and naturally I'm curious if she's here. I don't have her phone number, I don't have your phone number, and that brick wall with that gate is a mile high and impenetrable—and I don't even know for sure if she's here!"

"So you spied on her from across the river," Peter said accusingly.

DeKane looked at him. "I don't know what you're talking about! No, I borrowed a rowboat and came up to see if this is where she lived for sure." He shifted his feet. "Look, no disrespect, but would you mind terribly if I put my arms down? They're getting tired."

Dr. Grant gave a curt nod. He turned to look at Kyla, his phone still in his hand. "Would you like an officer on the scene?"

"Absolutely!" Peter said with fervor.

"What?" she asked.

"The police. Would you like to report this to the police?" Dr. Grant reiterated.

"Yes!" Peter repeated insistently.

Kyla stood with her mouth open, looking at her father in the dark. She was torn. "I—I don't know. It's true, what he said. There was no way for him to reach me."

Dr. Grant's eyes flicked to Peter, then back to Kyla, waiting with the phone. "It's your call."

She sighed. "I don't think so, not on my account. But he *was* trespassing on your property."

DeKane shook his head slowly side to side. "Mister, I certainly would have come right to your front door if I had only known for sure that she was here. I swear. If there had been any other way to get in touch with her."

Dr. Grant turned to Kyla again with a questioning look.

She brushed her palms together. "No police," she said softly.

He paused, then gave a nod. "Okay." He lifted the phone to his mouth. "Ma'am, I believe we have the situation under control. Our assailant turned out to be a family member." He paused. "Yes, that is correct. We would like to cancel our request for an officer." His eyes lifted to DeKane. "Yes. We're sure."

There was a pregnant moment of silence after he hung up. The professor slid his phone into his pocket, then gestured to the house. "Folks, I believe it's time to move this party inside."

Dr. Grant took Kyla's arm and walked beside her with her father on his other side. Behind her Kyla noticed Peter shining a flashlight into the woods, around the oak and into the ravine before he followed them up to the house.

In the light of the patio Dr. Grant took one look at how wet, muddy, and grass-stained Kyla was and sent her directly upstairs to change. When she came back down, the three men were sitting around the kitchen table, a glass of water in front of her father, who was wearing a short-sleeved dress shirt, black with tiny gray pinstripes, with dirt smeared across one shoulder. He seemed older than a few weeks ago when she had seen him, his face and arms weathered by the sun and his graying hair flat and uncombed. He looked sweaty and in need of a shower. He was staring at the ice in the glass when she joined them, and he was talking about her.

"—stick straight hair and such a cute way of laughing. Always happy. She used to bring me a pile of books to read to her every night." He looked up when Kyla walked in. "Ah, there she is!" He followed her with his eyes as she took a chair at the table. "My God, she's beautiful! The spittin' image of her mother with those long legs and dark eyes. She wears her hair exactly how Eva wore hers." He turned to Dr. Grant in explanation. "That was my ex, Kyla's mother. She's gone now."

Peter was sitting a little behind DeKane on the same side of the table. A dark look descended on his face as he observed the thick, red welt on Kyla's jaw.

Kyla took a breath and laid her hands on the table. "We gotta talk."

DeKane smiled. "Great! That's what I was hoping for, baby!"

She gave a little huff, shaking her head. *Was he that clueless?* "Look, I think you owe us more of an explanation for what happened out there tonight. I mean, seriously—who does that?" She frowned at him. "I get that you didn't know if I lived here or not, but geez, what about coming up to the house in the daylight instead of jumping me in the dark? You scared me half to death! Why did you do that?"

Peter echoed from his chair, "Why didn't you just get her phone number from her dad and call her?"

Kyla threw him a look. "Well, that I get! He and my dad aren't exactly on speaking terms."

Peter closed his mouth and sat back, folding his arms.

She looked back at DeKane, waiting for him to answer. Dr. Grant's gaze followed.

"Oh, hell, I know! That was stupid, and I'm sorry." He shook his head apologetically. "What with the rain and everything, it was just bad judgment. Bad timing. Pretty much bad everything!"

Dr. Grant's eyes narrowed. "How many times have you been here?" He was leaning against the edge of the peninsula with his hands in his pockets, bouncing one leg agitatedly. He looked tired.

"Oh—" His eyes dropped to his glass. "Maybe a couple."

"A couple? How many is that?"

He fidgeted in the chair. "I came up maybe two other times. Didn't see her, though."

Behind him Peter was biting his lip, shaking his head.

"So, what—you just kept coming back?" Kyla asked.

He shrugged. "Well, of course! I was looking for you! It was you I wanted to see!"

Kyla gave a loud sigh and leaned her head on her hands. Dr. Grant suddenly moved to the kitchen and filled a water glass. He placed it in front of Kyla and resumed his place at the counter. She said thanks, taking a long drink.

DeKane continued, "Like I said, I'm in New Hampton on business. I've been staying in a little rat hole of a hotel in town, and I've had a day or two here and there between meetings with my clients." DeKane paused, looking down at his glass of water for a moment, then lifted his eyes to hers. "When I saw you last month, I knew I was a fool for letting seventeen years go by. I can't even *begin* to describe what that regret feels like." His lips became a thin line.

Kyla folded her hands, saying nothing. Dr. Grant and Peter were also silent.

DeKane cleared his throat, breaking the silence with a hushed voice, "How does the car drive?" His mouth twisted into a smile.

She gave a small smile in return. "Pretty nice."

He looked down, nodding. "Good."

She sighed again. "Look—" Once again, she didn't know what to call him. "Dad"? "Father"? "Robert"? She would have to figure that out later. "Um, look," she started again, "I'm flattered that you want to get to know me, and I'm all for it, but we're going to have to figure something out. My job here is—well, it's full time. It's not like I can just go spend Tuesdays and Thursdays with you, if you know what I mean."

"No, no—I understand," he said, a veil of disappointment descending on his face. "I know you have responsibilities." He took a drink, fingering the condensation on the outside of the glass when he set it down.

An awkward pause followed. Kyla looked to Dr. Grant for help where he stood, studying the two of them.

"I assume you have a car?" Dr. Grant asked.

"A car? Yes, of course."

Dr. Grant tilted his head. "Which is where—?"

DeKane rubbed his nose with the back of his hand. "Where? My car is over by the public landing. I parked there and walked to where I borrowed the boat."

"Who did you borrow it from?" Peter challenged.

DeKane twisted to look at Peter behind him. "From one of your neighbors, Anna Klein. I should be getting it back to her."

"Not at this hour," Dr. Grant said. "I don't think she would appreciate that!"

DeKane frowned, looking down at his watch. "Oh, right. Probably not. Didn't realize how late it is." He pursed his lips, looking at Kyla. "Perhaps you could give me a ride to my car tonight. I'll take care of the boat tomorrow."

"Not on your life," Dr. Grant said. "She's not going anywhere."

He straightened in his chair. "Oh, right, of course." He nodded. "Sure—I understand. I'd be very grateful for whoever could take me back. I know it's an inconvenience. And Kyla, I can give you my phone number, and maybe we can figure out a time to meet in town—sometime."

Kyla nodded. "Okay."

Dr. Grant rubbed his chin thoughtfully. "Where did you say you were staying?"

"I'm at the Circle Inn," DeKane said. "It's a dive, but affordable for long-term. I'm there for another week, maybe two."

"And you're out visiting clients during the day?"

"Most days," DeKane replied. "Working on my laptop the rest." He made a sudden noise with his mouth as he sucked air between his teeth.

Dr. Grant was silent for a bit, his eyes moving from Kyla back to DeKane. He took a breath. "Okay, this is going out on a limb, but what would you think of staying here instead? In one of our guest rooms. That way you could do your business and Kyla could still watch my boys, but you would have a little more opportunity to spend time with one another."

Peter sat back, dropping his arms, his mouth open.

Kyla blinked in surprise. "What?"

"Would you be okay with that?" Dr. Grant asked Kyla.

She frowned, staring at him.

"Just for a short time. You could connect. Get to know each other."

"Well, it never crossed my mind, but—I guess. Are you *sure*?"

"What do you think?" the professor asked DeKane.

DeKane was shaking his head in disbelief. "That's, that's"—his eyes were wide—"that's incredibly generous of you!"

Dr. Grant tipped his head. "Well, good."

"I'd pay you, of course," DeKane added.

The professor gave a small laugh. "We'll figure something out. But for now it's time to call it a night. I'm tired. Are you okay if we deal with the car in the morning? Or do you need to be somewhere early?"

DeKane was scratching his head, his face still amazed. "Tomorrow? No appointments tomorrow. That would be just fine."

"Well, all right then. Peter, will you show him upstairs to the guest room across from yours?"

Slowly Peter rose, his eyes on Dr. Grant and his jaw set hard. "Sure," he said stiffly. "Come with me."

DeKane stood, reaching to shake Dr. Grant's hand across the table. "I really can't thank you enough."

"No problem," he replied. "Good night."

"Make sure he has a fresh towel," Kyla said to Peter, then to her father, "Good night."

Kyla was too adrenalized to go to bed. She paced in her room, reviewing the events of the night—the terror she felt being grabbed from behind, the shock of it being her own father! She shook her head in disbelief. All this time—all this time it was her very own father that was their stalker! It was as simple as that! Her own father! And all the expense and trouble Dr. Grant was about to go through to install a security camera system—all that would have been a waste! Part of her was glad for Dr. Grant's sake that it wasn't someone stalking Marilee, or worse, the boys. Another part of her was deeply embarrassed. This was *her father!* She held her face in her hands. Seriously, who did that? Who lurked around someone's house in the dark? She wondered how many times he had been up in the ravine, truly. And now he was *staying* with them.

She shuddered to think of what her dad, Kendall, would say about DeKane showing up like he had! She remembered the look on his face when she had told him about her father meeting her with the new car after her graduation. He had been livid! Kyla paused by the table in her room, staring absently at its surface. One thing that was clear was that her birth father was pretty clueless about social norms. That was twice now that he'd shown up in her life in a bizarre ways. Three times, if she counted their meeting at McDonald's, of all places. Plus the car gift. Kyla shook her head. He obviously had some strange ideas of how to do things!

Thinking of her dad reminded her of his news about Alex, and suddenly, for the first time, it didn't matter to her what he did. *So what! Go on—meet with my dad!* she thought. In many ways that was to her advantage—why not let her dad deal with him? She didn't really care. For once Alex Duvall seemed trivial to think about! *Have at him, Dad!* He was not her problem anymore.

As Kyla stood there, she suddenly noticed the empty cord on her charger dangling from the side of the table. *Her phone!* She had dropped it outside in the yard right before her father snatched her from behind! She knew she had better look for it right away. She hoped it had not gotten damaged or ruined from the wet grass. Grabbing a light jacket, she opened one of the French doors and stepped out into the hallway, noticing that the lights were still on downstairs.

"—oh, right!" Peter's angry voice carried up over the balcony from below. "You're telling me to cool my jets when you come waltzing out there with nothing but your phone! Did you even consider that the guy might be armed? What would have happened then?"

Kyla froze in mid-step, her arm halfway in her jacket.

"Well, he wasn't, but that's beside the point!" Dr. Grant fired back. "You scared me! You were over the line!"

"Oh, for heaven's sake! I was nowhere near the line! Did you hear her scream? Did you hear her?"

"Yes, I heard—"

"That scream told me she was terrified! I wasn't about to walk out there and ask the guy politely what he was doing here!"

"I'm not saying—"

"What happened out there was not right! I don't care what you say—I don't trust the guy!"

There was a momentary pause in the conversation. Kyla stood still, remaining where she was.

Peter continued indignantly: "And what are you thinking, letting him stay here? We have no idea who he is! That guy is—"

"That guy," Dr. Grant's voice cut in firmly, "is Kyla's father!"

"Ah, he is so full of crap! I don't believe a word he says!"

"Watkins," the professor returned with intensity, "when did I start needing your permission for what I do in my house? Here's my question for you, Peter Watkins: Did you grow up with a father?"

Kyla heard no reply.

"Well, that girl upstairs didn't! And yeah, I agree—DeKane might be a few cards short of a full deck, but he's still her father! I think this means something to her!"

Peter cleared his throat. "Okay. So what about the relative?"

"What relative?"

"The relative who knew about the house—the guy—"

"Yeah, yeah, okay. The friend of her father, or whoever it was."

"Yeah," Peter said. "We have no idea what her dad has been told or how long he's been slinking around the house. Or why."

Dr. Grant sniffed. "All right. I hear what you're saying. It's highly unlikely he knows anything, but we can—"

"But still! I think we shoul—"

"—can take some extra precautions!" Grant's voice rose irritatedly over his. "Stand down, Mr. Watkins!" Another pause. "Now—I'm home for the next few days, so I'll be keeping an eye on him, and we'll just see how things work out, okay? Is that all right with you? You seem to be pretty opinionated about this!"

"I'm just trying to be smart."

"Well, I wouldn't say what you did out there earlier was smart!"

There was another space in the conversation. Kyla waited, debating whether to sneak back into her room and wait until later or to make a bunch of obvious noise and go downstairs pretending she hadn't heard anything. Then it was quiet for so long, she wondered if they had left. She took a chance and started down. She was wrong.

"So is there anything else you wanted to discuss?" she heard Dr. Grant ask.

"No," Peter replied, "but I'd like to say something, just for the record."

"Okay, what's that?"

"I hear what you're saying about DeKane staying here. And I get what you mean about the two of them. But you're wrong about Kyla. She *did* have a father, and she had a *good* one too!"

At that moment Kyla appeared at the bottom of the stairs. The two men standing at the foot of the opposite stairs turned their heads in surprise. Dr. Grant was scowling. Peter's face was red with agitation.

"I, um, dropped my phone outside earlier," she said, pointing her thumb toward the door. "I'm going out to look for it."

Peter had it in his hand and held it out to her. "I was bringing it up to you."

She took it. "Thanks. Good night." She turned to go back up the stairs. After two steps she stopped. Since she had heard everything, she might as well face them. She turned, leveling her gaze at the two men. "Um, I apologize for the way my father showed up tonight. I don't understand anything about him, but I'm sorry that it happened. And I certainly didn't ask for him to stay here, so don't feel like you need to have him here on my account."

Dr. Grant shook his head and lifted his hand. "Your father is welcome here."

"I know, but if it's causing problems, then—"

"Miss DeKane," Dr. Grant broke in resolutely, as Peter's eyes dropped to the floor, "I seem to remember having a conversation with you the other day about the importance of fathers. I'm giving you an opportunity to move on that. That will be your prerogative. Everything else is on my shoulders and is not your concern. Period."

Kyla hesitated, glancing again at Peter. "Okay. Thanks." She nodded. "Well, good night."

"Good night, Miss DeKane."

She turned and retreated up the stairs to nothing but the sound of her own footsteps. At her room she paused with her hand on the lever before entering. Sure enough, the discussion below resumed.

"Okay, just one more thing," came Peter's voice again, more hushed this time. "I'm not sure if you noticed, but that man upstairs in the guest room does not have a beard."

Dr. Grant's reply was muffled and diminishing, like the two of them were moving their conversation elsewhere.

Kyla showered and got into her pajamas but sat on the settee, her knees up below her chin, a strange feeling stirring within. Concern for her had been the subject of an argument. It was clear that Peter did not like her father, but the professor had stood up to him—all because of her. All because of their conversation last week. He remembered what she had shared with him and was considerate of her feelings about her father showing up in her life. She sniffed, hugging her knees, the details of the night flitting back through her mind—the way Dr. Grant had taken charge in the yard and helped her up and took her arm on the way back to the house, even going so far as to invite her father to stay here in his house. She sighed, dropping her forehead onto her knees thinking about him. He was such a great guy—intelligent, capable, and kind. And a great dad. Not to mention handsome. But married. And completely unavailable. If only he were single. And younger.

Kyla held her hands over her cheeks. There was once a time when she had looked to Alex to feel special. With him she had felt sought-out and desired, but now she had no one. In her heart she longed to be cared for, watched over, and truly special to someone—*God, I want that*, she called out in her heart—but it wasn't a reality now. And she dared not let herself think that way toward Dr. Grant. She didn't need to have a mother to know how very destructive that would be. Her dad would kill her. Sweet Mrs. Gordon would kill her too. She recalled her first day at Wynnbury when Dr. Grant pulled up the photo of his wife between the two of them. Yes, Dr. Grant was a closed and locked door to her. End of story. Kyla sighed. She supposed she should go to bed and at least try to sleep. There was much to be figured out tomorrow with her birth father in the house now.

She had barely drifted off when she heard the sound of crying from the boys' room. It was Hank. *Oh, Hank.* Kyla rolled over tiredly, waiting to see if he would go back to sleep. *Please, please go back to sleep*, she begged internally.

He didn't. He showed up at the side of her bed with his blankie and bear.

"Come on," Kyla said, pulling him up and in. Without a doubt, this was becoming a very bad habit.

"Drink," he whined, hugging his blanket.

Forcing her body to move, Kyla crawled out of bed and fetched his cup from the bathroom. He pushed it away.

"Want my milk!" He started to cry, rubbing his eyes.

"We just have water, Hank," she said, offering him the cup again.

"Want my milk!" he persisted, pushing it away so that it splashed onto the sheets. He threw his face into the pillow with a tired whine.

"Shhh! Stop crying, Hank!" The last thing she needed was both kids awake.

He wouldn't stop. The boy wanted milk, and that was all there was to it.

"Hank," Kyla bargained, "I'll get you some milk if you stop crying."

Immediately he hushed. Wearily, Kyla searched for her slippers beside the nightstand. Previously she had been too wired to go to bed. Now every fiber in her body was exhausted and screaming for sleep. Quietly she opened her door and stepped out into the dark hallway. As she turned toward the stairs, a sudden movement in the Great Room below startled her—a figure in the dark! Kyla lurched with fright, and a cry stuck in her throat as she stared. Immediately it was apparent that it wasn't a ghost, but a person walking down there. Someone was pacing in the dark and murmuring in a low voice, and it gave her the chills. With her heart pounding she silently approached the rail, peering downward. In the dimness of the moonlight through the Great Room windows she could see by the glint of light on his hair that it was Peter.

What the heck was he doing? Her breath quickened as she watched his strange behavior. Was he sleepwalking? She observed his erratic pacing, the thrusting of his fists out in front of him, his urgent whispers. Suddenly he turned and raised both hands up toward the balcony. Kyla shrank back into the stairwell beside her, trembling, holding her breath. Had he seen her watching? She stood frozen in place. It was then that she could make out some of his words. Kyla shivered. Peter was praying. With a guilty curiosity, Kyla inched forward to peek around the corner and between the rails again, where she saw that he was back to pacing. Goosebumps prickled her arms and the back of her neck, and Kyla tiptoed backward until she felt the handle of her door to let herself silently back into her bedroom.

Shaken, she stood there in the dark for a moment, bewildered at what she'd just seen. Why was Peter doing that? And suddenly—she wasn't quite sure why—but suddenly she felt as if she could cry. As she made her way back to her bed she realized that she had forgotten all about Hank's milk. But he had fallen asleep. Gently she slid his little body over to the other side of the bed and crawled in beside him, her heart still racing in her chest, thinking of Peter in the Great Room below and wondering what was so important to warrant that kind of prayer.

Chapter Nineteen

Kyla was embarrassed at how late she slept the next day. Even Hank was up and downstairs before she stirred. Seeing the clock, she shot out of bed and hastily dressed, hurrying down to a sunny kitchen, with breakfast long over. The sudden jarring of metal and an engine's loud rumble drew her eyes outside, where out on the patio Dr. Grant stood with Hank on his hip observing an enormous excavator in the yard cutting a hole into the earth with a sharp bucket, the house vibrating with its action. Surprised, she watched it for a moment, craning her neck to look for her father, but she couldn't see him. Snatching a yogurt from the refrigerator, she went to join them. Dr. Grant turned when he heard the deck door close, and Hank immediately wriggled to be put down to run to her.

"I'm so sorry," she called loudly over the grinding of the heavy machinery, tousling Hank's hair as he hugged her leg. "I couldn't fall asleep last night, and then I overslept big time." The machine throttled down in the middle of her sentence, and her last few words were quite loud.

"Morning!" Dr. Grant replied. "I'm not surprised! Don't worry. You're entitled to a late morning after last night!" He grimaced, noticing the bruises on her cheek and jaw, his eyes rising to hers. "Does it hurt?"

She shrugged. "Not really. My wrists are a little sore, but other than that I'm fine. Where's my father?" She looked around, her hand over her forehead shielding her eyes from the sun. "And what's all this?" The smell of diesel hung heavily in the air.

Dr. Grant jerked his head to the other end of the patio. "He's down there, looking around."

Her father stood against the white concrete spindles of the patio, looking up at the house, unaware of her presence. Between them Howie played with his toy dump truck.

"And out there," Dr. Grant was saying, "we're preparing to run water and electric out to the fountain site. We have to dig a trench. I must have forgotten to tell you, with everything else going on. We were hoping to get a lot done this weekend if everything came in as expected. Haven't heard on that. And I don't know—the ground is pretty wet. This rain might have set us back."

"Ah," she nodded. "I thought maybe it had to do with the new security system." She squinted at the operator. "Is that Peter in there?"

"Our one and only Mr. Watkins," Dr. Grant replied, his voice betraying no residual irritation from their argument last evening. "And our security plans are temporarily on hold. Out there, at least."

Kyla glanced over at him. "I wondered about that."

Howie suddenly spied Kyla and began pushing his dump truck at nearly a full run down the length of the patio, purposefully ramming into a planter that blocked his way.

"Howard David, what did I say?" his father scolded. "You are done playing with that truck!" He pointed sharply for him to set the toy aside.

Howie scowled and abandoned his truck, plopping into a chair beside Kyla, who had just sat down at the table. He folded his arms in a pout, asking accusingly, "Where were you?"

"I slept late," she answered. Hank was backing into her, trying to get onto her lap, eager to share her yogurt.

Howie was very cross. "Well, did you know that guy over there is your dad? He slept at our house last night!"

"You, sir," Dr. Grant interjected, "will call him Mr. DeKane—do you understand?"

He wrinkled his nose. "Mr. DeKane?" He looked back at Kyla. "He's got the same name as you!"

Dr. Grant rolled his eyes. "Yes, they're related, Howie! You and I have the same last name too—remember?"

Kyla saw her father walking over to join them, and butterflies stirred in her belly.

"I'd appreciate any coaching for getting to know this guy," she said hastily to Dr. Grant.

"There's no formula. You'll figure it out," he said.

"I hope so." Turning to her father, she called out over the putter of the equipment in the yard, "Good morning! I hope you slept well."

He was wearing the same clothes as last night, but he had showered, and his hair looked much better—cleaner, at least.

"Very well, thank you!" he said, smiling as he approached. "Quite a project here!" He nodded toward the rumbling excavator, pushing his hands into his pockets. Then seeing her cheek, his smile suddenly grew plastic. Uncomfortable, he looked away from her.

"We're putting in a fountain," she told him, then realized it sounded like this was her house and corrected herself. "Dr. Grant and Peter are."

"So I hear," he said, peering out at the yard.

Dr. Grant spoke up. "Kyla, I told your father that when you were up, we'd give him a tour of the house. You up for that?"

"Of course," she said. Hank was just finishing the last bite of her yogurt.

"Can I come?" Howie asked.

"If you can remember your manners, yes," his father said.

The tour was much more streamlined than the one Kyla had gotten when she had arrived at Wynnbury, but she had come to the house as an employee, she reasoned, and not as a guest. Dr. Grant started at the far end of the long hall, showing her father the cozy theater and the game room, plus the fitness room, where Peter worked out. He made a point of showing him how to work certain machines and recommended following specific workout tables on the wall that highlighted different muscle groups on various days. Kyla was surprised at his thoroughness, since she'd never seen him use the room even once, and she mentioned it.

Dr. Grant's shoulder lifted in a shrug. "I'm busy this summer. And outside. It's yours to use too, you know."

"I know," she answered, though she clearly chose to avoid it. This was Peter's domain. Plus, most evenings she was just plain ready for bed at the end of the day.

Hank tapped her hip, pointing to one of the machines. "Be careful! Get pinched!"

Kyla nodded, not surprised that he remembered.

In the library Hank and Howie knelt, pulling their favorite books off their shelf, thinking it was their time to read. They built a stack in the usual place by the large armchair. Kyla had to tell them they would have to wait until after lunch. Meanwhile her biological father walked the perimeter of the room, fascinated by the books and the woodwork, examining the mantel top and bottom and running his hand over the oak doors, peering upwards in the door slots to the tracks on which they were hung.

"This is my favorite room," Kyla told her father, but he was focused on the door.

"I just love these old houses," he said.

"Yeah?" Dr. Grant said. "Well, this one actually isn't that old. Built in the late '40s is all. Of course, we've updated most of it—new electrical, everything basically. We kept the old-style woodwork, as you see."

"I'd love to hear all about it," DeKane said. "It's such an unusual style for this location—I hear it's modeled after a house in England."

"Yes, I've heard that too," Dr. Grant replied, waiting for Kyla and the boys at the door.

"It must be an interesting story," DeKane said, looking curiously across the hall toward Dr. Grant's office.

"No doubt. I've been meaning to look into it," the professor replied. "That's my private study, so if you'll follow me, we'll swing through the upstairs briefly."

He turned away from his study and motioned for Kyla and DeKane to go before him up the stairs, where he pointed to indicate Kyla and the boys' suite, his own room, and Peter's room, across from DeKane's. The boys immediately started playing with their toys in the playroom.

Dr. Grant turned on his heel and continued down the hall. "Back down here, past the balcony, are more guest rooms, but we've closed these off so we don't have to air condition them."

"And what about this? What's in here?" DeKane asked, still hanging back near Peter's room, trying the door to the third floor.

Lingering back with him, Kyla began, "That goes to the third floor—"

"—which we never use," Dr. Grant finished for her from his place on the balcony. "It's scheduled for a remodel next summer, but we keep it locked up. A bit of a bat infestation up there."

Kyla closed her mouth and looked at Dr. Grant, who evenly returned her gaze.

"How interesting!" her father said. "I would be curious to see it in its original condition before the remodel."

Dr. Grant pursed his lips and nodded. "Yeah, well, we might be able to arrange that sometime." He jerked his head toward the other end of the hall, where he had previously been headed. "I want to show you a shortcut down to the side entrance, which you might find handy."

"Come on, boys," Kyla called.

Howie's face appeared in the doorway. "What? We didn't even get to play one thing yet!"

"They're fine," Dr. Grant told her. "Let them play!" He was moving along quite determinedly.

She trailed behind her father to where Dr. Grant waited for them at the back steps and followed them down the dim stairway to the side entryway beside the carport.

"What a handy little set of stairs!" her father said. "In the olden days the servants' quarters had their own set of stairs."

"I know what you're describing," Dr. Grant replied, "but these are more your standard fire exit stairs. This house had no special servants' rooms."

"Really?" Her father was studying the walls of the side entry room. "Huh. I would sure love to see the original blueprints to this place."

Dr. Grant was silent.

"Are you an architect? Or builder?" Kyla asked.

"Oh, I've dabbled in lots of things," DeKane replied, "a little of this and a little of that. And I see there's a cellar." He pointed to the set of stairs leading downward.

"Indeed, you are right," Dr. Grant said. "And down there is nothing of interest, unless you have a fascination with boilers."

DeKane laughed, rocking on his feet. "Boilers, no. But I do have a fascination with wine!"

Kyla backed out of Dr. Grant's path as he made his way back into the main part of the house again, finishing the tour by indicating to DeKane the laundry room, the back restroom, the formal dining room, and finally ending in the Great Room.

"What a fantastic house!" DeKane declared, looking all around him. "You have an amazing amount of space—you could host a small convention here!" He laughed.

Dr. Grant smiled modestly. "Well, that's an exaggeration. But my wife and I do enjoy entertaining."

"I don't believe I have met your wife," DeKane said, with a turn of his head toward Dr. Grant.

"No, you haven't," Dr. Grant said, rearranging some pillows on a nearby chair. "Mary is out of town on business for a while. Which is why we hired on Kyla as our nanny."

Kyla's eyes lifted first to Dr. Grant, then automatically across the dining room beyond him, where she noticed an electric coffee grinder and a small canister in place of Marilee's framed portrait beside the coffee pot on the kitchen counter. Kyla pursed her lips. It had been quite an educational tour of the house for her this morning.

"So—" Dr. Grant tipped his head toward Kyla. "I'm sure you two will want some time to visit. Don't worry about the boys. I'll let you know when Peter is ready to take your father to pick up his car."

"Thank you," she said, watching him round the corner and go back upstairs to his kids.

Kyla and her father stood together in the middle of the Great Room, looking at each other.

"Shall we sit down?" she asked.

He held out his hand, gesturing to a nearby chair, where she sat; he took the couch across from her. Over his shoulder she could see Peter working with the machine, pulling buckets of dirt from the ground and dumping them to the side as he cut the trench through the yard. Her eyes flicked back to her father, but he was gazing at the fireplace wall and the long fabric art hanging above it.

"So here we are," she said.

"You have one helluva job here," he said in a low voice, his eyes rising to the balcony. "These people are crawling in money!" DeKane swore under his breath, shaking his head.

"Well, they do work for a living," Kyla offered. "And it's actually been a lot of work for me too."

He cursed again. "Freakin' gold mine here! You have no idea!"

She was silent, studying him as he moved agitatedly on the couch, looking around the room. She wasn't sure where this was supposed to go.

"What do you do?" she asked finally, trying to bring some focus.

"Me?" He looked surprised at the question.

Kyla leaned back, sliding one of the pillows near, fidgeting with the cord along the edge of it. She looked at him directly. "I guess from my perspective you must be crawling in cash too. Not many people just outright buy a car like the one you gave me for my graduation."

"Ah, you're right there!" He held his finger up at her with a broad smile. He seemed pleased that she had brought it up.

"So what do you do?" Kyla repeated.

"I'm in investments," he said.

"Investments. You mentioned that before. But what does that mean? Like investing your own money or other people's money?"

His eyebrows lifted. "Kinda both." He leaned toward her, his elbows on his legs, spread wide. "I dabble in the market here and there. Securities. I mostly broker precious metals. Coins, and the like. And other things. I've done well for myself."

"Well, do me a favor," she said. "Don't try to make Dr. Grant one of your clients, please. Or Peter for that matter."

His fingers lifted briefly. "Right. Gotcha. Of course not."

"Are you part of a larger company?"

"No, just on my own." He reached for his wallet and pulled out a card, handing it across the gap between them. She glanced at it and set it on the end table beside her.

Kyla waited a second while they sat looking at each other, giving him a chance to initiate more conversation. He didn't. She pressed on.

"Where do you live?"

"Illinois."

"Illinois is a pretty big place." She fought to keep the annoyance out of her voice.

"Yeah, sorry. I have a small house in the Champagne area." He gestured with his hands. "For most people there's Chicago, and then there's Illinois, which includes everything else."

"Ah, I suppose. And do you have"—she hesitated, not knowing how to ask, wondering if it was too soon to ask, wondering if it would hurt to ask—"do you have a family there?"

He looked down at his hands, then back up at her, shaking his head slowly. "No family."

An awkward silence passed between them.

"I mean, I've had girlfriends here and there," he continued, looking off to the side. "I haven't been alone all my life. But no one right now."

Kyla swallowed, plunging ahead. "Do *I* have any family?"

"You?"

She let out a breath, throwing her head impatiently to the side. "Any random siblings I should know about? Grandparents? Aunts and uncles maybe?"

"Yeah, yeah, right—I get it! You want to know who I am."

She gave a small snort, unable to hold it back. "Not just you! I want to know who I am!"

"Ah. Okay." He leaned back with both hands behind his head, looking upward toward the balcony. "I was born around that area, the youngest in a family of three boys. We had a farm. My parents are both gone now. And I haven't been in touch with my brothers since"—he frowned, thinking—"oh, for a long time now."

Kyla made a little sound. "What? Why not?"

He blinked, his face expressionless. "It was a mutual parting of ways."

"Why? Over what?"

He closed his lips and looked away. Kyla waited, but he didn't answer.

She frowned. "You're not going to say?"

The corner of his mouth lifted. "Save your strength for paddling up a different stream, baby."

Youngest in a family of three boys. At least she had discovered she had two uncles, Kyla mused. And possibly cousins.

"Well, I want their names," she said firmly. "Of my grandparents too. It's my family tree."

He nodded. "Yeah, we'll do that sometime."

"So I have no other siblings out there in the world?"

He shook his head. "Not to my knowledge. Although"—he gave a smug smile—"it's not beyond the realm of possibility. But as far as I know, there's just me and you."

Kyla winced at the statement. "Just me and you? You make it sound like we're some sort of close-knit pair. It hasn't *ever* been 'just me and you'!"

He gave an exaggerated nod, holding up a hand. "Of course! I only meant that you are my only living relative."

"Apart from the ones you choose not to talk to."

He lifted his hand again in assent. Kyla shifted in her chair, crossing her feet, forcing herself to settle down. Again she gave him an opportunity to talk, taking a few deep breaths while she waited. He remained silent.

"Where did you go to high school?" she asked next.

He paused, his eyes flicking to her face. "Delano, Illinois."

"Graduating in the class of—?"

Another tight-lipped smile. "Didn't graduate," he said simply.

"And how did you meet my mother?"

"We met on a job." He brought his arms down, folding them in front of him. "We worked together. We had a good thing going for a lot of years. And then I had to leave."

"Yeah. Because of me."

He looked away.

Kyla narrowed her eyes. "And you won't tell me why." She remembered this part of the conversation from before.

He grimaced. "Sorry, baby. Can't."

She surveyed him thoughtfully, tapping her hand on the pillow next to her, determining how far to go.

"You had to give up your parental rights in order for my dad—

Kendall—to adopt me. Do you have any idea of how that feels?"

His face fell as her words sunk in, and he scooted forward on the couch, pointing to his chest. "Yeah, I know what it feels like! I know what it feels like from *my* end of the deal!"

She nodded bitterly. "Uh-huh, right. No protest. No fight. Just a quick signature on the paper once my mother found you. Ba-da-boom, done."

He shook his head, heat moving up his neck. "It wasn't that I didn't want you."

"Well, it kind of felt like that!" She glared at him. "And no contact with me ever. Ever! For all my growing-up years!"

DeKane stood and moved about agitatedly. "It wouldn't have made a shred of difference. Not a shred."

"Maybe not to *you*."

He turned on his heel, appealing to her, "Kyla, you will never understand. It wasn't that I didn't want you! I was not *allowed* to have you!"

Her eyes narrowed again. "And why was that? I suppose you're going to blame my mother. Go ahead—tell me all about it!"

He shoved his hands into his pockets, shifting his weight on his feet, looking at her, his lips tight. Then he spat another curse word and ran his hand through his hair, turning to look outside. "Where *is* that kid? We were supposed to get my car a while ago. I sure as hell could use a cigarette!"

"Well, there you go," she said with a lift of her hand, as if he had just indicated how much she was worth to him.

DeKane took a step closer, leaning in and shaking his finger in her face. "One thing you need to understand—" He caught himself and straightened up, his pointing hand moving to rest on his hip. Taking a deep breath, he continued, "One thing you need to understand is that I kept my word to your mother. Every last thing I promised."

"Uh-huh." Kyla couldn't stop herself. "'Till death do us part'—tell me what that means to you!"

He blinked, unable to respond. Then he turned toward the window, looking out, with his hands in his pockets. "There's so much you don't know," he muttered.

"And I won't know until you tell me," she replied to his back.

The machinery outside suddenly became quiet, and Kyla saw Peter get out of the cab. Her father looked down at his wristwatch and back outside.

"So here we are," Kyla said, filling the uncomfortable silence.

He turned. "It's obvious you're irritated. Are you giving up on us already?"

Kyla fiddled with her earring.

"I suppose you're going to want me to leave—to not come back here when I get my car."

She lifted her chin. "No, you can come back. I've barely started with the questions I have for you!"

He looked at her, then gave a sudden laugh. "Ah, you are definitely like your mother!"

Kyla turned her face away. *Everything felt so forced,* she thought. So forced. Across the house she noticed that Dr. Grant had entered the kitchen. She watched him open the refrigerator door and peer in for a while, then close it to do something on the counter. After a few seconds he was back searching in the refrigerator again.

She took a breath, turning back to her father. "It looks like Peter will be ready for you soon. If you don't mind, I think I'll go help feed the kids. And maybe this afternoon we can, um, do something."

"Okay." DeKane gave a nod. "Would you mind then if I went out for some fresh air?"

"No. I'll show you the way out." She led him out of the Great Room through the main foyer to the front door. "If I see Peter I'll tell him you're waiting out here. But he'll probably see you himself."

"Thanks, Kyla." He reached down for her hand and squeezed it softly in his. "I know this is really awkward now, but I think things will get better between us. We just need time."

"Perhaps," she replied.

When he left, Kyla leaned against the back side of the door, blowing out air through her cheeks. She might have to talk to Dr. Grant. She didn't know if she could handle his staying there. Already she had a headache! She rubbed her temples, looking off to the side, then straightened suddenly, noticing that the photos of Wynnbury and Mr. Kennedy and his family had been replaced by one larger painting of an old English hunting scene. She stared at it a moment, then joined Dr. Grant in the kitchen, who was still leaning into the refrigerator. Howie was sitting cross-legged on the rug in front of the sink, pouting, and Hank was in his chair, eating part of a banana. Hearing her approach, the professor straightened, looking past her down the hall for her father.

"He's outside. Waiting for Peter," she said, observing Howie on the floor. She waved Dr. Grant out of the way and took over the preparation of lunch for the boys.

"Can I talk now?" Howie asked his father glumly.

"No," his father replied, "I said five minutes, not thirty seconds!"

Howie huffed and folded his arms, turning back toward the cupboard.

"Well, I see that *everyone's* cheerful today," Kyla said lightly.

Dr. Grant moved to the peninsula. "One morning and I'm worn out from these guys! I'm overtired and out of practice. How did it go?"

Kyla presented him with two plates and an expression on her face that said "Don't ask."

"Okay, Howie," Dr. Grant said, "you can come off the mat and talk now. But it's time for lunch, so go get in your chair."

With the boys occupied, Kyla turned to her employer. "So what's the deal—you have a new wife now? Mary?" Her eyebrows rose, gesturing to the missing photograph of his wife.

"It's probably best your father doesn't know some things, if you know what I mean."

"I've been deducting little things all morning! Like this, for one." She indicated the missing photograph. "You don't want him to know who you're married to—that's understandable. And I haven't told him anything. But the door we suddenly keep locked upstairs? And your refusal to talk about the house in England, and the pictures in the foyer gone, not to mention—"

"We're keeping it simple, Kyla. He's here for you. The waters don't need to be muddied. There's no reason he needs to be up there. No reason he needs to know anything about this house."

Apparently, these were some of the extra precautions he and Peter had discussed last night. She nodded toward the boys. "How are you going to get these guys to play along with all of that?"

He shrugged. "They call her Mom."

Kyla frowned. "It just seems strange. Dishonest."

He sighed tiredly. "I tend to view it as safe and simple."

Kyla tipped her chin down. "Was this by chance Peter's idea?"

At that moment there was a small commotion in the side entrance behind them, and Peter poked his head around the corner, holding up his keys.

"We're heading out," he said to Dr. Grant. Then he noticed Kyla. "Hey."

"Good morning," she said, then seeing the clock, "er, afternoon, I guess."

As he left, Dr. Grant gave a small whistle. "That just bought your father some time."

"What? What do you mean by that?"

"Well, it's apparent Peter didn't see your jaw. 'Cause when he does, I guarantee your father will be missing some teeth."

She gave him a sharp look. "He better not do anything foolish! He was a downright bear last night! I don't know why he's suddenly so overly zealous."

Dr. Grant said nothing.

Kyla turned to make sandwiches for the rest of the household. "So I was surprised that my father didn't just take the boat back this morning and get his own car. Why'd you have him wait around for Peter? He was dying to have a smoke! I think he was almost ready to *swim* back to his car!"

"Peter towed the boat back early this morning with ours."

"What?" Kyla turned to look at him. "Why'd he do that? That seems like a lot of trouble."

"So he could talk to Mrs. Klein." He was rubbing the morning stubble on his chin. "Who, incidentally, knew nothing of loaning out her boat to your father."

Her hands fell limp. "Why does that not surprise me?"

"And to see if he really did have a car there, which he does. Quite a nice one."

She gestured, spatula in hand. "I guess that doesn't surprise me either." She gave a heavy sigh, shaking her head. "You know, you don't have to have him stay here. In fact, it might be best if he doesn't. He already lied about the boat. Plus it was pretty brutal trying to talk to him this morning."

"Well, I'm sure he doesn't have the slightest idea of what to do with a daughter."

"You've got *that* right!"

Dr. Grant folded his arms, leaning back against the counter. "We're here. We'll keep an eye on him—you can count on that. But I think you need to give him a chance. A fair chance, that's all." When she said nothing he added, "How else can it happen? You can't get to know him if you don't try."

"I know." She bit her lip, looking down.

He was quiet for a moment, watching her. "Are you afraid of him?"

"No." She shook her head.

"What then?"

She hesitated.

"Are you embarrassed by him?"

Reluctantly she met his eyes. "Does it show? Yes! Kind of. He's just—just—" She shrugged. "I don't trust him. Not at all."

"Understandable. I get it." Dr. Grant nodded, observing her thoughtfully for a bit. "You know, ever since we talked that day here in the kitchen, I've thought about what it must be like for you with what you've been through. So hear me out. One of my biggest regrets in life is that I waited too long to get to know my father. He was there all along, but I never even *tried* with him. Everybody talks about how important fathers are. I always thought I didn't have a very good one, but in hindsight, I never bothered to find out who he was. I only believed the negative I had heard about him. I know it's hard for you with your father showing up like this, but hey—it's gotta be pretty tough for *him* too! You might find things get a little better once you get past the initial awkwardness of getting to know each other. I think you'll figure things out if you keep trying. I think you should give it a week."

Kyla's eyes widened. "A week?"

"That's when he said he'd be done with his business here. It's only seven days. How long has it been since he's been in your life? Seventeen years?"

"Well, yeah, but—"

"Then I think you owe it to yourself to give him more than a few hours of your time."

She sighed. "I guess. Since you seem pretty determined to make it happen!" She shot him a look.

He held up his hand. "Hey, I'm not *making* you do this! I'm just saying you might be surprised—things could turn out good! You never know unless you try!"

Kyla raised her eyebrows dubiously.

Dr. Grant chuckled. "Well, we'll see how it goes."

Chapter Twenty

Kyla was relieved that afternoon when her father insisted on helping the men with the fountain project outside, although the expression on Peter's face was one of displeasure when Dr. Grant agreed to his help. It didn't take much to see that Peter did not like Robert DeKane at all, and he did little to hide it.

A little earlier Peter and he had come home from getting his car and checking out of his hotel. DeKane parked his black Mercedes Benz behind Kyla's red-and-black Mustang under the carport, leaving Peter's truck now out on the driveway, open to the elements. The two newcomers joined Kyla and Dr. Grant in the kitchen, just in time for lunch. At the sight of Kyla's bruises, however, Peter pulled her into the narrow pantry, declaring to her that what DeKane had done last night ought to have been reported.

Kyla jerked her arm away from his hand and backed into a shelf of breakfast cereal, conscious of how close he was to her, his eyes intense as he leaned over her.

"Okay, I hear you," she said quietly so the others wouldn't hear, "and last night scared the daylights out of me, but I don't think it was premeditated or anything. I'm all right, and he's not going to hurt me again. I think we can just chalk it up to one really weird evening."

Peter shook his head. He was filthy with dirt and sweat, and he smelled like machinery grease. "No one does that to a girl, even if it was some kind of mishap!"

Her hackles were raised. "Well, it's clear that you don't like him, but he's my father, and I can't help who he is and what he's like!"

Peter placed his hand on the edge of a nearby shelf. "Your dad would not like him being here at all. Have you called him about this yet? You *need* to! And you need to talk to Grant about having DeKane leave!"

Kyla stuck her nose up in the air at him. "Oh, and you probably have already tattled!"

His face contorted. "What?"

"Is that what this is about?" she asked. "You—standing in for my dad? You know my dad doesn't like him, and it's easy to see why. But you—why do you think you need to take up my dad's case here?"

He huffed. "Well, it's about a lot more than *that*!"

As he leaned in, Kyla pressed back farther into the shelf, her hair snagging on the rough edge. "Well, consider this! My dad is never going to want a relationship with my birth father, Robert DeKane. So if *I* do, then that's something I'm going to have to make happen myself!"

At that Peter was silent, breathing hard.

"And that's what you want?" he asked finally.

Kyla's expression sobered. "I have to at least try, I think."

He nodded, looking down at her face.

He was way too close. She turned her head away. "Look—can we get out of here before someone gets a weird idea about this?"

After the briefest hesitation, Peter turned abruptly and left the pantry. Kyla stood alone, catching her breath and trying to interpret what just happened. She wasn't sure. She only knew she hadn't seen Peter like that before. When Kyla came out, he was in the washroom cleaning up. She joined her father and Dr. Grant, who were eating off paper plates on the patio, looking out over the muddy cuts and piles in the yard, discussing the project. Filling her plate, she wandered down to the canopied patio set to sit alone and watch Howie play with his truck. Nearby, Hank sat on his knees and lined his plastic animals up in long rows. Peter came out after a little while to join the men. Sour-faced, he ate in silence, but Kyla noticed him glance around until he saw her.

Shortly after that was when Kyla's father brought up the idea that the three of them could make a huge headway on the project by the end of the day if they all contributed. Dr. Grant was only too eager to comply, as this was his summer goal for his days off, and Peter unhappily had to make the best of the situation. Kyla, however, was thankful for the space and time away from her father for a while. The boys were glad to have their nanny back for the afternoon and kept her busy enough not to think about her father too much.

Later on Mrs. Gordon stopped by briefly, dropping off a Crock-pot of food and a few miscellaneous groceries.

"Hi, sweetheart," she said. "David said you had company this weekend and could use a little help."

Whatever she had brought smelled heavenly, and Kyla thanked her, plugging the oblong appliance in on the counter.

"My father is here," she explained.

"Oh, how nice of him to pay you a visit!" she said warmly.

"It was unexpected," Kyla responded. She wanted to ask if she had a month to talk about it, but clearly she was in a hurry. Perhaps next week when she came they would have a chance to talk.

"And here, hon—I brought you this too. It's for you to keep if you're interested." Mrs. Gordon handed her a plastic bag in which Kyla could feel was a book. "It was my daughter's," she said. "I hope you don't mind that it's not new. But I've gotta run. It's Friday, and my granddaughter's dance recital is tonight."

Kyla thanked her, and with a brief hug Mrs. Gordon was on her way.

Friday, Kyla thought, looking around the airy kitchen in which she stood, her two charges busily coloring activity sheets at the table, arguing over whose turn it was to use the blue crayon when there were several blue crayons within sight of them both. Friday used to be a milestone, the end of a week of class and the beginning of the weekend with Alex. But not anymore! Every day ran together now, and Fridays held little significance to her here. They simply meant that Dr. Grant was home, which wasn't necessarily a break for her.

The thought of how much her weekends had changed brought a wry smile to her face. She wondered how her old roommates were and what they were doing. No doubt they were very busy with their wedding preparations. How ironic that she, who had dated the longest of them, was now single, with zero prospects for dating on the horizon. Kyla leaned her elbows on the counter, absently watching the boys, glad to be busy enough not to think about it too much. The last eligible bachelor she had seen since college was Justin Marsden, the security rep, which seemed like a week ago, and she was pretty sure she wasn't on his radar, considering her awkward appearance in the foyer. She chuckled to herself. What he must have thought of her!

Kyla slid the plastic bag from Mrs. Gordon over closer to her. Mrs. Gordon. She had found a new friend in her, and she was thankful. A very motherly and safe friend. Kyla opened the bag and peeked in to see what book she had given her, and her breath caught in her throat. *What?* She frowned in confusion. *It was her Bible!* Not just any Bible, but Kyla's own Bible from her early high school years! She stared at it in disbelief. How on earth did Mrs. Gordon get it? Kyla's brain tried to connect the dots—did Mrs. Gordon also know her dad somehow, like Peter did? How was that possible? Carefully she took it out of the bag to examine it, the floral embossing on the lavender cover and the deeper purple strip along the binding exactly as she remembered it. *How on earth did she get this?* Intentionally she opened the cover, expecting to see her signature scrawled across the upper right edge in her fourteen-year-old handwriting.

There was a name there, but it wasn't hers. *Samantha Gordon*, it said. Kyla let out a breath, her hand over her mouth, marveling at the coincidence. Mrs. Gordon's daughter! *I hope you don't mind that it's not new.* Of course, Kyla realized. But what were the odds of this, she asked herself, gingerly paging through the book, observing the woman's underlining of verses and her handwritten notes in the margin? *What were the odds of this?* She closed the book, again examining the familiar front and back, then, resting her hands on the soft cover, wondered how long it had been since she had looked at her own copy at home.

Feeling slightly lightheaded, she put it back in the bag to take upstairs on her next trip up. Then for the rest of the day she couldn't stop thinking about it resting on the tile end table in her room. It was as if God himself were sitting there, waiting for her.

That night after dinner Kyla ended up in the carport with her father admiring their cars together. He had bought his Mercedes on the same day he'd bought her Mustang, he said. *Who does that?* she asked herself. But he was beaming proud—proud of the cars and proud that she was happy with hers. Apparently his business was doing extraordinarily well.

She offered to help her father bring his things in, but there were only two items, a hard, black leather briefcase with metal protectors on the corners and a fancy combination lock near the handle, and a large black suitcase. So she simply walked with him up the back stairway and down the hall past her own room to his, next to the locked door of the third floor. He was covered in dirt from working outside and was eager to get cleaned up.

"Thanks, baby," he said, his eyes bright.

She gave a little wave and went downstairs. He seemed comfortable calling her that. She was comfortable with nothing yet.

Dr. Grant had taken the boys outside to play with them before their bedtime, and Peter was in his corner of the Great Room with his leg up on his other knee, his head tipped back in his chair. Kyla realized he was asleep. She sat by herself at the peninsula waiting until her father, all showered and fresh, came downstairs and asked her to go for an evening walk. She agreed, but at that moment she heard Dr. Grant calling in through the side entrance door.

"Kyla, where'd you put the kids' bikes?"

She moved down the hall toward the side entryway, calling to him, "They should be in the carport!"

Behind her swiftly came Peter, jarred awake, who slipped though the doorway beside her.

"I got it," he said to her.

Kyla opened her mouth again, but Peter repeated with emphasis, "*I got it!*" and left through the side door. She stared after him, remembering then that the bikes were still on the third floor.

"Shall we?" she asked her father, who joined her in the side room.

"He sure shot out of there quick-like," DeKane said. "I thought he was sleeping."

"Me too," she said.

Kyla asked him if he would like to walk up the driveway around the bluff, and he was game. As soon as they were out of the house, he pulled a cigarette out of his shirt pocket and lit up, drawing deeply on it. Dr. Grant and Peter were already kicking a soccer ball around with the kids on the front lawn as they made their way down the blacktop path. DeKane held his cigarette down by his hip as they passed the crew in the yard.

"Ah, just so you know, Dr. Grant doesn't care for smoking at all. He doesn't want it around the kids," she told him.

"Oh, believe me—your guard dog already made that clear."

She shot him a look. "Guard dog?"

"The younger fellow, what's-his-name."

"Peter Watkins?"

He drew long on the cigarette, releasing in a breath of smoke, "Peter Watkins."

As they rounded the bluff on the pavement path, Wynnbury and those in the yard were now out of sight behind them. The evening was lovely, the thick and lush foliage of the woods alive with squirrels and birds, a beautiful wilderness. Kyla, however, found it hard to relax, unsure of what to talk about with her father. They walked together in silence, and while she tried to think of something to say, she scanned the back side of the bluff, searching for that climbable area to come back to someday.

"Is there something over there?" he asked, observing her looking back.

She gave him a questioning look.

"Did you see something in the woods?"

She shook her head. "No, just looking at the bluff. Something about it just says, 'Climb me'!" She gave a little laugh. "It's straight out my window, and I see it every morning. Some days I imagine myself climbing to the top and finally having decent phone reception!" She laughed again.

He gave a small chuckle in return. "It is a curious place for a house, tucked behind a steep bluff like that. They need their own cell tower here." He looked over at her. "But you would think that up on that third floor the reception should be all right."

"Well," she said, "I've been told that it's good"—she was going to say in the room above Peter's, but at the same second she remembered Dr. Grant's evasive techniques that morning. *There's no reason he needs to know anything about the house*—"out in the yard by the drop-off," she finished smoothly. "You know, by the wooden staircase. That's where I make my calls."

He nodded. "I see. I'll have to remember that. Have you ever been up there?"

"Up where?"

"The third floor."

Kyla quickened her pace slightly. "No." She felt uncomfortable lying, but thought it was probably best.

"Why not?"

She shrugged. "I don't know. They keep it locked."

He glanced over, keeping step with her. "And you're not curious?"

"Why? Should I be?"

He spread his hands out. "Holy cow, this whole place decked out like it is, and they keep an entire floor locked and out of reach—? I for one would be curious!"

"Dr. Grant says it's dusty," she made up without thinking, "and he doesn't want it to get into the rest of the house."

"Dusty?" His forehead puckered. "From what?"

Oh, brother. She was hoping to get off the subject, but now she had made it worse.

"I don't know," she answered. "Because it's old, I guess. I haven't been up there. But I do know they're planning a remodel next summer. Perhaps they've started the demo." There—it was a mix of truth and fabrication consistent with Dr. Grant's cagey spin.

Kyla slowed, then stopped walking, leaning forward, as if catching her breath, though she was breathing just fine. DeKane paused, turning to wait for her. He took one last draw on his cigarette stub and flicked it to the road.

"I'd like you to get me up there," he said boldly.

"What?" She straightened, flipping her hair back behind her shoulders. "Why?"

"Because I want to see it. Why else?"

She brought her hands to her waist. "How would I do that? I don't have the keys."

He smiled, reaching into his breast pocket for another smoke. "Easy! All you have to do is ask. You have those two eating out of your hand, if you haven't noticed." He raised his eyebrows as he held the lighter to the cigarette, then popped it back into his jeans pocket, shrugging. "You just say, 'I would like you to show my daddy and me the third floor,' and watch what happens." He winked at her.

He had a very charismatic way about him, Kyla had to admit, but never in a million years could she see herself calling him her "daddy." She swung her hand to brush away the gnats that had begun to gather around them now that they had stopped moving.

"I don't know." Kyla shook her head. "I mean, I respect Dr. Grant a lot, and if he says something's off limits, then—"

"Oh, come on!" His voice was smooth, charming, and persuasively persistent. "They probably have some amazing art collection or something up there. Think about it. Is the basement locked up? No. Is the dining room locked up? No. Is the game room or theater room, whatever-you-call-it, locked up? No. Everything's open, open, open. Except for the upstairs. Now why is that, do you think? Because it's dusty? Uh-uh. I don't think so." His foot tapped a stone in front of him, which zinged off into the brush.

Kyla blinked. Why indeed, she thought, as she stood with her hand on her hip, pretending to stretch back from the waist. It was confusing even to her, for it had been, as he said, open—until her father arrived. There was absolutely *nothing* up there, and Dr. Grant had had no problem with her going up, so what was the deal? He trusted *her*—why not her father? *Keeping it simple*, Dr. Grant had said. What was that supposed to mean? *Peter*, Kyla thought suddenly. It had to be because of Peter. Peter was suspicious of her father, an attitude no doubt borrowed from her own dad, Kendall.

"It's just—I don't know," she said to him again.

"Well, I'd like you to get me up there. You ask that Grant fellow tomorrow." He smiled and gave her a curt nod.

"I'll see what I can do," she said, turning away from him.

She didn't want to betray Dr. Grant's desire for privacy, but her father's questions had a way of pressuring her. Where would he go next? It was uncomfortable being caught in the middle.

"Ouch," she said suddenly, stepping around gingerly, feigning an injury.

"You all right? What did you do?"

"Um, my foot. It's kind of bothering me. I think maybe we should go back."

He eyed her, puffing on his cigarette. "You can go back. I'm enjoying it out here. If you don't mind, I think I'll go on a little farther. I'll be back after a while."

"Oh, sure. That's okay," she said and left him there on the road, heading back in a careful stride that didn't make it look too obvious that her foot was fine.

No one was in the yard when she arrived back at the house, but the boys' bikes were back in their usual places in the carport. The sun had just set, casting a golden hue on everything. Entering the house, she could hear Dr. Grant chasing the boys upstairs. Peter sat lounging in the professor's study with the door open, waiting for him. He rose when he saw Kyla by the stairs, coming out into the hall.

He looked around, and seeing that she was alone, asked, "Is your father still outside?"

She gave a wry smile. "Smoking. Making up for lost time this morning."

His lip curled up, and he nodded.

"I see you got the bikes," she said. She wondered if she should ask him right then and there about the third floor being locked up. It was a perfect lead-in. Perhaps he would bring it up himself.

"Yeah," he replied simply. "You going out to call your dad?"

She shook her head. "Too tired. I think I'm just going to go to bed."

"Me too," he said, brushing a hand wearily through his hair. "It's been a long day. Grant and I are about to meet, and then I—"

"Another one of your secret huddles?" Kyla leaned in dramatically, unable to help herself.

He cocked his head. "What do you mean by *that*?"

She tossed her hair behind her back. "Well, it seems like the two of you are always meeting behind closed doors like you're planning or conniving something!"

His tired eyes brightened, and he gave a small smile of amusement. "I'm sure if Grant knew you were interested in trench-digging or picking up a load of crushed rock in the morning, he'd let you sit in on our 'secret' meeting. We hope to lay the water line out to the site tomorrow, and we're trying to schedule the delivery of the fountain pieces and other stuff."

She felt a bit foolish. She hadn't thought about that part of what they did. Of course—there was a lot of planning that went into their project. She cleared her throat, trying to save face. "Huh. Well, then, I'm not the only one with false assumptions."

Peter's eyebrows rose. "Yeah?" He folded his arms, leaning his back against the door. "I guess that might be a possibility."

Kyla nodded, challenging him, "I'd say it's a likely possibility! Look at all the progress the three of you made out there today, thanks to my father helping you!"

He tipped his head. "You're right. That we did."

"I think you'll see that my father isn't as bad as you think he is."

Peter's cheek twitched. "I hope so. You may be right."

"Well, you've been very antagonistic toward him."

He looked at her a moment, then nodded. "Yeah, okay. Sorry. I apologize. I owe you."

"Thanks," she said, looking down from his gaze, remembering his nearness in the pantry. She wasn't sure what else to say, so she gestured toward the stairs. "Well, I'm going up."

"Yeah. Good night."

She turned and started up.

"Just for the record," he called after her, "I think it's good that you want to get to know him."

She paused, glancing down. "Thanks. Good night."

"Good night," she heard him reply.

Peter. Kyla couldn't stop thinking about him in her room while she got ready for bed. He was—he was—she struggled to identify what he was like. He was strong. But it wasn't so much that. It was more like he was *powerful*, she thought. But that sounded so lame. It was like he was both— strong and powerful, physically, of course, but more so on the inside. It was the way he carried himself. And then she felt silly—he was just Peter. And why was she even thinking about him?

Your guard dog, Kyla mused. That was probably the most accurate description of what she was trying to describe to herself. Peter was like that—like a guard dog, threatening and bristling around her father. Kyla looked at herself in the mirror while she brushed her teeth. She could see why her father had called him that and wondered if he had seen Peter pull her into the pantry. But that's what he was—a guard dog. Her father had inferred that it was about *her*, but she knew what Peter was like, and Peter was that way for everyone, not just for her. For Dr. Grant and the boys too. All of them. Peter was—he was—he was sort of like an older brother—someone bigger, smarter, protective. Brotherly. And even slightly annoying, although he had been less so lately. Sort of. She was getting used to him. Yes, Peter was like a brother. Both to her and to the boys. Even to Dr. Grant he related more like a brother than an employee.

Kyla had long finished in the bathroom but still stood in front of the mirror reviewing the evening. Her father certainly had some strange observations—that Kyla had Dr. Grant and Peter eating out of her hand! She frowned, trying to think of where that was true, and if so, she wondered if it was a good thing or a bad thing.

Howie suddenly appeared at the bathroom door, squinting into the light, needing his nightly drink. She helped him and then tucked him back into bed, kissing him on the forehead. He smiled at her and hugged her and said good night. Hank was already out, sound asleep.

Back in her room Kyla nestled into her spot on the settee before the fireplace, eyeing the new, old Bible on the end table before her. She felt as if it were eyeing her as well. She lifted it to her lap with mixed feelings, its cover a reminder of such a painful and confusing time in her life. Those were the early days of grief, when it was just the two of them, her dad being new to fatherhood and new to widowerhood, probably doing the best he could, taking her to church with him because that's where he had found comfort in his pain. Those awful early days, when every moment was numb. And then the days flowed like liquid into months and years, and there was never an outlet to communicate what it was like to be without a mother, no language to give voice to her loss, no place for her anger to go, except for the daily aching thought that if she had a mother, then a million other things could have taken place. Kyla brushed away a tear, staring down at the soft embossing.

She saw the progression. Her bitterness toward God had begun with sadness. A sadness that wouldn't go away. And that deep sadness had given birth to the beginning of those millions of *ifs* and the million corresponding *thens,* and all those scenarios had gradually soured in her over time, until bitterness had become a way of life for her, an outlet of anger that was directed toward God. Kyla reached for a tissue and blew her nose, wishing Mrs. Gordon was there to talk to right now. The older woman had helped her so much. Already she was starting to see things more and more clearly.

Now Kyla wanted to ask her how to clean all this anger out of her heart. Was that even possible? She hoped so. She could see where it had started. Did she need to go back there? To start over at the beginning and grieve again a better way? That sounded ridiculous.

Yawning, she shifted in the chair, pulling her feet up under her. For starters, she wanted to list out a hundred wonderful real things she remembered about her mother. *Actual, real things*. But maybe not tonight. She was tired. Perhaps she would ask her dad to send her some pictures of her and her mom together. No, she would like a photo of *all three* of them. Perhaps she would listen to all the video clips her mother had done for her, even repeating those she'd already seen.

Kyla yawned again, looking down at the Bible in her lap. It suddenly hit her that she hadn't even opened it yet. Simply looking at the familiar purple cover of the book had taken her down an emotional path. But reading it—*that*, she realized, would be a different story altogether! That would be a bigger undertaking, truly stepping back in time for a redo, and did she want to go there? It would be like giving God another chance. Kyla frowned considering it. Yet what were the odds that Mrs. Gordon would give her *this particular used Bible*, out of all the used Bibles in the world? She was probably meant to read it. Kyla sat staring at the cover for over five minutes until finally she closed her eyes, flipped the book open to the center, and paged four large chunks of pages to the right. Then she pointed and looked down to the place on the page.

Colossians. She knew it was a book of the Bible, but she didn't know what it referred to or how to pronounce it. The words on which her finger rested were underlined in blue ink, and she read them. *Once you were alienated from God and were enemies in your minds because of your evil behavior. But now he has reconciled you by Christ's physical body through death to present you holy in his sight, without blemish and free from accusation—*

Kyla pondered the verses. *Alienated from God*—she could definitely relate to feeling that way, although she wouldn't necessarily call her behavior *evil*. She knew she had sinned, but was she *evil*? And what did it mean to be reconciled by Christ's physical body? That just sounded strange. Very strange. It must have something to do with Jesus dying on the cross, she figured. And how could she be holy, without blemish, and free from accusation? There was no way she could live up to that. How could *anyone* be free from accusation? It was all so confusing.

Kyla frowned, reading the whole thing again. Well, not much had changed since the last time she read the Bible, she realized. She still had no clue as to what any of it meant. She thought about her dad and Peter, who read the Bible every morning, and wondered what this would mean to them.

As she turned off the lights on her way to bed, Kyla thought about Peter again, wishing there was a way to ask him about how to read the Bible—things like where to start and how to understand it and stuff. He apparently had it figured out. Yet at the same time she was scared to even get near the subject with him. He did have a way of stirring her up, of making her so irritated and angry. As she stretched between the sheets and made herself comfortable, she had an idea—sort of like a coin toss, where the outcome was put into higher hands, but different. Kyla decided that if Hank woke up and crawled in with her that night, she would get up to see if Peter was up praying in the night again. And if he was, then perhaps she would get up early in the morning to see if he was downstairs in his usual place. And if he was again, then perhaps, *perhaps* she would ask him. Perhaps.

Just before midnight Kyla felt tapping on her arm. Hank was at her bedside with his blankie and bear. She helped him in and snuggled him back to sleep. Then, keeping her promise to herself, Kyla crept out to the balcony to check. Sure enough, Peter was there, standing in the darkness with his hands raised, whispering, even singing softly to himself, and pacing quietly in the night. She sat on the top step, watching him through the rails for a while, until sneaking back to bed.

Kyla set her phone alarm to go off early that morning and, with extra care not to disturb Hank, dressed quietly before stealing downstairs alone for breakfast. Predictably, Peter was there nested in his Great Room corner with his Bible, pen, and notebook, looking awake and engaged. Surely he must be very tired, she thought. Kyla bit her lip, wondering if it would be an invasion of his privacy to say something about seeing him up the last two nights. She wondered how many nights he had been up praying before she had discovered him.

"Good morning," Peter said across the room to her. "*You're* up early."

Her eyebrows lifted. "So are *you.*"

The coffee was made and fresh, so she poured a cup and turned to make herself toast. She felt a little nervous, recognizing that she was putting herself out there as bait. The thought occurred to her that perhaps he wanted to be left alone, but it was fleeting, for sure enough, Peter came over to refill his cup, bringing his Bible with him, which he set facedown and opened to save his page. Then he slid into his seat at the peninsula, clearly waiting for her. The great eagle swooping in on the frightened rabbit. She brought her plate to the counter and stood opposite him, not wanting to sit on the same side.

"Thanks for making the coffee," she said to fill the silence, reaching her knife into the jam jar and spreading a thin layer on her toast.

His fingers lifted slightly in reply.

"Don't let me interrupt you," she added, nodding to his Bible, a small brown leather one. "Go ahead—do your thing."

"I'm good," he said quietly, drinking his coffee, watching her eat.

She crunched on her toast, self-conscious at how loud it seemed, abandoning it after a few bites.

She blurted the first thing that came to mind. "So you do this every morning?"

Peter lifted his hand again. "Most days. Sometimes it doesn't happen." He studied her over the rim of his mug.

"Why? What do you get out of it?"

His eyes narrowed and he tilted his head. "Are you okay?"

Kyla shrugged. "I'm fine. Why do you ask?"

He leaned to the side in his chair, watching her. "You're just, I don't know, up really early, and seem sort of—tense. Don't you want to sit down?" He waved his hand to a chair.

"No, I'm all right," she answered.

He nodded, fingering the handle of his cup. After a while he asked, "Any big plans for the day with the kids?"

"Not really," she said. "You?"

He looked up at her, his forehead wrinkled. "I'll be working on the foun—"

"Fountain, of course," she said. "Will you finish it today?"

"I doubt it, but we'll see how far we get."

Kyla took a deep breath. He was right. She *was* tense. Perhaps she should abandon the whole idea. He seemed to be content just sitting there, leaning peacefully on the counter with his tan arms. She took a smaller bite of toast, debating whether to stay or go, stay or go. She decided to plunge ahead anyway.

"So what are you reading about?" she asked. There. She had taken the step into unfamiliar territory. Then she turned back to her coffee, as if she didn't care too much.

He said nothing at first but only looked at her. Then slowly he turned his Bible over, pulling it nearer to him.

"About the love of God," he said.

"Ah," Kyla said, looking down at his Bible.

Peter glanced down at the open page before him. "Specifically, the apostle Paul praying that people could truly understand how wide and long and high and deep the love of Christ is, and to experientially know this love." He looked back up at her. "Love that surpasses knowledge. Beyond what we can even understand."

Kyla had the distinct feeling she had just placed her own foot firmly in a snare. She could feel her pulse quicken. She set her cup down onto the granite countertop. "And you know what he's talking about?"

Peter gave a short laugh. "Well, I know what he's talking about, but I can't say that I have fully experienced it. I've had a taste of it, though. Enough to make me want to pursue it."

"To pursue what?"

"To pursue knowing the love of Christ." He pushed the Bible slightly away with his arm. "It's my life goal."

She laughed out loud. "Your life goal? Seriously, I think you need to lift your sights a little higher!"

Peter simply smiled.

Kyla turned back to her toast.

He sat quietly, leaning his arms on the counter, tapping his thumbs lightly. "Mind if I ask you something?" he asked finally.

"What's that?" she replied.

"Have you ever felt close to God?" He folded his arms in front of him. "Like, *really* felt his love for you?"

Kyla pursed her lips. *Was this a trick question?* she wondered—one of those questions that led to another question, and then to another, and then all of a sudden she would be dying uncomfortable, wishing she had stopped while she was ahead? Would he corner her? She could feel the anxiety moving in. She frowned. "Didn't you just ask me this a few days ago? Or something similar?"

He shook his head. "I don't think so."

"Huh." It was Mrs. Gordon, Kyla realized. She looked down at her coffee, debating whether to deflect the question with a smart remark or to answer him. Peter seemed unhurried, waiting for her. Again she decided to take a chance. "Well, in all honesty, no, I can't say that I ever have."

Peter was silent at her answer, expressionless.

"I've never felt close to God," she said, "or felt his love, as you say. I don't know if it's even possible. For me."

His head tipped to the side. "Of course, it's possible!" He paused a moment, watching her, then shifted in his seat, folding his hands in his lap. "God loves you, Kyla! He knows exactly who you are, and he has loved you since the day you were born!"

Kyla said nothing. She had walked into this herself, and now, like she anticipated, she was unable to back up. This is not what she intended would happen when she had the idea last night. She was simply going to ask him how to read the Bible and get something out of it, and instead had invited a stream of words now flowing out of Peter, words that seemed so foreign to her, words that made her want to cry.

He was leaning forward, speaking eagerly. "Do you know how amazing our earth is—how all our ecosystems are intertwined and work together? And our solar system—it's so complex! It's incredible how our planet is situated just the perfect distance from the sun to sustain life on earth. And look at our bodies! The way the human body works is mind boggling! The same God of the universe who created all those things made *you*! And he knows you intimately—all of who you are, all the thoughts of your heart and dreams for your life, every heartache and disappointment you've ever had, every question you've ever asked. And his love is so much greater than the love of people—he's much more patient, much more kind. He's not selfish, and he loves you perfectly, more deeply than you can imagine! He longs for you to know him—to be his friend, like *he* wants to be *your* friend!"

His words blurred together, making Kyla think of a river or a waterfall. She tried hard to hold herself together, looking down at her toast, which lay untouched on her plate.

"That coffee mug—" He pointed to the mug beside Kyla's plate. "How much do you think Grant paid for that?"

Kyla raised her shoulders, confused at what he was asking.

"He probably bought it for, say, fifteen bucks—it's a nice one." He gave it an appreciative glance. "If you tried to sell it to me, I'd offer you about three. Maybe five." He paused. "But if I offered you a thousand dollars for it, you would look at it differently and wonder why. You would suspect I knew something about its value that you didn't know."

She frowned. "What are you saying?"

Peter opened his hand. "I'm saying that you have no idea how valuable you are to God! The price he paid for you was extravagant! He loved you so much that he gave the most precious thing he had—his only son, Jesus—to pay the penalty for your sins. He took the punishment we deserved. Jesus gave his own life as a sacrifice for you, dying on a cross for your sin. His love cost him his life!"

He stopped talking, and the two of them were silent for a moment. She didn't trust herself to say anything. The cap on her heart was suddenly loosened, like when her dad would open the pickle jar that she couldn't open herself, and he would twist it and pop—it opened right up, always sloshing juice down the side of the jar. Right now her confusing emotions wanted to spill over, and it frightened her. Her throat was tight. *Don't cry*, she told herself. *Do not cry!*

"What's going on? What are you thinking?" Peter asked, studying her.

"Noth—" Her voice caught. "Nothing."

He paused, rubbing his chin thoughtfully. Finally he spoke. "Here's the deal, Kyla. God gave his everything to bring you to him, but to come to God we must come on *his* terms, not our own."

She shook her head. "I—I think we should stop talking about this." There always came a point where she couldn't take talking about God anymore.

His face, she thought, his face was so eager, so sincere, and she was so far, far, far away from what he was like. Kyla could feel the panic rise in her, like steam at the corners of her mind, building pressure and wanting out. She closed her eyes, fighting her habitual angry response—to snap at him, to hurt him, like a trapped animal that only knew to snarl and bite. She held up her hand, determined that she would not blast him.

"He won't reject you, Kyla."

"No, just stop!" she repeated. "I can't—I can't talk about this now!"

"Okay. Why not? What's wrong?"

"I just—can't." Her hands were shaking.

His eyes rested on her face, waiting.

"Look," she continued in a hushed tone, "you talk about God and his love—that's all fine for you! The way I see it, I have *never* been loved! I don't even know what love is! All I've ever known for my whole life is people leaving me. And people pitying me. So I'm sorry, but I have a very hard time with talks like this. They're just—just painful! It's another reminder of how pathetic my life is. It's like rubbing salt in a wound—"

Peter's mouth opened, and he reached across the counter toward her. "Whoa, hey. I didn't mean—"

"Good morning, fine people!" came Dr. Grant's cheerful voice as he entered the room.

Kyla jumped. Peter leaned back suddenly too, neither of them having heard him approach.

"You two are up early," he said, moving toward the coffee pot. He looked between the two of them, adding, "I hope I'm not interrupting anything—?"

Kyla took a deep breath. "Good morning," she said. "Nope, I was finishing up my breakfast and going upstairs." She dumped her toast into the trash and put her plate and mug into the sink, then turned to go.

Dr. Grant turned to Peter, who was looking downward, shaking his head.

Chapter Twenty-One

What is happening to me? Kyla asked herself, running up the stairs to her bedroom. It was like every time she turned around, God was right there in her face—almost like he was pursuing her and she couldn't get away from him! As she neared her door, her shoulders fell as she realized the boys were still asleep inside. She closed her eyes. Where could she go? She wanted to—*needed* to—be alone to yell or cry or something. Her mind was like a shaken can of soda ready to blow. Downstairs the tones of the men's voices carried through the house, and she didn't want them to hear her. Nor did she want to hear them talk right now either. She just wanted to be alone. Without thinking, Kyla turned to the long hall of unused guest rooms and picked the one beside her room, immediately dropping to the center of the floor in a flood of tears. She held her shirt over her face to muffle the sound as much as she could.

She had not seen that coming this morning, nor could she understand it. She wasn't even sure exactly what all he said. All she knew is that Peter's words had felt like electricity, painful and alive, and she couldn't keep from crying. How could she be of that much value to God? How could that possibly be true when he had allowed such pain in her life? How could a loving God do that? Why would God be so against her if he loved her?

What is happening to me? Here she was, an adult—an adult!—having one emotional crisis after another! Her life was in an upheaval, and it wouldn't stop! Everything just seemed to stir her up more inside—the conversations she'd had with Mrs. Gordon, receiving the "coincidental" Bible yesterday, the conversation with Peter that morning, dealing with her biological father and his embarrassing behavior—everything! Ever since, ever since—Kyla tried thinking back to when everything started. Ever since she had come to Wynnbury. No, she realized, even before that. Ever since Alex had been a jerk to her. It was because of him that she was working here. Because of him she had talked to Mrs. Gordon, because of him—Kyla made a little sound. *Everything* was because of her breakup with him, and she didn't even want him anymore! It was like breaking up with Alex had snipped a thread in her life, and it wouldn't stop unraveling!

After a time she collected herself and took a deep breath. Sitting up cross-legged, she leaned against the side of the bed looking around at another stunning room decorated by Ms. Marilee. English roses were the theme, as evidenced by the lovely floral quilt hanging down off the bed. The walls were papered with a striking ivory linen texture, which made the soft pink upholstery of the furniture look so rich. On an antique dressing table sat an old-fashioned porcelain pitcher and basin, beside which was a photo of a mother and daughter—certainly Marilee Montayne and her mother. Rubbing her fingers absently through the plush rug, her default thinking automatically kicked in: *If I had a mother I would ask her if it would be possible to be connected to God, to know his love.* Then the jarring realization followed that her very own mother had left her a video about God. Why, oh why, oh why was it so difficult for her to just watch it? Probably the same reason she couldn't listen to Peter! Something in her just shut down or shut off. She had barriers against God.

Kyla heard a thump on the floor next door. Hank was up. She was glad. Crying was hard work, and she was ready to move on. She wanted to change her shirt, to wash her face, to go get another cup of coffee and start the day over, hopefully without Peter nearby. She was too embarrassed to face him right now.

There wasn't any particular reason that she opened the door of the guest room so very quietly to let herself out—habit, maybe, as she was accustomed to doing so in her bedroom when the boys were asleep there—but she did, and when she looked up, she was surprised to see her father down the hallway near his room. She was about to greet him for the morning, but right at that moment she saw him bend down to peer closely at the lock of the third-floor door. Kyla paused. He hadn't noticed her yet, so she continued watching him as he cocked his head at odd angles carefully examining first one side and then the other of the latch. She frowned. She had hoped that he would have forgotten about the upper floor since he had pressed her to ask the professor, but it was clear that it was still very much on his mind. She knew he would eventually notice her, so she spoke up.

"What are you doing?"

He straightened up quickly, his face breaking into a smile. "Hey! Morning, baby!"

Kyla cringed. She did not like him calling her that. "Good morning. What are you doing?" she repeated.

He had on the same soiled work pants from yesterday, but with a clean T-shirt. He passed a hand through his hair, gesturing to the lock. "Someone's been up there since yesterday."

Kyla moved her hand to rest on the lever of her bedroom door. Indeed. It would have been Peter. Getting the bikes. Her eyes narrowed. "How do you know that?"

He walked toward her, giving her a wink. "Oh, I know! It's not that hard to tell."

"Da—" She had almost said "Dad." She still hadn't figured out what to call him, but for sure it wouldn't be that! "Um, this isn't your house," she stated, "so it's none of your business if someone's been up there!"

He paused beside her, his lips curling into a smile. "Hey, chill out, baby! I was waiting for you to get up, so I was just killing time in the hallway." He lowered his voice. "But I'll tell you—I think this house has some secrets! We need to talk!"

She sidled back against the door. "I'm the nanny here. That's my job. That's what I'm paid to do. You're—you're a guest. A guest!"

He made the little sound with his teeth. "Ah, now, don't you worry your pretty little head!" He gave another wink. "Shall we go down for breakfast? I'm hungry, and I was looking forward to spending time with you this morning."

She hesitated. "Um, I need to get the kids." She gestured toward her room. "They're just getting up."

His head lifted in a nod. "Oh. All right. I can wait." He folded his arms, looking out over the balcony.

Kyla shook her head. "No, no, that's okay. You go ahead. I'll meet you in a bit."

"Okay," he said. "If you don't mind, I think I'll just poke around and try to find something to eat."

This is my father, Kyla thought, watching him start down the stairs. That man was irrevocably connected to her. She stared at the turn in the stairwell where he had disappeared. There was no choice in the matter. She had to figure this out. It was still hard for her to wrap her mind around the fact that he was staying there! She gave an inward sigh and turned to push open her door.

Hank wasn't in her room, but his bear was still on her bed. Kyla went to check if he had gone back to his own room, but when she passed the bathroom, there he was, sitting on his knees in his little pajamas on the rug in front of the sink, with every drawer and vanity door wide open. All around him the floor was littered with washcloths and soap, hair product containers, hairpins, body lotion bottles, rolls of toilet paper—every item that had been in the vanity was now on the floor of the bathroom.

"Hank!" Kyla said in surprise.

He jumped, dumping a box of tampons.

"I'm working!" he announced happily.

"I see that!" Kyla replied. "And it looks like I'll be working with you for a little while!"

The patter of little feet sounded in the next room, as Howie jumped out of bed and threw back the door to see what was going on. He began giggling crazily. Soon all three of them were laughing.

"All right, fellas," she told them. "Let's clean up this mess and go down for some pancakes."

At the mention of pancakes the workers were suddenly too hungry to concentrate. Kyla abandoned the mess until later. Plus, it was probably better to feed her father than to have him foraging around in the kitchen for food by himself. He had said he was looking forward to spending time with her. She wondered if her second breakfast that day would be more or less uncomfortable than her first one with Peter.

That day the men worked outside again, her father a willing part of the fountain installation crew. This left Kyla back to her regular job with the two kids for the day and no father to entertain. She had to admit she was relieved that he was busy. And yes, she knew her attitude toward him was rather negative, but she was trying to work on that. Dr. Grant had checked in with her privately right before the guys went outside to ask her how it was going, encouraging her that sometimes chemistry in relationships took some figuring out. *No kidding*, she mused. Ironically, her father had also checked in with her before they went outside too, right after Dr. Grant. He reminded her that he wanted to see the third floor, however she was able to make that happen. She told him she would see what she could do.

Since the weather was perfect, she took the little ones down to the waterfront for the entire morning, again slathering them thoroughly with sunscreen before they even left the house and tossing the tube in her bag for later. And also this time she took plenty of water and plenty of food with her to see them through until lunchtime. She halfway expected Peter to show up, but he didn't. No doubt all the men were very busy with the yard project.

At lunchtime she spread a little blanket out under the tree, and they picnicked on fruit and cracker sandwiches made from little cheese and meat squares. In her imagination she had pictured Hank becoming sleepy afterward and taking a long outdoor nap, but just the opposite happened. Instead, the two brothers ended up embroiled in a competition of flicking sand onto each other, which, of course, escalated into throwing sand—to the point that Kyla raised her voice to declare that it was time to pack everything up and go.

They took the long way up to the house by way of the trail. Kyla let the boys meander as much as they wanted, carrying the beach bags at a snail's pace while they stopped to pet toads and look at pretty rocks and shoot their pretend stick guns at squirrels. When they made it up to the side yard, she could see Dr. Grant and her father in the back with shovels. Howie wanted to go help them, and Kyla conceded. There didn't appear to be any dangerous equipment running nearby, and the boys hadn't seen their father yet that day.

"Probably good timing," Dr. Grant said to her, setting his shovel aside. "We got the conduit buried this morning, and we're kind of killing time until Peter gets back from town. They can hang out with me for a while. You go on."

Kyla went up to change into a cooler shirt, then stayed to tackle the mess in the bathroom, reorganizing the drawers as she put things away. Every now and then she would step out onto the balcony and peer outside the Great Room windows, making sure Dr. Grant wasn't waiting for her, but she could still see him with the boys out on the wooden platform overlooking the river. Peter wasn't back yet, and her father was out of sight.

After she had finished reorganizing the bathroom, Kyla went downstairs to hang out in the Great Room and rest until she was needed. She lingered near Peter's corner, reminded of her dad's study at home and how similarly Peter kept his Bible and notebook on the end table as her dad did his. As she sat, her mind replayed their conversation in the kitchen that morning. She had asked Peter what he had been reading, which is what had started their conversation. He had said something about God's love being high and deep—or something like that—but he had not read her the actual verses. Eyeing his Bible, she wondered if she read it for herself whether she would be able to understand more about it. She was curious to know at least. Dare she?

Glancing around her, Kyla stood and stepped over to Peter's chair to take the book in her hands. Something like this hardly qualified as being nosy, she told herself, holding it loosely by the binding to let it fall open at its bookmark, knowing it was the most natural way to find where someone had last read. As she looked down, a quiet exclamation left her throat as she observed the small card holding his place. Her father's business card! *RDK Investments.* Instinctively Kyla glanced over to where she had put it on the other end table when he had given it to her the other day, but it was gone. She pursed her lips. Peter. Why did he have her father's card tucked in his Bible? What was he doing with it? It was hardly an accident, as it was obvious what it was. Of course, he would know it had been given to her. How could he not? When he came in she would ask—

Behind her from near the stairs Kyla heard a small noise. *Oh, geez! Peter was coming in!* She hadn't realized he was back! Hastily she closed the Bible and slid it back to where it had been on his notebook, then whirled around guiltily to face him before he entered the room.

She stared in surprise. It wasn't Peter. It was her father. And he was out in the hallway, unaware of her presence, bent over, quietly examining the lock on Dr. Grant's office doors. She stood with her mouth wide open. What on earth—? Was he trying to break in? Suddenly he glanced around and, observing her across the Great Room, rose to face her.

"Ah, there you are!" he said.

Kyla brought her hands to her hips, asking with irritation, "What are you doing?"

He backed a step. "Heck—you startled me!" he said. "I was trying to find you—"

"Were you trying to break into Dr. Grant's office?" she asked directly.

He drew his head back. "What? Break in?" He gave a confused glance at the door and back to her. "I was looking for that fascinating little library! Is this his office?"

She stared at him.

He spread his hands. "We were taking a break, and I was trying to find you. I thought maybe you were lying down in the library or something. I was seeing if there was a crack I could peek through and not wake you by opening these doors." He gestured.

"That's his office."

He glanced at the door again with a sheepish look on his face. "Oh. I got turned around, I guess." He sniffed. "Well, where were you? I called for you a couple of times."

Chapter Twenty-One

Kyla blinked. "It looks like you're snooping around the house!"

"What?" His brow furled. *"Snooping?"*

Inwardly she rolled her eyes. "Well, that's twice I've seen you with your nose in a keyhole!"

He raised his hands innocently. "Hey, now! That blond kid runs to town for the stuff we need, and we finally get a break! I figured I'd go find the one I'm here for! Didn't you hear me? I was calling your name!"

Kyla regarded him carefully. Was he telling the truth? She supposed it was possible he had called for her while she was upstairs in the bathroom cleaning up Hank's mess, but still, it seemed so weird. "Okay," she said finally. "Well, what did you want me for?"

DeKane let out a heavy sigh, shaking his head. "Nothing. I didn't want anything. Just to hang out is all." He looked past her through the window. "But it doesn't really matter at this point. I think you're about to go on duty again."

Was he disappointed? Kyla glanced closely at his face. It almost looked like he was disappointed. Defeated. She turned to look outside. He was right. Holding Hank's hand, Dr. Grant was topping the patio steps, with Howie bouncing up them on his other side. DeKane made his way through the Great Room toward the sliding doors, and Kyla followed too, feeling a tiny bit bad. Perhaps she had misjudged him.

"Okay, I'm—I'm sorry I didn't hear you," she said to his back.

He turned, giving her a small smile. "That's all right, baby. Maybe we can spend some time together tonight—like after dinner or something."

She nodded. "Yeah, I'm good with that."

"And look, Kyla—" He reached up to scratch his ear. "I don't want to cause any problems for you with your job and all, so for your sake, I think it's best if we keep my blunder between the two of us." He gave her a playful wink and pulled open the door for her.

"Here we are!" Dr. Grant said cheerfully, handing off Hank to Kyla. He reached up to rub the back of his arm over his perspiring forehead. "Whew—it's warming up out here! Peter's back now, and we're going to prep the site and get that baby level!"

Kyla watched her father and Dr. Grant cross the yard to pull the shovels aside from the area where they had been working. She wondered how it was for the three of them to work together and hoped her father was actually helpful and not a nuisance. Both Dr. Grant and he stood side by side facing the same direction, and without looking, Kyla knew that they were waiting for Peter. She could hear the idle of a diesel engine from somewhere near the front of the house. The kids, too, anxiously watched for the truck to come around to the back yard, but it was taking a while. Kyla dragged two chairs over to the concrete railing for them to stand on so they could see over. They both happily climbed up, leaning their arms on the white concrete surface, when finally from around the side of the house they heard the engine rev. Just as the truck came around the side of the house, however, Hank slipped off the front of the chair, bumping his chin on the railing and biting his tongue—not horribly, but enough to bleed a little and make him cry a lot. Kyla lifted his little body out from where he was stuck between the chair and the rail and carried him toward the house.

"Can I stay out here?" Howie called to her.

She pointed her finger at him. "If you promise to stay right there on that chair and not go anywhere else!"

"Okay," he said.

With wide eyes he watched the large flatbed truck backing in through the side yard, beeping noisily as it approached. Attached to the bed by chains were large concrete pieces and a squatty metal container near the rear. A crane jutted out near the cab.

Kyla swooped up crying Hank and took him in to get him a frozen juice bar for his tongue. As she stepped into the house from the patio, she was met with the heavenly aroma of coffee. Alone on the peninsula was one large coffee from a coffee shop sitting on a napkin with her name scrawled on it. She stopped short, staring at it in surprise for a moment before a smile spread across her face. *Well, for once Peter Watkins had done good!*

Hurriedly she got Hank his juice pop, easing him down onto the edge of the peninsula and keeping him close to her while she removed the plastic wrapper. At first he was unhappy and reluctant to try it, but when she finally convinced him to hold the stick and put the icy treat into his mouth, he calmed down quickly. With a tissue Kyla wiped his tears and the drool from his chin and helped him blow his nose. At last, when the little boy was content, she reached over to try the coffee, which was not her usual order, but it was hot, sweet, and wonderful. She closed her eyes, savoring it. It was really nice of Peter to get it for her. Really nice. She slid Hank to the other side of the counter, where they could watch him in the truck unloading crushed rock onto a pile near the fountain site, the two other men leaning on their shovels nearby. One thing that was clear to her was that Peter hadn't gone through the drive-thru with that truck to get this order.

Howie suddenly appeared at the door, complaining that the truck was too loud. He spied Hank's frozen pop. "Hey! How come he gets one of those? Can I have one too?"

Kyla got one for him.

"And can I sit up there too?"

Kyla sighed. Neither kid should be up there, but it was kind of hard to explain that to Howie with his brother enjoying the privilege. "Okay, just for a bit," she told him and lifted him to sit on the edge of the peninsula.

He eyed her drink. "What do you have? Where'd you get that?"

"It's a special coffee treat. Peter brought it for me."

"Why?"

"I'm not sure. Maybe because—" she hesitated, not really knowing how to answer him. Because he said he owed her?

"Because he's nice?" Howie asked.

"Yeah," she replied, "because he's nice."

He nodded. "Yeah, I like Peter!" He squinted and pointed to the cup. "What does that say?"

"What does *what* say?" Kyla held it out, suddenly noticing there was permanent marker in Peter's handwriting atop the printed design on the cup.

"There's writing on it!"

"I see that." She moved the sleeve and turned the cup to read it. *Yes, you have—you just didn't know it,* it said. She swallowed, knowing exactly what it was referring to. On the opposite side of the cup she read, *Ask him, and he will show you.*

"What does it say?" Howie repeated.

"It just says some nice things," Kyla answered, her cheeks growing warm. She had let Peter see her heart, and she felt vulnerable and embarrassed.

"What nice things?" he insisted, his lips and tongue orange as he slurped his frozen pop.

"It says, 'I hope you have a really great day,'" she told him.

Howie nodded. "That's a nice thing to say. Maybe you and me and Hank could do an art project today and write that on it for my dad."

Kyla smiled. "Maybe."

Hank suddenly shivered from his cold juice bar. His tongue apparently felt better, but his mouth was purple, and his belly was soggy with grape juice dripping down his chin and arm. She dabbed him off, hoping his shirt wouldn't be ruined, as it was a cute one, one of Kyla's favorites. It was too bad his mother was missing out on seeing him in it.

She sipped her coffee slowly, noting the time on the clock above the sink. The day had been an odd one, but surprisingly, compared to how it had started, it was going pretty well. The coffee gesture had been thoughtful. Her eyes followed Peter, who now had the door of the truck cab open and was hanging partially out, shouting directions back to her father and Dr. Grant, who stood near the rear of the vehicle with their shovels. Peter. She was learning that he wasn't so totally weird. He could be really nice. He was mostly just very religious. And obsessed with her dad. Obsessed with her birth father too, for that matter. She cupped the warm coffee, absently inhaling the aroma, thinking about the business card in his Bible. Certainly Peter would have had a fit if he had seen her father poking around Dr. Grant's office, even if he knew he had mistaken it for the library!

Her gaze flicked to her father, who was at the moment signaling to Peter to pull forward. Slowly she shook her head. So far they hadn't had one conversation together that had actually gone well, but it appeared that he was trying. Maybe. Apparently he had wanted to be with her and had come looking for her. And he had actually looked disappointed that it hadn't worked out. That was something—if indeed he was sincere. So maybe Dr. Grant was right. Maybe they would break through the awkwardness in their relationship after all. It was just—hard. He always seemed to be doing strange things that made her feel uncomfortable—which reminded her of his curiosity with the third floor. She sighed. It might be a nice gesture on her part to talk to Dr. Grant about it. It might show her father that she was trying too. Perhaps Dr. Grant would take him up there if Peter didn't know about it.

She asked him before dinner, right after he had finished talking with his wife in his study. The boys were running out to their places at the table on the patio, where Peter and her father waited, and Kyla was alone with Dr. Grant in the kitchen.

He frowned at her. "He wants *what*?"

"He would like to see the third floor. He asked me to ask you to take him up there."

"No," he said briefly, "I don't think that's a good idea." Then he also went out onto the patio, leaving her to carry dinner out all by herself.

For a moment she felt insulted. Yet what could she say or do? This was his house. And judging by Dr. Grant's reaction to her request, maybe her father's advice was right to leave unmentioned his mistaking Dr. Grant's office for the library.

The men were in a celebratory mood over dinner that night, discussing animatedly together the next steps necessary to complete the project in the yard. Kyla sat quietly and listened, still a little piqued at Dr. Grant's rebuff. The more she thought about it, the more it bugged her—after all, what could her father get into up there? The rooms were empty! When she had an opportunity she thanked Peter for the coffee he had brought her, and he seemed pleased that she liked it. Nothing was said about their talk that morning or the note on the cup. Overhearing their conversation, Dr. Grant drew back in his chair, dramatically declaring that he was no longer king of his own castle and that the servants were now enjoying greater privileges than he was. Kyla's father simply raised his eyebrows and held out his palm when Dr. Grant and Peter weren't looking. She bit her lip and looked away.

As they were nearly finished with their meal, Howie spilled his glass of milk onto his lap, the sudden icy wetness making him quite upset. While Kyla ran to the kitchen to get a towel, Dr. Grant stripped off his son's wet shirt and pants, but then he cried even harder, ashamed to be standing in front of everyone in milk-soaked underwear.

"I'll take them up now," Kyla said, pulling Hank out of his booster seat. "We were going to have baths tonight anyway." She glanced at her father, hoping he would understand if their time together was delayed.

"Thank you, Kyla," Dr. Grant said. "You're a gem." He seated himself again and turned to her father. "DeKane, what do you say we try that brandy you've been talking up all day?"

"Yeah? I'm game! I'll go get it," her father answered, rising from his chair. "Did I tell you it's imported?"

He opened the patio door for Kyla and the kids and waved them through ahead of him.

"I'll be busy for a little while with the kids," she told him, "but I'll be down later."

"Yeah, yeah—no problem," he said, following her to the stairs. "The professor and I are going to sit and chat. We'll be occupied for a little while."

The boys' routine that evening felt like it was in slow motion. The baths took longer than usual, and afterward Howie couldn't find the specific pajamas he wanted to wear to bed, and no other pair would do. Then his stuffed monkey got wet on the bathroom floor, and finding another stuffed animal to replace it was not an easy task. One book apiece was not enough to read that night, nor was one drink of water for each of them sufficient after they were put to bed. After the last time Kyla turned their lights off, she had to change her shirt. It had gotten soaked during their baths.

When she finally got downstairs, she poked her head out the door, discovering that her father and Dr. Grant had not moved from the table on the patio, on which now sat two glasses and two bottles of booze.

"Hold that thought," the professor said to her father, twisting to look at Kyla with eyebrows raised. "Yes? Did you need something?" His eyes were bright, as if he were very happy—or as if he were perhaps feeling the effects of their drinks.

She hesitated. They were obviously in the middle of a conversation. "Um, I can come back later."

"That'd be nice, baby," her father said, reaching for his glass.

"Sorry," Dr. Grant said. "Your father is telling me about some of his adventures."

Kyla shrugged. "No problem. I'll—come back." *Right,* she thought flippantly, *because I wouldn't want to be included in hearing about any of his adventures.*

As she was about to close the door, her father called over his shoulder. "Hey, baby—"

She paused.

"Would you mind terribly if we moved our talk to the morning? We'll both be more rested."

She blinked. *More rested?* "Yeah." She gave a stiff smile. "Yeah, I could do that."

Right. She should have expected it, she thought, tromping up the stairs again to her room. Her father had initiated a time to chat and then had blown her off. She slumped down on the settee and put her feet up onto the tile table. *More rested?* Totally lame! Well, it was easy to see how important it was to him to spend time with her!

She sniffed, eyeing the Bible on the table, which seemed to be begging her to open it. Sometimes it felt like it was alive! She wondered if she could find the verses that Peter had read that morning. For a bit she debated searching but changed her mind, busying herself with straightening her room and putting away clothes. *Maybe later,* she told herself. At the moment it would be too hard to concentrate with how irritated she was with her father.

Later while cleaning she noticed on her phone that her dad had called her four times in the last two days, the most recent call earlier that evening. She sighed. She had been putting off calling him because she knew how the conversation would go. She could hear his voice in her head. He was going to be very unhappy to hear that her biological father, Robert DeKane, was there. Very unhappy. Slipping on her sandals, she grabbed her phone and decided to go get it over with. Besides, given that her birth father had bumped their time together, it might make her feel better to talk to her dad. She hoped so.

As she returned downstairs again, this time Kyla was surprised to find Peter in his corner of the Great Room reading. He was freshly showered and in athletic shorts. As she approached the dining room, he rose and came to join her beside the table. A pang of anxiety hit her as she remembered handling his Bible. She hoped he hadn't noticed it had been disturbed. And she hoped he wasn't moving in to start a "part two" of their morning conversation.

"What are you doing here this time of night?" she asked lightly. "You typically disappear after dinner."

He smiled. "Just hanging out."

"Ah." She lifted her head in acknowledgment, reaching for the patio door. *Just keep moving,* she told herself. "Well, enjoy your evening."

His long arm swiftly reached over to rest on the latch. "I don't think you should go out there."

She looked at him in surprise. "I'm calling my dad."

"Yeah, I know. But you shouldn't go out there right now."

Kyla made a small sound of protest. "What do you mean? Why not?"

Peter shifted his feet, shaking his head. "You just—don't want to go out there—right now."

He could be so annoying. "Okay. What's going on?"

Peter moved again, blocking the door, reluctant to say. Kyla looked at him, then peered past him to the lighted patio where she could hear her father and Dr. Grant laughing, their table cluttered with more bottles.

She tossed her hair back, looking up at him. "They're drinking. Is that it?"

"They've been at it since dinner."

"I know that, Peter."

"But they're—" He stopped.

She blinked. "Drunk? Seriously? Is that what you're trying to say? You could just say it—'they're drunk'!"

He scowled. "Can you just give them some space and use the door in the fitness room?"

Kyla rolled her eyes. "Oh, for heaven's sake, Peter! It's not like I haven't been to my share of parties!"

He folded his arms, his expression cross. "It's not that. Dang, are you stubborn!"

"Dang, are you bossy!" she flung back at him. "Why do you think you can tell everybody what to do around here?"

His eyes narrowed, and she returned his stare.

"Fine!" Peter replied, throwing up his hands and walking away. "Do what you want. I just think there are some things you don't need to see about people." He gave a wave as he left the room. "Good night."

Kyla stood on the edge of the rug, feeling both guilty and disappointed that he left. At the same time her jaw was tight with irritation. Oh, did he bug her sometimes! He was like the life police—always right, always good, always—! She huffed in frustration and pulled back the patio door.

Regret hit her before she was even off the deck. Robert DeKane, her father, was obnoxiously drunk and was droning on in a loud and slurred monologue in the direction of Dr. Grant, who sat opposite him across the table. At the sound of the door he turned in his chair to see Kyla come out, who acknowledged the men and voiced her intention to call her dad. As she crossed the deck to the stairs, her father's voice grew more animated as his subject changed to her. However, what was intended as accolades and flattery came out as an embarrassing jumble of anatomical descriptions pouring from his mouth. With her jaw hanging open, she looked back at him from the top step, while Dr. Grant, also inebriated but a bit more in control of himself, waved at her to go on. Her father raised a half-filled glass in her direction, a broad, toothy smile covering his face.

"Here's to you, baby!"

"I think you've had enough of that," she told him tartly.

Dr. Grant waved again, and this time she left, cutting a wide swath around the dirty ruts in the yard on her way to the wooden staircase, but even there she could still hear the drone of her father's voice from across the yard. It both perturbed and embarrassed her. How could Dr. Grant sit there with that? Yet *his* glass was filled with whatever they were drinking too. She had not seen him like that before. She fingered her phone, wondering if she could even talk to her dad with the two of them there on the patio within sight. Kyla opted for a text, telling him that she loved him and would call him soon. Then she cut through the side yard to the door by the carport, taking the back stairs up to her room. Yes, she was learning more and more about her father. And she was discovering other things too. Certainly that patio scene had knocked her admiration of Dr. Grant down a few notches.

308

All night Kyla tossed and turned, so disturbed by her father that she could hardly sleep. In the morning she determined that she would ask him to leave. She didn't care about building a relationship with him anymore. She was done, *so done* with him! There were just too many things that made her uncomfortable about his staying there, and his behavior last night was the last straw. *You know, this is just not working out,* she wanted to say to him. *Why don't you leave me your phone number and address, and we'll try this in another seventeen years.*

She didn't really mean that, of course, but she *thought* it, then rehearsed nicer ways to say pretty much the same thing, but with less of a time gap. Maybe just two years. Possibly one. Granted, it was nice that he had helped with the yard project while staying with them. But that wasn't the goal of his staying there. Kyla knew what she had to do. And hopefully she would be able to talk with Dr. Grant about it too—without Peter nearby. No doubt she would have plenty of time this morning before her father was out of bed! Peter would be off to church soon, and she would grab Dr. Grant after he left.

Two mornings in a row now Kyla was able to sneak out of bed and get dressed without waking Hank. Stepping out onto the balcony, she realized she had just missed running into Dr. Grant in the hall, for she could hear him on his way down the stairs nearest his room, his voice booming tiredly at the bottom.

"Good Lord, Watkins—pull those blinds!"

Kyla heard Peter answer, his words indistinguishable.

There was a shuffling sound below, and Dr. Grant's voice continued: "Cripes—I haven't had a hangover since—heck, I can't even think to figure out when! Tell me that coffee is for me, please! No kidding! Peter Watkins, my man, you are worth your weight in gold! Thank you!" There was a short pause. "Okay, I'm here—let's talk, let's talk! Sorry to have made you wait."

"Well, you wanted to mark where I've been digging—"

Peter's words faded as Kyla heard the rumble of the door being pulled shut. Annoyed, she rolled her eyes. What was it with those two? Always a private meeting! Shaking her head, she started down toward the kitchen. No one was even up to disturb them—why the closed doors? However, when she reached the foot of the stairs, she realized they weren't entirely closed, only partially this time, and the men's voices carried out into the hall. She paused as Peter's voice became clear.

"—not smart to have him around! What if he stumbled onto something? And I'm a little surprised at the two of you last night!"

The beginning of Dr. Grant's reply was too quiet to make out, but she heard the end of what he said. "—couldn't believe it! I knew what he was trying to do, so I played him at his own game! I couldn't get much out of him, but he definitely has information. He was dancing all around the subject trying to bait me. He's looking for it, all right!"

Curious, Kyla stood very still. Peter responded, but she couldn't understand him. It sounded like his back was to the door.

"Well, for one, it only confirmed to me that what we know is true," the professor said. "He most definitely knows something."

"In my opinion—" Again Peter's words were muffled, the rest of what he said lost.

"Yes, maybe. But I played dumb, and I think he believed me. As far as we're concerned, he thinks I'm ignorant of anything about the Kennedys. You—you're just the gardener boy. Sorry, that was his terminology, not mine."

"Okay, but was that necessary?" Peter asked, his voice suddenly clear. "You don't know what you're getting into. I think he needs to go!"

"Naw, I think he's a harmless good 'ole boy who's heard some rumors—" His voice faded out and back in. "—as long as one of us stays with him."

"What—babysit the guy? No, I'm not doing that!"

"Well, what if he finds it? We don't want him poking around by himself!"

"With all due respect, Grant, I think you would be wise to consider your kids. And Kyla."

"I *am* thinking of her!" His voice rose. "For heaven's sake, Peter—let the girl get to know her father! What do you have against it? I think he's harmless as long as we stay on him—that's all." He sniffed. "If I could have gone just a little longer. Just a little bit longer. I tried to ask as many questions as I could, like I was interested, but he was evasive with me. Then there came a point that I thought he was going to lose it and get sick on me. I had to close it down, get him upstairs."

Kyla's heart was pounding. She couldn't believe what she was hearing. Her cheeks were burning as she marched over, appearing sideways in the doorway.

"You!" she said with accusation, zeroing in on Dr. Grant. "You got my father drunk last night—on purpose!" She pushed the heavy door back further with her body.

The professor's head drew back where he sat on his leather couch.

Peter twisted in his chair, then closed his eyes and turned away, a hand covering his face.

"Good morning, Little Miss Sunshine," Dr. Grant said with an edge of irritation in his voice. "If you're going to eavesdrop, you might as well come in and get comfy. But keep your voice down. I have a killer headache."

Kyla's jaw tightened.

"This was not my idea," Peter announced from where he sat.

"Why would you do such a thing?" Kyla asked angrily.

The professor furled his brow. "Sheesh, girl—cool your jets! We don't need him down here too."

Kyla slipped the rest of the way into the room, squaring her shoulders at him. "I want to know what's going on here! You tell me!"

"Lordy, Lordy—the nanny is having a fit," Dr. Grant said under his breath, glancing briefly at the ceiling. "Why don't you have a seat? Please." He gestured to a chair.

"No," Kyla said firmly. "I'm going to stand right here, and you're going to tell me why you got my father drunk last night."

He spread his hands. "Suit yourself. But maybe the better question is why your father tried to get *me* drunk last night."

Kyla folded her arms, shooting a stern look across the room. Dr. Grant securely met her gaze. His eyes were bloodshot.

"Got any ideas on that?" he asked.

"What do you mean?"

He leaned forward in his chair. "Oh, all day long he talked on and on about sharing his wonderful imported liquor with me. Then again before supper he was very eager to invite me to have a couple of drinks afterward, even when I said I needed to be in my study for the night. But since he kept insisting, I thought, heck, a few wouldn't hurt. So then I see that he's trying to pour it down my throat! Now why would someone do that?"

Kyla couldn't speak.

"So I decided two could play at that little game—that's all." He opened his hands. "That's all!"

She dropped her chin, giving him a knowing look. "I'm pretty sure there's more to it than that! I overheard what you said earlier. You were trying to get information out of my father by getting him drunk. I heard you say it. Don't deny it."

His eyes narrowed. "Yes, but he was doing the same to me first."

Peter shook his head, holding up his hands. "None of this was any of my idea!"

"Oh, right!" Kyla snapped, shooting him a piercing look. "No, you just stood guarding the door so that I couldn't see him being taken advantage of!"

His eyes widened. "That's *not* why I was there!"

Kyla turned back to Dr. Grant. "So what is all of this about? What are you trying to find out? What is this information my father supposedly knows? You said it confirms what you know about—about—about whatever. I want to know what this is about!"

Dr. Grant folded his arms. "That's beyond your job description."

Peter jerked his head up. "Grant, you should—"

"We keep the circle small, Peter," he said stiffly. "Especially now."

Peter looked down, shaking his head, his cheeks pink and his lips tight.

Kyla stepped out carefully. "It has something to do with the third floor, doesn't it? With all those holes in the walls."

Dr. Grant unfolded his arms and reached for his coffee, taking a sip. "Maybe."

She eyed him carefully. "I'm right, aren't I? I saw how you guys looked at that postcard Howie found, like it was some big clue to something. And when my father came you totally locked up the third floor. Why? What's up there?"

Dr. Grant cradled his cup with both hands. "Have you talked about this with your father?"

Kyla paused. "No. But he's tried to with me. He wants up there in the worst way. He says this house has secrets!"

Dr. Grant gave a slow nod. "And?"

"And what?"

"What did you tell him?"

"I pretended I didn't know anything about it, which is kinda difficult, given how freakin' odd it is to have holes punched in the walls everywhere! Would someone please tell me why? What's up there? What don't you want him to find?"

Dr. Grant was silent. Kyla looked from him to Peter, who sat closed-mouthed with a look of frustration on his face.

She exhaled loudly. "I hate you both!"

Dr. Grant laughed. "Oh, come now! Look, Kyla—you did the right thing to pretend you didn't know anything."

"Why?" She tilted her head. "What are you hiding?"

He pursed his lips thoughtfully, not answering right away. "Okay—

here's the deal," he said finally. "We don't really know what is up there. We suspect that there may be—some sort of a time capsule or something."

"You don't know?"

His head jerked a bit, but he said nothing.

"Why don't you just go tear the place apart until you find it?"

He sighed, giving her a tired look. "Because, Miss Smarty Pants, I've spent last two years of my life repairing the first two floors of this house, and I'm tired to death of holes in walls. It's our year to dig up the yard."

Kyla frowned. "Dig up the—"

"To put in the fountain," Peter interjected.

"It's our year to put in the fountain," Dr. Grant reiterated, casting a glance at Peter.

Kyla exhaled loudly again. "So this time capsule thing, or whatever it is—does my father know about it? Did he ask you about it?"

"We're not sure what your father knows," Dr. Grant replied slowly.

She leveled her eyes at him. "So you decided to get him drunk and try to find out."

"Ah, but it was the other way around—remember?" He touched his fingertips together. "You understand you can't say a word about this. Not one single word."

"That's crazy!" Kyla said, shaking her head. "Seriously, why can't we just get everyone together in one place and have everyone share what everyone knows and all look together for this stupid thing? I don't get why it's this big secret!"

Dr. Grant shook his head. "Not a word. I need your trust on this."

She tipped her head, adding, "And don't you think pretending you don't know something would make someone who knows you know something more curious?"

Both men looked at her.

She sighed. "Okay, okay. Not a word. I promise. But I think this whole thing is dumb! It's completely asinine!"

"I need to get going," Peter said apologetically to Dr. Grant, rising from his chair. He had on fresh jeans and a white-and-blue cotton shirt.

Dr. Grant nodded, lifting a few fingers to acknowledge him.

"I think you owe my father an apology," Kyla continued.

The professor made a sound of protest. "Oh, now, now—the way I see it, the guy owes *me* an apology!" He also stood, his shoulders slumped a bit. He held out his hand toward her. "Kyla, admittedly for your sake, I am sorry. I apologize. That wasn't pretty last night. I wish you hadn't come out there. You didn't need to see that."

Peter raised his eyebrows, meeting Kyla's eyes on his way to the door.

She looked back at Dr. Grant. "Well, nevertheless it happened. And I'm asking my father to leave today."

His eyes grew large. "What? Because of me?"

She shook her head. "No. Because of *him*! I can't do this. He's—he's—I can't do this!"

Dr. Grant set a hand on his waist. "Look, Kyla," he said soberly. "I take full responsibility for letting that happen out there last night. I should have turned him down. Should've never let it get out of control like that. Like I said, I apologize."

"No, it's—"

"And beyond that," he continued, "the whole idea of your father staying here was for you to get reconnected with him, and instead I've used him as my labor force. That was really insensitive of me. You've barely had any time together."

"I know. But—"

"I don't think you should ask him to leave quite yet," he said earnestly, shaking his head. "Now that we're almost through with this behemoth fountain, you'll have more of a chance to get to know him. I promise to give you more time. So try again—will you? I think you won't regret the effort. And then in a couple of days he can be on his way as planned."

"Why do you care so much?" she asked. "Why are you pushing so hard for me to spend time with this guy? I'm trying, and it's not working!"

Dr. Grant spread his arms out. "Because I blew it with *my* dad, and I don't want *you* to do the same!" He paused, bringing his hands down and shoving them into his pockets. "I'm sorry. There're things you understand when you're older that you don't get when you're young. *I* don't need Robert DeKane at my house, but *you* do! I don't care how difficult this is for you—I'm telling you—your father needs this, and you need it too! Or this will be an unsettled issue that you will carry with you for the rest of your life!"

Kyla stared at him.

"That's why!" he added tiredly.

"Even if you feel you have to watch him so he doesn't find your precious time capsule?"

"It's a risk I'm willing to take!"

Kyla nodded, biting her lip.

"Now get out of here," Dr. Grant finished, waving her off. "My head is aching. I'm going to lie down and try to sleep till noon. Then I'm going to correct tests and prepare for my class tomorrow."

So the kids are mine, Kyla thought, leaving his study. With resignation she rolled the heavy door shut behind her. Peter was waiting for her beside the dining room table in his crisp shirt, the light color accentuating his sun-darkened skin and the blue of his eyes. His hair had gotten quite sun-bleached in the last few weeks and had grown out, curling around the edges. He looked good.

"Come with me," he said to her, his keys in his hand.

"What?" Kyla asked.

"Come to church with me."

A light feeling stirred in her stomach. "No, I have the kids."

He didn't move, studying her face. "Go tell him you will be out for a couple of hours. You'll like it. The music's really great, and I always learn a lot. I'll introduce you to some of my friends."

She hesitated.

"When's the last time you got away from here?" he asked. "Come on—come with me! I'll tell him for you. He'll manage."

"No," she said quickly, rubbing her forearm nervously, "I can't do that. Not today. Not when he's—like that. And my father. He'll be up soon, probably with a hangover too."

He gave a small nod. "Okay," he said simply, fingering his keys. "Okay."

He didn't move, and Kyla shifted uncomfortably.

"Don't you need to go?" she asked.

"Yeah," he said with a sudden deep breath. "See you after a while."

Chapter Twenty-Two

A thin layer of hazy clouds was moving in, competing with the blue sky above them. Kyla had the boys playing outside on the patio while it was still comfortable to do so, for the humidity was rising and she knew that by afternoon it would be hot, even with the steady breeze that stirred the air. Howie was lying in the grass at the foot of the patio steps, putting in a make-believe fountain in one of the flower beds that Peter had planted. Kyla let him pretend that the mulch was crushed rock, which he hauled with his dump truck from place to place in the corner. Hank, who liked to stay near Kyla, had been playing with his animals, but then had gotten distracted by the ice in her water glass, which had now become his glass by virtue of his little hands being unable to stay out of it. He held an ice cube up to her where she sat under the canopy, the chilly water running down his arm. She smiled at him, but inside she was still stewing, having unhappily just cleared Dr. Grant's and her father's drinking debris off the patio table from the previous night and swept up a pile of cigarette butts from the patio deck. That was where she was when her father joined her.

"Morning," he said casually, coming out on the patio. He had on a dress shirt with jeans and looked surprisingly rested. Making his trademark sound with his teeth, he stood with his hands in his pockets looking out at the fountain basin that the crane on the flatbed truck had lowered onto the crushed-rock fountain bed the day before.

"Good morning," she replied and waited for the excuses he would give for blowing her off both last night and this morning.

"Hot one today," he said, squinting toward the sky.

He retrieved a cigarette from his shirt pocket, lit up, and began drawing deeply on it, blowing smoke out through his nose. Then he turned, surveying Kyla where she sat with Hank in his soggy shirt and shorts. He stared at the boy for a bit, looked up at her, then away.

317

"You should put that out," she said. "The kids are here."

"Ah, he's okay. It ain't gonna hurt him any." He simply moved the burning stub behind his back, out of Hank's sight. She watched him, still waiting, but it was evident his failure to show up wasn't on his mind.

"It's almost noon," she said.

"Is it?" He looked at his watch. "Naw, it's only eleven."

She hit it directly. "I thought we were going to talk this morning."

Recognition dawned, and his shoulders sagged a little as he let out a breath. "Shoot!"

"You forgot, huh?"

His lips pressed into a thin line. He gestured with the cigarette in his hand. "Yeah, I guess I did."

She lifted her chin in assent but didn't respond.

He sighed again, shaking his head apologetically. "Kyla, I'm sorry. I—" He paused, looking down. "I guess I more than forgot. I blew it. And I guess I got a little carried away last night too."

Well, at least he acknowledged it. "Yeah. I guess you did." She leaned back, folding her arms and crossing her legs. "You embarrassed me last night. You were out of control and vulgar."

His expression—Kyla remembered the same expression on his face after her graduation, when he was leaning down, tapping on her car window, the guilty, regretful look on his face that had made her feel sorry for him then—he wore the same expression now. He puffed on his cigarette, speaking through a breath of smoke, "Yeah, I—I'm sorry. I'm really sorry." His eyes flicked down to where Hank sucked messily on his chunk of ice and back up to her. He shifted his feet, turning his head to look out toward the yard.

She frowned. That was it? What in the world—he just turned away from her! *This guy,* Kyla marveled, *this guy is unable to have a personal conversation!* She could think of a thousand things she would rather be doing at the moment than talking to him. Yet her employer insisted that she keep trying. What the heck was she supposed to say or do with a guy like this? She studied his forlorn figure staring out at the fountain site, unnerved by the fragments of her own facial features she recognized in his profile. Tapping her hand on her leg, she debated about where to go now. She fell on a question. "Is this a problem you have on a regular basis—'getting a little carried away'?"

"What?"

"Drinking too much."

He frowned. "Drinking too much? Ach—" He dismissed her comment with the wave of his hand. "We just enjoyed a few drinks too many. I'm okay. Don't worry about me. I'm not an alcoholic or anything, if that's what you're wondering."

Certainly she was wondering about more than a few things. Like if it was true that he had intentionally tried to get Dr. Grant drunk and what information he had about Wynnbury House that had made Dr. Grant so curious. And yet she didn't know what would be at the end of the road if she went there with him, so she couldn't ask. *Not a word*, Dr. Grant had requested. She bit her lip, sorely tempted.

The two of them were silent while her father finished his smoke. Hank had dropped his last piece of ice and was now experimenting with pouring small dribbles of water out onto the deck, giggling as he stamped his feet in the tiny puddles. Suddenly he poured the entire remainder of the glass onto the deck all at once, splashing Kyla's feet. Shrieking with glee, he squatted down to rub his hands in it. DeKane turned to give him a disapproving look.

He sniffed, leaning back against the rail. "So where is everyone?"

She slid across the love seat, away from Hank's water mess. "Dr. Grant is in his study preparing for his class tomorrow."

"And the younger fellow?"

"I'm not sure." She didn't feel like telling him where Peter was.

DeKane made a face. "He is something, that gardener boy! One of those born-agains. Can't have a conversation without him talking about his Jesus."

"Peter's a nice guy," Kyla responded defensively.

"Oh, he's a nosy, religious nitwit if you ask me!" He mimicked in a nasally voice: "'Does it concern you that your sins must be punished?' That's what he asked me yesterday! I got quite a lecture on my need for a savior! Can't keep his religious trap shut for nothing!"

"Dr. Grant hired him to do a job here, and he definitely knows his stuff."

"Yeah? Well, we could've had that done today!" He jerked his head toward the yard. "Could've finished that project for sure, but that bum kid won't work Sundays! Damn if he'd work for me for very long! I'd have him fired!"

"Well, even if they had worked today, they would've had it all finished before you were even out of bed," she jabbed coolly.

His eyes narrowed. Taking one last puff on the cigarette, he flicked the butt over the railing into the yard, then folded his arms, studying her. He made the sucking sound with his teeth.

"All right, all right," he said after a moment. "I'm sorry, baby. I'm being a jerk. I didn't mean to get you all riled up over that kid. Do you think we could start this conversation over again?"

She took a breath, not knowing what to say.

"That professor, now, he's a good guy," her father continued. "He's got a head on his shoulders. Likes you—that's for sure!" He gave her a wink. "In fact, he thinks it's a good idea for you and me to spend time together. He says a father should know his own children and the other way around."

How was this starting their conversation over?

He gave a small chuckle. "Although it's a bit ironic for a rich guy who has a nanny who does everything for him to lecture me on getting to know my daughter! That guy has it made with you here—"

"You can stop it right there," Kyla said curtly. "His name is Dr. Grant, and he is a good dad to his boys. And he pays me very well to watch his children. Please don't talk about him in front of them!"

"Hey, hey, now! Don't overreact!" He held up his hands. "I meant that as a compliment! Seriously. I—I respect your job. You do a lot around here!" His eyes dropped again to Hank.

Her anger was simmering, and she took another breath to calm herself down. Her father patted his chest pocket, reaching for another smoke. He lit up and took a puff, then held the cigarette in midair, his elbow resting on his other arm. Tipping his head back, he looked upward at the exterior of the house.

"This sure is a curious place," he mused. "It's nice, but certainly not the most beautiful house in the world."

Kyla said nothing.

"You would think that a guy who had the money to build a place like this would have at least made it beautiful, huh?"

"I think it *is* beautiful. In its own way."

He laughed. "It's odd—that's what it is!"

"Well, it's modeled after a place in England." *Not one word,* came Dr. Grant's voice in her head. "Um, I saw it online before I came here."

He nodded. "Yes, yes. That's what I've heard. But why? That's what I wonder." He turned to look at her. "Have you asked about getting me up there yet?"

She shifted uncomfortably. "No. Everyone's been busy." She knew he would not accept a no from Dr. Grant.

He puffed out a lungful of smoke, cocking his head at her. "What about right now? Now would be a good time." He rose from the railing.

Kyla shook her head. "Dr. Grant asked not to be disturbed this morning."

DeKane smiled, rocking on his feet. "'Dr. Grant' this, 'Dr. Grant' that. Forget about him! How about *you*?" He pointed the cigarette at her. "*You* take me up there! You can't be that restricted around here!"

"Me? How would I do that?"

He shrugged. "You get the keys, baby, and the two of us take a quiet little tour while your professor sleeps off his liquor."

She drew herself up taller. "Um, that would be the four of us. I'm working—remember? And that could happen only if I knew where the keys were, which I don't. So—sorry. It's not happening today. And anyway, Dr. Grant is the one you need to talk to about it. Why do you want up there so badly? I think you need to drop it and forget about it!"

His mouth twisted into a smile. "Ah, Dr. Grant. Nice guy, yes, but I tell you—I don't think he's all you think he is. I think he's holding out on you!"

She frowned. "What do you mean?"

"That man has a pocketful of secrets!"

"What would make you think that?" She squirmed uncomfortably on her chair.

"Isn't it obvious? There's things he doesn't want known around here." He paused, eyeing her carefully. "Baby, you should know that things aren't always what they seem to be."

This felt dangerously close to crossing Dr. Grant's line. With her pulse quickening Kyla raised her chin. "I was hired to nanny these two boys. It's not my job to go prying into someone's secrets or go poking around in things that aren't any of my business! And you shouldn't be either! You can't stay here if you're going to do that. Seriously."

"Oh, Kyla—chill out! Don't worry, I'm not going to put your job in danger. I'm just curious."

"This is not about me and my job," she clarified stiffly. "This is about *you* and your behavior if you want to stay here! Why are you here anyway?"

"What do you mean, why am I here? Because Dr. Grant invited me to stay."

Kyla laughed. "Right! Because you're such great friends!"

His head jerked, and he made an impatient sound. "Of course, I'm here for you, baby. That goes without saying."

She shook her head. "Well, this isn't working for me!"

He blew out a breath of smoke, flaying his hands. "What's there to work? What's it supposed to be like?"

She glared at him, unable to answer.

The patio was suddenly too quiet. Hank's little brow was furled as he gazed up at Kyla's father. Kyla also noticed that Howie had stopped playing with his truck and was standing at the top of the patio stairs round-eyed, staring at them. He was certainly getting an earful. But she would have to deal with him later.

"I would like you to leave," she said to her father.

DeKane's mouth opened in surprise. After a moment he nodded slowly. "Okay. And when would you like me to leave?"

"Today."

He pursed his lips, giving another nod. "Okay." He sniffed. "I guess I can honor that."

A silence passed between them. Taking one last draw on his cigarette, he flicked the butt to the patio deck, twisting it with his toe.

Shoving his hands into his pockets, he cleared his throat. "Can I mention one thing? I'm not bucking you or anything, but I have an appointment in town this afternoon at two, and I wasn't planning to be back until late. And I also have to be gone all day tomorrow on appointments. Would it be terribly rude to ask you if I could leave Tuesday morning?"

Tuesday was her birthday. It seemed cruel to make him leave on her birthday. Kyla gave an inward sigh. It was like she had a genetic obligation to let him stay. What else could she do?

"All right," she said, rising from her chair, "You can leave Wednesday morning. That gives you one extra day. So if you want to know me, here I am." She spread her arms out wide. "You better get busy, 'cause your time is running out. And I think I'm being more than generous!"

"Thank you," he said humbly. Awkwardly he shifted his feet, adding, "Look, Kyla—I'll be the first to admit that I'm not good at this relationship business. I suck at it! It's easier for me to throw shovels of dirt around out there"—he gestured toward the yard—"than it is to talk to you. Every time I see you I'm reminded of my failures, and every time we talk I screw it up. I'm sorry. I really am." In a nervous gesture he reached up and ran a hand through his hair. "But just being around you and seeing you makes me feel better about myself. I think you're beautiful and smart. Very much like your mother. But I'm not good at—at talking."

She bit her lip. That was probably the most authentic he had been since he showed up at her graduation. He wore that expression again that made her feel sorry for him. How could she fault him for what he admitted was difficult for him to do? Inwardly she sighed. It was just so complicated!

"Okay," she said. "But I need you to mind your own business about this house."

"Right. Done," he said, reaching for another cigarette in his shirt pocket.

"And stop!" she said sharply.

His head drew back in surprise.

"That's your third one already! Give it a break! No smoking anywhere near the kids from now on, okay? And absolutely no drinking. Got it?"

His mouth twisted into a smile. "Yes, ma'am! Little Eva." He winked.

She threw a glance at Howie, who was still watching them from the stairs. "I need to make lunch for the kids now. You can—join us if you want," she offered. She thought of adding that they would be having canned ravioli and stewed green beans, two of the worst foods she could think of, hoping he wouldn't oblige, but she didn't say it.

His hand twitched a wave, as he turned back to look at the fountain project in the yard. "Naw, you go ahead. I'll be leaving soon. I'll get a bite in New Hampton."

Taking Hank by the hand, she led him to the door, gesturing for Howie to come too. Behind her she heard DeKane make the sound with his teeth.

"You want my opinion?" he asked after her.

She turned with a questioning look.

"I think you need to get out of here for a few hours. Take that new car of yours for a drive or something. You're just too—uptight. That fella needs to give you a break."

She could think of nothing to say, so she simply nodded and went inside. As she busied herself with preparing lunch, Howie hovered nearby, pumping her with questions. What happened? Were they fighting? Was something wrong with their house? Who was "Little Eva"? Was she a kid? Was Kyla mad at her father? Why did she tell him he had to leave? Had her father done something wrong?

"I bet I know what he did that was bad," he added with a knowing look.

Kyla popped the lid onto Hank's sippy cup and handed it to him to take to the table.

"He was smoking," he whispered.

She gave him a grim smile but didn't reply. "Do you want milk or water?"

"Is he going to die?"

"What?" She frowned, setting the jug of milk down on the counter.

"Dad told me my grandpa died because of smoking."

She looked down at his upturned face. "I don't know, Howie. But everything's okay. You don't have to worry about my father. I'll talk to your dad about it so he knows, but you can let us grown-ups take care of things, okay? There's nothing for you to worry about."

DeKane left within the hour, right as Kyla had finished cleaning up the kitchen. After she got Howie situated in the library and put Hank down for his nap, she grabbed her phone and went out to call her dad, knowing she would probably catch him at home, since it was Sunday afternoon. The phone call was overdue—it would be the first time she had talked to him since the night DeKane had arrived, and she predicted that he would freak out at the news. On the other hand, judging by his repeated attempts to call her, she suspected he already knew.

She was right on both accounts. He scolded her.

"Kyla Evangeline, didn't you see that I called you? Why didn't you call me back? I found out everything from Peter, and all you did was send me a measly little text that said nothing!"

"I've been busy! You can't imagine how crazy it's been here!"

"Those kids have to go to bed sometime!"

"Yes, but there's a lot going on around here!"

"You should have called last night instead of texting. Texting is not a good form of communi—"

"Well, take my word for it—I couldn't talk last night!" Kyla said, cutting in. She wasn't going to explain the scene on the patio. He didn't need to know. "But we're talking *now*!"

"Well, I'm worried about you! Peter has expressed some concern for your safety!"

"What?" She rolled her eyes. "Oh, Dad—it's not like that. There's no danger. He's just a jerk."

There was a stiff pause. "Honey, I wish you wouldn't talk about him like that. Peter is a fine—"

"No, Dad—I'm talking about Robert DeKane, my biological father. He is a jerk!"

"Why? What has he done?" She could hear his voice grow tight.

"I don't know. Just—I don't know. Stuff." Kyla rubbed her forehead, debating what to tell him. There was no way he could understand. "He's—he's—well, he has very poor social skills, for one. It's been challenging trying to talk to him! Stuff like that."

"Well, he shouldn't be staying there!" Kendall declared. "That was absolutely wrong of him to show up like that! Unbelievable and inexcusable."

Kyla wondered how much Peter had told him. She glanced over to her tree at the eastern edge of the yard, where her father had grabbed her in the dark. It was still so bizarre to her.

"I know, Dad. You're right. But he's here, and Dr. Grant invited him to stay a few days so that he and I could get to know each other."

"That astounds me!" he growled. "I *can't believe* he was asked to stay!"

"Well, he was. And I'm an adult, Dad, so you're going to have to deal with it."

He let out a long breath. "I know, hon. I'm just—I don't know. Just be careful. I don't trust him. And Peter doesn't trust him."

"Yeah, well—Peter doesn't trust him because *you* don't, that's all," she said impatiently. "Believe it or not, he's actually helped the guys here with the fountain project in the yard. Quite a lot! But he's not staying long. He's leaving soon, so don't worry."

"Good. I'm glad he's not staying long."

"So do me a favor, Dad. Stop getting Peter all worked up about him!"

"I'm not—" He paused, letting it go. "Okay. All right, then."

He was silent for a moment before changing the subject, telling her that he sent her a package for her birthday. She thanked him and said she'd be watching for it. That reminded Kyla to ask him to send her their old family photo of them before her mom passed away, the one of the three of them together. He was surprised but quickly agreed and said he would send it right away too. Then he caught her up to date on his week's activities and asked her how things were going with the kids. Kyla deliberately didn't ask about Alex, and he didn't offer anything. After a while it was time to go.

"Honey, I want you to be smart about your time with your father," Kendall said.

"Of course, Dad!" she replied. "And I want *you* to quit worrying about me!"

"Ah, you're right," he admitted. "I know, I know—"

"I should probably go. I won't wait so long until I call you again, okay?"

"Okay. Thanks. I love you, Kyla, and I'm praying for you."

"Love you too, Dad."

Kyla hung up and let out a long breath. Her dad's attitude against Robert DeKane was glaring, but equally mystifying was that she had found herself defending him! She lingered there for a bit, untangling herself from the conversation as she leaned over the rail of the wooden staircase, gazing at the tiny beach below. She could understand her dad's angst—a good share of it was definitely warranted, for her biological father both confused and disturbed her. But she had to navigate this by herself. Just two and a half more days, she calculated. And who knows—maybe she would have an emotional breakthrough with him after all. *Wouldn't Dr. Grant be pleased about that?* she mused. Then his vicarious bond-building efforts would not be in vain. But it would take a miracle.

Kyla was in no hurry to go back to the house. As predicted, the day was hot and humid, but the sun felt good on her back, and it was nice to have some time to relax by herself in this peaceful spot. The squawking blue jay was back, and a slight breeze stirred, sending bumpy ripples across the water and making a pattering sound in the leaves of the trees. She scanned the island for the eagle's nest, wishing she had Peter's binoculars. No doubt the eaglets were out of the nest by now. She recalled that it was Peter who had first spied her father on the opposite bank, though her father had denied it. Kyla had been so mad at him that day. But Peter had simply been on guard. *Your guard dog.*

Moments later she heard her name called from behind her. She could hear voices coming out onto the patio, waiting for her. She sighed. Dr. Grant was both very crabby and very busy today. Part of her wished she had taken Peter up on his offer this morning. A few hours away would have been nice, even if it was at a church. She turned to see Howie with his arms hanging over the railing watching for her, waving to her, calling to her across the dug-up lawn. Dr. Grant was standing by the door, waiting for her too. Some days work felt like work, she thought, heading back to the house. And today was one of those days.

As he had said, Kyla's father was gone all day Sunday until late evening and all day Monday too, leaving first thing in the morning with briefcase in hand shortly after Dr. Grant left for his summer school class.

Kyla, who was up early, offered him breakfast but he declined, saying that he was in a hurry and would not be back until evening again. Meeting with clients all day, he said.

"But we'll have tomorrow," he told her. "We'll have some time together then. We'll talk."

Kyla wasn't sure if that meant he actually remembered her birthday or if he was just stating a fact. She didn't ask, watching him drive away in his fancy black Mercedes Benz.

Secretly she called her birthday "Invisible Day," as that's what she wished she was on that day most of the time. Her father—biological father—had never acknowledged her birthday. Her dad, of course, always remembered it, but since her birthday was in the summertime, her classmates and friends rarely did, unless she brought it up, which she didn't like to do. Or unless her dad made a big deal out of things and invited her friends over, which was then awkward, since it was during the height of vacation season, camp season, ball tournament season, what-have-you season, and out of the half-dozen girls he would invite, only two would actually be able to make it. That only lent itself to another opportunity for Kyla to feel pitied by others, a feeling she hated. So she grew to prefer to keep her birthday a secret and remain invisible, celebrating it as quietly as her dad would allow.

Of course, "Invisible Day" had also been annual fodder for all manner of reasons she was bitter against God for taking her mother. If she'd had a mother, then every birthday of her life would have been glorious. Standing on the step by the carport that misty, overcast morning, Kyla recognized again that what Mrs. Gordon had said was true. It was crazy how much anger she had expended on things that weren't actual realities! At the moment she was also trying not to be angry with her biological father in advance for not acknowledging her birthday. After all, it hadn't happened yet.

Peter also left early that morning, having to return some of the rented equipment they had used over the weekend for digging the trench to run the water and electric to the fountain. He was just leaving as Kyla was coming into the house from the carport. He told her he would be back later in the morning to start installing the water pump and asked if she would like anything from town. She said she couldn't think of anything. He left, and Kyla was alone in the house with the boys still sleeping, a rare occasion for her.

A further miracle was that Hank had slept the whole night in his own bed. So after a leisurely breakfast by herself, Kyla took her coffee up to her own room to sit quietly in her own space, taking some time to further explore the Bible Mrs. Gordon had given her. Once again, she wasn't exactly sure what to do with it, but since Samantha Gordon had underlined words and verses in a lot of places, Kyla thought she would start there by looking at those. Apparently those words must have some greater importance.

She opened the Bible to the middle, then paged to the first part she saw underlined. Psalm 139. She skipped over most of it, going directly to the part inked up.

For you created my inmost being; you knit me together in my mother's womb. I praise you because I am fearfully and wonderfully made; your works are wonderful, I know that full well. My frame was not hidden from you when I was made in the secret place, when I was woven together in the depths of the earth. Your eyes saw my unformed body; all the days ordained for me were written in your book before one of them came to be. How precious to me are your thoughts, God! How vast is the sum of them! Were I to count them, they would outnumber the grains of sand—when I awake, I am still with you.

It surprised her how appropriate and well-timed those very verses seemed, in light of her birthday the next day. Obviously the person who wrote those words was very close to God—probably someone like Peter or her dad. Someone good. Someone God approved of. With her life track record, there was more evidence for God being against her, but it would be nice to be on the other side of things. It would be nice to know that good verses like this applied to her. She wondered about the concept of one's days being written in God's book before they even happened. Apparently God had a book of some sort, and apparently he knew everything about everyone in it. Was that for real? Or was that a symbol or metaphor for something else? And if it were real, she wondered if God did indeed know all the days ordained for her. How was that possible?

It was a little difficult holding the Bible on her lap while drinking coffee, so she moved to her table, sliding out of her way her computer and the paper coffee cup Peter had given her Saturday. She had saved the cup because of what he had written on it but put a few pens in it so that it didn't look weird or so that Mrs. Gordon wouldn't throw it away. *Yes, you have—you just didn't know it.* She knew that he was making reference to her saying she had never felt loved by God, and strange as it may seem, his words meant something to her. She wanted it to be true. *Ask him, and he will show you.* That was something she was still considering.

Returning her attention to the Bible, this time she flipped farther back in the book, finding a spot where a huge portion of the page was underlined.

"All right, Mr. Romans—what do you have to say?" she breathed quietly, beginning to read.

And we know that in all things God works for the good of those who love him, who have been called according to his purpose. That, she decided, sounded great. Kyla had heard her dad say this very thing before. It was a verse she liked, but again, she didn't know if it could apply to her since she didn't exactly love God. After all, it did look like there were stipulations to the deal. She sighed and read on.

What, then, shall we say in response to these things? If God is for us, who can be against us? He who did not spare his own Son, but gave him up for us all—how will he not also, along with him, graciously give us all things? Who will bring any charge against those whom God has chosen? It is God who justifies. Who then is the one who condemns? No one. Christ Jesus who died—more than that, who was raised to life—is at the right hand of God and is also interceding for us. Who shall separate us from the love of Christ?

Kyla skipped ahead.

For I am convinced that neither death nor life, neither angels nor demons, neither the present nor the future, nor any powers, neither height nor depth, nor anything else in all creation, will be able to separate us from the love of God that is in Christ Jesus our Lord.

She sat, chewing on the edge of her thumb, thinking a long time about that section. That was the same love of God that Peter had been talking about. She didn't understand all of it, but it definitely made God sound very good, like an advocate. Giving and not condemning. Again, these verses were a great piece for those who were part of the "us" in it. But how did one get in the "us" club—and was it even possible to get on the inside? And how could a person know for sure they were on the good side of God? How did Peter know? What made him so sure? And what about her, when God's love seemed so contrary to her life experience? What was so wrong with her? So far she'd only felt like God was against her, like he disapproved of her for some unknown reason, like she was off his radar, completely cast off from him, alone, making her life a series of one bad event after another.

The old, familiar, and awful feelings of shame settled down over her. Often it seemed like the things that were supposed to make her feel better actually made her feel worse. It was like a voice shouting in her head that she could never be good enough for God or never be worth his time. Like she would always be on the outside looking in, never a part of the favored "us" who enjoyed the benefits of love.

A little hand touched her arm, making her jump. "Gah, Howie! I didn't hear you come in!"

Howie giggled, leaning on the table. "Ha, ha! I scared you! Are you reading?"

How she loved his obvious questions! "Yes," she said.

Behind him came the scrunch of Hank's diaper as he crossed her room to join them, his blankie trailing him. She greeted him and pulled him on her lap, kissing his neck.

"What are you reading?" Howie asked.

"Nothing. Are you guys hungry?"

"Are you reading the Bible?" He poked his nose over the table to see. "Can you read it to me?"

"Yes, I am, and no, we can't read now. It's time for breakfast."

"I like it when Peter reads his Bible to me. Can you read a little part? Please?"

"No."

He frowned. "Why not? Not even a little?"

Kyla sighed. "Oh, all right. Just a little bit." She looked down to read from the page before her.

"No, I pick! I get to pick!" Howie said, moving to sit on her other leg. He turned several pages and pointed to an underlined area. "Read this, right here."

Kyla read out loud from 1 Timothy 1: *Here is a trustworthy saying that deserves full acceptance: Christ Jesus came into the world to save sinners—of whom I am the worst. But for that very reason I was shown mercy so that in me, the worst of sinners, Christ Jesus might display his immense patience as an example for those who would believe in him and receive eternal life.* The words caused a little twinge in her stomach. Then why had God cast her off and abandoned her? If God could show mercy to the worst of sinners, then why had he been so cruel to her? The Bible seemed so contradictory!

Howie was waiting, looking at her with folded arms.

"There. We read a little," she said.

"No." He shook his head. "Now we talk about it! Peter always talks about it after."

Kyla moved in her chair, bumping Hank off her lap. "Then you'll have to ask Peter. Come on, boys—let's go downstairs."

Howie gave up, and the three went down to breakfast.

Mrs. Gordon showed up later that morning bringing groceries and the special treat of a gallon of homemade freshly squeezed lemonade, made from a case of lemons she'd been given and needed to use up. She quickly put the things away and with regret told Kyla that today she had to get right to cleaning because she couldn't stay very long. Her granddaughter had sprained her ankle playing soccer the night before and was staying at her house for the day while her mother was at work.

"Always something," she said with a laugh. "I know God is up to something good."

That wasn't what *she* would have said about the situation, Kyla observed. But it did make her think about the Bible verse she had read earlier that morning—that all things worked together for good for those who loved God. Mrs. Gordon definitely loved God, so that would apply to her for sure. That reminded Kyla to thank her for the Bible, and the older woman apologized again that it wasn't new.

"But you can have it, sweetie," she said. "Samantha got a different one quite some time ago."

Then she asked how Kyla's visit was with her father over the weekend.

"Actually, he's still here," she told her, following her down the hall into the laundry room.

Mrs. Gordon set a clothes basket on the washer and started to sort the clothes on the floor. "Oh, that's nice."

"Actually," Kyla said, "it hasn't been that nice. It's been weird. Very confusing to me."

"What? What's going on now with your dad?" Her voice sounded concerned. "I thought things were good with him!"

"Things *are* good with my dad, but this isn't him. This is my father—my biological father. He left when I was five and then showed up about a month ago at my college graduation. And then here, out of the blue, last weekend."

Mrs. Gordon paused at the washer to shoot a look of surprise over her shoulder. "Whoa—you never told me about this! Okay—let's hear the full story!"

Kyla stuck to Mrs. Gordon, talking and assisting her as she cleaned, while the boys tagged along and played nearby with their toys. She shared how her father had arrived and how awkward their conversation attempts had been so far, and the pressure she felt from him to get him up to the third floor.

"So what's the problem?" Mrs. Gordon asked. "You don't want to go up there with him?"

She shook her head. "No, we aren't supposed to. Dr. Grant has it all locked up."

"He locked it? Oh. Okay. So then you let David know what he wants, right?"

"Yes. Sort of." Kyla frowned in thought. "I mean, Dr. Grant knows. I don't know. It's more than that. It's just that my father acts strange sometimes. Like he's more interested in this house than me. I wish we could have a real talk. One in which I could learn about him, and he could learn about me."

They were in the Great Room, and Mrs. Gordon stopped her dusting to look at her.

Kyla closed her eyes and shook her head. "It's just so hard! I'm still waiting for his first question about my life. It would be nice if he asked about even *one* thing. Anything. Like ask me what my major was in college or what I got my degree in. It'd be nice if he asked if I had a boyfriend or something, even though I don't, but it would at least be a normal question. Or what my hobbies are, or what I like to do."

"Oh, honey!" The older woman came over and took Kyla gently by the shoulders. "I'm so sorry. That must really hurt."

Kyla felt stiff and unsure of how to respond to Mrs. Gordon's warm and sympathetic touch. "It probably *should* hurt," she answered, "but he's such a stranger. I've had teachers and coworkers that I'm closer to. It's more frustrating than hurtful. And disappointing. Very disappointing! And confusing. I don't know. It's hard to describe."

Mrs. Gordon squeezed Kyla's shoulders softly. "God can come in and heal your wounded heart, sweetie. He can be a true father to you."

Kyla blinked. "I'm okay. Really. I'm used to it." The older woman's concern was starting to feel a lot like pity, and she could feel herself drawing back.

Mrs. Gordon's head tilted as she studied Kyla's face. "Hon, can I tell you something?" Her forehead was creased with care. She motioned, and the two of them sat on one of the love seats. Mrs. Gordon flipped her dust cloth to rest on her shoulder and reached for Kyla's hand. It felt good to have someone hold her hand, Kyla thought.

"God intended from the very beginning that fathers and mothers would be a channel through which he could pour his love into the hearts of children. That's their job." Her eyebrows lifted. "Do you get that? A father's responsibility before God is to *love, nurture, care for,* and *protect* his children." She separated each of the words for emphasis.

Kyla nodded, listening.

"And to show them how to follow God."

"Okay," she answered.

"Your heart, hon, is like a stretchy reservoir made to hold love. God's love. It's made to expand and stretch because God's love is ever increasing. And limitless. But when an important person like a father or mother fails us, we close our heart because it hurts. Over time we learn to close off to others, and our heart becomes like a rusty bucket of pain instead. A bucket of sludge. And sometimes that pain sits in there for so long that we just get used to it and think that it's normal."

Kyla gave a little snort. "It *is* normal."

Mrs. Gordon shook her head. "No, hon—it's not. It's just all you know."

"So what can I do about it? Or is my heart just wrecked?"

"Well, hon," Mrs. Gordon said kindly, "the hurt's gotta come out, and God's love has to go in."

"And how does that happen?"

"Well, it's about layers and layers of forgiveness. And then learning what God is like as your *real* father."

Kyla looked down thoughtfully. "At least my dad—my dad who adopted me—at least *he's* okay. Things are good there."

Mrs. Gordon gave an understanding nod. "I'm glad. I'm sure he's a great guy, honey, but I guarantee that your dad, too, has come far short of giving the kind of love God wants you to have. That's why we all need God himself to come in and heal us. Everyone's wounded, Kyla, hon. You're no exception. We all need to be filled with the love of God. And until we find it, we'll look for love and approval in anyone else we can find."

"I don't know," Kyla said wearily. "You don't really know me. I don't think it's possible with me."

"Of course, it's possible!" Mrs. Gordon chided. "You were *made* for his love! You will not be complete until you have it."

Hank let out a loud shriek of laughter across the room. Kyla turned to look at the boys, where they were pretending to be worms, wriggling under the furniture in Peter's corner.

"Dr. Grant is a really good father," she said, "and he isn't 'pouring God's love into their hearts,' as you say." She tipped her head toward the boys.

Mrs. Gordon sighed, squeezing her hand again. "Kyla, Dr. Grant is a good, good man. I highly respect him. But in his heart he longs for the same thing you do. Those sweet little boys right there have a lot going for them. Their daddy does love them. But someday they will be grown up young men searching for significance and meaning in life too. David is a good father, honey, but he's missing the most important thing."

From a distance they heard the sound of the dryer buzzing. Mrs. Gordon looked down at her watch, then reached up to scratch her eyebrow.

"Golly—I wish I had more time today." She patted Kyla's leg. "I have so much more that I'd like to share with you."

Kyla smiled weakly.

Absently the housekeeper pulled the dust cloth off her shoulder and folded it on her lap. "I tell you what," she said. "I can't make it back out here until Thursday morning, but when I come I'll plan a little more time, and I'll bring my granddaughter with me. She can watch the boys, even if her ankle is still bothering her, and you and I can go somewhere to talk and pray."

Kyla felt a lurch in her stomach. That sounded like a bigger deal than their normal talks, and it made her a bit fearful. Talk and—pray? Pray? What would *that* entail? Prayer was something her dad did without her. Something that Peter did at night after everyone else went to bed.

"I'm fine, really," Kyla told her. "My biological father's been gone so long it doesn't bother me. I don't think I'm carrying around quite a load of pain as you're describing. It's just a little disturbing having him here. But he'll be gone in a couple of days. I'll be all right."

From down the hall the dryer buzzed again.

Mrs. Gordon smiled at Kyla. "Okay. Well, let's talk on Thursday."

Chapter Twenty-Three

After Peter had gotten back from town that morning, he spent the rest of the day outside in the fountain basin trying to get the pump working correctly. The other tiers of the fountain were laid out on the scarred lawn waiting to be installed, but first the pump needed to do its job.

"It's got to be a faulty pump," he told Dr. Grant when he arrived home from work that afternoon. "I'm tired of messing around with it. I'm going back to town to get a replacement."

It had misted all morning and early afternoon, and Peter's clothes were damp and his hair curly from working in the humidity. Kyla heard Dr. Grant ask him about the timing of the sod coming later in the week, and the two men talked for a bit while Kyla kept the kids at bay waiting for their dad. Finally they were through, and Peter left. Dr. Grant set down his briefcase and put on his dad hat, waving her off for a little while to have some time alone.

Although the clouds had cleared somewhat, the humidity was still very high, and it was uncomfortably hot outside. Kyla retreated to the comfort of her room, where, after being away from it for as long as she'd been at Wynnbury, she started up her computer and went online. She figured that since her time with Robert DeKane, her birth father, was limited, now was the time to record any information she wanted to know while he was here to ask in case she ever wanted to search out her relatives. She plugged the DeKane name and the Champagne zip code into a search and waited for results, discovering first that the Wi-Fi was painfully slow. Finally up popped two words in the search bar: no results. *Did you mean DeKarne?* She tried again, yet still no results. *Did you mean Delaney?* Frustrated, Kyla broadened the search geographically and found a few DeKanes in Missouri, but they spelled the name differently—with a lowercase *k*. On a whim Kyla then switched her search to "Delano High School," but no such place was found. No town of Delano, Illinois. No Delano High School anywhere in Illinois. *Had it closed down?* she wondered. *Now there's a question for our little talk tomorrow*, Kyla noted. She closed her computer and took a nap.

They grilled for dinner but ate inside because of the heat, sharing Mrs. Gordon's lemonade, which was delicious—though not without gross amounts of sugar, as Mrs. Gordon had warned her previously. Kyla found it especially pleasant eating with just Dr. Grant, Peter, and the boys. After they had finished dinner, her father arrived home, and they moved outside "to get some fresh air," which, she realized, meant that Dr. Grant had agreed to let her father smoke on the patio. After his day away, he seemed very cheerful and especially friendly to Dr. Grant and Peter, although Kyla had to remember that they had worked together for two days already getting ready for the fountain install and had gotten to know each another a bit, so it wasn't entirely strange. Peter seemed especially happy too and had to share with the others a play-by-play of his fountain pump troubleshooting. Kyla was hot, and so were the boys, so she offered to take them in for extra-long baths before bed.

"Yeah, fine," Dr. Grant said, engrossed in the pump saga.

A couple hours later, when the boys were asleep, Kyla ran downstairs for another cold glass of Mrs. Gordon's lemonade before it disappeared. She poured it over a tall glass of ice and set the pitcher on the counter beside the refrigerator. While she sipped from her glass, Kyla could hear an animated discussion outside between the three men. Suddenly Dr. Grant appeared at the door, sliding it open to enter the house.

Kyla heard Peter's voice calling from the deck, "I'm just saying to consider it! I mean, what good would it be to gain the whole world and lose your soul?"

"You've got a one-track mind, Peter Watkins," Dr. Grant replied, his voice laced with irritation. "Is that all you can think about? Maybe there's no such thing as eternity, huh? Have you ever thought of *that*? There are other views in the world, you know! Maybe when you die you just die, and there's nothing! Boom—dead—nothing! Think about *that* for a change!"

"I respect your opinion," came Peter's reply, "but what if you're wrong? Just consider—"

With a sound of exasperation, Dr. Grant closed the door firmly behind him, cutting off Peter's voice. He started when he saw Kyla leaning against the sink.

"God, that kid can get under my skin!" he said, his face flushed. His dark hair was tightly curled and damp from the humidity. He blew out a long breath, shaking his head.

"So, Miss DeKane, what do *you* think happens when you die?" He turned to face her across the peninsula, his brow furled and his eyes intense. "Peter seems to have his undies in a bundle about my soul! He is completely obsessed with this coming 'Day of Judgment'!" He made quotation marks with his fingers. "It's all hellfire and brimstone! It's like he's stuck on this Dante's *Inferno* sort of tortuous hell that he says all sinners are destined for. Sinners—you know, *bad* people, like me! Good grief! What's *your* take on all this?" He touched his head with both hands, then popped them off, making the small sound of an explosion.

Kyla held up her glass, as if indicating she was just there to get a glass of lemonade.

Dr. Grant slapped a hand on the granite as he moved around the counter into the kitchen to get himself a glass. She turned the handle of the lemonade pitcher toward him.

"I can take it in the classroom," he continued in aggravation. "I like it there. It, you know, it livens the discussion with the other students. Stirs things up, makes things interesting, and then class is over. But this kid has overtaken my *life*! I can't escape him! He's getting into my brain!"

He exhaled loudly again, pouring the lemonade and taking a drink. He smacked his lips from the tartness, glancing briefly at the glass.

"He actually asked me if I died tonight, would I be ready to meet God. Can you believe that? Ha! I told him I'm not going anywhere anytime soon!" He downed half his glass, then turned to fill it up again from the pitcher. Shaking his head, he leaned back against the counter, looking back at Kyla. "Seriously, Miss DeKane. Do you think about this stuff—like being ready to die? Do you? Wouldn't it just be smarter to focus on having some goals for your life? What do you believe? Do you agree with our Mr. Watkins?"

Kyla opened her mouth and shook her head, not knowing what to say. "Sorry—I didn't hear your conversation."

The professor gestured to her with his glass. "I'd still like to know where you stand. And don't worry—you can be honest."

Kyla hated being put on the spot like this. "Um, I'm not quite sure *what* I believe," she said evasively.

"But you *do* believe in God."

She hesitated. "Yes. Yes, I do. But I'm seeing how much I don't know about him, how much I thought I knew, but I'm seeing that I've been wrong about a lot of things. I'm—searching. I have a lot of questions." Her own words surprised her. Yes, she thought, it was true—she *was* searching.

"Interesting," he replied flatly.

She continued, "I read somewhere"—she didn't want to say that it was in the Bible—"that God can make everything work out for good. I'm not exactly sure what that means, but I would like to believe that with God whatever problems we've had could benefit us somehow in the long run. And that he could maybe do the same for the whole world—like somehow fix it and make everything right. You know, bring justice in the end."

Dr. Grant regarded her a moment, then shook his head. "Pfft! That's a religious fantasy! Can't happen. That would be impossible!"

Kyla closed her mouth, her cheeks pink.

He swirled the lemonade in his glass, brooding darkly. After a bit he looked up at her. "Sorry—that was rude. I asked your opinion. Sorry."

She shrugged, uncertain of what to say or do.

He shifted his feet. "So Peter says there's only one way to heaven. Only one. That you must put your trust in this Jesus Christ fellow—the 'Son of God, come to earth,' as he says—who can forgive us of our sins and give us eternal life. What do you think about that? I tend to think there are many roads to God. It doesn't matter what you believe—it's all the same God."

"So you're saying you *do* believe in a God, then?"

He stared at her. "No, I don't. I'm just—well, I don't know. Speaking from an anthropological standpoint, it just sounds more logical to me. You know, for people who say they do. For those who need religion. Sheesh—!" He rubbed his forehead. "This is what I mean! He's in my head!" Suddenly he straightened, his expression changing. "I'm sorry. I apologize. I shouldn't even be talking to you about this."

He finished his lemonade, put the glass into the sink, and stood gazing into his reflection in the window, its glass tinted blue from the evening light. Kyla looked at his back, awkwardly waiting, wondering if she should leave.

She swallowed, sharing candidly, afraid she would appear foolish but wanting to say it for her own sake, "Like I said, I don't understand all that much about God. All I really want to know is love. And although God is very confusing to me and seems far away, it seems to me that he's the place to find it. That's where I'm at anyway."

"Oh, I've found love," Dr. Grant said toward the window, "I've found love." He turned, his face etched with lines of fatigue. "But she's a third of the way around the world from me and surrounded by a hundred lusty bulls panting over her. Love is a fragile thing, Miss DeKane. You have no idea."

Kyla felt a pit in her stomach, slightly embarrassed at his vulnerability. She was suddenly fearful for him.

He took a deep breath and blew it out. "Well, on that cheerful note I'm going to my room. Good night." He started for the stairs, then stopped, calling back, "Oh, yeah. Tomorrow I have to make a couple of stops after work, so I'll be home a little later. It's my turn to cook, so I'll bring dinner. Just letting you know."

Nice, Kyla thought. "Thanks. Good night."

She had just put the lemonade back into the refrigerator and their glasses into the dishwasher when her father came in from the deck, a look of annoyance on his face.

"I've had quite enough," he muttered, closing the door and gathering his briefcase from the corner of the Great Room where he had left it. "I'm calling it a night. See you in the morning."

As he disappeared, Kyla half expected the door to open again, but Peter did not come in. Out of curiosity she peeked out to see what he was doing, but apparently he had left another way, for he was gone. On the table, though, she spied a few dishes left out, and she went outside to collect them. Pouring the leftover water from a glass onto a plant in one of the patio pots, she scanned the yard but didn't see him there either. The air was still quite humid, but it was beginning to cool off a little and felt good on her skin. She paused, reflecting on the conversation with Dr. Grant. *I can't escape him! He's in my head!* She could definitely relate to that—only for her it was *God* who was in her head. And who would have ever thought that she—Kyla DeKane—would be open to God and trying to figure it all out!

On a whim she set the dishes back on the table and headed out to the wooden staircase where she usually talked to her dad, but rather than hanging out on her perch at the top, she went partially down the staircase until the lights of Wynnbury disappeared behind her. There, halfway down, she stopped to sit on the top step of the middle landing, looking out over the river in the dark. It was a perfect place to think, and she had a lot to think about. Her fingers curled absently around the rough edge of the step. What Mrs. Gordon had said earlier that morning had made sense—again. Kyla had learned to appreciate the older woman's wisdom. She had given her an accurate picture: Her heart was a rusty bucket of yuck. And that was an understatement!

So what can I do about it? Or is my heart just wrecked?

Mrs. Gordon's response had been so kind. *The hurt's gotta come out, and God's love has to go in. It's about layers and layers of forgiveness.*

Yeah, Kyla got that. She could see it. The hurt needed to come out. But how was that supposed to happen? She didn't exactly know what the hurt even was, much less how to get it out. And what did "layers and layers of forgiveness" mean? Did that apply to her birth father and all his issues? And if so, how? The idea of having a relationship with him was overwhelming to her, given what he was like! He was just—well, he was different—that's for sure! And it was not likely that he was ever going to change. Was she supposed to forgive him for being strange? Or for being a jerk? Is that what she was supposed to do? Did it mean accepting him for who he was—was that forgiveness? She wasn't sure she could do that. Or was it more than that? How could you forgive someone when they weren't sorry for anything? She closed her eyes. Everything was so complicated!

God, whatever happened to the "one great thing" I asked you for? Kyla asked silently. The hot car her father had given her wasn't so great after all. She could live without it. Nor was having her birth father in her life. She could live without him too, she thought wryly. Maybe those things weren't from God after all, she considered. Had they simply been a coincidence?

Her thoughts were interrupted as suddenly across the way the lights in the neighbor's house lit up, as if someone over there had just come home, or as if they were on a timer and all came on at once. The illuminated windows looked lovely radiating out on the black bluff. Like a little needed reminder of life beyond Wynnbury. She leaned forward with her elbows on her knees, fixing her eyes on the glow on opposite shore.

That's kinda what you're like, God, she mused. *It's like you're the bright and perfect one over there, and I'm over here. We're in two different worlds. And I have no way to reach you. I can't fly over that river, I can't swim that river, and I can't wade that river. And furthermore, I'm afraid of water. But I'm supposed to figure it out. You're like that, God. I don't know how to reach you.*

How was God's love supposed to fill her heart, as Mrs. Gordon had suggested? And as Peter had referenced too. What would she have to do to earn it?

In the darkness on a nearby tree Kyla suddenly heard loud hissing and an exchange of growls, followed by the scraping of claws as some kind of animal scampered to the ground. Raccoons possibly? She shivered, rising to her feet, peering into the black to make out its form. It was too dark to tell, but creeped out by it, she decided it was time to go in. As she neared the top of the staircase, she suddenly heard Peter's voice and noticed him walking across the yard toward her in the dark, unaware of her presence. He was talking on his phone.

"Yeah, I know! It concerns me too! I agree, and I'm on it!" He paused, listening before he continued. "Definitely. So take a look at that email as soon as you can and see if your friend would check into that for us. And I don't want to pressure the guy, but the sooner he could do it the better." He paused a moment. "Yes, I would like that—please do." There was a longer pause as he turned back to face the house. "Yes, Jesus. Yes! Amen. I agree in Jesus's name! Thank you, Kendall. And don't worry about your daught—" He stopped. "I'm sorry, what was that?" He gave a laugh. "Right! Well, we'll see, won't we? All right. All right—you have a good night. Yes, you too. Good-bye."

Kyla knew there was no way around startling him. She gave him a moment before speaking. "Hello, Peter."

He whirled. "Kyla! What—what are you doing out here?"

She stepped off the staircase onto the lawn. "Sorry—I didn't mean to scare you. I was sitting on the steps down there having a little time to myself. I was just coming up."

He gave a little grunt.

"You were talking to my dad, weren't you?"

He hesitated. "Yes."

She nodded. "Thought so. Was he—praying for you just now?"

He held his phone out, as if guilty. "He was."

Her brow furled. "Why?" He didn't ever pray for *her* over the phone! His mouth opened, but he didn't answer.

"Is everything okay? Is anything wrong?"

He met her eyes. "I—everything's okay. We were just—chatting. Are you okay?"

Kyla frowned. "Me?"

He shrugged. "I don't know—I'm surprised to see you out here. What are you doing? You weren't calling your dad."

"I'm all right." She rubbed her arm. "Like I said, I was just having some time alone. I'm just—I don't know—processing stuff with my father. Biological father."

"Ah." He nodded his head sympathetically. He glanced at his phone a second, then slid it into his front pocket. "Your dad said he had a nice talk with you yesterday."

Gah! Her dad and his talking about her! She raised her chin. "Yeah, we did. So what?"

He held up his hands. "Whoa! Just making polite conversation! I wasn't in your business. Honest!"

Kyla was silent, eyeing him. He seemed especially tall where he stood, with Wynnbury behind him.

"I didn't mean to offend you at all," he added.

A small smile spread across her face, and she looked down.

"What?" he asked curiously.

"You could have been three for three."

He shot her a questioning look.

"You have to admit—you've had offending people down to an art this evening! First Dr. Grant, then my father—" She laughed. "You should have seen the expression on my father's face when he came in!"

Peter gave an embarrassed smile.

"Good night, Peter," she said. "I'm going in."

"Good night," he replied after her.

As she expected, Kyla's birthday was quiet and under the radar, for she hadn't told anyone about it. Everyone was up that day around the same time, except for Dr. Grant, who had already left for school, so Kyla made a special breakfast for all of them, but it didn't seem out of the ordinary to anyone but her. Afterward her father approached her, regretfully explaining that the night before while they were talking on the patio, Peter had asked him to help set the tiers on the fountain basin that morning. He told her they hoped to be done by noon, and would it be okay if they could have their promised talk then? Kyla obliged him and offered to do his laundry, since she was starting to recognize his wearing the same clothing often. He took her up on the offer, dropping a pile of smelly clothes onto the laundry room floor for her to sort and wash. But he didn't mention her birthday at all, at which she was simultaneously relieved and bugged. At least he was consistent with the last seventeen years. She was invisible—wasn't that what she wanted?

She took the kids down to the waterfront for the morning. It was very hot, but they stayed cool playing in the water. Kyla made them wear their swim shirts for protection from the sun. Afterward they came up to the house for an early lunch, where from the Great Room she and the boys watched Peter and her father lift the second tier of the fountain in place, with only one left to go. She hoped Hank would nap that afternoon. Then perhaps she could occupy Howie with an activity or send him with Peter, while she and her father hung out on this, their last day together.

She was wiping down the table and the countertops when she heard Howie call her from the library, where he and Hank were waiting for reading time.

"Miss Kane! Hank's going upstairs!"

"Okay," she called back.

That could be a good sign, she speculated. Perhaps an indication that Hank was tired and ready to lie down. She finished up and checked in on Howie, who had gotten out a bead kit and was at the table stringing them onto a plastic cord.

"Can I do this?" he asked guiltily.

"Of course," she answered. "Just remember to ask first, just in case. Some things are too little for Hank when he's around."

She told him she would be back in a bit and ran upstairs to fetch Hank and put him to bed. When she got to the top she groaned, for both Peter's and her father's doors were wide open. She peeked into Peter's room and closed the door, for no little intruder was within. Then she stuck her head in her father's room, spying the top of Hank's blond head on the other side of the bed, where he was sitting on the floor.

"I'm working," he said, smiling up at her.

Kyla remembered the boys standing on the chair at the window in this room before her father arrived, looking at the deer in the yard.

"Are you?" she said, coming around the bed to see him. "What are you working on?"

Kyla's jaw fell open, and she instantly felt sick. There on the floor was her father's briefcase, jackknifed and upside down, his papers scattered everywhere. Hank was sitting on top of them, kicking them with his feet, wrinkling and scattering them wildly.

"Oh, no! Hank—what did you do?" she moaned, glancing back at the door. Oh, her father would not like this at all!

"It falled off the bed!" he said, pointing to the briefcase.

"Oh, goodness!" Kneeling down by the mess, she scraped some of the pages together and started gathering them up, but Hank was having great fun spreading them out with his kicking as fast as she could pick them up.

"Hank, stop! That's enough!"

He gave a squeal of delight, whipping the papers up with his hands.

Hastily she snatched him up and took him to his room, tucking him into his bed with his blankie and bear, instructing him sternly to stay there until she came back. It wasn't very likely that a nap was going to happen, but at least he was contained in a safe place for a bit. She shut the door and hurried back to the disaster in her father's room.

Righting the briefcase, she propped it open against the nearby dresser and began carefully gathering the papers as before, stacking the obvious groupings into piles as neatly as she could. All the while her imagination played out her father's irritation when he discovered the mess. What would he do? Yell at her? Yell at Hank? She had almost finished pulling the last of the debris from under the bed when a small, lumpy manila envelope in the middle of the pile flapped open, and its contents slid right out, dumping onto the rug. Kyla looked down in surprise at a collection of what looked like at least twenty various credit cards and identification cards. That was a lot! She picked one up, her mouth opening in amazement as she studied the card.

What? Bewildered, she reached for a few of the others, examining the pieces. One was a driver's license that had her father's photo on it—but the name read "Robert Alan Morrow." On another card was a different photo of her father with the name "Robert D. Sandquist." And another—"Robert Michael Dewey." *What?* Kyla fingered them in confusion. Then her heart began to race as she spread them out on the floor, categorizing them by name. He was five different people! She bit her lip, shaking her head. *What in the world was this guy into?* Five different names, with matching credit cards and various photo IDs—even a library card for one of the names! Stunned, she stared at the array on the floor, wondering what her father really did for a living.

Put them back right away! she told herself. She did not want to confront this! She did not want him to know that she had seen any of it, and Dr. Grant was going to be told about this the very second he got home! She would tell him immediately! Although—Kyla glanced at the open briefcase and piles of papers—although it would be pretty obvious that someone had gone through his stuff. Perhaps she could hide the manila envelope somewhere in the center of the pile and pretend she knew nothing about it, pretend it hadn't opened. The idea also occurred to her to mess all the papers up again, as it had been when she had walked in on Hank. The more she thought about it, the more reasonable a solution it seemed to be. She would simply pretend she didn't know anything at all about the mess! Hank would be in trouble, certainly, but he was a baby, and DeKane's secrets would be safe.

Yet—Kyla chewed her thumb—yet she wanted to remember these

names. Quickly she repeated them in her mind: *Morrow, Sandquist, Dewey, Springman, Perkins*. Then she realized that all of the driver's licenses also had addresses. She definitely wanted those too, but—she frowned—how could she ever remember them all? *My phone,* she thought. *I'll grab my phone and take a photo of the cards.*

Right that second, behind her, before she could even move, Kyla heard the little sucking sound her father made through his teeth. A blanket of dread descended on her, and she closed her eyes, knowing he was there in the room, right behind her. Remembering how cruelly he had grabbed her in the dark that first night, she braced herself for his reaction and, feeling panicky, she wondered if she should call for Peter right away. But he was probably outside and wouldn't hear her anyway.

Nervously she turned to look up at him. He was standing in the doorway with his hands in his pockets, rocking on his feet, watching her. She wondered how long he had been there. With all her might she wished she hadn't gone looking for Hank, wished she hadn't found him and this mess in her father's room! It would have been much easier to blame it on an innocent toddler. Quickly, while the pile was still out of his sight, Kyla pushed the ID cards unobtrusively around the side of the briefcase, hoping he wouldn't notice, hoping that she would possibly have another opportunity to hide them somehow so that he wouldn't find out she had seen them.

"Oh, man—I was just about to come and find you!" she said, shaking her head. "I need to apologize to you! Wait till you see it—Hank got in here and made one terrible mess! I'm so sorry!"

DeKane stepped in and clicked the door shut. Kyla felt a pit in her stomach.

"I really let him have it," she continued breathlessly, "and he's now in his bed. I've been trying to straighten things up a little for you, but, as you see—" She made a face, gesturing to the papers before her.

He walked over to observe the floor on her side of the bed, then wordlessly sat down on the chair, facing her.

"I just hope I don't get fired for this!" she added, trying another angle. "I should have been watching him when he came upstairs!"

His face was flushed, and he was breathing hard. Kyla couldn't tell if it was from exertion, having just come up the stairs, or from being outside, for it was beastly hot out, and he was sweaty too. Or if it was because of her, sitting there beside the dumped briefcase. He rested his arms on the side of the chair, just looking at her. After an awkward full minute of silence, he stretched out a leg to slide the briefcase to the side, exposing the plastic cards spilled from the envelope. Kyla met his eyes, her lips pressed tightly together.

"I suppose you'll want an explanation for that," he said quietly.

Kyla's mouth was dry, and she couldn't think of one thing to say. Again they sat without speaking.

"Howie is downstairs," she finally croaked. "I should probably—"

"Never mind Howie," he cut in. "The gardener boy is with him, probably indoctrinating his little mind with religious nonsense at this very moment. I asked him to give us a little time together, and we need to talk."

She swallowed, relieved to know that Peter was in the house at least. Her father gave a long sigh, then made his signature sound through his teeth. She decided to face him.

"Yes. Okay then—let's talk!" She acknowledged the pile of plastic cards before her, gesturing with her foot. "So who are you?"

He opened his hands. "I'm Robert DeKane, your father."

"Really? Huh. Well, there seems to be a whole pile of other men who look *exactly* like you!" She waved to the cards.

"And as I said, there's an explanation for that." He leaned back and crossed his legs, pressing his fingertips together in front of him, studying her thoughtfully. "Kyla, Kyla—you're wound up so tight. Tight as a spring! You don't have to be afraid of me, you know. I'm not happy about my stuff being knocked over and the mess, but mostly I was really hoping we wouldn't have to go here. I didn't want to have to pop your fairy tale bubble, but I guess it's gotta happen. I hope you are an open-minded girl. Are you prepared for your world to change?"

Kyla wasn't prepared for anything. She stared at him, unable to speak, waiting for him to continue.

He watched her a little while longer, then tiredly rose to lift the briefcase from the floor, setting it on the edge of the dresser. With nimble fingers he fiddled with the combination lock until she heard the distinct pop of a compartment opening. Reaching in, he retrieved a thin black leather wallet and handed it down to where she sat against the side of the bed.

"This might help for starters," he said.

She opened the wallet. It was a badge, a very official-looking gold metal badge, and beside it a signed and stamped photo identification card with his name spelled out and *Federal Bureau of Investigation* written across the top. Kyla's jaw dropped as she shot him a look.

He sat back down in his chair, watching her.

"I—I don't understand," she said, scrutinizing it more closely. How could this be? The badge looked legitimate. It looked real. It looked *real*! Finally she lifted her head, her forehead scrunched. "You gotta be kidding me! You work for the FBI? Seriously?"

He smiled at her questioning look and gave her a wink. "Actually, no. It's a fake, but you wouldn't know that, would you? I think it's rather impressive. It comes in handy!"

Kyla blinked in surprise. "Wha—?"

"But I *am* a detective," he said. "A private investigator. Robert DeKane, PI." He paused, letting his words sink in. "Depending on what I'm doing, I have to take on different roles. I have a couple personas. I use props like that as a regular part of my job." He gestured toward the pile of identification cards. "And sometimes the badge, but sparingly since it's bogus."

She looked down at the badge again, then closed the wallet and set it with the cards.

"Things aren't always what they seem," he said.

She narrowed her eyes. "Then you lied to me! You said you were an investment broker!"

He made a sound of protest and jerked his shoulder. "I do that too!"

There was another long pause. Kyla rubbed her forehead. Was he telling the truth? A detective? For real? He looked so unlike any private investigator or detective she'd ever seen on television or in movies. The image in her mind did not fit him in the least.

"How—how long have you been doing detective work?"

He tipped his head. "A long time, baby. A long time. Longer than you've been around on the planet."

"My whole life? So when I was a kid, this is what you did—you were a detective? And are you now? Are you, um,"—she wasn't sure how to ask—"um, active? Like, you still work? You're not retired?"

"Still at it."

"What does that mean? What do you actually do?"

"Lots of thing! But basically at the bottom line—I catch bad guys."

Kyla studied him thoughtfully. "Does this have anything to do with how you met my mother?" She remembered he had told her they met "on a job."

He did not answer, his face expressionless. Kyla knew it must be close to the truth.

She probed deeper, taking a shot in the dark. "And does this have anything to do with why my mother asked you to leave?"

Again he was silent.

"It does, doesn't it? Was it because your job endangered the family? Mom and me?"

He answered carefully, "My job was dangerous and very stressful at the time, yes. And safer for you that I go."

Kyla gave a little exhale, looking down again at the disheveled pile of ID cards. For a split second she was five years old and in her childhood home, watching her mother cry hysterically, except that now she saw it from a new angle. She looked up. "So why couldn't you tell me this? Why couldn't you be honest with me about all this—about what you do?"

"That's what we need to talk about," he said simply.

"Well then, let's talk about it!"

He fingered his chin, hesitating.

"Well, what's the problem?" she asked after he still didn't respond.

"It's about a situation that's been in process for some time now."

"Yes? What does that mean? You're on a job right now?"

He made the sound with his teeth. "Yes. I'm working as we speak. In fact,"—he shifted in the chair—"right under your nose."

Her eyes grew large. "Here in New Hampton?" Then she gave a little exclamation, holding up her finger. "So *that's* what you're doing. Your clients. That's why you've been in town the last two days."

He raised his brow. "Closer than that!"

Kyla cocked her head. "Closer than New Hampton? How could— what, like here at Wynnbury?"

DeKane nodded slowly.

"What would be going on *here* that would need investigating?"

He leaned forward, resting his elbows on his knees. "I'm glad you asked, but you have to understand that if I tell you, it brings you on the inside of things. It's a game-changer."

Kyla blinked, goosebumps suddenly spreading up her arms at his grim tone.

His face was earnest. "I'm going to need you to be level-headed about this. And I'm going to need your full cooperation."

"Cooperation—with what?" Kyla shook her head, confused. "What's going on?"

"Hold on," he said a bit impatiently, "I'm about to tell you!"

She faced him, waiting.

He pursed his lips, hesitating again. "I'm sorry, baby. This may be difficult to hear." He sniffed. "There's just no easy way to say it. It's about the professor."

Her head drew back.

"I'm afraid your professor isn't as upright as he appears. Your Dr. David Grant is under investigation for a serious crime."

She gave him a dubious look. "No. There's no way."

The corner of his mouth turned up. "That's what I mean about being open-minded, baby. Things aren't always what they seem to be."

"Well, it's not true. Can't be!"

DeKane held out a hand. "That's what I mean. I'm going to need you to engage with me here. I can't tell you if I can't trust you to handle this."

Kyla stared at him in disbelief, shaking her head. "But for what? What did he do? I have a very hard time believing Dr. Grant could do anything—bad."

Her father was silent.

She paused, fidgeting nervously as she looked up at him. Was this for real? Or would he wink at her again and tell her it was all a joke? But his face was completely serious. And he kept looking at her, waiting for her response.

"This is crazy!" she said finally, "Just so—crazy!" She took a deep breath, letting it out in a controlled way, and tried to relax her shoulders. "Okay—I understand. You can trust me. I want you to tell me what's going on."

Her father folded his hands together. "Okay. It is believed that Dr. Grant has possession of some very valuable stolen property."

"Dr. Grant a thief?" Kyla shook her head. "Never! Like what? What did he steal?"

DeKane tilted his head. "Well, we're pretty certain he didn't *steal* what we're looking for, but we are pretty certain that he *has* what we're looking for."

This would explain her father's nosiness. "What are you looking for? And who's 'we'?"

"My partner and I." He slid down in the chair, crossing his legs. "This is where it gets interesting. One of my specialties as an investigator is finding stolen art. And artifacts. There is reason to believe he has some very valuable items that are missing from a museum in London. As you know, he and his wife, Marilee, travel back and forth from there frequently. We are investigating the possibility that these items may have been transported and hidden here."

"You're not serious. Stuff stolen from a museum? Like paintings or something?"

"Possibly. Or artifacts. Or other things."

A sudden soberness settled over her. "This is all speculation, right? I mean, do you know this for certain?"

He gave her a sad nod. "I'm sorry, baby. It's my job. Like I said earlier, I was hoping you and I wouldn't have to go down this road, hoping you wouldn't have to know anything about this. Professor Grant has been under investigation for over a year now. We have suspected that the items have been brought in and hidden somewhere here on this property for some time, but there was no way we could get in here without raising suspicion. You, my dear, were an incredible stroke of luck in the game. You were my ticket in!"

She frowned, considering his words. "Me? How was I—?" She stopped. "Wait—are you telling me that your visit here was planned? The stalking—that was for *this*?"

He chuckled. "Stalking? Baby, I wasn't stalking you—I was *watching out* for you! When I knew you would be here, I felt obligated to keep an eye on you to make sure you were going to be safe."

"Pfft! Dr. Grant is hardly dangerous!"

He shrugged. "That's what I needed to find out! And that night in the woods—I was going to try to talk to you, but unfortunately it didn't go down that way." He gave a twisted smile. "As I said, things aren't always as they seem."

She leveled her gaze at him. "Then that means you've been *pretending* you're here for me."

He threw his hands together with a smile. "Well, now, that's the beauty of it! I haven't had to pretend at all! I might act like a fool, baby, but I know how to do my job!"

Kyla regarded him for a bit, then put her head down on her knees, her mind reeling with the information she had just learned. She wouldn't have suspected that of Dr. Grant in a million years! How could it possibly be true? After a while she pulled herself up off the floor and sat on the edge of the bed. "Sorry, I'm just—just struggling to believe all this!"

"Yeah." DeKane heaved a heavy sigh. "Kyla, I know it's been tough reconnecting after all these years. It's only natural that it's going to take some time to build our relationship. But I care about you. I wouldn't want anything to happen to you!"

She swallowed. His sincerity surprised her.

"The last thing I want to do is make life more difficult for you, but I think it's pretty evident that someone's got some secrets around here! You're my daughter, my own flesh and blood, and I believe you're smart as well as beautiful. I won't insult your intelligence—you can look around for yourself and see it. Grant skirts questions, keeps things locked up tight, and keeps me on a short leash with a chokehold grip! Haven't you noticed that I've had next to no time away from the two of them? There's barely been a moment when I haven't been asked to 'help' them with something!"

Was that true? Kyla stared at the pile of papers on the floor, considering his words. He definitely had been drafted into the fountain construction. And yes, she knew that Dr. Grant had something clandestine brewing, but she could never imagine him into anything illegal. And yet in the back of her mind she remembered his words from her first day at Wynnbury when they had talked in the kitchen. *You know, this would be the perfect little spot if you were into anything illegal. You could train a terrorist army here, and no one would ever know....*

Resigned, she looked up. "So what now? What am I supposed to do, now that I know all this?"

DeKane sat forward. "Yes, we need to talk about that! First off, we certainly don't want to alert the professor that we're on to him, so you're going to have to act as if you know absolutely nothing about this. You must not say a word."

Kyla bit her lip. This was becoming a theme. "Yeah, okay."

"Second, if we find the goods, we've caught him."

"You want to get on the third floor," she stated simply.

He raised his eyebrows, giving her a *good girl* nod, as if he thought her very smart.

She shook her head. "I've been up there. There's no art up there. There's *nothing* up there!" She added candidly, "He told me he was searching for a time capsule." Then she suddenly felt guilty, like Dr. Grant himself was there in the room, invisibly peering at her. *Not a word!* But what was she supposed to do?

His chin rose. "Is that right? I believe that's called throwing you a bone—giving you an answer to make you happy while still protecting himself. But don't worry, baby. As I've mentioned before, this house has secrets, clues! I believe Grant has a strategy in what he does, and he hasn't locked up the third floor for nothing."

"What do you mean? Do you think there's a secret passageway or something?"

He chuckled. "You never know. It wouldn't surprise me!"

"Well, he never had it locked up until you came."

"Is that right?" DeKane's head tipped in interest. He nodded slowly. "Well, I suppose he trusted that you were ignorant. You certainly wouldn't be looking for anything."

"But why for *you*?"

"That's a good question now, isn't it?"

Kyla gave a tired sigh. "Okay," she said reluctantly. "He'll be at work tomorrow again. I'll see what I can do. I'll have to figure out how to get the keys."

DeKane clapped his hands together. "Thank you. I'm also looking for some information that I believe would be somewhere in his study. I'd like you to either get in there or get me in there to look for it. Information on a man named Michael Kennedy or on Wynnbury House—like a book or a file or anything that would contain verifying evidence of what we're looking for. Anything."

There *was* a file—Kyla's mind flashed back to the morning she had walked in on Dr. Grant and Peter in the kitchen, remembering him immediately closing a file folder on the counter. But again, this was Dr. Grant! How could he possibly be involved in something like this? She shook her head. "I don't know. It feels so wrong!"

"Hey—his *hidden loot* is what's wrong! And"—he gestured to her with his hand—"you're like a teacher's pet! He favors you! If he notices anything out of the ordinary, you can make up any old excuse and he'll roll with it. You have that man eating right out of your hand, baby." He smiled at her and winked.

Kyla looked down at her feet, shaking her head again. "This is unbelievable." She looked up at him suddenly. "What about the kids? If this is true, then this puts them in a terrible position! Dr. Grant could be in big trouble!"

He pointed his finger at her. "That, baby, is what an intelligent professor should have thought of before getting into this! It is indeed a big problem, but this is *his* big problem, not yours."

Her heart ached thinking of Howie and Hank. "Yeah, but still—it's terrible!"

"Yes, it is." He made the noise with his teeth. "But on the other hand, it doesn't have to be messy. He could easily turn himself in. The kids *do* have a mother. Or there's foster care. It's not our problem."

Not *your* problem, Kyla thought. But it was very much *her* problem.

She cared about those little boys! They were both silent for a bit. Then DeKane spoke.

"Kyla, you have to understand one other thing—"

She looked up.

"We're so close to solving this, but I need to be here for this to work. I can't leave."

Kyla nodded. "Yeah. I get that."

Peter and Howie were still sitting together, snuggled in the large armchair in the library when Kyla came down. Peter looked up from reading to Howie.

"By the look on your face I take it your talk didn't go very well."

Kyla gave a little shrug and made herself smile, trying to lighten up. "Oh, well—you know my father."

Peter had his arms around Howie, who was nestled cozily against his chest on his lap, their book held out in front of them. The two looked comfortable, and Peter made no move to leave, like he was ready to hang out and chat. Kyla knew she couldn't talk to him right now.

"Do you need to go quite yet?" she asked him. "'Cause if not, I wouldn't mind some time alone. That is, if you don't mind watching him for a while longer."

"Sure—I'll hang out here. We're good. Are you sure everything's all right?" He eyed her closely.

"Yes! I get to stay with you!" Howie gave a fist pump, beaming up at Peter.

Kyla smiled tiredly and answered, "I'm okay. I just need to take care of a few things."

She went upstairs to her room and sat before the tile fireplace, numb. Her head hurt with trying to make sense of everything. It was impossible to believe what she had learned about Dr. Grant, but yet all the mystery, the meetings behind closed doors, the sudden moving of the pictures from the foyer wall—those were just a few of many things that were admittedly odd. She wasn't sure what to make of it all, but something was definitely up with him. Kyla shook her head in disbelief. Valuables from a museum! She wondered what they were. And what did he intend to do with them? How could he possibly be involved in harboring stolen items? And what was Peter's role in all of this? They worked together so closely. She wondered how much he knew.

Hank! Her eyes grew wide as suddenly, out of the blue, Kyla remembered the toddler. She had thrown him into his room and closed the door. Hurriedly she went to check on him, peeking in through the door that adjoined to her room. She gave a start, then groaned at what she saw. Every single dresser drawer in the room had been opened and emptied onto the floor, like a violent volcanic eruption of little clothes had occurred, and there, right smack in the middle of the floor, was Hank, sound asleep on the rug, his blankie and bear neatly tucked under his arm.

Chapter Twenty-Four

Kyla was in a fog for the rest of the afternoon. Her father was exactly right—her bubble had burst. Her small world had been turned upside down.

At dinner that night Kyla was not hungry and could hardly concentrate on the conversation. Despite the stifling heat and pressing humidity, they ate outside because Dr. Grant said that everyone should spend some time outside every day—and apparently her morning at the beach didn't count. He was in a talkative mood and was in deep conversation with her father about the various dynamics in the current Middle East conflict, happy to have at least one person to discuss a topic he was very interested in. Kyla was amazed at how her father could play his part at the table, leaning in toward the professor, asking questions that drew him out. Every now and then he would glance at Kyla with a small smile.

Peter, on the other hand, was not himself. Kyla wasn't sure what had happened since she had seen him in the library, but he barely talked, eating in silence, stealing furtive looks at her father and looking out toward the fountain frequently. Anxiety gnawed at her. Her world was one of second-guessing now. What did he know? How much did he know? Was he right in there with Dr. Grant? Did he know that *she* knew?

After dinner Dr. Grant excused himself to the kitchen, then stuck his head back out the door to ask Peter and DeKane for some assistance. Kyla sat alone listening to Howie's incessant talking and tried to keep Hank from hitting his brother with his spoon. She was completely caught off guard when the door opened and her father came forth carrying a small birthday cake, setting it before her. In the angst of the afternoon, she had completely forgotten her own birthday! Her father was followed by Dr. Grant carrying a large rectangular gift and matching gift bag, and by Peter, who set a medium-sized brown box beside her place at the table, on top of which was another small package wrapped in plain brown paper.

"Surprise, baby," her father said, squeezing her shoulder warmly. "Happy birthday!"

Embarrassed, Kyla held her hands over her cheeks while the men sang her a very out-of-tune happy birthday wish. She thanked them, relaying her genuine surprise, and looked at her father in amazement. He hadn't let on all day about this! He smiled back.

She served the cake first, since Howie was already leaning across the table with his fingers in the side of it and Hank was flapping his arms and crying out that he wanted some too. Then after everyone had enjoyed some and the boys were sufficiently "sugared up," as Dr. Grant termed it, he encouraged her to open her gifts.

Shyly she turned to the presents and took the plain one from the top, on which was scrawled "From Peter." As she moved the package, it revealed a letter underneath. A jolt of adrenaline shot through her as Kyla recognized the handwriting and saw the name "Alex Duvall" boldly inked on the return address. Quickly she placed the letter in her lap to open later, glancing around the table. Dr. Grant and her father were talking and didn't see it, but Peter met her eyes, his face expressionless. Kyla looked away and turned back to his gift.

It was a journal. A white leather journal with the phrase *His mercies are new every morning* stamped on the front in gold. The pages were bright white and lined, with a Bible verse on the bottom of each page. It was beautiful. She recognized that it was a risky gift on his part, but she liked it, not minding so much that it was religious. Rubbing her hand over the smooth cover, she thanked him, to which he responded with a brief smile and a nod.

The box underneath Peter's gift had been mailed from her dad. He had sent her a bag of her favorite candy, a body wash and lotion set, and some earrings. Tucked in the side of the box was a birthday card with a gift certificate to a favorite chain restaurant, "for whenever she was able to get away," he wrote, plus a collection of mail from home. She opened the candy and gave a piece to the boys, because, Kyla declared that they needed "just a little more sugar" for the evening, at which Dr. Grant rolled his eyes.

The professor and the kids gave her an aquarium set and two goldfish in a bulging ziplock bag. The boys could hardly contain their excitement, staring and poking at the fish in the plastic pouch.

"I got the idea from Howie," Dr. Grant said apologetically, gesturing to the tank. "They'd been begging. I figured you'd either love it or hate it. I understand it means a little work."

"I love it," she said. She told the boys they could help her name the fish.

After she had finished opening her presents, Kyla thanked everyone for their kindness, but Peter interrupted her.

"We have one more thing," he said. "Hold on."

He rose from the table and left the patio. Kyla saw his back as he leaned over, doing something on the other side of the concrete spindles. Then he returned to the deck, smiling.

"Well, would you look at that?" Dr. Grant declared, rising to his feet. "We have a fountain, up and running!"

Everyone stood to look out across the yard at it, even the kids in their chairs, who clapped their hands and shouted.

Dr. Grant smiled broadly, moving from his seat to shake Peter's hand. "Nice job, Peter Watkins! She's a beauty!"

The two of them stood side by side, looking out over the rail at it, exchanging talk about the new challenges Peter had had with it just that morning. Kyla's father sat at the table, glancing at his watch.

"Well, my dear," Dr. Grant said, turning back to the table, "since it is your birthday, you have the rest of the night off. Come on, boys—let's go try to burn off some of that sugar before it's time for bed."

Everybody disappeared except for her father, and although the clouds in the sky had grown very dark and threatening, Kyla asked if he would like to walk out to the fountain with her. She wanted to get a closer view. As they crossed the yard gouged by the machinery, Kyla's father explained to her how he and Peter had hoisted on the tiers one after another and how the plumbing threaded up through the center. She really didn't care. She just liked how it looked, spraying out from the top in a perfect arc, filling the first tier, which elegantly dripped over to fill the second tier, which overflowed into the larger third tier, to finally pour into the broad pool basin at the bottom. She sat on the edge, passing her hand through the water below, its coolness refreshing on such a horribly sticky day.

"Here," her father said, handing her a small bundle of cash. "I didn't want to do this at the table in front of everybody. I hope you aren't offended. I'm not good at shopping for girls."

"No, please," Kyla said, shaking her head. "You don't have to give me anything."

"Hey—I want to," he said, placing the cash into her hand. "Happy birthday, baby."

"Thank you," she said, taking it and placing it in her pocket. "I just want to say"—she swallowed, feeling on the verge of tears—"um, to tell you that tonight—the cake—that was really special. Thank you." For a first-ever acknowledgment of her birthday, he had done very well.

He smiled again and looked away, placing his hands into his pockets, gazing out toward the river. The air was ominously still and heavy. In the distance they could hear the foreboding rumble of thunder. DeKane made his little noise with his teeth and said they should probably go in, as it looked as if the sky could open up on them at any moment.

Kyla assembled the fish tank alone in the kitchen. Her father had gone upstairs, and Peter was working out. She could hear him on one of the machines in the fitness room. From upstairs she could hear screeches of delight as Dr. Grant played with his children, and her new revelation of him invaded her mind again, distracting her to the point that she had to read the directions on the bottle of drops for the tank water three times before she knew what to do. What would happen to Dr. Grant? What would happen to this man she had grown to love and respect, who felt like her family? What would happen to his children? What would happen to his wife, Marilee Montayne, and would this be everywhere in the news? Once again Kyla's world was crumbling.

I didn't want to have to pop your fairy tale bubble, she heard her father's voice say. *Are you prepared for your world to change?* No, she was certainly not.

She finished preparing the aquarium and put the fish in, keeping them inside their plastic bag until they adjusted to the new water temperature. Leaving them on the peninsula, she took the box that held her presents upstairs to her room. This had been one of the oddest birthdays ever, she mused, with the sweetness of the surprise at dinner paired with the shocking discovery not only of Dr. Grant's secret thing but also of her father's secret occupation too. What a day! She took Alex's letter out and tossed it onto the table near her purse, unwilling to open it. She'd had enough to deal with today without adding him to the equation.

Pulling the new journal out of the box, she admired its snowy-white pages with their gilded edges and opened it to read a few of the verses at the bottom.

He who did not spare his own Son, but gave him up for us all—how will he not also, along with him, graciously give us all things?

She remembered that one from yesterday in her new Bible. She flipped to another page.

Call on me in the day of trouble; I will deliver you, and you will honor me.

And on the page next to that, *The Lord is gracious and compassionate, slow to anger and rich in love.*

The Bible verses made her think of her dad, and Kyla sighed. She wished she could call him to talk about everything that had happened that day, but she knew that was impossible. She wished she could ask him to pray, but she knew she couldn't. He couldn't know anything about what was happening. He would freak. In her mind she saw his face and missed him. He was always strong, always happy. He always knew what to do. She remembered weeks ago when she had asked him to pray that she got this job at Wynnbury how he had flung it back on her—*You pray*, he had said.

You pray. She bit her lip. The verse in her journal did say to *call upon him in the day of trouble.* Okay, she thought. Courageously, Kyla got up and took the journal to the table, where she took a pen from the cup from Peter.

"Dear God," she wrote in her neatest handwriting, "I don't exactly know how to pray, so I hope that you will be able to figure me out and understand what I am saying." She paused, wanting to write out all the detailed specifics of her dilemma, yet she debated. What if Hank accidentally walked off with her journal, and Dr. Grant ended up with it? It could happen. Kyla thought a moment and put the pen back to the page. "I love those kids," she continued cryptically, "and I don't want to see them hurt. I want to protect them, but I can't. I can't do anything about what's happening. It's like a flood has rolled in, and the water's too deep for me, and I'm afraid. I feel helpless, like I'm being swept away by all of this. God, will you help me?"

She drew back and read over what she had written, suddenly feeling very foolish. How lame her metaphoric words sounded! And childish. She had just marred the first page of her perfect journal. Wasn't that just like her *life*? So much beautiful potential that unfolded into disappointing and flawed realities, like these stupid words on the page. She fought the urge to scribble it all out or rip out the page, suddenly perturbed at God. Did she actually think God was going to read her journal?

With her stress level completely topped out for the day, Kyla drew a hard line across the page with her pen, then under it, in larger, angry handwriting, wrote, "God, where are you? Why are you so against me? Why is it that you have cast me off like I don't exist to you? Why is it that you have taken every person that I've loved away from me? First my father, then my mom, then Alex, now Dr. Grant and the boys." A teardrop plopped onto the page. She wiped it off with the back of her hand, continuing, "I feel like I'm trying to reach you, trying to figure you out, trying to get on your good side, but I can't. What do I have to do to earn your love? What do I have to do to earn a moment of your attention? Why is it that Peter and Mrs. Gordon and my dad can find you, but I can't?" Kyla paused, fiddling agitatedly with the clip on her pen. It snapped off and popped against the paper cup on the table. It reminded her of her time out on the wooden staircase in the dark last night.

She continued writing: "It's like you're the lights on the far side of the river and everyone—Dad, Peter, Mrs. Gordon—are over there with you. And I'm stuck by myself here on this side trying to figure things out. It's like I'm separated out, alienated for some reason, and I can't get across. The more I try to find you, the worse it gets. Is there no way to get to where they are? Is there no way to get to you?"

Kyla set the pen aside, leaning with her face in her hands over the journal, her elbows on the table, thinking. She sniffed, looking at the page, then picked up her pen. "My life keeps unraveling, and I don't know what to do. I feel like my feet are stuck in mud and the water keeps getting higher and higher. Can't you see me down here? I'm this speck—this crumb that you've brushed off your lap onto the floor! Look at me—I'm drowning, God!" She paused, then wrote in large letters across the bottom, "If you are real, then show me! And will you please help me somehow?"

She closed the journal and pushed it up on the desk, setting the paper cup on top of it. Peter's handwriting on the cup faced her with its words: *Ask him, and he will show you.*

Well, we'll see about that, she thought.

Her shoulders were tense. Kyla stretched her arms out and twisted first one way and then the other. It had been such a strange day, and she was wound up tight. She needed to relax. Eyeing the gift from her dad, she decided to draw a bath before bed so she could use the new body lotion afterward. It was a small way to feel connected to him. Even though he hadn't been there for her birthday, he had always tried to make her feel special on her day and thinking of him was comforting to her. After filling the tub with water, she sank down into the hot, bubbly water and put her feet up, crossing them on the front edge, breathing deeply.

Less than five minutes later, Kyla heard the sound of Howie's small fist on the door.

"Miss Kane, I have to go potty."

No stinking way! Seriously? "I'm taking a bath, Howie," she called.

"I have to go really bad," he said in a worried voice. "I forgot to go before bed. Hurry!"

Of course, every other night he remembered—but not tonight! At this point it was comical to her. Toweling off, she grabbed her robe from the back of the door and belted it around her waist, letting Howie in, who rushed to use the toilet.

"Could I have a drink too?" he asked while he washed his hands.

"A small one," she said, handing him the cup.

"It smells good in here," he said, sniffing the air.

"Thanks." He looked really cute in his little pajamas with his dark hair and light freckles, and she couldn't help smiling at him.

He smiled back. "Guess what? I already have names for the fish."

"Oh, yeah? What have you come up with?"

He handed the cup back, wiping his mouth on the nearby towel. "'Goldie' for the plain gold one, and for the other one that has a little white on it, 'Spot.'"

Kyla nodded. "'Goldie' and 'Spot.' I like your names. Come on—I'll tuck you in again."

She took him back to bed and covered him up, tucking the blankets in around him.

"I love you, Miss Kane. You're nice," he whispered.

"Love you too, Howie." She kissed his forehead.

He sighed happily. "I'm so glad Peter told my dad it was your birthday, because now we get to have fish!"

Kyla cocked her head in the dark. "Peter told your dad it was my birthday?"

He nodded. "Yeah, last night. Peter asked my dad to get you a cake. Then Dad got you the fish too."

"How do you know this?" she asked quietly.

He yawned. "He told me tonight when we took a bath. Do you like the fish?"

"Yes, I do. I like them a lot. Good night, Howie." She kissed his head again.

Back in the bathroom she abandoned the bath and drained the tub, then stood looking at herself in the mirror. Peter. Peter, not DeKane, had made the evening happen. She shook her head, biting her lip. Then later, while brushing her teeth, she concluded that it was more likely that her dad Kendall had reminded Peter about her birthday so it wouldn't be forgotten. Definitely, she thought. It had to be. Her dad was like that. So truly, her dad had made it happen. She was sure of it. Part of that made her feel really special, yet part of that made her feel like a little kid. She was twenty-three now, not thirteen. The evening whisked through her mind from the new perspective. Her dad had obligated Peter and Dr. Grant to buy her things. How embarrassing! She wondered how much Dr. Grant had spent on the fish tank and goldfish.

Then she frowned, remembering the conversation with her biological father beside the fountain. Why had he not said anything when she thanked him for the evening? Instead, he had taken credit for the night! She let out a little breath. What a total rat he was! Her head hurt from thinking about him. Tired, she used her new body lotion and went to bed.

Not too much later Kyla was awakened from a deep sleep by the sound of pounding on her door. Groggily she glanced at the clock, noting that she had only been asleep for a little over an hour. Again the knocking sounded. Sleepily she lifted her head right as the door opened and an outline of a head appeared in the light of the hall.

"Kyla, it's Peter. Are you awake?" He was talking in his normal tone, not a whisper.

She pulled herself up onto her elbow, alarmed. "What is it?"

"Sorry," he said, "Grant asked me to wake everyone. There's a bad storm, and he'd like everyone downstairs. Quickly!"

She sat up the rest of the way, jarred awake. "What? Downstairs?"

"Yes, down to the cellar. You go. We've got the boys." He disappeared.

Kyla had never been asked to take shelter from a storm before, and it frightened her. Hastily she pulled on her robe and stepped out in the hall, squinting in the brightness. She hurried straight on toward the back stairs, taking the shortcut down to the side entry where the cellar steps were. Her father was already there in his jeans and shirt, sitting on the floor against the stone wall, clutching his black briefcase. He greeted her tiredly and patted the concrete floor beside him for her to join him. Dr. Grant appeared shortly after with Hank in his arms, and behind him came Peter, carrying Howie and some blankets.

"Here—sit on this," Peter said, handing one to Kyla, casting a hard glance at her father.

She took it and sat on it, grateful for the padding. Hank stirred in Dr. Grant's arms, waking enough to see Kyla and reach for her. He handed him down to her, and she tucked his blanket and bear in his arms, snuggling him immediately back to sleep. Then Dr. Grant folded another blanket to make a bed for Howie on the floor, where Peter carefully laid him down, covering his face to keep the light out of his eyes. Then the two men stood at the bottom of the stairs, waiting. Peter had on shorts and a tank top, and Kyla could finally fully see his arm tattoo from across the room. It was the earth—a round earth with a wooden cross that covered and extended beyond it on the top and bottom. Underneath the earth was a scroll with words she couldn't read from where she was. He stood with his back to her, with a hand on his hip. Beside him Dr. Grant sat wearily on the steps, murmuring to Peter that old Mother Nature was sure releasing her fury tonight.

In less than twenty minutes everything was over. Dr. Grant went upstairs to check the weather and returned to announce that the storm had blown over. Everyone plodded sleepily back to bed. Hank, however, was unwilling to part with Kyla, so she let him sleep in her bed.

Kyla awoke early, and despite feeling bone-tired from the interrupted night, she was unable to go back to sleep, having yesterday's conversation with her father weighing heavily on her mind. She rolled over, hugging her pillow, still trying to take it all in—the new discovery about her father, along with the new discovery about Dr. Grant. All still so unbelievable. Again she wished she could call her dad at home and talk to him. But what could he do about anything? And Peter, she thought, surely he must be involved with what was going on in some way. He was far too close to Dr. Grant to be ignorant. They did everything together. Her mind sifted through the days since she had come to Wynnbury, pondering their interactions. Every conversation between the two of them that she'd overheard confirmed it. Most certainly Peter had to be involved.

And yet at the same time, that would be so foreign to who he was! Who did she know that was more upright than Peter? He was the guard dog, the protector. Mr. Nice Guy. He was like her dad, who had mentored him—good, wise, and trustworthy. Restlessly she tossed and turned, though conscious of Hank on the far side of the bed and trying not to wake him. Trustworthy. She pictured Peter in the morning in the Great Room reading his Bible, like a powerful eagle in a great invisible nest. Peter would never deliberately do anything wrong. Never. He was like her dad in that respect. He *couldn't* be involved with Dr. Grant. At least not knowingly. She rolled onto her back, looking at the ceiling in the dim morning light, knowing what she had to do. She must talk to Peter about what she knew concerning Dr. Grant. Kyla turned to check the time on the clock. It was early, and he was very likely in the Great Room right now.

To her surprise Peter was not downstairs, but Dr. Grant was in the kitchen pouring the last of some cereal into a bowl.

"Good morning! Coming to join the excitement, I see." He folded up the box and dropped it into the recycling bin.

"Excitement? What's going on?" Kyla paused by the peninsula, where his briefcase sat beside the fish tank. She reached in and opened the plastic bag, freeing the fish to swim in the tank water.

"Apparently you haven't looked outside. Our carport is in the backyard!" He pointed out the window.

"What? Oh, no!" Kyla went to the patio door, surprised to see a mess of twisted metal and vinyl. She swiftly turned back to him. "Our cars!"

"Miraculously okay," he replied, pouring his milk and starting in on the cereal, standing by the kitchen island. "Except for a healthy scratch up the passenger's side of my SUV, but you know, if it wasn't from the storm, one of the kids might have put one there before too long anyway." He looked up at her. "Peter says God answered his prayers. I think we got dang lucky!" He tipped his head at her and took another bite.

"Where is Peter now?" In the corner of the Great Room the lamp was still on and his Bible opened and face down on the chair. She added casually, "He's always up early doing his thing." She didn't want Dr. Grant to think she had come down just for Peter.

"Cutting me a way out of here," he said through a mouthful of cereal. He swallowed. "Apparently you haven't seen the front of the house either! Go look. We've got two trees down across the driveway, another across the front yard farther over, and several down in the ravine. Thankfully no damage to the house. Haven't checked the boat or the dock."

"The fountain?"

"Full of leaves but otherwise okay. Our Mr. Watkins has his work cut out for him for a while!" He raised his bowl slightly. "Perhaps your father could help him out." He finished his cereal and looked at his watch. "I gotta get on the road."

"Yeah, maybe," Kyla said. Yes, she realized, they were keeping him near.

She walked out with him, observing with amazement the anomaly of the five vehicles neatly parked with the carport torn clean off and away from them. The boys' bikes were parked in their usual spots beside the house, untouched. Peter, chainsaw in hand, was around the corner of the bluff, barely visible to her as Dr. Grant drove away through the parted branches on the road. She watched him for a minute, then turned to go back into the house, for the morning air was cool.

She jumped. Her father was standing on the step behind her.

"Oh! You startled me!" she said, a hand going to her chest. "I didn't hear you come out! Good morning."

DeKane made the noise with his teeth, nodding towards Peter. "Looks like the gardener boy gets to play lumberjack today."

Kyla was immediately annoyed. "Don't be insulting!" she said, walking past him into the house. She was overtired and perturbed with him for being dishonest about her birthday. And for ruining her life at Wynnbury, for that matter! She wished she was still ignorant of everything.

He followed her to the kitchen. "You seem to be rather defensive about that boy."

"Nooo." She shook her head, turning into the kitchen. "I'm not being defensive—I'm just being nice. Everybody deserves respect. It's a common courtesy of life."

He chuckled, watching her roughly open the bread bag and pop a slice in the toaster.

"Make one of those for me too—would you, baby?"

He rummaged through the cupboard, got himself a mug of coffee, then sat at the counter, facing her. Kyla stared at him, then went over to fill her own mug.

"Respect," he said, looking down at his cup. "You say *everyone* deserves respect?"

"Yes. Of course. Don't you think so?"

DeKane cleared his throat. "I've always thought that respect is earned."

Kyla's impatience was growing. Private detective or not, the guy sure could be a jerk. "I know what you're getting at. Peter is well worthy of respect. He is a really nice guy." Except that he didn't like her father. But she wasn't going to say that. After all, she was struggling with liking him as well.

"Huh," he replied, looking at her over the top of his steaming brew.

The toast popped.

"Butter or peanut butter?" she asked.

"Either," he replied. "I'll be right back." He left the room.

Kyla leaned on the counter. She wished he were gone. She wanted everything about him to go away. She wished her world were back to normal.

He returned very quickly with his briefcase and pulled a file folder out, laying it on the counter and pushing it wordlessly over to her. Then he pulled the plate of toast closer to him and started in.

"What's this?"

He waved his hand. "See for yourself!"

She hesitated, afraid of what she would find. Timidly she opened the file and stared in dismay at a newspaper headline and photo before her. *Local man sentenced for assault.* Her mouth fell open as she started to read, *Local New Hampton man, Peter Anthony Watkins, age 24, was sentenced to two years in—*

Kyla looked up. "Where did you get this?"

"Does it matter?" DeKane said over the rim of his cup. "You see, baby—things are not always as they seem."

Kyla stared at him a moment, then turned back to the file. Underneath the newspaper were copies of police reports, court proceedings, mug shots, more newspapers. Someone had thoroughly done their homework on him. She flipped through the stack in disbelief. *Possession of drugs, breaking and entering, assault with a deadly weapon.* She felt sick. There was no doubt that it was Peter. Did her dad Kendall know about all of this?

DeKane sucked air through his teeth. "Your Peter isn't as saintly as he lets on. He's got a few secrets in the bag, I'd say. Why do you think your rich professor hired him?"

"He's not like this anymore," Kyla said, studying a mug shot photo of a much younger, angrier-looking Peter.

"Maybe, maybe not," he replied, tilting his head. "But he undeniably has a secret life."

Kyla looked at her father squarely. "So you're saying that whatever Dr. Grant is into, Peter is too."

"Oh, yes," he said gravely. "Absolutely! I have not a shadow of doubt."

Behind them came the sound of the entryway door opening. Kyla snapped the folder shut, and DeKane lifted it from her hands, depositing it neatly into a fold in his briefcase, latching it quickly shut as Peter entered the room.

"Good morning!" he said cheerfully. He brought a waft of fresh air with him.

Kyla couldn't look at him. She greeted him while she turned to the sink and began rinsing cups and loading them into the dishwasher.

"Morning," Kyla's father replied. "Quite a storm last night! Looks like you've got your work cut out for you!"

Peter nodded. "Yeah, you got *that* right! Two trees down on the driveway. I got part of them cut up, but I need a little help getting them off the road. Came to ask if you'd lend a hand."

DeKane swallowed the last of his coffee and set the mug heavily on the counter. "I was just on my way out to ask if I could help." He looked at Kyla with a smug smile. "The two of us will be busy outside for a while, baby. See you later on." He gave her a knowing look and a tip of his head.

"See you," she said as they left.

Busy outside for a while. His hint was clear. Kyla knew what he wanted her to do. He wanted her to search Dr. Grant's study while they were out of the house. That was the last thing on earth she wanted to do. She looked up at the clock. It was barely past seven, and already the day seemed out of control! But soon the kids would be up, so if she was going to do it, she should do it now. Reluctantly she started down the hall to the study but halfway there stopped. Of course, the pocket doors would be locked. How would she get in? No doubt Dr. Grant kept his keys with him. She thought for a moment, then on a whim went to grab Peter's truck keys from the key rack by the back door. There were other keys on his key ring. Then she hurried down the hall to try each one in the study door. Sure enough—he had a key that fit!

After unlocking the doors, she pushed one all the way open so that she could hear if anyone approached, whether adult or child. Then trying to hurry, she went directly to Dr. Grant's desk to start in the most logical place. She was nervous. The whole room smelled like him, and it felt as if he were there. She would die if he walked in on her! *Don't think about it!* she told herself. Sitting in his leather chair, she decided to move clockwise around his desk, starting at the top right drawer. With a tug, she pulled it open. A jolt of fear snaked through her as she exposed a black metal handgun lying on top of a pile of disorganized papers. Stunned, she stared at it a moment, then slowly closed the drawer to sit back in the chair. Her mouth was suddenly dry, and her heart pounded in her chest. Why in the world would Dr. Grant keep a pistol in his desk drawer? There was nothing safe at all about keeping it there—right within the reach of his children! But more than that, why was there a need for a gun in the first place? Was he simply an irresponsible gun owner? Was he keeping it handy for protection? Or was he guarding something? Kyla shuddered, her worst fears about him reinforced.

She was afraid. She wanted to be done and out of this room! She had better hurry. Her eyes traveled around the room, scanning his shelves of books neatly lining the fireplace on either side, the leather furniture around the wooden chest that served as his coffee table, the drapes, the rug, his pictures. *Breathe*, she told herself, *breathe*. Steeling herself, she turned back to the desk, opening to the hanging files in the next drawer down. Carefully she tabbed through them reading the labels: birth certificates, health insurance, travel clubs, appliance receipts, household warranties — the list went on. Closing the drawer, she moved to the hanging files on her left. Bill files. The next drawer up on her left. Taiton College files lying flat in the drawer. She pulled them out and fanned through them quickly. Nothing. The top left drawer. Stamps, envelopes, stapler, pens.

Finally she drew out the center drawer. Staring up at her was the framed portrait of his wife, Marilee Montayne. *Are you aware of all this?* Kyla silently asked the photo. Carefully she lifted it, searching underneath, finding nothing of interest. Along the inside of that drawer, though, was a little lip for pencils and pens, and in that space were several sets of keys, each with a circular tab label. She went through each of them — front door, side entry, garden shed, office, library, third floor, classroom annex, Mannon Hall back, Mannon Hall front, Mannon custodial. Kyla sighed, placing the third-floor keys onto the desk. She turned back to the drawer with the gun. She had never even touched one before. Gingerly she lifted it and set it on the desk. Carefully she then searched between layers of papers, passports, and miscellaneous travel documents, credit cards, and the like. When finished, she repositioned the gun and closed the drawer.

On the far right corner of Dr. Grant's desktop were three black, wire-mesh paper trays stacked together. Standing to get a closer look, Kyla's breath caught with surprise as she spied a file with her name on it at the very top of the stack. She opened it, seeing her photo and online job application with Dr. Grant's notes from her phone interview. She closed it and put it back. Under hers was Peter's. His job application was filled out by hand. She lingered, examining his photo, comparing it mentally to the one DeKane had shown her previously. Lifting the page, Kyla recognized her dad's signature on one of the references stapled to his application, "Kendall R. Lee." For a moment she paused, reading his comments about Peter. Then she stopped and made herself shut his file and put it back. She would think about him later. In the middle mesh tray were items related to Peter's work — fountain receipts, equipment rental papers, nursery receipts, guarantee certificates, warranties, hardware store receipts. The bottom tray contained Dr. Grant's classroom notes.

Kyla glanced at the clock, trying to hurry. Frowning, she leaned on the desk, looking around the room. Where would *she* put a file if she were hiding it? Then she noticed that the desk mat she was leaning on was slightly thicker on one side. She lifted the corner, and there it was! A thin file with *Wynnbury House* inked across the tab. Opening it, she found the postcard that Howie had discovered positioned on top of a half a dozen sheets of notes, some of them with drawings of Wynnbury, some photos of the Tynnbury Hall in England, some notes regarding the American soldier Joseph Kennedy, and an old photograph of his family, similar to the one that had been hung in the foyer. Swiftly she glanced around the room, wondering if the hall portraits were nearby, tucked away in Dr. Grant's study. Also in the file was a hand-drawn grid of the yard with certain areas shaded in. She bit her lip, pondering the grid, then closed the file. *What was all this?* she wondered. *What made it so important? How was it related to stolen museum loot? And how could it possibly warrant an investigation?*

Bewildered, Kyla set the file on the desk and leaned her chin on her hands, thinking. She felt so uneasy. So uneasy about *everything!* She wished there were *someone* she could talk to about this, but she could not think of one single person she could tell! In her desperation Kyla did something that surprised herself—she prayed!

"God," she whispered out loud, "what should I do? I need you to show me what to do!"

Suddenly—so quickly it made her wonder—she got an idea. Promptly she emptied the folder before her and inverted it, turning it inside out so that the writing on the tab did not show. Reinserting the contents into the inverted file, Kyla then placed the whole thing inside of Peter's file in the mesh basket, burying it behind his job application. She tucked Peter's file back underneath hers. Then she opened the desk drawer, took out the Mannon custodial keys, and switched the tabs with the third-floor keys. Putting the fake third-floor keys into her pocket, she hastily left the study, closing and locking the doors behind her in perfect time to see the boys coming down the stairs.

Chapter Twenty-Five

Kyla felt miserable all morning. The small glimpse of the file about Peter that her father had shown her was so disturbing, and she couldn't stop thinking about it. Those newspaper articles had reported some pretty awful stuff about him—stuff that should have probably been revealed to her as a female coworker! That someone could be that violent was frightening to her. Furthermore, she was plagued with guilt. Through all her morning routines of feeding and dressing and playing with the kids, Kyla felt like a traitor, the burden weighing heavily on her that she had deliberately trespassed and snooped through Dr. Grant's studio. Certainly he would know that someone had been there, and eventually he would discover that the Wynnbury file was missing. She wondered what would happen then. Would this blow her father's cover? Wouldn't DeKane have thought of that? Would this cause Dr. Grant to do something foolish? Her mind played through all kinds of scenarios.

On top of everything, Kyla also felt guilty that she was unable to turn the file on Wynnbury over to her father. She just couldn't do it. He stopped in the house briefly during the morning to look at her questioningly. She shook her head, holding up the jingling keys to the third floor.

"All I got is this. The kids got up so early that I didn't have time to look," she told him.

Eagerly he took the keys and shoved them in his pocket.

She knew he would probably find a way to search the office on his own anyway. It was just a matter of time. After all, that is what a detective did. The question was whether he would know what she did, for he was smart, she realized. He might find the file on his own. He might know instantly that she switched the keys. She would have to wait and see how it played out. Her stomach churned with worry. Whether with Dr. Grant or DeKane, she was probably in trouble.

After the boys were finished pressing their noses against the fish tank to watch Spot and Goldie, they turned their fascination toward the downed trees in the front of the house and the mangled carport sculpture in the back. They begged to go outside. Since the storm had blown through, the humidity had dropped and the weather was much more comfortable, the sky cloudless and brilliant blue. Needing a diversion, Kyla dressed the boys in their swimsuits and declared that they could help her clean the leaves out of the fountain. She had an ulterior motive in this, for she brought her phone with her, and when the boys were busy sloshing around in the makeshift pool, she called her dad, hoping he would answer. He did.

"What's going on?" he asked. "You never call me in the morning!"

"Hi, Dad! I'm surprised you answered. You're usually at work," she countered.

"Well, I *am* at work, but we're closed today. We're having our new computer system installed here at the clinic this morning. So what's up? Everything okay?"

"Yes, I'm fine. I'm outside with the boys, and I felt like calling you."

He paused. "All right. Did you have a nice birthday? I had a meeting; otherwise I would have tried to call."

"Yes, Dad, very nice. Thank you for the package. I loved everything."

"I'm glad. I hope you get some time off to enjoy it soon."

"Yeah, I'm sure I will."

He cleared his throat. "So, hey—I hear you got a letter from Alex."

Kyla could instantly feel the heat of irritation crawl up her neck. "And how would you know that?" she asked sarcastically, knowing full well the answer to her own question.

"Peter called me. Last night late. He wanted to know who he was."

Kyla made a sound of protest. "How is that any of his business?"

"What did Alex say, may I ask?"

"And how is that any of *your* business?" she snipped. "I don't know! I didn't open it!"

"You didn't open your letter?"

"Not yet," she replied.

He made a little sound. "Well, then throw it away! I told him not to contact you!"

"Dad," she blurted out, "did you know that Peter has a criminal record?"

There was a space of silence. "Yes, sweetheart, I did know that."

She huffed. "Well, why didn't you tell me that?"

He paused. "Is that what this call is about? Kyla, I don't tell the stories of the young men I work with. That's up to them. I told you that if you want to know Peter's story you should ask him. Remember me saying that?"

Kyla peeked back at the boys to check on them, then turned away so they wouldn't overhear.

"He was, like, in prison or jail or something! For assaulting someone! Don't you think I should know something like that? You should have told me!"

Her dad answered quietly, "Kyla, that was part of his past. It's not like he's dangerous. I would trust Peter with my life." He let out a breath. "Look—what brought this on? Why are you so interested in Peter's background all of a sudden? Why don't you talk to him about it?"

She dug her toe absently in the dirt. "And another thing, Dad. Why did you tell him it was my birthday? I'm twenty-three now! I'm embarrassed that they had to throw me a party!"

"What are you talking about?"

"Dr. Grant and Peter both got me presents and a cake."

"That was nice of them."

She shook her head, looking upward. He didn't get it. "Well, next year, you don't have to tell my friends it's my birthday so that they get me stuff and throw me a party! I'm not a little kid!"

She heard him made a sound in his throat. "Kyla Evangeline, what is wrong? You are not yourself! Are you okay? I don't quite understand what you're saying about this birthday business. I didn't talk to anyone about your birthday."

"You talked to Peter!" Her voice escalated.

"Not about your birthday! For heaven's sake, Kyla, what's the problem?"

Kyla couldn't say anything.

"Has DeKane left yet?" he asked. "I thought you said he was leaving today."

She looked back at the great house behind her. "Not today. He's—he's helping Peter clear out some trees downed from a big storm we had last night. He'll probably leave in the morning."

Her father started to reply, but she cut him off. "Um, look, Dad—I think I need to go. Sorry. The kids need me right now and I can't talk. Sorry to have to drop you so abruptly."

The kids were fine. Kyla was just struggling with what to say. About everything.

"All right—I'll let you go. But honey, I want you to stay alert. Don't you be taking any foolish risks with those kids!"

Kyla cast a nervous glance behind her at the boys. "Dad, knock it off! You're scaring me! Of course—what do you think? I'm being *paid* to keep them safe!"

"And you can call me any time, day or night."

"Okay, Dad. I know that. Gotta go. Love you!"

"I love you very much, Kyla. And I'm praying for you."

His words had made her feel uneasy, and she returned to watch the boys at the fountain more carefully. As she had predicted, they had long forgotten about the leaves and were simply playing in the water, crawling on their bellies after each other in a circle, pretending to be sharks. Preoccupied with her thoughts, she watched them far enough back so that she didn't get soaked by their splashing, until she looked up to see Peter determinedly on his way across the yard toward them. Immediately she tensed. His eyes looked bright and his cheeks rosy from the fresh air, and he greeted her, commenting on the gorgeous day.

"Good morning," she replied lightly. "Yes, it's very beautiful today. Quite a relief from yesterday's brutal heat." It was still hard to look at him.

He smiled and looked off across the river for a second, then back at her. "Um, I hate to be the bad guy, but I need to tell you that the kids can't play in there."

She raised an eyebrow, as if asking if he were serious. "They're helping get the leaves out," she said, gesturing.

He nodded, watching them splash. "Yeah, well—it shouldn't be used as a pool. If the kids hang on those tiers, it could pull them off balance. It was a bugger to get them set in there just right."

"Oh, all right," she said. "They're going to *love* hearing this news."

"Sorry."

The boys groaned in protest as Kyla called them out. Peter stepped in to help them out over the side of the pool basin, explaining to them why. Kyla didn't know what to say or where to even look. Everything felt even more strange and awkward with him now. She had finally begun to trust him a little, and now this!

"It's okay," she told the boys, picking the debris out of their hair as they shivered in the morning air. "We'll pack a lunch and go to the beach instead."

Peter said good-bye and left. As he strode away, Kyla closed her eyes and rubbed her forehead. How absolutely surreal! Her summer had taken yet another major turn. *Here I am*, she thought, *stuck in another crazy, weird situation*. She shook her head, sliding her phone into her pocket. Tiredly she directed the boys to the house, where they could collect their things for the beach. Soon, however, she caught a second wind of energy. She had to admit that it was a good place to go today. Not only was the weather very pleasant, but it was a place to keep her distance from both Peter and her father for a while and think.

Down at the waterfront Kyla discovered that in the aftermath of the storm the boat and the dock were surprisingly fine, but they had obviously taken a beating from the wind, for they were covered with small branches and leaves. The beach also was littered with branches and mossy weeds that had blown in or washed up on shore, and one of the Adirondack chairs was floating in the river. She was glad she had worn her swimsuit, for she waded out nearly ten feet to get it, but the water was not deep there, and she could easily pull it in. Afterward she gave the boys the jobs of clearing the weeds away and cleaning the mud off the backrest of the rescued chair. In no time the beach was back to looking almost normal, and the boys were delightfully and thoroughly occupied with "washing" the dirty chair by pouring bucket after bucket of water over it for a long time.

Angling the other chair near it so that she would be perfectly in the sun, Kyla donned her sunglasses and tried to relax, keeping her eyes on the boys while she lounged. Eventually, when they had finished cleaning the chair, they asked for lunch, and despite the fact that it was early, Kyla fed them anyway since the excitement of their picnic was the next prominent thing on their minds. She made sure to set aside a few snacks and some water for later.

After only an hour into their time there, Kyla was surprised when Peter came down to join them, assumedly during his lunch break. He carried with him a Coke and a lemonade and two frozen juice pops for the brothers, who eagerly rushed him to enjoy them. She was immediately on edge, unsure of what to talk about and still bothered by what she had learned about him. Mr. Nice Guy apparently had a mean streak.

"Would you like one?" he asked, offering her a choice.

"Thanks," she said, taking the lemonade. She knew he preferred Coke.

He twisted the lid off his bottle and took a long drink, then buried the bottle halfway in the sand. Pulling his shirt off, he straddled the other chair beside her and leaned his head back against the slats, closing his eyes and breathing in the air. Kyla inhaled too. She was growing to love the sort of fishy smell near the river.

"So nice today," he murmured. "Gotta enjoy it."

She looked at him, her eyes lingering on his chest, his tan arms, his hair creased from his hat. He was muscular, both from working out and his job. His jeans and work boots were covered with a grainy layer of sawdust from the chainsaw, and Kyla thought that it was no wonder he was enjoying the break in the weather, having worked out in the nasty hot weather throughout all last week.

"You got another package from your dad," he said with his eyes still closed. "It came a bit ago. I left it in the kitchen."

He turned his head toward her, and she looked away toward Hank and Howie, where they dug little trenches for pretend fountains they were installing on the beach.

"Okay, thanks," she replied, sipping the lemonade.

His presence was always so powerful, twisting her stomach into knots. She wished she knew more details about his past, his history. She wished that she and DeKane hadn't been interrupted this morning in the kitchen so that she could have read the contents of that file more thoroughly. Of course, her dad—Kendall—said that she should just ask him, but she didn't know how in the world that would ever happen. She glanced at him out of the corner of her eye, glad for her sunglasses. He seemed normal again today, back to his happy self, like he was glad to be sitting outside on a perfect, sunny day.

"What does your tattoo say?" she asked. Since he was shirtless, she assumed it would be okay to ask.

He moved suddenly, as though the question surprised him, lifting his arm and looking down at it. "'All creation groans awaiting the adoption of sons,'" he answered.

Awaiting the adoption? Kyla made a face. "What's *that* supposed to mean?" She hated when people threw around the word *adoption* without understanding what it was like, like it was no big deal.

He shook his head slightly. "I'll explain it some other time."

"You weren't adopted," she stated with an edge of irritation.

"No," he replied. "Although spiritually speaking, yes—but never mind."

"Is it a Bible verse?"

Chapter Twenty-Five

"Sort of."

Peter placed his hands behind his head, looking out over the river where a family of ducks swam, bobbing their heads for food. "Haven't seen our eagles for a while."

She let him change the subject, following his gaze. He was quiet for a bit, absorbing the view of the river before him.

"It would be a good day to be out in the boat," he said, interrupting their silence. "Maybe I'll take it out later on this afternoon. Maybe fish a little. Care to go with me?"

Her eyes traveled to the boat beside the dock. "Um—I don't know. Maybe. If Dr. Grant—"

He gave an impatient sound, interrupting her, "We can take them with us—I don't mind!"

She was embarrassed, not wanting him to know she was uncomfortable on water. Plus, he made her nervous. "Okay," she said. "We'll see."

At that moment Hank came running to Kyla for a drink from his water bottle, resting a sandy hand on her leg as he drank. Howie followed him for a drink too, parking his seat on the edge of Peter's chair to be near him. Peter held up Howie's skinny arm, pretending to admire his muscles.

"Can you come and swim with us?" he asked Peter. "Please?"

"Not right now, buddy," he replied. "I want to talk to Miss Kane. But I've got a good idea! Why don't you guys go make a river and build a bridge across it with some little sticks?"

Howie's face brightened. Kyla sent them off with a little baggie of snacks, and they rushed off to collect sticks for the bridge. While she had her tote bag open, she grabbed the mesh cotton dress that she had worn over her swimsuit and pulled it over her head, the tropical scent of suntan lotion lingering heavily on it. Then tidying the bag, she shoved it back under her chair out of the sun.

"So you want to talk to me?" She took her sunglasses off, wiped them with her towel, and returned them to her face, sitting back in the chair.

"I don't know if I do," he said with a short laugh, folding his hands across his stomach, "as I see you're kind of in a mood. Have I done something to you? Or are you just mad that I chased the kids out of the fountain?"

"I'm not mad."

He raised his eyebrows. "Well, you're *something*."

Kyla tightened her ponytail, feeling the stir of adrenaline in her body. She thought about her phone conversation with her dad. *If you want to know*

Peter's story, then ask him. But how? That was the question. There wasn't any easy way to go there.

"Well, I'm not mad."

"You sound irritated as heck."

She squirmed in her chair, fiddling with the edge of her towel. "I'm not mad," she repeated. "I'm more confused, is all."

"And why is that?" He shot her a look.

"Because I know your secret."

His brow furled. "My secret? What secret would that be?"

Kyla nodded her head toward his arm. "Let's just say I'm guessing you had that done recently, because it sure doesn't look like your typical prison tattoo."

Peter's lips became a thin line. He turned away and lifted his face to the sky, nodding.

Kyla held her fingers up making quotation marks. "'Everybody has their secrets,'" she said, mimicking him from when they had talked in the kitchen a while back.

Peter was unfazed. "If you're referring to my criminal history, that is certainly not a secret—I got to have my picture in every newspaper in the area multiple times! My dad was thrilled—it was great advertising for the family business. I even got to be on TV!"

She folded her arms. "So what'd you do?"

He threw her a look. "Thought you said you knew."

Kyla closed her mouth, turning to watch the boys.

Peter focused his gaze out on the water again, not speaking for a while. When he did talk he took his time. "I was a dumb kid. Did okay in high school, but the end of my senior year I did a lot of messing around doing stupid things with bad friends. Really stupid things." He gave a sheepish smile. "Though I can't blame *them*. I was just as bad, I guess." He sniffed. "Anyway, I turned into a real troublemaker. One time me and this other kid got caught breaking into this business. Got busted before we actually took anything, but I got arrested for possession of drugs. Ironically"—he tipped his head—"that event turned out to be a good thing, because my parents freaked and tried to get me straightened out. Wasn't charged with anything. Got my hands slapped mostly. Ended up being a good wake-up call. For me anyways."

Kyla remembered the headline she had seen in the file—he'd gotten definitely more than a hand slap! She wondered if he were lying or simply minimizing his crime. Or if there was more he wasn't saying. "And then?"

she asked, testing how he would respond.

"Yeah." He gave a heavy sigh. "The other thing was a bigger deal." He paused for a bit before continuing, as if hesitant to talk about it. "So in a nutshell I was an idiot," he said. "I lost control of myself and beat the snot out of a guy and put him in the hospital. Spent sixteen months doing time to pay for it. Got the minimum, purely by the grace of God." He turned to look her in the face, as if judging her reaction.

She looked away, unable to hide her shock and revulsion, unable to say anything for a long while. He turned back to the waterfront, quiet too. The sound of the boys playing rose as Hank let out a scream, reaching for a stick that his brother had. Howie yelled back that he *needed* it for his bridge, and they fought over it until Howie finally gave him a different one.

"What I don't understand," she said finally, "is how you can do that kind of thing, and then be so religious. You're always so 'God this' and 'God that' to everybody. That's two-faced if you ask me. How can you be like that? Don't you have a conscience?"

He winced. "Ouch! What do you mean, don't I have a conscience? You don't think I felt terrible about what I did? *Of course,* I felt bad! I still do! I could have killed the guy! But, Kyla, I'm not that person anymore. That's who I *was* and not who I am now."

She shook her head. "It's not that easy, Peter. Look—I've dealt with enough hard things in life to know that you don't just wave the magic wand and have it all go away. That's called denial. There's still consequences."

He turned in his chair, spreading his hands. "Absolutely. Of course. You don't have to tell me that! I'm not denying anything. I did the crime, and I'm not proud of it. But I can freely talk about God because I've been washed. I've been forgiven. And more than that, I've been made new. The old Peter Watkins has died, and I'm a new creation in Christ Jesus."

"Oh, geez," she breathed, rolling her eyes. "Now you're sounding just like my dad."

He pointed his finger at her, irritated. "I'm *honored* that you say that."

She turned away. She could hear him tapping his fingers on the side of the chair.

"So why did you do it?" she asked finally.

Peter shrugged. "It doesn't matter why. I did it. I committed the crime, and I paid for it. It's over." He turned back in his chair, crossing his feet, leaning back as if he were done talking about it.

"Were you—were you on something? Were you drunk?"

He chewed his lip, looking out over the water as if debating what to say. She deliberately waited.

Finally he answered. "Okay. The guy I beat up worked for my dad. Like, for a long time. They were really good friends. It looked to me—I am required to use that exact terminology—it looked to me like he was about to molest my sister in one of our greenhouses. So I took a steel pipe and let him have it. Then as things turned out, he hadn't actually done anything to my sister yet, so I ended up being the one who was charged, and there was no evidence against him for any wrongdoing." He paused. "But that doesn't take away the fact that I did what I did. I deserved more than I got—that's for sure. I wasn't innocent."

Kyla shifted in her chair, thoughtful, pulling her knees up. "Thus the 'trust issues' with your father. You said that once—that you were earning back his trust."

"Correct."

He sighed, absently brushing sawdust off his jeans. "This all went down when I was twenty-four. I'm twenty-nine now. Last year was a big year because he started talking to me again. This summer he's letting me borrow equipment. I'm believing someday he'll have me back."

"To the family business?"

"Perhaps eventually to the business. To *him* is what I want! I want him to forgive me. Like, *really* forgive me. But I'm praying." He turned and gave a small smile. "I'm not sure if you know it, but it was through this whole mess that I met your dad."

She frowned. "My dad? How's that?"

"When I started college I was still on probation, and my parole officer connected me with your dad because I was moving to Stanton. He took an interest in me and listened to my story, invited me to church and over to your house. He's a good man. I owe him a lot. He led me to Christ."

Kyla stared at him a moment, then looked away. There was a lot she didn't know about her dad since she had been away at college and spending her summers with Alex and his family.

"That's kind of why I wanted to talk to you," he continued. "Sort of. I mean, I wanted to finish the conversation we had that one day in the kitchen. About knowing God's love."

Kyla felt the familiar jab of stress. She folded her arms and looked away, murmuring under her breath, "My favorite subject."

He frowned. "I don't get it with you. Why do you get mad when we talk about this? You, like, either clam up or react. What's with that?"

She exhaled, leveling her eyes at him. "Just look at my life—that's what! My life has sucked! My life is a history of one bad thing after another. I don't know why God is against me! You tell me! All I know is that every time I listen to you or my dad talk about him, I ended up feeling worse and even more convinced that I'm on God's bad side. Like I could never ever be good enough. You talk about things that sound so great—God is wonderful, God is this, God is that—but somehow it's all out of reach for me!" She sat up and turned in the chair toward him. "It's like you say, 'Here—look at the yummy candy that I have. Isn't this great? You should have some!' But it's all kept in a sealed glass case, like it's taunting me—'You can't have this! You can *never* have this!'"

"Whoa, whoa, whoa!" Peter sat up, facing her. "Hold on! Where's all this coming from?"

She wasn't finished. "It seems like even *if* I wanted God, it couldn't happen. I'm not like you! I'm not like my dad! I just can't make it work. As much as I try, I just can't do it right. I can't be good enough. I'm on the outside looking in. I'm always on the outside. Like when I was born, God just dumped me somewhere on the side of the road and said, 'I don't want her'!"

"Kyla, stop!"

Kyla clamped her mouth shut. Her cheeks were burning.

Peter shifted in his chair, his brow creased. He brushed an insect away with his hand. "No, I'm sorry," he said quietly. "Go ahead and finish. Say what you need to say." He looked down at the ground, clearly disturbed.

"I'm done," came her curt reply. She turned her face toward the boys.

The silence between them was long and uncomfortable. Before them Howie was making motor sounds while he drove his equipment over the bridge he had just constructed. Hank sat piling handfuls of sand on top of his legs.

"Can I say something?" Peter asked.

"Whatever," she replied. "You don't need my permission."

He breathed out loudly. "Kyla, I don't want you to take this wrong, but part of what you're feeling is appropriate."

She shot him a hard look.

"You *are* on the outside—"

"See!" she said, lifting her hand.

"No, please listen to me!" He leaned toward her. "I was on the outside too! But here's what I learned—it's sin that separates you from God."

"Oh, so I'm a bad person now!"

He rolled his eyes. "No! You were born with it, like I was—me and every other person. And your sin, my sin, it becomes a way of life for us, through deliberate choices and unconscious ways we're not even aware of." He paused for a breath. "Did you know the Bible says that we're actually enemies of God because of sin? We are all on the outside!" He tilted his head toward her. "Kyla, no one can be good enough, no matter how hard we try. That's why God sent Jesus. He sent his only Son to live the perfect life before God and to be the perfect sacrifice for your sin. He didn't have to do it, but he loves you! *He wants you,* Kyla. You can be sure of that! It's through Jesus that your sins are forgiven, actually taken away. When I came to Christ, I was given his righteousness and his nature. I was made alive."

All her defenses were rising. Kyla sat quietly, trying to listen.

"I didn't always know all this," Peter went on. "I used to think I was a pretty good person. Even with beating up my dad's friend, I justified myself because of what he tried to do with my sister. I could not see that I had done anything wrong because I felt he deserved what I gave him. But there were laws that I had broken, and I was judged by a court of law higher than my own opinion, and I was declared guilty. There were legal consequences, whether I agreed with them or not, and I had to do the time." He gestured with his hands. "I learned it's the same way with God. He has laws that I have broken, and there is a court coming, a time of judgment before a holy God. There will be a penalty for sin, and I won't be judged by how good I *think* I am.

"But here's the incredible thing about all this," he continued, shaking his head. "I know what I deserve!" He held his arms out wide. "But Jesus paid my penalty for sin. He did my time. And someday when I stand before the Great Judge, I will be declared innocent by his blood. Of all my sins! In fact, I can say that about myself right now, today. I am innocent by his blood." He blew out a long breath. "'This is a trustworthy saying that deserves full acceptance: Christ Jesus came into the world to save sinners— of whom I am the worst.' That's one of my favorite Bible verses, because it describes *me*."

Fidgety, Kyla leaned back in her chair, arranging her towel under her legs. She recognized the verse. It was the same one that Howie and she had read.

"I can understand how it might be frustrating for you, Kyla." Peter gave her a sympathetic nod. "I'm sure you've probably heard all this before many times, knowing your dad. But the Bible says you can't *see* the things of God unless you're *in* the kingdom of God—unless you're born again.

It's not a matter of a bad person trying to live better. It would be impossible to live up to God's standard! No, it's a matter of someone *dead* coming alive. A dead person cannot see, cannot understand. I was *dead* in my sin but was made alive in Christ—that's in the Bible. You actually come alive inside when you give your life to Christ. His Spirit connects with your spirit, and you receive his life. God loves you, Kyla. All you need to do is acknowledge your guilt to him—you know, be truly sorry—and believe that Jesus paid for all your stuff through his death on the cross. Then ask him to make you new."

He stopped then, looking at her in her chair, where she sat staring expressionless out over the river. He leaned back. "Okay—I'm done talking for a while."

Kyla said nothing, but her heart was beating faster and her mind racing as she mulled over his words. She had never seen it that clearly before. Not like that. She understood. Yet once again the dark anger stirred within her, the unexplainable, deep anger that was like an iron bar clamped across her heart and locked, keeping her from opening to God. She could not get past it. It owned her. She was its prisoner. She felt hopeless, stuck in muddy, murky waters getting deeper. Beside her she could see Peter glancing over at her now and then, and she knew he was waiting for some kind of response from her, but she didn't know what to say.

"I don't know. It's just hard," she said at last. "Hard for me to trust."

He nodded and reached for the Coke under his chair. It hissed open, and after a long drink, he replaced the lid and put it down. He looked at the ground thoughtfully.

"Okay—I know I said I was done, but can I offer you my opinion?"

She looked at him tiredly. "Look—don't you have work to do, trees to cut up? I can hardly believe that this is worth your time."

He frowned. "This is way more important than that! *You* are way more important than that!"

Kyla shifted uncomfortably, folding her hands in her lap. Once again the great eagle had swooped down upon her. She felt so exposed, so vulnerable, and inside her heart was poised to run, to flee. Her mind flashed back to earlier in the day when she had seen his picture in the file in the kitchen. How did DeKane's summation of Peter and this conversation fit? Her mind could not put the pieces together. Then, reminded of her father, it occurred to her that at this very moment he was alone in the house, probably rifling through Dr. Grant's study as they spoke.

"Ok, what's your opinion?" she asked. Her eyes dropped to his chest for a second.

"I think—I think that you have believed a lie about God," he declared.

"Yeah? Like what?"

"You're probably going to get mad at me for saying this, but since he's been here, I've talked to your dad about your father. Your biological father, DeKane."

What a surprise, she mused. "And?"

"Please hear me out on this, okay?" He sat up again, facing her.

She wished he would put his shirt on. She was so distracted.

He leaned forward, resting his elbows on his legs, folding his hands. "Okay, look—one of the major ways we learn what God is like is through our parents. God made it that way. You know, families. Fathers are meant to model to us what God is like." He passed his hand briefly over his chin. "Your father, Robert DeKane, made the choice to leave you. I don't care what excuse he's probably given you—he *abandoned* you." He emphasized the word. "That was wrong. He abdicated a truckload of responsibilities that he was called to perform concerning you."

Kyla was reminded of her conversation with Mrs. Gordon.

"I get that people make mistakes," he continued, "but I think that your father's leaving you programmed your mind to think wrongly about God. It gave you a messed-up view of what he's like. You think that God abandons children, casts them off, and doesn't come back. You think God isn't interested in you. You think he can't help you, that he leaves you on your own to figure things out, dumps you onto the side of the road, and wants nothing to do with you. God's not like that, Kyla."

Her cheeks grew warm, and her throat tightened. She was unable to speak.

"You've believed a lie about God. And when push comes to shove, you think that God's going to bail out on you." He paused for a moment, then went on. "And I think you're mad at God for your mom's death too, but here's the thing—your mother didn't want to leave you. That was out of her control. But because you already think wrongly about God, you blame him for her death."

Tears filled her eyes behind her sunglasses. That was something she already knew about herself.

"The irony of all this, Kyla, is that your dad, Kendall, who is not even genetically connected to you—he *wanted* you, adopted you. He *chose* to have you! You know in your head that he loves you, but you have a hard time receiving his love because of that same lie. You hold him at a distance emotionally because you're afraid of being abandoned."

"That's because he adopted me out of pity," she replied stiffly, bringing the neck of her dress up to wipe her eyes. "Because he felt sorry for me." She was embarrassed to be crying in front of him.

"Oh, come on!" Peter huffed. "That might have been a small part of the equation at first, but love grows when you do the right thing. He did the right thing! He did the courageous thing, the loving thing! Your dad adores you through and through—he'd give his life for you!"

Kyla had that same feeling the morning they talked in the kitchen. He spoke with authority, and his words had power over her beyond what she could hear, like electricity on her body, and she could feel it in her arms and legs.

Peter shifted in his chair. "Let me ask you something, Kyla. After you lost your mom, were there ever single women who hung around your home—you know, kind of helping your dad out?"

Kyla scrunched her nose at him, wondering what he was getting at. "What? You mean, like women pursuing him?"

He sighed. "I guess what I'm asking is, did your dad ever date? A young, single widower with a daughter—"

"Maybe a few times. But not really. What are you getting at?"

He lifted his hand, as if she had made his point. "Have you ever wondered about that? About why your dad never remarried?"

She shrugged. "I've never thought about it. Probably because he didn't want to."

"Oh, believe me—if he's a man, he wanted to! Especially with a daughter to raise." He gave her a knowing look.

She frowned at him. "Are you telling me that you've discussed this with my dad? I can't believe this!" She stood up, setting her hands on her waist.

Peter stood too. "No, I haven't. It's just a guess. But I've thought about it lately. Have you ever considered that maybe he never remarried because of *you*?" He tipped his head to the side with his question.

Kyla's face twisted. "What on earth would that have to do with me?"

He reached out to tap her arm. "I think he never remarried *on purpose* because of you. Because of your abandonment issues. You were abandoned by your father; you lost your mother. To bring in a stepmother when he's already not your biological father—I think he knew you wouldn't be able to handle it emotionally. I think he gave you the steadiest childhood he could give you under the circumstances." He let go of her arm and pointed his finger at her. "Your dad would do anything to protect you. Now, *that's* what you need to believe about God!"

She took a step backward, the calves of her legs tight against the chair. "This—this is way beyond any of your business! You think you have me all figured out! Me and all my issues! And this stuff about my dad—how can you even say that? You don't know that any of that is true! Somehow you think you have suddenly become the expert on him—like you know him better than me! You don't own him!"

"What?" Peter's head drew back. "Wait, Kyla. That's not what I'm saying! Don't be jealous."

"You're saying I'm *jealous*?" She raised her chin. "Look—I think this conversation is over! And since it looks like you have nothing to do today but sit around, I think I'm going up to the house, and when you're finished hanging out here, you can bring the boys up with you!"

Kyla grabbed her bag from under her chair and headed toward the stairs.

Peter went after her, catching her by the arm and turning her around. "See—this is what I mean! You close off! Please, Kyla—I'm not against you! Let's finish this! Don't run away!"

She couldn't look at him. He dropped her arm.

Howie and Hank suddenly noticed the two standing by the staircase and abruptly stopped their play. A look of anxiety spread across Howie's face as he rose to his feet.

"Miss Kane, where are you going? Wait! Don't leave me!"

Peter turned. "We're staying here with you, Howie. No one's leaving. We're just talking."

"Where are you going, Miss Kane?" he asked again.

"Kane!" Hank echoed, looking suddenly from his brother to his nanny.

"To the house, Howie," she replied, shooting Peter a challenging glare. "You get to stay with Peter. He'll bring you up after a while."

Kyla turned and climbed the staircase.

Chapter Twenty-Six

Kyla cut straight across the yard past the twisted metal mess of the carport to the patio. Her heart felt raw, throbbing as if a wound she hadn't known was there had suddenly burst open. Her thoughts were tangled in her mind, and she wished Mrs. Gordon was there right now, although Kyla knew she probably wouldn't even be able to talk about anything yet. It was all too jumbled, too new, too sore. She knew Peter was right about so many things, and it frightened her.

The kitchen was empty when she entered the house, and she took a tissue and blew her nose, glad for a moment alone. Near her on the peninsula was the box from her dad. She knew it was the family photo she had asked for and got a scissors from the drawer to slit the tape. Hearing a little noise, she looked up in surprise as Dr. Grant unexpectedly appeared in the hall, coming from his study. He was home a lot earlier than usual. Kyla was immediately tense, guilty from having snooped in his room that morning.

"Well, here's *someone* at least!" he said, spreading out his hands questioningly. "Where the heck *is* everyone? I come home, and there's no one here!"

Kyla lifted her thumb, pointing in the direction of the river. "We were down at the beach."

He looked around. "Where are the boys?"

"They're still down there. With Peter."

"You left the boys at the beach with Peter?"

She shifted, embarrassed. *Way to shirk your job,* she told herself. Despite the mesh dress she wore over her swimsuit, she still felt uncomfortable and wished she had clothes on. She pulled off her sunglasses.

"Peter came down to hang out for a while."

Dr. Grant eyes narrowed. "Were you crying just now?" He straightened. "What's wrong? What's going on?"

A new batch of tears slid down her cheeks. "Nothing. Just a weird talk with Peter. I'm okay."

"You don't look okay." He approached with concern and moved the tissue box nearer to her. "All right—what's going on?"

She shook her head, dabbing her eyes. How could she even say? She didn't want to talk about it and couldn't think of what to say. She tried to brush it off with light babbling. "Just—I don't know. Peter. He's suddenly the expert on my life and acts like he knows my dad better than me. He came down to talk to me, and we ended up having this awkward conversation about God, and then—"

He held up a hand, interrupting dryly, "Say no more! I know *exactly* what you're talking about!"

Right then Peter appeared at the patio door with Hank on his shoulders and Howie under his arm. Both the little boys were giggling wildly. He swung each to the ground and slid back the door, stepping in. His eyes went immediately to Kyla, searching her face.

"I hear you've been harassing the nanny," Dr. Grant stated bluntly.

"Wha—?" He inclined his head with a look of surprise at Dr. Grant, then Kyla. The patio door remained open behind him.

"Mr. Watkins, I think it's clear that everyone in the household respects your strong views on God. I'd like to ask the same courtesy of you—that you respect the rest of us and stop pushing your opinions so aggressively!"

Shooting an incredulous look at Kyla, he turned back to Dr. Grant, who was still talking.

"Are we completely out of projects that you have nothing better to do than sit on the beach and make her upset? Last I saw, there were still trees down in the yard and a wrecked carport to contend with! Not to mention a load of sod arriving in a day or two!"

Peter's neck was turning red, his mouth becoming a hard line. He gave a stiff nod to Dr. Grant. "Yes, sir. Understood."

Casting another glance at Kyla, he left through the patio door, closing it forcefully behind him. A wave of guilt washed over Kyla as the door smacked shut, and she felt sick, like the strength was sucked out of her. She stood hollowly beside the counter, her legs like water.

"That was overdue," Dr. Grant said crossly, watching him leave. "I should have said something to him long ago!" He shook his head. "But I can't say I've ever seen him with an attitude like this!"

Howie's face was distraught, looking from the door to his father. "What happened to Peter? What's wrong?"

"Peter went outside to do some work," he told him, lifting Hank to his hip, who had been patting his leg and reaching for him. "What'd you get?" He gestured to the box in front of Kyla. "Another birthday gift?"

Kyla couldn't speak. Her mouth was completely dry. Numbly she finished cutting the box open, folding back the flaps to reveal the dated family portrait she had requested from her dad. In transit the glass in the frame had shattered into tiny pieces, the shards of glass everywhere in the box, covering the images of Kendall, her mother, and herself as a girl. Kyla put her hands over her mouth and started to cry.

Dr. Grant looked on, dumbfounded. "Hey, hey—it's okay! It's a piece of glass! We can replace that. I can fix that for you!"

She couldn't help it. The dam had burst. Then confused by everything that had happened in the last several minutes, Howie's lip began to quiver, and he also burst into tears.

Dr. Grant frowned down at him. "What the heck? Why are *you* crying now? Everything's all right, Howie—Peter is fine. Go upstairs. I'll be up soon."

He didn't move, bawling loudly.

"Go on!" he said more firmly, setting Hank on the floor, who clung worriedly to his leg.

Howie moved toward the stairs, his wailing echoing through the house.

Carefully Dr. Grant pulled the picture frame out of the box. "Look, Kyla—this is an easy fix. It's just a matter of buying a new piece of glass from the hardware store."

She nodded, trying to get a grip, but the tears flowed unchecked.

He stared at her for a moment, then set the frame down. "Okay—I can see you have definitely blown a fuse. I think it's time you got out of here." He turned away from her, calling loudly through the house, "DeKane! DeKane!" He waited for a moment, then turned back to Kyla. "Where the hell is your father? DeKane!" he shouted again.

Kyla's father suddenly appeared at the bottom of the stairs, his eyes wide, his face pale. He walked jerkily toward them.

Agitated, Dr. Grant turned to him, gesturing to Kyla. "We have a minor crisis here, and you are needed. This girl needs a break from this place, and this is a job for a dad! I want you to take her to town. I want you to take her someplace nice to eat and buy her some clothes or whatever she wants. Get her a massage or a pedicure or something, but don't come home until she is buffed and puffed—do you understand? This kid needs a break!"

DeKane gave a nod, waving his arm toward her like he agreed that it was long overdue.

Dr. Grant turned to Kyla. "Young lady, you are done for the day. Go change and get your purse."

Kyla started for the stairs.

"Wait!" he called, holding out the box. "Here—you forgot this."

There was a letter on the bottom of the box that had been under the frame. A sticky note with her dad's handwriting was attached to the front that read "For Peter." Underneath the note the letter itself was addressed to Peter in care of her dad's address in Stanton. In the upper left corner was the name "Amy," followed by a hand-drawn heart. Kyla looked at it and set it on the edge of the table.

"It's for Peter," she said.

Dr. Grant watched her leave the kitchen. "I'm giving you tomorrow off too," he called after her, trailing off more quietly, "even if I have to call in sick."

They took her car. She hadn't even driven the Mustang since she had come to Wynnbury, and before they left the driveway Dr. Grant insisted on her putting the top down.

"There's nothing like the feel of the wind through your hair," he said, patting her door. "It will do you a world of good."

He was somewhat right. By the time Kyla and DeKane got out to the main highway, she was feeling slightly better. The road construction she had driven through on her way to Wynnbury had moved eastward toward New Hampton, causing her to have to drive through it again, but she didn't mind. Her associations with the smell of asphalt and diesel fumes were good, reminding her of city driving in college, and she needed the time to think. But although the fresh air and sunshine were indeed medicinal, they still could not dispel the dark cloud hanging over her from what had happened in the kitchen.

They went to a deli attached to a city mall and split a sandwich in the outdoor seating area at a table off to the side where her father could smoke. He sat quietly with his legs crossed, looking absently over the parking lot while Kyla finished her iced coffee. Neither of them had said much to each other, apart from his initial curiosity during the drive there as to why she was so upset. She had told him she was hormonal, ignoring his look of male amusement.

Kyla swirled the liquid in her cup. All she could think about was Peter's face as he stood inside the patio door. He had been completely taken by surprise, and she felt awful. His expression, the way he had looked at her—she stared at the stains on the concrete floor thinking about it.

DeKane spoke into the silence. "Those keys you gave me this morning were no good."

Kyla set her coffee on the steel mesh table. "Seriously? They said third floor."

"Seem to have been switched with another set in the drawer."

"Huh," she commented. "Why would he do that? Paranoid, maybe. Might be a good sign."

He was expressionless, blowing smoke out through his nose.

"Were you able to find anything else?" she asked.

"A few things," he said ambiguously. He made his noise with his teeth and looked at his watch. "So. You're supposed to go shopping. Or something." He made it a statement.

Kyla sipped her coffee through the straw without replying.

"I'm not much into shopping," he continued.

"Did you have something else in mind?"

"No, no. No, you go ahead," he said, lifting his hand in protest. "But if you don't mind, I might just hang out here or perhaps take the car for a little drive."

"This is hindering your investigation," she remarked.

He nodded grimly. "Well, I have a few things I can do while we're here."

She gave him her keys, and he handed her an extravagant wad of cash. Then they made a plan to meet up several hours later "to go someplace nice for dinner," he said. And suddenly Kyla was alone.

In college she had spent a lot of time at shopping malls. Today it felt strange. Almost foreign. She started at one of the anchor stores, looking randomly through the racks of women's clothing, finding nothing that interested her. Then on her way out of the store she passed through the children's section, where she stopped to buy two pairs of shorts, two shirts, and a set of pajamas for each of the boys. She knew they would love them, plus Howie was growing—he needed a few things. She wished he were here with her to try on a pair of shoes his size, which she held in her hand, debating whether or not to buy them. Perhaps if they didn't fit Peter could return them for her. Peter. That sick feeling stabbed her again as she pictured the pained look on his face. She put the shoes down, moving out into the main part of the mall into the dim roar of mall noise and food court aromas.

Since it was summer the mall walkways were crowded. All around her, people were walking determinedly in various directions, most of them talking on their cell phones. Directionless, Kyla walked slowly down the wide corridor peering into the stores, but she had a very hard time being interested in shopping. She wasn't in the mood. And furthermore, every male mannequin in every store became Peter with that blindsided look on his face. Kyla gave a miserable sigh. He had barely made it in the door before Dr. Grant had reprimanded him. He hadn't deserved that. And it was her fault.

Wandering through the avenues, Kyla finally stopped, as suggested by Dr. Grant, for a pedicure and to get her hair trimmed. She was glad for the chatty beautician who filled the time with stories of her last vacation cruise with her husband and in-laws. When she was finished, Kyla scooted out of the shop in the temporary foam flip-flops to a shoe store across the way to find a new pair of sandals that would not wreck her fresh pedi. It was nice having money to spend, and her father had given her a lot.

Farther down in the center of a widened area of the mall Kyla noticed a half-wall topped with plants, which trailed down the side, and as she neared it she realized that there were four half-walls that formed the sides of a small sunken waiting area with padded seats built into the backside of the walls. In the center of the space was a little oasis, a beautifully landscaped area with a little rocky waterfall trickling down multiple levels into a rock goldfish pond at the bottom, the fish giants compared to Spot and Goldie. The exotic plants around the waterfall made her think of Peter, and she wondered if his father's nursery had designed it for the mall. She found a seat on a padded bench near the pond, across from an elderly gentleman reading a newspaper with several shopping bags around his feet.

It was the word *issues* that had put her over the edge. He had used the term *abandonment issues*. She—Kyla—was a girl with abandonment issues. He had thought enough about her to have a label, which was humiliating coming from someone like Peter who was—who was someone like Peter. Kyla wasn't even sure what abandonment issues were, much less having someone point out that she had them. Were they glaringly obvious to the entire world? *Whoa—that girl has abandonment issues! Stay clear of her!*

She was glad she knew about his past now. He didn't seem as dark and evil as her biological father had made him out to be with the file he had shown her in the kitchen. And at the same time, he didn't seem as squeaky clean and priestly as she had first thought either. He definitely had a shady past. Yet, as he had said, he was not that person anymore. How does a person change like that? she wondered. How does a person become—like Peter? *So I took a steel pipe and let him have it.* That wasn't the Peter she knew.

Since the little area she had discovered wasn't crowded, Kyla put her packages onto the floor and sat sideways on the padded seat, stretching her legs out across the bench. The move reminded her of the Adirondack chairs on the beach—it had been a miracle that the boys had played so well together this morning, that she and Peter hadn't been interrupted a dozen times. She had needed to hear everything he had said. What Peter had told her about God—she could get it now, understand it. The way he explained it was clear, and she knew what she needed to do. But she was scared. It was hard to take that step. Hard to trust. Kyla bit her lip, watching the goldfish swim. He was probably spot-on right about the business with her believing a lie. Peter was always right. But what now?

And then there was the business about her dad. Kyla always found it hard to listen to Peter talk about her dad. It was true—she *was* jealous. She was very jealous of Peter's relationship with her dad! In some ways she knew the two of them were closer to each other than she was to her dad. Peter loved God, which was clearly the most important part of her dad's life. They had common ground there. By her own choice, she was on the outside of that. For so many years she had looked down on her dad, ignored him, dishonored him in a million ways, loving him on the surface from a place that was safe *for her*, a place that served her *own* interests. Did she have difficulty receiving his love, as he had said? Was that true? Probably, she thought. Probably.

Kyla pondered Peter's theory that her dad had not remarried because of her and frowned. The idea seemed outlandish to her! Of course, he could have remarried—he just hadn't found anyone! Her mind reflected on the past, wondering if indeed any of the ladies who had helped him out had had ulterior motives, trying to remember. Then for a second she imagined what it would be like to get a call from him now, announcing he had found someone. Even the thought of it stung. Or what if, on her next trip home, she found him excited to introduce her to *someone special*? Soberly Kyla decided that she probably wouldn't die, but it might definitely feel like it. It would be a difficult adjustment. Very difficult.

She wanted to call her dad right now and sat up, realizing that for once she didn't have to walk any distance to do it! Kyla pulled her cell phone out of her purse and pulled up his number right where she sat.

"Okay—what's going on?" Kendall's voice was filled with concern that she had called him a second time in one day, again at an unusual hour. "Kyla Evangeline, are you okay? Is everything all right?"

She explained to him where she was, telling him that she had been given the afternoon off and that she was sitting with her feet up thinking about him.

"Well, that's nice of you, but I'm still at work. I just happened to see your call, and it's out of character for you to call again in the middle of the day."

She apologized but asked if she could ask him a quick question, to which he was more than willing if she kept it brief since he was needed in the office. So Kyla asked him flat-out why he never remarried.

He laughed out loud. "Holy cow! I would have not guessed that was your question in a hundred years! What in the world is this about?"

"Nothing. Just thinking about stuff—that's all. Were there just no women around? No one who was right for you?"

"Oh," he laughed awkwardly, "there were some ladies. I don't know. It just never really seemed right."

"Why not? They didn't love God enough?"

"No, not that. It was more like a timing issue. Seriously, Kyla— where are these questions coming from?"

"I just want to know, Dad. What kind of timing issues?"

"I don't know—just life."

"Work schedules? Like that?"

He made a sound, as if searching for the words. "No, not that. It was more like—more like the season of life we were in. You were having a tough time adjusting, and it just didn't feel like the right thing to do at the time. Make another change, you know. And I guess that's the way it stayed. Just the two of us. I think that's how God intended it to be."

Kyla could feel the lump in her throat. "Huh," she said. "Okay. Well, I just want to tell you that I think you were a really great dad. And I love you a lot."

He was silent for a moment. "Thank you."

"You're welcome. Okay, since you're still at work I'll let you go."

"All right, sweetheart. And Kyla?"

"Yeah?"

"If you call me again today with another strange question, I'm getting in my car and coming down there!"

They both laughed.

Kyla sat with her phone in her lap, a deep warmth spreading in her belly, almost like the feeling when she learned for the first time that Alex loved her, only this was better. This was pure. *Your dad would do anything to protect you. Now that's what you need to believe about God.* More than pitying her, her dad had sacrificed his own happiness for her good. For her "emotional stability," as Peter had put it. At the moment it wasn't as offensive as it had been when he said it. She hoped she could learn to see God like that.

Okay, she thought, sitting up and bringing her feet to the floor. *So I have issues. How does one address issues?* Pulling the tissue paper out of her shoebox, she folded it to make a smaller surface to write on. She would make a chart, her own personal spreadsheet of issues to navigate. She drew a line, making a heading and then columns across the page. *My Issues.* First column: *birth father.* Second column: *mother dying.* Third column: *adoption.* Fourth column: *Alex.* She paused, reflecting on Alex. She had brought his letter in her purse. Perhaps she ought to read it. She got it out and opened it up.

Kyla: Hey. I wanted you to hear what's happened first from me. Your dad probably told you we got together a few times. I'm struggling with some of the things he says, but you know firsthand what he's like. I guess I don't necessarily agree that a person needs religion to get their life turned around. Anyway, I wanted to tell you myself that I am going to be a father this fall. One of those little accidents, I guess. It's no one you know, and we are not together, but I will be taking responsibility by paying child support, etc. So now it's out and you know.

I also want you to know that I still meant what I said. I have never loved anyone like I love you. I want you back so fiercely. I need you, Kyla. I'm so sorry for all the ways I've hurt you. I realize it's probably hard to get news like this, but I would do anything to have things back to the way they were last summer. Maybe you could take a weekend and meet me at the cabin and we could talk, try to work things out. Please call me, baby. Alex.

Kyla reread the letter and held it in her hand, staring at it. Oh, how greatly perspectives could change in just a short time! What a relief she hadn't opened it at the table with her other birthday presents, she thought. Without hesitation Kyla walked the letter over to the nearby trash can.

God, thank you for saving me from that relationship, she breathed, realizing that it might have been the most heartfelt prayer she had ever prayed in her life.

Back at her seat she crossed Alex off her chart, deciding that tomorrow when Mrs. Gordon was out at the house Kyla would ask her again about the "soul tie" thing. She wanted an official, clean break from him. She thought his attitude about her dad interesting, in light of her own discovery today about him—that he had laid down his life for her. What would be so hard that Alex would struggle with regarding her dad? Her dad was a man of integrity and completely trustworthy. The vast character difference between Alex and him was never clearer to her. Kyla knew that in the future, any guy she dated would have to be more like her dad. And like Peter, who was definitely like her dad in many ways. In fact, she would have a hard time with anyone who wasn't like Peter.

Exactly like Peter.

She closed her eyes, feeling a flutter in her stomach. Peter. He was— he was—he was so much older than her, so good, so far above who she was, a spoiled little brat with "abandonment issues." He knew things. He was smart. He worked hard. He was nice to everyone, even her birth father. He—Kyla thought about him with the grill tool in his hand the night her father grabbed her in the woods, and the night her father had been drunk, and the night of the storm—he was a protector. She had zinged him, stomped off on him, been so very rude so many times, and Peter—Peter was steady. He was steady. She wanted someone like him. Kyla breathed a long sigh. She wanted—him. *Oh, God*, she moaned internally, *I will have to make a column on my spreadsheet just for this!*

Kyla knew she wasn't anywhere close to being someone he would ever notice. She was mean. She was angry. And this morning—this morning she had been just plain cruel! She had not defended him in the least but had in fact caused the whole scolding from Dr. Grant. His face. Kyla chewed the side of her thumb. Just the thought of the look on his face pierced her.

She wanted to call her dad again, but she had just talked to him. And what could he do anyway? She sighed, checking the time on her phone. She still had an hour and a half before she would meet up with her father. Then they would go to dinner. She calculated what time it would be when they got back to Wynnbury. Would she have time to talk to Peter then? Would he have anything to do with her after what had happened that morning?

Why should he? she thought. She—she—she had been to Peter like Alex had been to her. Hurtful. Insensitive. Clueless. Self-centered. A soberness settled over her. She wasn't any different from Alex. They both had the same problem. Her problem was her own character. Her problem was *herself.* Nothing or no one would change the way she was inside. But— she dared to hope—if God had changed Peter, couldn't he also change *her?* She wished very much that she knew how.

Kyla stared absently at the fish swimming in the pond, trying to remember all the things that Peter had told her about God. In her vulnerability she decided to step out. *God, I am dead and dark inside. I am a sinner. A bad one. I am arrogant and mean. I'm as mean as Peter with a steel pipe. Am I a candidate for your forgiveness? Can you make me alive inside and change the way I am too? Can you work with people who have "issues"?* She hoped so. She hoped so.

Checking the time on her phone, Kyla got up from the bench and gathered her bags. She knew that tomorrow Dr. Grant would ask to see what she bought for herself, so she had better get busy finding something.

Her father was late. She waited at the deli for half an hour before she saw the Mustang enter the parking lot.

"Traffic," he said when he picked her up at the curb.

Kyla threw her bags into the back seat and got in. She had bought a cute and summery cotton knit dress, two summer tops on sale, a new swimsuit that was her favorite color of blue, and with it a white cover-up shirt of sheer, light gauze with tiny gold buttons on it, besides the sandals she had already purchased after her pedicure. Right before the time she went to meet her father, she changed into the new dress in the mall restroom for their dinner together. Her father hadn't noticed. Or at least he hadn't said anything about it.

They went to an Italian restaurant, and her father ordered an entire bottle of wine to go with their meal. *To celebrate their time together,* he told her.

"Just one glass is fine for me," she said, but he persisted, for this was a special occasion.

The waiter filled their wine glasses and left.

DeKane held up his glass, smiling at her with his dark eyes. "To our coming success!"

Kyla cocked her head. "To what?"

"Our coming success—at Wynnbury. I think we're close!"

She lifted her glass slightly, then set it down on the white tablecloth.

"What's the deal? You don't look happy," he said after he had taken a sip.

"I thought perhaps we'd toast to *us*."

His head drew back. "Of course, baby!" He raised his glass toward her with a smile. "To us!"

Kyla spread her napkin onto her lap and turned her attention to her plate. Would he initiate any conversation? She waited, and they ate in silence. *Just one question. One question* about her life.

"You're quiet tonight," he observed, moving his lips to clear food out of his gums. He took a drink of wine and swished his teeth. "You can't be missing those kids now, are you? I don't know how you can do it all day! They get on my nerves!"

She blinked, reminding herself to breathe. "I was hoping that perhaps we could talk about your family again," she said calmly. "I've had a difficult time locating any DeKanes in the Champagne area."

"I'm not surprised. Most have moved away from there."

"But not you."

He frowned. "What? No, but I travel a lot."

"To meet with clients?"

He winked at her, helping himself to another roll.

"Where do you really live?" she asked, toying with her salad.

"That's classified, baby."

She wondered if the location of Delano High School in the Champagne area was also classified. Who knew if any of it was true?

Kyla filled her fork and paused, balancing it slightly off the plate. "I was wondering if you would tell me the name of your parents—for the sake of my family tree. It would be nice to know who they were, where they came from."

He gave a short nod. "David and Shirley DeKane," he replied.

She blinked, surprised at the ease of his answer. "And your brothers?"

"Darryl and Derek." He took his knife and began cutting his meat.

Kyla looked down at her plate. "And your sister?"

DeKane said nothing. She looked up to find him studying her face. "I have no sister," he said.

"Oh, I must have remembered it wrong," she said, resuming her meal.

Chapter Twenty-Six

He observed her a little longer before turning back to his plate.

The waiter checked in again at their table. He was blond, but Kyla noted that he was not as tall as Peter, certainly not as well built as Peter. And Peter would have been much more personable. In her mind she saw his smile and his blue eyes.

They finished their meal making small talk about the weather, and the trees that were downed last night, and how they would have to cut the carport up to remove it from the yard. Kyla wondered if Peter had gotten the leaves cleaned out of the fountain or if they were still there. Perhaps tomorrow she would go out by herself and clean it. If he hadn't already.

DeKane ordered her dessert, but she could only eat a few bites and asked for a box in which to take it home. She would put it into the refrigerator and have it tomorrow. Perhaps she would share it with Mrs. Gordon. That made her think of the kitchen, which reminded her of the card that had come for Peter in her box. She wondered who Amy was and if her dad would know and if he would think it strange if she called him one more time just to ask him about it.

On the way home Kyla asked her father again to leave Wynnbury. She was driving the Mustang with the top up because the evening air was chilly. She brought up the subject when she pulled into the entrance gates alongside the keypad. She punched in the code, and the gates opened wide and then closed behind her.

"Baby, I don't understand," DeKane said. "Why would I leave now when I'm so close to solving this case? I can't."

"It's too stressful for me!" Kyla said. "Isn't it a bit hard for a detective to focus with his own daughter involved? What if things got dangerous?"

He shook his head. "I don't have an issue with focus."

"Yeah, but wouldn't things get weird if you felt you had to protect me? Like what if my life were in danger?"

He made a sound of protest. "Kyla, baby, you're a key part of the success here! It's just not an option right now for me to leave."

Kyla nodded, looking away.

The lights in the kitchen were left on for them, but the rest of the house was dark and quiet, including the equipment in the fitness room. Kyla thanked her father for the evening and went straight to her room. She turned on her lights and plopped the bags onto the tile table near the fireplace, setting her purse on the table by the window. A small movement startled her, and she turned to see Howie's sleepy head rise from her pillow. Quickly she turned off the overhead lights and clicked on a small lamp on the end table.

"Howie, you're in my bed," she said to him softly.

"Can I sleep here with you?" he asked. "Please?"

Kyla sighed and nodded. "Okay. But you have to sleep, not talk."

He nodded, giving a tired yawn. "You have new clothes," he breathed. "They're nice."

"Thank you," she said.

She put her pajamas on in the bathroom and then crawled in with him.

"This is kinda special," she whispered. "Like our own little slumber party. I missed you today!"

"I missed you too," he said, sliding up next to her. "I was afraid you left. I was afraid you wouldn't come back." He broke out in a sob.

Kyla hugged him and kissed his head.

A little before midnight the second one came in with his bear and blanket. Kyla pulled Hank up into the bed and kissed him good night too. As soon as he was asleep, she crept out into the hallway to peer down into the Great Room.

At first she thought he wasn't there. There was no one pacing, no one standing with arms raised, no urgent whispers. But then she noticed the glint of his hair in the glow of the yard light through windows. Peter was there, but he was sitting in his chair, motionless and looking straight ahead, his hands resting on his thighs. She watched him for a bit, then went back to bed.

As she was falling asleep Kyla heard footsteps in the room above her. She knew it was her father. Someone ought to know about this, she thought, but who could she tell?

Chapter Twenty-Seven

Kyla opened her door to the aroma of eggs and sausage in the morning and was surprised to find Mrs. Gordon and her granddaughter sitting at the table in the kitchen visiting with Peter when she and the boys came downstairs. Peter had his back to her as she approached. Her eyes rested on his broad shoulders and the back of his head. Mrs. Gordon's granddaughter, who looked to be about thirteen or fourteen years old, with long, blond hair and too much eyeshadow, was gawking at Peter from across the table where she sat beside her grandmother.

"*There* she is!" Mrs. Gordon said cheerfully, looking up when she saw Kyla. "Good morning, hon!"

"Did I miss something?" Kyla asked, looking at the three of them, then at the clock above the sink. "You're here super early!"

While she was talking, Peter rose quickly and reached across the table to shake Mrs. Gordon's hand. "It was nice to have met you finally," he said to her, and then he acknowledged the younger girl too, who blushed deeper. "Kyla," he said with a short nod in her direction and strode out the room.

Kyla swallowed, her face feeling warm. Peter hadn't even looked at her. She watched the boys run after him to the side entryway.

"This is my granddaughter Julia," Mrs. Gordon was saying. "She was going to come out with me today anyway, like we planned. Then when David called yesterday afternoon and said he wanted us out here before the kids got up, she just spent the night at my house."

Kyla turned back and greeted the girl. "David—Dr. Grant—called you?"

"Oh, yes, hon! He said he wanted you to have the whole day off. That's why we had to be here before the kids got up. I went into their rooms to wake them up, but neither of them was there!"

She gave an embarrassed smile. "Sometimes I let them crawl in with me."

Down the hall Kyla heard the side door close, and the boys returned to the kitchen, checking eagerly to see how the new goldfish were doing.

"Well, I made an egg casserole for breakfast," Mrs. Gordon continued. "I hope the kids will eat it. I left out the mushrooms."

Kyla fed the boys, and while they ate she coached Julia on some things to do with them, showing her the library and where the games and crafts were kept.

"Can we go outside?" Julia wanted to know, peering out the Great Room window to where Peter was hauling away cut-up brush.

Kyla told her yes but not to the beach and that they had to stay well away from any of the men working. That made it sound like there were more guys than Peter, while still setting a boundary.

Julia had brought a bag of activities that she pulled out immediately after breakfast, so it was easy for Kyla and Mrs. Gordon to slip into the formal dining room, which seemed especially beautiful with the morning sunlight pouring in the window. Kyla brought her leftover dessert from the night before with two forks to share with Mrs. Gordon over their coffee and tea.

"How did the day go with your father yesterday?" she asked, leafing through the tin of tea and selecting one. "Are the two of you getting to know one another?"

Kyla shook her head no. "No, not really. I—I asked him to leave."

"You did? Is he leaving today?"

She shrugged. "Um, he's got some—things to take care of first, but then hopefully he'll go. Soon."

The sober truth was that *she* possibly would go too. If her father was what he claimed to be, it meant that it was possible that any day now Kyla could be out of a job. All of Wynnbury would shut down. No more kids to nanny. No more housekeeper. No more Peter. She would have to go back home.

Mrs. Gordon clicked her tongue. "You know, some folks just aren't good at relationships. Sounds like your father is one of them. Is that why you look a little down today?"

Kyla sighed heavily. *Down* was an understatement! Where did she start? Her biological father and his strange behavior? The crazy thought of Dr. Grant and what he was hiding? Her emotional "issues"? Or Peter. Everything was jumbled into one big mess.

"That's part of it," she replied. "Yesterday I was having a conversation with Peter—"

"Oh, isn't Peter a nice man?" Mrs. Gordon interjected. "What a wonderful guy!"

"Yes," she said softly, "he is." She stared at her coffee, thinking of him.

Mrs. Gordon waited. "And you were saying?"

Kyla looked at her.

"You said you were having a conversation with Peter—?"

She forgot what she was going to say. She looked up at Mrs. Gordon. "So what do you do if you have abandonment issues? What *are* abandonment issues anyway?"

Mrs. Gordon leaned back in surprise. "Goodness! Well, you tell *me*!"

Kyla's eyes widened a bit. "Me? How would *I* know? I asked *you*!"

"Well," the older woman said gently, "why don't you tell me what it feels like to be abandoned? Let's start there."

She blinked. "I don't know! It doesn't feel like anything. I have no feelings of hurt from my birth father. He's like a stranger to me. I don't even like him! I don't even know what to call him. Certainly not *Dad*. Do I call him 'Robert'? 'Hello, Robert—this is Kyla, your daughter.'"

Mrs. Gordon gave a slow nod. "That would be difficult."

Kyla took a small bite of the dessert and a sip of coffee. Mrs. Gordon sipped her tea.

"I keep thinking that *perhaps today* he will be interested in me, that he will ask me a question about my life. That he will tell me I look nice in a way that isn't insulting. That he will care about something in my life. *Something!* It would be nice to receive a gift that isn't just a roll of money. One that takes some thought. Don't get me wrong—I didn't mind the cash he gave me for my birthday and yesterday for shopping. And the car. But—"

"But that's not love," Mrs. Gordon said quietly.

"No. It's not. At least it doesn't feel like it."

"Hmm." Mrs. Gordon paused with her fork balanced in her hand. "What did it feel like when you were a teenager?"

"What did *what* feel like?"

"Being abandoned."

Kyla shrugged. "I don't know. I guess I didn't think about him. I mean, a couple of times I took his picture out and looked at it just because I wondered if I looked like him. But I seriously didn't think about him much.

I was mostly embarrassed by my other dad—Kendall—who I considered to be my *real* dad. Or as close as you could get to a real dad. He at least was in my life!"

"Do you remember what it felt like when your father left home? Back when you were a little girl?"

She looked at the table, thinking. "Not really. No, I don't remember."

"Hmm. Fathers are pretty important." Mrs. Gordon stirred her tea with her spoon, then set it on her napkin. "How do you think Howie would handle it if his daddy walked out of his life today?"

Kyla grimaced. "Oh, my! He would be devastated! The bottom would fall out of his life!" She met Mrs. Gordon's eyes.

"He's probably near the same age you were."

"Yeah. Almost exactly the same age."

Mrs. Gordon sipped her tea.

Kyla looked down, considering the question. "He would wonder why. He would long for him to come back. He would be confused. He would wonder if it was his fault." She bit her lip and shook her head. "Last night he thought I had left and wasn't coming back. He was such a wreck that he slept in my bed waiting for me and then cried when I came home."

"So it doesn't exactly feel like nothing."

She sighed. "No, it doesn't. The hurt just gets turned off after a while. It goes numb."

Mrs. Gordon waited.

"It's just confusing," Kyla continued, staring down at her dessert. "You live in this great big 'why.' You try to figure out why you're not wanted, why you're not worth his time or worth his interest. Why you were just forgotten. Why you were cast off, rejected, not worth even knowing. Okay, yes—it *does* hurt. It hurts a lot!"

"Ouch. That sounds like abandonment. It makes me wonder if those might be the same questions you have about God."

Kyla's eyes rose to look at the housekeeper, then dropped to the table.

Mrs. Gordon paused. "How do you think this affects your life?"

She was thoughtful for a moment, then shook her head. "I don't know if it does that much. I seriously didn't think about him until he showed up. I think it's just an issue when he's around. Probably mostly a thing of the past that I need to get over."

Mrs. Gordon nodded, her brow furled. "So let me ask you a question. Say you have a loss. Or say you're talking to someone and something comes up that makes you feel insecure about yourself—like maybe you're not good enough or not wanted for some reason—how do you respond?"

Kyla shrugged. "I don't know."

"Hmm." Mrs. Gordon pursed her lips, thinking. "So tell me what kinds of things you struggle with."

"*Struggle* with? What do you mean?"

"Your weaknesses—"

"I don't know. I can't really think of anything."

Mrs. Gordon sat up quickly and blinked. "Nothing? Well, good then." She took a chunk of the dessert and savored it, then turned back to her tea.

Kyla looked down thoughtfully. She wasn't sure where Mrs. Gordon was trying to lead the conversation. She decided to speak what was on her mind. "Peter said he thinks my abandonment issues have caused me to believe a lie about God."

"Huh."

"That God casts me off and discards me. Because my father did."

"Do you think he's right?"

Kyla opened her hand. "I guess I could see that some. It *is* hard for me to trust God. Hard to believe that he would take the slightest interest in me. I know I tend to think that God's against me."

"And that he's completely left you on your own."

She nodded. "Yes. Like he wants nothing to do with me because—I don't know—there must be something-the-heck wrong with me! It's like you said—I have all those same 'why' questions about God."

Mrs. Gordon made a little noise with her tongue. "I would agree with Peter. Those *are* lies about God."

"Well, whatever it is, it's sucking the life out of me, and I don't like it!"

The housekeeper nodded. "That's what those lies do! Lies keep people bound up. Lies keep people from knowing who God is and what he's like. Once you start understanding what he's *really* like and how he feels about you, you'll feel so free. Honey, God is good! He is never the bringer of evil! The devil wants you to believe that God is *not* good and that he's against you, but the devil is a liar—yes, he is! He doesn't want you to know the love of God—no, no, no!"

Mrs. Gordon set her cup down on the ring of moisture on her napkin, continuing: "I'll bet those lies affect your relationships with people too. I would guess"—she cocked her head at Kyla—"I would guess that you have a great deal of fear in your relationships. I would guess that you're uncertain where you stand with people, and you wonder if you're worth their time."

Kyla's mouth opened.

"You probably have a hard time believing anyone could love you for who you are. You probably don't even think you're worth knowing."

She stared.

"And the other thing that I would guess is that you have some kind of protective barrier that keeps people out. You know, like if you drive them away with your tough behavior first, then they can't hurt you by leaving you. It's a way to keep your world safe, because you need to fend for yourself."

Her eyes dropped to the table.

"That's thinking like an orphan. You know—like someone who has no Heavenly Father watching out for her. You have to fend for yourself. You think, *No one is going to take care of me, so I have to take care of myself. No one's going to watch over my heart, no one's going to protect me, so I have to protect myself.* You probably feel like you always have to fight to defend yourself."

"How—how do you know all this?"

"Oh, honey." Mrs. Gordon gave her a sympathetic smile. "I've *lived* it! I had really great parents, but our family was so big that I kinda got lost. My mother was physically there, but she was busy and preoccupied with what seemed like everyone else in the world but me. I felt like she was clueless as to who I was on the inside. You might call it 'emotional abandonment.' I'm sure it wasn't intentional, but my perception was that I didn't matter. I felt like she was completely disconnected from me emotionally, and I was left to figure out life on my own. Every part of it! She had way too much going on in life to think about my emotional needs—my parents were pastors, for heaven's sake! They were important people working hard to help a lot of other people! Well, let me tell you—I didn't do so hot when I was a teen! I went looking for love and comfort in all the wrong places. Sometimes I still have to fight my preprogrammed thinking that says I don't deserve love. And still—at times—it's hard to be open with people. Emotional intimacy scares me because I'm not sure people really mean what they say. I tend to expect them to be too busy for me, which proves the old lie that I don't really matter. See how that works?"

Kyla sighed. "I feel that people love me only because they feel sorry for me."

"Well, there you go." Mrs. Gordon spread her hands. "Where does that get you? You're guaranteed to never receive love then—you won't allow yourself to! That's abandonment, self-pity, and hopelessness all rolled into one toxic package!" She reached out to touch Kyla's arm. "You know, I'm not required to visit with you, Kyla. No one's making me do this. I'm here because I like you and I care about you. Not because I feel sorry for you. Self-pity will frustrate and kill your relationships. People can't get past it because, like I said, you won't allow them to. You turn away their love and then blame it on them, but it's *you* who has the issues with pity."

Kyla was silent.

"Dads are important, hon. And there's fallout in your life from a dad who didn't take the responsibility to love you."

"I guess I can see that. But it's not like no one loved me. My adoptive dad did—Kendall. He loved me. *Loves* me."

"Yes. Yes, I know he does, hon! Of course. But our early life experiences set us up for how we experience life, and I would guess you receive his love through that same abandonment filter. I'm sure he wasn't perfect raising you either. Most dads don't know what to do with teenage girls. He may have failed you a few times. Look—I'm not trying to prove anything negative about him. I could be wrong. I'm just saying that no one can completely love us the way we need to be loved, except for God."

Kyla let out a long breath. She had no interest in her coffee and pushed it to the side. "Okay, I do have a problem. You're right about feeling like I'm fighting inside. I struggle with anger. I—I get so defensive. And very angry."

Mrs. Gordon nodded, placing her hand on top of Kyla's. "Well, then let's find out why. Pain and anger are connected. We'll do some talking. We'll ask God to reveal where it's coming from; then we'll ask him to heal what's causing it and take it away."

She let out a little breath. "Is that—possible? You can help me with this?"

She squeezed her hand. "Why, of course it is, hon! But we don't have to be in a hurry. I'll be coming out here all summer. I'd be happy to meet with you like this. Perhaps I could even bring Julia with me on Thursdays. She could watch the boys."

Kyla thought of her dad meeting with young men regularly, like he had with Peter. She wondered if it was a lot like her time with Mrs. Gordon.

"I just have to tell you," Mrs. Gordon interjected, "that today I need to go as soon as Hank goes down for his nap. I told my neighbor that I would let their dog out this afternoon. But Dr. Grant said Howie can hang out with Peter until he gets home."

"I don't mind having Howie this afternoon."

"And also, I do need to clean today. I didn't get much done on Monday."

Kyla turned back to her dessert, taking a large bite, followed by a wash of tepid coffee. She continued thoughtfully: "I do want to find out where this anger is coming from. I can be so mean. I don't want to be mean anymore. And I don't want it to keep me from God—I really do want to follow God."

Mrs. Gordon placed her hand over her heart. "Remember what we said the other day? Your heart was meant to hold the love of God. There's a world of hurt sitting in your heart, honey, and it's no wonder. I'm not surprised you're angry. Where there's hurt, there's anger. Or depression—same thing, just anger turned inward. But it doesn't matter which—God can heal it and take it away."

"Good. How?"

The older woman reached out for Kyla's hand again. "Oh, it's so very, very simple. And yet it can be so very, very difficult. You just need to keep doing the same thing over and over and over until it's gone."

"Which is—?"

"Forgive, forgive, forgive. And when those hurts come back to bite again, you forgive *again*. You just keep forgiving until it doesn't hurt anymore. Remember? All the hurt and lies need to come out, and the love and truth of God need to get in there to fill up its place! Keep doing that and you'll find yourself walking right out of hurt and into healing. But forgiveness is key. Sin and hurt *out*, truth and love *in*—that's the simple recipe for healing."

Kyla gave a forlorn laugh. "I don't know—this might take a while! My life is pretty messed up!"

Mrs. Gordon laughed too. "Oh, come now! You're no worse than anyone else! Listen, everyone's born as a sinner, Kyla. Everyone's a spiritual orphan—unloved, unwanted, and lost. We're all hurt and wounded in some ways. But 'though our sins be as scarlet, he can make us white as snow.' We can be forgiven and washed clean by the blood of Jesus. This is what the good news is—that Jesus came to forgive us our sins so that God can adopt us as his very own children! And then we get to learn what God is really like as our Father! You've been fed a bunch of lies about God. It's time to sort the truth from lies. That's your homework!" She pointed kindly at Kyla. "But don't be overwhelmed. I'll help you with that."

Kyla thought about what a jerk Alex had been. "Here's a question: what do you do if someone doesn't deserve forgiveness?"

Chapter Twenty-Seven

"Honey, no one deserves forgiveness. Do you?"

"Well—I haven't done anything all *that* bad!" Nothing nearly as bad as Alex!

"Oh, I see." Mrs. Gordon's eyes widened a bit, and she nodded. They were silent for a bit until she cleared her throat and looked at Kyla. "You've never lied to anybody, never said bad things, never dishonored your dad? You just said a minute ago that you didn't want to be mean!"

Immediately she felt a pang of guilt. Of course. Hadn't she realized just yesterday how much she was like Alex? Even right at this moment she felt the nagging guilt in regard to Peter. She looked down at her hands, remembering Peter's comments in their conversation yesterday about how much he hoped for his father to forgive him for what he had done. Who knows? Perhaps Peter's father felt that his son didn't deserve forgiveness.

"Okay—never mind. That was stupid to say. I've done plenty wrong, and no, I don't deserve forgiveness, but I do want to be forgiven. And I hope"—her voice caught—"I hope I *can* be forgiven."

"Well, forgiveness is the starting point of change," Mrs. Gordon said. "If you want to be forgiven, you must learn to forgive others. Maybe next time we can talk about that more." She looked at her watch, shifting in her chair. "I'm feeling like I should maybe get the sheets in the washer. David said to be sure you had plenty of time to yourself today. I don't want to take up your whole morning. You better go outside while the weather is nice—I hear it's supposed to be very hot and humid again this weekend."

Kyla thanked her for her time, and Mrs. Gordon hugged her warmly and left to start stripping the beds. After tidying up the formal dining room, Kyla closed it off from the hall and stood there with her back against the doors, feeling a little disappointed. She had hoped that talking to Mrs. Gordon would fix everything today. She wanted her issues solved *now*! Yet there was still so much to talk about, still so much she didn't know.

Not quite sure what to do with her time, she went to her room and putted around, straightening things up. Her floor was littered with price tags and shopping bags. She had given the boys their new clothes when they had woken up, and their discarded pajamas were strewn across her floor from their excitement to wear them.

Her new swimsuit was also on the floor. She tried it on again and decided that she still liked it a lot. It was very flattering—a shiny blue, ribbed fabric, with a tiny silver buckle in the center of the scooped neck—and it covered a little more than her other suit. She kept it on and put her shorts on over it and her new gauze shirt. The cover-up was pretty, the sheer fabric providing modesty while still showing a bit of her suit underneath. She loved the long shirttails and the tiny buttons. Perhaps it would be a beach day. She paused by her window, where the bluff before her beckoned her. On the other hand, perhaps today was the day to finally climb that bluff. She had hours to herself. But in the back of her mind she considered that if she went to the beach, perhaps Peter would come down again. She doubted he would. But just in case. She wanted to see him, to talk to him so badly. She sighed. It was a beach day for sure.

Finding a large tote bag, she packed up her Bible and her journal and her laptop, then made herself a lunch in the kitchen. It was strange to make something for only herself. Part of her wanted to make a bunch of extra sandwiches for the boys. And for Peter. Of course, there was Mrs. Gordon and Julia too. Kyla decided not to make the extra sandwiches so that Julia would have something more to do than drool over Peter. Oh, and there was her father too, she remembered as she headed out the door. She hadn't seen him all day, but she could guess he was in one of two places—in bed from his late-night exploration or still up on the third floor looking for whatever he was looking for. She didn't want to think about him.

She left out the patio door and made a point of walking slowly across the yard, hoping that Peter might see her from where he was cutting up and clearing out the downed trees at the edge of the ravine. It looked as if he were almost done. The carport debris was almost entirely gone too, she noticed, and the skid loader was out, parked near the edge of the house. They had probably used it somehow to get rid of the carport. She paused at the top of the staircase, looking back one more time, but he did not look up from his work. She noticed that the rest of the yard needed mowing again. Peter did a lot around the place—that was certain.

It had been just yesterday, Kyla thought, arranging her towel and belongings on the beach and making herself comfortable on the Adirondack chairs, less than twenty-four hours ago when Peter had come down to talk to her. It seemed longer because of her time away yesterday afternoon and evening. Would he join her today? She hoped they could talk soon. She hoped he would forgive her.

She opened the journal he had given her. It was time to use it. She didn't want to forget all that she was learning. Carefully she wrote out what had come out in the conversation with Peter yesterday, including all that he had said about Kendall, her dad. She took her time with it, thinking it through. She wrote about all that she had learned during her time at the mall too, including a whole page of all the qualities she admired about Peter, which made her heart ache with the desire to make things right with him. Closing her eyes, she leaned her head back against the chair, daydreaming about him, how strong he was—inside and out. How dependable and trustworthy. How—handsome. Finally she pulled her thoughts away from him, and she wrote about Mrs. Gordon's wisdom from the morning and the point Mrs. Gordon had made about learning what God was really like as a father.

Kyla didn't know the Bible very well, but she started to list out things she knew for sure were lies about God. *He doesn't know who I am. He doesn't care about my feelings. He is aloof and not very loving.* All lies. She wrote for a while, then glancing at the page, Kyla began to discover that most of her negative thoughts about God were also connected to her father, Robert DeKane. And she also started to see that where she was angry at God, she was also angry at him. *God did not dump me on the side of the road and say, "I don't want her."* But her father did, practically speaking. *God is not distant and disinterested in me.* But her father was *very* distant and quite disinterested in her. Nor did he provide for her growing up. Kyla's list began to grow. She kept writing and writing the failures of her father, growing angrier with each one until she looked up, wondering, as she gazed out over the river, why she was even doing this exercise. *This is eating me up!* she thought. *This is consuming me and filling me with hatred!*

Kyla remembered Mrs. Gordon's statements. She had written them in her journal above already: "Forgiveness is the beginning of change. Forgiveness is the key."

Promptly she plopped the journal onto the other chair and pulled her laptop out of her bag. *It was time!* She would not wait another day to watch her mother's video for her on forgiveness. These video subjects were the top five things she felt she needed to leave with her own daughter before she died. And so far, she had been spot on with the one about boyfriends. Kyla only wished she had watched it and taken it to heart sooner. She decided that right now she would first watch Forgiveness, and then she would watch the one on God.

As Kyla opened her laptop, however, she found in dismay that the battery was almost completely drained. She groaned. Her charger must have slipped out of the outlet! An ominous red box popped up on the screen warning her of low power. *I don't care,* Kyla thought. *I'm going to play it until it dies.* She double-clicked on the icon. Who knows—perhaps she would make it all the way through.

Kyla could tell immediately that it was one of her mother's later videos, very probably the last. Her beautiful mother, Eva DeKane, was lying down, not sitting, in the hospital bed in their living room. Her cheeks were sallow, and dark rings encircled her eyes. There was an air tube in her nose with the accompanying hiss of air flowing through it.

"Okay, we're rolling," said her dad Kendall from somewhere off camera. "Take your time, love. It's okay—you don't have to hurry."

Eva's eyes widened a bit as she focused up on the camera. "Hi, Kyla," she said, offering a weak smile. She spoke very slowly in short, choppy sentences, taking a breath between each phrase. "I have one more video"—a breath—"for you. I think it's important. So bear with me. It might take a while—to get this out. I'll try to—get to the point."

Kyla observed that her mom was sober, not smiley and cheerful as she had been in the other videos. She looked like she didn't have the energy for it.

"It's about forgiveness," her mother continued. "One of the keys—of life. So important. Without it you become toxic, angry, and bitter." She lifted her head slightly, adjusting herself on the pillow.

"Some things happen—that are out of our control. Storms. Accidents. Sickness. People dying. Foolish mistakes of others. Tragic mistakes. Those are all beyond our control—but we get to deal with—with the pain and mess left behind. It's what I'm struggling with right now." Eva paused to rest, reaching up with a thin hand to wipe a tear. After a moment she took a breath and went on. "But I've chosen to trust that God is good—no matter what has happened—and whatever *will* happen. *God is good.*

"I could be bitter. I'm tempted to be. Awful things have happened to me. Awful. But I have made the choice—to forgive God. To stop blaming him for bad things." She swallowed, her voice becoming strained. "God is perfect, you know. He doesn't *need* to be forgiven ever. But sometimes—it's very hard to understand life."

Eva looked to the side and gave a nod, and Kyla saw her dad—younger-looking, certainly—bring a Styrofoam cup with a straw to her so she could drink. She lay back on the pillow then, with her eyes closed for a moment. When she was ready, she turned back to the camera to continue.

"The next thing—is that no one is perfect. Unless you choose to live all by yourself—you will have struggles with people. People can be annoying. Or maddening. But you will only pollute your life—if you carry it all—in your heart or mind. Forgive, darling. Forgiveness is like—like a scissors—to cut their baggage off of you. And their unhealthiness—off of you. Whatever they've done. If you don't forgive, you drag all of that with you through life—and it becomes part of you. I know this firsthand. It's hard to forgive—but worth it to be free."

Again she rested, her chest heaving as her breaths came audible and strained.

"Do you need to stop?" her dad asked.

Eva shook her head, opening her eyes to look at the camera. "Eventually, sweet girl, you are going to make—your *own* mistakes—and you will need others to forgive *you*. I have made some big mistakes—and have hurt people deeply. Sometimes by accident and sometimes not. Either way, for your own peace of mind—make things right with people as much—as you can." She paused to rest.

When she started again, Kyla had to raise the computer volume all the way up to hear her voice. "No one taught me how to do this—when I was young, so I'll tell you. It's simple, but it's hard. Go to them and ask them to forgive you. Tell them you were wrong. Most people will forgive—but not all. That's their choice. Don't second-guess what they will do. The important thing—is what *you* will do. So, honey, just do it. Just do it."

Eva closed her eyes again for about five seconds. Then she looked up fully into the camera, giving one last powerful push. "Most important, darling—is to start with God. I have lived a life of sin and deceit. Of selfishness and wickedness. But God"—she wiped another tear from her eye—"but God forgave me—when I didn't deserve forgiveness at all. If you ask—he will rush in with his mercy— and forgive—will forgive *everything*. It's true!" She gave a toothy smile. "It's a miracle. But it's not—a magic wand that takes away—all your problems. It's a key. A key to a door—that opens to *him*. To Jesus and all he is. All I can say, darling—is go through that door. He's worth it. Go in. There's new life—with him." She smiled briefly, then closed her eyes and lifted her hand to indicate that she was done speaking.

Kyla put her laptop aside and sat with her hands in her lap, her eyes resting on the water washing rhythmically up onto the tiny sandy shore, her mind at work. Strangely she was not an emotional mess seeing her mother again with cancer. Part of that was because she had already stopped blaming God for taking her mother from her. She still missed her, of course, but there was something much greater that was happening at the moment that she needed to zero in on. She figured the best way to honor her mother was to actually do what she said, and that was what she intended to do. She sighed, wondering where she should start. Forgiving her birth father would be a biggie. She could already see that. But her mother had said to start with

God, which sounded like a good idea. Yet she had no clue what to do—what starting with God should look like. It didn't matter, she decided. She was going to take a stab at things in her own way.

With courage, Kyla started in with what was most important to her. "God, I have blamed you for everything bad in my life, thinking that you were against me." Mrs. Gordon's voice played through her mind, *God is never the bringer of evil.* Yes, she needed to go there. "I've been so angry— *so angry* with you! I've falsely accused you, and I've *hated* you. Especially for taking my mom, but also for a hundred other things, and I'm sorry. I was so wrong. Please forgive me."

She had started with just voicing the words out loud but was immediately overcome with emotion, suddenly crying into her hands, ashamed at how wrong she had been. Then through the tears she didn't really know what else to pray, but she hoped God knew how much she meant what she was trying to say. He hoped he could hear her heart through the silence.

After a bit she wiped her face, wondering where to go next. Into her mind came what Peter had said about Jesus taking the penalty for sin.

"God," she continued without hesitating, "I know I have a lot of sin. A *lot* of sin. I know I haven't lived right, the way you would want me to, and I don't deserve forgiveness. But if Jesus paid the penalty for sin, like Peter said, could you also pay the penalty for mine, so that *I* could be forgiven? Would you bring me to life inside, like Peter talked about—like, make me new? New—on the inside. What I guess I'm saying is that I want to really live for you, like my mom did and like my dad does. I want to take the key and 'go in,' like my mom talked about. I'm not sure how that is supposed to happen, but I want it to be real." She paused, thinking. "And I'm not sure how this works either, but I want to be adopted by you."

Adoption. She remembered back to the awkwardness of calling the guy who used to be her mom's boyfriend "Dad," but she was glad now that he had insisted on it. Peter was right. Kendall had *wanted* her, and he had taken his role—his *responsibility*—very seriously. There was no denying it. And if he, a regular guy, had taken it to heart, Kyla knew that God would too if he adopted her. The thought that God would actually *want* her as his child was a mind-bender, but if it was true that he did, then she knew he would help her grow, help her change, protect her, provide for her, all the things good fathers do.

"I want that, God," she prayed. "I want you to be my Father, and I want"—she broke into a sob—"I want your love to fill my heart."

When she had cried herself out, Kyla took a deep breath and rummaged in her bag for her water bottle. She took a long drink, looking out over the river. A slight breeze was stirring up ripples on the surface of the water and rustled the leaves of the trees near her. It felt comforting to her, like God was letting her know he was there. Maybe, she thought, maybe she could ask God to be like a mother to her too. But she wasn't sure about that. She would ask Mrs. Gordon about it. Mulling on the idea, her mom's imagery of the scissors came to mind, and Kyla immediately thought of a few things that she wanted to cut off.

"God, regarding Alex. I forgive him for hurting me and being such a jerk. But I was also wrong in that relationship. I need you to forgive *me* too. And would you please cut us apart so that I can be truly free from him? And cut me free from Mike and—" Kyla listed out all the others she had definitely gone too far with. She wanted every soul tie broken. Even sitting by herself on the beach she was embarrassed doing it and felt like a kindergartener. Her prayers sounded so simple. Did God hear such prayers? Was she doing it right? She hoped so.

Up above her she could hear the rumble of the skid loader in the yard. It was pretty obvious that Peter wasn't coming down. He was working. But it was best that he didn't right now, she thought. She still had business to take care of.

Her biological father was next. She blew her breath out her cheeks and opened her journal to her list. Starting at the top, line by line, Kyla went down the page, item by item, feeling the hurt and anger of everything she had written, of all he had and hadn't done. One by one, she brought every hurt that she could think of to the surface, confessing the pain she felt about it and then releasing her father in forgiveness for it. Somewhere in the middle of the list she found herself bawling like a five-year-old little girl, but she was deliberate in keeping the focus—bringing each hurt to a place where she could say out loud, "God, I forgive my father for—" and then she would spell it out plainly. Each time she would finish a hurt, she pictured a little scissors cutting those things away from her—until finally she reached the bottom of her page.

She was exhausted. Perhaps there would be more to come, and perhaps she would have to address some of the same things over in the future, but for now Kyla leaned back against the chair tired but able to relax. The tissues in her bag had been carefully rationed, but all of them were now lying in a disgusting pile in the sand beside her chair. Lifting her arms in a stretch, she noticed that she felt different. The tension she was accustomed to carrying had loosened within, and she felt lighter. The air seemed fresher. The tree beside her was suddenly more beautiful, with its leaves dancing in the light breeze, and the sky above it more vibrant blue, with its random puffy clouds. Kyla inhaled the freshness of the air around her and let it out. The day was suddenly much more pleasant. Underneath the dock the water made sucking sounds. The boat rocked gently next to it, reminding her that just yesterday Peter had asked her to go out on the water with him. That was before.

She sighed. She wasn't done. Peter. He was her next item of business. This would not be fun, she presumed, for she wasn't good at apologies. She preferred not to go there at all. She was accustomed to getting her own way, of throwing a fit, stomping off, pouting, anything she could do to control her circumstances and keep people safely away from her. But not today. She needed to face him. Chewing the side of her thumb, she rehearsed what she would say to him when she saw him. And in her mind she thought about what he might say in return. She played out the whole conversation, then didn't like the way it went, so she changed it, then again. Finally she made herself stop it. There was only one thing that would do—she would simply have to go do it! She would have to actually talk to him. And she wanted to do it before Dr. Grant got home, just in case it went south, for she surely didn't want to get him in trouble again.

Without a mirror Kyla couldn't check what she looked like, but she figured her eyes were probably red and swollen from all her crying. With the water left in her water bottle, she splashed her face with one handful at a time, dabbing herself dry with her beach towel. At least she *felt* fresher. Then she put on her new gauzy shirt, packed up her things, and started up the wooden stairs. Halfway up, Kyla thought of something and stopped to make a decision.

"This is for you, God," she said. "And for me, so that I can be free. It's not to get Peter."

She liked Peter. She wanted Peter. But more than that, she wanted to do the right thing. She wanted to have the right motive in talking to him. She decided she would be sincere and honest, whatever happened, with no manipulation for her benefit. She had done him wrong, and it was only right for her to apologize, however it turned out. Everything in her, however, hoped for the best.

Chapter Twenty-Eight

At the top of the wooden staircase Kyla stopped to catch her breath, surveying the yard before her. In preparation for the new sod Peter was digging the old patches of grass out of the yard with the skid loader. A large portion of the area was now completely bare ground, the grassy debris piled at the edge of the cliff near where Kyla stood. The skid loader was running, but Peter was not on it. He was standing beside it studying something in the dirt about halfway between the fountain and her, with his back to her. Kyla stayed where she was. He would certainly see her when he got back onto the machine. She watched him kneel, digging with his gloved hands in the dirt for a bit, looking at the ground to the left and right. Then he stood and stomped his boot on whatever it was, kicking the dirt at the edge. Finally he got back onto the skid loader, and it started moving. He hadn't seen her.

With butterflies churning, Kyla stepped with purpose out onto the lawn—or the bare ground, as it was now. Peter was navigating the skid loader to dig in the place he had just been examining. She moved closer, putting herself more in his line of vision. Finally he did see her, standing there in the dirt in her white shirt, her bag over her arm, facing him, waiting. He looked at her but he did not stop. He waved her away.

A shot of disappointment spiraled down inside of her. Kyla's cheeks grew hot. He did not want to talk to her. Immediately the beast in her wanted to react—to throw something at him, to yell, to storm off, to do something demonstrative. But she caught herself. *I am not that girl anymore,* she told herself. At least she would *try* not to be that girl. She didn't quite feel like a new person, but she believed she was. With determination Kyla lifted her chin and stepped forward, approaching the side of the skid loader. He paused and throttled down, shaking his head as he looked at her.

"I'm busy right now," he called over the sound of the machinery.

"You need to go away!"

She shook her head and stood there. "I want to talk to you!" she called back.

Peter turned away from her, resuming his work.

Kyla felt a pit in her stomach. This wasn't at all what she had expected! He was deliberately brushing her off. He refused to talk to her. She wanted to run to the house crying, like yesterday, but she knew it would only delay what she knew she had to do. If she ran away she might chicken out altogether. Feeling humbled, she walked through the dirt to stand in front of the machine as it was moving forward. He braked, looking at her darkly. Finally he powered down and got out, facing her where she stood. He seemed especially tall.

"You're in my way," he said matter-of-factly. "I got stuff to do."

She swallowed. "Peter, please. Will you please listen to me?"

He didn't answer but wordlessly removed his gloves. Kyla wished he would look at her. She shifted her feet in the dirt, wondering how to start.

Finally he looked at her, folding his arms as if to challenge her. "You realize you're harassing a fellow employee. You're keeping me from what I'm being paid to do."

She winced at the jab but countered. "I know. But this is more important."

His eyebrows rose slightly, but he said nothing, waiting.

She took a nervous breath, looking down. "I—I want to ask your forgiveness for what I did to you yesterday." Her mouth was dry. "What Dr. Grant said to you was all because of me. I was angry with you, and I'm sorry."

He said nothing but simply unfolded his arms, transferring the gloves to the back pocket of his blue jeans.

Kyla was suddenly afraid. This didn't fit any of the scenarios she had rehearsed in her mind. She had thought saying she was sorry would be all she needed to say, all it would take to fix everything. And yet he stood there silently, looking at her, waiting for her to continue. She met his eyes.

"Um, I—I want you to know that I needed to hear everything you said to me down there. And what you said about me was exactly right. Everything. I do clam up or get mad when I don't know what to do. I do have 'issues,' and I talked with Mrs. Gordon about them this morning. Anyway, I felt awful for what Dr. Grant said, and I haven't stopped thinking of it since. You didn't deserve that. I was wrong, and I want to ask you to forgive me."

He made a little sound of disbelief and looked away.

Kyla looked down at the ground. "Well, as you can probably tell, I'm not used to doing this. So I would really like it if you just said yes, because if I keep talking, I'm probably going to mess things up and end up getting irritated with you again."

He looked back, the corners of his mouth turning up.

"I have been so—so *hostile* toward you. So mean. I don't know why. But I'm sorry." She paused, not knowing what else to say. "Okay—I'll go and let you work." She turned and started walking away.

"Kyla," he said, and she looked back. She couldn't tell what he was thinking, but his eyes had their normal shining look again. They looked very blue. "I forgive you."

"Thanks," she replied with a grateful nod.

She turned for the house, trying to walk gracefully over the uneven ground, hugely relieved, feeling like a weight had lifted off her shoulders. At least he said he forgave her. She had hoped he would have had more to say, some way of reassuring her that he didn't hate her now. She didn't want to be the psycho girl with issues that he had to put up with all summer. Behind her it was quiet, and she wondered what he was thinking, wondered if he was watching her now. She wished he would have said something. She wished—

"Kyla!" he called after her.

A surge of gladness swirled inside her. She turned again.

"Do you have your phone on you?"

"What? My phone?" she asked, surprised. "No, I hardly ever carry it here. And I think it's dead—I left it in my purse last night."

He gave a slight nod, moving toward her a couple of steps. Kyla walked closer.

"I'm wondering if you could do me a favor." His expression was sober.

"Sure," she answered, trying to be nonchalant. *Anything*, she thought happily, *anything you want!*

"I need you to bring me my phone." Then he glanced behind her at the house. "Um, no, wait," he said quickly, pursing his lips, thinking. "I need you to do something for me." He turned his face toward her again. "My phone is in my room on my desk. You'll see it. I need you to text Grant for me."

"Uh, okay." Kyla nodded, a bit confused. "Sure."

"I want you to tell him that I think I found something."

She frowned, glancing around her. "Found something? What did you find?" She looked back at him. "Look—I'll just go get your phone and bring it to you."

"No." Peter shook his head. "No, don't bring it out here right away. I don't want it to *look* like I found something."

Kyla crinkled her forehead. "To whom? *Mrs. Gordon?*" She knew there was only one person he had in mind, and it wasn't the housekeeper.

Peter closed his mouth, his head tipping to the side.

She narrowed her eyes and folded her arms. "Okay—what is this about? I'm not going anywhere until you tell me."

He looked down at her, a sudden grin spreading across his face. "I knew you'd be back!"

Kyla felt her cheeks grow warm, and she lowered her eyes. "Peter, please tell me. What did you find? I know about Dr. Grant having stuff that's hidden away here, but what's this?"

"I'm not sure yet what I found. There's a metal box-like thing buried over there that I hit with the skid loader just now. It's big. It may be nothing. And what do you mean about Grant? What stuff? What are you talking about?"

Confused, Kyla glanced again at the place where Peter had been digging. Did he not know anything about Dr. Grant? Did he still think they were trying to find a "time capsule"? How could he not know—?

She asked cautiously, "So why don't you want my father to know about this?"

Peter hesitated, shifting his weight to his other foot. "Well, uh, please don't get mad at me, Kyla, but I don't think—" He stopped, struggling to finish his sentence.

She cocked her head. "What?"

Peter squirmed uncomfortably. "I don't think your father is here at Wynnbury entirely for *you.*"

She blew her breath out, replying matter-of-factly, "I *know* he's not! That has become quite obvious to me! He's only here for his investigation!"

He looked at her strangely. "Investigation?"

"Of Dr. Grant!"

His head tilted. "What? Of Grant? What are you talking about? Why would Grant be under investigation? By whom?"

"Well, you know—for what he's hiding here."

Peter's head went back, his brow knit together.

Kyla looked at him bewildered. Seriously, how could Peter know nothing about this? She wasn't thrilled to be the one to have to tell him the news, but he needed to know.

"Peter, there's something I have to tell you. My father is more than he appears." She took a breath. "My father is actually a private detective, and he is here investigating Dr. Grant." She paused to let her news sink in. "Yes, I know—it's hard to believe! It's all about some stolen museum goods he has supposedly hidden here at the house!" There! What a relief that she was finally able to tell someone! It felt like another huge burden lifted from her shoulders.

He stared at her in surprise, then glanced over her shoulder to the house. "Your father told you this?"

At his expression Kyla closed her eyes, a sinking feeling coming over her. "He's lying," she stated flatly.

Peter nodded slowly.

She exhaled quickly. "I—I didn't know what to believe! He was so convincing—I mean not really, but still I didn't know! And you—you and Dr. Grant were always so secretive! I knew something was going on, but I didn't know what, and I still don't—"

He touched her arm briefly. "It's my fault! I'm sorry. I should have told you. I wanted to, but Grant—he just didn't trust that you"—he stopped, searching for the words—"that you wouldn't say something to your father, even by accident. He didn't want to put you in the middle."

"So Dr. Grant's *not* hiding stolen museum property here?"

"No!" Peter exclaimed, shaking his head.

Kyla breathed out in relief, her hand coming to her forehead. "Oh, thank God! I was so afraid for him and the kids!"

"No," he continued, leaning in and speaking more quietly, "Grant's trying to *find* the stolen property—and yes, it's stuff from a museum in London. He believes that there were some things hidden here at Wynnbury."

"What?"

"It's his hunch. But it appears that somehow your father knows about this too. We thought he was just kind of curious about wild rumors at first, but it's now become pretty obvious he knows something, and that's why he's here, and we're not sure what to do about it! Yesterday Grant finally came to his senses and is trying to think of a way to tactfully get him out of here."

She nodded. "It's true! He's been insistent on getting up to the third floor, and I know he's looking for *something*! He was up there last night!"

"I heard him," Peter said. He glanced again at the house. "He's probably up there right now as we speak. He's been in Grant's office too. Yesterday Grant noticed that a file had gone missing."

"I took it," Kyla said guiltily.

He looked at her sharply.

She put her fingers over her mouth in embarrassment. "He asked me to go in there and look for a file on Wynnbury. I found it, and I hid it in another file, one with your name on it. In the tray on Dr. Grant's desk."

He furled his brow. "You *hid* it?"

"I didn't know what to do! I didn't want Dr. Grant to be found out!"

"So you put it in *my* file."

Again her cheeks felt warm. "Sorry."

He looked glad, nodding. "No, that's good—that's good."

He lifted his arm to wipe his forehead, leaving a small streak of dirt behind. Kyla thought how utterly handsome he looked.

"So what is it?" Kyla asked. "What are we, er, you—everybody—what are we looking for?"

Peter glanced back toward the skid loader, as if impatient to dig out what he had found. "I think maybe we should talk about this later so I can get back to—"

"Dang it, Peter!" Kyla exclaimed, folding her arms and lifting her chin. "I am not leaving! I have been put off too many times on this one, and I want to know everything right now!"

He cocked his head, a smile tugging at his lips. "You are *definitely* back, Kyla DeKane! Well, all right—I'll tell you, but I'm going to have to breeze through it! We've been talking out here for quite a while already, and I don't want it to look suspicious."

"Then go! I'm all ears."

"Yeah, okay. So—remember there's a house in England that this one is modeled after?"

Kyla nodded. "Yes, Tynnbury Hall. On the postcard."

"Yes. Well, right before World War II they were evacuating valuables out of London, moving everything north to safer locations."

"Yes?"

"That house was one of the destinations in England for rare art and artifacts. Grant said there was a very sophisticated system of transport, with various possible destinations for things, and with fakes and copies made of certain valuables, decoy transports and everything. But some valuables still disappeared. Since then, certain authorities seem to be convinced that these items were hidden away somewhere at Tynnbury Hall. They have never been found.

"So when Grant—who was familiar with Tynnbury because of his wife—when he got his job offer at Taiton College, he randomly happened upon Wynnbury House here and learned that the builder, who was a World War II vet, had copied the house in England exactly. A house like this is very unusual for this area. The architecture doesn't fit in at all. Grant heard someone say that the man who had built it had been a farmer before the war. The comment intrigued him. The farmers around here didn't have money to build mansions like this."

"He thought it was out of character."

"Yes." Peter gave a slight nod. "So Grant did some research on this guy, Mr. Joseph Kennedy—"

"The guy whose picture was on the foyer wall."

"Uh-huh. Grant discovered that Kennedy had served in England before the United States entered the war. And guess what? He was on the evacuation team for the Museum of London."

"And you think he was the thief! That he used the money to build this place," Kyla finished.

"Well, one of the thieves at any rate. But not just to build this place. That would only be a tiny fraction of what was stolen. We're talking— we're talking something big. Something very valuable. Grant believes that what authorities thought was hidden away and lost at Tynnbury was actually brought here and hidden. And he thinks it's still here."

"But you don't know what it is."

He shook his head no.

Kyla scrunched her face. "It seems like overkill to build such a big house to hide something! Why not just hide it on his farm if he was a farmer?"

"That," Peter said, "is a darn good question! We think maybe this was a beacon to bring his accomplices to him eventually. We don't know. Or perhaps he just hid it somewhere until his only son was old enough to be told about it and have it. But he died too soon. We're not sure. That's the mystery."

"Huh." Kyla was thoughtful. "How can you be sure anything is hidden here at all? Maybe there's nothing. Maybe the guy just liked the way Tynnbury Hall looked."

"Yes, I suppose that's possible. But when Grant looked at this place to buy it, the first two floors were punched full of holes like you saw up on the third floor. You said yourself—it looks like someone's been looking for something. And it's also interesting that there's rumors floating around about something hidden here. Rumors come from somewhere. From something. And then somehow your father shows up with the same hunch that we have. It's no coincidence, I believe."

"Very strange." She looked up at Peter. "My father thinks what he's looking for is on the third floor."

Peter tipped his head to the side. "Perhaps. He could be right. But Grant noticed that the only difference between Tynnbury Hall and Wynnbury House is that there was no fountain put in here."

"What would that have to do with anything?"

"He thinks that perhaps it wasn't put in on purpose, so that whoever comes to claim their treasure would know where to look."

"So that they would dig," she concluded.

Their eyes met. Kyla shivered. "Do you think you found it?"

Peter shrugged. "We've been keeping track of exactly where we've worked the yard this summer. The grounds have been Grant's focus for that purpose. I surely didn't expect to hit something there."

"I should go text him," Kyla said suddenly.

Peter nodded, pulling his gloves out of the back pocket of his jeans.

"You know what else is weird?" he added. "Grant just found that in the U.S. Army records our same Joseph Kennedy was killed in action."

"He *died*? Well, then—who built this?" She took a sudden breath and nodded. "Ah! So someone else posed as him to build this?"

He shook his head. "No, it was him all right."

She frowned. "How strange! How could *that* be?"

From a distance they heard the patio door suddenly open. Mrs. Gordon appeared, waving to them and calling out that she was leaving. Howie bounced down the patio steps and began his way across the dirt to them. Kyla waved, calling good-bye back to her across the yard.

"I'll go text Dr. Grant," she said.

Peter put his hand on her arm again. "Please be careful, Kyla. I don't know your father, but I have some very specific reasons that I don't trust him."

His touch felt electric. "Okay. If it's any consolation, I've already asked him to leave—for my own reasons. But I'm not sure it will do any good."

He gave a little nod. "Well, try not to do anything that would raise suspicion. Just do your normal stuff with Howie. And if he's wondering about us talking here, can you pretend to be irritated with me about something? I don't want him to know anything of what we're talking about. Tell him I was shoving my faith on you again."

Kyla's cheeks turned pink, and she gave him an embarrassed look.

"I'm teasing you," he said. He squeezed her arm and let her go.

"Mrs. Gordon and Julia have to go," Howie said, running up to where they stood. "She told me to come out here with Peter. Hank is taking a nap."

Kyla looked down at him. "Sorry, bud, you have to hang out with me."

His jaw opened with disappointment. "Aww! Mrs. Gordon said Peter!"

"Not today," Peter said, giving him a pretend punch on the shoulder. "But hanging around with Miss Kane will be fun. She's nice. Most of the time."

Kyla shot Peter a look, and he laughed playfully. She reached into her bag for her untouched sandwich and handed it to him. "Here—would you like this?"

His eyes brightened. "Sure! Yes, I would! Thank you!" Eagerly he took it. "See you later, Kyla."

She smiled, her hopes kindled. She reached for Howie's hand and started back for the house. "Come on, kiddo. Let's go find something to do until your pop comes home."

"My *pop*?" he asked, looking up at her.

"Your dad."

"Why did you say my *pop*?"

"It's another name for dad."

"But why did you say it?"

Kyla looked down at his little face. "Because I'm happy—that's why."

He scrunched his nose. "Why are you so happy?"

She smiled to herself. There were lots of reasons. One was blond and stood six foot something. But at the core of all her reasons was one big one—a clear conscience.

"Because—because I've been forgiven," she told him.

That was surely an understatement for how she felt. She was elated that Peter had forgiven her, but most of all she felt light as a feather being right with God. And that reminded her that she had resolved to watch the other video from her mother today too. She didn't know what time it was, but she guessed she still had a little time before Hank woke up. She would do it now, as soon as she texted Dr. Grant. Then remembering her dead laptop, Kyla stopped.

"Hold on, Howie," she said, turning back to Peter, who was taking the last bite of his sandwich and about to get back onto the skid loader. She called his name, and he looked up.

"Can I borrow your computer?" she asked.

"Sure," he said. "Only one way—Jesus! Numeral one, all caps for 'Jesus.' My password," he added at her confused look.

Chapter Twenty-Nine

Kyla knew the very first thing she needed to do was text Dr. Grant for Peter. She and Howie went directly upstairs, stopping first at her room to drop off her dead computer and to grab the flash drive of her mother's videos from her purse. Her phone was in there too. She checked it, and as she had suspected, her battery had barely a charge. A missed call and a text from her dad popped up on her notifications. *Kyla, if you get this, have Peter call me right away. It's important!* She frowned. What was up with that? Why did he want Peter? What would be so important? She stepped out into the hallway, seeing him working on the skid steer below through the tall windows. She should probably just take him his phone right away if her dad's thing was so important. But then she hesitated. Peter had said not to. He had specifically requested her not to deliver his phone out to him directly. She pursed her lips in thought for a moment and decided that she would text Dr. Grant first, wait a bit, and then bring it to him so that he could call her dad. Then she slid her phone into the side pocket of her shirt in case Peter's wasn't charged either.

She turned toward Howie. "Do you have something you could play while I do some business in Peter's room?"

He wrinkled his nose at her. "Why are you going in Peter's room?"

"Because I need to use his computer. You can come with me, but you need to have something to do. Go get a book or something else to play with."

"I could make fish!" he said excitedly. "I'll be right back!"

She heard him run down the stairs to the library, and then he returned in a flash, holding a book in his hand with several small sheets of brightly colored paper.

"Miss Julia showed me how to make these," he said, holding up a little orange fish made out of folded paper.

Maybe Julia wasn't so bad after all, she thought, examining Howie's little origami creation.

Kyla decided not to try to be particularly quiet, as she didn't want to make it appear that they were sneaking around. She hadn't seen her father yet that day, and it was very likely he could be in his room across the hall from Peter's, still resting from his late-night activities. It was also possible that he *wasn't* in his room and was still searching up above them. It didn't matter. It had to be a regular day for Howie and her.

"Don't wake up Hank," she said to Howie a bit louder than usual as they moved down the hall.

"I won't," he replied.

"Come with me, Howie," she said. "I'm going to use Peter's computer for a bit."

He looked at her funny. "You already told me that!"

Kyla bit her lip. She should probably be careful not to overdo it.

Mrs. Gordon had apparently changed Peter's linens and had done some of his laundry, because his bed was crisply made and a pair of jeans and a short stack of clothes lay neatly folded at the foot, with his belt, his wallet, and some change neatly set beside it. Another stack of folded T-shirts rested on his chair. Kyla moved them for Howie, but he had already situated himself on the floor and was hard at work folding his first fish, humming and singing to himself.

She left the door open and went straight to Peter's dark wooden desk to find his phone, which was resting out where he said it would be. Her head jerked back in surprise when she noticed that he had six missed calls—all from her dad! She uttered a silent exclamation. *Holy cow, Dad—where's the fire? What is so important? Okay, okay—I'll get Peter his phone*, she told him mentally, *but you're going to have to hold your horses. Just a few more minutes!*

Opening Peter's texting app, she easily found Dr. Grant's name near the top and typed Peter's message quickly, the phone making a swoosh sound as it sent. Then she popped his phone into her pocket beside her own to take it to Peter as soon she reasonably could. Five minutes? Ten minutes? She wasn't sure how long to wait, but since she knew her mother's video on God wasn't that long, she decided to watch that and then run it out.

Turning back to the desk, she noticed the family photo her dad had sent her—complete with a few remnants of broken glass—sitting off to the side of Peter's computer. A little note in Dr. Grant's handwriting was stuck to the top. *Replace glass or buy new frame for Kyla*. She cringed. That must have been salt in the wound for Peter yesterday! She shook her head, so glad she had talked to him, so glad she had made things right! As she reflected on that awful moment in the dining room, her eyes were drawn to the edge of a piece of folded stationery sticking out from under the corner of the frame. Gingerly she lifted it, and as she had guessed, there was the note from "Amy" on the desk, with its matching envelope underneath it. Amy, with the hand-drawn heart. Inquisitively, she picked it up. *This, now, was officially snooping*, Kyla mused. Bravely she opened it.

> *Peter,*
>
> *You win the favorite brother award! Thank you for the funny card and birthday money! Will you be home for the Fourth? Jason and I plan to come home to do some wedding planning with Mom that weekend. Hope we see you—I want my fiancé to know my brother! Not sure this address is current, so I hope you get this.*
>
> *Love,*
> *Ames*

His sister. Kyla quickly put the note back where she found it, then sat with her hand over her mouth for a moment. She gave a little smile of relief. Amy was his sister.

Turning to his computer, she woke it up and typed in his password. After a couple of attempts she finally got in. She reached into her pocket for the flash drive, but as she was about to plug it in, she observed that he had left his email open. She moved the cursor to close the page when she suddenly noticed her dad's name—Kendall Lee—at the very top of his inbox. She paused, feeling the familiar pangs of jealousy. *What the heck!* Not only had her dad called Peter six times today, but he had emailed him too! She peered closer, noticing the little number fourteen beside his name. She gave a quiet exclamation. Apparently they emailed each other quite a lot! Fourteen exchanges!

Kyla bit her lip, knowing it was wrong to snoop *again*, wrong to read his emails, but her curiosity overpowered her. Besides, they were from her dad—it wasn't like they were *completely* none of her business! Daringly she double-clicked to open the long thread of communication between the two of them and searched for the earliest date.

Hey, Kendall. Just checking in. It's been a good first week. I've been in the Word every day.

Pretty tame, Kyla observed. Not surprising for Peter, certainly. She scrolled to his second message.

Your daughter Kyla arrived today. Apparently she didn't know that the email about the job here was from me. It kinda took her by surprise, and she seemed a little offended.

Kyla let out a little breath, checking her dad's reply.

That's my bad. I assumed she knew, since it was on the email. I probably should have said something. I still think it's wild you both ended up at the same place! I'm sure things will smooth out soon.

Peter's next email: *Things are going well. Steady reading the Word every day.*

Her dad's reply: *Awesome. Keep it up!*

Email number four: *Still steady in the Word. I've had a few opportunities to talk with Grant and your daughter about the Lord. I think she must be dealing with a lot of stuff. She's pretty short with me. I'm not too good at sharing my faith, I guess. Or talking to girls. Ha, ha.*

His reply: *Don't be too hard on yourself. Remember to listen before you speak.*

Yep, Kyla mused, *they definitely do talk about me!*

She scrolled down further, skipping a few exchanges, noticing one with more words: *Okay, it's been a while since I've emailed you. I'm doing good. A few unusual things have happened here that I have a check in my spirit about. I took your advice to start praying each night for everyone here. Praying for God's light and protection. On another note, I specifically want to ask you for prayer about something quite personal to us both. It's about Kyla. She is more than beautiful, to say the least, and I guess I've been smitten by her. It's pretty obvious she does not reciprocate any feelings toward me, and I'm trying hard to be the gentleman. I am definitely giving it over to God, but I'd appreciate your prayers too, and any advice.*

Kyla sat back in surprise, a smile spreading across her face. So Peter *did* have feelings for her! She pressed her hands over her cheeks, feeling terribly guilty for trespassing but also enormously happy to learn this little tidbit of information. Her belly felt the twinge of butterflies, and she read on to see how her dad had responded to his email.

Faith and patience, son. Faith and patience. You can ask and knock, but only God can open doors.

Kyla looked away. Things were really personal now, and she didn't know if she wanted to read any more. Her eyes flitted to the family photo beside the computer, her heart overflowing with feelings of admiration for her dad. For all this time he had known how Peter felt, yet he hadn't divulged anything during her phone conversations with him. He hadn't hinted, hadn't pushed her. He hadn't tried to play matchmaker. Her dad was—her dad was the *best*! He was wise. So wise. And Peter. She stared unseeing at the desk, thinking of him.

"Little fish! Here, little fish!" Howie's voice broke into her thoughts as he played on the floor by himself. "Here you go! Show this to your mother, little fish!" His voice became a different character. "My mother is not home. She is in England."

Kyla glanced at him where he sat, deeply engrossed with his little paper fishes. She took a breath and shook herself back to where she was. Focus! She was way off track for why she was there! She was borrowing his computer to watch the video clip on God from her mother, and as soon as she was done she needed to take Peter his phone. It was time to stop poking her nose in his emails.

One more—the thought tugged at her. Just *one* more.

Hesitantly Kyla looked back at the thread of email conversations before her. Timidly she clicked on a more recent one and peered at the words on the screen.

Kendall, I have to be honest. There's some things about Kyla's father that are making me very uncomfortable lately. Little things I've noticed. For one, I called the number on his business card, and it was out of service. And so many other things. Anyway, I have to get this off my conscience, so I'm telling you. I picked the lock to his room and went through his stuff. I felt crazy guilty doing it, so I want to bring it into the light. I know it was wrong, and I want to be clear that I'm not going back to my old ways. But Kendall, I found something important I need to tell you about. I found several ID cards—

No way! Kyla leaned forward in excitement. He had found them too! She peered intently at the screen as she read his words, when suddenly in the middle of his paragraph she heard the distinct ping of a notification. A new email suddenly appeared in Peter's inbox with the word URGENT written in the subject line. Kyla frowned. Another email from her dad! She checked the time on the top of the screen. Her dad was at work.

"What is going on, Dad?" she whispered to herself. "Why are you calling and emailing Peter like this? What is so doggone important?"

She hesitated with her finger poised to tap the cursor. Did she want to do this? If she opened it, and if it was indeed urgent and something he should know about right away, then she would have to tell him. That would mean she would have to admit to Peter that she had been reading his emails. That was embarrassingly over the line. But, she reasoned, since the subject said it was urgent and since it was from her dad, it would only be logical to do.

She clicked on it.

Peter, I've been calling you, but you must be away from your phone. I'm praying that nothing has already happened! If you get this, you need to get Kyla and the kids out of there as soon as possible!

She frowned, feeling a surge of bewilderment and alarm. *What?* The room suddenly grew quiet as Howie stopped talking to himself. Concerned, Kyla leaned closer to continue.

It's very possible you all may be in danger there! It took longer than expected, but I finally got my friend at the station to run the names you gave me. Got the results a few minutes ago. Will forward them. Alarming! It appears Robert DeKane is a fugitive from the law with quite a violent record. Four of the names you submitted are known aliases, the fifth was unknown, but probably another alias. The authorities in New Hampton have been alerted. I'm trying to reach Dr. David Grant. Will try Kyla next. It is imperative you call me as soon as you get this! Kendall.

A pulse of dread coursed through her body as she scrutinized the words, and she suddenly felt weak. Violent record? A fugitive with a *violent* record? Her heart began to pound. Her father was a criminal! A complete fake—which wasn't much of a surprise. She just hadn't realized the extent of it! *Violent record.* It made her sick!

"What a bold-faced liar you are, Robert DeKane!" she exclaimed under her breath. "A bold-faced liar and a deceiver."

She needed to find Peter *immediately*!

She turned straight into Howie, who had suddenly appeared at her side, patting her arm and looking above her. "Mr. Kane is here," he said.

Kyla's head shot up and she jerked back in her chair, crying out, for her father was directly behind her, bent at the waist, peering over her shoulder, reading the monitor, his head near hers. He made his sucking sound with his teeth and looked into her face with a smile. He was so close that she could feel his breath, and she repelled from him as far as she could in her chair.

"What—what are you doing here?" she babbled. "You scared— scared me!"

"Well," he said slowly, "hasn't this been a day of discoveries!"

Her heart slammed in her chest. Unable to leave her chair with him standing there, Kyla instinctively took Howie's arm and drew him close as DeKane leaned forward, squinting to finish reading the email. He nodded and pursed his lips when he was done, glancing down at her again. Then he reached over top of her and pulled Peter's laptop closed.

"A day of discoveries," he repeated.

Kyla's mind was racing. *Peter.* She needed to alert Peter! Somehow. And quickly. Beside her Howie pressed in, looking tense and confused.

DeKane straightened, staring thoughtfully out the window beside the desk for a moment, with Kyla still frozen in the chair right in front of him. Her head was practically touching his chest.

He sighed heavily and shook his head. "That gardener boy—he is something else. A pain in the hinder, but still a most useful person to have around. He has saved me a considerable amount of work." He looked down at her. "He's been most interesting to watch today, playing out there with his big boy machine, digging around, making discoveries." He looked at his watch. "I'm giving him a little more time to get what he's found up out of the ground." He shoved a hand into the pocket of his slacks, making the sucking sound with his teeth again.

"But it seems he has created a heap of trouble for you," he continued with a nod, his eyes brushing her. "And for himself, of course. Yeah, Peter Watkins—you should have minded your own business." He clicked his tongue, shaking his head. "So unfortunate."

Kyla stiffened as her father suddenly reached over top of her to roughly yank the cords out of Peter's computer, his side crowded against her shoulder. *Stay calm,* Kyla told herself. *Stay calm and think.*

"I'm going to need this," he said, lifting the laptop from the desk. "And I'm going to need your phone too, my dear." He held out his hand. His breathing came hard and fast.

Without protest Kyla reached into her shirt pocket and handed it over, leaving Peter's there where it was.

DeKane stepped backward into the room a few steps. "And now I'm going to need you to come with me." He gestured with his arm toward the door.

A sense of foreboding washed over her as she rose. "Where? Where are we going?"

"You'll find out, won't you?" he said.

Howie whined nervously, "I don't want to go with him. I want to go outside with Peter!"

Kyla took his small hand, noticing the look of disdain that DeKane sent him. "I think we'll just stick together," she told him softly. "You can hold my hand."

Maybe, she thought, maybe he would take them outside where Peter was working! She hoped so! But DeKane motioned them out of Peter's room across the hall to the door of the third floor, where they paused while he set the computer on the floor and dug a set of keys out of his pocket. Kyla threw a quick glance toward the balcony, debating. Beside her Howie had a tight grip on her hand and was watching DeKane warily, who looked at them with a cold smile as he inserted the key into the lock. She wouldn't get very far with Howie if she took a run for it, and leaving him was out of the question. She squeezed his hand back reassuringly.

DeKane chuckled, pulling open the door. "Got duplicates made yesterday in town, and now we won't even need them! After you." He sniffed, waving his arm for her and the boy to go before him.

Kyla glared at him. "Everything about you is completely phony. Everything! Your private detective career, all that stuff about Dr. Grant— everything you've told me! It's all bogus!"

"Sometimes you just gotta do what you gotta do," he replied smoothly. "Now don't get chatty. Just do as I say, please." He waved his arm again.

She didn't have a choice. Resigned, Kyla started up the stairwell with Howie in tow, wondering why he was taking them up there. Briefly she considered running up to the landing ahead of them to pound loudly on the window for Peter in the yard below, but she knew he was still on the skid loader and wouldn't hear her anyway. Her better judgment told her to keep calm and do as he asked for the time being. As she turned on the landing and continued without stopping up the stairs, her mind careened from one thought to another, trying to come up with something that she could say to reason with him.

Behind them DeKane paused on the landing to look out the window. "Making progress!" he said with a smile. "He's making progress!"

Kyla looked back, craning her head to see Peter outside. From where she stood she could see him below, still navigating the skid loader on his find. The object he was digging out of the yard looked like a big old box. A very large box. He had dug away some of the dirt from part of it, but the bulk of it was still buried. She wondered what was in it. And she wondered what Robert DeKane would do with Peter after he got it out of the ground. She also wondered what he intended to do with *them* once they got upstairs. Oh, she did not trust this man, and she had a terrible feeling about this! Howie was trembling, clenching her hand and looking worriedly up at her face, waiting for her to do something. *Think*, she told herself. *Think!* She needed to do something—*something* to distract her father or stall him from whatever he had in mind to do!

"Can I ask how you have evaded the authorities all these years?" she asked him suddenly.

He turned from the window with a look of amusement. "Hey—I'm good at what I do! Damn good at what I do!" He jerked his head for her to continue upward, starting up the stairs after her. "I've been doing this longer than you've been alive, baby, longer than you've been alive! I know what I'm doing."

His shoe scraped the last step behind them as they reached the third floor. Kyla glanced down the long hall, the dusty floor still streaked with tracks from Howie's bike. Strategically and swiftly she moved toward the large room in the center, the one with the taller windows overlooking the yard, hoping her father would let them stay in there, hoping for a chance to signal Peter, hoping perhaps he would look up at the house for some reason, hoping—

"No, no—over here! Over here," DeKane said gruffly with an impatient gesture, pausing before the small door in the hallway that led to the attic.

Kyla stopped, observing him take another set of keys out of his pocket and fiddle with the lock. What was he going to do with them up there? She had never been up there. The door stuck, and he yanked at it until it opened stiffly to a dark and narrow wooden stairway, a draft of musty attic air rushing down to fill the hallway where they stood.

"There now—up you go!" he said, ushering them on with his hand.

Whimpering, Howie balked, pulling fearfully away from the doorway. Kyla's pulse was racing. *Stall,* she told herself. *Just stall! Say anything!*

She turned to face DeKane where he stood beside the door. "I don't believe anything you say. How is that even possible—longer than I've been alive? You were with my mother until I was almost five!"

He smiled. "Yes, smart girl. You're right—I was! We were such a good duo. Your mother was damn good at what she did too. We were quite a pair."

"A pair?" Kyla retorted. "Right—a pair until you left her! Left *us!*"

He breathed a laugh, rubbing the back of his head. "No, baby—your mother was damn good at what she did even *after* I left her."

She cast him a confused look, trying to understand. Was he being crude? Her eyes narrowed. "Don't talk about her that way!"

DeKane tipped his head back and laughed out loud. Resting his hand on the edge of the door, he said, "You don't know the first thing about your mother! Haven't you learned by now that people aren't always what they seem? How many times do we have to go over that?" His eyes suddenly dropped to look menacingly at Howie, who skirted to cower behind Kyla.

Kyla stepped in front of her young charge, still holding his hand. "I'm afraid I don't know what you mean." *Just keep talking.*

He laughed again, looking at the ceiling. "She was so afraid for you that she made me leave."

"Afraid for *me*? Why?"

He didn't answer but simply looked at her.

Kyla felt her mouth grow dry. "Are you saying—are you saying that my mother was—that she was—"

DeKane gave her the "atta-girl" smile. "Oh, now you get it! Yes, that's what I'm saying! Your mother was my partner—in every way! My fellow, ah, *fugitive*, in your Asian stepfather's words, evading the law for"—he frowned, looking upward—"oh, heck, I don't know how long! Oh, we did have some exciting years together! That gal was one intelligent woman, and we were quite a pair." He shook his head nostalgically. "Until you came along, and I had to go solo. She started getting nervous and wanted out. With both of us together, the odds of being discovered increased. She said she just wanted to disappear, to melt away into society. And she *did*! She stayed under the radar until she died. See what I told you? She was damn good!"

Kyla shook her head. "You're such a liar! Such a stinkin' liar! My mother was a saint!"

"Oh"—he jerked his head back in amusement—"a saint she was *not*! But she *learned* to be! Later on, you know. She could put on religion really well. Everyone's got a sinful past in church, you know. Easy to hide there! You just throw out the word *Jesus* here and there, and you're good!"

Kyla was speechless.

He tapped the side of the door with his fingers, continuing, "You know what they say about a wolf in sheep's clothing? True story, right there in the flesh! That was Eva, all right, and no one ever suspected it." He laughed.

She let out a quick breath. "I don't believe you for a second! That's not my mother! What did the two of you do together? What crimes did you commit?"

A slow smile spread across his face. "Crimes? No crimes! It was all business. Investments, baby, investments!" His chin jutted out as he enjoyed his own humor.

She leveled her gaze at him. "Always vague."

"Don't believe me? Let me tell you something, Kyla DeKane! That car sitting out there in the driveway—that's a little payback to your mother! It's her half of the last deal we did together, and I promised it to her before I left. She refused to take it, and she made me swear to her that I would stay away from you until you were done with school. I'm a patient man, Kyla. I'm a patient man. You were done with school, and I kept my word on both accounts."

Kyla huffed, giving him a look of repulsion. "That almost makes you sound like a good guy! The only thing you're good at is lying! And *acting*! You were never here at Wynnbury for me for a moment! Everything you've done has been for your own devious purposes!"

He gave her a long look, his face suddenly growing sober. "All right—conversation over. I've had enough chatting." He turned to look up the attic stairway and back to Kyla, gesturing. "After you, baby!"

Howie pulled away and started to cry, refusing to go up. Kyla had to pick him up and carry him kicking and screaming up the dark and steep stairwell, and he was heavy. She didn't know what else to do—there was no way to get away from DeKane. She held him firmly against her, speaking to him softly, trying to calm him down, trying to comfort him. Briefly the thought crossed her mind to turn suddenly and try to kick DeKane down the stairs with her foot, like she had seen in so many movies, yet this was real life, not television, and with Howie in her arms she couldn't take any chances. At the top of the stairs they paused on a small landing before a narrow door. Behind her DeKane stepped up, pressing against the two of them in the tight space as he fumbled in the light of his cell phone to unlock it. The door creaked loudly as it opened inward.

"Here we are," he said, guiding her firmly with his hand on her back.

The attic was hot and dusty and smelled like creosote, old wood, and bat guano. Its side walls were lumber and slanted upward to the peak, making the shape of an *A*, but the walls in the front and back of the house were triangles of brick. An octagonal window high on each of the brick walls was the only source of light in the room. Kyla stepped cautiously inside the doorway, waiting for her eyes to adjust to the dimness. Wide-eyed, Howie clamped his arms harder around her neck. Hoisting him up a little she talked softly to him, patting his back while her mind sought desperately for something—anything—that would help them.

"You realize the authorities have already been notified," she declared, as DeKane stepped in beside her. "This may be the end of your running. Will you turn yourself in?"

He gave her a strange look. "Ah, no—I won't be doing that. No, baby, I'll be off again—the moment that boy gets the chest out of the ground. But it's such a shame about him! He's such an eager lad!"

Fear for Peter coursed through her body. "What are you going to do?"

"You just leave that up to me. Now go on over there." He pointed to the other side of the room.

She breathed a prayer as she tried to unhook Howie's arms and legs from her to set him onto the floor. He clung to her leg so tightly it hurt. *God, help me! Help me think of something, quick!* What could she do? What could she say?

She turned back to him where he stood in the doorway. "So is this good-bye, then? For you and me?"

He shot her a look, saying nothing.

"If it is, I want to tell you something. Something important."

DeKane raised his brow, looking skeptical. "What could you possibly have to say to me that would be so important?"

God, help me! Kyla took a breath, her hand pressing against Howie's shoulder for strength. "It is. I want to tell you that I forgive you."

His head drew back, and he was silent for a moment; then he scoffed, "You forgive me?"

"Yes," she said. Her heart was pounding like crazy. Surely he could hear it! "I've spent a lot of time thinking about our relationship. A lot! And just this morning I made some big decisions that I want you to know about. I unloaded a truckload of hurt from you onto God, so I want to tell you—to let you know that I forgive you for leaving me—for abandoning me. And for not providing for me or protecting me when I was growing up. I forgive you for being absent in my life—both physically and emotionally! I forgive you for not teaching me about life and about God. For not ever remembering my birthday and for not showing any interest in who I am as a person. I want you to know, Robert DeKane, my father who gave me birth—I forgive you!"

It was like he was frozen. He stared at her, stunned.

Emboldened, Kyla lifted her chin and continued, "I will not let your failures toward me be a poison that ruins my life, so I do—I forgive you! I release you! I'm not going to live hating you and being bitter. Your absence will not define me! I have a father now who is good and perfect. And he loves me!"

"Hell—oh, he's so perfect, huh?" DeKane jerked and swore viciously, kicking the door beside him violently, which smacked loudly against the wall and bounced back. "That man your mother married is a religious *fool*!" He stepped toward her, his face dark.

Kyla winced, shrinking from him, and Howie cried out, clutching her leg harder. "I'm not talking about Kendall—I'm talking about *God*! He's my father now! I belong to him, and he's watch—"

"Oh, shut up!" he spat. "I've heard enough of you!" Roughly he pushed her further into the room. "Get over there! Sit on the floor by the far wall!"

Kyla hurried Howie across the room and kneeled at the edge of the angled wall, pulling him down to the floor beside her. He was crying in an odd, high-pitched whimper, his arms clutched her around her waist and his head pressed into her side. DeKane glanced around the attic briefly, then returned to the door. Reaching behind his back, he drew out a small black revolver, a metal-on-metal click resounding as he brought his other hand over to cock it.

A chill ran through her at the sight of the gun, and she flinched, staring at him in horror as he stared right back with his steely eyes, raising the handgun to level it at her. She had not noticed it under his shirt and in a split second wondered if it was the one she had seen in Dr. Grant's desk or his own. How could he do this to her, his own daughter? Had he intended this all along? Or had she set him off, making him lose his mind in the heat of the moment?

"Your little speech just made this a lot easier for me," he rasped, holding his aim. "I *hate* religion!" His face was hard and his eyes cold.

Instantly a thought flashed through Kyla's mind from one of her conversations with Peter, and in panicky desperation she blurted out wildly, "Wait! There's something else!"

Without waiting for his response, she spoke swiftly and steadily, "You're right! I didn't know any of that stuff about Mom—but there's something *you* don't know about her either! She may have been like you said she was at first, but she changed! Her religion wasn't put-on. She became a new person. She was genuine, the real deal!" In her head Kyla could hear Peter's exact wording about himself and knew it also applied to her mom. "The person that she was with you died, and she became a new creation in Christ. In her life and in her death, my mom was declared innocent by his blood."

DeKane's face contorted. "Blood? What the hell are you talking about?"

"Jesus' blood. My mom—she was washed and made clean by the blood of Jesus!"

There—she said it. She braced herself, holding her breath, waiting. She knew her father would hate her answer. She knew he would be enraged, and it would be the end of her. It was crazy, but at that second all Kyla could think about was Peter beside the skid loader, happily eating the sandwich she had offered him, calling out his computer password to her: *Only one way—Jesus!* She was okay with dying. She was ready. And someday she would see her dad and Peter again.

The silence in the room was pregnant with tension. Her shoulders were tight around her neck, her lungs screaming for air. At last, hearing a scraping sound, Kyla cracked open her eyes in time to see the attic door slam shut, followed by the scratching of metal on the door plate as DeKane fumbled with his keys to lock it behind him. His footsteps diminished down the attic stairs. Numb, Kyla sat still for a moment until she was sure he was actually gone. Then her body let down in relief, and she pulled Howie, who had begun to wail, onto her lap, wrapping her arms around him.

"I want my daddy!" he bawled, his body trembling. "I want my daddy! I want my daddy! I want my daddy!"

Kyla rocked him, crying silently with him. "He's gone, Howie. He's gone now. He went downstairs. It's going to be okay." She was physically and emotionally spent.

"I want my daddy!" he cried over and over until his breath came in hiccups. His face was wet with tears and snot.

With her cheek pressed against his head Kyla held him firmly in her arms, while from their huddled location she studied the room, knowing full well from the layer of tiny black pellets scattered on the dusty floor what was hanging above them asleep on the sloped beams. She couldn't think about that now and didn't even look up. The dark, triangular room was completely empty and void of furniture except for a large old trunk resting on the wooden floor in the center of the room. It was the old-fashioned kind, an antique metal steamer trunk, darkened with age, with curved wooden slats up the front and back and cracked leather handles on the sides. Beyond the trunk, on the wall beside the stairway door, was another shorter door to what looked like a small closet, for the top of it did not go to the ceiling. She would explore that in a bit, Kyla decided, rocking Howie and stroking his hair.

When he finally began to calm down, Kyla brushed her own tears off her cheeks, then wiped his nose with the tail of her new gauze shirt that she had worn over her new swimsuit.

"I want my daddy," he breathed shakily to her. "I want to go downstairs to my daddy."

"Yes, Howie," she said, looking into his eyes. "You'll see your daddy soon. Mr. DeKane is gone now, so we're safe, but he locked the door. We can't get out without a key. We have to wait. Your daddy or Peter will come and help us, but right now we have to be very brave. I'm right here. I'm not going to leave you."

He gave a jerky breath. "Okay." He gave a stifled whine, reaching up to rub his eyes.

"And you can help me be brave, all right? We can help each other."

"Okay," he replied, but he was struggling hard not to cry.

Kyla reached for Peter's phone, bulky in her pocket. Dr. Grant had answered her text.

"On my way," it said.

She breathed a sigh of relief and touched his name to call him, putting the phone to her ear. He must be warned! She waited. After hearing nothing, she held the phone out to look at it. No signal. With an impatient groan she stood up. Howie scrambled up beside her with a cry of panic.

"It's okay, Howie. I need to find a place where the phone will work. We're going to walk around a little, okay?"

She held his hand as they moved from place to place, trying every corner of the room. Nothing. Exasperated, she returned the phone to her pocket. Together they went to the attic door and tried it. Carefully she examined the lock and searched her clothes, his clothes, their shoes, for a pin or something to insert into the lock, something. Then she turned to the hinges, using her sandal to try to pound one upward, but they were rusted and stuck.

The other shorter door was indeed to a small closet, empty and creepy, with narrow rough-cut boards for walls. Kyla closed the door and stood looking around the room, feeling helpless. She wondered about Peter in the yard, about Dr. Grant on his way home, and about her father. Robert DeKane was cunning, unfeeling, and unstable. A sense of foreboding came upon her.

With her hands on her hips, she eyed the octagonal window above them.

"I just wish I could see outside!" she moaned in frustration.

"You could stand on that box thing," Howie suggested, pointing to the trunk.

She'd had the same thought. The trunk was light and slid easily across the rough floor to the brick wall beneath the window. Crawling onto it, the top of Kyla's head came to the bottom of the glass.

"Maybe there's something in there that you could stand on," Howie offered.

They looked. The inside of the trunk reeked of mothballs, and nothing was in it but an old woolen army uniform of olive green and a key that she found underneath it. She pulled it out, and they tried the key in the attic door to no avail. Kyla tossed it back into the trunk and dropped the lid closed. Kneeling, she rolled the smelly suit up tightly and then climbed up onto the trunk again to stand on the bulky fabric. It gave her enough height to bring her forehead to the bottom pane.

"Maybe we could tip the box sideways," Howie said, right as Kyla had the same thought.

"Great idea!" she told him. "This box is called a 'trunk.' They were sort of like very large suitcases in the olden days."

It was harder to climb up and stand on, and it wobbled on its leather handle strap, but Kyla could now see the tops of the trees outside. They were getting closer!

"Maybe I could climb up there and hold you up!" Howie suggested next, and Kyla wanted to hug him for his sweetness.

For a moment she considered holding *him* up, but then she sobered at the thought of what he might see. She jumped down and shook the uniform out, laying it on the floor as a makeshift rug for them to sit on while leaning against the trunk. There was nothing to do but wait, which was very difficult for Howie.

After about two minutes he turned to Kyla. "I'm tired of this. Why can't we just go downstairs?"

"Because the door is locked—remember?" she said.

He scrunched his nose. "Why did he lock it? That's your dad! Why was he so mean to us? Was he mad? He was very, very bad!"

Kyla gave him a serious nod. "Yes, he was! I don't know why."

Howie let out a long breath and sat back, folding his small arms. "Well, how will Hank know where to find us when he gets up from his nap?"

Hank! Kyla's heart turned over. She hadn't even had time to think about Hank!

Chapter Thirty

Kyla felt nauseous at the thought of Hank alone in the house downstairs. What if he woke up from his nap and wandered out of his room? It was terrible to think of him finding no one there. It was worse to think of him finding DeKane! She breathed a desperate prayer that he would have a long, long nap. Not wanting to alarm Howie, Kyla told him she needed to walk around, and then she tried calling Dr. Grant again with Peter's cell phone, holding it in every square inch of the room, hoping for a signal. She knew it was because of that stupid bluff. *Why did that stupid guy have to build this stupid house so close to that stupid bluff?* she grumbled to herself, so irritated. In despair she gave up and instead texted both Dr. Grant and Mrs. Gordon to let them know that Hank was alone and in danger. As expected, her texts did not send. She wanted to throw the phone against the wall. There seemed to be no rhyme or reason to the phone signal in this place!

Agitated and feeling powerless, Kyla settled down again on the mothball-stinking uniform beside Howie, who was holding his stomach complaining that he was hungry. He asked Kyla if she had brought any snacks with. It was almost laughable—like somehow this had all been planned! Yet there was nothing to laugh about. He then asked if they could play one of Peter's games—"God's Creation"—except that out of all the living creatures on the planet, the animal he picked to start with was an eagle.

For a moment Kyla was unable to speak. All she could think about was all the times Peter had tried to talk to her about God and how nice he had been to her when she hadn't wanted to listen. Peter. Strong, powerful, and good. She knew she couldn't go there.

"Um, let's start with a different one," she said.

Howie sighed. "Okay. How about—um, a turtle?"

She nodded. "That's better." Knowing she was supposed to come up with some way it described God, she thought for a second. "Well, turtles help us see that God is very patient."

He nodded, looking up at her, waiting. Then he frowned. "That's all? You don't play as good as Peter. He says a lot more stuff!"

No doubt, she thought with a little smile, continuing on with the game. But now she couldn't stop thinking about Peter. He was smart. He would figure out some way to help them. He had been ahead of DeKane all along. Yes, he had known something was up from the very beginning. Peter would know what to do. He was always watching, always protecting. He would have a plan, and he would get them out of this somehow. She prayed for him between her turns with Howie as he talked about beaver teeth, goldfish scales, and giraffe necks.

After what seemed like hours, Kyla pulled his phone out of her pocket and checked the time. Less than an hour had passed since they had been locked in the attic. She shifted on the woolen uniform, trying to find a comfortable place for her back between the wooden slats on the side of the trunk. The awful smell of the scratchy wool was overpowering, but she was thankful for it to sit on.

It was then that she heard the commotion outside, though it was muffled through the walls. First there was yelling that sounded far away, followed by more shouts, faint and distant. And then she heard a loud and distinct crack, followed by another, then a third. Then nothing. It had been so brief, so quiet that Kyla thought surely she had imagined it, but Howie looked up at her questioningly.

"What was that?" he asked. "Firecrackers?"

Worry jarred her. "I don't know," she answered, keeping her voice calm. "Could be. I should look."

She stood up, her legs feeling like jelly. She *had* to see out that window! She absolutely needed to know what was happening out there! Just another four, maybe five more inches was all she needed to be up far enough to see. Desperate, she looked around for something else to stand on. There had to be something! Anything!

Jerking the closet door open, she peered into the dark cavity again for anything on the floor, but the tiny closet was completely empty. Reaching ahead, she felt the rough boards of the closet walls. Perhaps she could tug one off. She pulled at the slats. Nothing. Systematically she went from one side of the wall to the other, wedging her fingers between the boards and giving each a tug, pulling on the boards one by one, until she noticed one of them give in to a little pressure. Wiggling her fingers further into the narrow crack, she pulled with all her might. It came loose!

Victoriously she set the board on the floor. That would give her less than an inch, but at least she was going in the right direction. The board above the vacant space was nailed on tightly and wouldn't budge despite her efforts to loosen it. Determinedly, Kyla gave a hearty yank on the board below the one she had removed, and to her surprise it gave way easily, and with a cry she fell back onto her seat, bumping her head and shoulders against the opposite wall of the closet. Simultaneously something heavy fell out of the wall and crashed with a bang onto the floor in front of her. At her exclamation Howie gave a whinny of fear. Immediately she called to him that she was okay, and he sneaked forward to peer into the dark closet.

"What happened?" he asked, standing in the doorway. "What did you do? What was that noise?"

"Something fell," Kyla replied, backing out of the dark closet on her knees. She reached back in to retrieve a small, black metal box about a foot square and six inches deep. It reminded her somewhat of one of her dad's toolboxes, and it had a lock on one side.

"What's that?" Howie asked as she climbed out of the closet with it. "I don't know."

She turned it and moved closer to the light of the window to read the faded white letters stenciled across the top of the box, making out the words "Human Remains." With an involuntary cry she threw the box down and away from her, repeating the same crash as before, which terrified Howie, who also screamed and ran to the other side of the room, starting to bawl again. Trying to catch her own breath, she went to calm him down, rubbing his shoulder as she steadied herself. He wiped his eyes with his fist, asking her what the box said.

Kyla hesitated. "Um, it says—it says 'old photographs' on it. You know, like the pictures on your dad's phone, only older. Printed out."

He sniffed, unconvinced. "Why did you throw it?"

"A spider was on it," she told him. "A big one!"

With her heart still racing, she went back to retrieve the box, carefully picking it up. It gave her the creeps. Near the bottom edge of the metal top, the name "US Army Pvt. Joseph P. Kennedy" was stenciled in smaller letters.

"Mr. Kennedy," she breathed, "you freaked me out!" One mystery about Joseph Kennedy was solved, Kyla mused. He had definitely been dead!

Kyla realized that the box, the two wooden boards, and the rolled-up uniform were probably all that she needed now to see outside. Howie helped her turn the trunk onto its side again, and together they rolled up the uniform into a tight log. She would definitely have bruises on her knees tomorrow, she thought, climbing up again. With the trunk sitting on its leather handle, her perch was unsteady, but sure enough, she had enough height to see down into the yard.

Beside the quiet skid loader a large rusted metal box lay completely out of the ground. Around it in the yard there was no one in sight. Kyla gave an uneasy sigh. She felt like she could explode with the anxiety of not knowing what had happened. She wished there was something she could see, something that would give an indication that Peter was all right. And Dr. Grant too, who surely should have been home for a while already.

With apprehension Kyla pushed herself up on her tiptoes to see farther down, closer to the house. Now she could see a sliver of the concrete deck railing below. Craning her neck, she spied something in the grass toward the stairs of the patio, but she couldn't quite tell what it was. With another mighty stretch to pull herself up as far as she could, she peered down farther and instantly felt a punch in the gut. It was someone's legs that she had seen, the jean-clad legs of someone lying flat on the ground, unmoving, and she could not see the rest of the person. She blinked, stunned, and pulled herself up once more, trying to determine who it was, trying to see anything else—his shoes, his shirt, his hands. Then, suddenly, without warning, someone appeared in her view near the patio stairs, a man she did not recognize. From her upper position she could not see his face, but she could see dark hair and a round balding spot on the top of his head. He held a large white cardboard box in his arms.

"What the heck?" Kyla murmured softly, straining for a better look. "Who are you, and what do you have there?"

The stranger started across the yard toward the wooden staircase on the cliff, then paused, turning to call back to someone else near the house. Kyla gave an exclamation, recognizing him now from his chunky build and the dark beard—her father's friend, Rich Connors! Of course, Kyla thought. It all made sense now! The man with the beard! Rich Connors must have been the man peering at her from across the river with the binoculars way back at the start! Then, noticing more movement below her, Kyla craned her neck to see her father, Robert DeKane, immediately appear in her view, walking determinedly down the patio stairs following his friend. In one hand he carried his black briefcase, and on his other arm was Hank—*Hank!*—who was red-faced and crying, his arms reaching back toward the house.

Spontaneously Kyla reached her fist to bang furiously on the window. "No!" she choked. "No!"

With her sudden motion the trunk wobbled, causing the boards beneath her feet to shift, and her footing tottered out from under her. With a metallic scrape, the small box on which she stood slipped off the trunk, shooting out to bang against the wall and loudly crash again to the floor. With a cry Kyla fell with it, jumping out past it at the last second so that she didn't land on top of it. Howie cried out, watching her tumble, then ran to her.

"Are you okay?" he asked. "Was my dad outside? Could you see him? Is my dad home from work yet?"

"I couldn't see anything," Kyla answered, but a wave of nausea hit her, and she began to retch uncontrollably. She went down onto her knees. *Hank. He had Hank. He had Hank!*

Howie stood motionless, his face filled with horror, having never watched a grown-up vomit.

"I'm okay," Kyla breathed when her heaving finally subsided. She brought her shirt up to wipe her face. "I'm okay. I just—got sick. Maybe we should sit down."

She tipped the trunk down onto its bottom and laid out the stinky uniform rug again so they could sit beside it. Howie drew up closely to her, studying her face with reserve.

"How come you threw up?" he asked. "Does your tummy hurt? Is that why you're crying?"

She nodded, churning with anguish inside.

He leaned against her with concern. "Do you want to play Peter's game again? Maybe it would help you feel better."

"I think we should just rest a bit," she replied. Her chest hurt. It felt like her heart had been wrenched right out of her.

"You don't feel good?" he asked.

She shook her head no, trying to contain herself for his sake. He was quiet, but she could read the stress and confusion on his face. To distract him, Kyla offered to scratch his back, and he lay down on the jacket next to her. Her technique worked. Relaxed, he began to yawn, and after a while his eyelids grew heavy. Before long he was out, and Kyla's tears streamed unhindered down her cheeks as she was unable to stop thinking about his brother. Hank was just a baby! What kind of madmen would take a baby? What were they going to do to him? And Peter. She hoped to God that it was not him lying there. Or Dr. Grant either. But it was someone.

Kyla sniffed and wiped her her nose on her shirt. Everything was out of her control. *Everything!* What else was there for her to do? Surely the authorities would arrive soon. Why weren't they there already? Hadn't her dad said in the email that he had contacted them? Then surely Peter would come and find them. Oh, God—she hoped he would. Unless—

She tipped her head back, resting it on the trunk. There was nothing for her to do but sit and think, her imagination taking her down horrific paths. She shuddered, her mind picturing a dead body lying there where Peter had just planted the shrubs. She had seen death before. She had watched the life recede from her mother bit by bit, until she took no more breaths and her body grew cold and stiff. A beautiful life that could never come back ever. A lovely voice that never again would speak. A life gone. Gone. Oh, she hoped it wasn't Dr. Grant! How could the two little boys live without him? And she hoped it wasn't Peter. How could—

Her eyes gazed unseeing across the room. Would she be angry at God if Dr. Grant was dead? Or if Peter was dead? Yes, Kyla decided. Absolutely yes! Yes, she would definitely be angry at God. She would be furious! She would hate him forever! And she would hate Robert DeKane forever too. She clenched her teeth, infuriated at them already. But as she sat there churning in her mind, she was surprised by tiny foreign thoughts that came wisping in, one at a time, like invisible feathers falling, touching her mind and heart. Thoughts of her pronouncement of forgiveness to her father, thoughts of herself at the beach, snipping his baggage off herself. To hate her father again would make meaningless all she had done. To hate him would mean taking back all those hurts and all that anger again. Kyla let out a sober breath, seeing the choice that lay before her. How could she take it all back on and start all over with it?

And if she hated God for taking Peter, how would that be any different from what she had been through in the last ten years with her mom? Hadn't she already experienced the dead-end road of bitterness? She closed her eyes, considering it. Awful as it was, she couldn't go back—she didn't want to be filled with all that anger anymore! One of the Bible verses from her journal came to mind—that God causes all things to work together for good for those who love him. She *did* now. She *did* love God! At least she was *trying* to! She *wanted* to love him—so could that verse really be true for her? Even now? Gently untangling Howie's arm from her leg, Kyla turned, got on her knees, and leaned onto the trunk.

"God, if you are real," she whispered, then stopped, ashamed of herself. She started again. "No, God, I'm sorry. You *are* real, and I believe it. And I believe that you really do love me, and you really are for me. And I want to tell you right now that if Peter is dead down there"—her hand covered her mouth as she choked back a sob—"if he is dead, then I will *still* believe that you are real, and I will *still* believe that you love me. And I will trust you. God, it would be really, really hard, and I can't promise to do it perfectly, but I will *try* to trust you, no matter what!" She quit trying to hold back her sorrow then and had a good, hard cry.

The hard part was the waiting. After she prayed, she got up and walked around the room quietly for a while. She checked the time on Peter's cell phone again; the minutes were ticking by agonizingly slowly. It was easy to pray a prayer, but the trusting part—*the trusting part*—she was struggling with that! What did trust look like when you were locked in a dark room and all you could do is sit and wait and think?

When Howie woke up from his nap, he asked Kyla if his dad was home from work yet. Kyla said she didn't think so and asked him if they could play God's Creation again. It kept her mind busy so that she didn't think about the new possibility that had started tugging at her mind—the possibility that perhaps *both* Dr. Grant and Peter could be lying unresponsive down below. Perhaps neither would be coming for them. A weight of worry settled on her heart.

And seriously, where were the authorities? Her dad said he had contacted them! Shouldn't they have been there by now? She hoped when they came they would think to look beyond the abandoned third floor. She hoped they would see the attic door when they searched the house. If they searched the house. If they came. Surely they would come.

Another hour passed. And then another. Howie was complaining again that he was hungry. And then he complained that he was bored. Kyla felt like she would go crazy if she had to make up one more story to tell him. She urged him to tell *her* a story, but he shrugged and said he didn't know any.

Then Howie suggested they do like Peter and pray.

"That's probably a good idea," she told him wearily.

She sighed. She had already prayed. Sort of. And she didn't really know what else to say. *God*, she asked him in her mind, *what am I supposed to pray?* She didn't know where even to start. She sat quietly beside Howie on the woolen uniform as he looked at her and waited. Suddenly Mrs.

Gordon flashed through her mind. She saw the two of them standing in the Great Room, and Mrs. Gordon was telling her, "A father's responsibility before God is to love, nurture, care for, and protect his children." Her words resonated within—*protect his children.*

Kyla had a sobering thought. It came like an epiphany, another revelation about herself as it occurred to her that she looked to *Peter* as the one with the eye to protect. *Peter* was the one who was always watchful, always standing guard. Had she trusted Peter more than God—just as she had looked to Alex to meet her need for love? Perhaps, she thought, perhaps she should stop waiting for Peter and look to God himself for her rescue! Perhaps she should go to God in prayer as if he were a good father who did not abdicate his responsibilities. And as if he were a father who was actually capable of doing something!

Kyla reached for Howie's hand and closed her eyes. She knew very little about praying, but she did her best, praying that God would protect each one of them, keep them from danger, and bring them all safely through their crisis. Her words sounded extremely sterile to her, but she hoped God could understand what she meant inside.

"What's a 'crisis'?" Howie wanted to know after she had finished.

Kyla looked at him. "A crisis is a difficulty. A trouble. You know, like we're locked in this room and can't get out."

He had his knees up under his chin. He rocked a bit, turning back to Kyla. "Why don't we pray for someone to come and unlock the door?"

Kyla gave a short laugh. He would be annoying if he weren't so cute. She gave him a quick side hug. "Good idea. God, would you please send someone to let us out of here? Preferably soon, thank you! Amen."

"Amen," he said.

They sat together in silence again for a several minutes, with Howie leaning his head against her arm. The room was slightly brighter now with the early evening sun shining more directly in the high window from the west. Kyla decided she would stop checking the time on Peter's phone.

Howie sighed loudly. "Would you scratch my back again?"

He spread out the jacket and laid on it where Kyla could reach under his shirt and draw out little adventure stories on his back, all the while fighting the wave of fatigue that had just come over her. She wished there was somewhere to lie down besides the hard, dusty floor.

Suddenly Howie lifted his head. "There's yelling in the floor!" he said.

Kyla eyed him tiredly. "What?"

"There's someone yelling in the floor! Yelling for you!"

In a flash Kyla was on her hands and knees, putting her ear to the dusty floorboards. She heard it too and hopped up.

"Howie, it's someone looking for us, and we need to make some noise. A lot of noise!"

Kyla yelled and stomped her feet, and then got the boards she had stood on from the closet and banged on the floor with them. When she stopped to listen again, she could hear a faint buzzing sound below, like the sound of an electric tool. They yelled again, until before long they heard footsteps coming up the attic steps.

Kyla went to the door, pounding and shouting, "We're in here!"

She heard a voice. "Kyla! Is everybody all right? Is anyone hurt?"

She paused in amazement. It was her dad—*her dad!* What was he doing here all the way from Stanton?

From the other side Kendall hollered for them to be careful while he cut the door open, and the buzzing started up again. Soon a little saw blade poked through the wooden door, making an arc around the knob and latch, until the door swung open, revealing Kyla's dad holding a jigsaw. He all but dropped it to embrace Kyla.

"Oh, thank God you're safe!" he exclaimed, hugging her hard. "Thank God I searched again!"

Releasing her, Kendall looked down at Howie, who stood near Kyla with a guarded expression on his face. Then he glanced around the room, holding his palm low. "Where's the other one?"

Kyla shook her head, wiping her tears with her sleeve. "DeKane—" She pointed down at Howie, then made a walking signal with her fingers. "And there was another guy with him!"

His eyes grew wide. "Took him?" he mouthed the words. His jaw set hard when she nodded.

Kyla sniffed and put her hand on Howie's shoulder. "Howie, this is my dad. His name is 'Mr. Lee.'" To his confused look she continued, "He's my other dad—my *real* dad, actually, and he's a very good and wonderful man! You can trust him." She wiped the tears from her face with the arm of her shirt.

Howie's voice quavered, "Can we go downstairs now?"

"Yes, Howie—we can!" she replied, and turning to her dad added, "I saw your email to Peter earlier today—about my—about Robert DeKane." Then suddenly remembering Peter, her face grew concerned. "Dad, please tell me you've seen Peter! Is he downstairs? Is he okay?"

Kendall spread his hands and shook his head. "I don't know where he is. Haven't seen him. He wasn't here when I got here. But Kyla—" He stopped, touching her arm, the pained look on his face again. He glanced down at the boy then back up at her, speaking very quietly. "The professor. He's been—"

"Shot?" she asked.

He gave a grim nod.

"We heard it. Did he—is he—?" Kyla's hand went to her face as she felt the wave of nausea again.

Kendall shook his head. "No, but it doesn't look good. They had to really work on him. He lost a lot of blood. They took him by ambulance a few hours ago."

Her heart sank. "Oh, no! That's awful!"

She looked down at the top of Howie's head where he stood beside her, thinking of Hank and Dr. Grant. And Peter. How would she explain any of this to him?

Kendall gestured to the stairs. "Come on."

Her father talked as Kyla carried Howie down the attic stairway to the third floor, continuing on down to the main floor. "It took me a while to find this place and then forever to get in through those gates! I had to hack into your email to get the code! It was completely quiet when I got here. Absolutely no one around. So I went in and saw that something happened down there—the place is a wreck. And then I found"—his eyes dropped to Howie's head—"the guy outside, and I called 9-1-1. Barely conscious. He asked me to find his boys, and then he passed out. Then the police got here. They've been here for hours—five, six hours already. They're almost done with processing everything already."

"I had no idea. We were totally isolated up there."

"They looked for you! They did an initial search of the house right away, but I decided to come up and look again. That's when I heard you up there."

"Thank you, Daddy," she breathed. "And thank *God*."

The main floor was a mess, as her dad had warned. A chair was on its side in the Great Room, and the carpet was badly stained with dirt. Dr. Grant's office was in shambles, the furniture also overturned, and the rug pulled back off the floor. His desk drawers hung open, and papers were strewn everywhere.

Howie gaped at it round-eyed and visibly upset. "What happened? Where's my dad?"

"I'm not sure," Kyla answered simply, "but we're safe. There's some police that are here to help us. Let's go talk to them."

He gripped Kyla's hand more tightly as they walked toward the kitchen, where three police officers stood by the island speaking to Mrs. Gordon. They could see more officers outside through the patio window.

The officers looked up in surprise when Kyla entered the room. Mrs. Gordon rushed to her, and the two embraced and cried together about Dr. Grant.

"Thank God, you're safe! I got your text that Hank was alone and in danger, and I came out right away!" She looked down at Howie. "Did you find him, hon? Is he okay?"

Kyla started. "What? No! I've been locked in the attic—" She looked from her to the staring police officers, suddenly fearing that no one there knew Hank had been taken. Her voice rose. "Someone needs to be out there looking for Hank! There's a little boy out there! He's only two years old!"

Mrs. Gordon laid her hand on her arm. "Hon, they know! I told them! They've been looking for *all* of you! I just thought maybe he was with you."

She shook her head, feeling panicky. "No. Two men took him—a man named Robert DeKane and his partner Rich Connors. I can describe them both! They went that way toward the river!" She pointed. "A long time ago! I saw them take him when I was looking out from the attic window! Is someone looking for him? Please—you need to find him right away! Right away!"

"Yes, Kyla, they're looking for him," Mrs. Gordon affirmed, and the officers nodded in agreement.

Howie threw Kyla a frightened glance. "What happened to Hank? Who took him?" His little arms started to shake as he looked around, unsure of what was happening, unsure of why his home was filled with strangers. "Where is he? Why did someone take him? Where is my dad?" His face began to pucker. "I want my daddy!"

One of the officers skirted quickly out the back door, while another, a female, drew near to Kyla, holding out her hand. "Calm down, ma'am— we're on this! We've got officers in pursuit of the suspect, and if the child is there, they'll find him. We will advise them of the situation, but we need you to stay calm."

Another moved forward, holding out a chair for her. "Here you go, ma'am. We'd like to take your statement if you'd have a seat, please."

Kyla wanted to pace, but Howie was trembling and clinging to her side. She sat and pulled him onto her lap, wrapping her arms around him.

"I want my daddy," he whispered urgently under his breath, "I want my daddy."

She held him securely. "It's okay, Howie. It's gonna be okay."

"What happened to Hank? Did bad guys take him?"

"They're going to find him," she reassured him, berating herself for not having been more careful in front of him. "They're looking for him. Everything's going to be okay." Oh, she hoped so. *She hoped so!*

Her father sat down on a chair to her right, while the policewoman sat down on the other side of her, setting on the table an official-looking clipboard filled with forms. Another officer joined them, looking kindly at Howie and sliding in beside her father.

"I'm Officer Parker, and this is my partner, Officer Hanson." She gestured across the table, and gave Kyla a sympathetic smile. "We have someone from Child Protection on their way. He'll go with them tonight. They'll be here soon."

Kyla's mouth opened, and she gripped the boy tighter. "No. No, he stays with me."

Officer Parker pursed her lips, glancing at her partner.

"It's required," he said. "He needs to be removed from this environment until the investigation is completed."

Kyla shook her head. "I'm his nanny. I can't send him with a stranger. He stays with me."

"Yes, but he can't stay here."

"Where he goes, I go."

"But there's another factor," Officer Parker added. "You're a relative of the suspect, and we need to ask you some questions. It's better for the boy to go, but you, ma'am, need to stay where we can reach you for anything if we need to. It's truly better for the boy."

"What?" Kyla gave her an incredulous look. "Yeah, I'm a relative, but I'm also a victim here! No, I won't let you take him!" She turned to her dad for support, but he was looking downward, his eyes closed. She knew he was praying. Kyla shook her head no again.

"I'm sorry, ma'am," Officer Hanson continued in a firm but kind manner. "It's best. And it's standard procedure."

Behind her Mrs. Gordon cleared her throat. "My daughter does foster care, and she's taken emergency placements before. Could he go with her? It's Julia's mom," she told Kyla.

Kyla looked to the female officer who paused, then nodded and spoke to Officer Hanson, "Okay—check it out. Get her name and contact Child Protection to find out if she's an option for us. See if you can make it work."

Mrs. Gordon gave the officer her daughter's information, then offered to take Howie upstairs to distract him and to pack an overnight bag. Kyla didn't think he would go, but surprisingly, he took the older woman's hand and left. When they were out of the room, she remembered he hadn't eaten since lunch, and she asked her dad to take Howie some food.

"And make sure he washes his hands really well," she added, remembering how filthy the attic floor was.

Kendall set a plate of fruit and cheese beside Kyla too, but she didn't touch it.

"Does anyone know anything about Peter?" Kyla asked the officers. "Peter Watkins. Has he shown up anywhere? Has anyone found him?" She was beside herself with worry and frustration.

"Our officers are searching for him right now," the woman said, sliding her chair in closer to the table, her pen in hand, indicating that she was ready to take notes. "We'll let you know if we find him. Now, I need you to tell me what happened this afternoon."

Running a hand through her hair, Kyla gave a loud sigh and then started in with her statement. She hadn't realized how much it would entail. Though her story started with what happened that afternoon in Peter's room, it led to disclosing so much that had happened before then—all the way back to her father's strange arrival at Wynnbury, the discovery of the various identification cards in his room, his asking her to search Dr. Grant's office—more and more details kept coming out, which then led to her telling of his fascination with Wynnbury house. The officer gave her a scrutinizing look.

"You're saying there's believed to be something of great value hidden here on this property? Like what?" She cocked her head. "I'm going to need some details on that too."

"Well, I'm not exactly sure what it is."

At that moment one of the officers on the patio poked his head in the door. "Good news! They just radioed back that they have the little boy! He's okay!"

Kyla heaved an enormous sigh of relief. Surely Hank would be traumatized by this, she thought, but he was alive, and he was okay!

The woman beside her smiled, laying a hand on her arm. "We'll make sure the Grant brothers are together tonight at your housekeeper's daughter's house."

Kyla was too relieved to correct her. "What about Peter?" she called to the officer at the patio door. "What about Peter Watkins?"

He gave her a blank look. "Who?"

Kyla stood up hastily, her chair tipping to the floor. "Peter Watkins!" Her voice was loud with aggravation. "He's still missing! Is anyone even *looking* for him?"

Her father, who had been pacing softly in the hall behind her, moved up, laying his hand on her shoulder.

Officer Parker rose to her feet too. "Ma'am, we're doing all we can to find him. When we—"

"—Well, it doesn't sound like it!" Kyla snapped.

Kendall gently squeezed her shoulder. "They're working, Kyla. They're doing their job." He bent down to pick up her chair and gestured, indicating that she should finish with the officer.

Resigned, she sat, leaning her elbows on the table and biting the side of her thumb. Everything about this was moving so slowly! Her whole afternoon had been like an edge-of-your-seat action movie—*minus* all the action! In movies you saw everything happening quickly—bam, bam, bam—one thing after another and from every angle. You knew where everybody was and what they were doing. Here she sat in a chair, waiting, waiting, waiting. And this was after already sitting for hours in a dark attic, waiting, waiting, waiting. So much waiting! She couldn't take it anymore!

"Dad," she said over her shoulder, "would you tell Mrs. Gordon to pack a bag for Hank too? Tell her not to forget his bear and his blanket." Her voice rose agitatedly as she added, "Tell her she *absolutely* must not forget them!"

"Yes, I'll tell her," he said calmly and left the room.

"They're on my bed!" she called after him. "In my room!"

Officer Parker called after him, "Child Protection is here now too, and they're ready to take the boy!"

She turned back to Kyla, glancing down at her notes. "All right—you were going to tell me some business with something about this house—?"

Inwardly Kyla was conflicted. That was exactly what she didn't want to do. No more privacy, no more tight circle. The mystery that Dr. Grant suspected would now be common knowledge. There might even be an official investigation, a search of the property. Of course, Dr. Grant wouldn't be suspected of wrongdoing, but his private search could certainly be over. She felt so guilty. Dutifully she shared the little that she knew with the officer, all the while miserably distracted with her thoughts about Peter, wondering where he was, hoping he wasn't lying somewhere in the woods, or worse, floating out there in the river somewhere.

Staring absently ahead, she noticed her goldfish in their tank on the counter and realized they hadn't been fed that day. It was just a tiny thing, but it made Kyla think of the many, many changes ahead from here on out. The normal routine of life at Wynnbury would not be the same. She wondered about Dr. Grant in the hospital—how he was doing and if he would pull through. She wondered about the boys. About a lot of things.

At last the officer was satisfied with the information she had compiled and said Kyla could go. *Go where?* Kyla thought, rising from her chair. There was only more waiting to be done.

"The children will return to the house tomorrow sometime to be with their mother," Officer Parker was telling her, collecting the papers before her and sliding them into the clipboard.

Kyla shook her head, explaining, "Their mother is away. She's not here. She's in London shooting a movie."

"Oh, she's on her way already!" Officer Parker said with certainty. "Ms. Montayne has been notified and is in the air on her way. But she'll still need you here, no doubt. I would think she'd want to be with her husband."

Kyla nodded soberly.

"Also," the officer said, returning her chair to the table, "they pulled a few items out of the fountain that I'd like you to take a look at for me. A couple of computers and a phone. And a flash drive. They're on the deck."

She knew whose they were without looking, but she went out to identify them anyway. The bare dirt of the yard and the silent skid loader beside the metal box brought the awful pang in her gut again. She wished they would hear something. She asked again for them to tell her as soon as there was any word about Peter. All but one of the police cars had left. Officer Parker gave Kyla her card and said that she and Officer Hanson would be leaving shortly and that they would be in touch.

Kyla hadn't seen her dad since Howie had left, and she went to find him. She looked in the Great Room, observing again the dirt ground into the carpet. Probably from Peter's shoes and clothes from working in the yard. She wondered what had happened there.

She found her dad in the library, seeing him first from a distance as she approached from the hall. His back was to her, and he was walking slowly to and fro, his arms extended in the air. Praying. Just like Peter. She stood still, watching him for a moment, the realization settling in: he was Peter's teacher, Peter's model. Peter prayed like her father prayed. Kendall turned as Kyla entered the room. She went directly to him and hugged him tightly.

"Daddy, I love you," she said with deep emotion. "I love who you are. I love everything about you!"

He held her long and hard. She buried her face in his neck and clung to him, so grateful for him. So grateful for his love, his care, his protection. So grateful he had come here for her sake. He had come for *her*. He kissed her cheek and urged her to go outside with him to get some fresh air.

The sun had set, and in the dusky light he showed her where he had found Dr. Grant, the telltale blood smears still on the grass. She cried again, and he steered her away. Sniffling, she showed him the fountain Peter had put in, telling him about how they had had to dig up the yard for it, and the many steps it took to finish it. Gesturing to the partially excavated ground, she told him that Peter had been preparing for sod that they were expecting very soon. They walked to the large metal box askew on the scraped ground, and she stared at it sadly. It had all been over this—this dirt-caked, bent up, four-by-five-foot metal box—and what lay mysteriously inside. This was what they had been searching for. This was why Dr. Grant was in the hospital, why Hank and Howie were in a stranger's home, and why Peter was still missing. All because of this. With the illumination of Peter's phone flashlight, Kendall stepped across the lumpy dirt to pull the latch and raise the rusty lid.

Kyla knew they would find it empty.

Opened, the box smelled like old leather and horse liniment. It wasn't completely empty, but almost. In the light of the flashlight they could see a few things sitting on the bottom—a couple of horse brushes and a bridle, the leather straps dark and brittle from age. Whatever else had been in there with it was gone now, no doubt taken by DeKane and Rich Connors. Would it ever be found again? Kyla bit her lip, wondering for the first time about her biological father. Where was he? Had they caught him and Connors? What had he done with the museum items? What had he done with Hank before they found him? What had they done with Peter? Kendall dropped the lid shut on the box and came to stand beside Kyla. She looked out toward the blackness of the river, the horizon now completely darkened.

"I wish we knew where Peter was," she said.

Her dad nodded. "Yeah, me too. But we've prayed, sweetheart. Now we trust. And keep praying."

"It didn't even sound like anyone was looking for him."

"I'm sure they are. They know what they're doing. They have their system."

"I just don't like this waiting! I want to do something. I want to go look for him myself!" Kyla turned to her father. "Dad, I like Peter."

Kendall exhaled, nodding. "I know, honey—I like him too. He's such a fine young man."

Kyla shook her head, a tear slipping down her cheek. "No, Daddy," she said miserably, closing her eyes. "I *really* like Peter. We have to find him!"

He was silent a moment, looking at her. "Well, come on then. Let's take the car. I don't know where we'll go—"

"We'll go to the landing," Kyla said, taking his arm and starting quickly for the house. "The public landing. I want to go look there."

"Okay," he said, keeping step with her, "but maybe you should put something on."

Kyla looked at him. "What?"

"That shirt is really dirty and super thin, and"—he frowned—"are you wearing a *swimsuit*?"

She looked down at herself. The sheer gauze cover-up over her swimsuit was filthy with mascara, dirt from the attic, and tears and snot from her and Howie's faces. Hastily Kyla ran upstairs to whip it off and throw a sweatshirt over her suit, moving Peter's phone to the new pocket.

Chapter Thirty-One

There were six vehicles on or near the slab beside the house where the carport used to be: Dr. Grant's two, Peter's truck, DeKane's Mercedes, her Mustang, and her dad's Toyota.

"We'll take my car," Kendall said. It seemed logical; it was parked at the end behind all the others.

"Mine's faster," Kyla said.

He looked at her strangely. "We barely know where we're going, Kyla, or where we're going to look. We won't need speed."

"But what if we get a call?" she countered. She wanted to be prepared for *anything*.

He conceded, and although she had previously been blocked in, without the carport there they were able to drive straight off the slab and curl around through the grass to the pavement of the driveway. Kendall insisted on driving, and Kyla pointed him in what she thought was the direction of the public landing.

"When DeKane was stalking us, he brought a boat in from the public landing," she explained. Kyla had seen him and Connors leave with Hank by way of the waterfront, and she assumed they probably had taken a boat again—possibly even Dr. Grant's boat.

Her directional guess was correct. Before long they passed the sign to the landing and turned onto the gravel drive down to the waterfront. With the light of their headlights they could see several sets of fresh tire tracks cut into the surface of the approach. "But this is a *public* landing," her dad reminded her, "and they could be anyone's tracks." Kyla had her dad turn the car to the left, its bright headlights revealing in the distance Dr. Grant's boat, roughly tied to a nearby dock with other boats.

"See! I knew it!" she said.

They parked, and together she and her dad walked along the shore, aiming their flashlights into the nearby underbrush, trudging through the woods, searching for quite a distance in both directions. Finding nothing, they returned to the landing where Kyla checked Dr. Grant's boat, then stood on the dock, looking dismally out at the black water in the dark, fearful of what she might see.

"This isn't doing either of us any good," her father said behind her.

"I know." Kyla sighed, reluctantly walking with him to the car.

"I think we should just go back," he said, and she quietly agreed.

They drove away in silence, and Kyla felt defeated. More waiting, she thought. How much more could she take?

"Kyla," her dad said after they had turned onto the main road, "there's something else that came out of this whole thing with your biological father that I've been putting off telling you. But it's something you need to know. Something about your mother." His voice was sober.

Kyla turned her face toward him in the dark.

"You told me earlier that you read the email I sent Peter this afternoon," he said.

"Yes," she replied.

"So you know about DeKane—that there's several warrants out for his arrest."

Kyla nodded. "Yes."

He cleared his throat, looking straight ahead, his hands on the wheel. "Well, one of the detectives at the station in Stanton is a close friend. He was doing some research for me on your father. And he discovered some alarming things. DeKane's got a long history with the law that goes back pretty far. And Kyla, your mother"—his voice suddenly grew raspy as if it were hard for him to speak—"your mother was right in there with him." He turned his head to look at her.

Kyla met his eyes, then looked back at the road. "So it's true."

Kendall shot her another look.

"He told me," she said. "Today when he was taking Howie and me up to the attic, he told me. I couldn't believe it. I didn't want to believe it."

They were silent again for a bit.

"It blew me away," Kendall said finally. "I had no idea. She never talked to me about her past. Never. I finally stopped asking her. I always figured she must have had a rough time in her relationship with DeKane, but I would have never thought this. Never in a million years!" He shook his head in disbelief.

"What did they do?" she asked. "What were they involved in? She didn't kill anyone, did she?" The memory of being held at gunpoint lingered unpleasantly.

He let out a quick breath. "I sure hope not! I don't think so. From what I learned from my investigator friend, they had quite a sophisticated operation. The two of them were drawing money out of large corporation bank accounts using a combination of computer hacking skills coupled with several shady investment firms that they used as cover. My friend said your mother was a genius. They were successful for a long time. I guess the two of them were quite good at what they did."

"Investments," Kyla said flatly.

"Very large sums," he added. "Just unbelievable to even think of her in that way."

Kyla patted her hand on the creamy leather seat beside her leg. "This car, Dad—he said this car was her share of their last job." She spoke quietly, reflecting on her mother. "He was paying her back through me. He told me Mom made him promise not to have any contact with me until I was finished with school." She sniffed, continuing matter-of-factly, "We can sell it. Perhaps we could find out who the money was stolen from."

There was another pause in the conversation as Kendall navigated the road in the dark. Far ahead the headlights of an approaching vehicle appeared as dots of light.

"After they split up, there was no record of her involvement again," Kendall concluded.

"Because of me," Kyla said. She looked at him in the dark. "He told me she was afraid for me. That she wanted to disappear into society and be a normal person." She sighed. "You know, some things make sense now. I always wondered why Mom had no family. None whatsoever. She was living in hiding!"

Kendall gave exclamation. "Ah! That's all part of this too! I found out something else about your mother, Kyla! Get this—you *do* have family!"

"*What?*"

"Yes!" he said, braking and weaving on the road as he slowed. He hit the steering wheel with his hands in excitement. "You're right! She lived in hiding away from her family, but the authorities knew who her family was! You would never believe this! 'DeKane'—'DeKane' was an assumed name! That was not her name! Or his! And she and your father were never legally married!"

She turned in her seat. "What?"

Kendall pulled haphazardly over onto the shoulder of the road. He stopped and slipped the car into park, the rear of the car still jutting out onto the road. "Oh, I can hardly believe I forgot this detail until now! Your mother's name was Delano—Evangeline Delano. And she has been 'missing' for over twenty-five years! Kyla, you have grandparents! David and Shirley Delano. And more than that, you have two uncles and cous—"

"Derek and Darryl," she said, recognizing the names.

His head went back. "How could you know that?"

Kyla looked down, shaking her head in wonder. "He told me those were the names of *his* parents and *his* brothers." She bit her lip, wondering if he somehow wanted her to know. She looked back at her father. "From Champagne, Illinois."

He looked at her incredulously. "Yes!" They stared at each other.

The approaching vehicle passed by them on the other side of the road, and suddenly behind them red and blue lights began flashing. Kendall looked up through the rearview mirror, watching the car take a U-turn behind them. He groaned, dropping his hand from where it rested on the steering wheel.

"Oh, for heaven's sake—what next?" he said impatiently. "Haven't we had enough for one day? I supposed it's how I'm parked. I should have used my flashers."

He popped his seatbelt off as the police car pulled up swiftly behind them. Kyla looked back, waiting for the officer, when she saw the rear door of the squad car fly open and a familiar head appear. Peter's tall figure straightened and started for their car.

"Dad, it's Peter!" Kyla shouted, barreling out her door toward him.

They met between the two cars in the glaring of headlights and police flashers. He threw his arms around her, and she hugged his waist.

"Kyla, thank God!" He pulled her tight. "You're okay? You're not hurt?"

"I'm okay," she said, crushed into his chest.

After a brief moment he released her and turned to her father, who approached from the other side of the car.

"Kendall, thank God you're here," he said simply, but his voice was filled with emotion. The two of them reached as if to shake hands but grasped forearms, standing eye to eye. And Peter's face—his face said a million things in that moment. "Am I ever glad to see—" His voice broke, and the two of them embraced. Kyla's throat grew tight as she watched.

Pulling away, Peter drew his arm across his eyes and turned back to Kyla. "I didn't know where you were," he said, shaking his head apologetically. "You and Howie were just gone, and I didn't know where! And then they took Hank—" He put his hand on his chest. "I had to go after Hank. I had to! I'm so sorry, Kyla. I'm so sorry I left you!"

"He locked us in the att—"

The static-filled sound of police dispatch cut into the night air, drowning out her voice. Kyla was suddenly aware of the police officers standing near them in the road.

"Please step to the side, folks. It's not safe standing out here," one of the officers said, waving them to the side of the road. "And I'm sorry, sir—you're going to have to move your car."

"We were on our way home," Kendall replied, lifting his hand to point down the road. "Just down the road here."

"So am I," Peter said to her dad. "They were taking me. I'll ride with you."

He shook hands with the officers, thanking them for the ride. Kyla crunched into the back seat of her car, leaving the front seat for Peter and her dad.

"They were just delivering me to the landing," Peter said, getting in after her and buckling his seatbelt. "I was going to get Grant's boat and bring it home. Were you at the hospital?"

"No," Kendall answered. "We were out looking for you."

"For *me*?" Peter shot a look toward Kyla in the back seat. She was glad it was dark and he couldn't see her blush.

Kyla's father pulled the car out onto the highway, resuming the short drive to the Wynnbury gates.

"I saw Grant," Peter said. "For about two seconds only. They wouldn't let me stay. He had just come out of surgery and was pretty sedated, but they said it went well, and they think he'll be all right. He was pretty bad off."

Kyla felt a wave of relief pass through her body.

"DeKane?" Kendall asked. "Any word? Did they get him?"

Peter shook his head, casting him a look of disappointment. "No. Not that I've heard anyway. He was working with someone else, and they had a car waiting for them at the landing. All planned out, for sure. This was definitely not by chance. They took off, but I got Hank! That's all that matters. But you—" He pumped his fist. "Thank God you called the station when you did! And with the information you called in it won't take long, and they'll have them both. I'm sure of it! You blew this thing wide open!"

Kendall gave a modest exclamation. "No, it was all God's timing.

I just got the right information into the right hands. If you hadn't sent me those names when you did—"

"—Holy cow! I felt like I was back at my old craft, breaking into that room!" Peter interjected with a sudden chuckle. "I had visions of my old probation officer freaking out on me! And of you having to come and bail me out of jail!"

The two of them laughed and continued their talking while Kyla watched them from the back seat, waiting once again. She loved the sound of their voices together, loved their laughter, and she didn't mind the waiting too much this time.

Back at Wynnbury Kendall parked her car with all the others. Peter got out and stretched, exclaiming loudly what a long day it had been and how glad he was to be back home.

"I smell like the river, and I'm starving!" he said. He bent down to move his seat forward, reaching for Kyla's hand to help her out of the car. "I need a shower, and I need some food, and I need—"

"—and you need to tell me *every detail* of what happened today!" Kyla said, drawing herself up as she stepped out of the car. "I've been waiting all day long for any word on you, and I've been going crazy!"

"Same here," he said quietly, holding onto her hand for a moment.

While Peter showered and changed, her dad made them dinner. Kyla righted the furniture in the Great Room and began the process of cleaning up Dr. Grant's study by gathering up loose papers. She rubbed her forehead at the thought of how long it would take to organize everything again, for every drawer had been emptied and scattered. The wire mesh baskets from the top of his desk were lying empty behind Dr. Grant's desk, one leaning against the bookshelf, the other two in the corner beside the wall. She knelt beside the bookshelf, picking up and sorting through the mess of papers fanned out on the floor, searching for Peter's file among the debris. She found it. And there, still tucked inside, was the file on Wynnbury. A sense of gratification spread through her, even though she knew it was too late anyway. She set the tray on Dr. Grant's desk and placed the file on it, a token of at least one way in which she had actually helped him.

When their food was prepared they gathered at the table, but it felt strange without Dr. Grant and the boys there. Kyla's dad had them join hands, and Kyla took her father's hand and self-consciously placed her other hand in Peter's. Her father expressed his gratefulness to God for his protection over each of the household members before also giving thanks for their food. He prayed so naturally, Kyla thought. She recalled her stiff and formal prayers in the attic, still shocked at the possibility that God might have heard them and that they actually may have made a difference.

Releasing her hand, Peter asked to hear Kyla's story first. "Ladies first," he said, but then he winked at her. "That way I can eat while you talk." He was happy, his blue eyes twinkling.

"There's nothing much to say," she said. "I missed everything that happened down here! I went to your room and texted Dr. Grant, like you asked. Then DeKane walked in on Howie and me while I was reading"—Kyla was suddenly embarrassed to divulge that part—"um, while I was on your computer. He took us up and locked us in the attic—the one above the third floor. We were stuck in there until Dad came and got us out. Then the police were here, and I had to give a statement. That's about it. I missed it all!"

"You were *protected* from it all!" Kendall said into his plate.

Peter gave her a knowing look over his fork. "Were the bats terrible?"

"All asleep in their little attic beds," she said with a small smile. "I didn't look up or mention anything to Howie. You have *no idea* how brave I was!"

The three of them laughed together.

Then Kyla shared with him what she had learned about her mother from her biological father. Kendall filled in the details from what he had learned that day from his detective friend at home. Peter's face was somber.

"I'm very sorry about that," he said to both of them. "That must have been very difficult news."

"It was," Kyla agreed. "It was shocking. But I told Robert DeKane to his face that my mother wasn't the same woman that he knew. She was a new creation in Jesus Christ. And by his blood she was declared innocent in her life and in her death."

Kendall looked up suddenly from his meal. Peter stopped his fork in midair, turning his face slowly toward her, his eyes bright.

Kyla looked down, embarrassed. "It's true," she said.

"Yes, it is," her father affirmed. "Yes, that is most certainly true."

Kyla felt awkward that Peter continued to look at her.

"So what happened here?" she asked, trying to divert his attention. "Ms. Montayne might not be happy when she sees the Great Room carpet!"

"Yeah." Peter turned back to his plate and set his fork down, taking a break from eating. "I was working so hard trying to get that box out of the ground that I wasn't even aware of anything happening in the house—to you or to Grant. I didn't even hear Grant come home. It looks like he must have walked in on DeKane ransacking his study—you can tell by the looks of it that there was some sort of scuffle in there! Anyway, all I know is that I had finally gotten that box out of the ground and had just gotten off the skid loader to open it when Grant came out of the house waving and yelling at me, telling me to get out of there fast, that DeKane had gone crazy. Then here comes DeKane out of the house right after him, pointing a gun at him!"

Kyla made a noise and raised a hand to her mouth.

Peter flicked a look her way, continuing, "I didn't know what to do! I started praying like crazy and hollering his name. I thought maybe I could try to talk to him or distract him." He looked down at the table with glazed eyes. "That was awful, seeing him raise that gun and watching Grant crumple like that. He shot at me twice—which is a freaky feeling! Never had that happen to me before, and never want it again! Then he went back into the house."

He pushed his plate to the side a bit, leaning on the table with his arms. "So I'm out there in the yard, thinking about you and Howie still in the house, so I tore in here after him." He glanced at Kyla. "I caught him in the Great Room and took him down. Got his gun away from him and pinned him. I had him—I definitely had him! I asked him where you were, and he said I'd never find you. I wanted to choke that son—" He stopped, pursing his lips and looking down for a moment. "Anyway, behind me I hear a noise, and all of a sudden there's another guy standing there—this big guy with a beard. I'm pretty sure it was the same guy I saw across the river with the binoculars—"

"I'm sure it was!" Kyla interjected. "I saw him up above through the attic window. His name is Rich Connors, my father's friend. I met him when my father gave me the Mustang."

Peter nodded. "Ah. Makes sense. Well, I had no idea where he came from, but this guy's also got a gun, and he's aiming at me on top of DeKane telling me to let him go. I was about to make a reach for DeKane's gun, but right in the middle of everything, Hank walks in! Hank!" He shook his head, looking away. "So I let him go. I let DeKane go, and Hank came right to me where I sat on the floor."

Kyla fidgeted uncomfortably in her chair.

"So I'm sitting there with Hank on my lap, and there are now two guns on us."

He paused, raising his water glass to his lips. Kyla and her dad sat still, listening.

"The two start talking now between themselves real quietly, and I'm straining to hear what they're saying. I hear the older guy say something to DeKane about the box in the yard—the one I just got up out of the ground—and it sounded like he'd been looking in there. I figure he must have come up from the dock right when I headed into the house. Anyway, they're talking, and then DeKane cusses something fierce and tells the big guy to watch us. DeKane disappears into Grant's office for a bit, and I can hear him throwing stuff around in there while Hank and I are sitting on the floor out there." He jerked his head to the Great Room behind him. "There was nothing I could do but sit tight.

"Eventually DeKane comes out of Grant's study with this box of stuff—like the size you would carry files in. I have no idea what he took. Who knows, maybe even some of Marilee's stuff from their room upstairs—I don't know—but he has this white box with a lid. He set it down and got out his gun again. I really thought it was all over. I thought he was going to shoot us both right there, like he had done Grant." He took a breath, his eyes far away. "The big guy duct-taped my arms and legs together, then took the box and left out the patio door. Then DeKane"—he paused, closing his eyes for a second—"then DeKane walked up and took Hank. He said something like 'maybe they'd make a few bucks out of this after all,' and then he yanked Hank up from the floor by his arm and carried him out of the house down toward the dock. He took him right before my eyes! He took him, and I couldn't do a thing about it! That was the hardest part—seeing Hank's face. And I couldn't do a single thing." His eyes grew red.

Kyla pictured the moment herself as she had viewed it from the window in the attic.

He cleared his throat and sniffed, taking another drink. "It didn't take me long to get that tape off, and I ran upstairs first to call 9-1-1 for Grant, but DeKane had taken my phone. It was one of the hardest decisions I've ever made, but I had to leave Grant lying there. And I couldn't look for you—I had to go after Hank." He gave her a rueful look. "I had to go after Hank."

"It was the right thing." Kyla nodded, reaching in her sweatshirt pocket for his phone. "It went up to the attic with us. Sorry." She set it on the table. "I put it in my pocket to give it to you after I texted Dr. Grant. I didn't even get a signal up there, but somehow Mrs. Gordon got my text."

"It's all right." Peter looked at the phone and back to her. Meeting his eyes, Kyla felt a sudden warmth in her belly. He glanced away to her father.

"So I took off after them," he continued. "They were long gone. They had their own boat, a good one. But I had Grant's. They were gone by the time I got to the landing, but somehow they must have known I was behind them because they abandoned Hank in the boat. Thank God!"

"What?" Kyla exclaimed. "He was left in the boat all by himself? He could have—"

He held up his hand to cut her off. "But he didn't," he said. "He didn't. He was safe. Crying, yes, but he was safe. I brought him with me to the nearest neighbor, where we called 9-1-1 for Grant and for ourselves, and then we waited there for the police. The police wanted to take Hank to the hospital and get him checked out, so we did that, and then they wanted to put him into some kind of special care for children, but I wouldn't let them take him from me. He went with me to the police station, and he stayed with me the whole time while I made my report. That took quite a long time, because we got into the things you sent." He nodded at Kendall. "I was able to pull up my email there and show them what we had learned about DeKane.

"Anyway, eventually some lady came in and said that Hank could stay with his brother at some woman's home who was a relative of Mrs. Gordon. I had no idea who that was, but I was overjoyed to hear Howie was found and figured if Howie was there, it would be okay to leave Hank with him. I went there with him personally, just to be sure. Met Mrs. Gordon's daughter. But I still hadn't heard anything about you." He looked toward Kyla. "And no one knew anything. I had no phone, and there was no answer on yours. I just had to believe that if Howie was all right, you were too. The officers were nice enough to offer me a ride home, but I begged them to take me to the hospital first to check on Grant. And then we were on our way to the landing to Grant's boat when we passed your car."

Kyla couldn't talk, and the three of them sat in silence. Finally Peter looked at his plate, then slid it over to resume eating. After a bit he paused, holding his fork in his hand.

"It just bugs me that they got away," he said. "I know it was right to let them go for Hank's sake, but it bothers me just the same."

"No one *ever* gets away," Kendall said quietly. "No one ever gets away. He may have evaded the law for a time, but there's coming a Day when he will answer for this. You can count on that."

"I suppose," Peter said. "Still, I hope they catch them soon."

Kyla silently watched Peter finish his meal.

He looked over at her. "I had to tell them about Wynnbury."

Chapter Thirty-One

She returned his sad look. "Me too."

He nodded, looking down.

"So what was it?" she asked him.

"What was what?"

"In the box you dug up. What DeKane took. What everybody was looking for."

Peter gave a short exclamation, straightening in his chair. "Nothing! That was nothing but an old tack box buried in the ground! There was nothing in it but an old bridle and a couple of horse brushes. I'm pretty certain that's not what we're looking for!"

Her eyes grew round. "You mean you didn't find it? And DeKane didn't get anything?"

Peter shook his head with a smile. "No and no—apart from whatever he took in that white box, of course. I'm pretty confident from the sound of his frustration that he was expecting the same thing we were in that tack box out there in the yard. He was pretty disappointed."

Kyla breathed a huge sigh of relief. "Thank you, God!"

"You've got *that* right!" he said. He finished his plate and set his knife and fork down. Then lifting his arms in a stretch, he added happily, "Oh, I can't say how glad I am to be home! And Kyla"—he raised his eyebrows at her—"your dad can cook!"

She narrowed her eyes at him. "I hope that isn't some kind of backhanded commentary on *my* cooking!"

They all laughed, and Kendall rose to his feet, beginning to clear the dishes.

"No, no—I got this," he said to his daughter as she moved to help. "You two have had more than your share to deal with today."

Peter turned to Kyla. "Care to sit on the deck?"

The air was cool, and Kyla was glad for the sweatshirt. Stepping off the deck momentarily, Peter turned on the fountain and its lights, then came up beside her where she stood by the concrete railing watching it. He leaned his arms on the rail next to her, looking out.

"It's really hard for me to have the boys gone tonight," she said. "I hope they're all right."

"Yeah, I hope so too," Peter said. "It was pretty tough to see Hank so scared. It might take some time, but I think they'll be okay. At least Grant—" His voice cracked, and he stopped, looking away.

Kyla nodded. "Yeah."

They stood together in silence for a while. Behind them they could hear the sound of Kyla's dad singing to himself in the kitchen as he cleaned, and both of them chuckled a little.

"He's a better cook than a singer," she commented.

Peter turned to her. "I called my dad today. From the station."

She looked at him in surprise. "You did? Why?"

He gestured toward the yard. "I asked him for help. We've got a load of sod ordered that will be delivered tomorrow, and I'm not ready. I don't have any help, and I just can't let it sit there."

"What did he say?"

"He said he'd be here with his crew in the morning. And he was great about it."

Kyla gave a happy nod. "Nice. I'm glad."

"I'll introduce you to him."

"I'd like to meet him."

They looked back out toward the fountain, quiet again for a while, the sound of water trickling mixed with the sound of crickets and frogs in the woods.

Finally he spoke. "That was really something today." He stared out unseeing into the yard. "It was like a bad dream that kept getting worse. First I see Grant fall like that; then DeKane takes Hank right out of my hands. Just one unbelievable thing after another. And you"—he turned his head toward her—"you had vanished, and my imagination was going berserk. I didn't know if he had done something to you and Howie too, like Grant or what! All day I just kept waiting to hear that you had showed up, kept hoping that you had hid or run away or something! When I saw your car and you pop out of there"—he shook his head, letting out a heavy breath—"I can't tell you my relief!"

"I know," Kyla said, leaning beside him. "It was horrible being up in that attic, not knowing what was happening! Not being able to warn you of anything. Having a phone but unable to call out. After a while I piled some stuff up so that I could see down from the window, and I saw someone— someone lying on the ground so still that I thought for sure whoever it was must be dead." She stopped, shaking her head, looking down at the hydrangeas below. "I was so afraid it was you. And then I had to wait and wait, and no one had heard anything. It seemed like forever!"

"You came looking for me." He was still leaning on the rail but turned his face to look at her.

In the darkness she could feel her cheeks grow warm. "We went to the public landing. Just a hunch. Glad we didn't find you the way I'd imagined. That would have been awful."

Peter straightened. "So. What's happening here?"

She met his eyes, answering slowly. "Something."

"Yeah, something," he murmured.

Shyly she looked away. Gently Peter reached for her hand and pulled her into an embrace, hugging her warmly. She felt him kiss the top of her head. As he loosened his hold, she raised her chin and closed her eyes, waiting. After nothing happened, she opened them to find Peter looking down at her.

"Are you going to kiss me?"

"I'm thinking about it." He gave a small smile.

She drew back. "Thinking about it?"

Peter shifted awkwardly. "Sorry. I guess I'm trying to be careful not to lead your heart down a road you're not ready to go down. It's been an emotionally charged day, and believe me—I want to kiss you. But that might only complicate things and hurt you in the long run."

Kyla stared at him, unsure of what to say.

"I'm not going to push or manipulate you into anything," he finished.

"What? What would you have to push me into?"

He was silent.

"You mean your faith in God," she said.

"I—" He hesitated, letting her go. "Yes. It's an important part of my life. Of who I am. Sorry."

Kyla stepped back, looking up at him. "Is this because I have issues?"

He frowned. "Issues? Who said you have issues?"

"*You* did! At the beach."

He closed his eyes, turning his head away. "Oh, geez, Kyla—everyone has issues! I didn't mean—I wasn't putting you down! I was just trying to help you see why you might have a hard time trusting God. That's all. I'm sorry." He gave a sigh, running a hand through his hair. "Grant's right. I need to lighten up. I've been way too pushy, and I'm sorry."

"Well, if this is because of what Dr. Grant said to you, as I told you yesterday—um, this morning or whenever that was—that was all my fault, and I'm sorry. I wish he would have never said what he said. You need to know that I don't feel the same way as him. I needed to hear—"

"Hey, hey, now!" he said, holding up his hand. "I've forgiven you! No, Kyla—it's me. I've had ulterior motives in wanting you to come to Christ, and it's just not right. I won't push you anymore or make you do something just for me."

The glow from the Great Room windows on the patio illuminated half of his face. Kyla studied him in the dimness, then took a breath. "Peter, this is all pretty new to me. I don't know as much as you, but I've stepped into this—this God-life on my own, all by myself. You've helped me see some things I needed to know. So it's too late—I already want your road!"

He was silent, looking down at her.

"I already want your God! I want to know him like you do. Truly I do." She swallowed, adding quietly, "and I want—I want *you*."

He didn't move for a moment. Then he reached for her hand. "Is this for real? Because if this is where you're coming from, this is really good news!"

She leveled her eyes at him. "I told God in the attic that if you were dead, I would still trust him. But I don't know the first thing about following God. I mean, Mrs. Gordon is helping me with some things already, but I don't know very much. I need someone to show me what I need to know—like how to read the Bible and all that stuff. I was kind of hoping that you—"

He gave a quick breath. "Yeah. Yes. Definitely yes!"

Then he made a soft sound and pulled her forward to kiss her on the lips, but much too lightly and much too briefly. Kyla rested her head on his chest, disappointed again. She could feel his heart pounding.

"What was *that*? Payback for my being so mean to you?"

Peter gave a groan and an awkward laugh. "It's called self-control. It's late, and"—he separated himself from her, but took her hand again—"and now is not the time for this. Both of us should probably call it a night. Come on—let's go in."

Kyla's dad was gone from the kitchen, and the lights were off. Peter walked her upstairs to her door and said good night, kissing her on the forehead.

"Tomorrow sometime we'll go see Grant together," he said.

"Yeah—I'd like that," she said. "The boys are coming back tomorrow too. And Dr. Grant's wife will be arriving."

"And the sod. A busy day. With lots of changes."

"Yeah."

Their eyes met and held. She smiled, and he squeezed her hand. Then he opened her door for her, said good night again, and left her there as he continued to his room.

Chapter Thirty-Two

Kyla closed her door and leaned back against it with a smile that would not leave her face. Every inch of her body felt alive and light, as if she could float up to the ceiling. She closed her eyes and reveled in it. At the moment she wasn't crazy about "self-control." She loved Peter. She wanted Peter. She wanted all of him. But she knew he was right. He was absolutely right. Self-control was right. She sighed, thinking about how much waiting she had done today, waiting, waiting, waiting. And now more waiting. But this waiting was good. This waiting was right—a waiting that honored God and each other. She would need God's help for sure.

Too adrenalized to even think about going to bed—or even to sit down—Kyla wandered about her room, her mind brimming with a million thoughts and feelings from the day. The tile around the hearth felt cold on her bare feet as she restlessly paced in front of the fireplace trying to process everything. In one single day every relationship in her small world had changed in a significant way—her relationship with her dad, her birth father, her mother, Dr. Grant, and Peter! And most important, her relationship with God!

Plus—she had family now! The discovery was like a dream! If she had her computer, she thought, she could try to Google her newly found grandparents and uncles to see what she could find out—perhaps even find their homes on a satellite map, but both her phone and computer were toast. She tried to recall if she had lost anything valuable on her laptop. College projects, she knew, but that was okay. And lots of college photos. But those were peppered with Alex, so it was okay to lose those too. And the videos of her mother. But her dad still had those on his computer too, so they weren't actually lost.

Her mother. *Evangeline Delano*. With new eyes, Kyla wondered what it had been like for her mother to live with such a dark, secret past.

What a burden of guilt she had carried! Kyla sighed, understanding now that there had come a distinct point in her mother's life when her decisions had changed to doing what she thought was best for her daughter. In Kyla's eyes it was another picture of sacrificial love—like what she had come to realize about her dad's care of her after her mom was gone. But it was also a tangible expression of the sovereign care of God over her life too. God had never abandoned Kyla. He had been there all along, *keeping her*, watching over her during her childhood. As Peter had said, she just hadn't known it!

How wonderful it must have been for her mother to experience the forgiveness of God! By then she already carried the death sentence of terminal cancer in her body. Had her mother not been dying, Kyla wondered if she possibly would have turned herself in to the authorities. Perhaps, Kyla considered, perhaps even her mother's death may have been an expression of God's grace, protecting Kyla from what may have been a brutal decision for her mother! She marveled at the possibility. It was all speculation, of course, but nevertheless she could see with clarity that God had not abandoned or rejected her during her childhood. He had been carefully watching over her to lead her to himself!

The weirdest part for Kyla was realizing her entire life as a "DeKane" had been built around a made-up identity! For a moment the anxiety of abandonment overtook her again, the feeling of floating in space tied by a fragile thread. *Who was she?* What was her biological father's *real* name? Would she ever know? Could she go on with her life being a "DeKane," knowing it was a fake name? Would she now be considered a Delano? Should she change her name to Delano? Would the Delano family have anything to do with her? *Who was she? Where did she belong?* It was an awful feeling not to have roots!

And then, like a light snapping on to illuminate a room, Kyla remembered that in her legal adoption by Kendall Lee, her new stepdad had insisted on her keeping "DeKane" as her name—but only because it sounded better than "Kyla Lee." She knew then exactly what she would do. She would have ample money from this nanny job to change her last name to Lee! And that's what she would do—no matter what the cost, no matter what it sounded like, no matter that she was in her twenties, no matter that her diploma said *Kyla Evangeline DeKane*, no matter that it might eventually change again—she hoped. Maybe.

Still antsy and pacing her room, Kyla paused near the table, observing the tangled charger cords and the disposable coffee cup from Peter on top of her journal. *Yes, you have—you just didn't know it.* The words made her heart turn over again, knowing it was true about God loving her for her whole life. And for Peter. It was nice to discover that you were loved.

Setting the paper cup to the side, she picked up the journal from him. It had been a perfect gift. Adjusting the chair, she sat down and opened it to read her first journal entry. *I'm drowning, God! Will you please help me somehow?* Kyla shook her head in awe. *He had! Yes, he certainly had!* Her eyes dropped to the bottom of the page to read the printed Bible verse, and then she gasped in amazement. She hadn't read the verse when she had vomited her thoughts on that page—*He reached down from on high and took hold of me; he drew me out of deep waters.*

Did it really say that? *What were the odds of that?* But it was so true—when she felt as if she were drowning, it was as though he had reached down to pull her out of those deep waters! She wondered what else it said around that verse. Eagerly she slid her new Bible from Mrs. Gordon close, paging through it until she found the Psalms, then searched for the right Psalm. Then drawing her finger down along the page, she found the verse and began reading from there.

> *He reached down from on high and took hold of me; he drew me out of deep waters. He rescued me from my powerful enemy, from my foes, who were too strong for me. They confronted me in the day of my disaster, but the Lord was my support. He brought me out into a spacious place; he rescued me because he delighted in me.*

She sat back. Delighted? Because he *delighted* in her? Seriously? *Delighted* was a strong word! Kyla closed her eyes, feeling that she could hardly contain God's love for her. Her heart felt as if it were expanding on the inside of her, and she sat there still, enjoying the deep feeling of love and peace surrounding her. She didn't want to move from there and couldn't wait to tell Peter about it in the morning!

At last Kyla began feeling a little tired. She shed her clothes in the bathroom and showered, glad to be out of her new swimsuit finally. When she was ready for bed, Kyla went to the boys' room and sat on Howie's bed. What a trooper that kid had been throughout their ordeal, she thought. So brave. She loved him—she loved him so much! She loved both of the boys and missed them so much that her heart hurt. In her new and feeble way she prayed for them and thanked God for bringing her here to Wynnbury for the summer. She prayed for Dr. Grant too, and for his wife, whom she would meet tomorrow. That she was a famous actress was the last thing Kyla cared about. She was a *person* first—Dr. Grant's wife! Then she thanked God for her dad—and for Peter.

Peter. She sighed dreamily. Finally, feeling very, very happy, Kyla went back to her own bed and fell asleep as soon as her head hit the pillow.

It was all her fault. She was to blame for everything.

She was having a nightmare, Kyla realized, waking from her sleep with a sob, drenched with sweat, a horrible, horrible dream, but it lingered heavily. Like a crushing weight, a pervasive feeling of guilt and dread pressed down on her as it replayed vividly in her mind.

In her dream she was at the airport waiting, having driven there to meet Ms. Marilee Montayne, waiting and waiting for her arrival there with the awful task of telling her that her husband and her two little boys were dead—all of them. Robert DeKane, her biological father, had murdered them all in cold blood right before her eyes. Her legs shook as she stood waiting to do her morbid task. She could hardly stand under the burden of guilt and regret, for Kyla knew their deaths were all because of her. *Entirely* because of her. Had it not been for her coming to Wynnbury, Robert DeKane would not have been there and none of the tragedies would have happened. But there she was, standing at the busy airport, waiting for the beautiful woman to arrive, waiting for her to come down the escalator and through the glass doors, waiting to give her the horrible news that she knew would send her into a spiral of grief.

She sat up in bed, lifting the sheet to wipe her tears in the dark, trying to separate reality from the horrible unreality, but the residual feeling the dream left was so awful that she felt as if she could cry forever.

God, I'm so sorry! Forgive me!

It wasn't her fault, of course. She knew it was just a dream. Even in reality DeKane's presence at Wynnbury had been beyond her control—not her fault—yet at that very moment the professor lay gravely wounded in the New Hampton hospital, and at the heart of what had happened was an undeniable connection to her. With her face in her hands she shed more tears, so sorrowful for what had happened and so thankful that things hadn't turned out any worse.

Sleep was gone now. Her mind was awake. She glanced at the clock to see it was barely five. The first of dawn's light drew a faint line of light around the window shades. It was awfully early, and she was so tired, but she knew that if she stayed there, the nightmare would replay over and over in her head. She decided to get up. Certainly Peter wasn't up yet, but he was always up before her, so eventually he would be.

Quietly Kyla went downstairs and made herself coffee in the dark. Clicking on the lamp in the corner of the Great Room, she curled up in Peter's chair, waiting for both him and the sun to rise. Eyeing the furniture in disarray and the spot on the carpet, she reviewed the events of the previous day and prayed for everybody. Gradually the ugly images of her dream began to fade and the web of guilty sadness loosened its grip on her.

Peter's Bible and journal were in their places on the end table, and she picked them up. His journal was the same size as hers, but his was brown leather, not white, matching his Bible. It was about halfway filled, his writing very small and neat, and the content very businesslike, listing out what he had read in the Bible with a few brief notes that went with it each day. His last entry was the day before last, just a few short sentences after the date.

God, I give up. I die to this and give her to you.

She stared at the words, a wonderful swirl of happiness stirring in her belly. She took his pen and wrote the new date underneath his handwriting, scrawling after it, "You are wonderful, Peter Watkins. And I love you." Then she put his journal away and opened his Bible.

His bookmark was in Luke, so Kyla began there, reading about Jesus healing a paralyzed man, and the tax-collector Matthew becoming his disciple. Then came the Beatitudes, and words about loving your enemies—which made her think about her birth father. It was apparent that another deep layer of forgiveness would be in order there, and she wasn't crazy about the thought. But it was the way of God, she realized, her eyes lingering on the page. He would help her through it.

She read on. With no one else up the house was quiet, and she found she could focus and take her time. It was nice. She could see why Peter liked getting up early. After every paragraph she would pause a bit to reflect about what she had read and what spoke to her the most in the words. Then she would move on again to the next section, overjoyed that for once the words actually made some sense to her!

Eventually she reached a story of a dead man being carried out of town—the only son of his mother. She stopped, reflecting on her awful dream again. The dread she had felt waking up had been so terrible— having to break the news to Marilee Montayne about her sons and husband.

Her eyes rested on the paragraph. This Bible story had more meaning now after that dream. How terrible it would have been for that mother to lose her son—for *anyone* to lose a child, truly! She looked out across the room, remembering the metal box of Joseph Kennedy's remains in the attic. What an awful day it must have been when his poor mother received that box! A brief and tragic scene played out in her imagination. Oh, how very awful for any family whose son's remains were brought home in a box!

Shaking herself from her morbid thoughts, she turned back to the story, reading how Jesus approached the funeral procession and raised the young man from the dead. *The dead man sat up and began to talk, and Jesus gave him back to his mother.* Incredible, for sure, but what a relief and joy to have her son back! Kyla tipped her head to read the notes Peter had penciled in his margin beside the verse. *Postcard verse*, it said. Kyla frowned, reading the verse again. The postcard verse. The postcard that Howie had found up on the third floor. The postcard that had been sent to Joseph Kennedy's mother so long ago. She stared at it in thought for a moment, then dropped the bookmark in the page, rising rapidly off the chair. *Peter! She had to tell Peter!*

Bounding up the stairs, she hurried to his room, knocking urgently on his door in a way that she hoped wouldn't wake her dad.

"Peter! Peter, wake up!" she called softly.

His door jerked open, and he leaned out, shirtless, looking both ways down the hall. "What's wrong?" he asked with concern, obviously jarred awake.

"I found something very important!" she answered, breathless from the stairs. She stepped past him into his room, holding out his Bible.

"Is there an emergency?" He glanced down the hall again and back at her in confusion.

"No, but this is very, very important! I found something, and you need to come with me—upstairs, right now!"

Running a hand through his hair, he strained to look at the clock. "What time—? Holy cow, Kyla! What are you doing up so early?" His eyes dropped to his Bible in her hands. "What's going on?"

"The verse!" Kyla couldn't keep the excitement out of her voice. "The postcard verse! I know what it means!"

Hastily Peter snatched a shirt and pulled it over his head.

Kyla pointed her finger hard against the Bible in her hand. "Jesus raised the boy from the dead and gave him back to his mother! The mother got her son back!"

"What?" He frowned in confusion, untwisting his shirt around his waist.

"You don't bury a dead person in a wall," she continued, gesturing wildly with her hands. "You put them in the ground! And even if they're cremated, you still don't put them inside a wall like that! I mean, you can keep them somewhere—but not in a wall!"

"What are you talking abou—"

Kyla held the Bible up. "I was reading your Bible this morning, and I saw the postcard verse. I think I found it, Peter! I think I found what we're looking for!"

At his stunned look she continued, her words running together. "Joseph Kennedy wasn't really killed in action, and we know that because he built this house! But his *mother* didn't know that! And she would be receiving a box of his remains delivered right to her door! That's why he sent her the postcard ahead of time with that verse—the mother got her son back alive! He was telling her, *hinting* to her that she would get her son back—because he wasn't really dead!"

He frowned, trying to follow. "Wha—what'd you find?"

"Peter, come with me! Bring your phone—we'll need a flashlight!"

"Okay—I'm there!" He snatched his phone from his desk and met her at the door to the third-floor stairs.

She started up, chattering excitedly. "I woke up with a nightmare that my father had murdered Dr. Grant and the boys, and I had to give Marilee Montayne the news—"

"That's awfu—"

"—and I couldn't sleep, so I got up and went downstairs. I was reading your Bible, and I saw this story and thought about that poor mother—and then I thought about Joseph Kennedy's poor mother receiving his remains, and it all became so obvious! I think I've found it! I just know it!"

"What'd you find?" He kept stride beside her.

"Well, I'm not exactly sure, but I'll bet it's what we're looking for, and I think you'll agree when you see it!"

He shook his head, his smile broadening. "Okay—I'm not sure which is more of a surprise—that you think you found Kennedy's stash or that you were up before me reading *my* Bible! I've never seen you like this!"

She gave a giddy laugh, leading him down the hall to the attic door. "Just wait till you see what I have to show you!" She leaned in and kissed his bicep.

He smiled down in surprise, then turned, suddenly frowning at the strange cut in the attic door around the lock. "What the heck happened to this door?"

"Same thing that happened to the door downstairs across from your room! DeKane locked them and took all the keys. The police had to use a jigsaw to cut the door open. But they missed looking in this attic! Dad came back later with the jigsaw and cut us out of here!"

"Wow!" He pulled the door open and glanced upward, whistling at the dark and narrow stairs. "I can see how the police missed it. Thank God your dad thought to look up there."

"We prayed," she said simply. "Howie and I prayed, and God sent him to find us."

"You," he said, looking down at her, "are acting like a believer!"

She gave him a little smile, then let out a breath, gazing up the stairs. "This is where it gets kind of creepy. There's another door at the top that Dad had to cut open too. I'm a little scared to go up there again. It was a frightening experience."

Peter shot her a look. "Then you stay right here." He shone his flashlight upward. "I'll go. Just tell me what I'm looking for."

"A metal box. About this big—the size of a tool chest. It was boarded in the wall of the closet." She held out her hands to show him. "It's on the floor on the far side of a trunk now—to your right. You'll see it, and you can bring it down."

"Interesting," he said curiously.

She laid a hand on his arm, adding, "Ah, before you go, we might want to pray that all the bats are back to bed already."

"This time of day?" He chuckled. "Um, I'm not sure God's going to answer *that* prayer! Okay—" Peter took the stairs and disappeared at the top as he pushed the door open and hunched over to enter the room. "Oh, whoa! Yeah, stay where you are," he called down. "Our friends are up, all right!" In a few moments he had retrieved the box and hurried down the stairs to where Kyla stood.

He gave a sour look. "How long were you guys locked in there? That place reeks like—"

"—bat guano and mothballs?" She raised her eyebrows. "Hours! Felt like forever!" She tapped the metal box. "See what I mean, Peter? Let's take it into the big room."

The sun wasn't up yet, but the eastern sky was bright enough to see with natural light in front of the tall windows. Peter set the box on the floor and knelt, examining the stenciling on the cover.

"Human remains, huh?" he mused, shooting her a look. "Well, now, isn't this interesting? What did you find, girl?" His lip curled up in a smile.

Kyla gave him a knowing nod. "I stood on the trunk to try to see out the window, but I didn't have enough height. But when we heard the gunshots—I knew that's what it was—I just *had* to see what was going on out there somehow! There was nothing around, so I tried to pull some boards off the closet walls to put onto the trunk to stand on, and this fell out of the wall."

"Huh. A *closet* in an attic like that?" he asked.

"Right!" she said. "And who boards up human remains in an attic closet wall?" She patted the box. "Joseph Kennedy wasn't dead! These aren't his remains. He sent something else home in here!"

They looked at each other for a long time. Then Peter looked back at the box.

"Okay—it's locked," he murmured, tipping it up for a closer look. "I suppose we'll have to try to pick it open somehow. At worst we could try to *cut* it open—maybe with the jigsaw. Unless there's a key hidden up there too. I could go look arou—"

"Oh, duh! There *is*!" Kyla lifted her hands excitedly. "There's a key in the trunk! It was under this old smelly uniform. I tried it in the attic door, but it didn't work, so I threw it back in there."

Peter's shoulders sagged dramatically, and he made a face. "Are you kidding me? You're going to make me go back in there *again*?"

She batted him, and his blue eyes danced. He told her he would be right back, and she heard him take the attic stairs two at a time. In a moment he returned with the key in his hand and knelt beside her. Again they locked eyes. Peter's face spread into a broad grin.

"Can you believe this?" He shook his head in disbelief.

"I know! We found it!"

He pointed at her. "*You* found it."

Kyla pointed upward. "All too amazing for me to get the credit!"

Looking back to the box, Peter tried the key, which easily slipped into the lock. He hesitated, biting his lip for a second. "You know what I'm thinking?" he asked.

"I think so," she said. "And I agree. Dr. Grant should open it."

He nodded. "Exactly!"

Peter removed the key and carried the box as they hurried down the stairs.

"I have a large tote bag I can put that in," she said to him over her shoulder, "and we should tell my dad where we're going."

"Yes, good idea," Peter replied, immediately going to Kendall's room to knock.

The door opened, and Kyla's dad peered out sleepily into the hall.

"What's going on? Is everything all right?" he asked.

Kyla quickly explained that they were about to go to the hospital to see Dr. Grant, and Peter added that they had found something valuable, something Dr. Grant had been searching for a long time. Kendall listened intently, looking from one to the other with his narrow Asian eyes.

"How long have you guys been up?" he asked finally, then with a hint of disapproval added, "And Kyla, what are you wearing?"

Kyla looked down, realizing she was in her pajamas. "I'll change," she said hastily.

By the time she met him in the hallway, Peter had changed too. He gestured to the end of the hall, indicating that they should take the shortcut to the side entrance.

"We should take your truck," she said as they paused near the key rack by the door.

"My truck?" he questioned. "Your car is faster."

Kyla shrugged. "I don't really care about that. I'd rather ride with you."

His lip curled up a bit. "Is that so?"

She smiled at him with sparkling eyes.

Peter shifted his feet, looking down at her. "Okay, true confessions," he said. "I have been drooling over that Mustang since the day you arrived, and I'm dying to drive it." He grinned sheepishly.

Kyla laughed. She took her keys off the hook and set them in his palm.

The sun was fully up when they arrived at the hospital, the nearly empty parking lot a clue to their discovery that the front doors of the main entrance were still locked. Redirected to the emergency room entrance, they returned to the car and drove to the other side of the building to park in the lot there. Kyla hefted the bulky box in her bag to her shoulder, and the two of them entered and were met immediately by a triage nurse.

"There's no emergency," Peter said. "We're here to visit someone upstairs."

Another nurse in the ER office came to help them. She frowned, looking Dr. Grant up on her computer. "Well, I can let you through, but it's on the early side. I don't think they're going to let you in to see him yet."

Pointing them down the hall, she indicated which elevators would take them to Dr. Grant's floor. The admitting nurse had been right. The head RN at the nurses' station looked up from her task to stop them in the hallway, emphatically shaking her head no.

She was matter of fact. "There's been a flurry of activity in there all night. He's finally resting now. You might try back in a couple of hours."

In disappointment Kyla turned to go. Peter, however, paused. With respectful determination he stepped up to the counter, resting his arm and tapping his fingers lightly. Kyla saw his eyes flick to read the woman's dangling name badge as she leaned over her task.

"Nurse Anne, I know these night shifts can't be easy, so I want to thank you for all you do as a nurse. We appreciate you caring for our friend. When would you say is the soonest possible time we could see him? It's just that we need one brief moment with him to finish tying up a small matter regarding something very important."

Expressionless, the woman studied them both. She hesitated for a moment longer, and then waved them on, pointing down the hall. "Room 414. Be *very* brief."

"Your dad would *so* confront me on manipulation if he were here," Peter said under his breath as they walked down the hallway.

"He might make an exception this time," Kyla replied, lugging the box in the tote.

The room was dim and quiet when they entered except for the soft clicking of machines near the bed. Dr. Grant was reclined with his head slightly raised, his body hooked up to various monitors and tubes. His skin was pale, his eyes closed, and his chest bandaged. Peter shot a look at Kyla, as if to ask if she was okay seeing him like this. The familiar smell of medical equipment gave her flashbacks to her mother's last days in their house, but she shook it off and nodded to Peter. This was not her mother. Peter rested his hand lightly on Dr. Grant's arm and waited. In a moment he opened his eyes. They brightened a little when he recognized who was there.

"Hey, Grant," Peter said softly. "How are you, my friend?"

He blinked in response with barely a nod. His eyes moved to Kyla, and she smiled at him.

"We came to see you," Peter said, "and to show you something." He took the dark metal box out of Kyla's shoulder bag and set it on his bedside table, pulling it over to rest in his line of sight. "See this? This was in an upper attic wall. Kyla stumbled onto it yesterday afternoon when she was locked in there by Robert DeKane."

Dr. Grant gave a blink and a nod.

Peter tilted the box up so that Dr. Grant could read it. "It says 'Human Remains,' but this girl figured out that people aren't buried in walls and that Joseph Kennedy probably wasn't in that box, since he built that house after the war." He held up the key. "Would you like to see what's inside this box?"

Dr. Grant's arm twitched, and he gave a nod. "Please," he whispered with a hint of a smile.

Peter held the key out to Kyla, but she shook her head. "No, Peter— you open it."

Peter inserted and turned the key, then raised the lid, revealing several bundles of small cloth bags inside, most of them of yellowed cotton flannel. Curiously he reached for the largest one lying on the top. Loosening a tiny drawstring, he slowly and carefully tipped the contents into his hand. Out tumbled a shimmering jewel-encrusted tiara, a rather small one, like for a child, and slightly tarnished with age but sparkling brilliantly nonetheless. Peter's breath caught and Kyla gasped, covering her mouth with her hands. Dr. Grant lay with a look of amazement on his face. His eyes moved to Kyla.

"Found it," he breathed.

Kyla stared, dumbfounded. "Is that—are those real?"

Covering his fingers with the fabric, Peter held up the little crown by the edge, turning it and watching the clusters of diamonds glitter in the light, even after it had been hidden away for so many years. He gave a little whistle.

"Stunning!" he said with awe. "Look at that setting!"

"It's amazing!" Kyla said in a hushed voice. "Absolutely amazing!"

"Elizabeth," Dr. Grant whispered with a smile. "Baby."

Peter studied Dr. Grant for a bit, then looked at Kyla. "I think he's saying that it belonged to Queen Elizabeth. It was hers when she was a baby. In his file there's a photograph of her as a little girl wearing it. It was one of the items that disappeared and was believed to be at Tynnbury Hall in England. It was what Grant suspected Kennedy had hidden here."

Dr. Grant blinked, giving a tiny nod. He closed his eyes.

Together they stared at the crown. There was no doubt in her mind of its authenticity, but she knew an official process of identification and authentication would be done eventually. Peter carefully returned the tiara to its pouch, pulling the drawstring closed. He selected another small bag and looked inside, then held it over for Kyla to see. It was full of what she presumed were loose diamonds, clear stones of differing sizes, cut in various gem shapes. One by one they began opening cloth bags, finding pouches and pouches of all sorts of jewels, and elegant necklaces and bracelets studded with rubies, emeralds, and diamonds.

Suddenly Peter stopped, jerking his head toward Dr. Grant. "He's asleep. I think we should take this home now. He knows. Hopefully he's not too drugged to remember this moment."

Peter closed up the box and locked it. Carefully he placed it back into Kyla's tote bag, and then moving close to Dr. Grant's bedside again, he placed his hand on Dr. Grant's shoulder and quietly prayed for him.

"Thanks," came Dr. Grant's soft reply when Peter had finished. His eyes flickered open.

Peter took his hand, and Dr. Grant squeezed it lightly.

"Want to talk," he whispered with effort, "want—"

"You want to talk sometime?" Peter asked, leaning closer.

Again a barely perceptible nod. "God," he breathed.

Peter squeezed his arm. "Yes, we will talk about God. You can ask me any questions you want. You get better, okay?"

Dr. Grant's eyes moved to Kyla. "Boys," he said. "Thank—" He swallowed, his eyes growing red.

"They're safe," Kyla said, her throat tight. "And they'll want to see you soon!"

"Yes," he replied quietly, closing his eyes again. Soon it was evident that he had fallen asleep.

They were silent walking down the hallway when they left. As they passed the nurses' station on the way to the elevators, Peter gave a salute of thanks to Nurse Anne.

"I hope he's going to be okay," Kyla said on their way down to the main floor.

Peter took the bag from her to carry it. "He's in tough shape, but he'll pull through. I can hardly wait until he's well enough to enjoy his discovery. He was so convinced that it was here somewhere and so determined to find it!"

"He's going to flip!" Kyla agreed. "He will definitely have something to look forward to when he gets out!"

He gestured to the bag. "I'll tell you one thing—his life is worth far more than anything in *here*."

"You're absolutely right about that!"

The elevators opened, and the two cut through the emergency room hallway on their way back to the parking lot entrance.

"I couldn't believe that tiara!" Kyla reflected in amazement as they stepped outside into the sunshine. "Did you see all those diamonds? I wonder how much just that one piece is worth!"

"No kidding! I know for certain that there's a museum that's going to be pretty excited to hear about this find! I can't imagine what all this is worth!" He gave a low whistle. "Kennedy had a pretty sneaky plan, didn't he?"

"What'll we do with it now?"

"I'll put it in Grant's safe until he comes home. Then he can truly enjoy the find and call the proper authorities himself. He's earned that right—that's for sure. He bought this house with that hunch, and he's searched for it for years."

He put the bag into the trunk and went to open her door. "You know, I can't help but compare Grant to the man who found a treasure in a field—in one of the parables. He found it and sold everything he had to buy that field to get that treasure. Grant's buying this place is so much like that. He was so sure that the treasure was here, so convinced of its great value—so sure that he made a huge investment to find it. His buying Wynnbury was like an act of faith."

"I take it that's something from the Bible."

"Yes. It's a story that Jesus told. To illustrate a point."

She nodded. "Ah, that's cool." She got into the car and waited for him to come around to the driver's side. "You know what that parable makes me think of?"

"What?"

She tipped her head. "Well, it's kinda like me this summer. I wasn't even looking for God, but I stumbled into finding him. And now I want to give up everything else to have him."

He looked at her. "Yes. It's exactly like that!"

Kyla sighed. "I just want Dr. Grant home."

On their way back to Wynnbury Peter stopped at a coffee shop to pick up two coffees for the road. Kyla confided to him that she had saved the paper cup from the time he had brought her the coffee a while back.

"It was what you wrote on the cup that was special," she replied to his questioning look."It was kind of a turning point for me. I started to warm up to you a little more."

"Huh," he said, nesting his coffee in the drink holder in the tiny car.

"But when I saw the look on your face after Dr. Grant came down on you—that's when I knew you were something more to me. I felt absolutely terrible! And then on top of that, there was a card in the box addressed to you from someone named Amy. Oh, I was so relieved to find out she was your sister!"

He furled his brow. "What? I don't have a sister named Amy."

Kyla's mouth opened in surprise.

He winked. "I'm teasing you. Yes, Amy's my sister!"

"You!" She smacked him playfully. She took a sip of her coffee, savoring it. "So when did you know you liked me?"

He shook his head, driving. "Wow—that is such a girl question."

Kyla rolled her eyes at him. "So I'm a girl!"

"Well, if you really want to know—" He shot her a look in her seat. "I saw your picture every week on your dad's desk in his office for a long time."

She groaned. "Seriously? That was taken in high school—like five years ago. I look like a little kid!"

"It's a great photo! Almost every week we would pray for you to meet Jesus as Savior."

"You did?"

"Yes. And I couldn't help hoping that I'd meet you some day too." He cleared his throat. "And then one day you walked into his office wearing this dress that—" His eyebrows rose, and a grin spread across his face. "It was black, and, well—wow!"

Kyla dropped her head, shielding her face with her hand. "Oh, geez, I'm so embarrassed! I could tell Dad was mortified!"

"No! You looked—you looked *good!*"

"I bought it for a class presentation and—"

"You don't have to explain anything! But to answer your question— that was when."

She threw him a look, her cheeks pink. "I expected something much more saintly of you, Peter Watkins!"

He laughed out loud. "Well, you certainly didn't make it easy for me!"

Chapter Thirty-Three

Peter's father showed up with his crew early in the morning as expected, and the abandoned yard began to flourish with activity. An hour later a truck full of fresh sod arrived, waiting alongside the driveway until the area was prepared and workers were ready for it. Inside, Kyla and her dad worked in Dr. Grant's office, putting all the furniture back and returning the books to the shelves. Kyla didn't even attempt to put his papers and files back, but she straightened them up and semi-organized them so that it would be easier for him when he eventually got to it. Glad to recover the framed portrait of Marilee undamaged, she cleared off the counter in the kitchen to restore it to its original place, with Spot and Goldie tucked right next door to her under the kitchen cabinet. A while later Kyla also found the framed photos of Joseph Kennedy in the overturned trunk in Dr. Grant's office and happily returned them to their places on the foyer wall.

While they were working, Mrs. Gordon stopped by with her carpet shampooer, informing Kyla that she wanted to clean the Great Room rug right away before the dirt got ground in any further. The two of them had a little time to talk. Kyla gave her details of the previous day and thanked her for offering her daughter to take the boys. She also told her briefly of her time on the beach doing the hard work of forgiving her father, and Mrs. Gordon cried a little and hugged her, telling Kyla how proud of her she was. Then Kyla shared what had transpired between her and Peter. Mrs. Gordon's eyebrows rose in surprise, but she told Kyla that he seemed like a nice young man.

"Just as long as he puts Jesus first, hon," she said. "Believe me—you do not want to be linked together with someone who doesn't love God or with someone who's only giving him lip service! The Bible calls that being 'unequally yoked.'"

Kyla agreed but made a mental note to ask her about it again sometime.

Late morning Kyla stopped in her room to take a short rest and ended up sleeping for over an hour, waking up to a grilled feast on the deck that her dad had prepared for all the yard workers. Peter introduced his father to her, who was tall like Peter and burly, with thick shoulders and dark blond hair. He was pleasant and asked her questions about her life and what had brought her to the New Hampton area. In turn, she told him that she had heard of his company, and they made small talk about that. Then Peter introduced his father to Kendall, and the two of them visited. During lunch Kyla learned that they were almost finished laying the sod. Peter and his father were now working on a temporary sprinkler system to keep the grass well-watered for the next week. It appeared to Kyla that things were going well between the two of them. Everyone working seemed in good spirits, and they were very appreciative of the good meal.

Around two o'clock Mrs. Gordon's daughter brought the boys home, much later than Kyla had hoped and expected them. Hank bounced happily up to Kyla to hug her and show her several new toys from the new babysitter. Howie had some new toys too, but he also carried a yellow sand bucket filled with origami fish that he and Julia had made.

He eyed Kyla soberly. "I hope your dad doesn't come back! He's bad! He hurt my daddy!"

Kyla got on her knees to be eye-level with him. "No, he's *not* coming back! Mr. DeKane is gone and not coming back!" She took his hand. "Howie, please forgive me for letting him stay here with your family. I'm so sorry he did all those bad things to you and to Hank. Will you please forgive me?"

Howie scrunched his face. "What does *that* mean?"

Kyla wasn't quite sure how to answer. She took a breath. "Um, it means you will still love me and let me be a friend in your heart. It means you won't stay mad at me and blame me for hurting you."

"Okay—I will," he said easily. He looked toward Kyla's dad in the kitchen. "Who is that guy again?"

She sighed inwardly. Another complicated question. "When I was little, Howie, my father Mr. DeKane had to go away for a long, long time. So this man, Mr. Lee, became my dad instead. He's a good dad, like yours. Very, very good."

"Mr. Lee." Howie nodded, ready to go play. "I just forgot his name is all."

Later on the sod was completely set in and finished, and the yard looked beautiful. Kyla brought the boys out onto the patio in their swimsuits to run through the sprinkler where the water sprayed slightly beyond the grass onto the concrete deck. Peter was going to move it but left it there for Kyla so that she could sit outside in a dry spot on the patio furniture and still watch them play in the water. She was glad, for then she could watch Peter too, who was also in her sight while he finished up on little details in the yard. Eventually he left to go mow the front and side yards of the house because they had been neglected for so long in all their efforts toward putting in the fountain and cleaning up from the storm.

The boys were still outside on the deck in their swimsuits when Ms. Marilee Montayne arrived, flanked by her two personal bodyguards, who promptly searched the house and yard while she came out to rejoin her children. Even after such a long flight and visiting her husband in the hospital for a few hours already, she looked fantastic, with perfect hair and makeup, wearing designer jeans with a smart designer top and shiny red heels. Feeling a burst of butterflies inside, Kyla stood up quickly from her patio chair while Howie flew to her excitedly, leaving a trail of wet footprints across the deck. Hank was more reserved, observing her guardedly but following his older brother's lead, soon approached her on his own.

Kyla stepped forward to introduce herself and tell her how sorry she was about her husband. She asked her forgiveness too, for the awful behavior of her birth father.

Marilee was as gracious as she was beautiful. "Don't worry about it, Miss Kayla," she said, mispronouncing her name. "Your father's choices were his own. David has had nothing but good to say about you, and he trusts you completely. I'm pleased to have finally met you."

Then she suddenly noticed the fountain behind Kyla in the yard and cried out in surprise and excitement, telling Kyla that her husband hadn't said *anything* to her about it. Kyla told her how hard Dr. Grant and Peter had worked on it, never imagining that she would be here so soon to enjoy it. She added that Peter and his father's crew had just finished sodding the yard only a few hours ago.

The boys clung to their mother the rest of the afternoon, and Ms. Montayne seemed eager to resume her role as mom, showering them with love and attention, playing with them, and doling out special gifts that she had brought for them. Kyla watched from the sidelines as the woman of the house had her things carried in and took her place.

Later in the day Kendall once again created a wonderful dinner, and they all sat around the table on the deck, where Marilee asked questions to get to know everyone while helping her boys with their meal. Afterward Peter and Kyla shared discretely what had happened the previous day from their perspectives. Ms. Montayne wept and expressed her sincere gratitude to both of them for their care of her sons.

After dinner Ms. Montayne and the two kids retired upstairs to her bedroom, where Kyla heard the boys' happy laughter as they interacted with their mother. Kyla was surprised at the sudden pangs of melancholy encroaching on her mood. She missed the boys. She knew how tired Hank was from having skipped his nap that day. He would lose it pretty soon, no doubt. If she were up there, she would be drawing baths for them right away, she thought, but she wasn't. They would have to be fine without baths for the night.

Peter came and got her when she and her dad were finishing up with the dinner dishes. He was smiling and carrying a blanket and a small paper bag.

"Come with me," he said, his eyes alive.

"Where are we going?" she asked, wiping her hands on the towel, casting a glance at her dad, who waved her off.

"You'll find out!"

Peter took Kyla down to the dock, where he had cleaned out the boat.

"I'm cashing in on a missed opportunity," he said. "You and me— floating out there, watching the sunset."

"Hmm," Kyla said, narrowing her eyes at him. "I'm pretty sure I gave you a 'maybe' and not a 'yes.'"

"Huh," Peter said. He was in the boat, reaching for her hand to help her in. "I thought for sure by now you'd be at a 'definitely.'"

Nervously she took a seat, admitting, "I'm just not crazy about water—that's all. Lakes and rivers—they're deep. And all the stuff that lives in them freaks me out!"

"Oh, is that it?" He untied the boat and pushed off. "No problem, then! Just stay right here in the boat, okay?" He gave her a wink.

They motored out a short ways, where he turned the engine off and came to sit beside her. He then pulled a small box out of the paper bag he had brought with. Inside were two large strawberries, double dipped in both white and dark chocolate.

He held the box out to her. "One for you, one for me! You get first pick."

Kyla's face lit up. "Yum! Where did you get these?"

"My mom answered the phone when I called Dad from the police station yesterday. I told her briefly what was going on. Then when he showed up this morning he gave me this box from her."

"Totally nice," she said. "What a treat! Be sure to tell her thank you."

They shared the strawberries while they drifted on the river, enjoying the quiet sounds of the evening and the gentle lapping of water around them. Together they replayed the excitement of finding the hidden museum loot, each telling the other from his or her own perspective. Peter teased her for busting down his door in her pajamas, waking him up from a sound sleep, rattling off what sounded like absolute nonsense at the time.

"And on top of everything, you were poking your finger onto my Bible, talking a mile a minute, and then holding it up in the air! I didn't know what to think!"

They laughed together. Peter asked more about her time with Howie in the attic, and she filled in the details, including playing the game of "God's Creation" together. He smiled at that but told her what a trooper she had been. Kyla reflected on how many times she had handled and dropped the metal box, clueless of what was inside.

"I kept thinking that poor Mr. Kennedy's ashes had no resting-in-peace with me nearby! I never dreamed what could actually be in there!"

Peter was thoughtful for a moment, then shook his head. "Wow—did you ever think you would find a treasure like that when you decided to come here this summer?"

Kyla blew out her breath. "Never in a million years!"

"Well, you found it! You actually found a genuine hidden treasure!" He threw his head back and gave a laugh of amazement. "How often does that happen to someone?"

She smiled, reminded of the parable he had shared with her earlier that morning. "I found more than one treasure here this summer!"

"Yeah," he agreed. "You've found the true treasure."

"But not *all* of him. It's just the beginning. I mostly found the door to the treasure room!"

"Yes, that's a good way to look at it—at *him*." He turned his head to smile at her.

Both of them were quiet. Kyla reflected that once she had asked God for *one great thing,* and he had answered her. Who would ever have thought that her one great thing would be God himself?

The sun was starting to set over the hill to the west, and Peter fired up the boat again.

"I want to show you something," he said.

He took her to the shore opposite their little beach at Wynnbury and tied off the boat on the neighbor's dock. He tossed the blanket over his arm and got out, reaching back to help her onto the wooden decking. Assuring her they had permission to be there, he took her by the hand to climb their neighbor's grassy hill, where they stopped halfway up to spread out the throw on the hillside.

"Have a seat." He gestured and plopped down beside her. "The light of the sunset on Wynnbury is really nice, and I thought you'd like to see what it looks like on the cliff from over here on this side. I discovered it when I was sleuthing for our binocular man."

Kyla gave him an appreciative look. "Thanks again for that. For being alert and noticing."

He nodded. "It was a God thing, truly. I have to admit, though—I'm ready to be done with strange and mysterious things happening around here! I wouldn't mind some relaxation. No doubt the summer will change for me as there's no need to keep digging up the yard looking for Kennedy's hidden loot."

"Yeah. Dr. Grant will have to come up with some new projects." She gave him a twisted smile. "Unless our Mr. Kennedy has another stash hidden away somewhere."

"Good heavens! I hope not!" he replied with a laugh. "Look—see what I mean?" He pointed across the river.

Peter was right—the sunset colors against Wynnbury House were indeed beautiful, a swirled mix of pinks, reds, oranges, and purples, shining on the brick and reflecting in the many windows.

"Gorgeous," she whispered, and they sat together in silence, watching the colors change against the house and the cliff across the way. The birds' evening chorus and the waking frogs and crickets offered a peaceful symphony behind nature's glorious show. Kyla filled her lungs with the cool air. It smelled like the river and freshly mown grass and Peter's soap. She sat with her arms wrapped around her knees. Peter was stretched out on the blanket beside her, propping himself up with one arm.

"You tired?" he asked after a while. "I'm guessing your early morning has caught up to you. You got quiet."

"Maybe a little bit," she said. "I'm thinking, mostly." Thinking about how she was struggling to warm up to Marilee Montayne. Here Kyla was, privileged to be in the close presence of a famous star actress—she should be overjoyed! But something about her didn't sit well inside, and she struggled to put her finger on it. Was it her perfect body? Her perfect teeth, perfect nails, perfect voice—perfect *everything*? Embarrassed by her internal battle, Kyla kept her troubled thoughts to herself, but the tide of her self-pity was rising.

Eventually the evening light began to diminish. The colors of the sunset faded to bluish grays, and Wynnbury House began disappearing in the shadows of dusk. Then suddenly, without warning, the lights around the fountain came on, illuminating it in the darkness. Even from the distance where they sat she could see the water dancing brightly and alive. Kyla gave an exclamation of delight.

"That was the other thing I wanted to show you," he said, watching her. "It's just a little thing—nothing too significant. I put the lights on a timer—that's all. I thought it would be kinda cool to have them automatically come on every night."

"Very nice, Peter," she told him with a nod, "very nice! I bet your father was really proud of you for the job you did over there!"

He gave a small smile. "Maybe. I don't know. He didn't mention it."

"He didn't mention it?" Kyla frowned. "Like, didn't say *anything*?"

He shrugged. "That's okay."

They watched the brilliant fountain in the darkness. Behind it now shone the lights of the Great Room windows, lighting up the center part of the patio outdoors. One by one other lights came on in the house, revealing the life within. Kyla thought about her father and Ms. Marilee and the boys.

She took a breath. "Look—can I be honest about something?"

"What's that?" Peter replied.

She sighed. "I'm having a hard time with Marilee Montayne being here. Really hard."

He looked at her in surprise. "Really? Why's that?"

Kyla groaned a bit, shaking her head. "I don't know! I mean, she's really nice and everything, but I'm just struggling." She gave a little scowl, thinking about it. "It's like she acts like she owns the place!"

Peter let out an involuntary laugh. "Ah, yeah—well, she does!"

She sighed again. "I don't know. Since she arrived this afternoon, it's like I don't exist to Howie and Hank anymore! They haven't wanted anything to do with me. They just cling to her!"

He gave her a look of surprise. "She's their *mother*! They haven't seen her in a month! That's how it *should* be!"

"I *know*," she said, looking away from him. "It's just that I feel so—so high and dry. So left out and displaced. So—I don't know—*jealous*!"

She was ashamed to admit it, but it was true.

"Hey—you're important!" he said. "Marilee said so herself! She was very grateful for all you've done for her since she's been away. I heard her say it, and you heard it too!"

She shot him a look in the dark. "Yeah. She called me 'Miss Kayla.' Twice! I'm so important that she doesn't even know my real name. And Howie didn't even correct her!"

Peter made a little sound and sat up beside her. He opened his mouth to speak but hesitated, as if searching for the right words.

"What?" she asked a bit sharply, looking back at him. She was feeling overtired and a bit cross.

Peter shook his head. "Nothing. I'm—listening."

She blinked. "You look nervous, like you have something to say. Just say it!"

"Well"—the side of his arm bumped against her shoulder—"this is where your life with God gets real, Kyla. This is what it's all about!"

"What's *that* supposed to mean?"

Peter put his hand on his chest. "You've got to get used to living with a new father. A heavenly father. You've got to learn how he sees you and take your value from him, not from others around you. With him *everyone* belongs, and *everyone* is important. There's no shortage of blessings. There's always enough love for whatever your need is, and more than enough attention to make *everyone* feel special." He squeezed her arm.

Kyla bit her lip, fighting the old urge to think God was against her, fighting the urge to get angry or be full of self-pity when things didn't go her way.

"God loves you, Kyla! You're his daughter, and he sees you. He knows how you're feeling. You have the full spotlight of his attention right now, and he understands. Truly. He cares about you! Don't be jealous of Marilee—God sees your value around here! And those boys adore you!"

She pursed her lips, thinking. "Well, I hear what you're saying. And I'm trying to believe it. But I'm not all there quite yet."

He nodded. "I know. I get it. I've felt that way plenty of times before too. Still do at times. But here's the deal. When you learn to see your value from how God views you, you won't be looking around at others wishing they would notice and validate you. And you won't be so disappointed when they don't meet your expectations. And you won't be so frustrated with them when they don't change. You can just know the calm reality in your heart that you are loved and seen and cared for, no matter what." He lifted his hand, gesturing across the river. "It would have been nice if my dad would have noticed the fountain and said 'good job'—or patted me on the back or did *something* at least! I spent a lot of time on that! In the past I would have been disappointed or hurt and gotten mad at him. But I'm okay. My Heavenly Father sees it, and I know he's proud of me. I'm not going to hold it against my dad."

Kyla leaned her head against his shoulder. "I'm beginning to see that I don't know the first thing about God's love."

He looked down at her, speaking to the top of her head. "Then stick with me. We'll make it our quest together."

They didn't speak for a little while.

Finally Kyla broke in with her thoughts. "You know, Peter, the other night when I was sitting out here—the night I surprised you in the dark—I was thinking about God. I was looking across the river at this house behind us all lit up thinking that God was like that—a perfect being of light far away on an opposite shore. It felt like he was so distant and so unreachable for me, impossible to get to. But look—here I am!" She patted the blanket on the ground, turning her head to look at him. "It's like the moment I asked Jesus to forgive my sins and God to be my father, it's like all of a sudden I was here! In a moment! It's not like I even had to take a boat—it's like Jesus invisibly carried me from one side of the river to the other!"

"That's cool," he said appreciatively.

"It was like I had to finally *surrender* to him. But I'm sure glad I did! It was such hard work resisting him for so long—and the whole time I was resisting love! Who knew? You have *no idea* of how good it felt—of how good it *feels* to be free from all that garbage!"

He smiled. "Yeah, I do know."

"Yes." She nodded. "Yes, I guess you do. Peter, I can't thank you enough for putting yourself out there to share your faith with me."

He gave a humble nod. "You're welcome. It's what your dad did for me." Then straightening his back, he turned toward her. "And speaking of your dad, I had a little conversation with him today. I wanted to tell you about that tonight too."

"All right," she said, turning her face toward him.

"Well," he started, "the whole reason I started meeting with him way back was to grow in my relationship with God. I asked him to help me in that. And as you know, we'd get together often and talk about the Word and stuff."

"Uh-huh."

"Well, our relationship is built on trust," he continued. "Kyla, I've chosen to be completely transparent with him. I can tell him everything. And he can ask me anything and count on an honest answer."

"Okay," she replied, wondering where this was going.

"Anything at all," he repeated.

Kyla listened, waiting.

"So today"—Peter took her hand—"I asked him for the official green light on this relationship, on pursuing you, although he's known for some time how much I liked you."

"Yep, you guys talk about me!" She smiled.

He laughed. "Okay—maybe we do!"

"So what did he say?" she asked shyly. She had never heard of any guy asking a girl's father for his approval to date her! It made her feel special and valued. She was confident her father felt honored by it too.

He looked at her soberly. "He asked me if I recalled what the boundaries of a gentleman were in regard to a woman, and I told him yes, and that I intended to honor them." He squeezed her hand. "And he told me that he would be very disappointed in me if I hurt you in any way, which I assured him I had no intention of doing."

Kyla waited as he paused.

"And then he gave me a nod and said that he hoped you and I would become great friends."

"So do I," she said, smiling back at him.

He kissed her hand and then moved to put his arm around her again. She leaned her head against him, looking out toward the dancing fountain of light across the way.

Kyla sighed. "Seriously, it wasn't too long ago that I felt like everything in my life was falling apart. I thought it was because God was against me. Now I see that he was *for* me the whole time, letting it all crumble so that I would find him."

"Sounds familiar," Peter said.

After a while Kyla yawned and admitted that her early morning had now caught up to her in full effect. Peter got to his feet and gave her a hand up. He pulled the blanket off the grass, shook it out, and offered it to her. Kyla threw it around her shoulders as they walked down to the dock.

"I'm really glad we took the boat out tonight," he said.

"It was very nice," she agreed.

"Well, for more reasons than that," he said.

"What do you mean?" She took the hand he offered to help her step into the boat.

He let out a breath. "For a second up there, I thought you were going to be mad at me and stomp off. But I knew that if you did you couldn't go very far, since you didn't have any other way home but with me on that boat." Kyla could hear the teasing in his voice.

She tossed her head. "Well, just for that I'm stomping off the moment we reach our dock!"

He laughed. "Oh, yeah? Then I think I'll let you off at the public landing!"

She folded her arms and tried to fake a pout but couldn't help laughing with him.

After they had made the short journey to Wynnbury's dock on the other side, Peter tied off and helped her out, and Kyla waited for him while he put the cover on the boat.

"There was one other thing I wanted to give you," he said to her when he finished and came to join her where she stood.

"What's that?" she asked, chilly from the night air. She pulled the blanket tighter, looking up at him.

He stepped close, pulling her near. "I want to redeem myself from botching this last night." Then taking her face in both of his hands, he kissed her, deliberately this time—a real kiss—and when he had finished, Kyla wasn't disappointed.

"How was that?" he asked her softly, leaning his forehead against hers.

"Much better," she said happily, "much better."

"Good," he replied, "'cause it's going to have to last you a while."

Then he took her hand, and the two of them walked together up to Wynnbury House.

About The Author

The daughter of a cattle rancher, Joan Crombie grew up in a small town on the prairies of South Dakota. In 1985 she graduated from St. Olaf College with a B.A. in English Education. She and her husband Steven Crombie have been married for thirty-five adventurous years and have raised five children—one daughter and four sons. Currently they reside in beautiful southern Minnesota where they pastor a church.

As an "empty nester," Joan has more time to pursue her love of writing, which she infuses with wisdom gained from ministry and raising a family. She has always liked fiction where an ordinary girl unwittingly steps into a mystery, and in her writing she seeks to couple that with helping her character identify lies she may have believed about God and combat those lies with biblical truth. Having experienced firsthand the freedom of a healed heart, her passion is to help women grow deeper in the love of God and knowledge of him as their very personal and caring Father.

Her hobbies include thrift shopping, reading, traveling, visiting historical museums, and spending time with her eleven delightful grandchildren.

To learn more about following God or about some of the concepts in this book, visit www.joancrombie.org.